The Magic Crystals

Corridors

by

Stephen Hayes

Corridors

Book 4 in the Magic Crystals series

Written by Stephen Hayes

Published 2015 by Stephen Hayes, Australia

Formatted by www.eBookIt.com

www.stephenhayesonline.com

This is the clean edit edition. For more
information, visit www.stephenhayesonline.com/cleanedit

Disclaimer: All characters in this publication are fictitious and any
resemblance to real persons, living or dead, is purely coincidental.

ISBN-13: 978-0-9944590-0-8

Table of Contents

Previously on the Magic Crystals...

Corridors is the fourth volume in the much larger 'Magic Crystals' series, and picks up about eight weeks after the last book left off; but don't worry, all the important stuff that you missed will be covered throughout the story, so there's no need to look so sad as you ponder these words on the page, screen, or whatever else you're using to read this. In fact, if you haven't read or even heard of 'The Seventh Sorcerer', 'Rock Haulter', or 'Hunt and Power', then what on earth are you doing here? Go back and read them, or you may find yourself floundering as you try to imagine what a bludginator is supposed to do, or why just about everyone hates Mr. Hall so much. Go on, go and read them now; I can wait.

...You're still here. Now why is that? Is it that you're too lazy to go and find them? Can you not afford the twenty-five dollars or whatever it is to get the Ebooks? Can you not even be bothered looking for a pirated copy? If it's the latter then good, 'cause it means I'll get to eat sausages for dinner tonight. Or maybe you have already read them and just want me to get to the point, or perhaps you're a daring soul who thinks they can take this mammoth tail on without the background knowledge. If so, I would tip my hat to you—or my headphones, as that's actually what I'm wearing on my head at the moment.

But since I'm so generous, I'll grant you a quick recap. In the beginning, a bad man by the name of Bernard Moran, who works for an even worse man by the name of Arnold Hammerson, was tasked with finding all of the Sorcerous Crystals—the source of all the Sorcerers' power. But Moran decided to doublecross his masters and take all the magic for himself, including that belonging to the Hammersons. If it hadn't been for his sons Marc and Lucien, and an army of their teenage friends, who knows what Moran might have achieved. Unfortunately, Marc turned out to be the Seventh Sorcerer, and only needed to hold all six Sorcerous Crystals to have magic at his disposal—it was the reason why the Hammersons had wanted him out of the way in the first place. With his friend Tommy's help, Marc was able to defeat his father's Beast of Magic, Fewul, and return the magic to its rightful owners.

The victory was short-lived, however, for as soon as the Hammersons got their magic back, they regrouped, broke Moran out of jail, punished him for his failure and betrayal, and hatched another plan—to steal the most powerful source of magic in the world: The Sien-Leoard Crystal. It was protected on an island called Rock Haulter, a strange place only accessible a few times a year from certain locations around the world. One of those times was conveniently near, and so Moran was given the job and a chance to redeem himself. Once again, he failed, this time because Marc had used his Seventh Sorcerer powers to call on Fewul, the same Beast of Magic Moran had used against him just days earlier, and was able to get to the crystal first.

Moran didn't make it off the island until weeks later, but news of his failure preceded him. The Hammersons decided to use Stella, Arnold's daughter and a not-so-secret traitor to her family, to lure Marc and his magic into a trap. Marc came willingly, but without his magic and with plenty of backup. After Arnold accidentally killed the wrong person, he was forced to take swift action against Marc and his friends before his opposite number, Frederic Woodward, took action of his own. A raid was launched, in which the Hammersons reclaimed five of the six Sorcerous Crystals, as well as took three teenagers—including Frederic Woodward's daughter Amelia— captive.

It took two days for them to escape, in which time the Hammersons captured eight more teenagers through Mr. Hall, their secret agent within the Chopville high school, and all eleven of them were subjected to unspeakable horrors. It was Stella who saved them, by first pretending to kill three of them so that she could take their bodies away, and then secretly restoring Amelia's nullified magic so that Amelia could break them all out. The very next day, the Woodwards stripped the Hammersons of their powers just as Moran had done, and gave them to the Fletchers. They also took the Hammersons and a few of their followers captive.

But the Hammerhearts, the army of loyal followers the Hammersons had been raising for years, rebelled spectacularly the very next day, launching an attack at the high school, killing many of the teachers, some students and a few of the Woodwards' soldiers. It was bad, but beyond that, they seemed like a rudderless pack of troublemakers. The Hammersons re-joined them quickly, though, either having broken out themselves or been broken out by a traitor within the Woodwards' ranks, and many suspected Stella of being responsible. And that was when John (how could it have taken me so long to mention his name) went into the Hammerheart base to attempt to recapture them, assisted by his friend Tulip. They were both captured, she was killed, and he only escaped because Moran chose that exact moment to return to base.

When we last left them, John felt terribly guilty for being responsible for Tulip's death, and had resolved never to try to be a hero again. But how long will that last? Given that he currently has possession of the Sien-Leoard Crystal, I'm willing to bet it won't be long.

Still have questions? The Light, Darkness and Villain Crystals? Agonators? Bludginators? Solid-outliners? The strange connection between John and Stella? The domination charm? The influential charm? The Hammerson base? The Woodward base? Well, if you're really curious, there are three lovely books just waiting for you to go out and buy them. If you still can't be bothered, well, neither can I. So without further ado, let's just pass it over to John Playman and get this ball rolling…

Prologue

The plan was made. The long preparation was complete. The moment of truth, after weeks of effort, had finally arrived. Was it any wonder that I was nervous as I knocked on the door and stood back, waiting for it to open? When I had been asked about what this job would involve, I hadn't been able to give much of it away, for who would really understand it, anyway. Basically, and it was true enough, I would meet someone, I would take something from him, I would give him something that he wanted (if I absolutely had to), and then I'd get the hell out of there. With a bit of luck, and not just for myself, I wouldn't have to give him what he wanted, but I had to be ready for him, because he would be ready for me this evening.

I stood for only ten seconds before the door flew open, and the man I'd hoped to see was standing before me. However nervous he made me feel, I was always extremely grateful whenever I saw him in good health, as he was almost the only person left in his family whom the Hammerhearts hadn't managed to kill. I gave everything in the doorway a cursory glance before looking at his face, making sure to note as much of his intentions by his surroundings as possible. He hadn't bothered to wear anything particularly special, which made my heart sink because it meant that he intended to waste very little time this evening. The room beyond was dimly lit and had a sensual smell to it that I'd never known a man who lived alone to be capable of manufacturing—not that I had been in many such dwellings.

"Hello," he said, smiling slowly and deliberately taking half a step back from me. "You're a little earlier than I expected. Come in."

"Thanks," I said pleasantly, moving carefully past him and into his apartment, swerving ever so slightly to prevent his free hand from making contact with my waist. Whatever happened tonight, I would only make it easy for him after making sure playing it hard wouldn't work.

He closed the door softly and turned to face me, raking me with his greedy eyes. I let him do it, knowing it was part of the ritual. He couldn't help himself, in any case, and I'd made sure to make the most of it when planning my attire for the evening. As though reading my mind, he said, "You do look nice tonight. As always, of course."

"Thanks," I repeated, wondering briefly if I should return the compliment, then deciding not to. He hadn't gone to any particular effort, after all. He was smooth talking, but that didn't mean I had to smooth talk. I would need a different kind of persuasiveness this evening, one I'd fortunately become practised at over the last few months.

Realising that I wasn't going to compliment him on his appearance and reacting before I could become awkward, he moved swiftly forward and hugged me, allowing his hands to roam wherever they so desired. This time I had to return the gesture and did so graciously enough. When he drew back from me, though not letting go entirely, he said, "Would you like anything to drink?"

"No thanks," I said, staring around over his shoulders and head, my eyes falling on the couch and fixing there, hoping he would invite me to sit down.

"You sure?" he asked. "I'm about to have one. Would you like to sit down?"

Poor, predictable young man, I thought, amused.

"That would be nice, thanks," I said in a tone I hoped sounded sweet to his ears, letting go of him and allowing him to lead me to the couch. "How was your day?"

"Busy," he replied, and I saw that whatever he had in mind for this evening, he did look pretty tired, and I had a feeling that whatever he said, some of it was due to nervousness as well as his work being busy. "The place has been a bit of a mess ever since—well, you know."

I did know. He was a secretary in the government, and the governments in this country, my own country, and several others had been thrown into turmoil a little over two weeks earlier when their leaders had been assassinated by the Hammerhearts. The prime ministers/presidents of some of the countries in the hostile takeover attempt had survived and were now more heavily protected than ever before, but so many had been unlucky. I nodded to show my understanding.

"Never mind that," he said, sitting down beside me and smiling again. "Work's dull. I'd rather not think about that just now. How was your day? Get much done?"

"A bit," I said vaguely, wanting him to think my vagueness was due to him putting his arm around me and not the fact that I hadn't done anything of the sort that day. I'd told him that I was an international exchange student, due to return home in June—although in reality I would be long gone by then. "It's a bit hard to study now, with everything going on. I'm—I'm worried about my—my family."

I didn't have to lie about that last bit. As it was, I had lost a family member less than two weeks earlier, and the others were all in constant danger back home. I was almost grateful for the embrace he gave me at that point, whatever I otherwise felt about him.

"I'd be worried about mine too," he said quietly. "Try not to think about it. It's easy to get depressed getting caught up in things you can't control. Are you sure you wouldn't like a drink?"

"I'd better not," I said. "I mightn't know when to stop, and I've got classes tomorrow."

He nodded. "Good point, that. I turned up hungover at school once a couple of years ago and it was one hellish day. Just make yourself comfortable. I'll be back in a bit."

He stood up and walked into the next room. I leaned back and listened to his footsteps moving around, thinking about the war and most particularly the events of the last two months. The whole war had been eventful enough, right from the start, but there had been a period where the Woodwards and Hammersons had been moving stealthily around each other, not giving anything away. There had been a few deaths in that time, like David Rockson and Craig Hardy, both killed while following orders from Mr. Woodward to attack the Hammerheart Highway (the international link between all the Hammerheart bases and homes around the world). Liam Stammerus had been in the same attack, and although he had escaped, he had not been the same since. Justin Time, who had briefly spied for us, had been killed when his cover had been blown, most likely by an opposition spy. Javelyn Richardson, a year-twelve student who'd been with us since the school battle and wasn't widely known in either circle, had taken over the spy role and had managed it for a whole month before she had been discovered and killed while attempting to escape the Hammerheart Highway. And Nicole, whose death had been the worst of all, at the same time as Javelyn's but much closer to where I had been at the time.

I started as he sat back down on the couch beside me, leaning forward and putting his drink on the table in front of us.

"Don't think about it," he said gently. "Whatever it is, don't think about it."

"I'm trying not to," I said, still vaguely. "What about you, though? Aren't you worried for yourself?"

"A little," he said. "If things get out of hand, then I'll go into hiding. I've been told to stay put for the time being, though, so I'm staying put. In any case, the Hammersons gave up looking for me ten years ago. Probably they don't know I'm part of my family."

His tone on the last word sounded extremely doubtful, and I couldn't be sure if it was because the Hammersons had long since killed almost everyone else in his family or because he was starting to doubt his position. The latter suddenly became so much more likely because he added, "A lot of people have been interested in me lately, though, like that bitch Lindsay, and did I tell you what happened to me a few weeks ago?"

"Not April the tenth, I assume?" I enquired, because that was the only thing he'd mentioned had happened to him a few weeks ago, and he'd mentioned that several times.

"About a week before that," he said. "I had five people knock on that door there, two of them very attractive young ladies—a little too young for me but still attractive enough for me to be interested. Would you believe it, they were Amelia Woodward and Natalie Fletcher. Sorcerers, come all the way across the world just to talk to me. That's how it seemed, anyway. I wanted them gone as soon as I worked out who they were, and the three boys with them; they looked a little dodgy too, even if they were teenagers—kids, really. That had me worried, though. If they're interested in me, and they can find me, then maybe the Hammersons can too. Like I said, though, I've been told to stay put."

"You just listen to that?" I enquired. "Even if it goes against your own judgement?"

"Never led me wrong before," he said, shrugging.

"What did they want?" I asked. "The Sorcerers. Did they say?"

"They wanted to find my grandfather." He scowled. "At least I'm pretty damn sure that's what they were after. Screw them. No one finds him except those he wants to find him. I might have given them too much to be going on with, though, because I let slip about my life assistant before I knew who they were. In hindsight, I wouldn't be surprised if they sent that Lindsay over here to try to get it off me. And here was me, stupid enough to let her use it."

"You let her use it?" I asked, my heart skipping a beat. Did that mean he might let me use it? I preferred to examine that gleam of hope than the lurch my stomach had taken at the mention of Natalie and Amelia, for I had received alarming news of those two that very morning.

"Just once," he said grudgingly. "She never told me what it told her either, except that once she'd tried it, she had no interest in me anymore. She gave good head, but otherwise she was too damn frigid for my liking. I don't wanna think about her, though. You're much more interesting."

"How do you use it?" I asked casually. "Could you show me?"

He hesitated long enough to make me wonder if I'd made him suspicious. "You won't give up on me once you have, will you?"

I shrugged and said, casually I hoped, "Or not, if it'll make you feel better. It's up to you."

He hesitated a moment longer, then stood up. Jackpot, I thought. If he brought it out here, I wouldn't have to give him anything after all. The only thing that had prevented me from just knocking him out and getting it myself was that I had no idea what to look for, but if he showed it to me, I would have no reason to hold back. He disappeared into his bedroom and returned less than a minute later holding—what? Whatever it was, it was very small. I couldn't see it at all in his fist, in fact.

"You're only the second person I've ever shown this to," he said, plonking himself back down on the seat beside me, "so I hope you understand what it means."

"Don't worry, I won't be like her," I lied smoothly, knowing what he was getting at. "I'm just curious. It's obviously something that means a lot to you, and you know, if there's anything for us, we should share in these kinds of things."

He looked mollified by this. "Hang on, let me just make sure he's there before I show you."

Now was the moment, I knew. I put my hand in my pocket and closed my fingers around the smooth surface of the invisible crystal that lay there. Knock him out for ten minutes, I thought, and the man beside me slumped back in his seat, out like a light. Something toppled from his slackened grip and fell to the floor. I leaned forward and scooped it up. It was about the size of my hand—a small, flat, rectangular object, completely plain except for a fingertip-sized pad of felt in the very centre of it. I pocketed it and made my quick escape, immeasurably thankful that I'd got through that episode without needing to take my clothes off.

Part 1: Recount

Chapter 1: The Crash

I could go anywhere I wanted. After all, the Sien-Leoard Crystal was the key to opening many things, not least those things that keys normally open—doors. The doors around the Woodward base weren't normal doors, but I could still force them open with a bit of magic. It was particularly useful on the morning of April 28 because I needed to enter an area to which my standard electronic key did not allow me access. If I could find a Sorcerer, then there would be no problem, but none of them seemed to be around, except, of course, within their living quarters. So, ignoring the breakfast goers as they tried to waylay me, I descended from the second-floor room I had been using for my now completed mission and headed for the rooms at the very back of the base.

Inside the Woodward living quarters, unlike the rest of the base, breakfast seemed to be winding down. That was a relief because I would have felt rather odd interrupting them while they were eating. I had distracted Amelia several times while she had been eating, but as I had been told several hours earlier, Amelia wasn't here, and Mr. Woodward was a different kettle of fish. The three of them—Mr. Woodward, his wife, and his mother—were in their dining room when I entered.

"Knock, knock," I called as I tapped on the wall beside the open door.

"Ah, good morning, John," said Mr. Woodward, looking around and smiling when he saw me. "I wasn't expecting to see you again 'til the end of the week. Did it go all right?"

"Not bad," I replied. "Did you still want to talk about it?"

"Yes, I would," he said, "unless you'd rather do it another time."

Part of me did. I was extremely tired at the moment, but I weighed up the situation and realised that if things kept going the way I expected them to, Mr. Woodward wouldn't have a lot of time later to talk about anything.

"Now's fine," I told him, "and I wanna know what's been happening around here, too. Marc said something about—"

"I know what Marc most likely said," said Mr. Woodward, his eyes widening slightly. "Can you wait for me in my office, John? I shouldn't be more than five minutes."

"Sure," I said, and I retreated back out of the room and headed for his office, feeling jumpy for some reason.

Once in there, I sat down in front of Mr. Woodward's desk and considered what I was about to go through. Since the last night of February, I had been working mostly independently of the Woodward army, asking advice of Mr. Woodward occasionally but mostly keeping the knowledge of what I was doing with those within the trusted circle—Amelia, Marc, Tommy, Natalie, Peter, James, and Nicole. Now that the job was done (or at least the first phase of it), Mr. Woodward wanted to be brought up to speed. He would continue to let us do our own thing, of course, as he always seemed to do, but considering what we were doing was quite likely as important as what he and his army were doing, he wanted to at least be aware of what was going on.

The main objective of what we had been doing was to work out why Arnold Hammerson wanted me dead, so that we could then work out the best way to keep me alive. Those who cared about me were obviously interested in helping out, and given that my life seemed so important to Hammerson, the Woodwards were happy enough to let me continue the investigation. After working out that a man called Rafael Smiley was the missing link between my real parents, the Woodwards, and my adoptive parents, we had decided to put our efforts into tracking Smiley down. We knew he was an old family friend of the Woodwards, and we also knew that he had been Tommy's Maahoo teacher. With those things to go on, Marc, Tommy, and I had decided to question Mr. Woodward on the afternoon of March 6 about everything he knew about his old friend.

Maybe we could have done it earlier than that, only the first week of March hadn't exactly been uneventful. We had been back at school, back amongst Hammerhearts such as Hall, Hignat, and Wilwog, and getting homework all over again. School hadn't been exactly the same, though. With such a large portion of the school staff having been killed in the school battle the previous week, they had been forced to call up all substitute teachers, as well as people who weren't exactly qualified to be teachers. Most were from Chopville but quite a few were from other smaller towns in the electorate. For me personally, the week had been eventful for other reasons as well. Tuesday had been the funeral day for those from the Woodward army killed in the school battle, and having to attend three of those funerals back-to-back had been a bit of an emotional strain on everyone. What had been worse for me was that nothing at all had been done for Tulip, as far as I knew anyway, and once I had become aware of a way to honour her myself, on the Thursday after school, I had used the Sien-Leoard Crystal to construct a monument in her memory in the main hall of the living quarters, directly opposite the lounge room.

One other thing that had been jerked around a bit that week was my love life. It had been a bit of a fiasco, a kind of soap opera for those who were aware of what was going on for several weeks prior to the first week of March. Admittedly, most of the trouble was caused by me being unable to work out which girl I wanted to be with. Natalie, Serena, Lena, and, up until that point, Stella all had a piece of my interest. Natalie was the one I really wanted, but at that stage, she had been dating Tommy, and when it looked like they would last, even though I had resisted at first, I had opened to the idea of dating one of the others instead.

Natalie and Tommy had had issues the previous week where Tommy had cheated on her with her sister, Rebecca, but their relationship had somehow survived it once Natalie had become aware of the fact—not that she had been particularly happy in the relationship (I knew part of that was due to her wanting me). They hadn't survived the second cheat, however. Rebecca, furious that Tommy had got so easily off the hook, had orchestrated the demise of the relationship by getting one of her year-eight friends to seduce him, and then she had brought Natalie to the room in question (accidentally it had appeared, although we all knew better) so she could see them kissing for herself. That had been on Friday, and she had dumped him on the spot.

That would have been good for me, if it hadn't been for one thing: Due to circumstances that had been partially in my control and partially not, I had found myself with another girl on Monday night, and this was more personal than my three-day fling with Tulip. It had been after dinner, and I had been feeling bored and introverted. The few people I had felt comfortable being around were off doing other things—spending time with their partners, mostly. There had been people in the lounge room (I could hear the twins in there as I had stood just outside the dining room), but it was still so soon after the events that had caused Tulip's death and I hadn't quite come back to myself yet. I had been thinking that maybe I would go upstairs, do a bit of homework that I had been given that day, most of it from Mrs. Worlker (I had no real connection with her but the idea that she was still alive had given me an enormous feeling of giddy relief), and use the Sien-Leoard Crystal to cheat myself out of depression if it threatened to take hold of me that evening. I had been just about to set off for the stairs when a voice spoke to me from inside the dining room.

"John? What are you doing?"

I had started and looked around. It was Serena, weaving her way between the tables towards me. She had been one of the last to finish dinner, I knew, because she had been one of the last to start it. Though why she had been late, I didn't know.

"I don't know," I had said truthfully. "Can't decide what I wanna do."

"Ah," she had said, stopping beside me and cocking her head slightly, apparently listening to the chatter issuing from the lounge room. She had looked a little awkward, most likely because she was still unsure how I was coping after the events of two nights previous. It hadn't helped me much, but it was better than what she had been like before my most recent encounter with the Hammersons—very flirtatious, always trying to get me on my own. I had to keep reminding myself that I may not have been the only person seriously impacted by this war. Serena hadn't given any signs of being too badly affected so far, except for the day of Daniel's funeral when she had been unusually quiet. I had reminded myself of this fact then and somehow felt an inexplicable upsurge of affection for the girl beside me.

"What about you?" I had asked. "What were you going to do?"

She had shrugged, glancing sideways at me. I wished she hadn't. "I'm not sure either. Homework, maybe."

"That's what I was thinking," I had said gloomily. The prospect of sitting upstairs, alone, History homework before me, was not very inviting at all. In fact, since Serena had joined me, that had become even less inviting than walking straight into the lounge room and engaging in verbal banter with Harry and Simon.

She had looked at me then, and at that moment she had looked exactly as she had the very first time I had laid eyes on her on our first day of school this year—awkward, confused, and nervous. It hadn't taken long for her to gain her footing in Chopville when she had arrived a month earlier, so seeing her like that again had come as something of a shock. That new feeling of affection had intensified, and I found myself resisting an urge—not a powerful one as yet but an urge all the same—to reach out and put my arm around her.

"You wanna—I dunno—hang out for a bit?" she had asked, offering me a slightly strained smile.

I had hesitated for only a fraction of a second, and only because it had become instinct for me to do so. However much Serena had bugged me before, however nervous she sometimes made me, hers was the kind of company I needed at that stage. All the things that had happened to me in recent days had combined to form a feeling of terrible loneliness, not at all helped by the fact that those I would have liked to be with were nowhere to be found, quite likely enjoying the sort of company I would have liked from Natalie. But Natalie was out of the question. She and Tommy seemed to have defied the odds, and now here was Serena, apparently wanting something similar to what I wanted.

"Yeah, why not," I had said, and once the words were out, I felt amazingly cheerful. "I didn't really wanna go in there, anyway." I had jerked my thumb at the lounge room as we walked past it.

"They're good," she had said a little vaguely, and when I looked at her questioningly, she went on, "Harry and Simon—I have no idea how they can stay so upbeat with everything going on. It's not what we need now, maybe, but I think, sometimes, if we're a little down, sitting with those two for a while would make us forget about all the bad stuff."

"I guess so," I had said, thinking that she was probably right. "Er, where are we going, anyway?"

"One of our rooms, I guess," she had said. We had already climbed one flight of stairs. "Doesn't make much difference. They're right next to each other."

We had ended up going to my room. It hadn't been a conscious decision of either of ours; we had just walked straight past Serena's door without stopping, without thinking. And so we had hung out in my room for most of the night. Nobody would have believed that not much really happened, at least at first. Not being alone, the two of us had found it a little easier to settle to our history homework and had worked through it together, as I had often done in the past with Peter and James. We hadn't finished it all but we had done enough. Certainly that put me ahead of the boys, and with the funerals the following day, I knew better than to expect I'd get a lot of work done. After that, we had sat together on the couches where I had sat with Stella only days earlier, and there, we had talked.

"I thought I heard someone say that you were using magic to block your dreams," she had said. "Is that true? I suppose it'd make sense after last week. I keep dreaming I'm back in that horrible Basement."

"I'm not," I had replied. "I thought about it, obviously, and I did do that on Saturday night, but I'm not going to anymore."

"Why not?"

"I'd rather not say," I had said regretfully. "I've got reasons, though."

And I had, for I hadn't had a single venture into Stella's mind since before her magic had been snatched by Natalie, or whichever Fletcher now had her crystal chip. Hammerson had believed that our connection still existed, magic or no magic, but I had been starting to become unsure. If it was true that our connection could keep me safe from Hammerson as long as it existed, then I dearly hoped it still worked, and that there was a good reason why I could no longer see into her mind but that it would reassert itself in the days to come. I had intended to use it to spy, now that I was starting to come to accept that Stella had betrayed us in some way, but for now I would just be happy enough to receive some sort of reassurance that the connection still worked. This had been days before Justin's appointment as spy, so I had no way of knowing that the cover Stella had worked for a week earlier had been blown.

"Right," Serena had said, looking confused. I didn't blame her, and part of me wanted to tell her, but I had felt that, at that stage, the knowledge of my connection with Stella ought to be kept in a very tight circle. "Well, I would, if I were you. All the stuff you went through last week can't be good for you."

There it was—careful flattery all over again, except this time it had been more like Tulip's style than the stuff Serena normally came out with. She was sitting very close to me, not quite as Stella had done—or what I had done, rather—but close enough that I could feel a certain intimacy between us, so that I could have turned and put my arms around her at any moment, and I had to wonder if she could feel it too.

"I could probably help you out, if you like," I had said, feeling rather more nervous than the conversation warranted and unsure exactly what I ought to say. "If you don't wanna have nightmares about the Basement, I mean."

"Really? How?" she had asked. She was looking at me now, and I could tell by her soft smile and the twinkle in her eyes that she had narrowly avoided adding words to the effect of 'by giving me more pleasant things to dream about?'

"Well, I've got the crystal," I had reminded her. "So I could probably use that to make you sleep dreamlessly—*probably*," I had added. "I've never tried it before, though."

"Could you make me have good dreams?" she had asked, and I wasn't sure if she meant by way of the crystal or by other means.

"Maybe," I had said, shrugging. "Not sure though. That might be a little more difficult."

"Oh, I don't imagine it would be that difficult," she had said, and her meaning became perfectly clear a moment later when she put her arms around me and kissed me firmly on the lips.

And so it had happened, just like that. The following three or four hours had passed in similar fashion to the nights I had spent with Tulip the previous week, except that we hadn't gone quite as far, not on the first night anyway (that time had come three weeks later), and the talk that had happened had been completely unrelated to the war. I hadn't been stupid enough to tell her of exactly how I had struggled with my love life the previous week, for that would surely make her jealous, but the newly found affection I had found for Serena meant that I hadn't needed to pretend to care for her as she cared for me. I had felt a small pang for Natalie, thinking that I had just made my chances of being with her any time soon slightly more remote, but I had also felt happier. I no longer had to be alone while watching her with Tommy, as well as the rest of my friends with partners. Also, and perhaps more importantly, I cared enough for Serena that I didn't feel like I was merely using her for my own ends. It wasn't the most moral of reasons for being in a relationship, I knew, but I was beginning to think that it didn't really matter. I didn't need to find my life partner at fourteen, but I didn't need to be lonely any longer neither.

It should have simplified things, being with Serena, but it hadn't. As well as Natalie becoming available only days later, making me feel that I could have gotten exactly what I wanted if I had only waited a little longer, a new player entered the game later that week. Thursday afternoon, when I had returned to the Woodward base after school, I had set to work using the Sien-Leoard Crystal to construct a memorial for Tulip. This kind of creativity wasn't normally one of my strong suits, but I had given it thought and had eventually decided on a larger-than-life model of a pendent, the same as the one Tulip had worn in her final days—I had become familiar with it when I had been with her. I had completed it and was standing several feet back admiring my work, holding back tears—I didn't want to cry for her now—when Amelia spoke behind me. I hadn't even noticed her presence, yet I felt sure she had been there for at least five minutes.

"It looks really nice," she had said quietly. "I think she would have liked that."

I had started and looked around, feeling a little embarrassed and defensive. Amelia had seemed to notice, for she had taken half a step back from me when I turned, looking a little tense, and realising that had quickly brought me to my senses.

"Thanks," I had said. "I—I wasn't really sure what to do."

She had smiled and moved slightly forward again, staring intently at me. I had stared back at her, feeling an uneasy mix of emotions. I had only really known Amelia personally since the second week of term, when we had worked together to wrest the

Sorcerous Crystals from Moran, but our friendship had grown steadily stronger in the four weeks since. In fact, I had considered Amelia one of my best friends, and certainly my best female friend (not counting Jessica or Felicity, who were like sisters) ever since we had depended on each other's support during the two days we had spent locked up in the Hammerheart Basement.

I had never considered her a potential girlfriend because there had always been too many others jostling for the position ,and because she had been into Marc that whole time and had been dating him officially since Stella's birthday party nearly two weeks earlier. The thought had crossed my mind then, though, simply because I had just stumbled over the realisation that I could cry now, in front of her, which was something I probably wouldn't be able to say for Serena, or any of the others—possibly even Natalie. Perhaps that realisation had been brought on by nothing more than the emotions I had been feeling right before she had announced her presence. Either way, I had to push the thoughts away. They would not do while she was with Marc and I was with Serena.

"Are you gonna be okay?" she had asked gently.

I had shrugged and managed a smile. "I usually end up being okay."

She had covered the remaining two feet between us and given me a hug, which I had returned, feeling enormously grateful. There still had been tears behind my eyes, and I thought that if Amelia continued being supportive, I probably wouldn't be able to hold them back. I could have handled her, but it was such an open area and not one I wanted a moment like this in. The lounge room and dining room had both appeared empty. Most people must have been up in their rooms, or perhaps in the Library, but that didn't mean I wouldn't be seen by someone other than Amelia. I had been lucky, though. As we had let go and been about to stare at each other again, at much closer range this time, Amelia's watch had beeped, announcing the presence of someone outside the base, and she had to hurry away to let whoever it was in. I had lingered a moment longer, admiring the monument a little more, before hurrying up to my room just in time; the dam had broken just as I shut the door, and I had thrown myself down on my bed, thinking of Tulip, and Natalie, and Stella, and Amelia, and feeling guilty for not having emotion to spare for Serena, the one I should have been thinking about.

Yet knowing that fact hadn't changed the way I felt. Amelia seemed to have taken up residence inside my head just as Natalie had done for many periods throughout my life. The following day at school, my thoughts had only drifted from her twice. Firstly, an episode had taken place during period three English between the Young Army members and the three Hammerhearts in there. It had been settled by Stephanie and Cassandra, two students who had bugger all to do with the war, who had reminded us that we were students and Hall was our teacher, and reminded Hall that he was our teacher and should therefore act responsibly. I had been invisible during the drama, as had Peter, James, and Erica, but all four of us had been close to launching our own attacks on Hignat and Wilwog, those two not-so-secret agents of the Hammersons, anyway. Then, in the evening, Nicole had told me what had happened earlier between Natalie, Rebecca, Tommy, and the other girl—that had taken my mind off Amelia for a good ten minutes. To top the day off, I had dreamt of Amelia that night, a dream I had needed to clean up after. It had made me feel both guilty and depressed because I knew I could neither stop myself from thinking those thoughts nor do anything about them.

There hadn't been any deaths within the Woodward circle in that first week, which was something to be thankful for, particularly after we had lost seven of our people in the school battle, but there were enough deaths the following week to make up for it good and proper, starting with David and Craig on the night of March 8. It must have been a terrible place to die, trapped in the darkness and not knowing where any of the tunnels were, knowing there were Hammerhearts around and not being able to see them, the constant danger of the Hammerheart carts (which travelled at superbly ridiculous speeds) tearing through them—although, in hindsight, I felt sure the carts would have been programmed to stay away from that area so as not to kill any Hammerhearts.

Liam had recounted the story only once, and once had been enough. I had been one of the lucky ones to have been present when Mr. Woodward made Liam tell him what had happened, the proof of the pudding coming the following morning when the two burnt and mutilated bodies were deposited unceremoniously on the Woodwards' front lawn. They were the first Young Army members to be killed since Lisa (less than two weeks later), and the way it had happened was more terrible than anyone could have predicted.

As always seemed to happen around the Woodward base, word of the three boys' job had got around smartly so that they had been given a rousing reception before they had left, which in this case was straight after dinner. Most times something like that had happened, nobody seriously expected that it would be the last time they saw them, but this was just nine days after the death of Tulip, and since then, the general view of the war around the base had become much more tentative.

Most people had gone off and done their own things (most people who had joined since the school battle had been given chances to go out and get more things since) but I was one of those to remain in the lounge room. Natalie had been the only Sorcerer present. As the day had been March 8, it was Amelia's sixteenth birthday, and the Woodwards had been in their living quarters having a small dinner for her. In fact, by the time Liam had returned, there had been only six of us in there.

The topic of conversation in the lounge room had been mostly about the events that had taken place over the last week: the reopening of Chopville High on the first; the various funerals that had taken place over the first few days of the week (Lisa's had been on the Tuesday); the return of Mr. Hall and several other Hammerhearts (including Hignat and Wilwog) to school on Wednesday; the altercation that had taken place between Hall, Hignat, Wilwog, and the year-nine Young Army members in English on Friday; the attack that the two Fletcher sisters had almost successfully launched on Candice Young, the girl who had killed Lisa and almost killed Tommy; Mr. Woodward's most unpopular request that Young Army members not attack Hammerhearts at school—it was not the right time apparently; and, the biggest news of all, the appointment of Justin Time as a spy against the Hammersons, and the news he had brought back earlier that day— that Stella had been killed because Hammerson and Tankom had discovered the truth of how she had not killed Peter, James and Erica.

The three Fletcher Sorcerers had been given several special privileges by the Woodwards a week earlier, including their own private living quarters opposite the Woodward living quarters (in which those Fletchers who weren't Sorcerers also had the honour of inhabiting) and, more importantly in this situation, full access rights to all areas of the Woodward base, including in and out of it. Natalie's watch had beeped around eleven o'clock, announcing the presence of someone in the study. She had returned in a few minutes, followed by Liam but not by David and Craig. Liam hadn't said a word to anyone, not even Natalie, but had slumped down in a seat in the lounge room and curled up in a ball, trembling. He looked pale, sore, and, for no reason I could think of, dripping wet. I had been glad that not many people were present at that moment; he had looked extremely pathetic. Natalie hadn't said a word either but had left us again and returned minutes later, followed by Mr. Woodward.

And so the storytelling had begun. It had taken ten minutes for Mr. Woodward to get Liam to say anything about what had happened, in which time Liam had looked around at the rest of us several times in annoyance, as though trying to tell us without words to get out of the way. I had stayed where I was, mostly because it was the lounge room and a public place. Mr. Woodward could have taken Liam anywhere if he had really wanted privacy. Eventually, though, Liam had sat up straighter in his seat and told us what had happened in the Hammerheart Highway.

Marc had seen the three of them on their way with specially designed one-man aircraft, designed to shrink and become invisible at the push of two buttons and with functions specifically designed to block up the tracks used by the Hammerheart carts. He had also given them instructions to enter the Highway via his house. Getting into the tunnel had been easy, and they had managed to create a barrier that would stall any Hammerheart carts that used the tunnel off which the Moran house branched, but then the trouble had begun. Apparently the Hammerhearts had been tipped off that three boys were launching an assault on the tunnel, for they poured into the tunnel the three boys were working in from both ends, guns and normalisers at the ready.

Liam had understood very little of how the Hammerhearts had coordinated the situation, but by his description, I had gathered that they had shrunk themselves as the boys had done, though not quite to the same extent, and unlike the boys they had come in on foot. None of the boys could see the Hammerhearts, but they could hear their shots and see the flashes the guns and normalisers cast. It was enough to tell them they were in big trouble. On top of everything else, Liam collided with one of the other boys, and the impact caused all three of them to lose their bearings. From that point on, it was confusion and mayhem.

Under the circumstances, Liam had coped rather well. He had deduced extremely quickly that the only way to reorientate himself was to simply fly, and if he hit a wall, then he was flying the wrong way. He had also known that he had to get down low, because the Hammerhearts had all been aiming upwards, but at the same time not hit any of them or any of their normalising magic on his way down. He couldn't have turned his headlights on because he would have given his position away. For all the good Marc had done, he'd forgotten to give the aircraft any weapons to use against the Hammerhearts. It had been a simple but monumental mistake.

The first hint Liam had of any of his friends' fates was when one of them was hit by a normaliser, and the expanding aircraft (which he had seen all too clearly, though not which person had been in it) had almost knocked him out of the air. Within seconds, the aircraft had been a fire ball, and although it had taken one of the boys' lives, it had given a lease on life to Liam, who could now see the tunnel perfectly clearly before him. Hammerhearts had been lined up all along the tunnel, guns and normalisers in the air (though Liam hadn't known exactly what the devices were at the time), shooting side to side.

Then the other aircraft had been shot down, this time by a bullet. Nobody had seen it, but Liam had seen the explosion out of nothing that could only have meant one thing. The Hammerhearts had seemed not to notice anything, and because no normalisers had hit it on its way down, it was quite likely never discovered, or at least not until much later when they had cleaned up. Liam had only had one option at that point—flee—which he had done, swerving and tumbling all over the place in his attempts to get into a safer tunnel, all the while heading into more uninviting darkness.

There had been Hammerhearts around, of course. Liam could both hear and see the fire of the guns shooting around him, but he hadn't seen them again nor had any other contact with them. Instead he had flown wildly through the tunnels, hitting the walls and even the roof at one point, trying desperately to find a way out. There had been periods of quietness, and then he would hear shooting ahead or off to one side, and he would turn in the other direction—anything to avoid the enemies. He had been forced to fly through the fire eventually, though, because he had seen Hammerhearts lined up along a tunnel with a station in it similar to the one at the Moran house. He had been in the Hammerheart Highway for hours by then and had become deliriously desperate for any means of escape, even something as suicidal as what he'd been forced to do.

In order to pull off such a dangerous stunt, Liam had done the smartest thing possible, which, if it had been me, I would never even have considered as a possible option. He had flown low, very low along the floor of the tunnel, straight down the middle of it between the two rows of Hammerhearts. When he had reached the escape, he had turned and flown straight through a pack of shooting Hammerhearts. The aircraft had been damaged, but by some miracle, it hadn't been normalised, and he was able to keep flying, even though he had given his position away and the Hammerhearts behind him were attempting to give chase. He had been faster than them and managed to get the aircraft out of the house of the unsuspecting Hammerheart before the aircraft had finally given up its ghost and plummeted to the ground.

Liam's work in the descent had been lifesaving in several ways. In the weeks that had followed, many people expressed the belief that he should become a pilot when he was older. The descent hadn't been very far, but given his shrunken size, it had been far enough for the aircraft. He had managed to make an emergency landing on the street nearest the address of the house he had come out of, but he had needed to become his normal size before the crash so that he would be able to get back to the Woodward base. The aircraft had eventually smashed through the steel rail at the end of the street and dropped, now falling to pieces, into the Jade River, at which point Liam had swam back to shore before making his way back to base.

Footsteps in the corridor dragged me back to the present, and a moment later, Mr. Woodward entered his office. He looked tired. The only time I'd ever seen someone look that tired was the first night of camp Rock Haulter, when Stella had admitted to using magic to keep herself awake, and I wondered if Mr. Woodward was now employing the same technique. He also looked stressed and worried, and given what was going on—what had happened the previous day—I couldn't blame him. Natalie and Amelia—two of the people I cared most about in the world, for my feelings towards both hadn't changed since that first week of March—where were they? What had happened to them?

"Let's see if we can get through this quickly, hey?" he said, managing a small smile. Mr. Woodward had always smiled in the early days of the war, except in the aftermath of a death of course, but these days he hardly ever managed it.

"How much do you need to know?" I asked him. "You know how it started? That day when me, Marc, and Tommy asked about Smiley."

That day had been warm—probably the last really warm day we would have that summer. It was the sort of weather in which we would normally spend the day in the park, jumping repeatedly off the foot bridges into the river, and indeed that was no doubt what a lot of people were doing that day. Not us, though. It was too dangerous for us to be seen in the park in broad daylight. We had therefore been forced to remain inside the Woodward headquarters, where you wouldn't have had the slightest inkling that it was a nice day outside, as no heat penetrated the place except for that which it created for itself.

Very little had been done that week in follow up of the meeting that had taken place on Sunday night, except for scattered conversations between two or three of us at a time. Through the disorganisation, we managed to schedule a meeting with Mr.

Woodward, which Marc, Tommy, and I would be sitting. It perhaps should have been me, Tommy, and Amelia, but Amelia had been having a birthday party that evening, which turned out to be similar to Stella's, only a bit smaller (her actual birthday was two days later), and she had been helping set it up, so Marc had taken her place. The purpose of the meeting was quite simply to ask Mr. Woodward anything he could tell us about Smiley that might help us locate him.

"You remember what you told me the other night?" I had said to Mr. Woodward once the four of us had settled down in the Sorcerer's office in the early afternoon. "About how I ended up a Playman, I mean?"

"Ah, yes, I remember," he had said, raising his eyebrows. "You're wanting to know more about that? I was playing it straight with you, but if there's anything further I can—"

"I know you were," I had cut in quickly. "I'm not looking for more information about what happened. You said that you got me from Smiley and passed me onto the Playmans. What we want to know is can you tell us any way we could possibly get in touch with Smiley?"

Mr. Woodward had looked surprised for a moment before lapsing into contemplation. Finally, he said, "I've had many dealings with him in the past, but our contact over the last ten years or so has been negligible at best. He could be dead now, for all I know. He would be getting on in years."

"We know he's alive," Tommy had told him. "Or at least he was as recently as a few weeks ago. He's my Maahoo teacher, see, but I haven't had any lessons lately."

Again, that moment of surprise, but only a moment. Mr. Woodward had nodded slowly. "He has been in great danger for a long time, so he always keeps contact on his terms."

"It's a little off-topic, maybe," Marc had said, "but why is he in danger? We sort of know why the Hammersons want us three, but according to Amelia, he's right up there with us—H1 to us being H2, H3, and H4. What did he do to get on their wanted list?"

"Several things, really," Mr. Woodward had said. "He certainly made a name for himself during the war. I suppose he was to my mother what Hank Cornish has become to Arnold Hammerson: not much of a fighter, but a great deputy—very loyal, great at managing other people, and full of ideas. It's only really been since the war that he's feared for his life, since—well, since he gave you to us, John, but there was also an incident about thirteen years ago. They hadn't been targeting him at the time, but they had almost caused his death, and it was his survival that day that made him what he has since become."

"When you say that," Tommy had said slowly, "are you referring to the danger he is in? Or do you mean his—how do I put it—"

"Both," he had said, smiling.

"What was this incident?" Marc had asked. "I mean, again I know it's off-topic, but we might as well find out as much as we can about him. It might help."

"I agree," Mr. Woodward had said, "although so much of it still remains a mystery. This is way back when we had been based in England. Two of our people had been in Germany, investigating a deal the Hammersons had done with a group of newly recruited German Hammerhearts, and they discovered something startling about Stella that we believed might have been related to you, John." The three of us had swapped significant looks that Mr. Woodward had appeared to miss. "But we never found out what it was because one of the Hammersons—I believe it to be Tankom, although I have no proof of that—used magic to bring down the plane that they had been aboard. Smiley hadn't been the target, as I said, but he had been on the plane, and he was one of only three survivors. I believe, and so does he, that it had been something in the impact—some loose magic floating around—that gave him the—er—special abilities he's had ever since."

"What special abilities?" Marc and I had asked almost in unison.

Tommy had laughed. "He would never tell me, but like I said, he always knows what's going on and when to turn up. I'll bet playing the Maahoo was one thing that came from it, though. That's not something just anyone can do."

"Quite right," Mr. Woodward had agreed.

"The two who they'd gone for," I had said, startled, for a curious connection had formed in my mind, "were they who I think they were?"

He had looked carefully at me for a few seconds before smiling. "I think so. They were the parents of your friends, Harry and Simon. If that's what you were thinking, then you would be correct."

"Blimey," Marc had muttered under his breath.

I had been dwelling on this as he spoke, but my attention had been caught at that point by the look on Tommy's face. "You okay?" I had asked.

"Three survivors," he had said slowly. "Three survivors. Er, what happened to the other two? Did they get any special abilities from the crash?"

"Don't know for certain," Mr. Woodward had said, smiling significantly at him, "but I suspect so. They had both been infants. Smiley had taken one of them with him because his parents had never been identified, either in the wreckage or in Germany or England, but that child had been abducted here in Australia only weeks later."

Tommy had still looked distant, and now I understood the theory that was forming in his mind, and my mouth fell open. "You reckon it was you? Both of them were you?"

"Blimey!" Marc had said again, this time looking really astounded.

Mr. Woodward had nodded slowly again. "I suspect it may have been you, Tommy. Your biological parents were identified in the wreckage—or at least the biological parents of the German you were —so you were sent back to Germany. Smiley had taken the other you —this you, which had no doubt been created in the impact—and had intended to hand you over to me to find a home for you the same as John, but you went missing before it could happen. We never found out what happened in the weeks between Smiley losing you and you turning up in Sydney, but we suspect Hammerhearts to have been involved and then to have stuffed it up somehow. That makes it sound certain, but we have never been completely sure that it was you because no DNA tests had been performed on the infants since just after the crash. And, of course, the authorities in Germany never considered that your two bodies could be related because of the obvious physical differences."

"Didn't you say once that you had DNA tests?" I had asked Tommy. "When you got your two bodies together, they did DNA tests to work out that you were the same person?"

"I dunno," Tommy had said. "I was really young at the time. It worked, though. That's how we worked out I was switching bodies in my sleep."

"Again, we don't know for sure," Mr. Woodward had insisted, "but it's enough to suspect. It certainly makes sense."

"And that's why you think it was Tankom more than Hammerson?" Marc had said. "Because she's the one hunting Tommy now?"

"Yes, but that doesn't help us much," he had said, "for we still don't know exactly why she wants him. If it was as simple as it looks, she would just let him go. The only powers Tommy gained from it were the ability to play the Maahoo and his dual lives, and while the Maahoo is useful, it's not something Tankom would hunt for without telling her son. After all, they certainly make no secret of why they want you, Marc. Furthermore, I'm confused as to how they know who you are, Tommy, after all this time. They certainly had trouble tracking John down over all these years until recently. I can only assume that either you weren't in the crash, that your strangeness—for want of a better word—was caused by something else, or that something else happened to you in that crash that only Tankom knows about."

"Blimey," Tommy had said in a low voice. "Blimey. Well, I was told my biological parents died in that crash, but if you're right, then there's still a chance it wasn't really me. But you think it was?"

"Yes, I expect so."

Marc had checked his watch and said, "Okay, that's all very interesting, but it's not really what we came here for. About Smiley, have you got any ideas of how we can get in touch with him?"

Mr. Woodward had shaken his head. "He's always turned up when we've needed him, but if he doesn't turn up now, then there would be a good reason for it. One thing I do know is that after we came to Chopville, he preferred to stay back in England. That was where all his family was and where he felt most comfortable. All of his family has since been killed by the Hammerhearts, though, so I'm not sure if he would still be there now. I know that he moved away from his home when he learnt of the danger he was in, and that was more or less the last I heard from him."

"England?" Marc had repeated quietly. "Geez. How are we gonna get over there?"

"The crystals?" I had suggested.

"Second-floor rooms have back doors," Mr. Woodward had told us. "You can navigate the location where they will open. They all open here in Chopville by default, but you can move them to anywhere around the world. For security reasons, those doors aren't accessible by ordinary keys unless those keys are specifically reprogrammed, but if you decide it's necessary to go to England, then you will be able to use that feature."

"There's another way out of here?" Marc had enquired. "Without going through the wall? Maybe the Hammersons used that instead of the wall."

"We checked all that out already," Mr. Woodward had said, "when we strip-searched the place, and none of those doors had been used."

"Okay," I said. "Thanks for that. I guess we'll let you know if we need to use those doors to go to England, but I expect we'll do some poking around here first."

Chapter 2: Photograph

"Yes, I do recall that conversation," said Mr. Woodward, "and I don't need the whole story to know that you did eventually take my advice on board, but it took a while. What was your next move?"

I had to think about that for a moment. There really hadn't been a move straight after that conversation. The next thing I could remember was another meeting with all of them (Marc, Amelia, Tommy, Natalie, Peter, James, and Nicole) but that had been on the thirteenth, a whole week later. The week between those two meetings had been a noteworthy one, with David, Craig, and Justin all being killed by the Hammerhearts (David and Craig while attacking the Hammerheart Highway and Justin while spying); luckily for Justin (I think), his body hadn't been harmed much. Javelyn, a year-twelve girl who I'd brought into the Woodward army after the school battle, had been appointed as the main spy the day after Justin's death and had immediately reported a new plan of the Hammersons', to have another go at attacking Chopville High. The day before her appointment, however, I'd had a most curious dream indeed, which, in my mind, disproved the information that Justin had provided the Woodwards days earlier. I'd also had two other dreams that week; the recurring dream about me and Stella in the main hall on Rock Haulter—both times it had been just the two of us and both times I had got progressively closer and closer to her without being able to touch her—but I held these dreams in little regard. Granted, it was weird that it should keep coming back to me, but surely it meant nothing set next to the dreams in which I actually entered Stella's mind.

"Well, I guess it was that day Marc and I went back to his place and—" I cleared my throat; thinking about that day always caused me to lose some composure. "But—um—the eight of us had another meeting a week later, partly to talk about what you'd told us and partly about Stella."

"Ah, yes," said Mr. Woodward. "You still stand by your theory?"

"Absolutely," I said. Mr. Woodward knew what I thought because Amelia had told him several times. It wasn't surprising that he would doubt me, though, because Amelia (along with everyone else) thought I was either making it up or otherwise mistaken. I knew better, though; I could now tell the difference between normal dreams and those that weren't really dreams but forays into Stella's mind, and if that didn't convince anyone, surely the note I had laid hands on only days earlier would.

"Very well," he said. "We'll come back to that then. I take it that you decided, at this meeting, that it would be necessary for you to go down to Marc's house?"

"Yeah," I said. "I suppose, in hindsight, there wasn't much sense in it. Marc told us that his father had a bunch of filing cabinets in his bedroom, which we all believed because we'd seen them before, that he thought contained a lot of sensitive information about the Hammerhearts. He thought maybe we could raid it to see if there was anything about the crash in there, or anything about the Hammersons' hunt for Smiley after it."

Hindsight was such a wonderful and useless thing, I thought, and yet I wasn't so sure it had been the stupidest thing we'd done during our hunt for Smiley. I couldn't remember laying a finger on the Sien-Leoard Crystal at all during the meeting, but perhaps it (or some other magic) had urged us in that direction, not because we would find any useful info on Smiley there, but because there was something else of importance waiting to be discovered, something that would, in fact, give us part of the information we wanted to get from Smiley in the first place.

Like the only other meeting the eight of us (who I was starting to think of as the *real* Young Army as opposed to the other fifteen or so who really weren't contributing much anymore) had so far had, and like all those that would follow it, the location of the meeting on the thirteenth was the rear section of my bedroom in the Woodward base, which contained a circle of couches large enough to fit the eight of us quite comfortably. It had started off with some awkwardness, for it was the closest Natalie and Tommy had been to each other since she had dumped him eight days ago, but thanks mainly to Amelia, we had been able to push on past that stage.

"I'm expecting none of you found out anything particularly useful about him," she had said, focussing on me, Marc, and Tommy —easy to do, given that we were all sitting together.

"We sort of did," Marc had contradicted her. "We found out why the Hammersons want him so badly, and we found out that he's always been based in England, so your dad believes anyway, and we could use a second-floor room to go over there if we wanted to check it out."

"Didn't we already guess that much?" James had asked.

"Not about the room."

"I could have told you that, though," Amelia had said. "What did you find out about why the Hammersons want him?"

The three of us explained what we'd found out about the plane crash that Smiley and Tommy had both survived. Everyone had looked completely stunned to learn about Tommy, even Natalie, who had refused to acknowledge his existence for the rest of the meeting.

"So can we assume," Peter had asked once we'd covered as much of what Mr. Woodward had said as we could remember, "that they want you for the same reason that they want Smiley?"

"Not if Mr. Woodward's right in thinking that something else happened in that crash that only Tankom knows about," Tommy had said, "and that's a fair bet since Hammerson himself doesn't know the whole story."

"It's probably just that she's the only one who knows about there being a you in Germany as well as here," Nicole had suggested.

"If that's the case, then wouldn't she be making a greater effort to capture me in Germany instead of here?" Tommy had pointed out. "I've got a hell of a lot less protection over there than I do here, after all."

"No," James had said, looking as though he was understanding something, "because if I've got this thing right, you're German body is your original body. If they wanted to undo whatever they did, which is probably what it's about—don't ask me why they'd wanna do that, I have no idea—but if I'm right, it would be this body they would want to sort out."

"What if Smiley has two bodies too?" Nicole had asked.

"Highly unlikely," Amelia had said dismissively. "Smiley got a lot of other talents from that. You two remember what my dad said about him when we asked him about William, Carl, and Lisa? That, I think, is a big part of what's happened with Smiley."

"Are you saying you think he's passed into a half-life too?" Peter had asked, horrified. "If that's true, then we're in big trouble. How the hell are we gonna catch up with him without killing ourselves and being brought back?"

"No, I'm saying that I don't think Tommy and Smiley came out of that crash looking the same," Amelia had said. "The ability to play the Maahoo is probably the only thing you both took from it. If Smiley had two bodies at the end of that, they would have found the other one, probably sleeping in the wreckage like one of Tommy's would have been."

"So what do we do about Smiley, then?" Natalie had asked; apparently she'd heard enough about Tommy for one day.

"I don't know if there's much point going to England," Marc had said. "I mean, I know we can, but your dad said the Hammersons killed all his family, so what would we be looking for?"

"Have you got a better idea?" Peter had shot back. "Maybe we should ask Mr. Woodward about the rest of the people Smiley dealt with over there. You know, old friends, places he might have worked, things like that."

"You think maybe he'd still be in touch with one of them?" James had asked him.

"Maybe not, but it's a way to track his progress over the years," Peter had replied. "They might know someone who can point us toward someone else, and each step may be a step closer to finding the bastard."

"Maybe so," James had said, "but there might be an easier way."

"Like what?"

"Like following the Hammersons' attempts to track him down over the years," James had told us.

"If that could possibly work, then don't you think Smiley would be dead by now?" Nicole had asked.

"Not if Smiley knows the difference between us hunting him down and the Hammersons hunting him down," Amelia had said. "It's like Tommy said last time, he likes to keep contact on his terms. It may be that he doesn't know about us wanting to get in touch with him yet, but if we go to the right places, speak to the right people, make the moves that he's come to expect of the Hammersons, and he recognises us for who we are, then he might offer us the rest of what we need to locate him."

A silence had followed this little speech. Finally, James had said, "Does anyone have any idea where the Hammersons might keep records of their attempts to track down their most wanted?"

"There were loads of filing cabinets in the den on the top level of their base," I had said, thinking back to the only time I'd got a good look at it—when I had been invisible and in search of the Darkness Crystal.

"That's probably true," Amelia had agreed. "Stella told me once that half of the top level of their Chopville Base—the part that only level-one- and level-two-ranked Hammerhearts can access normally —was a work area. If this den was on that level and it had filing cabinets in it, then those would surely contain the most sensitive information, too sensitive to put down in another room, like the one John says he captured them in."

"Do you think we should go back down there and try to gain access to their filing cabinets?" Natalie had asked, and she looked scared as she glanced at me.

"Maybe," Amelia had said, "but let's not make a decision to do that just yet."

"My dad had a filing cabinet in his bedroom," Marc had said at that point. "Do you guys remember it? I'm not sure how much he would have had to do with Smiley, but maybe we should check that out before trying to get into the base again."

"That's a starting point," James had said. "In fact, it's a good one. Amelia's right about the base, though. John got lucky when he went down there to capture the Sorcerers when they lost their magic, but since then, it's been all death and destruction. We don't want any more Davids, Craigs, Tulips, or Justins if we can help it."

"I doubt that would be a problem so long as nobody here tells anyone else we're going in," Peter had said. "It's that friggin' spy. Dad or Charlie, can't remember which one, said that Mr. Woodward was really good at working out who the traitors are, but until he works out who the rat is in here now, we have to move carefully."

"I think we all understand how we've made big mistakes with regard to everyone being allowed to know about raids on the Hammerson base," Amelia had said tensely. "Nobody's gonna know about what my father does from here, and they're certainly not gonna know about what we're up to. I like Marc's idea; maybe we should check those out first before trying to get into the Hammerson base again."

"What if we find nothing?" Tommy had asked.

"If we find nothing in the Moran filing cabinets," Amelia had said grimly, "it's onto plan B: raid their headquarters again. If plan B fails, I suppose plan C would be to go back to my father for some references over in England. How does that sound?"

There had been a murmur of assent, and then Peter had said, "So when should we go down into Marc's house again, then? And who?"

"I'll go," Marc had said, "and someone else, maybe. Doesn't really matter who."

"During the week," Amelia had said. "We can worry about a certain day or time pretty much on the spur of the moment. I'd say given that it's Smiley we're hunting, maybe John should be the one to go with you, Marc."

I had nodded. I still hadn't completely recovered from what had happened to me the last time I'd been involved in any action (not counting the conflict at school a week earlier), but I felt I was ready for more action now, particularly if it was to do with locating Smiley.

"Hang on, I wanna do it," Tommy had said. "If there's stuff on Smiley in there, then how do you know there won't be stuff about me in there too?"

"If there is, we'll bring it back for you to look at," Marc had said, grinning at his friend. "Let's face it, we may not have much time down there to do anything except look for what we really need. We might have to fight my dad or Lucien; I'm not sure if either of them still live there, but it's possible, isn't it?"

"Yeah, it is," Amelia had said heavily. "That's why it's dangerous. You two can probably fight well against either of those two."

"And I couldn't?" Tommy had shot back.

"Don't start, mate," Peter had said wearily.

"I meant compared to me or Natalie," Amelia had said quickly. "If Lucien sees us, he would have orders to try to hit us with those things that disable our magic, and then to abduct us. We don't need that."

"Yeah," Natalie had agreed, "but isn't that better than them getting their hands on the Hero Crystal?"

"They wouldn't," Marc had said quietly, and the look in his eyes made it all too clear that no Hammerheart would stand a chance against him if he was set on something.

"Okay, you two, then," Amelia had said. "You two go whenever you want, but don't tell anyone what you're doing. Don't even tell me —unless you need me to let you out of here, that is. If you can surprise us, then you'll surprise them even more."

"Okay," Marc had said, looking at me, and I had nodded.

"Right. Anything else?" Amelia had asked.

"Yeah," I had said, slightly nervously now (I always felt nervous discussing this with anyone other than just Peter alone). "Not got anything to do with Smiley, though. You remember, Amelia, when your dad asked me if I'd like him to put a spell on me that would make me not have any dreams when I sleep?"

"Yeah, I remember," she had said. "Would you like one of us to do it now? It's not like you need to keep an eye on your connection with Stella anymore; we know what happened to the dreams now."

"That's not it," I had replied, more nervously still. "I dunno exactly what Justin heard, or who he heard it from, but it's bull 'cause I saw her the other night. I dunno where she was, but she was well and truly alive."

There had been a silence while the others digested what I said. Then Amelia had said, "From what I understand, what Justin told my father was that the Hammersons announced to all their Hammerhearts that Stella had betrayed them by only pretending to kill Peter, James, and Erica—not that they knew all your names, I expect—and that they had killed her for it, now that they were able to kill her. They wanted it to be a lesson to all Hammerhearts that treachery will be dealt with extremely harshly."

"You don't reckon it could have been—you know—a dream?" James had asked me.

I had shaken my head. It hadn't been a dream, and I knew that because normal dreams were never quite that vivid. I had also known it for what it was because of what Stella had been thinking about at the time: reliving the previous day when she had snuck back into the base with an extender case and practically emptied her little hidey-hole in the kitchen of all the magical devices within it.

"Why would they say they killed her and not be telling the truth?" Nicole had asked.

"There could be a reason for that," Amelia had said, "but I can't see it myself. Let's face it, they could have killed Stella a hundred times before now if it wasn't for her being a Sorcerer. Now that she's not, I guess, last time pays for all."

James had shrugged. "That's probably right. Shame for her, really, that it had to go like that. If she had just stuck with us instead of leaving the base with them, things could have been very different."

"Now hang on a moment," I had protested.

"He's got a point, though," Marc had said reasonably. "I mean, I hate to think of how confused she must have been, but apparently in order to keep her ties with both sides, she had ended up betraying both sides and had been disowned by both sides."

"Are you saying that you still believe she had something to do with Tankom and Hammerson escaping from here?" I had asked heatedly. In truth, I believed Stella had been innocent of that now, but not innocent enough to stick to her story. We knew now that there was another spy inside the Woodward base who had probably had a big hand in all the escapes, but I was finding it hard to believe he or she could have done it without the cooperation of the escapees.

"It's possible," Marc had replied, with James, Amelia, Tommy, and Natalie all nodding in agreement, "but it doesn't really matter now. Look, what's your point, John? Are you saying we should go out and find her, see if she really is still alive?"

"No," I had said. I had wanted nothing more to do with her or the confusion she added to my life. "But come on, you guys—can't you open your minds to the possibility that she might still be alive?"

"Sure," James had replied. "If you open your mind to the possibility that you could have been just dreaming. I'll believe it when I see it, put it that way."

"I'm with James," Amelia had said. "Okay, I wouldn't be surprised if the Hammersons often bend the truth to their Hammerhearts, but my father can usually tell the difference between their truths and their lies; he's dealt with them for a long time, after all. He believed what Justin said, so I believe it."

"Not this again," I had sighed. "Look, Amelia, he's proven he can make mistakes. And anyway, don't you think the chances of him believing Justin depend on how much Justin believed, rather than anything the Hammersons might have actually said?"

Amelia had shaken her head. "I know that, but I trust his judgement. It's like James says: If she turns up, then obviously I'll acknowledge that we were all wrong and you were right, but until that happens, I'm not gonna deny all the facts that have been presented to me just to fall in line with a single dream."

I had felt stung by those words but had no answer to them.

"What exactly did you see, anyway?" Peter had asked.

"She was in some sort of barn, it looked like," I had told them. "She had a bag and it was full of stuff she'd stolen from the Hammersons—magical stuff. There were farm animals outside the barn, and she was deciding on the best way to take one, kill it, cook it, and make it taste reasonably good, and all that without letting the owners see her. I'm not sure where this was—could have been just outside Chopville—but it was very vivid. The only dreams I've ever had that vivid were when I connected with her mind, or that one where I found out you were the Seventh Sorcerer, Marc."

"Just out of curiosity," James had said, "that dream—do you think that had something to do with Stella's mind?"

"Possibly," I had said, "but it wasn't the same. For one thing, Stella was in it—I could see her on that cliff. For another, that place surely couldn't have been real."

"I guess we'll never know that," Amelia had said. "Stella may or may not have known Marc was the Seventh Sorcerer, but whatever she is now, I think she was helping us back then, and I'm sure she would have told us something like that if she had known."

"Not necessarily," Nicole had said shrewdly. "John and Peter knew and they didn't say a word—except to Tommy in bed in the night."

"Don't complain. He would have tried harder to kill us if he knew that everyone knew the truth," Peter had muttered.

"Okay, whatever," Amelia had said, exasperated. "What do you want us to do about that, John? Personally, I don't think we need to do anything."

I had shrugged, feeling immensely frustrated; I had just assumed that they would believe me. "I guess not," I had said, "but for the record, I'm gonna try to keep an eye on her, and if something shows up in the dreams that we have to respond to, I want you guys to take me seriously."

I hadn't seen a single face that had been particularly happy with the condition, but I glared at each of them in turn and eventually they all agreed. As it turned out, I hadn't dreamt of Stella again for over a week after that meeting, by which time plenty had happened. On the Monday following the meeting, the fifteenth that would have been, Javelyn had reported that the Hammersons believed the Woodwards were relaxing the protection around Chopville High. In actual fact, the security had been increased around the school, but it had also been made to be more difficult to detect from the outside, and the Hammersons had taken the line exactly as the Woodwards had meant them to. Justin's funeral had been on Tuesday, and Wednesday had seen Mr. Woodward and Mr. Fletcher attempt to enter the Hammerheart Highway again, but the attempt had failed due to whatever magic the Hammerhearts had set up stopping Sorcerers entering their headquarters.

It wasn't until Thursday, March 18, that Marc and I had separated from the others after school and gone to investigate his house. Neither of us had to attend school invisibly anymore, not for nearly two weeks now, and Peter, James, and Erica had begun to come visibly again since the start of that week. We had made ourselves invisible that afternoon, though, but done so that we could see each other in transparent form. Keeping an eye out most particularly for Lucien on the way home (for we knew he was also back at school), we had walked down Main Street toward Rail Street to begin a task that turned out not to yield the answers we were looking for, but which would otherwise be very informative indeed.

The entering procedure had been done very carefully. We had stood around the back of Marc's unusually small (on the outside anyway) house, and I had used the Sien-Leoard Crystal to separate from my body (as I had done a few times before) and investigated the inside of Marc's house, looking to see if anyone was down there. Marc had stood with me, watching the street, the plan being that he would tap me on the shoulder if anyone came who we didn't want to see. Nobody had come, but we both remembered how his father had made himself untraceable on camp and remembered how Fewul had been unable to use magic to locate him, meaning that the Sien-Leoard Crystal would quite likely be limited in the same way.

After about ten minutes that way, we had contented ourselves with the idea that the house was deserted and had teleported down into the living room. Both of us had our crystals out and ready to use magic, in case we had landed right in front of Marc's father, but the room was just as deserted as it had looked from above. Still invisible, we had gone to Moran's bedroom and parked ourselves outside the closed door where we had begun a procedure we had already discussed for opening doors behind which we couldn't be sure what would be. Marc stood in front of the door, crystal in hand, and it would be he that opened it. The moment it began to open, he would throw himself sideways out of the way of any magic that might come flying at him. I would stand just out of line of anyone's aims, but close enough to see if there would be anyone there, and I could use my crystal to disable them quickly and, hopefully, quietly. The job of listening in case we were approached from behind, of course, belonged to us both.

Marc had taken a deep breath and pulled the door open. He had dived, as planned, and I had focussed so hard on what I saw through the door that I thought I would probably have lines on my face in unusual places if I held the expression for any length of time. There was nothing there, nothing whatsoever. Moreover, what I could see of the bed gave me the impression it hadn't been slept in for a long time, probably since Stella had used it after camp.

"Well, that's anticlimactic," I had said quietly, feeling enormously relieved and trying not to laugh.

"Just get in and shut the door," Marc muttered, scurrying in through the door and only half getting up off the floor in the process.

I had done as he said, and once the door was closed, I'd felt much better—safer. We had agreed that we would only talk quietly, just in case Lucien or Moran did come home while we were there, but with the door closed, I knew that we would at least have some warning if someone were to come; they wouldn't be able to sneak up on us this way. We would hear the door open, and we would certainly hear the trapdoor if they decided to enter that way, especially if it was as squeaky as I remembered it being. Feeling more secure, we both made ourselves visible again, just to save us both some confusion.

The filing cabinet Marc had mentioned was directly opposite the door, on the near side of the large bed, next to a safe I thought we would do well to break into along with the cabinet. The trapdoor was on the far side. I had given the room a neglectful glance as I strode over to the filing cabinet, then two feet from it had done such a violent double take that I ended up on the floor, my teeth jamming together with my tongue between them.

"Whoops," Marc had said, helping me back up. "You okay?"

I hadn't answered. I couldn't have answered, and not just because my tongue hurt a lot and I could taste blood in my mouth. My breath had been temporarily stopped by what I was seeing. Directly opposite Moran's bed was a dresser, the mirror of which he had replaced with an enlarged photograph of a young woman. I had thought so long and hard about who that woman had been for weeks, and she had been right here all along. I was dumbfounded; not only had neither Marc nor Lucien bothered to mention her when I had asked them about any women their father cared about, but I had seen her here only a week before I'd seen her on camp, and I hadn't even recognised her. Eventually I had managed to unlock my throat.

"Who's that?"

"Eh?"

"That woman, that's the one he called back. Who is she?"

Marc had looked curious for a moment as he glanced at the picture. "No way," he had said finally. "That's Mum. He wouldn't call her back, no way."

"What? But Cornish said she was *my* mum. That's how they knew."

Marc had turned his attention to the filing cabinet as I spoke, but now he turned back to me. "What?"

I had no longer been listening, though. My mind had gone back to Moran, the way Moran had seemed to hate us all so much when we had been fighting him. And the woman, the Casper on camp who had preferred not to fight but stand and watch, supporting both the man who had called her and her son, whichever of I or Marc was actually her son. I'd thought of Cornish and wondered if he had been being sarcastic. The response "your mum" was often given sarcastically by a certain type of smart-arse in a situation like that, except that he had said "mother," not "mum," and he certainly hadn't looked sarcastic, and Hammerson had been filthy with him for saying even that much.

"Holy crap," Marc had whispered, and I could tell by his face that he had already raced ahead to the truth of the matter. "He—he mustn't have—have done it after all."

I had looked at him more closely now. Marc, Lucien, and their father all looked very alike, and now I knew it wasn't such a coincidence that I shared many of their features. Daniel had also looked a lot like Marc, but I supposed that really must be a coincidence, unless he was yet another part of this complicated spider web of relations.

"It was him?" I had finally rasped. "He was the one who gave me to Smiley?"

"Yeah," Marc had croaked back. "It must have been, and that's why they killed her. It was never him. He was just made to take credit—must have been Hammerson's idea of a punishment."

I had thought that over, but…yes, it made sense. Hammerson had told Moran before sending him on camp that he had blown two chances. We had known what the second of those chances was; now it looked like we had discovered what the first had been as well. That also explained why Moran had seemed to recognise me, both when we'd been fighting him in this house and again on camp. Then I remembered, with an enormous jolt of the stomach: Even Hal and Pol Maivis had been aware of what was happening, for they had referred to me as "your son" when talking to Moran about the encounter with me and Amelia. My mind had been reeling, trying to take in the enormity of what must have happened all those years ago.

"So," I had croaked, and then, clearing my throat, I had managed to regain my voice. "So—I'm—I'm really a Moran?"

"No wonder you're screwed," Marc had said, grinning at me, and just like that, the tension in the room had broken, and we both burst out laughing.

"But how does it work?" I had asked when we had pulled ourselves together. "I mean, what actually happened? Were they tipped off that Hammerson was after me, so they gave me to Smiley?"

"Probably," Marc had said. "And once Hammerson found out you were gone, he was probably so furious. Geez, I wonder what stopped him killing my dad? Surely he would have wanted to."

"Maybe he thought it would be a greater punishment to kill her and keep him alive and make him live with it," I had said thoughtfully. "Hey, what's her name, anyway?" I had added, realising that Marc had never mentioned it.

"Er, it was Cindy," he had said, smiling slightly. "Cindy Moran."

I had smiled too, but quickly turned my thoughts back to where they had been going before. "That's not the sort of thing I would have expected of Arnold Hammerson, but I suppose he was particularly on his game that day."

"Hmm, yeah," Marc had said, "and through all these years, he never told Hammerson where you were. Or maybe he didn't know. He could have told them he gave you to Smiley, but obviously they couldn't find him anymore. If you had never seen those ghosts, I reckon they'd still be looking today."

"That nips my theory in the bud," I had said. "I was thinking maybe she was also Stella's mum, and he wanted me 'cause I was a result of her cheating on him or something weird like that."

Marc had laughed at that. Then, considering, he shook his head. "Nah, me and her were born too close together for that. Not a bad theory, though; that'd explain why you and her get on so well."

"Got," I corrected him, looking back up at the picture again.

It was a good shot, I had thought as I looked at the woman. It only showed above her waist, with her arms folded below her breasts, that pleasant and slightly vague smile on her face, the same one I'd seen on camp when she had looked at not me, but everyone else; it had been more than pleasant when she had looked at me, and certainly not vague. She looked quite at her ease in this photo, and I had wondered who had taken it. Was it Marc's father? My father, I had reminded myself for the first of many times. And when was it taken? Had it been before or after my birth? Before or after they had given me to Smiley? In the case of the latter, I had thought it would have to be before; surely she wouldn't have looked so comfortable between my disappearance and her death—surely.

Suddenly, from nowhere I knew, I had felt extremely sad, more sad than I had ever felt in my life, so sad that it had cost me an effort not to break down on the spot and rely on Marc to drag me out of here and back to the Woodwards. I had no right to put that on him when this experience would be a deep one for him as well: He had just discovered the truth of how his mother had died after so many years of thinking his father (our father, damn it) had killed her. I had felt responsible—this woman was dead, and this family destroyed unnecessarily because of me. It had been difficult not to imagine how different things could have been, with a happily married couple and three sons, everyone getting on like a house on fire. Ah, but Moran had been a Hammerheart, I had reminded myself; even before I was born, he had been. He had hung around with people like Hignat and Wilwog Senior and Cornish in his heyday.

"It's not your fault," Marc had said quietly, and I jumped.

Had I been that obvious? No, more likely Marc had recognised the look on my face. I had worn it quite a lot lately, especially in the immediate aftermath of Tulip's death. I had been still trying to think of something to say when we were both distracted by a deep rumbling close at hand.

"Holy shit," Marc had hissed, jumping to his feet and gripping his crystal tightly. "That was the hidden quarters opening; someone must be here."

I had also gripped my crystal tightly and cast my mind outward, looking to see who was out there. Marc had been right; the hidden quarters were indeed open, although they were already beginning to close, but I had seen the four people who they were about to cut off from the world: Lucien and three Hammerhearts, one of whom I recognised as Candice Young, the year-eight girl from school, the friend of Rebecca Fletcher, who had first attempted to shoot Tommy, Kylie, and Natalie (hitting Tommy in the process) and then had killed Lisa in the Chopville High battle.

"There's only four of them," Marc had whispered when the hidden quarters had sealed them in. "You reckon we should try to take them in?"

"No," I hissed back. "The Hammersons will know we were down here if we do that, and I don't want them to have any idea of what progress we're making working out why he wants me dead. We gotta get out of here."

"The filing cabinet?"

"We'll do it tomorrow. Come on."

And, without giving him time to argue, I had teleported us both out of there and into the park close to the Woodward house.

Chapter 3: Vision

"And was there?" Mr. Woodward prompted me.

"No. Well, Marc and I didn't get much of a chance to look that day, you know," I said, "but he and Tommy went back the next day 'cause I—"

Because I wasn't up to it, but I couldn't bring myself to say that, so I just said, "Well, they didn't find anything useful in the filing cabinet, or the safe. The safe was empty actually, so we expect he used to keep the Light and Villain Crystals in it."

"That would be a reasonable assumption," Mr. Woodward agreed. "I take it that, after you got nothing from the Moran house, you decided you would have to go back into the Hammerson headquarters?"

"Yeah," I said. He already knew we had done that. "We went for the filing cabinets in the den I'd seen before, but we didn't get a chance to look through them all. What we found was all interesting but none of it useful. We also checked Stella's hiding place of weapons to see if we could nick anything else, but it was empty; she'd obviously taken everything with her when she left."

"Or her family cleared it out after she was gone," Mr. Woodward said, smiling slightly in spite of himself, "but again, we'll come back to that. Just as a matter of interest, how did you and Marc manage to search all the cabinets without getting caught?"

"We got pretty lucky, actually," I said. "We used the capsules to get in again—the same ones Tulip and I had used, with every normalising-repelling charm on them we were capable of doing with the crystals. We went all over the base, looking around for the Hammersons or anyone worth capturing again, but they all must have been at other bases, or out in Chopville, more likely, since that had been the day before the fight. We had to get out of them when we got up to the den, but we were never interrupted while we were in there. We had the crystals set up to warn if anyone was coming, but like I said, no trouble."

I had actually skipped a step in the progression of events after Marc and I had quite literally stumbled over the identity of the woman (our mother, I had to keep reminding myself; not just his, not just mine, but ours). Once back in the Woodward headquarters that afternoon, I had sought solitude in my room, where the emotions I had kept such a tight nose-peg hold on for weeks and weeks finally spilled forth. I had shut the Sien-Leoard Crystal away in a drawer, thinking that I had to go through this; I didn't deserve to have the privilege of magic after all the trouble my life had caused. Marc, who had been shaken up somewhat by the truth himself, had done me an enormous favour by telling only Mr. Woodward and those who usually attended our meetings the truth about the woman. Several people (Marc, Amelia, Natalie, Peter, Nicole, James, Serena, and even Mr. Woodward) had come up to my room throughout that evening, but I let none of them in.

The following morning, I had been confronted by a different emotion: separation. It was one I was no stranger to; I had felt it after fighting Moran the first time, then again on the boat back from Rock Haulter. This time, however, it was separation from everyone. A good night sleep had helped me realise that it wasn't really my fault; so much of it had been because of me, but that didn't make it my fault. I couldn't have done anything differently to change things, although that only applied to the events that had taken place when I was a child. Yet I still felt estranged. Would they understand what I was feeling? I doubted it, and I hadn't been able to face them that morning.

I had therefore slept in 'til about eight o'clock. When I had finally got up, I had taken the crystal from the top drawer of my desk once again (satisfied again that I would use it) and sent a short, sharp, telepathic message to Amelia. She had told me on more than one occasion that the Sorcerers were able to send messages to each other that way, and now I used it to inform her that I would not be going to school and not to worry that I had gone missing. I knew it had worked because Amelia responded to it at once; it wasn't her voice I heard, but I knew it was her, planting the message inside my head in the same way that I had felt Serena, Natalie, and Rebecca's thoughts inside my head when I had travelled into their memories. She was worried, not that I would go missing, but that I might do something to myself, but I gave her no reply and was grateful that she (and all the others) went off to school without me.

Breakfast in the Woodward base went from six until nine, and the procedure to get students out of the base and into the Woodward house was usually finished by half past eight. Amelia would go through first and stand guard, while Natalie went back and forth through the wall, bringing students through in twos, threes, and sometimes even fours, if that many could grab some part of her, anyway. What it had meant for me that morning was that I had about half an hour when I could go down to the dining room and have breakfast without having to face any students. In fact, most people were usually done by that time anyway, and the few that had still been in the dining room that morning were people I knew by sight but had never had any dealings with, which meant I had been able to escape interrogation.

I had headed back upstairs, thinking that I might as well use the crystal to attend school in spirit, just so that I wouldn't miss anything. I had been having a lot of trouble keeping my mind on anything that morning, and I doubted I would be capable of concentrating on whatever topics came up in the various lessons I would normally attend on a Friday, but at least with the crystal I would be able to pull out of it and do something else if I chose. It was a great freedom I wouldn't normally have.

I had moved absentmindedly along the row of rooms to number nine, slid my electronic key into the slot in the door handle, and opened the door. Trouble was, the door hadn't opened. I had slid the key into the slot again and wrenched at the door, but it didn't budge. I had heard a loud clang from inside the room at that point and, feeling horrified and thinking that the resident spy had got into my room and was probably using the Sien-Leoard Crystal to do God only knew what, I had spun around, intending to bellow at the top of my voice for reinforcements, anyone at all with more magic than I had on me at that moment, which was sweet bugger all. Then I had understood what had happened: I had been so distracted on the stairs that I'd only gone up to level two instead of three, and I was just thinking that maybe it was lucky I hadn't brought the crystal down with me (what would I have done in my panic?) when the door behind me opened.

"You all right, boy?" a gruff but friendly voice had asked me.

I had turned to see the owner of that voice and found myself facing just one of those I spoke of before, a Woodward soldier I knew by sight but had never dealt with before. This one (assuming it was who I thought it was) could often be seen in the library or gym, or standing around chatting with Rob, Bob, or Grillion whenever they dropped by headquarters. I had also seen him in the battle at school weeks earlier, though of course I hadn't been around long enough at that stage to recognise anyone. He had looked curious, but not annoyed.

"Sorry," I had said, a little abashed. "Wrong floor."

"Aren't you supposed to be in school, boy?" he had asked.

"Er, not going," I had said, preferring not to go into the details of it with this complete stranger. What business of his was it anyway?

"Skiving, eh?" he had boomed merrily. "Times never change, do they. You fancy a drink, boy?"

No wonder he gets on well with Rob and Bob, I had thought, and had to fight down a laugh. It had seemed very early in the day to be drinking, and I wasn't normally much of a drinker anyway. I could remember thinking to myself after the battle at Chopville High that maybe I would have my first drink that night. It had seemed a good time for it, given all the emotional strain I had been under at the time. I hadn't done it: I had ended up a little busy for that, although I had taken my first girl up to my room that night, so I suppose that made up for it. That moment had seemed a good time to have my first drink; it could have helped dull the feelings of responsibility I'd felt for such a long time, particularly those I had developed the previous afternoon.

"Yeah, why not," I had said, grinning. It felt strange to do so, but once it had formed on my face, I couldn't get rid of it. "Not normally what I'd do, but I guess it's no normal day."

He had let out a booming, jolly laugh and stood back to let me into his room. That was the first time (the first of many now) that I had been in a level two room. In all honesty, they didn't look much different from level three rooms (same size, same features, at least that were visible), and the only noticeable difference was that this room had the appearance of one that had been in use for a long time. When I had first come here, my room had felt comfortable but empty. That feeling had slowly changed as I came to think of it more and more as "my room," but this room would have been more to this man. It would have been his home, and it sure felt like a home.

"I was just doin' a bit of readin' before," he said, swaying across the room towards the back wall. "Best do it in the morning before I make myself dyslexic later, eh?"

He had let out a bellowing laugh, a smoker's laugh, I had thought, and hoped he wasn't about to offer me one of those along with the drink. He had gone into the couch area (not unlike the one in my room) and was facing the back wall. I knew there were buttons there, but I had never examined them; I'd only ever had time for the ones around the door and bed. He had pushed one and a small compartment opened in the wall. He had then put his hand over something else and stood like that for a few seconds, and I had just been wondering if he had forgotten how to do whatever it was he was trying to do when the bottom of the compartment in the wall suddenly vanished, then reappeared with two glasses and two bottles of beer on it.

"Wow."

"This stuff's good," he had said, carrying the bottles back to the table where I'd sat and seating himself down opposite. "Well, ya can't fault Freddy. 'E's a right old dog at keeping drinks in good nick with magic."

"Er, I'm assuming that means he's good at it," I had said, grinning.

"You bet he is," he had said, pouring me a glass from one of the bottles and pushing it towards me, then pouring himself a glass from the other bottle. "Bottoms up, eh? To good fortunes and skippin' school!"

We had drank. It hadn't tasted good, not that I had expected it to, but I had a strange desire to drink it anyway. Closet alcoholic, I had wondered, then decided I really didn't care. I had intended to use the Sien-Leoard Crystal to clear my head once I was finished here, always assuming I wasn't too stonkered to find my way back up to my room. We had both put our glasses down after a few seconds, although my glass had contained considerably more drink than his when they were both on the table again.

"What's ya name anyway, boy?"

"John Playman, and just for the record, I'm only fourteen."

He had chuckled and taken another swig. I had taken another sip as well, waiting for the unwelcome recognition. Surely he would know the name and connect it with half the crap that had happened in February, and sure enough…

"Playman, eh?" He grinned jovially at me. "Chester's boy? That explains it all, the skippin' school and early takin' to the grog."

Two minutes in the room and I had already felt comfortable enough with this bloke that I could have punched him for that little jibe just as I would do Peter or James in the same situation. Grinning in a most uncharacteristic fashion, I had said, "Not so sure he still holds to those values. He kind of fears for his life nowadays."

"'E does?" he had enquired, raising his eyebrows, apparently unsure if I was joking or not.

"Yeah. I mean, sometimes he would consider letting his guard down and being lenient, and then along comes Mum."

He had taken another swig while I had been speaking. Now half of that swig came flying back across the table towards me, missing both our glasses yet appearing to draw a liquid line between them. I had jerked backward, slightly disgusted, but also amused. That'll teach him to shadowbox insults with me, I had thought. He had also looked highly amused as he wiped his face.

"Good point, that. Awfully brave man to live his lifestyle and live with such a strict woman, but I'm sure 'e's found a way to balance it." He chuckled and drained his glass. "My name's Graham, by the way. Chester used to be an old drinkin' buddy o' mine, but lucky for him he found a woman and got settled down. Yep, the good die young."

He had boomed more laughter and poured himself a second glass from his bottle, which I now saw seemed to be a different blend from the one I was drinking—probably a heavier blend. I had grinned, trying to ignore the grief for my biological mother that was threatening to wash over me again at Graham's last words about the good dying young. Now I understood why I had seen this bloke in the company of Rob, Bob, and Grillion; they were all one of the same.

Graham had worked his way steadily through three more glasses of his probably never-ending supply of beer over the next half hour, finishing that first bottle and having to sway and stumble his way to the back wall to get a second, while I had worked my way steadily through my one and only glass. He had become expansive under the influence, which I figured would be enough to put him to sleep by lunchtime if he kept going at the same rate. I came to learn that he had met Dad and Charlie while fighting for the Woodwards in the first Sorcerous war; that he had maintained a good friendship with them both ever since, despite the age difference of twelve years; and that he was now a permanent resident in the Woodward base because his assets, immediately after the war, had come to a total value of around fifty dollars, and it was the least the Woodwards could do given that he had taken on some dangerous jobs for them. Those were his words anyway, and I believed them, even with all that drink going through his system. He'd done most of the talking in that time, mostly how it was in the old days with Dad and Charlie, and some of his stories were ones I would remember to bring up next time Dad tried to convince me not to do something stupid.

Another thing I had become sure of, although he didn't come right out and say it, was that he had never managed to pull his life back together after the war and had consequently become an alcoholic. He had confirmed that while my beer was light, his was a special kind that couldn't be bought anywhere because of its dangerous level of alcohol; it was custom made, and he only drank it because anything lighter just wasn't enough for him anymore. It had made me feel sorry for him, because I also happened to know that my own father had struggled with a similar problem immediately after the war, but at least he'd managed to get his life back on track (mainly with Charlie's help). War may kill a lot of people, but I had seen at that point how it does plenty of damage to those it leaves behind too.

After a while, even though I'd drank considerably less than he had, the alcohol had loosened my tongue just a little too. The pain I had felt since the day before hadn't quite left me, but somehow it became easier to deal with. Eventually, I had started to add more to the conversation, talking about how things were with Peter and James, and the twins (Graham had practically fallen in love with Harry and Simon by my description, and I had wondered about getting them in here to drink with him, and had almost choked on imagining the expression that would cross their grandparents' faces if they ever found out). Then, quite naturally, the conversation had moved around to girls. Graham had been surprisingly observant for a bloke who was downing a beer for every ten minutes of constant chatter. I had mentioned that I was in a relationship (some sort of relationship) with Serena (for that was still how I thought of it even though the two of us hadn't had a lot of intimate time together since that first night, which I mentioned without too many details). I had also mentioned Natalie, to account for my lack of dating experience up until that point, but Graham hadn't been fazed.

"You're only fourteen, boy," he had said. "'Ow much experience are you wantin' to 'ave by then? You've got a lotta growin' up to do and plenty o' time for it."

"I guess so," I had said, unconvinced. He was right, of course, but that didn't change the way my teenage feelings affected me.

He had known I was bothered by the way things were and had stated, correctly enough, that I still wanted Natalie. Later, I had blamed the drink for the way I had made the situation so much more complicated, by first dragging Stella into the equation, and then Lena, and then Tulip, and then Amelia. Graham listened to this, drinking through it. At the end, he had chuckled.

"Boy," he had said gruffly, "you got one unsettlin' mind. You know you can't 'ave 'em all, so just take what you want most and leave the rest."

"How do I do that?" I had asked, slightly stung. To me, it seemed like he was telling me I shouldn't care what these girls thought or felt.

"You reckon you still want Natalie? She's single, and you know she'd still 'ave you, most likely anyway?"

"I suppose, but—"

"Then grow up, boy. I know what it's like to want several women at the one time; you jus' remind yourself that you can't, and that they'll get by quite fine without ya. They're young. They'll find other guys and be 'appy."

I had considered this as seriously as I could under the conditions. It was true enough, I supposed; at least, it would have been for Tulip, and probably for Amelia and Lena too, assuming Lena got her act together and started looking at other guys. Serena, I thought, would do best of all; certainly she seemed the most independent of all those I considered on my "list." Stella, of course, wasn't even on the list anymore. That just left Natalie, but it didn't change the fact that I was on with Serena, and that I kept thinking about Amelia, kept looking at her, wishing that we could be alone together, in much cleaner ways than most fourteen-year-old boys would wish that. My fantasies about Natalie were sometimes clean, sometimes dirty (since I'd begun to have dirty fantasies about any girl), but for Amelia, they were only ever clean these days (apart from one very erotic dream), and I wondered why that was. Perhaps because my feelings for her had been brought on by close experiences rather than anything physical, I supposed, but I fully expected my teenage hormones to catch up with me there as well—only a matter of time, John.

So what was I supposed to do?

Graham had stood up once again and staggered towards the back of the room, now having downed eight highly toxic gasses from two bottles. He'd been far too tipsy to return to the table this time, so I had got up and followed him into the couched area, sitting opposite him with my first glass, now almost empty.

"But what's the right thing to do?" I had asked. "I know I still want Natalie most, because I think Amelia could do quite fine just as a friend, especially while she's with Marc, but Serena—I like her a lot, as a friend, and certainly physically she's real greatly, but I don't wanna leave a girl for another girl, ever."

He had chuckled. "You follow your 'eart, boy. You want the Natalie girl, you go get 'er, and Serena can deal with that."

"It just doesn't seem right," I had said, "to do that to Serena. I know she'll recover, and I know she won't like me much when it ends, but it seems"—I searched my mind for the right word, then just spoke the only one I could think of—"wrong."

He had chuckled again. "If that's how you feel now, then nature will take its course eventually. You keep thinkin' about other girls, Serena's gonna notice, and then things'll get bad between you and you'll end up breaking up anyway. You'd better 'ope Natalie's still available when you do."

I had considered this too. Natalie had been single ever since breaking up with Tommy, and she had seemed happier than she had been while she was with him. She still looked at me, though, and when she assisted me in entering and leaving the Woodward base, she would often hang on to me a little longer than was necessary, particularly when there was no queue behind me, and I didn't think it was only my imagination telling me these things. How long would that continue, though? Was I banking on the idea that she would wait for me to be single, then accept me when I came to her? What if, when I was ready for her, she didn't want me anymore? Graham had sure given me food for thought, but my mind hadn't been convinced. I still wanted to let my relationship with Serena, or whatever it was, run its course. Strangely, through all my analysis, the thought of my actions being dishonest hadn't even occurred to me until later on.

That was the last of any sensible conversation I had got out of Graham, but it had only been just after half past ten by that stage, and I didn't want to go back up to my room again just yet. I had finally finished my first drink and got a second one from the bottle I had left on the table. Graham made no objection; he seemed aware of what I was doing, but maybe he was too drunk to care, or maybe he was too drunk to register it. He had just kept on slurring and stumbling his way through whatever it was he was trying to tell me.

"I thought he was dead," he had mumbled, raising his eleventh glass to his mouth but seemingly unable to find it with his lips. "What's a man supposed to live through?"

"Um, yeah," I had said, trying to remember who he was talking about.

"And 'e came back up," Graham had gone on vaguely, his eyes rolling slightly in his head, and I made a mental note to try to catch the glass should he suddenly drop off to sleep. "Never seen anythin' like it in me life. Ya know how it is, boy, when you see something you never seen in your life. He been to hell and back."

"Hmm."

"I saw 'is 'ead first," he had said, "risin' as they were all lifted up out o' the hole. Ya know, it's one o' the mos' unbelievable things I ever seen in my life. Scary too; 'e was all burnt an' charred, and good old Benjy—God rest his soul—said somethin' like, "E's father Christmas climbin' out of the chimney after a run-in with the family dog.' Real insensitive-like, but 'e was smilin' and 'e was just 'appy to see us, and we was just 'appy to see 'im alive, and then we was all laughin' around on the floor like."

I hadn't heard much of the last part of what he said, though, for his words had brought on a powerful flashback that had distracted me somewhat, a flashback that had made me shiver. I couldn't remember exactly how long ago it had been, but it had been back in the days when I could sit in front of the television for hours on end, watching whatever Mum chose to watch during the day and understanding almost nothing of it (I would have been five or six, probably). This memory was one I hadn't realised until that point I even had, and I now understood more of what it had been about than I had as a child.

The television show in question had been one of those documentary-type programs, this one relating to how regular people narrowly escaped near-death experiences. I couldn't remember the name of it. The episode I had thought of was one where a woman, for reasons best known to herself, had attempted to enter her house via the chimney; maybe she'd been locked out and valued the glass in the windows too highly. Anyway, she hadn't been able to fit inside the chimney and had got stuck halfway down. I couldn't remember what had been done to free her, whether the chimney had been disassembled in the process; what I had remembered was the scene where the woman, completely blackened with soot, had been lifted from the chimney. The way she had risen slowly into view matched exactly what Graham had described, and I agreed with half of his assessment of it: scary, but not unbelievable.

That, however, wasn't exactly what I had envisioned this time, though; it was merely what I related what I had seen to. The scene I had imagined at Graham's words was considerably scarier, to me anyway, perhaps only because I knew not where it had come from or what it meant. It had been an outline of a person, blackened with soot just as the woman from the chimney had been, except that there were bursts of flame around the person, surrounding them but not so closely wrapped that the flames actually seemed to cast shadows upon the body, which surely had to be dead. Everything else was black…smoky…sooty…shadowy…deadly.

I had shuddered and wrenched my mind back to the present. Graham was mumbling about something or other, and my second drink was hardly touched. Suddenly I had felt put off by drinking and wanted to get back up to my room, to either ponder my disturbing vision or to find some way to take my mind off it. I had got up and put my glass down in the hatch (he can drink the rest of it when he's ready, I had thought) and had been about to sit back down where I had been when Graham suddenly stood up, causing me to start. He hadn't even seen me as he walked slowly across the room towards his bathroom. I had known what was probably coming and decided I'd better hit the road before I had to see it.

Up to my room I had gone and locked myself inside, where I had sat down and examined my current mental state. I had felt better after being with Graham, and I suspected it had much less to do with the drink than the fact that I had got so much off my chest that morning. Though, if I'd bothered to think more deeply about it, the alcohol had probably played a part in opening me up to chatting about some of that stuff, so I had to give it some credit. In fact, apart from the memory of fire and smoke and whatever else I was still seeing behind my eyes, I felt far more cheerful than I had any right to feel. I had, in fact, felt more cheerful than I would on most days where I had nothing to be unhappy about. Weird, I had thought, but I decided I didn't care about that particular aspect of psychology at that moment either.

The rest of the day had passed quite uneventfully after that. I had seen Mr. Woodward over lunch. He had walked past me where I sat alone at a table and asked if I was okay. I had said I was, and he had nodded and walked away, respecting my privacy. I had been extremely grateful for that, but that had been the point where I had started to feel a little nervous about the reception I would get in a few hours when they started coming back from school. I had dearly hoped I wouldn't have to answer too many questions. The important people in my life knew the truth, thanks to Marc, but others, like Harry and Simon, knew very little indeed, and they would be curious as to why I hadn't been at school. Then there were Natalie and Amelia—how would I be with them? Serena? Somehow, I had very much looked forward to seeing Serena again, being past the point of careful caution on her part and whatever would come after that for the two of us. I had apparently been in one of those moods where physical contact with a girl was even more exciting than usual.

I had spent the rest of the afternoon in my room catching up on homework, reading chapters out of textbooks, using the Sien-Leoard Crystal to spy on the Media class that was my elective on Friday afternoons, though it looked quite boring from what I saw, and only leaving my room once to stretch my legs. I had been up in there with the crystal in my hand when Amelia had entered through the wall at around half past three. I had actually been waiting for them to come where I sat, wondering if I ought to send another telepathic message to her or Natalie to let them know that I didn't mind talking to them. Natalie had been right behind her, and it had been delegated to her to help the rest of them through the wall.

I had hesitated a moment as Amelia hurried down the corridor, either to her living quarters or to ours, impossible to tell since I couldn't read her mind. In that moment, however, I felt her send her mind out to contact me in just the same way, hesitantly on her part because she couldn't know if I had the crystal in my hand or not. I had got her message, though, asking if I was okay, and I had responded to it at once that I was okay and that I was up in my room if she wanted to talk to me at all. The invitation had been left open because I didn't want her to think that I absolutely needed someone to talk to, because in truth I had felt quite fine at that moment. All the same, though, I had hoped very much that she would come straight up to my room with no stop-off (yep, apparently I still felt that way about her), and to my delight, that was exactly what she did.

"Come in," I had called when I heard her knock.

"Aren't you gonna open the door for me?" she had called back.

"I thought your key could open any door?"

"Yeah, but it's your door."

Respecting my privacy, I had thought, and I'd been pleased by that. If only it hadn't meant I had to get up and walk all the way across the room unnecessarily. Sighing, I had done so, and to my astonishment (though I hadn't really known exactly how she would react), the moment there was no door between us, she had stepped forward and thrown her arms around me. I had hugged her back, feeling enormously grateful for her presence, nudging the door shut with my foot in the process.

"Are you okay?" she had asked me after she'd pulled back slightly and had a good look at my face.

"Yeah," I had said. "Well, better than I was. Took a few drinks to sort me out," I had added lightly. "You wanna sit down?"

"Yeah, sure," she had said, allowing me to lead her over to the table. My sense of caution had been active enough to prevent us sitting on the lounges or the bed, though a small part of me certainly wanted to. What were you saying earlier about teenage hormones, I had thought to myself, and put a hand over my mouth to smother a smirk.

"There weren't too many—er—questions, were there?" I had asked, slightly awkwardly, when we were both seated beside each other.

"A few," she had said. "There were more last night than this morning, the ones who noticed you weren't around. Serena's been bugging us all since then too, so you're gonna have to do some explaining when she gets hold of you; she's really worried because we weren't sure if we should tell her. Well, we were all kind of worried."

"Yeah, I know," I had said, still a little awkwardly. "Sorry about that."

"Do you wanna talk about it?"

I had considered this quite seriously. I wanted to be able to talk about it with Amelia; closing myself off from her went against every desire I had. The trouble was, I wasn't sure exactly what there was to talk about. If Marc had already told her what he and I had worked out, then I couldn't add anything to what she already knew. When I said this to her, she had merely replied, "Which part of it bothers you? Is it the emotion of finding out who your blood relatives are?"

"No," I had said at once. "I mean, that's pretty big, but it's no more for me than it is for Marc, and he was okay with it—shocked, I guess, but okay. I can get used to that idea, all right. I think—" I had thought carefully, then said, "I guess I just hate being in the centre of all this, that so much of it was because of me."

She had nodded. "Yeah, that's what Marc thought was going on. It's not your fault, you know? That was all long before you were old enough to take responsibility for your actions. You couldn't have done anything to change things."

"I know that. I know it's unreasonable to think it; I mean, I'm much more responsible for Tulip's death than the woman." My mother, damn it! I was still having trouble adjusting to that idea. "But it doesn't change the fact that it happened because of me. I've been lucky to have the Playmans and Thomases when the only thing I had to grow up with was never knowing who my real parents were, yet, because of me, Marc and Lucien had to grow up without a mother, believing their dad had killed her."

"Marc doesn't blame you."

"He should, though. It doesn't change things."

"You sound like Stella." She had sighed. "You remember what she was like? How we all had to try to persuade her that so much wasn't her fault because she always took responsibility for anything that went wrong around her. I don't know about the others, but I'm not prepared to go through all that again."

"That's okay, I won't make you," I had said, not entirely sure if she was attacking me or not. "I'll learn to live with it; it'll just be a bit hard for a while, I think."

There had been a knock on the door at that point, for which I was grateful; the conversation had gone down a path with which I wasn't particularly comfortable. I had hoped that whoever it was wouldn't stay long, though. The longer I could prolong my alone time with Amelia, the happier I would be later on—unless later on would be romantic time with Serena, in which case I would have to wrap up my chat with Amelia before anything could happen. It never occurred to me at that stage that Amelia was still with Marc, so of course nothing would happen.

As I found when I had opened the door, I didn't have to wait 'til later to see Serena. She had thrown herself on me and hugged me much more tightly than Amelia had done, rather similar to how Stella had hugged me one time and how Tulip had the day before her death. She had kissed me as well, which I had allowed, though I didn't return it. Not on, I had thought, not in front of Amelia. Serena didn't look particularly happy to see Amelia in my room, though, and once she let me go, she turned to her and said, "You wanna give us some privacy?"

"I guess so," Amelia had said, standing up from the table, but she didn't look particularly happy about leaving.

"Hang on," I had said quickly, feeling unreasonably irritated with Serena. "Are we done? Was there anything else you wanted to talk about?"

"She's had her time," Serena had answered for Amelia, not looking at me but standing beside me, wrapping a possessive arm around my waist and staring pointedly at Amelia.

"Up to you, John," she had said. "Was there anything else you wanted to talk about? I should probably go, but if you want me to stay—"

"That's okay, but he can talk to me now," Serena had said sweetly. "I've been so worried about you," she had added, looking back at me again.

"He doesn't need a mouthpiece," Amelia had said coolly. "Well, John?"

I had dearly wished that I had the Sien-Leoard Crystal in my hand; it would have allowed me to smooth this whole thing over with no fuss. As it was, all I could have hoped for was a hole to open in the floor and swallow me. Not until later would I consider myself weak for even thinking to use the crystal to get myself out of that mess. Deciding on the spur of my emotions, I had turned to Serena and said, "You can have as much of my time as you want after dinner. For now, though, can you let me finish talking to Amelia?"

She had scowled at me. "So I come second now?"

"No," I had said quickly, and then, reconsidering, I had added, "You come 'later,' but like I said, you'll have as much of my time as you like, much more than anyone else is getting before dinner. Can you wait?"

"No," she had replied. "You've already made me wait long enough. I wanna come first."

I had sighed. I thought what I had told her was perfectly reasonable; she was certainly getting a better deal than Amelia, yet it still wasn't good enough. I had been in no mood to put up with such childish possessiveness as what I was now confronted with.

"I don't want to have this conversation now. I'll see you later on, okay?"

I had anticipated her drawback, and before she could move, I had taken hold of both her shoulders and turned her to face me so that our noses were less than two inches apart and we were staring into each other's eyes. "Do you understand what I'm saying, Serena?"

She could have said anything; she could have spat in my face—the range was certainly sufficient. Yet apparently she still had enough feelings for me not to shout, cry, or carry on too much. "I understand what you're not saying. You know we've been together for three weeks and we haven't done hardly anything together, certainly no dates to speak of, and now you're telling me to come back later so you can talk about stuff with another girl that you don't wanna talk about with me."

"I never said I wouldn't," I had said, trying to remain calm. "Just not right now. I'm not gonna go back on my word, if that's what you're worried about. Surely you'd prefer to be the one with me tonight, but you can't just tell me who I can and can't talk to. I'm not gonna stand for that."

"Fine," she had said, attempting to pull away from me, but I tightened my grip.

"Is it? Is it fine? You know I'll be very disappointed if you turn around tonight and tell me you want nothing more to do with me. That's the last thing I want."

"Okay," she had said, tears forming in her eyes now. "You'd better mean that, though."

"Of course I do," I had said, and I pulled her back into an embrace before turning her back to the door.

Once I had shut the door behind her, I simply stood there, digesting what I had done and wondering why the hell I had done it. Surely our relationship would be in much better shape if I'd just told Amelia to give us some privacy, as Serena had done? If I had, Serena and I could at that very moment be on the bed or couches doing who knew what. It was probable that even after all that, I really had finished with Amelia after all. What else did we have to talk about? Yet I knew I had done the right thing. That was a test that my relationship with Serena had needed; I shouldn't be required to let her dictate to me as she had tried to do then. If we survived the following week or so, we would be much better for it.

I had simply stood there, staring unseeingly up at the ceiling for what felt like several minutes, though it had probably only been one or two, when Amelia touched my shoulder from behind, causing me to jump. She had gone into my small bathroom while I had been dealing with Serena and run the tap loudly, God bless her, and apparently I had been so lost in my thoughts that I hadn't heard her return.

"Sorry," I had muttered, not looking at her, trying to pull my mind back to where I stood. "I didn't want you to have to see—"

She had silenced me by pressing a finger to my lips, and then she had hugged me again. This hug had been different from the others (in fact, it had been different from all but a very select few hugs I'd ever had in my life), in the way that, rather than feeling her arms around me and mine around her, I had felt her body against mine. Her head resting on my shoulder, she had said, "You don't have to say anything about that to me, okay."

"Thanks," I had muttered, feeling so touched, both by her understanding and the embrace, that I could have broken down and cried on the spot, but I mastered myself.

After maybe fifteen seconds, she had straightened up and stared at me. Our faces had been closer than mine and Serena's had been earlier, if that were possible. That position had held for maybe five seconds before both of us realised at the same moment how close we were to kissing, and we had both pulled back slightly. Amelia had looked strained and a little embarrassed, and possibly ashamed of herself, but her eyes told a different story. She had clearly enjoyed the moment as much as I had.

"I guess we'd better be a little more careful," she had said, smiling weakly.

I had shrugged. "Guess we had."

Right on time, another knock had sounded on the door. We had quickly let go of each other, and Amelia had opened it nervously. I had dearly hoped it wasn't Serena; she would be difficult to deal with so soon after what had nearly happened. It had actually been Natalie, coming to see how I was after she had finished letting everyone back through the wall. Easier to deal with than Serena would have been, but still slightly awkward, given that when we had hugged (a treat that had surprised me), I began noticing her body against mine just as I had done with Amelia's, and I had a feeling Natalie was thinking the same thing.

Chapter 4: Coordination

"Yes, very good," said Mr. Woodward, smiling slightly. "That was the twenty-first, and if my memory serves me correctly, you spoke to me again about your plans on the twenty-seventh. I take it nothing happened in between to lead you to that idea?"

"Well, it was plan C," I said, "after searching Marc's house and the Hammerheart base didn't answer any questions. We only had one meeting about it, on the twenty-seventh, earlier in the day before we spoke to you. There was too much going on during the week for us to meet any earlier than that Saturday."

There certainly had been a lot going on that week, although admittedly most of it had nothing to do with me. In fact, a lot of it, such as what the Hammersons had been doing and what the spy had been doing, were things that we hadn't found out about until later dates. Much of it that we had been aware of, however, had been the fallout after the Hammerhearts' second attempted and failed takeover of Chopville High that had taken place on Monday, March 22.

The first attack on the school, the one in which Lisa had been killed, had been coordinated by people other than the Hammersons, or even those who would normally take charge in this part of the world. It had been done at the very end of recess, in the time when students and staff alike would be least organised. Fortunately, Mr. Woodward had suspected a possible attack that day and had stationed some of his people around the school grounds, so that the students and teachers weren't completely defenceless when the fighting broke out shortly before the bell. The security around the perimeter of the school had been drastically increased since the attack, so that an invisible magical barrier prevented unauthorised people entering the grounds. At least, that's how it had been since the fifteenth, for that had been days after the newly appointed Javelyn had learnt of a second plan to attack the school. Prior to that, there had been sentries standing guard around the perimeter. The idea of the change had been to make the Hammersons think the Woodwards were letting down their guard when in fact they were doing the complete opposite, and it seemed to work—for a while.

In theory, the new protection should have been almost foolproof. There was some flexibility in it, though, to allow students to bring their parents through, for example, by holding onto some part of them as they crossed through the barrier. That made it like the Woodward headquarters in a way, but it also allowed for the same weakness that the Woodward headquarters had: You couldn't know if the people being brought through were trustworthy. In addition, you couldn't be sure that all those who were authorised were trustworthy. In fact, we knew the opposite, for Hammerhearts such as Hignat, Wilwog, and Hall were authorised. So, in practicality, the new protection sucked the big ones, but surprisingly, none of us realised just how badly it sucked until it had been breached.

The second attack on the school had been planned and coordinated, we later found out from Javelyn, by Hank Cornish, the number-one man below the Hammersons themselves. It had been almost the complete opposite of the first attack, in that it had been done much more quietly—at least at first. It had been timed for the middle of period three on Monday, when us year nines were in English with Hall, Hignat, and Wilwog—no coincidence, I had no doubt whatsoever. The year tens had been in their divided Maths classes, the three rooms all in a line, making them a single target in the eyes of the Hammerhearts; Nicole and Jane in Elementary; Natalie, Felicity, Jessica, Sebastian, and Darcy in Intermediate; and Amelia, Marc, Tommy, and Lena in Advanced.

In English that day there had been an oral presentation. Hall had given the class a few tasks that had to be completed at some stage during the semester, and one of them had been to perform an oral presentation on anything of our choice, and we had been allowed to work in pairs or groups of three for it. On that day, Harry and Simon had gone first; they spoke for a little over five minutes about Chopville's plumbing and sewerage systems. Many of the class had known they were doing that topic (they'd wasted no time in being vocal about it in the beginning), but everybody had underestimated the number of substitutes for "shit" the twins could come up with or the number of times they could drag it into the presentation. They had even printed a map of Chopville's sewerage system and marked on it (in brown) the areas most prone to clogging. I was sure they were exaggerating some of their points along the way, but Hall didn't seem to mind; it added up to one highly engaging presentation.

"I can tell you one thing, though, folks," Harry had told the class loudly. "These homes here"—he had gestured to the far southeast corner of Chopville—"are not where you'd wanna live. This particular area right along here has regular build-ups of excrement because the flow around the corners here towards the river isn't very smooth. The council doesn't tell anyone, but what it has to do is send troops down there to unclog it, but because it's very dark down there and no machinery can fit, you usually get at least one person emerge into the sunlight, covered head to toe in—"

"Don't forget to tell them the anecdotes," Simon had reminded his brother, "about how sometimes they accidentally get it in their mouths. Can you imagine some of the conversations that must go on down there? 'Wow, these guys must have been eating pizza not too long ago.'"

Ellie and Stephanie had been due to perform their oral presentation immediately after the twins, but as they were out in front of the class getting their notes all organised, Hall had moved oddly. Many of us had been on the alert for anything odd from Hall, Hignat, or Wilwog since their return to school, so we reacted in time to lower our heads so that the jet of pale light flew just over us, hitting the wall and disappearing.

Hignat and Wilwog had reacted at almost the same moment; they had both been seated in the back row so they had easy aim. Hignat's jet of light hit Erica, who was sitting on the other side of the room with Serena, Kylie, Holly, Anna, Cassandra, Matthew, and Anton. Wilwog's jet had hit James, who hadn't been quick enough to turn to see that Wilwog had aimed at him. Peter and I leapt away from James as panic erupted from the rest of the students, particularly those who weren't fighters.

In the next moment, the door had crashed open, and three more Hammerhearts had burst in. A fourth had done something in the doorway (sprung up an invisible barrier to seal us in, I had felt sure), then hurried off along the corridor. The three Hammerhearts that had invaded the room had lined up along the back wall, their solid-outliners (small devices that shot jets of thicky prison) poised. They had fired in unison; one had hit Ellie, who was completely without cover out the front of the room with Stephanie (Stephanie had screamed and tried to tear the white stuff spreading over Ellie's chest off her, only to have her hands swallowed in it and have it spread up her arms); one had hit Serena, who had just used her own solid-outliner to free Erica; and the third had narrowly missed Wilwog and hit Simon, who had just freed James from his prison. I'd had the Sien-Leoard Crystal in my pocket, but I didn't have a solid-outliner, so I had quickly sprung up an invisible shield around myself and Peter, then began moving us through the chaos towards the front of the room. It had been towards Hall, who was standing behind his desk. He had taken aim at us, but the crystal had been in my hand, and a moment later, he had fallen out of sight.

The five Hammerhearts in the room had overwhelmed the rest of the class for about ten seconds more before Peter and I had a chance to take charge. Nearly all of them had been trapped in thicky prison (a white spreading substance that immobilised everything it touched) by then. I'd used the crystal to knock them all out in turn; the last one had tried to make a run for it but been thwarted by the barrier his mate had erected. Peter had then freed the rest of the class from the thicky prison; they had all fallen about, sobbing and crying and panicking. With the reduced noise in the room, I could hear commotion throughout the rest of the school and knew that the same assault had been launched on all the other classrooms.

"Anyone got a spare solid-outliner?" I had asked the Young Army members.

"Use that thing to duplicate mine," Peter had suggested, putting his in my hand.

I had never tried duplicating something before, but to my surprise, it had worked fine—I just had to hope it would work when I needed it to. I had then used my crystal to levitate the unconscious forms of Hall, Hignat, Wilwog, and the other three Hammerhearts into a line at the back of the room. The whole class was watching me now, and their thoughts, written on their faces, were simple: The same person who took charge in the last battle had saved the day again. Apparently they were waiting for me to tell them what to do, like the good little sheep they were.

"You guys all stay here," I had said. "Peter, James, keep watch over them all. Take down any Hammerhearts before they can get too far into the room if they try to come in, and make sure they don't wake up—although I doubt they will. I'm going out there."

"What about us?" Katie had asked. "We have stuff too."

"Same thing. Anyone with weapons, be ready to fight."

I had hurried between the rows of desks and around the back towards the door, using the crystal to remove the invisible barrier as I went. Once out in the corridor, I had resealed it so that not even the Hammerheart devices they used could affect it; that ought to keep them in, and anyone else out, until I got back. Now, however, I had been in Hammerheart territory; it seemed that everyone had been trapped in their classrooms, and the only ones roaming the corridors were Hammerhearts. I had decided, on the spur of the moment, to attack this situation in a far different way to the previous battle, in a way I had never tried before but felt would work just as well.

I had quickly made myself invisible and taken off up the corridor towards the year-seven/eight locker bay, which was the nearest door out into the yard, looking through the open doors of classrooms as I went, seeing nothing in any of them except Hammerhearts (no more than three to a room) loading packs of joined students into extender cases (backpacks enchanted to fit anything of any size inside them while reducing the weight). There had been a few Hammerhearts hurrying around in the corridors, but I had dodged them, preferring not to alert anyone to my presence just yet. Into the locker bay I had run and through the doors into the schoolyard, looking around and again, seeing nothing more enlightening than Hammerhearts running here and there with bags over their shoulders. All I had needed to know was the location of their base of operations; it had been the gym in the first attack, but I had a feeling that Cornish would prefer to do it somewhere smaller—or Hammerson, if that part of the plan had been his—

Wam!

I staggered backwards as the invisible person I had run headlong into lurched forward. It was a girl, I knew, for I had heard the noise she had made on contact.

"Who's that? Amelia? Natalie?"

No answer had come from her. I had scrambled back to my feet and squeezed the crystal, sending my mind out to find the person. Natalie and Amelia had been in the staffroom, which had been at some point taken over by the Hammerhearts, probably prior to any of the classrooms being attacked. Marc was with them, and it seemed that they had found the centre of operations and were taking control of it. I searched for girls closer at hand, but whoever I had hit had scarpered pretty quickly. I had therefore returned to myself and hurried across the yard towards the new building, and the centre of operations.

Then I had seen the problem facing me. Hammerhearts had been being struck down on the other side of the yard—not just knocked unconscious, but much worse things. One had been turned inside out, parts of his (or her) clothing mixed with his (or her) intestines; another had been mutated, so that he was attempting to stand on one leg and one arm, his head sticking out between his other leg and arm, his clothes almost completely ripped off; another had been cut into at least a dozen pieces; and another simply lay dead in a pool of flesh and blood. Quite suddenly, the Hammerheart running about ten feet in front of me was hit by an orange laser from high above and in front of us; he had screamed, then melted, and within seconds all that was left of him was a foul-smelling puddle that was not flesh, blood, or anything else I recognised.

With the worst timing possible, the sight had drawn my attention back to that horrible vision I'd had the previous week. A body, a dead body, burning, mutilating, smoking, surrounded by bursts of flame and dark, obscuring smoke. No. I had shaken my head roughly, returning (not without effort) back to my surroundings and the more urgent issue at hand.

I had looked up to where I thought the jet had come from and quite clearly seen the person who had cast it. It was enough to distract me completely from my nightmare vision. My stomach dissolved; it might as well have been hit by that jet of light along with the Hammerheart. I couldn't have been sure if this was a good thing for our side or not. Bernard Moran, Marc's father (my father, for the love of all things fine and dandy), was standing on the roof of the two-storey building ahead, watching the commotion below quite impassively. I'm invisible, I had reminded myself forcefully. He wouldn't be able to attack me if he'd wanted to.

But as I had prepared myself to enter the fray ahead so that I could get to the doors into the building, Hammerhearts started coming out of it. In the lead had been Hank Cornish himself; he had stopped and stared at the battlefield before him even as another Hammerheart had been struck down. This one had writhed for a moment before his arms and legs had begun to stretch and reduce in density. His legs snapped under his weight and he fell to the ground, unable to move as his arms continued to grow, wrapping around him and eventually cutting off his extremities. Geez, my father sure was horribly creative, I had thought uneasily.

"What the hell!" Cornish had cried out, looking around for some sign of the source of all this mess, but Moran was way out of his range of vision.

"The bags!" a so far untouched Hammerheart had called to him. "He's killing anyone who has an extender case."

The offending Hammerheart had actually been bagless, but apparently Moran thought it prudent to deal with him as well. Seconds later, he had met a similarly horrific end, as many of his fellows had.

Cornish wasn't stupid enough to run out of the protection of the building's shadow to catch sight of Moran. Instead, he turned and ran back into the building. Abandoning my initial plan, for it didn't seem to matter much anymore, I skirted around the edge of the battlefield and headed after Cornish into the building. I hadn't kept an eye on Moran while I moved, so I didn't realise he had moved until he appeared right in front of me, his back to me, running down the corridor in Cornish's wake.

In the staffroom, when I had reached it, it had been a stalemate. Marc, Natalie, and Amelia were on one side of it (the latter two bearing rips in their clothing, the marks on their skin indicating that their magic had been neutralised clearly visible from my position), and Cornish and a few other Hammerhearts I recognised (3K17, 3A93, 3P69, and 3E57) were on the other side of it. In the middle, several bags had lain on the floor between the lounges, along with (my stomach dropped like a stone) Marc's Hero Crystal, which had somehow been rested from him without splitting into the six smaller Sorcerous Crystals. There had also been a magic door standing off to one side, which opened up to the entrance of the Chopville Basement; I could see it clearly in the narrow view I had been afforded. With all the magic on one side, the situation looked bad indeed. Normally in this situation, I would stand quietly and see what the situation was before acting, but that hadn't been an option this time; Moran appearing in the doorway had changed everyone's focus from wherever it had been before.

"Oh, shit," 3P69 had hissed, comprehension dawning on his face.

"Hello, Andrew," Moran had said jovially. "How's it hanging? Limp and floppy as usual?"

Both 3A93 and 3E57 had laughed in spite of themselves. 3P69 had glared.

"Oh, no," Cornish had groaned. "Get out of here, Berny."

Moran had smiled unpleasantly. "I wouldn't have made the effort to come here today if I was going to leave immediately."

Marc had been staring at his father with a face that could have been made of stone. Beside him, Amelia had put a resting hand on his arm.

"Just get out of here, all of you," she had said forcefully, "before my dad turns up. He is on his way."

"Oh dear, poor little girl crying for her daddy," leered 3E57.

I had carefully squeezed through the doorway at that point, past Moran (he may or may not have noticed, but he acted as though he hadn't), and headed for where Marc stood with Amelia and Natalie, all three defenceless.

"We'd better just take those three," Cornish had muttered to 3K17, and she immediately raised her solid-outliner and shot a jet of pure thicky prison at Natalie. It'd hit her before she had a chance to move. Marc jerked away from Amelia, but Amelia, whose shoulder had been against Natalie's, hadn't been quick enough to move aside, and the white stuff had begun to wrap around both of them.

I had raised my solid-outliner, intending to release them both before it could get a good hold of them, then changed my mind; they wouldn't get through the door, and this way they (magicless) couldn't get in the way. I had instead crouched there and begun to work on their crystal chips, performing the magic that would restore their own for when they were released.

"Dear me," Moran had said amusedly. "You really are on top of the situation now, aren't you?"

"Looks like it," Cornish had replied, moving forward to pick up the Hero Crystal at last. "If we take this, we should be able to deal with the remaining Woodwards and Fletchers if they—"

But he hadn't got a chance to finish, because the crystal leapt up into the air before he could lay a hand on it. Everyone in the room had stared at it in surprise, everyone except Moran, who hadn't looked surprised at all.

"Cut that out," Cornish had snapped. "What the hell are you doing?"

"Making the contest a little more…even," Moran had replied serenely, and with a flick of his eyes in Marc's direction, the crystal had hurled through the air towards him. Cornish had yelled in dismay as Marc caught it, and at the same moment, I finally snapped my solid-outliner at Amelia and Natalie, releasing them, their magic now in full working order. My presence had gone completely unnoticed, for all the Hammerhearts, and even Marc and the girls, had thought either Marc and the Hero Crystal were responsible for it, or Moran was.

All three of them had reacted at the same time. The wall behind the Hammerhearts was suddenly peppered with jets of light, but only one Hammerheart (3P69) had been hit. The rest of them, realising the game was up, had dashed for the door back into their basement, not bothering to stop and pick up any bags on their way. A moment later, they had gone. I had looked back into the other doorway and Moran had also disappeared, in his case back into the corridor. A silence had followed, before I decided to get the hell out of there too. Not bothering to let any of them know I was ever there (no reason for me to be praised as the hero this time), I had teleported out of there and back into the year-seven/eight locker bay.

The clean-up operation had begun after that. Marc had removed the door from the staffroom to prevent Cornish sending out any reinforcements. I had gone back up the corridor where my English class still waited for me, only to find that someone had been along before me, removing all the barriers from the classrooms, apart from my own, of course. Hammerhearts were still around, but Mr. Woodward and Mr. Fletcher had arrived by that stage and sorted them out quite easily. Once all the bags had been rounded up and all attendance logs for that day had been checked, they found that there were, thankfully, no missing students or staff. By the evidence of everyone in year-nine English, period three, Hall had been presumed to be the person responsible for bringing them into the school in his bag, based on the fact that he knew (by the minute) the exact time that the attack was supposed to start, and he had been arrested by the local cops and carted off to Shepparton. Hignat and Wilwog were also rounded up, presumed not to be responsible for the attack but to have had knowledge that it would be happening that day; they were questioned by the local police and released later that day.

Moran seemed to have vanished. The cops looked all over the school for him, but he had apparently achieved what he had wanted to and had run for it. The Woodwards and Fletchers dismissed the whole school after that, students and staff alike, while they began to add further enchantments to the boundaries of the school grounds. At some stage, the mess of Hammerhearts in the yard had been cleaned up. I never found out what the Hammerheart death toll was. I had been sent back to the Woodward headquarters along with all the other students, other than Amelia, who Mr. Woodward had held back to help with the magic, and we had spent the remainder of the day speculating on how the attack had happened, what the Hammersons would do about the failure of their Hammerhearts, what would happen to Hall now that he was locked up, and (most importantly for many) what had actually happened in the staffroom to turn things, for Natalie and Marc hadn't been clear on any of it. Nobody had mentioned Moran, so I had followed their lead.

I had spent most of that evening with Serena. We had been a little awkward since the episode the previous week, but on that night we had fully appreciated each other's company for the first time. She had fallen asleep very shortly before I had, and when I had dropped off, my dreams returned me to the worst part of what I had seen that day. I had decided, to make the experience of the battle easier to deal with, that Tulip's death had still been worse than any of the Hammerhearts' that day, but seeing all those tortured and contorted Hammerhearts again, even in my dream, had not been what I'd wanted that night. Except I hadn't really been seeing them in my dream: I had been remembering them in my dream; remembering how Bernard Moran had stood on the roof of the Administration building, attacking all those with bags on the ground below, and how I had watched a Hammerheart right in front of me shatter into a million sloppy pieces as a jet of light hit him; remembering how Cornish had come out, seen the Hammerhearts, and quickly retreated again, and how Moran had followed him into the building; remembering that I, at that point, had gone to make sure students around the rest of the school were okay; remembering how, as I had been assessing the situation when I had first spotted Moran, I had been run into from behind…

The shock of the realisation had been enough to wake me up completely. Serena had stirred beside me, muttered something, and slept on. I had sat up without realising it. I carefully lay myself back down in the bed, my mind full of what I had seen, and what I had just learnt. Stella, bloody Stella—she was the invisible person I had run into. She was the one who had gone and removed the barriers from the classrooms by the time I had got around to checking them. What on earth had she been doing there? Had Stella in fact been attending school invisibly every day since her exile from the Hammersons?

I hadn't seen anything of what Stella had been doing at that moment, but wherever she was, whatever she was doing, she was lost in memories of what had gone on that day. I hadn't been surprised that she had got into the school—she was probably still a registered student, after all. She had attended school visibly for just one day, between her exile from the Woodwards and her exile from the Hammersons. Had she in fact been coming back to school every day since? Or if not, how had she known that trouble would strike that day?

Despite the trouble that had been caused, Chopville High had been able to reopen again on the twenty-fourth, two days after the attack. The security measures had been improved even further this time. I had been most favourably impressed with the enchantment that disarmed people as they crossed the boundaries into the school, stripping from them any magical weapons, or non-magical weapons sparing the average pair of scissors, affecting absolutely everyone (except the Young Army, who were allowed to cross into the ground with recognised weapons). Hall hadn't returned to school. He was still being held, but there had been some doubt in the Woodward camp about the success of his charge because, most unfortunately, the only evidence against him was the word of a class of year-nine students that he had known when the attack was to take place before it had happened, and even that wasn't concrete. Hall could have easily said he had been launching his own attack, not knowing that another larger attack was happening at the same time. Mr. Woodward had doubted that he would even need to say that much. That had been the talk all through Tuesday that week, though my mind had been mostly on Stella. I had used the Crystal within the school grounds to discover if she were present, but I only achieved negative results.

On the twenty-fifth, Thursday, school had begun to return to normal (Hall had been replaced by a younger, more friendly bloke whose name was also Mr. Hall, which caused mass confusion and conflict among those of us who despised the original Hall), but the previous evening, Javelyn had returned from the Hammersons' base with some alarming news that I had been one of the very few people to find out about: Plans were being arranged and executed to take control of the Australian government, mostly by way of the influential charm but also by having some of their Hammerhearts placed secretly in positions of power, impersonating politicians. That last part of the plan had seemed unclear to me, but according to Mr. Woodward, Javelyn had looked very scared by the idea. Mr. Woodward had acted swiftly. The following day, some of his people were also placed within the government, not to control it but to protect it from the Hammerhearts. Unfortunately, as we were to find out later, the move hadn't happened quickly enough.

Then, the following night, Friday night, I had dreamt of Stella again, only the third time since her magic had been taken from her but the second time in four nights. The first thing I had thought upon waking was that dream had been a real disappointment compared to the one I'd had the night before, which had been about Amelia and had required me to clean up after myself. Then I had thought about what I had seen, and felt horrified. Stella had been hurt, very badly hurt, hardly able to move. She had been in hiding, nursing herself and expecting to be dead very soon. She had, at one point in the dream (which had been mercifully short), thought back to how she had acquired those injuries: During the day of the twenty-fourth, she had run into Moran, who had also been in hiding, and they had fought, she with her weapons of magical destruction and him with his Villain Crystal. She'd done her best, but for some reason she couldn't explain, even to herself, she had been utterly terrified of him. Her fear had been almost debilitating in its completeness, and although he probably would have beaten her anyway, her terror then had undoubtedly played a big part in causing her present condition. Nobody had died, but he had won the fight, and now Stella was not in a good way at all. The only trouble was I hadn't got a clear idea at all of where she was hiding. I had supposed it didn't matter too much; the idea that she had been trying to help the students of Chopville High was a good one, but other than that, there was still not a lot of evidence that Stella was on our side, only that she was on the outs with her family.

There had been another meeting in my bedroom the following day with the usual suspects (Marc, Amelia, Tommy, Natalie, Peter, James, Nicole, and yours truly), and the first topic of discussion had been the two dreams I'd had about Stella, for I hadn't mentioned either of them to anyone up until that point. I had known not too far into my recount that most of them weren't interested in taking this seriously, still believing that Stella was dead, and a couple of them looked positively exasperated that the subject had come up again. Nevertheless I had ploughed on until I had explained both dreams and what I had deduced from them.

"But what proof is there of any of this, John?" James had asked, trying to sound calm.

"The only proof," I had said through gritted teeth, "is that I ran into her. You guys don't have to believe it happened, but that's far more substantial evidence than dreams, even in my book."

"Okay," Amelia had said, also calmly. "Let's say, for the sake of argument, that Stella is alive. I can't see how she could have fooled the security around the school into letting her through—the security that had been there that day. She may have been a student before, but she would have been removed from the school's database when they had found out about her death. We know she couldn't have got in with the Hammerhearts, and if the second dream is also true, then she couldn't have been with Moran. Any ideas?"

"You don't know that she was taken off the school's database," Natalie had said, and I had been grateful for her support. "That's only guessing. And how do we know she didn't have a magical device that could poke a hole in that barrier? Because apparently she had one that could remove the barriers from the classrooms."

"Those were weak barriers by comparison," Amelia had said, a little less calmly now. "And you're right; I suppose we can't know for sure if she was taken off the database."

"I do know that she hasn't been back once since," I had said. "Maybe because she's too injured to or because she doesn't think she needs to. If it's the latter, though, what confuses me is how did she know she might be needed at school on Monday? How did she get the inside word? Do you reckon she could be spying on the Hammerhearts?"

"Wouldn't that be her death sentence if she was caught?" Peter had asked.

"I don't know," Amelia had said, "and since she really didn't make much of a difference on Monday that we know about, I don't really care. John, what's your point? Because, again, even if we take you seriously, I don't see how there's anything we can do about her."

"I'm just keeping you all up-to-date," I had told her, "because even if you don't believe me, it might be useful for you to know these things as they happen, just in case I'm right. Is that not a bad thing?"

"No." She had sighed. "It makes sense, I guess, but, John, you can't expect us to remember all these things. It's not us having these dreams or whatever they are."

"Okay," Marc had said pointedly. "So, Stella might have been at the battle on Monday; she might have gotten into the school somehow; she might have used a magical device to break down the invisible barriers around the classrooms at the end of it; she might have met my dad on Wednesday and had a fight with him almost to the death; and she might be lying somewhere now, you don't know where, gravely injured. Fine. Now can we talk about Smiley?"

"Yes, let's do," Amelia had said quickly, as eager as everyone else to get off the topic of Stella. "You guys found nothing, right?"

"That's right," Marc had said. "Nothing in the filing cabinet in my dad's house and nothing in the ones in the den in the Hammerheart base. What now? Are we gonna trace him back to England?"

"I guess that's what we'll have to do." Amelia had sighed again. "I didn't want it to come to this, but I suppose I'm not really surprised. It was never gonna be easy."

"Geez, where do we start?" Nicole had asked. "Any ideas, Tommy?"

Tommy had shaken his head. "Wish I could point us in some direction, but like I said, he always kept contact on his terms. Honestly, I've been hoping he'll come to us at some stage, but it doesn't look like that's gonna happen."

"What if—hey, what if he really is dead?" Peter had asked. "I don't think we talked about what we'd do if that was the case."

"We'll worry about that if we get to that stage," Amelia had said. "I certainly don't like the idea of us running around in circles looking for some sign of him and finding nothing because he's dead, but I expect if he really is dead, someone somewhere will know. We just have to find them."

"So where do we start, then?" Nicole had repeated.

"My dad, I guess," Amelia had said. "He didn't give us much last time, but if we tell him we're actually going over there, he might be able to point us towards someone they both knew or something. It's worth a try. If he can't tell us anything, I suggest we go over there anyway and poke around in people's minds, use magic to see if anyone has any idea what's happened to him or how to get in touch with him."

So, later that afternoon, about an hour before dinner was due to start, Amelia, Marc, and I had gone to see Mr. Woodward, who had been out and about for most of the day and had only just returned. He greeted us as he always did with his friendly smile and his gesture to take seats and join him for a drink. None of us had ever actually had a drink with him but I supposed, given that he was

Amelia's father, he wouldn't have given us anything more interesting than red cordial. He had still managed to smile at that stage—that would become much more difficult over the following two weeks.

"We need to talk about Smiley again," Amelia had told her father without preamble. "We've decided we're gonna have to go over there and check the place out."

"Ah," he had said, not asking the usual questions. They would come later. "That's a big decision. You're sure it's necessary?"

"Yeah, it is," she had replied. "Can you help us get started?"

"Hmm." He had deliberated for a moment. "Possibly, I can. Unfortunately, everyone who knew Smiley both during the war and in the years after the plane crash is either dead or living here and knows no more than I do. I do know that in the years following the war, Smiley worked in a law firm in London, which I should be able to find you the address of. I suggest you pay a visit to them and see if there's anyone there willing to talk. I know he retired in 1990, but that doesn't mean there isn't someone there who can point you in a certain direction."

He had got up and started looking through the many filing cabinets behind the desk, apparently using magic to help him locate what he was looking for. The rest of us had stayed silent, waiting and hoping that whatever he was going to give us would be helpful. It had taken about ten minutes for him to find what he had been looking for.

Turning back to us, he had said, "This should give you all the information you need. The address is here, and if you get there and find that the firm is no longer in business, this man"—he gestured to a phone number—"will know or know of someone who knows the people who were last in management there. I don't think that would be the case, though."

Chapter 5: The Survivor

"Very true," Mr. Woodward agreed, "and I know that you used a second-floor room, moving it to a location in London, and used that room to step into London on the evening of the twenty-ninth. That was only the first time you went over there, correct?"

"Yeah," I said. "We only went one other time, a week later."

"And how did it go? What did you find when you located the law firm? You never did tell me about that visit."

"Well, it was still in business," I said. "You were right about Smiley retiring in 1990, and nobody who works there now knows him personally. Amelia, though, she's great at getting people to give her what she wants. Eventually we managed to find a manager who was willing to look in the database and give us some names of people who had worked closely with Smiley in the latter years of his career. He gave us the name and address of Smiley's first understudy from way back; that bloke had retired in 2007, but the details on file were well up-to-date, so we went to pay him a visit too."

"Really? I didn't know he ever had an understudy."

"Well, apparently he did. This guy's name was Gerald Fick—looked way older than his age but seemed to still have plenty of smarts about him."

"And did he turn out to be any use to you?"

"Plenty," I said. "Actually, when he first saw Amelia, he thought you'd sent her to bring him in here to protect him. He was going on about how the Hammerhearts killed most of his family while they were trying to get him to tell them where Smiley was twelve years ago. He's scared shitless they're gonna come after him again. Anyway, he did have a useful name for us."

Mr. Woodward raised his eyebrows, so I went on. I was getting close to the sensitive part now. Hopefully I wouldn't need to go into absolutely all the details. "When Smiley disappeared, the Hammerhearts gradually tracked down and killed everyone in his family they could get hold of, but they managed to miss one person. They killed his three daughters fairly early on in the piece, but one of them also had a son who had been with foster parents at the time—name of Jacob Underwood. Fick had kept an eye on him through his job up until 2007. In fact, I think he played a big hand in helping his foster parents gain custodial rights over him as a child without the Hammersons picking up on the connection. He couldn't keep an eye on him after he retired, but he gave us the most up-to-date details on Underwood that he had."

"Very good," Mr. Woodward said again. "Did those details turn out useful?"

"Yeah," I said. "Well, we had time to get hold of his foster parents, anyway, and they gave us the address of his work and his apartment, but it was pretty late by then and we were all completely stuffed 'cause of the time difference—kind of like what I'm going through right now," I added, and he smiled at me.

"So I take it the second time you went was to visit Smiley's grandson?" he asked.

"Yeah," I said, "that's right. Well, he was far less helpful than everyone else we spoke to. If he had been, we could've been in touch with Smiley three weeks ago."

He certainly had been far less helpful, though of course he'd had his weak spot, and having Natalie and Amelia with us the day we went to visit him made that weak spot fairly easy to find.

The date we went to visit Underwood had been April 4, a Sunday. Easter Sunday, as it were. Quite a lot of bad stuff had happened in the week since our previous visit to merry old England. Before any of it, though, the first thing that had happened to me the following day, when we had all been sleeping off our all-nighter, was another trip into Stella's mind. It had been extremely brief. In it, she had still been injured but apparently mobile enough to attempt entry into the Hammerheart Highway, through whose house I didn't know —probably the Moran one, though. I had dreamt of Stella again a few nights later and, upon waking, had discovered that she was completely healed. I had asked Amelia at the meeting the following day (it had been on a Friday night, that dream) if she knew of any magical healing places the Hammersons might have that Stella could have snuck into, and she had said, to my surprise, that Stella had once told her of such a place. She had still showed no sign of believing that what I was seeing was real, but I wasn't prepared to give up.

Then, on March 31, a Wednesday that happened to be Tommy's sixteenth birthday (he had been allowed to go home and spend it with his parents), Javelyn had returned to the Woodward base with a most alarming follow-up to her earlier report of the Hammersons' plot to overthrow the Australian government. On the very day that she had delivered that report, and the day before the Woodwards had reacted to it, various highly ranked officials in both the upper and lower federal houses had been struck by the influential charm and had since been opening tiny holes for the Hammerhearts to worm their way into power and, most ominously, gain access to powerful military equipment. They had achieved this goal (or part of it) on the twenty-ninth of March. That same day, they had also been in operation overseas, beginning to do the same thing to the United States government and defence forces, along with a whole bunch of other unidentified countries. On the day that Javelyn had learnt all this (as she would learn the following day), the Hammersons had been in the US, taking possession of a number of weapons of mass destruction and using certain enchantment devices to make them even more powerful. Mr. Woodward didn't believe they would ever use such destructive weapons; the only purpose he could see for such power, assuming the Hammersons didn't want to kill everyone on the planet, was to intimidate the Woodwards and Fletchers and, in turn, all their other enemies.

Yet while all this had been happening, as hard as it might be to believe, something even worse had been happening right inside the Woodward base. At some stage between the school battle and April 1 (the day the Hammersons were believed to have learnt of the Woodwards' knowledge of their plans), the Darkness Crystal had been stolen and handed secretly to the Hammersons. Not even Javelyn had been aware of that plan. On the night of April 1 Pacific time, which had been the following afternoon for us, a powerful earthquake had struck the west coast of the United States, slightly south of San Francisco, killing more than two thousand people and causing billions of dollars' worth of damage. The timing of the earthquake had taken many scientists by surprise, and Mr. Woodward, suspecting there may be more behind it than science, had promptly checked the place he had chosen to store the Darkness Crystal. It was no longer there. He had been more shocked than anyone that the resident spy had managed to locate it and remove it without anyone's knowledge. In his shock, he had asked me if I would like to go into the Hammerson base and try to steal it back, but I had refused; I'd had enough goose chases in that place to last me a lifetime. Marc had gone instead. I had given him as many tips as I could and Javelyn, who had been in the Chopville base at the time, had texted him to let him know when the coast had been clear and nothing seemed suspicious. However, Marc had been unable to locate it, for it had not been put back in the same spot as last time. It was probably being kept on one of the Hammersons' person.

News of Mr. Woodward's discovery of the Darkness Crystal hadn't taken long to fall into the Hammersons' hands, and they had responded immediately. The following day, the Darkness Crystal had been put to further use; three more earthquakes had struck in China, Egypt, and Germany; a hurricane (Hurricane Cecilia, it had been called, although it had been known privately in both Woodward and

Hammerson circles as Hurricane Dorothy) had ripped through the area around the American city of Miami, killing at least two thousand people (though the official death toll hadn't been confirmed yet due to the enormous structural damage done to the city); and a tsunami (must have been about twenty feet high) had come crashing in along most of the western coast of Chile. The Hammersons had released a statement in the wake of these disasters, saying that more will come should their demands not be met in any area. That had been the first major hint of an attempted takeover as far as the general public was concerned.

Then, on the very day that we were to step through the back door of our second-floor room and back into 2010 life in London, Javelyn had reported a rare piece of good news. The Hammersons' whole organisation had been thrown into disarray by Bernard Moran, who had in one stroke achieved what the Woodwards had failed several times over. The previous day, he had entered the Hammerheart Highway and blocked a good portion of it, cutting the Chopville base off from the rest of the Highway for seven hours. Javelyn had also reported, separately (although everyone was sure it had also been Moran's doing), that the Darkness Crystal had been stolen from the Hammersons. None of us had been comforted by Moran having possession of the Darkness Crystal; knowing him, or not knowing him, nobody had any idea what use he might put it to. Him still having the Villain Crystal was unsettling enough.

So with all that going on, it hadn't felt pleasant, stepping into our second-floor room and halfway across the planet that evening. We had done it, though—Marc, Amelia, Tommy, Natalie, and me. It had been ten in the morning local time when we got over there, and on that lazy Sunday morning, luckily for us, Underwood had been at home when we came to call. Amelia had done the talking at first when he answered the door, taking us all in curiously and, in the case of Natalie and Amelia, eagerly. We had foolishly assumed that he would be prepared to help us in any way he could as soon as he came to realise he was in the company of two friendly Sorcerers. If we had not made that assumption, things might have gone far better for us that day.

"You're Jacob Underwood, aren't you?" she had asked.

"Yeah, that's me," he had said, his eyes roving over Tommy. He had clearly not wanted any of us boys there, but Tommy was the one he had been most uncomfortable with, for some reason. "What are all you here for? How'd you get past security? Damn fools, have they deserted their—"

"No, they haven't," Amelia had said quickly, slightly startled. "We just wanted to see you. Could we come in?"

"Who sent you?" he had asked suspiciously, half closing the door on us but still leaving enough for him to see through. "I have ways of finding out, you know."

"We sent ourselves, actually," Amelia had said, picking her words with great care. "We just want to talk to you about some things. Can we come in?"

He had studied her for a moment, his eyes wandering between her and Natalie on a regular basis. Marc and I had picked up on this undesirable trait of his at the same moment, and we both took a step back, leaving Amelia and Natalie closest to the door. Tommy had quickly followed our lead. Underwood spent a good ten seconds drinking in every bit of the two girls' appearances before finally saying, "How old are you folks? You look young."

"I'm sixteen. She's fifteen," Amelia had replied, and then to Tommy, Marc, and me in turn, "sixteen, fifteen, fourteen."

"Not that it matters, of course," Marc had stated boldly, and I nudged him hard to make him shut up.

"Ah," Underwood had said thoughtfully. "That's okay, then. I guess you can come in."

"All of us?" Natalie had asked, making it quite clear that she wasn't setting one foot inside the apartment without the three of us to back her and Amelia up. The fact that they were Sorcerers didn't seem to make a difference.

"If you say so," he had replied, most unwillingly, but he had pushed the door the rest of the way open and stepped back to let us pass.

The place had been small and reasonably tidy. It had had a cosy feel about it. The main room had served as a lounge/dining room. Through one door I could see into the kitchen. There had been two other doors that were both closed, but I had assumed one was his bedroom and the other perhaps a guest room or study. Underwood gestured to us to sit around the table. Marc, Tommy, and I had done this, for there had only been three chairs. Amelia and Natalie had taken the couch, also on Underwood's invitation. He, however, remained on his feet, his eyes on us three boys now and not at all bothered if we were comfortable. He hadn't wasted any time offering us drinks or anything.

"So what's the deal?" he had asked, his gaze returning to the couch and the two females sitting on it. "Why have you two come here, surrounded by henchmen, just to talk to me?"

His use of the word "talk" had made it all too clear that talking wasn't what he normally did when he invited young ladies he'd only just met into his home. His use of the word "henchmen" made it all too clear that he regarded Marc, Tommy, and me as protectors of the two girls. We hadn't been, of course, but that didn't mean we wouldn't stand up for them should the need arise. I could see that in Marc's face and felt sure mine had looked the same.

"Well," Amelia had said carefully, "firstly, we want to know if there's anything you can tell us about yourself."

We hadn't really discussed what we would do in a situation where the person we were trying to talk to was so unwilling to go along with us. We had just assumed that we could use magic to get the information we needed, but this man gave the impression (somehow) that he couldn't be taken in so easily by magic. Amelia's opening line had been a good one theoretically, but now that we were here, it wasn't at all surprising that Underwood had bristled at it.

"No," he had said shortly. "There's nothing. I don't just go telling people about myself."

"Why not?" Amelia had pressed him, smiling sweetly.

The smile had almost worked. Underwood had certainly been turned on for a moment, but it hadn't been enough. "Never you mind. I see no reason to share my life with complete strangers. Now, would you mind telling me what you people want?"

Amelia had glanced at Marc. The big mistake was about to be made; it had seemed all too clear at the time that Underwood was afraid that we were Hammerhearts, sent by the Hammersons to learn of any ties he might still have with his grandfather. Surely informing him that the two girls were Amelia Woodward and Natalie Fletcher, the two youngest Sorcerers, would ease his tension. Before anyone could speak, though, Underwood had broken the silence. "You guys all from Australia?"

"Er, yeah, we are," Amelia had said, surprised off her game. "How'd you know that?"

"Accent," he had replied, looking a lot more comfortable now that the conversation was on his terms. "I had an Aussie chick once, when I was about your age. You reckon you'd be as good as her? Can't see how, but I guess it's possible. I always had it from my life assistant that Aussie chicks are top-shelf."

"These ones aren't for touching," Tommy had said in a voice that reminded me forcefully of the big, bulky Hammerheart guards. A tone like that could only confirm Underwood's belief that we were there to protect the girls, nothing more significant than that.

"So all you're prepared to tell us about yourself is that you've got a filthy mind?" Natalie had asked, looking disappointed. "Is there anyone else we can talk to who might be more willing to give us more information on you? A friend or family member, perhaps?"

It had been clever to see if he would let slip anything about his family, but the way we were so determined to learn about him seemed to confirm his belief that we were up to no good. This had shown on his face for a moment, but rather than answer the question either way, he had turned the conversation on its head for a second time.

"I think I read somewhere that a lot of women who come across as prudish actually have dirtier minds than most," he had said, scrutinising Natalie closely. "I'd say, given the way you're sitting, you'd have to be pretty rich to accuse anyone else of having a dirty mind."

"What the hell are you talking about?" Natalie had snapped, going red. Big mistake, I had thought, and I'd been right.

"Have you had a look at yourself?" he had asked her, grinning slyly. "You look like you're wound tighter than a drum. I'd have to put the jack I use on my car between your legs to spread them apart, I reckon."

Natalie had gone even redder at that, stiffening horribly and looking quite as tight as Underwood had just described. He had noticed this and might have commented on it had Amelia not swiftly intervened. "Mr. Underwood, we're trying to help you here. Are you going to cooperate with us at all? Or should we find someone else to talk to instead?"

"I don't think this one is willing to help out anyone," Underwood had replied, gesturing at Natalie, his eyes now on Amelia. Beside me, I had felt Tommy stiffen, but thankfully he hadn't said anything. "You might, though. You don't look nearly as tight. In fact, you look pretty easy by comparison. I notice there's just enough space between your thighs to give a man's imagination enough to work with."

Amelia had gone almost as red as Natalie, but to her credit, she had kept a straight posture when replying. "Fuck you. We didn't come halfway across the world today to listen to shit like that."

"There's no need for you to be so disrespectful," Marc had added.

"Bullshit. You come into my home, you do things my way," Underwood had said dismissively. "And you ought to watch yourself," he had added to Amelia. "You keep talking like that to guys and they might just decide that 'fucking you over' is exactly what they want to do."

Amelia hadn't blushed; she had blanched, her eyes turning inward, and I thought I understood why. The incident in which she had been raped by Hignat and Wilwog, all under the supervision of Hank Cornish, had come about in exactly the way Underwood had just described. Amelia had dealt extremely well with the aftermath of the experience since it had happened a little over a month earlier, but apparently having the memory brought back so forcefully had affected her in a big way. I had been the only other person in the room who understood the significance of what Underwood had just said, for Marc, Natalie, and Tommy had never known about that incident and Underwood himself could have had no idea of what he'd just done, so it had been me to whom Amelia had looked desperately for help.

"Mr. Underwood," I had said curtly, the first time I'd spoken since arriving, and Underwood had looked around at me. "Does the name Gerald Fick ring a bell?"

"Gerald—" He had broken off, thinking, and then comprehension had slowly dawned on his face. "Old family friend. Why? Do you know him?"

"Yeah, we do," Marc had answered. Both girls had gone very quiet by this stage and neither looked like they wanted to speak to Underwood again. Amelia had appeared to be going through some sort of emotional turmoil, painful thoughts flickering rapidly across her face. "Actually, he was the one who gave us your address. We hadn't expected you to be alive, which is why we had to come and check on you."

"Who are you people?" Underwood had asked slowly. Something he should have asked some time ago, I had thought.

"Marc," he had said, pointing at himself, and then at the rest of us in turn. "Tommy, John, Natalie, Amelia."

His eyes had popped on the last word; the name Natalie had meant nothing to him on its own, but coupled with Amelia's, and not even Underwood was stupid enough not to understand who the two girls were. He had seemed to struggle with himself for a few moments, glancing at least twice at one of the closed doors. Then he had returned his gaze to the two girls. Amelia had been staring at her lap, lost in thoughts that looked too painful to voice, but Natalie had been brave enough to meet his eyes, and that had been enough to confirm in his mind that she was also a Sorcerer, and since she could now control the mind reading gimmick, Natalie knew it.

"You haven't had any trouble in recent times, have you?" I had prompted him.

"Not until now," he had replied quietly. The fun had well and truly gone out of his eyes. "I don't want you people in here. If they track me—"

"They won't be able to track you if you can assist us," Marc had told him.

"Assist you? Hang on, am I helping you or are you helping me?" Underwood had asked nervously.

"A bit of both," Marc had said. "Depends what sort of help you want to accept."

"None," he had replied at once. "I've done fine on my own for ages. If I start mixing with these magic folk now, I might as well sign my own death certificate, and if that's your idea of paying me back for what I think you want from me, then you might as well get walking."

There had been a silence in which Underwood had stared us all down, and all of us bar Amelia had stared back defiantly. Underwood won.

"Very well," Marc had said, getting to his feet, and the rest of us followed suit at once. "I'm disappointed, Mr. Underwood, but I can see your point, and I'm not gonna waste an afternoon trying to change your mind. We might return, though, or others like us, to make sure you are okay. The Hammerhearts are gaining in momentum, so the safety you've managed over the last ten years can't be guaranteed now, even if you don't change anything. Come on, guys."

Underwood had seen us out of his apartment without a word, leaving us to contemplate one hell of a dilemma. He had known, eventually, what we were about. He had known, without needing to be told outright, that we were looking for information about his grandfather. Yet despite the fact that we were on his side, that we were against those who had ever been a threat to his family, he had not wanted to help us. So what were we to do? We all knew that the search for people was over, at least until we could learn what Underwood knew. The question now was how do we get answers out of him?

Around two the following afternoon, Marc had held a meeting in his bedroom to discuss this complication.

"I've been thinking about it all day," he had told us. "I've been thinking about what he was like. I thought that his grandfather— thinking about his grandfather was a bit of a weakness of his. You saw what he was like when John mentioned Gerald Fick."

"I thought his weakness was magic," I had said. "He wanted nothing to do with it, 'cause of all the trouble it's brought on his family. In fact, if he's been raised for so long by foster parents, he's probably grown up blaming the Woodwards as much as the Hammersons."

"You guys are on the wrong track," Tommy had said. "Those might be sore spots for him, but bringing them up just causes him to put up his shutters and block us all out. Can you think of any way to use that against him?"

"Get him drunk?" Peter had suggested.

"Er, yeah, that might help," Tommy had conceded, "but that's not what I was thinking. We need to get him comfortable so that we can worm our way in and get what we need. Can you think how we can do that?"

"Get him drunk?" Peter had suggested again, and several people laughed.

"That might be part of it," Tommy had said, impatiently now. "No, his weakness is women. I reckon he'd do just about anything for a girl if he could get what he wanted out of her, and I'm fairly sure he would have tried that on you, Amelia. You noticed how he asked about your ages before letting you in? If you'd both said you were fifteen, he probably would have said no because you're underage—unless he's into that sort of thing too."

"So what are you suggesting?" Marc had asked angrily. "Are you saying that Amelia should go back over there and seduce him?"

"Wouldn't work." Tommy had shrugged. "He knows who she is. It would have to be someone who looks about eighteen or so, someone he won't recognise and who's good-looking enough that he'll wanna try his luck. I'm not sure there's anyone like that in the Young Army, though."

"We could go back to England and look for one," Natalie had suggested, an edge in her voice.

"And what?" Marc had asked. "Put the influential charm on her, give her the mission, and tell her to go for it? I'm not sure I'd feel right about that."

"Neither would I," Amelia had agreed.

"You got any better ideas, then?" Tommy had asked edgily.

"I don't know, but I refuse to use magic against a woman who is unwilling to surrender her body," Amelia had said in a flat voice. I had known full well what that was about, as had Peter, who knew about the incident, so neither of us had disputed Amelia's decision.

"Couldn't we find a woman and just have one of us use her body, so that she doesn't have to do it herself?" James had asked.

"I suppose for Amelia that would come to the same thing," Tommy had replied, "unless we actually ask her if she's prepared for one of us to take control of her body and make her sleep with that filthy prick. Can you think of any woman who would be prepared to do that?"

"You never know," Peter had muttered. "Honestly, you'd be surprised how low people are prepared to sink these days. I suppose most women would consider that rape; it would be like a man having sex with her while she's unconscious. We'd have to offer her a pretty damn good deal for her to be tempted."

"A prostitute would probably be prepared to do it without needing to be enchanted," Natalie had said, smiling slightly. "If we promised a hell of a lot of money, anyway."

"But that wouldn't be good enough," James had reminded us, "because the woman who does it has to be talented in other areas as well. We can't rely on just anyone to worm information about Smiley out of this guy."

"So what can we do, then?" I had asked. Circular arguments like this grow wearisome after a while. "If we're gonna satisfy all the arguments you guys have come up with, we have to find a young woman—either from over there or one of the year-twelve students here—and educate her. Then we have to get her to agree to have sex with Jacob Underwood and try to use that to get him to talk about Smiley. Does anyone else see how thin that plan is?"

"Yes," Marc had sighed. "Blimey, I can't see how we can possibly pull that one off. John's right. I honestly don't think we could get it to work, no matter how smart a woman we could find out there. A woman smart enough to deal with him wouldn't want to have sex with him, and vice versa."

"So it has to be one of us?" Nicole had suggested. "Well, since he would recognise Amelia and Natalie if they did it, I guess that leaves me to clean up the mess, huh."

"Very funny," Peter had said, quite as sarcastically as our sister. "You fail in the age requirement; you're only fifteen, and you look it, too, which is the more important point."

"Excuse me—"

"Look, maybe we should just give it some thought," James had suggested. "Er, some more thought, in case one of us has a bright idea. We might have a starting point with what we've got, but it clearly needs more work."

"Hear, hear," Marc had agreed. "I know it's immoral, but it could be so much more important for the world in general if we can get it done, even if it means using magic to make a young woman do something she wouldn't normally do of her own free will. We can always use magic afterwards to make sure it has no effect on her at all, so it really shouldn't be too bad."

"No, no, no," Amelia had said flatly. "If we're going to use someone from outside, she has to agree to it. It would be necessary for one of us to be using her body at the time to deal with Underwood—because John's right, nobody who hasn't been in this from the start could do it properly—but she would have to agree to that too. I know most women would flatly refuse to share their body with a complete stranger, but if I've got any say in it, then that's how we're doing it."

"To that, I'd say that it's probably easier dealing with Underwood as we are than finding a woman prepared to fall in line with that plan," Peter had said. "Couldn't you just use magic on one of us to make us look like a hot, sexy eighteen-year-old chick? It would really simplify things."

"See," James had gloated. "I knew if we gave it more thought, a bright idea would come up. Great one, Pete."

But Amelia had been shaking her head even as James had been speaking, and I couldn't blame her; I certainly wouldn't be brave enough to do that sort of magic on one of my friends.

"That's extremely dodgy," she had said. "I've tried to do that once before. You have very little control over what you make the person look like. I could probably make you look like a woman, Peter, but you'd probably end up with horrible warts all over your face and breasts the size of beach balls, and of course, if Underwood undressed you and you still had a penis, that would really screw things up."

"Do it to yourself, then, or Natalie," Nicole had suggested. "There would be far less to do since you're already a girl."

"Or you," Peter had said, grinning at her.

"No," Amelia had said firmly.

I had to force myself to be sympathetic. Amelia was going through a very tough time; it had been quite clear by her face that the pain she had suppressed for such a long time was finally rearing its ugly head and wriggling far too much for her to control. Yet she had really made things more complicated than they needed to be.

"Why don't we leave it for a few days and come back to it," James had suggested. "Perhaps Thursday or Friday we meet again, or sooner if anyone comes up with anything good."

I had listened to all this without a word. I'd noticed that none of them had paid any attention to my suggestion of the woman in question being someone from within the Woodward army, but I hadn't forgotten the idea. She only had to look like she was eighteen or so; she didn't necessarily have to be eighteen. She had to be reasonably knowledgeable about the war so that we would have a lot less explaining to do. She would have to be willing to give up her body for a short amount of time, and despite the sensitivity of the issue, I thought that such a woman could be found with the right incentive. It would also be good if, like Tommy had said, she were physically attractive. Lena Tuck fitted the bill almost perfectly—she was tall and athletic with a very pretty face; long, blond hair; long, strong legs; long, slender fingers; slim waist; great arse; and what my dad (my Playman dad) would have called "bountiful bosoms." Very curvy indeed, and delicious. Just the sort of girl Underwood (or any red-blooded male) would love to get on top of. She would be perfect if we could get her to agree to the job, and on that score, I thought that I had a better chance of persuading her than anyone else.

So, the following afternoon, I had taken Lena up to my room to inform her that she might soon be involved in top secret Young Army business. It had been difficult to get her to be serious; it had been the first time I had ever invited Lena anywhere alone, and she seemed to take it to mean that I was finally showing interest in her, and she had certainly acted accordingly, flirting quite as intently as she had done on Rock Haulter, trying to touch me, trying to get me to sit on the bed with her. I had done my best to keep the conversation where I wanted it to be, but remembering Tommy's words from the day before, I had kept her behaviour in mind; her still being interested in "doing things" with me may be useful in getting her to cooperate. Later in the week, on the eighth, I had asked Amelia's opinion of using Lena's body to seduce Underwood, making it clear that I hadn't yet told Lena exactly what she would have to do. Amelia had agreed that it would be okay if Lena agreed to surrender her body to one of them, which made me feel considerably better. If Lena didn't let us down, we may have taken a big step in picking her.

The next day, the ninth, I had called another private meeting. There would be one the following day, because Saturday seemed to be the standard day for meetings, and I had wanted to bring Lena along to it, but we had needed to discuss the idea without her first. Predictably, there had been arguing over the suggestion.

"Are you sure it's such a good idea to bring Lena so far into all of this?" James had asked. "I mean to say, if we get her involved now, wouldn't we have to keep her involved in everything from now on?"

"I don't see why we would have to do that," Marc had said. "We could always just wipe her memory of it once it's done. That way, she'd know none of it and we wouldn't have to be responsible for her."

"I don't want to wipe her memory of something like that," Amelia had said as flatly as at the last meeting. She'd had a very bad week since the Underwood experience. "We would have to put fake memories in place of the real ones; otherwise, she would be incomplete. If she agrees to do this, I think she has the right to be allowed to remember it. We'd just have to make her understand that she's not to go shooting her mouth off, and if I know Lena, I don't think she would—she hardly ever opens her mouth. If we have to let her be involved in what we're doing from now on, that seems like a fair enough price to me."

"How do we know she won't be tricked or enchanted into spilling the beans?" Tommy had asked.

"How do we know you won't be enchanted into spilling your guts about all this?" Peter had retorted.

"We can look after ourselves okay," James had said. "How can we be sure that she can do the same? The way I see it, we can make sure of that only if we make her one of our number. Do we all want Lena coming to all these meetings and to be involved in our decision making?"

"I don't," Natalie had said quietly. "I trust her, but the only reason she factors into any of this is because of her looks. That's not enough for me. I dunno if that makes sense but—"

"It does," Peter had said heavily. "Okay, how's this for a suggestion: We don't make her forget what happens, but we instead put a spell on her similar to the one John said the Hammersons put on some of their Hammerhearts to make them not speak of certain things. She'll remember what happens, but she won't be able to speak of it to anyone."

"Wow, that's a damn good idea," Marc had said, mightily impressed, as was everyone else, including Amelia.

"One other thing, though," James had said soberly. "What if we tell Lena all this, and she refuses to have a bar of it. What do we do then? The same thing—not let her speak of what we tell her?"

There had been a short silence. Then Tommy had said, "If she doesn't agree to help us, then I don't see why we shouldn't make her forget what we tell her. It's not like she would deserve to know."

Everyone had looked at Amelia at that point, apparently in agreement that she was the only one who might disagree with this suggestion. She had given it some thought, then said resignedly, "I guess Tommy's right, but that's all the magic we'll do. No more than that."

So that had been two-quarters of the plan achieved. The next step was to bring Lena fully into the picture, so for lunch on the tenth, I had found her in the dining room and asked her to come join us in my room. She might have been excited by this, but she was a smart girl and had picked up on the plural, and had taken it accordingly to mean that this was business, not pleasure. She had looked around at the seven people sitting around the lounge area of Marc's room (for that was where this meeting was held) with considerable scepticism, and a touch of distaste, as though wishing they were gone and it was just me and her here. Well, that was what I took it to mean, but that could have been just me knowing what Lena had been like with me.

"Sit down here," I had told her, gesturing to a spot beside Marc and sitting myself down on her other side—any little thing to make her a little more persuadable. "Right, you probably know how the eight of us have been working secretly away from the rest of the Young Army for about a month now, but we think we might need your help with something, so we're going to tell you a few things that none of the others know about, things that you may need to know if you agree to help us. Can you promise not to tell anyone what goes on here?"

"Sure," she had said eagerly. Good sign, I had thought, not that the promise mattered; we had already agreed how we would make sure she kept her silence.

"Good," I had said. "Well, what we're trying to do is contact a man who used to be part of the Woodward army but has fallen out of touch since. He has some—er, important knowledge about the Hammersons that we need to know—stuff about why they want to kill me, and possibly Tommy too. We've located his grandson, who seems, to us anyway, to be the only person still in touch with this old guy, but he's extremely difficult to deal with, as we found out last weekend. Er, this is the awkward part: We need you to help us with him because—er, you're the sort of person he would be more willing to submit to."

"Er, okay," Lena had said cautiously. "What does that mean?"

We had all looked at each other. I should have been the one to explain it to her, and we all knew it. The only trouble was I hadn't been sure exactly what to say. Thankfully, as he'd been known to do in times like that, Peter had jumped straight to the point. "This guy we're talking about likes women. We all know how good-looking you are, and you're the only one who looks like she might be old enough."

"Oh," she had said, her face falling slightly. "You want me because of what I look like. Wow, I'm just flattered."

The sarcasm in her voice had been unmistakable, and I hadn't been at all surprised.

"You don't want to help, huh?" Marc had said, watching her closely.

"What exactly are you wanting me to do?" she had asked, her eyes on me, but again it had been Marc who had answered.

"We think if he believes he can get what he wants from you, he will be more willing to give us what we need from him. We don't expect you to have to reason with him; in fact, you won't actually need to do any of it. Isn't the plan that one of us take your body so that we can deal with him while trying to seduce him at the same time?"

"That would be the easiest way," James had said.

"What?" Lena had said, startled. "Hang on. What do you mean, 'take my body'? I'm not sure I like the sound of that."

A few of us had exchanged unsurprised glances at that point.

"You wouldn't feel it," Marc had told her, trying to sound reassuring. "You wouldn't have to experience any of it. I think one of us—probably either John or Tommy, since they're the most involved in this whole thing—would take control of your body so they can get this guy where we want him. You wouldn't have to do anything except spare a few days or so out of your life."

"Are you gonna make me have sex with this guy?" Lena had asked, and as soon as the words were out of her mouth, we all knew that this would be the make-or-break straw of the deal. Amelia had glared at all of us very quickly and sharply in that moment, making it quite clear that only the truth could be spoken.

"You wouldn't be having sex with him," Marc had said, "because like I said, you wouldn't have to do it yourself. You won't feel it or experience any of it."

"That's not what I meant and you know it," she had said flatly. "Are you going to make my body—if that's all it is to you—have sex with this guy?"

"Well—" Marc had hesitated, but Amelia had glared at him again, and he had conceded, "I guess we would do what is necessary. It may be that whichever of us is doing it can get him to do what we need first, meaning that we wouldn't have to put you through much of anything, but if not—we would do what is necessary."

Fairly put, I had thought, as had everyone else in the room. Lena hadn't looked at all impressed.

"So can you help us at all?" I had asked her. Again, a little thing that may or may not help our cause. "We really need this."

"No deal," she had said flatly. Her eyes were on me, and they were burning; she looked pained by something. "I wish I could help you guys, but I'm not going to do something like that, not now. You only want my body and not the rest of me."

My insides had shrivelled at that. She had never taken her eyes off me when she said that. The implication that it was me who wanted to use her for her body and pay no respect to who she was as a person hurt; there was so much more to this than that. A silence had followed these words, which was eventually broken by Natalie. "Well, I can't say I'm surprised. I would have said the same thing. Thanks anyway, Lena. Maybe we should put this meeting on hold for a while so we can do a bit more thinking?"

That was all good for them, but I hadn't quite given up on Lena. I had felt quite sure that there was something she hadn't explained at that meeting; perhaps it was something she had only wanted me to know, and not the others. Her points had all been fair and I didn't blame her for any of them, but all the same, I still felt I could bring her around if I understood a little more of what was going on in her mind. So, that evening, I had gone to see her again, in her room where she was completely alone, apparently studying.

I had felt wrong-footed before I'd even begun because I didn't have the Sien-Leoard Crystal with me, which only showed how I had come to rely on it more than I should have. This was on the evening of the tenth, and it had been only hours earlier that the Hammersons had launched their worst assault yet—the assassinations of many of the world's most powerful leaders. All the Sorcerers, plus Marc, Tommy, and many of the Woodward army soldiers, had been called out to increase the security around those who had been missed and to prevent the Hammerhearts putting their own people in positions of power in all the confusion and fear. I had flatly refused to go out (I was done being a hero), but Mr. Woodward had insisted that I at least hand over my crystal to someone else so that they could have as much magic on their side as possible. I had wondered at that point if he had asked Marc to call Fewul, the Beast of Magic with unrivalled powers that would obey the Seventh Sorcerer, then decided I didn't want to know.

"Hi," Lena said when she had opened her door and seen me standing there. "I hope you're not here to use your crystal to get me to do what they wanted, are you?"

"No," I had said truthfully. "We agreed before we even approached you that we wouldn't use magic against you, and besides"—I had waved my empty hands—"I don't even have the crystal with me anymore. Mr. Woodward made me hand it over to help with all their protecting work tonight, you know."

"Oh," she had said, taken aback. "Yeah, that would make sense. Why aren't you out there with them? They always used to get you to do the big jobs."

"They wanted me out there," I had said, "but I'm done with the 'big jobs,' at least for a while. I wanted to talk to you about this afternoon. Can I come in?"

"Do you really expect me to change my mind?" she had asked, but she had stood back to let me pass her. Her room was a mirror image of mine, with all the same furniture in it arranged all the same way, though in reverse, of course. I had taken a seat at the table, and Lena had sat herself down on her bed, facing me.

"Possibly," I had said, unsure exactly how best to proceed.

"Oh, really? What are you gonna tell me that would make it sound even a little bit bearable?"

"I don't know, but I can tell there's something," I had said, thinking very fast. "I understand everything you said earlier, and they're all fair points, but I just had a feeling that there was a bit more to it than that. Am I right?"

"Maybe," she had said cagily.

"You wanna tell me?" I had pressed her. "I won't tell the others if you don't want me to, but if there's any deal we can make on this— it's really important that we make one somehow."

"I guess," she had said slowly. "This is really important to you, is it? You think it will help you stay alive?"

"Probably," I had said. "It's hard to know, but we expect it would pay off."

"Why me, though?" she had asked. "You could have picked anyone. Why me?"

"Well, Peter said why," I had reminded her. "Amelia says we can't use magic to change one of our own appearances to suit, and we agreed not to use magic to force someone into it, and it would be just about impossible to get someone from outside to agree to it; they wouldn't know any of what's been going on. At least you've been in the Young Army before. You really are the best one for the job."

"It's the most demeaning job you guys have ever given me," she had said solemnly.

"We're not going to make you do anything," I had told her, "although I should let you know, if we can't change your mind, we will have to use magic to make you forget what we've already told you about it, and if you do agree, we'll use it to make sure you don't speak of it to anyone."

"But I promised—"

"I know, but just in case the other side uses magic to attempt to wheedle it out of you. I've already done that to a Hammerheart once; it's not too difficult if you know what you're doing."

"I hate it. I don't wanna do it. It's just so—so dirty."

"I know, but then I guess just about everything about this war is dirty. This is just a different kind of it."

She had closed her eyes and considered my words for some time. I had waited, thinking that maybe this was the closest I could get to convincing her to do it or to finding out what part of it was putting her off most. Eventually, she had opened her eyes again and stared hard at me for a few seconds. It had been the stare that she always gave me, the one that always made me squirm, because I felt sure I knew what she was thinking about.

"I suppose if it's as simple as you made it sound," she had said carefully, "then perhaps I would be honourable enough to do my bit in this war—if you can call something like that honourable. In fact, I think I'd like you to use magic on me to make me forget the unpleasant parts of it if it's such a bad thing."

"Which we can do," I had assured her, "and for all we know, you mightn't have to give up anything along the way, but it's not as simple as I made it sound, is it?"

"Not for me, no," she had said quietly.

"No?" I had prompted. "Why not? Am I allowed to know?"

She had shrugged, looking awkward. "I suppose so." She had taken a deep breath and forced herself to look me in the eyes. Apparently, doing so had somehow given her courage. "The thing is, I'm a virgin, and I don't know if the first time's as big a deal for you guys as it is for girls. Perhaps for you, you could do this thing unconscious, then go out and have sex with someone else and it would still feel like the first time because you wouldn't remember the real first time—it would have been someone else having it the first time, if you get my meaning. That's more or less what Marc was saying, so I suppose that really is how it is for guys. But it's not like that for girls, and I've gotta say I'm surprised none of the other girls pointed it out—they must have thought of it. I guess what I'm trying to say is I don't want this thing to be my first time, because I won't remember it. And even if I did remember it, well, that would be even worse—I don't wanna live my life with that as my first time. Can you understand that?"

"Yeah, I can," I had said heavily. That was a damn good reason, I had thought, good enough to make me think that it probably wasn't worth continuing down this track. "And I guess we just don't know how it would go, so I can see why you wouldn't wanna take the chance. You don't think there's anything any of us can do to make you feel better about it?"

"Possibly," she had said quietly, and my heart had skipped a beat. Maybe all hope wasn't lost yet.

"Such as?"

For answer, she had smiled and licked her lips at me. Comprehension hit me with the force of a charging bull. My stomach sunk to somewhere around my knees.

"No, I don't think so."

"You don't wanna meet me halfway on this one?" she had asked, smiling sweetly. I had to give her credit; she had really turned the tables on me this time.

"Well, I don't—I can't."

"You sure?" she had persisted. "That's a lot less than I really want, but at least for now, I'll be much more agreeable if I don't have my virginity to consider, and if you really want to do what you can to make me agreeable…"

"Blimey, that's blackmail if I ever heard it."

"It's not blackmail; it's a compromise."

We had stared at each other for several seconds, in which time I had looked over and thought geez, Serena doesn't know just how lucky she is to have a guy who can look at this woman and refuse to have sex with her. Or maybe Serena does know. After all, since Serena and I had been on our most eventful first date earlier that week, she and I had become better in our relationship than ever before. I didn't want to screw up what I'd had so much trouble getting by doing the deed with Lena, even if it was for the good of the war. I had understood better at that point exactly what I was asking from Lena, and I had to hand it to her, she'd got me good. Our sacrifices were just about equal in weight.

But something else had happened while I had been in the room. Memories of several weeks ago, of fantasies (many of them about what I could be doing with Lena should I choose her over Natalie, Stella, and Serena), had come flooding back to me. I could have stood up and jumped on Lena then and there; she had quite deliberately sat herself on the bed for the purpose of allowing that possibility, I had felt sure. Apparently, part of me had still wanted her, after all this time of having very little to do with her, of having nothing more than the occasional flirtatious glance pass from her to me. That, on top of my desire to work out what the hell my whole life had stood for by finding Smiley, had opened the door for me to do something I had always promised myself I would never do.

"Put it on the table. We'll come back to it. I don't ever wanna cheat—and if you were in Serena's position, you would appreciate that—but this may be more important than a single relationship. We'll talk again about this."

"I look forward to it," she had said softly, extremely seductively, and I had left the room, hardly knowing what I was doing.

Chapter 6: Changing Hands

"Maybe so, but that was on the fourth," said Mr. Woodward, "and today is the twenty-eighth. There was a considerable time when you made no move against Smiley's grandson. How come?"

"Well, the delay was because of Lena," I said. "You know Lena Tuck?"

"Yes, I'm familiar with Lena."

"Yeah," I said. "Well, and because there was a lot of other stuff happening then. Things moved very quickly after those assassinations. You know what I mean."

People had their own opinions about when the Hammersons stepped into the open. Some said it was their attempted takeovers of Chopville High, but that was on such a minor scale compared with the sort of things they had done in the previous war and were planning for this one that many people (I among them) didn't count it. Some said it was when they used the Darkness Crystal to create those natural disasters; I liked to think of that as Operation Hammerson, step one. Operation Hammerson, step two, was the events of April 10; that was the day I meant when I had referred to the assassinations. Some people, such as James, considered Operation Hammerson, step three, as the date the Hammersons began a full-scale takeover; that date hadn't come yet, but we all knew it was close. I had no idea that, as I sat there in Mr. Woodward's office thinking about it, that moment was mere hours away.

"Yes, I do," he said heavily. "I take it you're referring to the more personal things that happened to you around that time? That would have been around the time of the fire, and the contact with Moran—"

"It wasn't Moran," I said quickly.

Mr. Woodward raised his eyebrows. "What do you mean?"

"I know who that was now," I said. "It's part of the Underwood business actually. It had nothing to do with Moran."

The incident we were talking about had actually been earlier in that week. On the Monday after Easter, April 5 that would have been, the day Marc had called us to his room to discuss the complication Underwood had left us with, Serena had followed up on the displeasure she'd had with me the day Amelia and I had almost kissed—that she and I still hadn't gone on a proper date as yet. It had been after dinner, but the place had been unusually quiet. It had been getting more and more so as those who lived here regularly became so accustomed to the place that they spent much of their time doing their own thing or hanging somewhere other than the lounge room. We had been in the main hall, just outside the dining room, and the only person close by had been Sebastian Williams, a jerk in year ten who struck me forcefully as a slightly younger version of Underwood, leaning against the wall and texting away on his phone.

"You said ages ago that you would take me out for dinner sometime," she had complained. "We've been dating for over a month now, but we haven't even gone on a date. I know stuff keeps coming up, but we can't let that control our relationship, can we?"

"Of course not—"

"I really wanna make this work, but you've gotta help me here."

"I know that—"

"Don't you care about me? About us?"

"Yes, but—"

"Or are you more interested in all these other people who keep wanting to get between—"

"Are you gonna let me get a word in or not?" I had snapped. Above many things, I despised being talked at rather than to.

She had frozen, biting her tongue, waiting for me to say whatever I was going to say (I had no idea what) and looking ready to interrupt at any moment. Welcome to dating, John, I had thought, and had to work very hard not to laugh. I couldn't have picked a worse time to laugh if I'd tried.

"I know what you're saying," I had said cautiously, "and I do wanna make this work, believe me. How about tomorrow night? I'm fairly sure the world won't end in the next twenty-four hours. Not completely sure, but fairly sure. How about I take you out to dinner, so we can actually have a date for a change?"

"Ooh, dinner," she had said excitedly. "Where? You got anywhere in mind? I haven't been around Chopville long enough to know of half the stuff in the town central."

"I might ask around, but I think I may know a good place," I had said carefully.

"And, and," she had pressed eagerly, "what comes after dinner?"

"Er, I hadn't thought that far ahead," I had admitted, feeling like an utter fool. Ah well, Johnny boy, you're only fourteen, and if you stumble along this rocky road often enough, you'll eventually learn where the potholes are. That sounded like something Harry or Simon would say in their ridiculous attempts to sound wise and worldly, and I'd had to force down yet another laugh.

"Oh, you," she had laughed, slapping my arm. "We come back here, of course. We wouldn't be allowed out too late anyway, given how dangerous it is. We can entertain ourselves after dinner—or more like entertain each other."

She had grinned roguishly at me and slipped away up the stairs and out of sight, leaving me standing stock-still, hardly knowing what I'd just gotten myself into. Sebastian had just snapped his phone shut at that moment; now he looked over at me, grinning broadly. "Blimey, John, that was the weirdest display of asking a girl out I've ever seen."

"Oh, shut up," I had said wearily, but I had still felt close enough to laughter not to be angry with him.

"It'd be easier to manage with sweet little Nat, you know that," he had said daringly. "You know she's single now. I'm surprised you haven't jumped on her."

"Because I'm with Serena," I had said pointedly.

"Really? Wow, I could never have worked that out. Seriously, though, I can't see why you'd have any trouble. She still looks at you often—I see it all the time. I'm surprised she hasn't used magic to spell you over to her, now that she has the power."

"I guess because she's an honest person, unlike some," I had said, pointedly as ever, and left him there.

I had indeed asked a couple of people (well, Harry and Simon counted as a couple of people, I supposed) about good places to take a first date for dinner. They had both recommended the place I had already thought of, which made me feel fairly good. At least I had some taste to start with; it didn't all have to come from experience. I'd had no way of knowing, however, what the consequences of speaking of the location of the date would be. I hadn't told Serena where we were going—I'd wanted it to be a surprise—but the twins had told Katie and Sophie, and they'd spread it like no one's business. Not until Serena and I had been there in the restaurant had I realised, the hard way, that the Hammerson spy had also learnt of the time and place I would be out and about, and unprotected. I wasn't completely unprotected, of course. I had the Sien-Leoard Crystal with me, but that was all, and in a small and cosy place like the one we had been in, there was only so much I could do with it.

The evening had started fairly well for a date. I had been worried that Serena might have found out that I had taken Lena into my room earlier that afternoon (for that was the day I had first informed her that she might have some business with us), but if so, she had acted as though she didn't know. There had been only one other possibly bad moment, when Amelia had just assisted us out of the Woodward headquarters; all three of us had frozen, believing (without any proof whatsoever) that someone was lurking close by, watching us. Amelia had done several spells to flush the person out, but they had all failed. Moran, I had thought, the untraceable one, but if it was only Moran, then we would probably be okay. I'd hoped, anyway.

Adding to the good stuff, Serena had neither seen nor heard of the little restaurant I had chosen, which was tucked away behind the supermarket in the northwest corner of the town central. Even better, when we had entered, only one of the six small tables had been occupied; one solitary woman, her face covered by a veil, was sitting alone at the table farthest from the door, turning her head from side to side like a metronome. When Serena and I had entered, however, she had fixed her gaze on the counter, but I had seen her eyes for maybe half a second, and had thought, I know her, I've seen those eyes before. I had felt sure of it, because…whatever I had picked up from them and the gaze hadn't been long enough for me to quite identify it, but those eyes had been like no others.

We had taken the table closest to the front of the restaurant. Serena's choice, because I would have preferred one where I could get a better look at that woman over there. The server (the place was small enough that it only needed one) had brought her meal out to her, and she had thanked him in a very quiet voice that was almost completely inaudible from our position—far too quiet for me to place, although I had still felt sure I'd heard it before. The server had then come and taken our orders, and when he had gone, Serena and I had been left staring at each other.

"I think this is the part where we're supposed to learn a bit about each other," Serena had said, smiling slightly.

"Yeah, but we already know each other. Well, sort of," I had said, also smiling. Talking had felt easier than sitting in silence.

"I wonder why," she had said, winking at me.

"I know, I know, but we're here now. You like it?"

"Yeah, this is perfect," she had said softly, smiling slowly and looking several times prettier than usual. She had certainly gone to pains to look her best tonight; in fact, I thought she'd looked better that night than she had even on Stella's birthday night. She was wearing a long, blue dress—that was all I had noticed about her attire because I was more interested in looking at her face, and the ample amount of cleavage she had shown when I couldn't prevent my eyes from dipping downward. I had worn black pants and a white shirt, but that was the extent I had gone to. I wasn't good at dressing up at the best of times, and what did it matter when the best part of the night would be taking all this stuff off? At least I'd had the sense not to voice that last thought.

The door had opened at that point and another couple had come in, hand in hand. They had been not much older than me and Serena, eighteen or nineteen at most. The bloke was about James's height and looked tough enough to lift his lady friend off her feet and spin her around in the air over his head. Then again, that wouldn't have been too difficult, because she had been roughly the size of Katie, who was very small indeed. They had looked wrapped in each other and had taken a table two farther back from the one Serena and I had been at. The server hadn't had a chance to come out to them because the bloke had left his little girlfriend at the table and gone up to the counter to place their orders. The woman had looked around her in this time, taking in the solitary woman as I had done, then meeting my eyes over Serena's head and looking curious—probably thinking Serena and I looked too young to be serious.

The guy had come back and sat down with his back to Serena and me, blocking his girlfriend from my view. He had leaned across the table, and I had heard him say very quietly, "I don't think old tubby over there likes people walking around in his shop." The woman had said something even more quietly, but I had not been able to pick it up.

"What are you thinking, John?" Serena had asked, making me jump.

"Er, what?"

"What are you thinking?" she had repeated. "I can tell you're thinking about something."

"Oh, I don't know," I had said, uneasily. "Maybe it's just how things have been lately, but I'm feeling a might jumpy tonight. Don't worry about it. I don't want my mental problems to ruin our evening."

She had laughed at that and reached across the table to hold my hands. Even better, I had thought; having some kind of physical contact seemed, for the time being, to mean we didn't necessarily have to continue talking. The server had come at that point with a couple of non-alcoholic drinks to get us started and the opposite to get the other couple started.

For maybe ten minutes after that, Serena and I had sat in silence, apart from the occasional comment from either of us about something or other. Mostly we had just held hands and stared around us, at the table, at the surroundings, at the three other diners, and always back at each other before too long. I had wondered at around that point at what stage would we kiss. We had kissed plenty of times already, but the first kiss tonight seemed to mean much more, as though it would make our relationship more official than it had been before. I had supposed it wouldn't come until after the meal; if we were older, it would be over the wine. Or maybe it wouldn't come until we were leaving. Or if we could have had a date in more normal times, it might have come at some stage during the walk along Achior Stroll, which stretched between Main Street (the north-south route through the centre of Chopville) and the far west edge of Chopville right along the Jade River, making it one of the more spectacular views in town, particularly at sunset, or at twilight, lit by the towering street lights that stretched high into the air on the sides of the Coleman Bridge. Corny, maybe, but I thought even I would find the idea of enjoying a scene like that with a girl particularly romantic.

Our meals had been brought to us shortly after I had mentally lamented my lack of freedom to make this date what I would have liked. After that, we had let go of each other's hands and eaten in silence for some time. The server had already returned with the other couple's dinners before Serena decided to break the silence.

"How far do you reckon you and I can go anyway?" she had asked. "I mean—I don't mean realistically, 'cause I don't wanna think about the war tonight, but just—I'm not sure how to say it."

She had looked imploringly at me. "Do you mean how far would we like to go if it's up to us and no outside factors?"

"Yeah, yeah," she had said eagerly. "How would you like it to go?"

I had hesitated for only a split-second, wishing that she hadn't seized on this topic. I imagined it was one blokes the world over dreaded. The truthful answer was that I wanted it to go however it went, because of course, breaking up with Serena would open the door to a possible relationship with one of the others—Natalie or Amelia, both of whom I cared about in a different way from Serena (Amelia had looked a little more likely earlier that day, as I had observed her and Marc having a heated argument in the lounge room earlier that day), or Lena, whom dating would probably have felt like a wet dream impossible to wake up from. Saying that, however, would not have been sensible, so I had said the closest thing to the truth that I could.

"I'd like it to go as well and for as long as we can possibly make it, which I guess is supposed to mean 'forever.' I can't see how we can make it if we're trying to foresee the end, and if we're thinking like that, then there's no point being together at all. I suppose it mightn't work out—I keep feeling like I'm blundering along with no idea what to do—but if it goes wrong, it goes wrong. We don't have to look forward to that."

My words would come back to bite me, I had felt quite sure, and my stomach had dropped horribly. Damn, inexperience sucked big time. I had looked over Serena's shoulder at that point at the other couple, wishing I could do things as well as that guy over there was doing them. Temporarily (or completely) abandoning his dinner, he had got up from his seat, walked around the table so that he was behind his girlfriend, and was on his knees behind her, massaging her shoulders and back through and around the back of the chair.

"Forever," she had repeated, her eyes wide and bright. "You serious, forever? You're not interested in—er—experimenting with other girls before you settle down?"

"No," I had said automatically. "I mean—well, we don't have to settle down as such, but what's the point in us taking our relationship seriously if it's just an experiment?"

"No point at all," she had said. "So it's not an experiment, then?"

"No. I'm not into that. Haven't you worked that out?"

I had said the wrong thing, I knew it. I had just stopped myself mentioning all the other girls (most particularly Lena) who had clustered around me over the last couple of months, but that was surely not a sensible thing to do on a first date. Telling Serena that she should have worked out I would be faithful by observing how I am with other girls had been no better. Okay, John, that was a stuff-up—better luck next time.

"Well," she had said, pulling herself together. She had no more wanted to argue than I. "That's good, then. For the record, I'm the same—I'm not interested in anyone else anymore."

"Aw," I had said. "I'm so glad to hear you say that."

What I'd wanted to do was get things back on positive terms. I'd wanted Serena to think about now—not the past, not the future, not the crap that was going on in the present, but right now. I had reached across the table and taken both her hands again and given them a small squeeze, not minding either of our dinners for the time being. Taking a tip out of the book of the bloke two tables away, I had supposed; that one had progressed considerably. He had one hand down his girlfriend's dress, his other wrapped tightly around it while he pashed her. She, meanwhile, had her hands in his long hair, running her fingers through it. My gaze had been mostly for Serena, but I had noticed, out of the corner of my eye, that the server was observing this scene with something like alarm; perhaps he was worried about just how far they would go right here in the restaurant.

"This has been a great night, John," Serena had said softly, drawing my attention back to her, ignoring the sounds of slurping and the occasional moan from behind her. At least she didn't have to see it, as I had to over her shoulder.

"With a bit of luck, it will get better," I had said, just as softly, as we had both leaned forward.

Was this the moment, I had briefly wondered, for the kiss I had been anticipating? I'd been with Serena long enough to recognise when she was about to make contact, and at that moment she had looked ready to wrap her mouth around mine and replace the meal on her plate with my tongue. I had been a little nervous, not scared that she would be too passionate for me to handle but that this kiss might be different, more important than any of the others we'd had, and that I might not be up to it. I had wanted it, though, very much.

We had been staring into each other's eyes, only inches apart, both our mouths puckered, ready for the moment, when it happened. There had been absolutely no warning, no sign of movement, no sudden sound, and if the aim had been true, Serena and I would have both been down without a single chance to defend ourselves. As it was, the bloke two tables away had saved our lives; he had been so determined not to straighten up to give himself away that his girlfriend had been in a position far too awkward to efficiently aim a solid-outliner. The jet of white light that should have hit the back of Serena's head had soared inches over both our heads, giving us both the fright of our lives. We had let go of each other, and Serena had spun around so that we could both see our two assailants. They had both straightened up now, and the woman, the only one armed at that second, had fired again. The second jet had hit Serena squarely in the chest; she had let out a yell and then sat stock-still, letting the stuff take her and apparently trusting that I would save her—that had actually been the smartest thing to do in that situation.

"Oi! Oi!" the server had cried. "You stop that right now! You—"

The man had turned and shot his solid-outliner at the server. It hit him in the face, and he fell to the floor. The manager and two kitchen staff had come running at that stage, and all three had got themselves caught up in the thicky prison too. In all the confusion, nobody had noticed the solitary woman who'd spent all this time at the back of the restaurant; I had forgotten about her, but as I had jumped to my feet and withdrawn the Sien-Leoard Crystal from one pocket and extracted my own solid-outliner from the internally extending pouch I carried in the other (it was something I had stolen from the Hammerhearts when I had been abducted by them and had carried it ever since the second school battle—these things were useful to have in addition to the crystal), I thought I had heard (or perhaps felt) her pass close behind me. I hadn't been at all surprised that she was making a quiet exit from the place.

The situation hadn't taken long from that point to defuse. The woman had had enough time to fire a shot at me, but I had dodged it, thinking as I did, knock her out for twenty-four hours, and the crystal had obliged as always. The bloke had also got a shot at me, and his had hit my left hand, the one bearing the Sien-Leoard Crystal, and thicky prison had begun to spread over it, up to my wrist. Knock him out too, I had thought as he had advanced on me, me worried that the crystal wouldn't work while it was trapped in the thicky prison, but no such bad luck; the man had dropped to the floor, almost bringing down a table as he fell. I had quickly used my own solid-outliner to release my binds, then Serena's, before hurrying around to the back of the counter to attend to the friendly staff who had been guilty of nothing more than being in the wrong place at the wrong time. Serena, who hadn't once lost her head in the confusion, followed closely behind.

"What the hell was that?" she had fumed. "My God, we can't even have one romantic evening without Hammerhearts trying to have a go at us. Are there any more hanging around?"

I hadn't considered that, and as the three men and one woman before me had struggled together, trying to stagger back to their feet, I had hurriedly used the crystal to check. No, they were only the two who had been sent after us. That woman who had been in before seemed to have disappeared altogether.

"What are you people doing?" the manager had asked, the first to regain his feet.

"Saving your bacon," I had said. "Those two"(I had jerked my thumb over the counter at the two prone figures separated by one table)—are apparently Hammerhearts. They thought they'd have a go at us. We did nothing wrong, as he can probably testify."

I had looked at the server, who nodded but said nothing. The two kitchen staff—a young male chef, by the look of it, and a dishwasher lady—were also on their feet now. They both thanked us timidly and had hurried back through the bat-winged doors into the kitchen. The manager had also disappeared into another room without a word, leaving me and Serena staring at each other, the server forgotten.

"What do we do?" she had asked me. All the passion we had been feeling prior to the would-be kiss had been snuffed out by the attack, and I had felt angry about it.

I had looked over at the two Hammerhearts, wondering how much of what they had done had been an act for my benefit, for I had felt quite sure that they had been sent to capture me and dispense with Serena if she got in the way. Were those two really a couple? Well, either way, I had thought, I could learn from them; that little act of intimacy had looked effective, however genuine it had been. I would bear it in mind, since there was little else I could take out of the evening.

"I'll take them to Mr. Woodward," I had decided. "He can either keep them or hand them over to the police."

"How did they know we were going to be here?" Serena had asked as I began working magic with the crystal to create an internally extending bag (like the pouch, which wasn't big enough) to carry the two unconscious bodies in. "They were only a few minutes behind us; how could they have come so quickly?"

"I don't know," I had said, but no sooner were the words out than I knew the answer. "The spy!"

"What?"

"The spy—the one who's been causing the Woodwards so much trouble, the one who stole the Darkness Crystal. He or she must have heard about us coming here tonight and let the Hammersons know, so as soon as we left, these two were sent out after us."

Her eyes had widened in comprehension. "At Amelia's! We all thought there was someone in the house with us."

"Yes! Yes! It must have been them! They must have followed us all the way here! Probably invisible!"

We had stared at each other in horror for several seconds, before I pulled myself together. "Let's get out of here. Come on."

We had left our meals on the table, as well as those of the Hammerhearts, and without asking for the bill, I had tipped the server twenty bucks; hopefully, saving his life, as well as the manager's, would compensate if the bill had been more than that. I had then walked Serena home, back to the Woodward headquarters, intending to enjoy the rest of the evening with her, regardless of the way dinner had ended. I had kept both the crystal and the solid-outliner out of my pocket, feeling that to put them away would be to invite attack. Serena, who hadn't thought to come armed (not that her pretty dress appeared to have pockets to store arms in, anyway), stayed close to me, her arm around my waist. There had been no further attacks.

"You're a little early," Amelia had said when she had materialised in the Woodward study to find the two of us standing there. "Oh, shit—what's happened?" she had added, spotting the bag on my back that hadn't been there before and the solid-outliner in my hand.

"Hammerhearts," I had told her. "We reckon the spy tipped them off where we were going. Can we come in? I've brought them in so that Mr. Woodward can see if they know anything useful."

"Oh, shit," she had repeated. "Are you both okay?"

"We're fine, nothing major," Serena had said curtly, holding her hand out to Amelia. "I got hit by a solid-outliner, but I'm fine now. John's sorted himself out as he always does."

Amelia had sighed and led us both through the wall into the headquarters. I had told Serena to go and wait for me in her room, and then I had hurried to find Mr. Woodward, locating him, as ever, in his office, where he had been talking intently with Javelyn. Amelia had followed me eagerly. I had handed over the bag and briefly described how they had tried to attack us, neglecting to mention what they had been doing before the attack and completely forgetting to mention the attack on the restaurant staff and the other woman who had been present at the start of the attack. Amelia had stayed to listen, biting her lip and looking lost in worry. Javelyn, who had also stayed, had shaken her head, looking shocked; she had been in the Hammerheart base earlier that day and apparently she had heard nothing at all about this plot. Perhaps it had been concocted in minutes, which would explain why there had only been two of them and not a whole army, strategising against me.

When I had been excused, Amelia followed me again. The door to Mr. Woodward's office was only feet from the one back into the main corridor, and as soon as I had shut the office door behind us to give Mr. Woodward and Javelyn some privacy, Amelia had thrown her arms around me and held on for dear life, resting her head on my shoulder.

"Amelia—"

I had hugged her back, feeling surprised, grateful (for my attraction had sparked in me again at her touch), ungrateful (because I had still wanted to finish the night with Serena the way it had almost been in the restaurant, and Amelia wasn't helping that cause), and a little indignant—how often did I have to put up with girls crying their hearts out on my shoulder? For when Amelia let me go and before she had turned and hurried away in the direction of a bedroom (a room I hadn't been in at that stage), I had clearly seen tears in her eyes. Feeling dazed, I had left the Woodward living quarters and proceeded up the corridor into our living quarters, up the stairs to the third floor, and along to my room—just a quick stop-off before joining Serena in the room next door and, hopefully, staying there for the rest of the evening.

There, in my room, I had finally been able to take the pouch back out of my pocket and return the solid-outliner to it. I had been on the point of putting the pouch in the top drawer of my desk where it usually resided when I wasn't using it when I stopped. I had felt something unusual as I was putting the solid-outliner in the pouch, like it was a little fuller than it was supposed to be, and I hadn't registered it until several seconds after the event. Curiously, believing that it had been my imagination, I had raised the pouch to my eyes and looked carefully inside it. What I had seen made my heart stand still; the light above my head should have illuminated the items on top, or at least reflected off them, but there had been nothing inside the pouch but darkness. Even the solid-outliner I had just put on top of everything was concealed in it. Unbidden, my mind flashed back to that vision of fire and blackness around a dead body that kept popping up unexpectedly behind my eyes, but for now, I shook it off. This was only darkness, after all; there was no fire involved.

I had bent closer, trying to penetrate the unusual darkness with my gaze—there was far too much of it in there. With my nose almost touching the edge of the pouch, I had just been able to see the solid-outliner, still hidden by the darkness. Then I had seen the outline of the thing crouched beneath it, hidden almost completely by the darkness. My stomach shot up into my throat—any more and it would have come spilling out of my mouth. I had scrambled backward, groping around for the Sien-Leoard Crystal, which I had put down, eventually locating it with my free hand and gripping it tightly. I had put the pouch down on my desk; then, carefully as ever and still gripping the crystal tightly, I had put my hand gingerly into the pouch, pushing the solid-outliner aside and withdrawing the other crystal (the one that had been the source of the unusual amount of darkness) from its depths.

As my fingers closed around it, I had felt my knuckles scrape something else that shouldn't have been in there. I had carefully placed the Darkness Crystal on my desk beside the pouch and put my hand back inside it, groping and eventually locating the thing I had felt. It had been attached to the crystal at some stage, but the magic of the crystal seemed to have broken the tape; it was a short, handwritten note. Feeling stunned and hardly breathing, I had read the words.

I am watching out for you, John Playman.

There had been no signature.

I had stared at the note for maybe a whole minute in something quite close to horror. Watching out for me? Watching me? Was that a good thing? Who was this person? When I had got over some of the shock, I had carefully placed the Darkness Crystal back in the pouch (I would give that back to Mr. Woodward tomorrow, but not tonight) and taken the note back to my bed, where I had sat down and pondered it.

One thing I had zeroed in on almost at once was that the handwriting looked vaguely familiar. I had cast my memory around for possible candidates and had quickly landed on the veiled woman I had seen in the restaurant. Her eyes had seemed familiar, her voice had seemed familiar (not that I'd been given a good look at either); was it so unlikely that this note had been from her? She had passed very close to me on her way out, and I had been far too distracted to notice if she'd tampered with the pouch; that was an unsettling thought. If it had been she who had put the crystal and the note in the pouch, though, who was she? How did she know me? How was she keeping an eye on me? Why hadn't she wanted me to see her face?

My active imagination had, for some strange reason, focussed on my ghost mother, who was probably still wandering around somewhere, perhaps still following Moran, or lurking in the caves of Rock Haulter. Could it have been her? I had only considered this for a few seconds before disregarding it. For one thing, I'd seen enough of the woman in the restaurant to register that she was quite tall, taller than the ghost of my mother had been. For another thing, that woman had definitely not been a ghost, and I wasn't at all prepared to entertain myself with the idea that my mother had been brought back from the dead as William, Carl, and Lisa had.

Then my mind had finally clicked on the answer it should have right away. Moran—he had done this. He was the one who had stolen the crystal, so instead of giving it to me himself, he had hired someone else to do it. Or maybe that had been him; maybe he had attempted to change his appearance by magic and stuffed it up, and had been forced to hide his face because of it. Was he watching out for me? That had been almost as unsettling as the idea that my pouch had been tampered with. And if that had been Moran, or Moran had been involved somewhere along the line, how the hell had he known where and when Serena and I would be out? Surely he didn't have a spy in this joint too…

I had put the note away at that point, with the Darkness Crystal, and gone next door to where Serena was waiting impatiently for me. She and I had continued our date in her room, and not left until breakfast the following morning. After I had eaten, I had returned to business, locating Marc and Amelia and dragging them along to see Mr. Woodward. I had retrieved the two items of suspicion from my room before going down to breakfast; once in Mr. Woodward's office, I had shown them to them. They had all been as shocked as I had been the night before. Amelia hadn't said anything at all on the subject, but Marc had examined the note very closely for some time before saying that he didn't think it matched his father's, although he could be disguising it. Mr. Woodward had told us not to tell anyone about the Darkness Crystal; he had wanted his followers to think that they still didn't have it, that way the Hammersons couldn't know it had been returned either.

Chapter 7: Forbidden

"Really? Who was it, then?" Mr. Woodward asked.

"The same person who wrote this," I said, and I showed him the note I had found, with the aid of the Sien-Leoard Crystal, days earlier, on the other side of the planet. Mr. Woodward read it quickly, his eyes widening with every line.

"Lindsay," he said, very softly. "Lindsay. But, surely, that has to be—"

"Yes, it is," I said, triumphantly. "I actually knew what she was doing as early as the Monday after all the assassinations, but nobody took me seriously. I wasn't sure if she was trying to help us or not until I found this. She must have written it once she knew she could never get the life assistant from Underwood. You have to admit, unless there's some unlikely twist in this thing, that she must be on our side after all."

"Yes," Mr. Woodward agreed, "although as you've seen for yourself, most unlikely twists have a way of happening these days."

"I guess that's true," I conceded.

"So go on, then," Mr. Woodward prompted me. "We were speaking of the delay that your friend Lena caused."

"Oh, yeah," I said, feeling awkward again; I still wasn't sure how much I ought to tell him about what had happened over the two weeks following the assassinations: The arguments; the conflicting advice; the emotional upheaval; the betrayal. "Well, to cut a long story short, we needed Lena because we knew from our earlier visit that Underwood was interested in good-looking women, and I'm sure you've seen Lena—she's as good as they come. The delay was because she wasn't happy with her part in the plan, and none of us wanted to use magic against her to make her do what we wanted. That's why it took some time for her to agree."

"What changed her mind?" Mr. Woodward asked. I wished he hadn't.

"I had—er—met her halfway," I said, going red. I hated to think about it. "She had something she wanted from—from me in return."

"Ah," he said, and I knew he knew; he had seen the way Lena was around me, had probably seen her fantasies about me directly out of her mind. "I understand."

I supposed the sequence of events that eventually led to my meeting Lena's demands had been set in motion before the night she and I had discussed it in her room, for the main factor that had caused me to betray Serena, as I had tried so hard not to do, had been the actions of Serena herself. There had been other factors as well; it had been only days after Nicole's tragic death, for one thing. Amelia had been another major factor; since the meeting with Jacob Underwood on April 4, the psychological wounds caused by Hignat and Wilwog's violations, which she had done so well to contain for so long, had reopened in a big way.

It had started with her being noticeably subdued for a couple of days. Marc, who had never been told about Hignat and Wilwog's crime, had been hurt and confused because she wouldn't open up to him. When he tried to ask her what was wrong, it had escalated into an almost out-of-control argument, Amelia crying and claiming that Marc was getting too pushy and not giving her space. That had been on the sixth, the day Serena and I had gone out to dinner with most remarkable results. The following day, after Marc and I had left Mr. Woodward's office, Amelia had (I had found out from Amelia herself) spoken to her father about Hignat and Wilwog that day for only the second time (the first had been a little over a month earlier).

Amelia hadn't come out of the Woodward living quarters at all that day, and Marc and I, both worried sick for Amelia (for far too similar reasons), had eventually gone to find her. There, we had found her in her bedroom, lying on her bed and practically in pieces. I had, with considerable effort, kept my distance, letting Marc do the bulk of the comforting—being her boyfriend, he surely had first right to that sort of thing—but when Amelia had got enough of a grip on herself to actually speak to us, she had invited me to come closer.

"Amelia, please," Marc had said, quite desperately, holding her in his arms and staring into her face. "It doesn't take a shrink to see you're falling apart, and I honestly have no idea why. Is it something Underwood did?"

"No. Well, yeah, a bit," she had said uneasily. Either she didn't want to tell him the truth, or she wanted to tell him but didn't know how, I had thought. If it was the latter, that would make it my duty to speak of it, which I did not want. But, for Amelia's sake, if that was what she wanted, then that was what I would do.

"Marc," I had said quietly, and he looked around at me quickly, his face hard with concern and resentment. He wanted to be the one to sort this out, I had felt certain. I didn't blame him; if Amelia had been my girlfriend, I would want the opportunity to do this alone too. "Can I take her for a moment?"

"Why?"

"You'll see in a minute—I hope."

He had hesitated for a moment, but after a glance at Amelia's face, he relented. I had taken his place beside Amelia on the bed and put an arm around her (only one), ignoring Marc for the time being.

This wouldn't last very long, not nearly as long as I wished it could last.

"Is it that you don't want to speak of it?" I had asked quietly. "Or is it that you want to speak of it but don't know how? Either way, I think Marc has a right to know, don't you?"

She had nodded, her face tear-streaked.

"What do you want to do, then?" I had asked her, for I knew that if she spoke of it herself, she would be better for it in the long run, but I wasn't at all qualified to make her feel comfortable doing so, and I didn't want to force her into further discomfort without knowing what the consequences might be.

She had thought for some time, looking at me, at Marc, at nothing in particular. Eventually she had shaken her head, looking disgusted with herself. "I don't think I can speak of it."

"Can I say it?" I had asked, hating that I had to do this.

She had flinched, but she nodded, looking down at her lap. I had released her and made space for Marc to join Amelia on the bed again, but he was standing stock-still, frozen, watching me and looking angry.

"You're not gonna like what you're about to hear," I had warned him.

"I'm already not liking what I'm hearing. Are you saying it gets worse?"

He had feared I'd slept with Amelia; I couldn't read his thoughts, but I had known them all the same. For answer, I had gestured to him, then pointed at Amelia, making it clear that I wanted him beside her (Amelia deserved some sort of comfort during the telling), but Marc, hot-headed and clearly thicker in the head than was usual for him, hadn't got the message. I had given up.

"Right. Well, not many people know about this. Even Amelia's dad didn't know until he found out from someone else. I guess the reason why you don't know is because Amelia has never felt comfortable talking about it with anyone, and those of us who knew about it respected her right to tell who she wanted to know."

"I get it. What's going on then?"

I had taken a deep breath and told him. "When we were stuck in the Hammerheart Basement back in February, the night I had escaped for a little while, Amelia had been several floors below me, getting raped—by Hignat and Wilwog."

Marc had jerked convulsively. He had looked sharply at Amelia, who was still staring into her lap, trying to look small and insignificant and succeeding only in making herself look utterly pathetic. Marc had struggled with himself for several seconds, still jerking, looking like he wanted to kill someone, and with the Hero Crystal in his pocket, that made him rather dangerous to be around. I had hurried to say a little more.

"Cornish had been supervising. It was just Hignat and Wilwog's way of taking advantage of things. You know—she said 'fuck you' to them, and they jumped all over it. I guess the reason it's hurting so much now is because of what Jacob Underwood said the other day, about how guys will do things to her against her will if she keeps showing them too much attitude."

"Those two," Marc had said very quietly through gritted teeth. "Those two—if I ever see them again—"

"Control yourself, man," I had said urgently. "I tell you, Peter and I wanted to rip them apart the day we went back to school, but we controlled ourselves; you have to do the same."

"I don't care—I'm gonna kill them! Them and whoever gave them permission to do that—thing!"

"That would be Arnold Hammerson himself, then," I had told him. "Look, I'm gonna go—(Marc had really been scaring me by then)—so control yourself, man, and for God's sake, help Amelia. Her well-being is more important than chasing after Hignat and Wilwog."

Marc had looked hard at me for several seconds, but then he had looked down at Amelia, and his face had softened. He had gone to her and sat down beside her. She had flinched away from him at first, but soon allowed him to take her in his arms. Feeling as though I had a hole in my heart, I had left them to it. To my later disgust, Amelia had then been driven out of my mind for the rest of the afternoon by Serena, who had quite deliberately cornered me, dragged me upstairs, and done all matter of things to me, right up until dinnertime. That afternoon had been quite incredible, even more so than the nights I had spent with Tulip; it had even topped the last one Serena and I had spent together. I had known why she was doing it— to put herself at the fore of my mind, in front of Amelia and all the rest. But at the time, I hadn't minded one bit, not, at least, until my mind had returned to Amelia, and I had felt terrible guilt for enjoying myself while she was suffering so badly.

I had seen Amelia again the next day, this time without Marc. The purpose of that meeting had actually been about Lena, but I had observed her closely in that time to make sure she was okay. Thankfully, she seemed to have slept off the edge of her depression, at least for now, and I had inwardly thanked Marc for being there for her when she needed him most, trying not to wish it were me that had been there for her instead.

My next private meeting with Amelia had occurred on April 11, in the afternoon. All the Sorcerers, plus Marc, Tommy, and some of the other Woodward Army soldiers that had been deployed the previous day to control the balance of power in the wake of all the assassinations, had returned around lunchtime, stating that they had done all they could for now. Mr. Woodward had gone to organise some of his own security around other political targets around the world, assisted by Mr. Fletcher, while the others had been allowed to sleep. I, however, had been concerned for Amelia's mental well-being, considering everything else she had been going through on top of having to use magic to keep herself awake all night.

So I had gone to see her, again in her bedroom, and this time without Marc. First, however, I had sought the Sien-Leoard Crystal, eventually taking it from Mr. Woodward himself, who told me wearily that it may have made all the difference in the end. I had then done something I had wanted to do since my most stimulating encounter with Lena the previous night. I had used the crystal to tap into Serena's mind; I had been in my room at the time and she had been in the lounge room, chatting with Kylie and Erica, but the magic had worked fine even with three floors between us. What I'd wanted to know was what would be her most likely reaction to me asking her if I could have sex with Lena just once; I did not want to know what her reaction would be to finding out I'd already done it just once. It made no difference, however—I got nothing more exciting than a thick wall of complete disapproval. I'd hoped for something more, but that was all. That had left me feeling very disappointed; if I could have gotten permission from her, it wouldn't have made it completely right, but it might have made it considerably better, but sadly, not to be—not that I had been surprised by that.

Having the Sien-Leoard Crystal in my possession again had made getting into Amelia's room an utter breeze, but I had still knocked and made sure I was allowed first—common courtesy, after all. Once she had let me in, Amelia had crossed back to her bed and lain down on it, watching me with unfocussed eyes.

"How are you feeling?" I had asked, propping myself beside her, more or less where Marc had been the last time, but I hadn't made physical contact with her this time, again with some effort and regret.

"Tired," she had yawned, curling up beside me, closer than I had intended, but that had been her doing, not mine, so I didn't chastise myself for it. "That was a really long night. You know, I don't think any of us realised just how disorganised we are compared to the

Hammersons. They've got people everywhere, and loads more than us."

"I'm starting to see that too," I had said. "You know, I thought Sebastian was just being a prat for stepping in and criticising your dad's handling of things, but he was right; we've been far too reactive lately. We haven't done nearly enough to prevent the Hammersons doing something like this. Having Javelyn in there wasn't enough to prevent this."

That had been three days earlier. Sebastian had approached Mr. Woodward and asked him why he hadn't made any plans lately to recapture the Hammersons themselves again, and a few of their closest minions. Many people (me included) had assumed Sebastian was just trying to make a name for himself (as he had been known to do), but he had been spot on. Mr. Woodward had given up being proactive some time ago, settling for tiptoeing around, trying to wrong-foot the Hammersons. Clearly, he had failed big time. The Hammersons hadn't taken control of things yet, but they were closer to it than we had realised up until now. The Darkness Crystal hadn't been enough; it had taken a political assault to awaken us to how tenuous our position was.

"Yeah, I know," she had said wearily. "Hey, John?"

"Yeah, Amelia?"

She had wriggled a little closer, and I realised that what she wanted was a hug. I had obliged, leaning over her so I could get my arms around her.

"You should sleep," I had told her, carefully disengaging from her. She had reluctantly let go, but as she had rolled over, I had kept a hand on her shoulder and gently ran my hand up and down her back until she had fallen asleep.

The following day, I had returned my mind to the ongoing Serena and the relationship versus Lena and the war debate. What I had wanted to do was ask Amelia's opinion of cheating on Serena; it would be cheating for a good cause, after all. I had decided against talking to her about it though because, again, of her current mental state; she and Marc had had another fight that morning, this time because Marc didn't want me and Amelia alone in her room together. It made him uneasy, and I honestly hadn't blamed him, even though I had felt resentful towards him for it—it made him sound just like Tommy had been about me and Natalie. Amelia had ended up in tears by the end of that, and their relationship had been even more in the balance that evening than mine and Serena's. So I had gone instead to Nicole for advice. She had been shocked that I would even consider Lena's request and thought that I should immediately give up on her and look for some other good-looking chick to use instead, saying that potentially losing my girlfriend in exchange for satisfying Underwood was hardly worth the trouble. I had figured she hadn't thought how many steps backwards that would put us, but I hadn't argued about it with her; she had her moral opinion, and I knew I couldn't change it.

Then, right on cue, just after dinner, Serena had come to me in a fit of indignation, complaining that I talked too much to other girls and didn't spend enough time with her. I had relented and spent the rest of the evening with her, but only because of what was going on between Marc and Amelia. I hadn't wanted to be in that position. All the same, though, I'd made a mental note not to take her possessive behaviour so lightly next time. Even if I wasn't getting up to anything dodgy with them, Natalie and Amelia, particularly, were still very important to me.

The next day, April 13, I had gone to see Amelia again first thing in the morning, Serena frowning at me as I had gone. Amelia had been most happy to see me, hugging me and hanging on to me a little longer than she ought to have, chattering away about nothing in particular, something most unlike her. I had put my hand in my pocket, around the Sien-Leoard Crystal, and although I couldn't use it to read her mind (her mind, like mine, was shielded from mind reading), I had nevertheless discovered from its wisdom that Amelia's behaviour was due to an exotic dream she'd had the previous night, a dream in which I had starred. I had quickly forced my mind away from that and focussed on the reason for my coming to see her, for I'd had another voyage into Stella's thoughts the previous night, but to my displeasure, Amelia still hadn't taken me seriously.

Later that afternoon, I'd had one last shot at trying to convince Lena to go along with our plan. We had argued, or more like debated, for neither of us had lost our temper; it had been more like something you would see in a courtroom than in a bedroom. Sadly, Lena had been much better at that sort of arguing than me.

"There's still a good chance you won't have to go all the way with him, though," I had pointed out; that was my only good point to use against her now. "How about I promise to meet you halfway only if it's necessary to go all the way with him?"

She had smiled and shaken her head. "That won't help me much if I've already given it away."

"I tell you what," I had said, wanting to leave the room; even while debating, she had never missed an opportunity to attempt to seduce me, and it had been starting to work by that stage. "I tell you what. I might consider sleeping with you—*might*—but only if you consider sleeping with someone else. I don't want to ruin my relationship with Serena—you must understand that."

She had only smiled. "Sleep with someone else? Someone other than this Underwood, in addition to him? I can't think of a single thing appealing about that. You know"— she had lowered her voice then, both looking and sounding more seductive than I would have believed possible, "you could solve all this, all your worries about being unfaithful to Serena, by just dumping her and switching, if you get my drift."

I had smiled pleasantly and left the room at that point, but the deal still wasn't done. That night, I'd had a startling dream in which I'd gone ahead and done it with Lena, only to have Serena discover us. I had woken in a sweat, remembering quite clearly the way Serena had yelled at me, how offended and angry she had been, how happy Lena had been, never letting go of me even after Serena had arrived, determined to destroy as much of our relationship as possible so that she could have me all to herself. I hated dreams like that because they weren't fair, although this one wasn't entirely untruthful either. I knew full well that Lena liked me, and in a strange way, I appreciated her honesty about it, but it irritated me that she didn't care enough about me to respect my current relationship. She was simply looking out for her own interests, never mind how they impacted the bigger picture.

Wednesday, April 14, hadn't been a particularly good one for me on the female front. We had still been in the Easter holidays (they had actually begun the previous week), which meant that Lena had as much freedom as she liked to follow me around all morning, flirting with me all the while, no matter what was going on. I had begun to think that she really wanted to do this thing, not because she wanted to play a part in the war but because she wanted to show me that she would be prepared to help me when I needed it; this was just one time she would need something in return. Or perhaps she would ask me to have sex with her every time I wanted something from her—that would be unacceptable. What made things even worse that morning was that Serena had been with me for a lot of it too, and things had got rather frosty between the three of us by lunchtime.

Afterwards, when we had managed to shake Lena off, Serena had argued furiously with me, telling me that I should just tell Lena to "fuck off and leave us alone" because it was making her uncomfortable. She had also reminded me of what we had talked about on our one and only date. I had told her that it shouldn't be an issue if she trusted me, and never mind Lena, but even as I had spoken the words, I didn't really believe that I deserved Serena's trust. I had been pretty down after that argument and had, for the first of a few times, considered finding Lena and doing the deed while the emotions were still fresh, but I had fought the feeling off and later had been glad I'd done so.

That evening, I had gone, once again, to Amelia, to seek from her the advice I'd wanted a day earlier. She had been considerably more helpful than Nicole had been, telling me that I should sleep with Lena once if I absolutely had to and not to let Serena know about it, to use magic to keep Lena quiet if necessary. More important than trying to be moral, or faithful, or practical, Amelia had told me, "You should use your best judgement, not mine, or Lena's, or Serena's, or Nicole's, or anyone else's—yours." If only I could trust my own judgement.

The next night, the fifteenth, I had, for only the third time since arriving at the Woodward headquarters several weeks earlier, gone home to our house on Lopher Lane, the one that was still linked to the one next door by an underground tunnel. In my absence, an argument had erupted in the lounge room, one that I wished I could have been there to sort out before it could get way out of hand. Typically, Serena's insecurity had been the instigating factor. It had been her and Lena at first; Amelia had tried to break up the fight and had only been drawn into it herself; Natalie, who hadn't even been present in the beginning but had arrived to find the place in an uproar, had been pulled in the same way. It had been Marc, Tommy, Peter, and James who had eventually pulled the four girls away from each other. It had almost got to the point of nails, hair pulling, and bitch slapping by that stage, so Peter had told me, although I doubted it had really been that bad—he was prone to exaggeration. Along with Harry and Simon, he had taken great amusement out of the event.

I'd had much to sort out upon my return, much of which I hadn't been up to one bit. My sister had been killed that morning, and the last thing I'd wanted to worry about was sorting out a bunch of girls who couldn't seem to get their act together. With highly inflamed emotions (no pun intended), I had tracked down Serena and let her have it for starting the fight, for all witnesses said that it had been her. I had reiterated what I had said two days earlier, that she should trust me even if she didn't trust anyone else. Her insecurity had been a massive turnoff, though, and for the second time, I'd seriously considered tracking Lena down and just getting it all over with. For the second time, though, I hadn't, this time because the idea made me feel extremely guilty about going against Nicole's advice so soon after her death.

All the same, this drama had to end sooner rather than later, and I had been beginning to think that it would require multiple confrontations. If so, though, who should they be with? Did I really want to potentially ruin other friendships for Serena's comfort when at the end of it all, she wasn't actually my first choice for a girlfriend? It was all just so confusing, and despite what people like Peter thought, there was no enjoyment to be had in being wanted by more than one girl.

Another thing that had been incumbent upon me to do that day was console Natalie. Felicity and Jessica had been there to support her the previous night and that morning over her part in the "cat fight," and they had too been there for her upon learning of Nicole's death, for they too had been mourning. Later in the evening, though, Natalie had come to see me in my room for only the second time ever; the first had been the day I'd almost kissed Amelia. I'd had very little comfort of my own from anyone that day other than Peter and James, who had been going through much the same things I had been. My two main regrets with regard to Nicole's death had been firstly, that Daniel had probably foreseen this, and so brought about his own death. I had to wonder if that thing he'd wanted to tell me on my way out of Stella's birthday party could have possibly changed things on that score, although I doubted it would have made a difference. The second had been that Peter had too foreseen this; he had said, and not very long ago, that this could possibly be how Nicole met her end. He had only been joking at the time, though, which only made it worse. Due to my own mental state, I hadn't been able to do very much for Natalie, nor had she been able to do much for me, but we had hugged and held onto each other for some time, the first time I could remember doing so, and that (after years of wanting her so badly) made the whole thing worthwhile.

Javelyn had also met her end in the wee hours of the sixteenth, so the following day, Mr. Woodward had called on me and Marc to find a new spy for him. He had told us to go to America to do it instead of anywhere local or England; being Americans themselves, the Hammersons might less suspect one of their own kind of being a Woodward spy—that was Mr. Woodward's theory, anyway. We had called a meeting in the second-floor room we would use to go to the States, not the same one we had used to go to England, with everyone who usually attended being there, except for Nicole, of course. Amelia had asked us to look around over there for women to use against Underwood; incredibly, she seemed to think that was more important than the work her father wanted done, which she'd just wanted out of the way.

That meeting had been in the late morning, and after lunch that day, I had been accosted once again by Serena. There had been another argument; this time, she was indignant that she hadn't been allowed in the meeting with me, that she felt as though I was hiding something from her by not letting her get involved. It had been perfectly true, of course (she hadn't known any of what was going on in the hunt for Smiley), but that didn't mean she ought to know. I had almost lost my patience with her completely, telling her that it was none of her business what we were doing, that Kylie and Erica hadn't been brought in just because they were Peter's and James's girlfriends respectively, that it had nothing to do with her and that she should just focus on the war from a Woodward perspective like everyone else. At that point, she had reminded me that she was on my side, a claim that had made me feel extremely guilty. I hadn't caved in, but I had decided to spend the rest of the day with her to make up for it.

The second-floor room, which we had set to travelling from the moment we'd first entered it, had reached the west coast of the United States by that evening. Marc and I had used the crystals to make very minor changes to our appearances (nothing a good normalising charm wouldn't fix) so that no Hammerhearts in disguise could recognise us, or word could get back to the Hammerhearts that we had been on the other side of the planet. Marc had done as Amelia had asked, but I had told him that I believed I could still bring Lena around to our side in perhaps not too much time. We'd had time to talk while scouring, only having problems with a very small minority of women who believed we were trying to chat them up; one had followed us for twenty minutes before we had managed to shake her off by ducking into a public toilet and then teleporting to a location three states away. Eventually, after some persuasion from Marc, I had confessed Lena's demands, and just into the bargain, how frustrated I was becoming with Serena's behaviour. The decision had been very much in the balance at that stage, but Marc had said the thing that seriously began to tip things in Lena's favour: "I won't pretend to approve of being unfaithful, but how much accusation can you take before you might as well do the thing you're already suspected of doing?"

We had ended up going back without a suitable woman, which both Amelia and Natalie had been most displeased about, but we had maintained that we hadn't seen any way to bring them around to our way of thinking without using dark magic against them. Amelia's moral objection to the idea had been beginning to fray by that stage. I hadn't seen Serena in the hours before we had gone to sleep for half the day, but I had decided, after what Marc had said, that one more uncalled-for outburst from her and I would find Lena and then we would just see what came next. It had been put off, though, because over lunch on the nineteenth, Serena and I had had a chance to talk and re-establish a thin resolve. In a terrible way, it had been disappointing; apparently, I had half hoped for an excuse to have sex with Lena, thereby living a magnificent fantasy, and I had chastised myself mentally for thinking that way. But all the same, I couldn't deny it. Lie to the others if you must, John, but for the love of God, don't lie to yourself....

It had only lasted one day. The following morning, Tuesday, April 20, just eight days before my recount to Mr. Woodward, depressed and sleep deprived, Amelia had almost broken down again. A lot had happened in the Woodward camp since the night of the fifteenth, and it had been beginning to take a terrible toll on everyone involved. Marc, Tommy, Natalie, Peter, James, Felicity, Jessica, and I had all spent the morning with her, not in her bedroom this time but in the private Woodward lounge room. The other Woodwards had respectfully given us youngsters some privacy. I had been somewhat distracted early in the morning by the dream I'd had the previous night, which had been the most disgusting venture into Stella's mind I'd ever made. Before too long, however, the seriousness of Amelia's situation had taken priority. There had been too many people around for me to get close to her, but thankfully the amount of support she was getting had made that unnecessary. Most of these people didn't know the full story of what was going on with her—perhaps they assumed that it was a result of the war—but they could see that she was struggling with something and assumed it was a result of the heavy responsibility she was carrying as a young Sorcerer. That wasn't quite true, but it hardly mattered; the support she was getting helped. All we had to do was sit around, chatting about cheerful things and making sure that Amelia participated. By lunchtime, although she still wasn't quite right, she looked a bit happier.

That hadn't made a difference, though, because Serena had come to me at lunch, displeased again. Later, I had been deeply ashamed of what had happened next. When analysing my behaviour that day, I decided that I must have, on some subconscious level, been looking for an excuse to be unfaithful to Serena, to do exactly what Marc had said, to sort all this business out once and for all. Serena had asked me, more kindly and patiently than she had done on previous occasions, that I not spend so much time around Amelia. I had snapped.

"Now listen here," I had hissed at her; there were people around and I hadn't wanted them to hear what this was about. "I am perfectly entitled to spend as much time as I like with whoever the hell I choose. There were loads of us in there with Amelia earlier; in fact, you yourself should have been there. You know what this is about, what Hignat and Wilwog did to her." Serena had been present the next day when they had taunted her about it. "Would it kill you to try for a bit of sympathy?"

Serena had been stunned. "I didn't say that. I know what Amelia's going through isn't good—"

"But that's not enough, is it? You reckon she should just be left to her own devices and I should just be left to you? That I'm not allowed to help her out at all, even though I was the one she went through a lot of that stuff with?"

"John, please, I didn't—"

"For crying out loud, Serena, I've seriously had enough of you trying to control who I talk to. Why the hell don't you trust me?"

She'd had every reason not to trust me, and I knew it, but I'd been so steamed up with rage that day that I hadn't bothered to consider that, or ask myself what I could do to make things better. I had stalked away, leaving her in tears, and not seen her again until the following morning, prior to Nicole's funeral. I'd been emotional that day; ashamed of how I had treated Serena and sad for Nicole, I had tried to make things right between us. She had still been very upset with me, but she had given me another chance because, as she said, she still liked me very much and wanted to make it work. The greatest shame, however, had been because of what had happened on the night of the twentieth, what had finally happened.

Word had a way of getting around quickly within the confines of the Woodward living quarters. News of my argument with Serena had taken some time to spread to Lena's ears, perhaps because I'd told nobody, Serena had told very few, and those who had seen it wouldn't have heard enough to understand what it was about. When Lena had heard about it, however, at about half past nine that evening, she had come straight up to see me in my room. I'd let her in unwillingly but graciously enough; I had felt rather introverted since the argument. Something about having Lena in my room, late at night, with my emotions in such a tailspin, however, had been stimulating, which, as per usual, had probably been Lena's intention.

"I'm not here to cause trouble," she had said firmly, and to prove her point, she had taken a chair from the table in the centre of my room and pulled it up to my bed, where I was sitting, toying with the Sien-Leoard Crystal, trying to convince myself that using magic to worm my way out of all these problems was a coward's way out. "I only thought I should come and see how you are. I heard about what happened earlier with Serena."

"I'll bet," I'd said drily. "What's on the rumour mill now? Who are they saying is the guilty party this time?"

She had frowned at me. "I think some of them aren't sure how interested you are in her, but most of them haven't forgotten what Serena was like last week—you know, what happened with her and me."

She had looked a bit embarrassed, having to bring up the cat fight that she herself had been so prominent in.

"I see," I had said tonelessly. "Well, thanks for coming. I appreciate it."

Did I, though? I hadn't been entirely sure.

"Always welcome," she had said, smiling and patting me on the arm. "I just figured, 'cause I've seen how lately you've been trying to be everyone's rock, Amelia especially, but when this stuff happens to you, nobody bothers to come to give you a shoulder to lean on."

I'd considered this; it had been true to a certain extent. Nobody had come to be my rock lately. Amelia, Natalie, and Serena had all wanted to in the wake of my learning my parents' identities, and there had been a few people, like Natalie, Peter, and James, who since Nicole's death had come to me seeking as much comfort as they were prepared to give. There hadn't been anyone like Lena, though, coming out of her way to give me comfort without needing any herself. The gesture had been touching, even though I knew she was still looking out for her own interests as much as anything else. That last one hadn't been easy to keep in the fore of my mind, though, not on that night.

"Hey, thanks," I'd said again. "Honestly, though, I'd never actually thought of that."

"That just makes you all the more deserving of it," she'd said sweetly.

I'd reached out, taken her hand in mine, and squeezed it. I hadn't been sure where this would go, but my body wanted it to go as far as Lena would let it, and given my emotional state, my mind hadn't been too far behind. She had returned the squeeze, watching me with avid interest. I'd kept a hold of her hand but made no further moves towards her. She had actually made the next move, bending forward, reaching across me and plucking the Sien-Leoard Crystal from my other hand (apparently seeing my fingers wrapped around nothing had confirmed to her that I was holding it) and placing it carefully on my bedside table. She had then taken my other hand in her other one, pulling me slightly towards her to make it possible for her to remain seated in the chair. Now we had been facing each other completely.

"What do you want me to do?" she had asked softly, smiling seductively, and I had almost shivered. "This is your party, after all."

"Er, what do you mean?" I had asked, my voice just short of being even.

"Well, how best would you like me to comfort you? I don't wanna overstep my bounds if you still wanna set things to rights with Serena. Well, maybe I do a little, but I wouldn't if you say so. It's up to you."

"I'm not sure what I want," I had said, and the complete honesty in that had been a little startling. "I've had a lot of fights with her over the last few weeks. I don't think our relationship has turned out how she imagined it when she was chasing me a while ago."

I'd watched her for a reaction to that, wanting her to understand that, if ever she and I started something down the track, she might find herself in the same position as Serena. I doubted that any of the girls around me now could change me to the point that I wouldn't speak to any others; those girls would just have to learn to accept it. If they couldn't do that, then that made us incompatible. I'd thought all this through while staring at Lena's face, and perhaps she'd seen some of it in my eyes. The fact was, I'd just realised, as I hadn't at any point until then, that Serena and I were wrong for each other.

"That does tend to happen," Lena had said softly, drawing my attention back to her. "I've read plenty about this sort of thing. When someone becomes attracted to someone else, they often assume that they will learn to live with that person's faults or that person will iron out those faults. It's not until they are actually together that they realise it's a lot more difficult than they'd first thought."

"I guess so," I had said. That was close enough to my own train of thought after all. "I decided quite a while ago that I would only take so much from her, that if she didn't grow up, I'd have to—give it up, I suppose. I'm not sure I thought that far ahead, actually. And now, every day it feels like, she's still trying to control me."

I'd paused, marshalling my thoughts. Lena had sat in silence, holding my hands and watching my face, letting me reach the conclusion on my own. I had a moment to marvel at the fact that I was speaking so openly about my relationship to someone other than Peter or James.

"Maybe I'll have to end it," I'd said more quietly. "I don't like it. We were only saying a couple of weeks ago that we both wanted to make it last, and I'd said that we could if we wanted it more than anything else, but I guess that had been a little too simple to work."

"You don't have to be unhappy," Lena had told me, quietly but firmly.

"I know that. Trouble is, sometimes, happiness is real hard to find."

"You can find it, though, if you look hard enough."

I had stared at her. Was this it? Was this the moment? I had felt quite sure that it was, and I wanted to take it with both hands. I had known only one way to do that.

"Lena, what exactly do you want from me, anyway?"

She had stared at me, not hard, as though she wanted to drill holes in my head with her eyes, but firmly, wanting to make sure she had my whole attention. She hadn't needed to do much to manage that.

"You know what I want," she had said quietly, squeezing both my hands in unison. "You know, but since this is more about you than me, let's settle it to say—I'll take what I can. I don't mind looking for happiness. I know where I want to look, so I'll take any chance I'm given to have a little peak. The rest, I guess, is up to you. Whatever you decide to do shouldn't be what someone else wants. That, I think, is the reason why you're in this mess with Serena to start with. Why don't you do what you want this time?"

Wow! Now that, I had thought, was full on smooth. Who said you needed experience. Lena had probably never done something like that in her life, but she had positively nailed it then. She had continued to watch me, her head tilted slightly to one side, and I had thought. And then, without any conscious decision to do so, I had stopped thinking altogether.

"Sit beside me?" I had asked her quietly, letting go of her hands at last (noticing they had both become rather sweaty) and patting a spot on the bed beside me, turning myself so that I was once again facing the foot of the bed and the desk several feet beyond it.

Lena had got up and scrambled over my outstretched legs, then stretched her long frame out beside me. She had taken me in her arms and held me to her, and so the deed had begun like that. There had been no further discussion; talk hadn't been necessary anymore. By the end of it, when we had been lying together on the bed, our clothes strewn around the floor beside it, I had thought again, as though for the first time, as though every thought I'd ever had before that had been nothing but blinding ecstasy—which, in fact, it had been. What Lena had given me then and there, perhaps because it had been wrong to do it when we had, however right it had felt, had been beyond anything either Tulip or Serena were capable of. She had been less skilful than either of them, being her first time (I'd seen for myself her honesty), but she had been magnificent anyway. With practise, she would get better, but when I had regained some sanity, I had begun to think that it wouldn't be with me. If I followed her advice, went after what I really wanted, both Lena and Serena would have to look elsewhere.

"Lena?" I had said quietly, placing my hand beneath her chin to make her look at me. "Now will you help us? Will you do what we need you to do?"

Unlike me, Lena hadn't quite come back to her senses, probably because it had been a long time coming for her. She had said, almost completely breathlessly, "I'll do whatever you want, John."

That was how the deal had finally been done. I had sacrificed my fidelity, something I had always assumed was far more solid, but I hoped from then on that it would be the only time, and it would be worth it.

Chapter 8: The End

"That occurred on the twenty-second, correct?" Mr. Woodward asked me.

"No, the twentieth," I told him. "I spoke to Lena about it, told her exactly what would be happening on the Thursday morning. Part of it was actually to make people think the deal had only been done that morning. I don't want anyone to know what I had to do to get her on side, if possible."

"Ah, I see," he said, seeming to understand. I supposed it was his lifetime of mind reading that had made him less judgemental of people's actions. "So go on. What happened then?"

Storyteller, that's me—big John the storyteller.

"Well, we had a meeting about it that day," I said. "All of us involved in the search, plus Lena. We decided there that we would leave on Friday night, after checking it with you. You know what happened next."

That had been something of a surprise, not that Mr. Woodward would make us clear it with our parents first, but that they took it so easily. Mum and Dad had accepted it rather quickly; they had thought it unlikely that I would be hunted all the way across the planet if the Hammerhearts didn't know I was over there, but they were also adamant that I should return quickly should anything go wrong. Lena had also been given permission easily, for she had told them she would be with me and one of the Magic Crystals. The only person who had been really unhappy was Serena; it had been the day after I had been granted a second chance. After the meeting, I had told her I would be going to England with Lena for a few days on Woodward business. I hadn't told her any of the details of the plan. She had wanted to come along with me, but I had told her, truthfully, that it would be inappropriate. I had asked her, before she could accuse me, to trust her, that I was not going to do anything dodgy with Lena, that I wouldn't be given a chance to do so, which had also been truthful. She had accepted, but unwillingly.

"Yes, I know," he said. "What about when you went over there, then? What did you and Lena do?"

"Well, we used the same room we'd used the last time we went to see Underwood," I told him, though he probably already knew that. "What I did when Lena and I were alone in there was use the Sien-Leoard Crystal to leave my body and take possession of hers. Had to put my body in stasis—is that what you call it? Anyway, I locked it in the wardrobe in that room—glad to see nothing bad happened to it while I was gone. We thought she would have to be knocked out while I did all this, but I found when I actually did it that while I had the Sien-Leoard Crystal in my hand, or in Lena's hand when I was in her body, I could control her mind separately from her body. I could choose if she was conscious or unconscious. I could give her small amounts of control when I needed her to do something to herself that I wasn't familiar with—you get the idea."

That had actually been pretty neat, although thankfully it had come about because of the magic I had performed to get into her body in the first place—given that I would have to give her the Sien-Leoard Crystal throughout the duration, I didn't want to risk her using it to take control of the entire mission. Once I was in her body, I was able to read her mind separately from my own, while she wasn't able to read mine, and I had learnt a couple of things very quickly: She couldn't have cared less about the Sien-Leoard Crystal; but she was rather annoyed that I wasn't taking my body to England with us, partially because she would have liked to minimise the amount of time I would spend inhabiting her body (just for the sheer invasiveness of it), and partially because during the down time when it would have been just the two of us, it might give her an opportunity to try to seduce me again. I hadn't wanted to take my body with us just in case Underwood found it stashed in a closet, thereby blowing the whole plan.

"Anyway, when we got over there—I'd been in control then—I'd rented an apartment for a month in the same building as Underwood. Don't worry, I had the crystal, so money was no issue. I think the crystal might have been at work then; I hadn't been deliberately doing magic with it, but maybe I'd been thinking about those two last dreams I had about Stella, though, 'cause I somehow ended up in the apartment she'd lived in when she was over there. I'd sussed it out with the crystal when I got in there; I'd just had a feeling I ought to do so, and I found this"—I gestured at the note, still on the desk between us—"hidden in one of the kitchen cupboards."

The note read:

His name is Jacob Underwood.
He calls it his life assistant.
It is a magical connection with his grandfather.
He is proud of it but he keeps it secret from everyone.
He will do just about anything for sex.
I could not take it from him; I would not have sex with him.
He hit me and threw me out of his room.
To him, I was Lindsay, my mother's name, I had once been told.

"And you're sure it was Stella?" Mr. Woodward pressed me.

"Yes, I am," I said certainly. "The dreams I had, this note; it's true because Underwood himself mentioned Lindsay. I think he said she gave good head, so God knows what she had to do to him." I had known that before Underwood had mentioned it, though, because I had entered her mind at the worst possible time. "But he also said she was frigid, which would explain this note. And that other note—do you still have it?"

Mr. Woodward opened his desk drawer and extracted the note that had come by way of the Darkness Crystal, the one about watching over me. He placed the notes side by side, and we both saw that although the notes were clearly written by two different pens, the handwriting on both was identical.

"Of course she could watch over me," I said, "the same way I was watching her. She must have seen our plans in my mind and gone over there. It would have made me think she was against us if she hadn't written this, but if she really wanted to help—maybe she was trying to get back in our good books by doing something so huge for us."

"She was gone by the time you got over there?"

"Yeah," I said. "Actually, I know where she is. I dreamt of her, not last night but the one before. Lena never found out about that, thank God. I could read some of her thoughts, the stronger emotions, but she couldn't read any of mine—maybe 'cause my mind's been protected for months. Anyway, Stella's not alone anymore. She's joined forces with Moran and Lucien."

Mr. Woodward swore. I knew there was plenty of shock value in that statement. Other than his appearance in Chopville High and his attack on the Hammerheart Highway, Moran had been very quiet between that second last night in February and the night of the assassinations. In the two and a half weeks that had followed, however, he had become much bolder, beginning with another attack on the Chopville base. It had been the day after the assassinations, many of which had succeeded but a few of which had failed. Governments all over the world had been in disarray, and none of them had been well enough equipped to deal with the weapons that the Hammerhearts had been using to take control—small magical devices that probably had a name that I hadn't known at the time, but they put the influential charm on those their beams hit. It had therefore been up to the Woodwards, Fletchers, and others to cover the slack.

The Sorcerers hadn't been the only ones working hard, though. The Hammerhearts had been in a position where the magnitude of what they had done was greater than even they were able to control. It had been difficult for them to know which assassinations had succeeded and which had failed, for some of them had been in private places with no witnesses, and in some cases the assassins hadn't survived either. The other problem the Hammerhearts would have had was that they didn't want too many of their people to be taken by the Sorcerers, when the Sorcerers caught up with them, anyway. The Hammersons had therefore worked very hard to make sure all their troops were well ahead of the Sorcerers.

It had taken an enormous amount of concentration, and so, unsurprisingly as it were, the Hammerhearts had been sucked into another attack. Moran must have heard about the assassinations on the six o'clock news (or more likely the late news, given the times the assassinations had taken place) from wherever it was he had been camping. He had therefore taken it upon himself to do something about it. So, that day, he had entered the Chopville base and, by waving his hands around and with the aid of the Villain Crystal, he had murdered as many number-two- and number-three-ranked Hammerhearts as he could find. He hadn't got any of the important ones, like Cornish (oh, how I wish he'd got Cornish), but he may not have hurt him, anyway; Moran and Cornish had been old mates in their day.

Javelyn had been in the Chopville base at the time, trying to learn as much about the Hammersons' follow-up plans to the assassinations as she could find. She had started off a number-four-ranked Hammerheart when she had joined almost a month earlier, and she hadn't been around long enough or done enough to be promoted to a number-three ranking, despite the fact that she was a few months older than Lucien, who had been promoted earlier in the year. Her low rank had saved her that day, though; Moran hadn't recognised her from a bar of soap, and being a number four and likely of no importance, he had spared her life. This meant that she had been able to report all this back to Mr. Woodward that very evening.

In the immediate aftermath of the assassinations, the worldwide media had gone completely nuts, for want of a better description. The Hammersons, who had released their first public statement in more than twenty-five years in the aftermath of the natural disasters caused by the Darkness Crystal, had released another one on April 13, claiming responsibility for the assassinations and stating in no uncertain terms that all those terrorist organisations who had been coming forward over the last forty-eight hours would be severely punished if they continued to take undue credit. There was some amusement value in that since the Hammerhearts themselves could have been considered a terrorist organisation. The Woodwards had released a statement of their own a mere ninety minutes later, confirming the Hammersons' claims but saying no more than that.

The media had come down hard on the Woodwards. Many people had believed that the Woodwards weren't doing enough to ensure their safety. I hadn't cared about that; what was Mr. Woodward going to say? "We have the matter under control now, and we know we have all the resources to prevent a recurrence." That would have sounded way too political for my liking. The Woodwards cared far more about walking the walk than talking the talk, it had seemed. The trouble was, as Sebastian had rightly pointed out, the Woodwards hadn't done nearly enough walking either.

Although that had begun to change. A day earlier, the twelfth, Mr. Woodward had called on Sebastian, Jane, and Darcy and given them a mission. The three of them would be on standby because he had wanted the timing of it to be unpredictable, just in case the spy got wind of the plan, and he had chosen those three because they would have been difficult to associate with the Woodwards. It would involve the three of them infiltrating the Chopville base as I had done, at a time when Javelyn could assure them that the Hammersons would be there. The aim had been simple: Bring them in, dead or alive, but don't be seen by anyone. They were to also attempt captures of Cornish, Lucien, Hall, and the people coded 2L11, 3K17, 3P69, 3A93, and 3E57; they seemed to be prominent around Chopville, those Hammerhearts.

On the fifteenth, just hours before her untimely demise, Mr. Woodward had sent Javelyn into the Chopville base, giving her freedom (should that freedom be granted by her Hammerheart superiors) to travel to other bases around the country and even the world should that be necessary to learn what he needed her to find out. The earliest the Hammersons were known to have had people in the Australian and American governments and militaries had been March 29. They'd had plenty of time to gain access to who knew what weapons and other resources. It had been imperative that the Woodwards at least have an idea of the scope of how much the Hammersons had recently gained. Many in the Woodward base feared the Hammersons would throw away all caution and drop a nuclear bomb somewhere.

Javelyn had come up empty-handed as far as that went, but she had returned to Woodward headquarters with some alarming news.

The previous day, on the fourteenth, the Hammersons had tested a powerful explosive weapon in remote desert lands in Western Australia. The fact that this news had taken a whole day to reach the Woodwards was terrifying. How could the Hammersons have achieved something so monumental without anyone noticing? Could it possibly be bogus information, fed to Javelyn to trick the Woodwards? Mr. Woodward hadn't wanted to take that chance, and a good thing, for it had been true.

Mr. Woodward had acted swiftly, calling on the three (Sebastian, Jane, and Darcy) to be ready. Sebastian, unfortunately, had told Mr. Woodward hours later that he couldn't do it; there had been a family tragedy and he had to go home for the night, possibly two nights. Mr. Woodward had granted him this, but with some regret. Could Jane and Darcy do it alone? With Javelyn's help, they could.

And so they had. Javelyn had scoured the Chopville base that night, searching for signs that the Hammersons were in. They had been, and she had texted Mr. Woodward with this information at once. There had been more in her text, though: The Hammerhearts had plans that night, right here in Chopville. The Woodwards had instantly gone on alert, for I had also gone home that night. The tip-off to a possible attack on me had been Javelyn's last great act, for shortly after that, she had been murdered. Her body, along with a note from Arnold Hammerson, had been deposited on the Woodwards' front lawn. Keeping up with tradition, it seemed.

Jane and Darcy had gone ahead with their attack, unknowing of what had just happened to our spy, and it had been a success—not a complete success, but good enough. They had managed to capture Arnold and Dorothy Hammerson and Hank Cornish before any of them knew what had happened to them. They had also seen Lucien, but Lucien had been much quicker, and he had made a break for it. Where the Hammersons had strictly told their faithful Hammerhearts to stand up to them should they be overwhelmed, Lucien's faith had failed. It hadn't completely broken the influential charm that had been placed on him, but perhaps it had lessened its effect slightly. Jane and Darcy had attempted to chase him, but Lucien's flee had been successful, against all the odds given that Jane and Darcy had been as microscopic as I had been the last few times I'd entered the Chopville base. I knew not how long it had taken Lucien to reunite with his (our) father; it could have happened that very night, or perhaps it had taken a few days, but no longer than that. Stella wouldn't join forces with them for at least another week yet.

With the Hammersons in custody, on the evening of the sixteenth, the Woodwards had released a public statement to the media, which quickly spread throughout the world. The release had stated that the Woodwards had taken an upper hand in the war, but it had urged the public not to relax just yet. The Hammerhearts, we had found out later, interpreted this to mean that the Woodwards were relaxing in spite of themselves. The following day, however, the Hammerhearts had tested another explosive weapon in remote desert lands in Western Australia, and this time it hadn't gone unnoticed. They had been forced to quickly release a public statement, which turned out to be completely honest: They were in possession of and were testing powerful weapons, preparing a mass assault on the world, which could only be prevented if the Woodwards met their demands. Having this statement in the public domain had caused societies all over the world to cower in fear, and the Woodwards had been forced to release a follow-up statement, reiterating that they had things under control. In fact, I had doubted, even then, that Mr. Woodward had even sat down long enough to hear what the Hammerhearts' demands were.

Meanwhile, with Javelyn dead, the Woodwards had needed a new spy. Having the Hammersons safely locked away in the prison block, which had been secured more tightly since they had broken out two months earlier, didn't mean that they could afford not to have a spy within Hammerheart ranks. Mr. Woodward had therefore asked me and Marc to find him a new spy. He had wanted an American, because the Hammersons themselves were Americans and he had believed that an American would be assumed not to have any Woodward ties—a dangerous assumption, but really no worse than any other spy. Marc and I had used a second-floor room that night to travel to the United States to search.

We had placed the secret door, which backed against thin air, in the shadow of a rock in the desert lands of California, returning to it only when we had found someone to take back home with us. We had brought the Sien-Leoard and Hero Crystals with us, enabling us to teleport around the country as we searched, meaning that we didn't have to make the door appear in a new location in every city or town we wished to search.

I had lost count of the number of places we searched by about a dozen, but we had teleported plenty of times across several states before we finally struck gold. In a bar in a small city in Kansas, we had listened to a bunch of blokes talking about the war. This had been at about lunchtime local time, so they were sober, thankfully.

"Well, I say they've got the right idea," a big bloke with a scary looking beard had said defiantly. "The world's going to shit as it is, you know. Sure, the Hammersons would make themselves all high and mighty, but at least they'd bring everyone together—make us all one, instead of many."

"You think you'd be happy with that? Living under their rule?" another man had asked. "You really think the Hammersons will make a better world than this one? Haven't you been listening to their media releases? Did you see the news this morning? They're saying they're testing weapons of mass destruction."

"Yeah, that's not great," Mr. Beard had conceded, "but they wouldn't have to worry about stuff like that if there wasn't so much resistance. People just don't like change, but if they gave it a chance —got used to it—"

"Personally," a third man had said, and just the serious tone of his voice made me feel sure we had finally stumbled upon gold, "I think that even if the Hammersons were to gain power, they would remain as cruel and deadly as they are now. I hope the Woodwards show them where to go, I really do."

"Yeah, right," the second man had said. "I wouldn't want to live with the Hammersons in charge of the whole world, but I tell you what, if the Woodwards go ahead and fight them like they did thirty years ago, I'd hate to see the world at the end of it."

"You don't trust the Woodwards?" the third man had enquired. "You've lost faith that they know what they're up against?"

"I just think that the Woodwards have forgotten how to fight," the second man had said. "The Hammersons would never have forgotten how because they've been furious for thirty years, but the Woodwards probably thought their little treaty would hold, that the Hammersons would keep to themselves or risk the Woodwards' complete wrath, as though the Woodwards believed after thirty years that the win they had then would still hold now."

"That just shows how much more organised the Hammersons are," the first man had said. "They've got any government beat before they even get going, and the Woodwards—are you kidding me? They're too soft to be relied on."

"At least the Woodwards are humane," the third man had said. "I only wish people like us could do something about it, but up against magic—we would have no chance."

That's it, I'd thought; that's what we needed. Marc and I had waited, invisible, in the bar for the man to separate from his two disagreeable mates and head out alone. Eventually, at around two o'clock, he had told them that his shift was about to start and he had to leave. Marc and I had followed him out of the bar and down the street for a couple of blocks. We had then ducked behind a wall and made ourselves visible, before ducking back out and catching up with the man at the next street corner.

"Hey, mate," I had said as Marc and I crossed the road with him.

"Hello, boys," he had said cheerfully enough. "Enjoying the weekend? Can ya feel summer coming?"

"Yeah, can't wait for it," Marc had lied. "Listen, can we have a quick word? We've got a business proposal for you."

"A what?" he had asked, stopping in his tracks just above the curb.

"A business proposal. You're not too busy, are you? It won't take long."

"How old are you boys?"

"Old enough," I had said, wishing we had made ourselves look older instead of just a little bit different.

"Of course he does," Marc had said, and as we had discussed already, he had taken hold of the man's arm and I, my hand in my pocket around the Sien-Leoard Crystal, had teleported the three of us back to the magic door in California.

"Jesus Christ!" he had bellowed, spinning around to take in his surroundings. "Where the fuck are we? What's going on? Who the hell are you boys?"

"Marc Moran, John Playman," Marc had said, gesturing to himself and then me. "We've been looking around for someone like you to help us with something really important."

"You're shitting me."

"It's a nodder," I had joked. "Just go along with it until you come back to yourself, okay."

Marc had nudged me hard to make me shut up. "What's your name, sir? What do you want us to call you?"

He had hesitated, still looking completely astonished by what had just happened to him. "Luivic," he had finally said. "Frank Luivic."

"How old are you?"

"I—thirty-two," he had said weakly.

"Right, you're perfect," Marc had said decisively. "Listen, Frank, how would you like to make a difference in the war against the Hammersons?"

That had gotten his interest. He had stared at us, some comprehension dawning on him. "Was it magic, what just happened to me?" he had asked.

"Course it was," Marc had said brightly. "As is this." He gestured at the door in front of us, which showed another door through it, and beyond that second door, the interior of the second-floor room we had used to get here.

"Yes, I wish I could make a difference," he had said quietly, "but I don't know how. Crossing the path of magic—that's a death sentence."

"You can," Marc had told him, "if you've got the courage to, if you're prepared to place yourself in the company of potentially dangerous Hammerhearts, or possibly the Hammersons themselves. Are you prepared to give up everything you have here in the US to come back to Australia with us? The Woodwards need a new spy, and we think you would be great for the job. You'll only ever be seen as a Hammerheart—you'll be invisible at all times in Woodward headquarters, so hardly anyone on our side will know you're working for us."

He had thought about it for some time. We let him; it wasn't like he could make a decision this huge without some consideration. Then he said, "Can I go back home and get a few things first?"

"Sure," I had said, noticing that Marc had looked disapproving.

"Do you have a family?" Marc had asked.

"No. Well, none I get on with."

"Good. Okay, John, you go with him. I'll wait here."

Prior to April 19, two days after bringing the new spy in (one day when you take the time difference into consideration), Mr. Woodward had spoken twice to the Hammersons and Cornish, the second of those times using his discomfort device that I had been forced to use on Stella on the last day I had been physically face-to-face with her, not counting the school battle or the date with Serena. On the nineteenth, however, two events, one good and one bad, had combined, with our new spy being the only connection between the two.

It had started with his text to Mr. Woodward at around seven o'clock in the evening. Shortly after his arrival at the Chopville base, everyone who was there had been trapped. Moran had launched another attack, along with Lucien (though we hadn't realised it at the time), not just blocking the Chopville base's Hammerheart Highway connection from the rest of the Highway, but blocking in the entire southeast of the country, including the links between Sydney, Melbourne, Brisbane, Adelaide, and everywhere in between. Without their leaders present, the Hammerhearts had been trapped and powerless with no organisation and no plan to turn the situation.

Mr. Woodward had gone to tell the Hammersons what had happened, just to gage their opinion, and then…calamity! They, and Cornish, were gone. The base had been locked down again while the

Woodwards and Fletchers had searched high and low for signs of magical concealment. I had been in the lounge room at the time, along with many other Young Army people, waiting for updates. Eventually, late in the night, Mr. Woodward had returned to inform us that, once again, the Hammersons had escaped.

But this time, they had three early leads. Firstly, the security footage taken from the newly installed cameras in the cells had showed the door opening, and then several things in quick succession: Firstly, wherever the prisoner was in the cell at the time, they had been knocked unconscious; secondly, as they fell, they had flown through the air towards the door; and thirdly, at the point of the door, they had vanished into thin air. There had been fluctuations of movement as the offender had moved across to push the button, releasing the red line before the prisoner could cross it. The door had then closed. Secondly, studies that had been done on the keymonatic, a device stored in a secret location within the Woodward living quarters, showed that an unauthorised key had been created days earlier. That key had been used to open the door to the prison block. They had teleported the key to them and found that it had also been programmed to grant access to the Woodward and Fletcher living quarters (including the location the Darkness Crystal had been in, which covered another previously unanswered question), plus several secret locations within each of Marc's, Tommy's, and my bedrooms and a number of other locations that residents weren't supposed to have access to. Unfortunately, however, the key had carried no identification of the person who had created it. The Woodwards had then destroyed it. Thirdly, after investigations of all the second floor rooms, it was found that Room 2-94 had been moved recently to a location within Hamster's Stretch Reserve and, most notably, had been accessed by the offending key they had destroyed. Again, though, there was no identification of who had used it.

Two days later, before Nicole's funeral, Mr. Woodward had held a meeting with his closest advisers (the Fletchers, me, Marc, Tommy, and several others) to discuss the second breakout. He had told us that he had a plan to secure the prison block even more tightly, but he wanted to keep it close to his chest for now. It would make getting new prisoners in there a bummer, but unfortunately, it had got to the stage where they had to put up with the inconveniences in order to keep the prisoners locked up. We had found out later, when he had done it, that his idea had been to replace the door altogether with a wall that only a Woodward or Fletcher Sorcerer could pass through. It would work as the wall in the Woodward study worked.

We had also discussed the ongoing issue of the spy, who was still active within the Woodward army. Nobody had any ideas as to who it could be, and the best anyone could come up with was to ask Luivic to keep an eye out for anyone familiar in the Hammerheart Chopville base. It would be less dangerous for him to get close to the spy than it had been for Javelyn; the note Arnold Hammerson had left with her body had been cryptic, but Mr. Woodward had read into it that she must have seen the spy and been attempting to escape the base in order to confirm his/her identity when she had been ambushed and killed.

Luivic, however, had been otherwise occupied that day. Moran and Lucien had followed up on their attack on the Chopville base the day before, not just blocking the Hammerheart Highway tracks but sealing all the exits, locking all the Hammerhearts in, the plan being to starve them or something similar, no doubt. At some stage in the day of the twenty-first, possibly during Nicole's funeral, Moran and Lucien had entered the Chopville base again, protected by enchantments designed to repel both magic and non-magic attacks on them. They had used cages not unlike the ones I had been transported around the Chopville base in during my captivities to capture many Hammerhearts and leave the base with them. Some of the Hammerhearts had managed to escape the base during the distraction, but Luivic had not been one of them. When Moran and Lucien had left, he had texted Mr. Woodward again with a desperate plea for help.

Mr. Woodward, clearly not wanting to leave Luivic to his own devices as he had done with Justin and Javelyn (not that either of them had faced something like this), had set Marc and I to yet another mission together. Marc and I had always worked fairly well together, but since learning of our blood relation, we had been something close to dynamic in a partnership. Late in the evening, by which time we had both put the funeral behind us, we had forced entry into the Chopville base through Marc's house and, by way of the Hero and Sien-Leoard Crystals, had teleported every Hammerheart we found in the base into a secure box hidden inside the prison block in the Woodward base. I had done something similar when freeing prisoners the Hammersons had taken from the first school battle. When we were done, the base had been completely empty, but we hadn't recaptured anyone of any particular importance. On the advice of the Sien-Leoard Crystal, on our way out, we had forced entry into Marc's hidden quarters. Moran and Lucien had anticipated our approach and scarpered, but there were plenty of prisoners still being held captive in cages all around the walls. We had teleported them into the same box before heading back to base, leaving Moran and Lucien to discover for themselves what we had done.

Mr. Woodward had been the one to organise the new prisoners into their separate cells. He had taken Luivic aside from the rest of them and, making sure he was invisible, had taken him into their living quarters. Luivic, in his time of captivity, had acquired a weapon that would be most useful for the Woodwards to understand. It was a device that altered the mind of the person its jet hit, feeding certain thoughts into their heads that will make them far more agreeable to the Hammersons' desires. In other words, it put the influential charm on them. Luivic had informed us that such a device was called a boggler. Mr. Woodward had taken it with the intention to create a counter-device.

The last news I had heard out of the Hammerheart quarters had come two days later, within hours of our departure for England. The Hammersons had called in a large party of American Hammerhearts. Apparently they had entered their Chopville base the previous day by some secret entrance only to find it deserted. Luivic had been able to join up with the American Hammerhearts, meaning that he had managed to get quite close to the Hammersons without them suspecting a thing. That, Mr. Woodward had considered a massive win for our side. Luivic had texted Mr. Woodward late in the evening with some news that wasn't so good: The damage that Moran had done to the Hammerheart Highway had now been completely repaired.

I'd had some time to think of how Stella must have joined with Moran and Lucien in the time since then. She would have almost certainly used the Hammerheart Highway to get to and from England, but if she'd returned to the country while the southeast was cut off, she would have had to wait a few days somewhere else, perhaps over in Perth, for the situation to clear. I could only assume that when she had returned to Chopville, she had used the Moran house to leave the highway, only to be caught by its residents. Perhaps this time, she decided it would be better to join rather than fight, and after the brief look I had been given of the three of them, that seemed to be a good decision; while she was with them, she was in no danger from either of them.

"So you believe me?" I now asked Mr. Woodward. "You believe that Stella is really alive? That she has been the whole time?"

"Yes, I believe you, John," said Mr. Woodward. "In truth, I half-believed you all along, but I had to lean towards the evidence. Now that the evidence has turned, I shall turn with it. Make no mistake, I am not perfect, I will make mistakes, and the way things are becoming now, I am likely to make more of them."

"So what's been happening here, anyway?" I asked. Now it was time for him to give me some answers. "Amelia gave me updates in the room every day while I was in England with Lena, except this morning—last night for you—I get Marc instead, and he tells me that she and Natalie have disappeared. What's happened?"

"We don't know," he said heavily. "A lot happened at school yesterday. Firstly, Hignat and Wilwog had been ordered to capture Marc, but Marc was able to use his crystal to catch them and bring them in instead. Candice Young, I'm sure you remember her, was ordered to block Amelia and Natalie's magic by way of those devices that tamper with the crystal chip. She succeeded, but she was noticed in doing so by Rebecca Fletcher, who launched her own attack; we now have all three of them in the prison block. After they lost their magic, though, the girls disappeared. Possibly not having their magic made them more vulnerable to another Hammerheart assault. That's all we know for sure. We went out using magic in the area, trying to detect signs of them or what happened to them, but we came up empty-handed."

I could get no more out of him. "Thanks," I said, feeling depressed. "Well, I'm really tired, but before I go up, did you want to see this?"

I pulled the life assistant from my pocket and held it out to Mr. Woodward, but he shook his head. "Save it," he said, getting to his feet and looking weary as ever. "The others who were in the search party will want to see it. I suggest you share the experience with them, and perhaps Lena too. You should go and get some sleep—you look as tired as you say."

"Thanks," I repeated, also getting to my feet.

I went up to my room, where I changed into my pyjamas and slipped into bed. I slept deeply, and when I rose seven hours later, the world as I had always known it was gone forever.

* * *

The town of Chopville, which had had a population of around two thousand prior to the Sorcerers setting up residence, had undergone sweeping changes in the thirteen years since. Unsurprisingly, tourism had boomed, rejuvenating an economy that had always depended entirely on the farmers in the Goulburn Valley. The population had swelled to more than seven thousand (that was the 2010 estimate, anyway) as more and more people had wanted in on the action. The skyline had evolved into something unlike any other country town I had ever seen, the identifying feature being the many bridges over the Jade River. The Chopville Luxury Inn, located on Achior Stroll overlooking the river and with a good view of almost the whole town, had grown to be the tallest building in town (six storeys) and had never failed to do good business since 1997. The hospital had grown too, not just in proportion to the population but now to include the world's only Magical Medicine Research Centre, which Lillian Woodward visited on a weekly basis.

Many things in the town had also evolved along with the town itself. Prior to the year 2000, the *Chopville Telegraph* had been just like any other local rag in any other country town all over the country—twice weekly with news of local events and economy. Now it had become a daily rag and a complete advertiser, with about a dozen different writers all working hard to provide the town with news and gossip. As technology had also evolved, they had started an online subscription service, and the only person I knew stupid enough to blow most of his pocket money on it was James (perhaps Lisa had done the same in her time).

I wasn't calling him stupid on April 28, 2010, though. For the first time in living memory, the Telegraph writers were working on the fly, posting their articles online almost as soon as they had finished them in order to keep up with the flow of breaking news coming out of Canberra. It was highly unlikely that any of them were actually in Canberra, but seeing as Chopville was such a desirable place to work for certain types of writers and the town wasn't big enough to accommodate too many of them, those working at the Telegraph were highly popular with writers from other papers. Normally it was the Chopville writers sharing information, but on this occasion, it was the writers in Canberra doing the sharing. James had printed three such articles from his computer, and they were among the first things I saw when I woke up.

SECOND SORCEROUS WAR DECLARED AS AUSTRALIA FALLS

The treaty that the Woodward and Hammerson Sorcerer lines drew at the end of the great war in 1981 was shattered on Wednesday afternoon when more than 1,000 heavily armed Hammerson soldiers stormed Parliament House, killing some upper and lower house politicians and capturing many others. Those held captive were gradually released back into the government, but it is unknown what they were forced to endure during their captivity, except that the end result is that they are all now doing the Hammersons' bidding. One correspondent was assaulted by a well-known Liberal seat when he asked a witness, who was leaving for the day, what may have happened.

The federal government has been highly disorganised since the attack against the Prime Minister, but many believe that even a highly organised government couldn't have stood up to such a premeditated assault. In the hours that followed the coup, other authorities, such as the military and police force, were also overpowered. The police officers that had previously been ordered to rest Parliament House from the Hammerson supporters were ordered, only minutes later, to retreat, by the same commander. Likewise, the military were given orders to stand aside.

The Hammersons' organisation, who call themselves the "Hammerhearts," have made it clear that they intend to reorganise the Australian government completely, making it independent of Great Britain and, most likely, not a constitutional democracy.

The only public statement that has come from Parliament House this afternoon was made by Arnold Hammerson himself. Addressing a large crowd, he stated that a Hammerson sympathiser by the name of Hank Cornish would be running the country in the immediate future, until such time as the country no longer requires a leader of its own. This ominous announcement has caused some stirring both locally and internationally. The president of the United States of America responded to this announcement almost at once, stating, "We will do all that is necessary to ensure the safety of the American people."

SWEEPING CHANGES ABOUND AS NEW ERA BEGINS

Hank Cornish, the newly declared Prime Minister of Australia, has wasted no time in stamping his authority on the country. Under the new rule that the Hammersons are beginning to establish, the Prime Minister can effectively do whatever he wants so long as his orders fall in line with what the Hammersons desire. Cornish has spent much of the afternoon making widespread changes to as many levels of authority as he can reach.

Some of the changes that Prime Minister Hank Cornish has already ordered and had approved by Arnold Hammerson include:

• The discontinuation of all other forms of government: By the end of the day, it is estimated that all state governments and approximately 60 percent of all local governments will be emptied and its representatives sent to Canberra for a stringent screening program to ensure that they are fit for positions of authority under the new rule.

• The discontinuation of the Australian health system: All hospitals and medical institutions around the country have been ordered to close their doors until such time as a full inspection can be performed on them to make sure they are up to "Hammerheart" standards. Cornish intends to have this done for New South Wales and Victoria by tomorrow, Queensland by Friday, and the rest of the country by early next week. Cornish has also ordered that up to 1.2 billion dollars be invested in the first "Hammerheart hospital" of Australia, which will be built most likely in Sydney's inner west. The criteria required to gain access to such a hospital is as yet unclear.

• The discontinuation of the education system: Cornish has ordered a complete overhaul of the education system, requiring all schools at primary and secondary level (public/private/ ethnic/religious/special) be closed indefinitely until new guidelines are drawn. Similarly, he has ordered that, aside from religious topics, all schools are required to teach the same materials, and any diversions from these materials will result in terrible punishments for the educators responsible, as well as those coordinators organising materials at that particular institution. The teaching of any anti-Hammerheart materials may also result in further charges of treason.

• An overhaul of the Australian police force: The new police force will be temporarily run federally, until such time as the same rules and regulations can be enforced on a global scale. Each officer must be sworn to regulations imposed by the Hammersons and enforce only approved laws. Once this overhaul is complete, the police force will be given new magical arms to use against civilians who show outward signs of contempt for the new regime.

• An overhaul of the Australian Defence Forces: All army, navy, and air force personnel and equipment have been ordered to return to base. Troops located overseas have been ordered to retreat immediately. Further to this, all airports in Australia have been closed since 2:00 under the order that they are to be

converted to major air force bases and not used for civilian aviation until the situation of the war is stabilised.

This last order has caused mass panic in the Australian public. Many civilians who attempted to flee the country have been taken custody by the Hammerson supporters and are presumably being either tortured, converted, or both. All this correspondent can say is: Sit tight, there is more to come.

NEW POLICE CHIEF RELEASES NAMES

Interim Prime Minister Hank Cornish has ordered a federal police chief take charge of the Australian police force during its overhaul. Dermot Hall, a Hammerson supporter who is suspected but not proven to have instigated an attack on Chopville's local secondary college at which he had taught, has been given the position as a trusted adviser of the Hammersons. Hall had only been in his position mere minutes when he began to flex his muscles.

Hall has already began reorganising officers all over the country, calling in those whose records he finds impertinent and moving those he trusts to greater positions of power. Many of these officers have been organised into a taskforce whose mission is to track down five men and put them behind bars. These men, former Hammerson supporters and local to Chopville, are known to have great bloodlust but no faith at all in the Hammersons. Bernard Moran, Lucien Moran, Marc Moran, John Playman, and Tommy Blue may be armed with magical weapons of great power and destruction.

"These men are extremely dangerous and should only be approached with great caution," Hall said from Parliament House, the current centre of all Hammerheart operations. "It is no secret what crimes these men have committed in recent times.

"Indeed, Moran, Bernard that is, has a list of previous charges as long as the Murray River. He was single-handedly responsible for the well-publicised attacks on all the Sorcerers and the worldwide weather alterations three months ago. His son, Marc, has been found guilty of the murder of Lisa Pont, a well-known Woodward supporter, and likewise, John Playman is known to be guilty of murdering a young schoolgirl by the name of Tulip Naval, and is suspected to have raped her as well."

When asked if he believed these men would join with the Woodwards' and Fletchers' resistance, Hall had been noncommittal.

"It's possible, but I doubt it. From my personal involvement with them, apart from Blue, with whom I've had little to do, I believe they would get the greatest thrill out of working against both sides.

"They could possibly turn on civilians, but I suspect that attacks on civilians will be only to make a point of their power. Mostly, I believe they would target the authorities."

Again, we reiterate, these men are most likely heavily armed and extremely dangerous, and whatever Chief Hall says, they should not be approached under any circumstances. Photos of the five offenders can be found on page twelve. If you see these men anywhere, do not confront them! A special hotline has been set up to track them down.

Part 2: Takeover

Chapter 9: Rescue

For his safety, or perhaps more for the protection of the Hero/ Sorcerous Crystals, Marc had been ordered to return to base. He was distressed by what was happening and the fact that he was now in even more danger than he had been before. Most of the teenagers inside the Woodward headquarters were culminated in the lounge room, but Marc didn't want to join their loud contemplation of what was happening in the world around them. He had therefore positioned himself in the hall outside it, directly opposite Tulip's memorial, so he was the first person I met when I came downstairs shortly before dinner that evening.

"Hey," he said when he saw me. "John, it's happened."

"What? What's happened now?"

For answer, he pointed into the lounge room where, clearly visible from where we stood, the television screen showed none other than Hank Cornish addressing a large congregation of people.

"You see what that is," he muttered. "They've taken over, and it's only the beginning. They've got arrest warrants out for you, me, and Tommy now too."

"Holy crap," I said in a hushed voice.

He nodded and silently passed me four sheets of paper I hadn't even noticed until then. Slowly, in a numbing sort of horror, I read the three articles James had printed from the Chopville Daily Telegraph. On the fourth sheet were the photographs referred to in the last article. There were three pictures, one large across the top and two more along the bottom. The top one showed me, Marc, and Tommy standing together, shoulder to shoulder and clearly laughing at something hilarious. There were other people on either side of us, but they had been blurred so that only we three were distinguishable. I had no idea when they could have taken that picture, but from the graffiti on the wall behind us, I knew it had been during recess or lunch at school. The pictures of Moran and Lucien were much blander and had probably been taken from some sort of Hammerheart database.

"They sent me back," Marc said when I looked up, "'cause of that. All the Sorcerers are out there, and practically everyone else from here. The only ones left are a couple of cleaners and a nurse."

"We've gotta go out there."

"We can't," he said quickly. "Mr. Woodward told me the crystals are now more important than ever."

"Yeah, important to use against them," I said heatedly. "What good are they here?"

"That's what Mr. Woodward said." Marc shrugged. "He thinks we'll have a chance against them so long as they don't have any of the crystals. If they get them, and especially if they get mine and take the Woodwards' and Fletchers' magic, well…it'll be so much worse."

I swore under my breath. Did Mr. Woodward actually want to win this war or what?

"So what are we supposed to do?" I asked.

"I guess we guard this place," he said, unsurely. "It's bad as it is, but Mr. Woodward seemed sure that they would still find time to go for us. If they can get in here, the Woodwards and Fletchers and all their people will have nowhere safe to lodge."

"Let's go and have dinner," I said grudgingly. "I dunno what I wanna do, except that I'm not sitting back here doing nothing, whatever Mr. Woodward says."

"Okay, fine," he said, following me. "Whatever you do, I'll help out. If we stay unconnected and we're careful enough with our magic, then we should be okay and not get them in any extra trouble. So how'd it go with Underwood?"

"Well, I've got the life assistant," I said quietly. "I feel bad now, though; Underwood works in the government over there. He's gonna have absolutely no protection now. Do you think we should go back and let him come here?"

"Do you think he would?" Marc asked doubtfully.

"Maybe. Things have changed since twelve hours ago."

"I haven't seen Lena yet. How's she going?"

"Fine, I think. She told me she was okay with it when I left her body. We didn't have to—you know—do anything with him, though, so it's easy enough to deal with. At least, I think so. She went to bed as soon as we got back. Don't know where she is now, but I reckon she'll be hanging around us a whole lot more from now on."

There was one thing that might be more difficult for Lena to deal with, I thought. It had only occurred to me since we had gotten back how self-conscious Lena would have to be around me now, after I had spent the last few days in complete operation of her body—how very familiar I must be with it. This was only partially true; I had allowed her to take responsibility for whatever physical maintenance girls needed—I had actually checked out during those times—so ultimately, I was no more familiar with her body now than I had been after I had thoroughly explored it a week earlier. Still, even though I hadn't needed to let Underwood have his way with her, I could now understand a little better how she would probably feel more self-conscious. What I couldn't predict, however, was how she would deal with it.

Marc looked around us, but the dining room was empty. He said, very quietly all the same, "Did you end up—you know, with Lena?"

"Yeah, I did, but I think you know what made it easier. Don't tell anyone, though."

"Sure. Oh, we've got company, speak of the devil."

It was Serena, which meant that discussion of Underwood was off the table. She latched on to me all through dinner and for some time after it, making her intentions clear; she wasn't letting me go anywhere without her for as long as she could get away with. Marc had hung around all this time, preferring to pretend that he didn't notice Serena's behaviour. Tommy also joined us shortly after dinner, clearly wishing to know how it went with Underwood but finding no way to ask me due to all the people hanging around us. Partly because of my disappearance for five days and partly because of the events of that day, just about everyone in the base wanted a piece of me, and it wasn't until about ten o'clock in the evening that I managed to get away from most of them.

On the stairs between the first and second floors, I was still surrounded by Marc, Tommy, Serena, Lena, Harry, Simon, Sebastian, and Rebecca. Peter and James were at the bottom of the stairs, apparently with the same wishes as Tommy but again seeing no way to go about satisfying themselves. What I eventually did was, as I had reached the second level, I created an invisible barrier between myself and everyone else so that none of them could follow me along the row of rooms on the second floor.

"Oi, John," Serena cried out. "Get rid of it. Come on."

"I will, a little later on," I tried to assure her. "I need to do something alone first, okay?"

"What's up, John?" Harry asked. "If you're trying to get up to your room, then you're on the wrong—"

"I know, I'm doing something along here," I said, and I turned my back on them, ignoring the muttering.

Along the row of rooms I went up to the divide, then through it another three rows. Along the fourth I went to the left until I reached Room 86 and slipped into it. This was the room that Marc and I had used to travel to the US to find Frank Luivic. It was still set to open in California (although non-existent while it was closed), and I didn't have time to bring it back to Chopville, but it would serve the purpose I needed anyway. I used the crystal again to open the back door and went through it into the control room. Without changing any settings, I opened the next door and stepped into early morning

California, where I used the crystal again to teleport all the way back to night-time Chopville. My mission tonight was quite simple. Whether or not it would actually be simple to accomplish was yet to be determined.

Chopville was very quiet, even more quiet than usual for night-time. It was also darker than usual; it looked as though the town central was completely closed down, everyone preferring to stay at home and stay safe. They couldn't have kept up with the news because since about eight o'clock, every single TV station in the country had been shut down. Even the hospital was practically dead, having been ordered to shut up shop earlier that day. All the houses I passed were dark and silent but not uninhabited; the people inside wanted to stay safe, and the best way to do that was not to draw attention to themselves.

I felt sure that, out of sight, resistance was being put up around me. People were fighting back, and the Hammersons (though I also felt sure that the Hammersons themselves were either sleeping or in another country, organising wider plans) would have their work cut out for them. Vigilante groups would be forming everywhere; in fact, I wouldn't be at all surprised if a single police officer had stayed in the area to prevent crooks taking advantage of the situation, or a makeshift hospital had been set up somewhere so that the ill and injured could be cared for until this new Hammerheart hospital could be established.

But Chopville was quiet, so I felt reasonably safe that I wouldn't be attacked here tonight. That wasn't to say I wouldn't be, though; it would make sense for the Hammerhearts to have left a few people behind just to have a go at getting those who still dwelled here. Wouldn't they just love to get their hands on some real magic, like what Marc and I had? With that in mind, I set off through Hamster's Stretch Reserve and along Main Street, both invisible and with an invisible shield around me.

Natalie and Amelia were out here somewhere, I felt sure of it. It wasn't the crystal (not at first, anyway) but a gut feeling that was telling me this. It would make sense, and as I walked along Main Street, I thought it all over. They had both had their magic taken off them, which would have made them an easy target for just about anyone; after all, those who normally had magic seemed to consistently make the mistake of not bringing any backup magical items to defend themselves. But if Hignat, Wilwog, and Young had all been caught and brought into the Woodwards, and it had been Young's job to bring the Sorcerers into the Hammersons, then who could have done it? Who, in fact, could have known that Young had failed, if Young never had a chance to report back, for, according to Mr. Woodward, Rebecca had retaliated immediately?

If there had been an army of Hammerhearts in the school, as there had been twice before, the answer would have been obvious, but if there had been, then that would have been obvious too. Was Hall a factor in this? I doubted it; if Hall had ever been brought back to school, even if it had been the day before, the only day of school I had missed while in England (thank you, Anzac Day), then Marc would have told me. That left only one possibility, and it was the one I wanted to investigate most: Moran, Lucien, and Stella, who had already done more to disrupt the Hammersons than the Woodwards and Fletchers had. Could they be behind this? What would be their motive, except to cause trouble and never mind which side it disadvantaged?

So it was to the Moran house I went, thinking of the last time I had been there. Marc and I had seen for ourselves the post that Moran and Lucien had set up within the hidden quarters. We had only gone about transferring their prisoners from those cages to the cells in the Woodward base, but there had been other things too that, given how well they had been going against the Hammersons, we had decided to leave intact. A new control panel had been placed against the side wall, between the two entrances, the ones I knew of anyway. On it had been a couple of TV screens, both blank at the time, and a number of other buttons, dials, switches, and levers, who knew what all did. It had looked efficient, and based on what they had done to the Hammerheart Highway, the way they had timed all their attacks on the Chopville base, it had certainly been as efficient as it had looked.

The first obstacle I met was the front door of Marc's house, which, as it had been the last few times I had come to call here, was locked tight. One touch of the crystal and a well-chosen thought solved that problem at once. I slipped quietly down the stairs, shutting the door behind me and listening carefully. If they were in the hidden quarters, which they surely would be, assuming they were here at all, then I wouldn't be able to hear anything they did, even if they were having a roaring argument. Likewise, they wouldn't hear me if I bellowed at them to come out and say 'howdy', but if those television screens in there operated as I expected they did, or if Moran's Villain Crystal was in a good mood if the screens didn't, then they would know I was coming anyway.

As I carefully descended the stairs, I wondered: What would the three of them do if I came face-to-face with them? Would they attack me? I had to chastise myself for thinking that they wouldn't. I might have softened slightly towards Moran since learning he was my father and he had tried to save my life when I was young, but I had to remind myself what else he had tried to do to me, that he had tried to kill me (and everyone else) when he'd been a Sorcerer; that he had used the domination charm on me, which had done more good than harm, as it turned out; and that he had tried to use an agonator on me and had hit Lena instead. If he had known I was his son, why had he done that? I supposed there was no mystery there—he'd treated Marc and Lucien very similarly.

Now, heart thumping in anticipation, I reached the bottom of the stairs and emerged into the Morans' hallway. It was lit as it almost always was. I had only once seen the lights in this house out, and that had been only after a flood had cut the power. Still invisible, still with a shield around me, I stopped and listened hard, my eyes roving around the room. There was no one in the lounge room, or the kitchen, which I could see part of over the counter through the lounge room door. There was definitely no one in the hallway with me; my hand was around my crystal and it was confirming that.

Moran, I suddenly remembered, had a distinct advantage over me: He was untraceable, and I wasn't. This surely meant that if he was in here with me, the Sien-Leoard Crystal wouldn't tell me, while his Villain Crystal would have no trouble detecting my presence. I prayed that my shield would be strong enough to protect me, and I wished to give it strength; the crystal went warm in my hand, granting the wish. Feeling slightly better, I turned my body towards the hidden quarters. It was hardly worth going anywhere else in the house before the hidden quarters, and if they thought of racing through the tunnels under the house to evade me, I would have to do something drastic to flush them out. What that was, I didn't know yet.

I approached the hidden quarters and stopped in front of them, still listening and not knowing why; there was still nothing to hear. Marc and I had done this before, and I had no reason to suspect it wouldn't work this time. I gripped the crystal in my hand and imagined the rock in front of me splitting smoothly down the middle, creating the opening through which I would step. The crystal did its magic, then some more magic, then some more. It grew very hot in my hand, not just warm like the Light Crystal had when it performed magic, but so hot that I withdrew my fingers from my pocket hastily, hissing in pain. The crystal bounced out of my pocket and onto the floor, where it rolled away, lost in invisibility.

My head spun in a panic I hadn't felt for a long time. So much had gone wrong. The Sien-Leoard Crystal had come up against a magic stronger than it had faced before—probably just the Villain Crystal, but it had put up a tremendous fight, for the rock still hadn't split (I hoped dearly that Moran's fingers had burnt as mine had done). Now the crystal was on the floor somewhere and I had to bend down and search blindly for it, while at any moment Moran could burst out at me, if he knew what had just happened. And there was a third problem: I could sense other movement around me and knew instinctively that Lucien and Stella were on the move. What they were doing, whether they were escaping or doubling around behind me, I had no idea, but either way, I felt extremely nervous.

I did the only thing I could do; leaving the Sien-Leoard Crystal was not an option. I crouched down and felt wildly around, trying to stay calm and make sure I didn't miss a spot on the floor. My shield was still around me—at least, it should have been—but that didn't mean a good curse from the Villain Crystal couldn't shatter it, and the person within it. This thought invariably made me stop searching and listen, and I could still sense movement close by, but for all I could make out, they could have been absolutely anywhere. I continued searching, and finally, I nudged the thing I was looking for. I felt some more 'til I found it again, got a grip on it, and gathered it up again. That had been way too close.

I leapt to my feet and backed against the wall. There, protected by the shield, which I again strengthened, I sent my mind out from my body and scanned my surroundings. Moran was untraceable, so I had no idea where he was, but the magic of the hidden quarters wasn't strong enough to keep me from seeing that Natalie and Amelia were indeed locked up in there. As for Lucien, he was currently sliding down towards the Hammerheart Highway; where he would go with it without being caught was his business, but if I was right in thinking that Stella had used it several times in recent weeks without getting caught, and with the Hammerhearts busy in far more open places than underground tunnels, he would probably be okay. As for Stella, she was nowhere. Had she left them, even if only temporarily?

Returning to my body, I turned back to the hidden quarters and tried again to make them open. They slid apart without any trouble this time, and I knew only then that Moran had never been attacking me; he had simply bided time to give himself and Lucien a chance to escape. I could still have gone after them, brought both of them back and questioned them about what they'd done, what they'd been doing, what their motives were, and where Stella had gone, but the two girls closer at hand took higher precedence in my mind. They were, after all, the reason why I had come out here tonight.

The cages that Moran had held his Hammerheart prisoners in were gone. In fact, the hidden quarters were almost completely empty. The control panel that had been there last time was still there, but anything else that Moran, Lucien, and Stella had used (I assumed they had lived in here for a good few days now), they had either vanished or taken with them. Natalie and Amelia were sitting against the wall opposite the control panel, but neither of them were in cages —they weren't even tied up. In fact, Natalie, who was closer and looking in my general direction rather more placidly than I would have expected, looked almost comfortable.

"Who's that?" she asked, getting to her feet and taking a tentative step forward. "Is that you, Marc? John?"

"Yeah, it's me," I said, gripping the crystal and making myself visible again, fairly sure that Moran was not coming back. "Are you two okay?"

"I am," said Natalie, but though she could see me, though she was not bound, she did not move towards me. Amelia, still sitting on the floor, didn't move at all, and as I caught a good glimpse of her, I understood why Natalie had said "I" instead of "we." Amelia was in a bad way; she hadn't been physically assaulted like she had been when the Hammersons had taken us in, but she looked a mess all the same.

"You don't have your magic, do you?" I asked, fairly sure that they didn't, but I was honestly thrown by this lack of reaction from the pair of them.

As I thought this, a horrible possibility occurred to me: Had Moran used the influential charm on them? Were they really on his side and not the Woodwards' anymore? But a moment later I understood as Natalie said, "No. I asked when we could have it back, but he said the time wasn't right. Look, can you get rid of this thing?"

I gripped the crystal again and suddenly realised—they were held by the same sort of shield I was using to protect myself, the difference being that it couldn't be moved. It only took about half a second to get rid of it, and when it had gone, Natalie finally leapt forward, as I'd been waiting for her to do. She tried to hug me but found herself impeded by my invisible shield, which I still hadn't vanished, and in some surprise, I found that Natalie didn't realise that it was the same as what had been holding her and Amelia hostage for the last thirty hours. Wanting the hug (why wouldn't I, it was Natalie after all), I vanished the shield, and a moment later, Natalie was on me.

"Oh my God, it's horrible," she said desperately, pulling back after about ten seconds and staring at me. "You have to fix us up so we can get out there."

"You've been following it?" I asked, slightly surprised. Moran and Lucien would surely have been following the progress of the Hammerheart takeover, but letting their prisoners do the same?

"Yeah, on that," she said, jabbing her thumb at the control panel. "John, we saw Stella."

"Yeah, I know she's with those two now," I told her. "Where is she? Not with them anymore?"

"Yeah, she is," said Natalie, raising her eyebrows. "Apparently she's untraceable now; something happened when she left her family. She was thinking about it a bit but didn't say much."

That sparked my interest. What sort of stuff would Natalie have picked out of Stella's mind? What had happened to her? Untraceable —that explained why I had been unable to locate her so much of the time, but I pushed it from my mind. There were more important things to worry about.

"Listen, what did they want with you two?"

Natalie grimaced. "Nothing, actually. I think they just wanted to prove that we can trust them not to hurt us. I suppose that's true enough, but they would have done a lot better to let us go when everything started happening earlier, but Moran wanted to hold on to us for longer. He said he would turn me and Amelia into his personal protectors or some crap if we kept protesting."

"Geez," I hissed. "Okay, well, stand still so I can fix you up. You okay, Amelia?"

Amelia still hadn't moved. She was staring at the opposite wall, at a spot a few feet to the left of the control panel. She looked blank, as though her brain had jammed.

"Later," muttered Natalie. "Just do the magic thing. I'll explain it later, or she can if she's up to it."

I quickly fixed her magic up, then Amelia's, without disturbing her motionless pose. I then did something I had done to the two girls in the aftermath of the second school battle. That day, I had recognised the great danger that those devices that blocked the Sorcerers' magic posed, so I had placed upon them both an enchantment of my own. I hadn't known at the time if it had worked, but I'd assumed that it must have because neither of them had lost their magic since. The enchantment placed a shield around their bodies, not one like the one I had placed around myself, but one that moulded to the body, like thicky prison did. This shield only blocked magic designed to attack the crystal chip. It wouldn't protect against anything else because I didn't want to make it more difficult for the Sorcerers to access their own magic, and I couldn't be sure that wouldn't be a consequence. Knowing that the spell would only last for twenty-four hours if I didn't give it a time limit, I had set it to last for a month. That had been on March 22, and the day that Candice Young had taken their magic had been April 27. I did the same again now, and this spell would also last a month.

"Cheers," said Natalie, waving her hands around herself. The spells she was casting over herself seemed to be for personal maintenance—apparently she hadn't had a chance to wash herself or brush her hair or anything for two days. She also performed the same spells on Amelia, for Amelia seemed unable to do anything at all. It made her look a little better, but it didn't change that expression on her face.

"I don't think she can go out there," I said quietly to Natalie, watching Amelia.

"No, I don't think so either," she agreed. "So—um—where should I go? The TV went out three hours ago; I've got no idea what's happened since."

"Just teleport to wherever Mr. Woodward is and let him tell you what to do. What's the latest you know, anyway?"

"Fighting," she said simply. "The military's trying to fight back —at least, parts of it are—and the Kiwis have sent some of their forces over as well. It's big 'cause remember what Javelyn said ages ago—they've already taken weapons from the military, here and in some other countries too. They were just saying when the TV went out that the US and UK are also sending jets over here, and Indonesia too 'cause they think they'll be next. I don't know where the fighting's happening, if it's around Canberra or somewhere else."

"Okay," I said, thinking. "I say you teleport to Mr. Woodward, and—hang on."

I concentrated hard on the crystal in my hand again. What I wanted to do was to ensure that none of the other Sorcerers would have their magic blocked; I was certain that the Hammerhearts had been ordered to attack the Woodwards and Fletchers with those devices should they be spotted. It would have been simpler for me to just go with Natalie and do those enchantments myself, but it could also be potentially disastrous if I should get in their way. I therefore wanted a device that Natalie could use on them, that she could ensure that they wouldn't have their magic blocked.

"Here," I said, handing it to her when it had landed in the palm of my free hand. "Take this and use it on the other Sorcerers; it will put that shield around them too. At least it will if it works like it's supposed to."

"Thanks," she said, looking impressed and pocketing the object. "Well, I guess I should—"

She hesitated, and I knew she was putting off the moment when she would have to teleport herself into the waiting arms of danger.

"Go," I said quietly, "before you lose your nerve. Don't worry about Amelia—we'll take care of her back at the base. Hopefully she'll be right to come out again soon. And we'll see you—"

I hesitated too. Now I knew what was going through Natalie's mind. When would I see her again? When would we see any of the Sorcerers again? Natalie ended my hesitation by hugging me again, and when she pulled back, I saw that her eyes were bright and watery.

"Good luck," I said quietly. "Marc and I will try to help out wherever we can. See you soon, okay?"

"Say 'so long,'" she said, smiling weakly. "It's supposed to mean better luck."

"So long, then," I said, also smiling weakly and touching her shoulder. She smiled and vanished into thin air. Teleporting was something Natalie had mastered only a week ago; I hoped, over what could be a very great distance, she wouldn't stuff it up.

"Amelia," I said quietly, approaching her nervously.

The only movement she had made since I had entered the hidden quarters was to rise to her feet, which she had done when I had unblocked her magic. She was now standing, still and stiff, staring straight ahead. She made no sign that she had heard me speak and didn't acknowledge my presence at all until I touched her lightly on the cheek with a finger. Her eyes rolled, found mine for about three seconds, and then she swooned, with just enough warning for me to reach out and catch her before she hit the floor.

With Amelia, even an unconscious Amelia, I could probably have got myself into the Woodward base through the main entrance. Well, it would have required me to push her halfway into the wall and then push myself through, not letting go of her. I didn't, though, because the door I had used to get out of the base was still wide open and accepting traffic, should any traffic find it. So I teleported the pair of us to California and, using the crystal to make my life a little easier, lifted Amelia into the air and carried her through the door and into Room 86. I lay her down on the bed, went back to close the door, and then sat myself on the bed beside her, watching her.

Given her recent imprisonment, her fainting could have been caused by just about anything—injury, blood loss, hunger, dehydration—but I had a feeling I knew what it was and what had been wrong with her before. If my suspicions were right, the nervous breakdown Amelia had been edging towards over the last three weeks may have been triggered by her most recent experience. I didn't think Moran had gone out of his way to be horrible to her, because if he had, Natalie would have been in a similar state. Never having been held captive before, she probably would have coped even worse than Amelia in that situation. Maybe having her magic taken off her and being taken prisoner against her will had been enough, even if the imprisonment itself could have been much worse.

If that were the case, then it would explain her current state. At least, I thought it would. I had never actually seen something like what had probably happened to Amelia, but if she had broken down into a storm of tears and insanity while in the company of Moran, who had about as much emotion to spare as the rock behind which they had hidden, it wasn't difficult to imagine him sedating her with magic or even drugs, if he had them. She had probably still been sedated when I had come, and then, when she recognised me, the emotional implosion (for it certainly hadn't been an explosion) may have caused her to faint. It sort of made sense to me, but I couldn't confirm any of it until she came around.

I tapped her lightly on the forehead, the cheek, the chin. She didn't stir, and I sighed. I really wasn't sure what to do for the best. Should I stay? Should I leave? If I stayed, how long would I have to stay before she came to? If I left, what would happen if she woke up and found herself here, alone? Would she remember me entering the hidden quarters and freeing her and Natalie from Moran's hold? How did I even know that it wouldn't be better for her to wake up alone? All these questions raced around in my mind, and the more I thought about it, the more I wanted to just use the crystal to wake her up and sedate her myself, as Moran had done, if necessary.

I didn't, though. What I did was inject some reason into my thoughts. If Amelia woke up alone, she might panic. If she woke up and found herself with me or Marc, or both, she wouldn't panic. She might be surprised, though, or relieved. She might burst into tears; she probably would burst into tears, and she might cry enough of them to fill a bucket. That, I supposed, would be better than sedating her. Whatever was inside her, whatever she had been trying to hold back and cover up for so long, was far better out than in, and if it had to come out tonight, even during this great time of trouble and with her parents so far away (for even Amelia's mother had gone out to help), it would still have to do.

So, making up my mind, I gripped the Sien-Leoard Crystal again, and Amelia disappeared from view. I then used the crystal to levitate her invisible body into the air, so that she would float along behind me, high enough that she wouldn't knock into anyone who might still be lurking on the stairs, waiting for me. I had only been gone for a little over an hour, so it was certainly possible. As I saw when I approached the stairs again, however, I had been wrong; nobody had bothered to wait around for me, at least not where I could see them. I could hear quiet, familiar voices in the lounge room, however, and knew that those who were waiting for me to return were congregated there and probably had someone lurking around up here, waiting to give them a signal that I had returned.

I decided I would save them some trouble and actually go down there, but only when I had deposited Amelia somewhere. The best place for her to wake up would probably be her own bedroom, but I honestly couldn't see a way of getting her there without being spotted; teleporting within the base felt way too risky, and I honestly felt I didn't deserve to have to make myself invisible to achieve it. I therefore went up, instead of down, and along to my room. I lowered her onto my bed, made her visible again, then went back downstairs to see who was waiting for me.

It turned out to be nearly all the same people who had made getting up the stairs such a task; Marc, Tommy, Serena, Lena, Sebastian, and Rebecca. If the twins were upstairs keeping an eye out for me, they had done a lousy job because the six in the lounge room got something of a shock when I walked into the room.

"John!" several of them shouted, and they all jumped up and hurried forward. Lena, clever as she was, had positioned herself so that she would reach me first, making it difficult for anyone else to get near me. I struggled to free myself from her clutches; Serena was about an arm's length away and she was the one I really wanted to hug now.

"What was that about?" Tommy asked. "Oi, come on, guys," he added, trying to pull Rebecca away from me. She lashed out spectacularly at him, almost whacking Marc across the face.

The struggle went on for about another five seconds before the group finally separated, the three guys putting in the effort. I looked around at them all, and my gaze lingered on Marc.

"You should probably come upstairs with me," I told him quietly. "And you," I added to Tommy, "if you've got the Light Crystal, anyway. Do you?"

"It's in my room," he said. "I'll go get it."

His room? That was careless, I thought, with a spy probably still in here somewhere, although the spy most probably was out fighting on both sides at the same time. Leaving it in a place where the spy has been known to have had access at some point—not a smart move. But if Tommy hadn't lost it, and wouldn't lose it from this point, I wouldn't judge him too harshly—yet.

"What's going on, John?" asked Sebastian.

"Er, I probably shouldn't say it all," I said carefully, "but basically, I went out just now to find Natalie and Amelia. Turns out Marc's dad had them, and Lucien and Stella."

A silence met this announcement. I could see their thoughts ticking over before me: Stella? What's he on about? Stella's dead. Even Marc didn't know yet about Stella. He would, though, because if Amelia had been in her right mind at any point during her captivity and she returned to it sometime soon, she would finally be able to confirm what I'd been saying for weeks.

"Anyway, Marc, can you come upstairs with me?" I asked him. "I wanna do something with the crystals. Er…" I hesitated, then plunged on. "Serena, can you come too?"

She would be of no magical use, but the moral support would come in handy, and I felt much better asking her than Lena, despite the intimate experience we had recently shared.

"Okay," she said, looking nervous but pleased. Lena looked disappointed, but to her credit, she said nothing.

"What was it you said about Stella, John?" asked Sebastian.

"She's with Moran and Lucien," I told him. "She's been with them for about a week, I think. I didn't see her myself, but Natalie and Amelia did and they told me so. She's been hanging around causing trouble the whole time."

"But—but I thought she was dead," said Sebastian blankly. "Didn't they kill her because of what she did with James and Peter?"

"Rubbish," I said dismissively. "They spread that around deliberately, but they didn't kill her; they just disowned her."

There was another silence, but I didn't wait for someone to break it this time. I held out my hand to Serena. She took it, and we turned and left the lounge room, Marc hurrying along behind us. We met Tommy on the stairs, and then the four of us proceeded up to the third floor.

"What's this about?" Marc asked as we left the stairs and passed his room, the first on that floor.

"Actually, there's something else," I said. I hadn't wanted the others to know about Amelia, but now that it was just Marc, Tommy, and Serena… "Amelia didn't go back out after I found them. I brought her back here. She's not in a good way."

"What—what's wrong with her?" Marc asked in a shaky voice.

"Not sure, but I've left her in my room. She's unconscious. I reckon it was just the stress of it that's got to her."

"Amelia," he muttered distractedly when I opened the bedroom door half a minute later, and he hurried over to my bed where Amelia lay, still unconscious. "Amelia. Oh God, what have they done to you?"

"I'm not so sure they've done anything at all," I said. "I don't really know, and Natalie didn't have time to tell me everything that went on in there. She had her magic taken off her, as you know, but she's got it back now."

"Nothing at all?" he repeated, stunned. "You serious, you actually think that? What on earth did he want with them if not to do something to them?"

"Natalie said maybe he wanted to show that he's on our side," I said, sitting down on my bed. It was big enough that I could sit quite comfortably without being too close to Amelia—for Marc's comfort. "I know Amelia looks bad, but Natalie looked quite healthy. They weren't tied up or in cages like we saw or anything; they were just behind an invisible wall."

"I'm missing a lot here," said Serena vaguely, sitting down beside me and leaning on me. "John, you knew about Stella, right?"

"Yeah," I said. "Long story, though; better you not ask, but just so you know, you remember that weird woman we saw on our date? That was her."

"Stella?" repeated Tommy. "Stella? You mean she's actually—"

I sighed and explained it all again, impatiently enough that I probably missed several points along the way. I mentioned nothing about the dreams or the note I had found in England; those were points that they didn't really need to know, and it would have involved explaining even more to Serena, and there just wasn't time for that tonight.

"Anyway, look," I said finally, "what I wanna do tonight, if you guys don't mind staying up late, is use the crystals to keep an eye on what's going on out there and try to use magic to turn things back in our favour. We've got enough magic in here that we should be able to make a difference."

The three of us took our crystals out: Tommy, holding a handful of blinding light that nobody could look at directly; Marc, holding a bronze-coloured stone slightly smaller than a tennis ball; and me, holding a fistful of what looked like thin-air. We set to work, Tommy making various wishes to ensure the safety of those out there and the failure of the missions the Hammerhearts were currently undertaking. Marc was using his crystal to discover what these missions were, by following the Hammerhearts around in spirit form, listening to their conversations and reading their minds, and informing Tommy whenever he learnt something worthwhile. I, meanwhile, was using the Sien-Leoard Crystal to cause major disruptions in the Hammerhearts' plans, clogging up their weapons and making them unusable, knocking Hammerhearts unconscious just before they were about to use their bogglers on people, or in the middle of battles, or even performing the influential charm (or something that resembled the influential charm, as I'd never done it before) on a male Hammerheart who had just murdered a prominent New Zealand military official and was beginning to impersonate him, making changes to the Kiwis' tactics.

We had been going for about twenty minutes when Tommy said, "Um, guys, we may have a problem."

"What?" Marc and I said in unison, and I added, "Has something happened to the Sorcerers?"

"No, they're fine, I'm watching them," Marc informed me. "Natalie's done what you told her to, by the way."

"Does anyone actually know where the Darkness Crystal is?" Tommy asked.

"It's locked up in here somewhere," said Marc. "You know it was given back to us, right?"

"Yeah, I know that," said Tommy, "but—"

"What? Hang on," said Serena suddenly. She'd been dozing on my shoulder before, but now she straightened up slightly and looked at us with bleary eyes. "We don't have it; it was taken ages ago, remember?"

"We got it back," I told her. "Mr. Woodward wanted it top secret so that the spy wouldn't be able to get it back. You remember when Moran stole it from the Hammersons?"

"Yeah."

"That was Stella," I told them; none of them would have known that. "That note, remember? That was from Stella. Don't ask how I know, long story. Mr. Woodward locked it up again but not in the same spot; he didn't want the spy risking another look there."

"Oh," said Tommy vaguely. "Well, trouble is, someone's using it now."

There was a brief silence.

"How do you know?" I asked, a sinking feeling in my stomach.

"I can feel it in this," he said, holding up his fistful of light. "The Light and Darkness Crystals counter each other, remember?"

"I've never felt the Villain Crystal being used in this," Marc retorted, shaking the Hero Crystal at his friend.

"You think I can answer for that?" asked Tommy testily. "Maybe the countering is more direct with these crystals. Look, maybe we should go and look around in the Woodward living quarters for it, see if we can find—"

"What good would that do?" I asked. "If we don't find it, which we probably wouldn't, we won't know if it's because it's been stolen again or because we just can't get to it."

"Let's wait 'til Amelia wakes up," suggested Marc. "She might not know where it is either, but she'll have a better idea of where her father might put it than we would."

We decided not to act on the Darkness Crystal for the time being, and although Tommy kept saying that he could feel it working against him, neither Marc nor I could detect any outward signs of its magic around the world, no earthquakes or other natural disasters, though I wasn't foolish enough to think that natural disasters were all the Darkness Crystal could do. We kept using magic from the crystals for another couple of hours. Tommy fell asleep at around half past one, and Marc about half an hour later. Their sleeping patterns being more normal than mine, I didn't bother to wake them up.

Serena, who had been dozing on and off since she had arrived in the room, now pulled herself together somewhat, and with those in the room with us asleep, we were able to enjoy each other's company for a little while. It basically just involved us holding onto each other and feeling each other up, careful as possible not to make a sound lest we wake up Marc, for Tommy would be in Germany now and beyond being woken. There were no sexual moments either for the same reason; based on what I knew of Serena when she was excited, any sexual thrill she received would wake him up straight away.

We actually did quite well for about an hour, with me still holding onto the crystal but not doing magic with it. We stopped right away when we heard a stirring close by, but instead of it being the boys, it was Amelia who was finally coming back to life. Marc jerked back to life at that moment too, and the three of us gathered around Amelia as she finally opened her eyes, looking far more on-the-planet than she had earlier.

Chapter 10: On the Stairs

While I had been in England, Amelia and Marc had kept me up-to-date with the happenings inside the Woodward base. There had been no news on the night of the twenty-third because it had been only hours after I'd left, and in Australia, all those hours had been in the middle of the night. I had met Amelia in the second-floor room that I had used to travel to England again on the morning of the twenty-fourth (British time), and then again twenty-four hours later, and she had told me (looking very awkward, knowing that she was speaking to me in Lena's body) what Mr. Woodward had organised in the aftermath of our raid on the Hammerheart Chopville base and the hidden quarters: He had created devices that would counter the ones the Hammersons used to place the influential charm on people. The official name for such devices was unbogglers, but I preferred to think of them as rebogglers just because of the exact magic they performed. An unboggler would have surely removed all traces of the influential charm rather than perform a new one to remove any loyalty that person might have to the Hammersons. He had assigned three people to begin talking to the prisoners, determine if they'd be affected by an influential charm prior to becoming a Hammerheart, and if so, bring them across to the Woodwards' side by way of the rebogglers. That hadn't begun by the twenty-sixth, though, and I hadn't heard any more about how that was going since, because the morning of the twenty-seventh, I had met Marc instead of Amelia, and the conversation had been about her and Natalie's disappearances.

I hadn't seen any signs of the conversion process since my return. I supposed that most of the ones who had been converted (about a dozen so far, according to Marc) had been called into battle like nearly everyone else. The day I had come back, there hadn't been anyone around who could get inside the prison block, so the conversions had been put on hold since. Only Marc had entered the prison block, while I had been asleep, not to convert the prisoners or in fact to do anything to them (apart from Hignat and Wilwog, who he had a few stern words with about Amelia) but to bring them food and water, since no one else could.

I had another concern, though. It seemed that each of us had certain things we worried about more than the others. Tommy was still fretting over the Darkness Crystal at dawn on April 29; Amelia had gone to look for it but had come up empty-handed, and now the suspicion was that it had fallen back into the wrong hands. Marc was worried about the prisoners; it had somehow become his responsibility to make sure they were looked after, and he was wondering if he should risk letting the conversions continue. He had felt uneasy about letting anyone else into the prison block in case something went wrong. I, meanwhile, was thinking about a few people who hadn't been seen at all since the Australian coup had begun.

Dad and Charlie were surely out and about, but what about Mum and Marge? And Hilda and Violet? Where were they? My guess was at home on Lopher Lane, but was that the best place for them? Where were Harry and Simon's grandparents? The two sets of Maivis twins were safely locked up inside the base, but what about the rest of their family? Where was Natalie's mother? She normally lived in the Fletcher living quarters with the rest of the Fletchers, but she worked during the day and apparently hadn't been able to get back into the base. Had she gone back to their home on Greenly Street? Was she safe there? I knew that Rebecca, who was now the only person living in the Fletcher living quarters, was very worried about her. There were several other sets of parents too, like Serena's, who might be in danger where they were. Lisa's mother was another who hadn't been seen. At the top of my worry list, however, was Jacob Underwood. He worked in the government in Britain; he would be in the direct line of fire if the Hammerhearts attempted a coup over there. Would the theft of the life assistant cause him to do something stupid to reveal himself to the Hammerhearts after such a long time of careful misleading by people such as Gerald Fick? And could doing so possibly give the Hammerhearts fresh clues as to the whereabouts of Smiley?

I resolved to do something about these people later on, but I had my priorities in order. At around nine o'clock in the morning, it was time for me to go to bed.

"Why don't you just use magic to keep yourself awake?" Serena complained. She hadn't been up very long, and apparently she'd been looking forward to spending the day with me. "Like Stella did that time? I mean, how long are you gonna be nocturnal for?"

"If I'd thought of that an hour ago, I probably would have done it." I yawned. "But right now, I doubt I'd get any sort of magic right."

"And I'm not brave enough to try," added Marc, grinning at me, apparently enjoying the look on Serena's face. I didn't enjoy it, though; I couldn't help feeling that, whatever my obligations to the war might be, I was being a lousy boyfriend.

"Okay," she said resignedly, "but then tomorrow—"

"What's the plan for today?" asked Tommy.

We were in the dining room having a late breakfast—Marc, Tommy, Serena, Peter, James, and I. There were other people around us, listening, like Harry, Simon, Felicity, Jessica, Erica, Kylie, Katie, Sophie, Sebastian, Lena, Rebecca, and, the first time I'd seen her around the Woodward base, Candice Young, who had at some stage since her capture been converted. She wasn't very popular, though, not with anyone who had known Lisa.

"I'm not sure if there is a plan," said Marc. "This whole thing's gone way out of our control now; I doubt that even the Woodwards could keep up with it all."

By way of the crystals, we had seen how the fighting had grown worse and worse overnight as the British and American air forces joined the fray. Indonesia also had jets flying around, seeking targets and causing destruction of their own, most of it apparently centred on the military facilities up north, the aim of all countries involved being to prevent the Hammerhearts from gaining enough control here to have attention to spare for them. The Hammerhearts had responded by firing a rocket at Indonesia, one that had apparently been enchanted at some point to find its targets more effectively. Its target had been the Halim Perdanakusuma Airport in Jakarta, and its aim had been true. Indonesia hadn't responded to that attack as yet. On top of all that, the Australian and New Zealand militaries had been completely taken over, so now it felt like we were at war with our own country. Tankom and Hammerson were out of the country, and Cornish, who had slept for six hours but returned to action shortly before we came down to breakfast, was continuing with his mad plans, only some of which had been covered in the Telegraph the day before.

"I tell you what we should probably do," I said. "Marc, Tommy, can you two keep trying to do what we were doing last night? The rest of you just—I dunno—keep things in order around here."

I could have laughed at myself. It really wasn't much of a plan at all, but I decided at that moment that it wasn't necessarily down to me to make a plan at that stage. I had my plan: go to sleep; wake up; have dinner; go out that evening and look for those I wanted to bring to safety. Once that was done, assuming nothing else drastic had gone wrong (outside the progression of everything that was going wrong all around us), I would finally turn my attention to the life assistant, which I had put away in my top drawer and hadn't touched since my return. I would prefer to have Natalie back before using it to contact Smiley, but hopefully she would understand if we couldn't wait for her.

Serena followed me up to my room after breakfast, apparently hoping she might be able to keep me awake for a while and enjoy a little more private time together. She had some luck in that regard, because the first thing I did when I got upstairs was jump in the shower, and of course, Serena joined me, even though in my tired state, I would have preferred she didn't. That was the extent of it, though, because after that, I was in bed, and even with Serena curled up beside me, I fell asleep almost straight away. Serena didn't hang around, but slipped out of bed and out of my room without disturbing me.

I slept for a little over six hours and had a few different dreams. One of those was yet another dream involving me, Stella, and the main hall on Rock Haulter. This time, Amelia, Natalie, Marc, and Lucien were all off to the sides while Stella and I were in the middle, feet apart. I wanted to give her a hug, to thank her for the assistance she'd given over the last month, but she was laughing at me as she continually evaded me.

Another dream that day was another detour from normal sleep into Stella's mind. The way I had come to distinguish between normal dreams and visions of Stella was not based on how vivid the dreams were, but how clear my thought processes were during them. Normally when I dream, I remember a lot more doing than thinking, and that is sometimes the case with Stella's visions depending on what Stella is doing at the time. This vision was like only one other that I could remember, and that had been the one in which I had learnt of her involvement in the second school battle. It was one where she did nothing but thought about everything, and I was astounded by how much I remembered of her thoughts when I woke up.

She, Moran, and Lucien were in a hole deep underground. A lantern was hanging from the low ceiling, swinging slightly on what was probably a never-ending rotation, given that there was no breeze to move it. The hole was accessible by a pipe that Stella was facing, though exactly how one was to climb up it and out was not on her mind. There was a television screen in the corner, currently blank but would illuminate with whatever Moran wanted on his command. He and Lucien were out of her line of sight, but she knew they were behind her, sleeping. It was her responsibility to keep watch until midday, when the three of them would conference again.

Stella was contemplating. She wasn't particularly happy with the turn her life had taken. For so long, she had looked forward to the day that her family would make her leave, but as that time approached, she had become used to the idea that there would be somewhere else for her to go. Plus, whatever she told herself to the contrary, it did feel a little debilitating not to have magic anymore, after having it for the first sixteen years of her life.

She hadn't banked on the Woodwards turning on her so suddenly. Moran and Lucien were better than her family, but not by a lot. Moran still showed far too many Hammerheart tendencies for her liking. He was against the Hammersons, of course, and she could tell that, deep down, he did care what happened to Marc and Lucien, but whenever she started thinking he was okay, he would say something so cruel that she would have to start all over. As for Lucien, he was still affected by Tankom's influential charm, and Moran hadn't been daring enough to use the Villain Crystal to change that; apparently there wasn't enough evil in the gesture. She was certain that Lucien was only here because, like her, he had nowhere else to go, but she was also sure that, unless someone could perform another influential charm on him sometime soon, his true loyalty was to the Hammersons, whereas hers was against them. Moran, of course, was loyal to neither side, so in theory the trio of outcasts was quite balanced.

The group's main priorities were: firstly, to stay safe; secondly, to cause the Hammersons as much trouble as they could; and thirdly, to demonstrate to the Woodwards that they were on their side, for as long as it took the Woodwards to accept it. The reason why the group leaned in general towards the Woodwards, what with about half of it not being loyal to them naturally, was fundamental: The Hammerhearts would kill them, whereas the Woodward Army probably wouldn't. This suited Stella fine; she had seriously begun to believe, with great resignation, that the Woodwards would never take her back as she had been prior to her being whisked out of their base.

This resignation had been because, in her lonely state, she had forgotten just how much she wanted it. It hadn't been Moran and Lucien who had changed this, though. They had given her a chance, a routine that she could fit into and give herself a better chance of getting back to where she really wanted to be. Her desire, however, had been restored by Jacob Underwood, or rather, the old man to whom Underwood owed most of his life. She'd had to do things to him that had sickened her, and given that she hadn't been able to take the life assistant, it could have been considered a waste of dignity. Stella didn't think so, however, for when Underwood had taken her hand and touched one of her fingers to the most sensitive spot on his life assistant, a thought had been planted in her head, a thought that had been sent from thousands of miles away. It had opened her eyes to what she should have known months ago, and what she should have taken with both hands while she had the chance.

Yet she couldn't help feeling that the chance had actually been taken right out of her hands. How often had she dwelled on those events over the last two months? Of how John and Amelia had turned on her that day, for no reason at all that she knew. They had believed she was hiding something from them, that she knew some information of how her father and grandmother had escaped. She hadn't known anything; the only thing she hadn't mentioned was a suspicion that might have incriminated someone else who could have been innocent, and all because they had told her to say what she knew, not what she thought.

That was as much as I had been able to register. I woke up at that point, wrote down as much as I could remember, went back to sleep, and returned to my notes when I woke up again at around three o'clock. What useful information could be gleamed from that? Well, it confirmed what Natalie had said, how they were trying to regain the trust of the Woodwards. It also confirmed what Underwood had said about her, though of course I already knew that. Her suspicion, the suspicion that had cost us so much—how different would things have been if we had accepted Stella's story that day? Why hadn't I just gone into her memories with the Sien-Leoard Crystal, like part of me had wanted to?

She hadn't been thinking hard during the dream about the suspicion itself, but a face had swam in her mind, and putting two and two together, I was able to work it out without too much trouble: Stella had believed that Sebastian had helped her father and grandmother escape to freedom. Why she had believed that was not information I had gleamed from the dream. An interesting thought, I supposed, but I couldn't see how Sebastian could have gotten them out without anyone working out what he was doing. Furthermore, if Sebastian was also responsible for so much that had happened since, I couldn't imagine how he could have done such things as stolen the Darkness Crystal.

I spent another hour or so in my room, during which time I had another shower (something was making me feel unusually dirty lately). When I went downstairs, I found a small group of people sitting in the lounge room (Marc, Tommy, Peter, James, Felicity, and Jessica), looking and sounding as though they were in a funeral.

"What's happened now?" I asked resignedly, plonking myself down in a seat beside Peter.

He gave a hollow laugh. "What hasn't happened?"

"Well, for starters, they're still looking for us," Marc told me. "They want to set people onto capturing the Sorcerers, and Stella too, but that'd be too obvious. They've coordinated coups in just about every country in the south Pacific now, and all with practically no violence at all apart from some casualties in the Kiwi military, but that's only 'cause they were fighting here."

"Have any other countries responded?" I asked, feeling slightly sick. How could all this be happening? We were the ones with all the magic (or almost all of it); how could they have such a tight hold on this part of the world now?

"The French want to," said Tommy, "since they have ties with a few of them, but they're too worried about what might happen to themselves if they send their troops away from home, and the Indonesians are having a whole load of fun with it all."

"Oh yeah," Marc laughed; it sounded as unconvincing as Peter's had. "They're sending loads of jets over. They're gonna destroy half the country if they're not careful. The rest of the world, though, they're preparing to defend themselves, but they don't wanna send troops off their own land in case the Hammerhearts attack them and they can't all get back. It's a little late for the Brits; they've come to help us out, and the Hammerhearts haven't gone for them yet, but they will soon."

"Too late for the US, though," said Felicity in a hushed voice.

They all exchanged looks. This, apparently, was the source of the great shock that seemed to have settled on the room.

"What's happened to America?" I asked nervously. "Don't tell me they've been taken over too."

"They've gone and used a weapon," Marc said quietly. "Not one they've stolen since a month ago, but one they created themselves when they still had magic. It's—(he swallowed)—just horrible. They've wiped out a whole load of government officials over there, and—and the White House is destroyed."

"Destroyed?" I repeated, unsure if he was referring to the entire government or the building itself.

"Yeah," he said with some hesitation, "by the same thing as— you know—what with Nicole and all."

My stomach dissolved. I understood exactly what he meant, and it made everything much worse. It would have been better not knowing what had happened to everyone who had been in the White House when the attack had happened. It would have been better to think a bomb had blown the whole place sky high; that would have been an immeasurably more pleasant death than what those people would have suffered through. I didn't want to think of how terrified they must have been as the Fire Man stalked them. Just thinking of the Fire Man again made me shudder.

"Where are the Woodwards and Fletchers?" I asked, not wanting to continue the subject of the White House, not wanting to think what else the Hammerhearts had already done to tighten their grip on the United States.

"Well, Mr. Woodward's in the US now," said Marc. "None of the Sorcerers were near enough to stop the attack, but he's over there now trying to get things back in order. The two old ladies are in Canberra, 'cause Cornish and Hall and a couple of other important Hammerhearts are still dismantling the country. Natalie's in the thick of the fighting with the Indonesians. Everyone else is on the Hammerhearts' side now. Her father—I'm not sure where he is, but I think he's trying to track down Hammerson and Tankom. I think that they think that if they can get the Hammersons back in custody, they can muck up the Hammerhearts' coordination."

"It won't stop them running amok," I muttered, remembering the first Chopville High battle. "What about Amelia? How's she doing?"

Amelia had seemed considerably more aware of her surroundings when she had returned to consciousness the previous night, but still not entirely normal. It looked as though she was in shock, not necessarily from what Moran had done to her but whatever emotional turmoil she had gone through while she had been there. She hadn't wanted to talk about it, perhaps because Serena and Tommy were there, or perhaps because I was there and she only wanted to talk to Marc, or perhaps the other way around, or perhaps because she knew her father wasn't anywhere near. She had sat with us for the rest of the night but said almost nothing and done absolutely nothing. Even when I was the only other one awake, she had kept her silence, and I was too preoccupied with the crystal to try too hard to talk to her.

"She's in her living quarters at the moment," said Marc quietly. We had all agreed that Amelia's presence in the base ought to be kept quiet, in case those who didn't understand her current mental state accused her of being weak or lazy. "Not sure what she's doing except that she wants to be alone. I think she's getting better, though; she did say before I left her that she would probably stay around here to keep this place in order, rather than go out into the fighting. She doesn't see the point, and honestly I don't blame her. One more Sorcerer wouldn't make much of a difference."

I sighed, but I supposed it was the best anyone could do for now. I made a mental note to go and see Amelia later on this evening; her sleeping patterns might be closer to mine than any of the others, which should make it easier to get her alone. Perhaps she would be willing to come with me to track down those missing people. I hoped so—there was something comforting about being able to do those things with Amelia.

"So what have you been doing, then?" I asked. "Trying to cause trouble like we did last night?"

"Trying to," said Marc, "and we've been able to make very small differences, but overall, we can't slow them down. We're having no greater effect than the Sorcerers are having. I was just saying to Tommy before you came in: Do you think it's time to take a risk? A big risk?"

"I think if we don't take a risk now, no risk will be big enough later," I said miserably. "What are you thinking of?"

"Calling Fewul," Marc said quietly. "I don't know if I could control it—it could be different from last time in ways I don't know. If I can, though, maybe Fewul can make a difference in a way the rest of us can't—kill all the Hammerhearts with a single spell, clear the minds of all those who have been bewitched into doing their bidding."

"I like the idea," I said at once. "I suppose we'll have to go outside to do it, but it's a great—"

"Hang on," said Marc quickly. "Hang on a second—I just said I don't know if it will work the same as it did last time."

"Why wouldn't it?" I asked impatiently. "You had no trouble controlling it on camp, and you'll call it the same way this time, won't you?"

Marc shrugged. "I've just got a feeling about it," he said quietly. "I'd like to ask Mr. Woodward about it first—get his advice."

"I know Mr. Woodward's all wise and knowledgeable and all that," I said firmly, "but I think you've got more experience with the Beast of Magic than he does, so why not just use your own judgement?"

"Because my own judgement says no," he almost whispered. "At least that's how I feel when I hold onto the crystal, and you know how the crystal sometimes gives you those feelings?"

I nodded; the Sien-Leoard Crystal had helped me out quite a few times in that way.

"Okay, okay," I said. "In that case, maybe you should ask him, but geez, Marc, we can't afford to sit around and wait for wisdom to hit us. If we do, we might miss our chance to make a difference."

I spent the time before dinner in the lounge room with the rest of them, in which time we were joined by Serena, Kylie, and Erica. The conversation mostly centred on Marc and the crystal in his hand, but

I spent the time mentally preparing myself for what I wanted to do that evening and how I would go about it without putting myself, or anyone else, in danger. Talk to Amelia first, hopefully put her in a good enough state to come out with me in the evening. If Marc objected, I would leave the decision up to Amelia, as she had done when Serena had objected. Those in Chopville would come first, Underwood second, and in the case of the latter, perhaps it would be better to leave Amelia behind.

So, when the time came, and three quarters of the people left in the Woodward base had already eaten and left the dining room, Marc, Tommy, Peter, James, Serena, and I congregated just outside the lounge room, along the short stretch of wall between its doors and the entrance to the stairs up to the bedrooms.

"We're going up there," said Marc, gesturing to himself and Tommy with one hand and jerking his thumb in the direction of the stairs with the other. "We're gonna keep working with the crystals; feels kind of pointless how things have turned out, but we can't just sit back and do nothing."

"You're telling me," I muttered darkly. "I'm gonna go find Amelia, see if I can get her to open up."

"Good luck," Marc said, just as darkly. "If you think she's ready to talk, come and get me, won't you?"

"Sure, no probs."

"Anything you want us to do, John?" asked Peter.

I considered. Peter, James, and Serena were right here, just ready to be useful somehow, but I couldn't think of a use for them off the top of my head.

"I dunno," I said finally. "Er, the prisoners—"

"Sorted," said Marc. "Amelia can start doing that once she's back to normal, but I've already gone down there and given them all their dinners."

"I don't think Amelia should have to face Hignat and Wilwog alone," Peter corrected him.

Marc considered this, then nodded.

"Hignat and Wilwog are still here?" I enquired. I had forgotten until that point that they had been brought in along with Candice Young.

"Well, they're not going anywhere in a hurry," said Marc, shrugging, "and I doubt they were ever magically influenced."

"Why not just convert them anyway?" I asked, deciding that Hignat and Wilwog had surely waived their right to make that decision after all they'd done, particularly to Amelia. "I don't like them either, but surely it's better to have them on our side."

"I guess so, but it means we don't have an excuse to keep them locked up," said Marc darkly, "and I don't like them. Using the influential charm on them will bring them over to our side, but it won't make them likeable people—they'll still be unpleasant as ever."

"Let's not be selfish about it," said James, but he was smirking. "Actually, I've got reservations about using those things at all. Have any of you tried to have a conversation with Candice Young since she was converted?"

Everyone shook their heads, and Tommy said, "Can you just imagine me having a civil conversation with her?"

"Well, I have," said James, "and I can tell you now—I don't know what she was like before, because I only have one memory of her, and you guys know what I'm talking about. I think all this mucking around with people's minds may have its negative effects. Candice seems—odd now, not altogether with it."

"If you mean what I think you mean," said Marc, and he looked scared, "then we could be in real trouble. You think it's because Young was already affected by an influential charm that another one on top of it might be too much for her brain to handle?"

"Possibly," said James, "but I expect it's even worse in this situation, because the two influential charms directly counter each other. I don't know how long we can get away with doing this before these people's minds become permanently damaged."

"A Normalising Charm?" suggested Peter.

"No good," said Marc dully. "That works on most things but not the influential charm because once it's done, it doesn't leave any traces of its magic."

"What you'd need," said James slowly, thoughtfully, "is a spell that returns the mind to the state it was in at a certain time, kind of like how you can use system restore on the computer to set it back to how it was at a certain time."

"There's just one tiny little problem with that, James," said Peter. "You'd wipe their memory of everything that happened ever since. John, didn't you say Young was cursed back in January?"

"Yeah, it was early in the year," I said.

"That—er—could be a problem," said Marc, "but I can think of ways around that, like what we were going to do if—well, let's just say we can restore those memories we want her to have if we can find a way to set her mind back to before she was cursed."

"We might have to do that with loads of people," said Tommy in a kind of groan.

"It'll be worth it for every one of those people," said Marc.

"Agreed," said James briskly. "Well, anyway, unless you guys can think of something I can do to help tonight, I might go and read for a while. I know school's out indefinitely, but that doesn't mean we should become ignorant of our studies."

"Have fun," said Peter, grinning at him. "I'm going in there for a while"—he gestured to the doors into the lounge room; at that stage, Harry and Simon were the only ones in there—"in case you need to find me. Serena?"

"Um—yeah, me too," she said, glancing warily at me. "If you're talking to Amelia, you won't want me around, right?"

"Guess not," I said, "but only because I don't think she'll talk if you're there."

She nodded, looking resigned, and followed Peter into the lounge room, leaving me, Marc, and Tommy alone. The two of them set off up the stairs, and because I wanted a pit stop before going to find Amelia, I followed them.

We were all exactly halfway between the first and second floors when the coordinated attack hit us. We had only a split-second of warning, as several sudden movements sounded behind us by people who had apparently been waiting for us just off the first floor landing. Then about half a dozen jets of red light shot down the stairs at us from the second floor; Marc and Tommy, in front, were hit, and both stopped dead in their tracks. The rest of them flew above and to the sides of me, hitting a few of the attackers at the foot of the stairs, but the jets that came at us from behind, all six of them, hit me in the back, and I froze, unable to move, my hands too far from the Sien-Leoard Crystal for me to defend myself in any way.

The invisible attackers, who seemed to know exactly where each of their fellows were, as though they could see each other, closed ranks around us, the three whose stunners had been true standing back in order to keep the three of us still. How many were moving? Not many. In fact, possibly only one. I had a feeling many of them were staying at the top and bottom of the flight of stairs, ready in case anyone else came up or down. And then, to my horror, I felt a hand reach into my pocket, feeling for the crystal. The crystal was actually in my other front pocket, but that didn't matter; we were in big, big trouble.

Impatient, the hand ripped itself out of my other pocket and felt for others. It nudged the crystal and then, to my horror, it reached into that pocket and closed around it. The crystal was withdrawn, the person moved on. Ahead of me on the stairs, I heard Tommy being searched, and I had room in my mind to wonder what was going to happen next. What would these people do to us once they had the crystals? Turn us in to the Hammerhearts? It seemed likely, even though I couldn't imagine how they would get us all out of here. Perhaps we would have to lie, wrapped in thicky prison, in the bottom of someone's backpack for several days before we had to face the real fireworks.

I saw the blinding gleam of the Light Crystal for a moment as the hand withdrew it from Tommy's pocket, before it was placed in the pocket of the assailant along with the Sien-Leoard Crystal. Now it was Marc's turn, and this would be the interesting part, because the moment the hand made contact with the Hero Crystal, it would split into the six smaller Sorcerous Crystals. Could this be our chance? Could this person possibly not know what was about to happen? Could one or two of the crystals perhaps roll away, down the stairs? Could that be enough to distract them, enough to muck up the coordination they had clearly planned so well?

Indeed, the disturbance came at that point, but it was not the Sorcerous Crystals that made the difference. Behind me, far behind and below me, well beyond the spot where the attackers stood guard, someone screamed. The attackers behind me leapt into action, and the scream was cut off quickly, but it was enough. Shouts echoed from inside the lounge room, and I could hear people running out, trying to look up the stairs to see what was happening. I could hear Peter, Harry, Simon, Serena, and several others shouting, none of them sure who was up the stairs but apparently unable to come up and see. I wished I could see who had screamed and raised the alarm for us; whoever it was, we were in her debt, for I was sure it had been a girl.

The chaos lasted perhaps ten seconds before the only person capable of making the difference arrived on the scene. The person on the stairs behind us screamed again, and I heard her leap back down to the ground, but she did not sound scared—she sounded triumphant, and I knew she had staged the whole thing, apparently when she had seen the three of us frozen on the stairs. At the same time, I could hear those attackers behind me dropping, unconscious, onto the first floor landing. Alarmed, the attackers at the top of the stairs began firing stunners down, apparently surprised, and I felt extremely glad that we hadn't made it public knowledge that Amelia was still in the base.

With the defeat of those at the bottom of the stairs, I was released from the magic binding me to the spot. I backed quickly against the rail, leaving space for Amelia to attack those at the top and deal with the one who was still on the stairs with us somewhere. I heard people falling unconscious on the landing above us, and one at a time, Marc and Tommy regained the use of their bodies. They too backed against the rail, leaving space for Amelia to attack the last few at the top. The battle, as suddenly as it had begun, ended a few seconds later. The one who had rested the crystals from us, apart from Marc's, which he hadn't been able to get a hand on in time, had backed against the rail when the rest of us had, but Amelia hadn't been fooled. Her spell, whether intentional or not, knocked him right over the rail, and he plummeted a storey and a half down to the floor below.

A ringing silence followed. Then the people at the foot of the stairs, who had been startled by the sound of the falling body, broke into murmurs once again. Marc, Tommy, and I simply looked at each other, hardly able to believe what had almost happened to us.

"What happened?" Amelia asked franticly. "Did they hurt you?"

"No, but that one down there, he's got our crystals," I said, looking over the rail and wondering if the invisible person down there was dead or alive.

"I've still got mine, though," Marc assured her, taking it out of his pocket.

Without another word, Amelia turned and hurried down the stairs, tripping over the invisible bodies on the landing and flying down the bottom flight, and only magic saved her from breaking her leg or worse. Marc raised his eyebrows at me and Tommy before moving carefully down the stairs, crystal out. He began revealing our attackers, and one by one, I recognised them: A year-eight boy who spent much of his time following Rebecca around like a bad smell; a year-eleven girl who spent most of her time in the library, not talking to anyone; George Tuck, Lena's brother; Robyn Lloyd, a year-nine girl I knew by sight but had only spoken to a handful of times in my life; a year-ten girl I recognised as the sister of Dean Abodi (an acquaintance who was not quite a friend) but whose name I didn't know; and Liam Stammerus. They all looked very odd because, for reasons that made no sense to me whatsoever, they were all wearing goggles, the exact goggles that Marc had created on the Rock Haulter camp, which had enabled us all to see ghosts. Marc turned and went to the top of the stairs, satisfied, but I was not. I stared, dumbstruck, at Liam's body, unable to believe it. Of all the people to turn on us, after what had happened to David and Craig.

That was when I realised the magnitude of the situation facing us, and the enormous positive that might just come out of it. The spy, it seemed, had smuggled a boggler into the base to recruit an army whose job it would be to bring H2, H3, and H4 into Hammerheart custody. This might mean that one of them could tell us who the spy was, with some persuasion. Or, even better, the spy could actually be one of the attackers—the one on the bottom floor, I hoped furiously.

I turned to watch Marc at the top of the stairs, revealing the bodies up there. Below, I could hear Amelia trying to disperse the crowd so that she could reach the person who had the Sien-Leoard and Light Crystals. By the time she was back on the stairs, the crystals in her hands and the body floating along behind her, Marc had revealed the bodies of all our attackers. I saw that there were an even dozen of them, and they were all teenagers. Ten out of the twelve were students I had brought after the first school battle—the other two were Liam and Sebastian. Marc, Tommy, Amelia, and I stood together on the stairs, looking at each other and wondering what to do.

"What's going on up there?" Peter called up the stairs at us. "Amelia, do you need any help?"

"Go back in the lounge room, all of you," Amelia called back down the stairs. "We've got it under control. We'll let you all know what happened when we've worked it out ourselves."

"Just out of curiosity," I said quietly, as those below began moving obediently into the lounge room, muttering, "who screamed before?"

"Lena," said Amelia shortly.

"I tell you what," said Marc, apparently straining to think straight, judging by the tight expression on his face. "Let's line them up along down there so we can check them out one at a time. Do we need to bring them around to work out who's behind it?"

"If you're wanting me to read their minds to work it out, then yeah," said Amelia. "Maybe you can read their minds while they're unconscious, though; I don't know."

"You should probably do it," I said, trying to think hard and straining as Marc had done. "That would probably be quicker. Once we've found the instigator, we can use the crystal to find out more about what they've done."

"Do you think we can use the crystal to work out if they've had their minds messed with?" asked Marc. "Because if we can find one of them who's acted of his or her own free will, that would explain a lot."

Amelia shrugged. "Not sure. Let's just do it John's way."

So we began, using magic to move them down to the first floor landing and along it, lining them up against the wall. Amelia handed me and Tommy our crystals back, and I used mine to magically bind them all to the wall, so that when Amelia brought them all around, they were unable to speak, move, or attack us. To top it off, I used the crystal to remove all contents from their pockets, teleporting them up to my bedroom so I could sort through them later. As Amelia began to read their minds, concentrating on each of them in turn as they stood there, unable to do anything but look straight back at her, I began experimenting with the Sien-Leoard Crystal. There was some merit in Marc's idea, and I wanted to see if the crystal could tell me if any mind altering spells had been performed on them recently. As it turned out, to my delight and slight surprise, it could. I then began moving along the line behind Amelia, testing this on each of them in turn, and it was by this method that I struck gold. Out of the dozen, eleven of them had been attacked by the influential charm in the last forty-eight hours. Out of the dozen, only one of them had acted of his own free will, and it was this realisation that made the bottom drop out of my stomach. Stella had been right: Sebastian Williams *was* the spy.

Chapter 11: Bitterness

I was done being a nice guy. I was done being all trusting and respectful. I was not going to make the same mistake twice. So, an hour after the attack, when the stairwell dozen (as Peter had dubbed them) were in new cells in the prison block, I volunteered to do the investigation alone. My plan was simple; to get the truth, the whole truth, no matter how long it took, I was going to do what I had been too soft to do to Stella. I was going to use the Sien-Leoard Crystal to browse his memories and learn exactly what he had and hadn't done. This way, if Sebastian turned out to be innocent of other crimes I now suspected him of, at least I would know for sure.

"It wasn't my idea," he said immediately when I entered his cell.

"Save it," I said shortly. "If it really wasn't your idea, you won't have anything to worry about, but since you're the top suspect, and the only real suspect we've had since Stella, I'm gonna do whatever's necessary to find out."

Sebastian raised his eyebrows. "How so?" he asked, and there was no trace of fear in his voice, merely curiosity.

"Nothing you need to worry about," I said. I was standing on my side of the red line, the line that Sebastian was magically trapped behind, though I could pass through as easily as if it were nothing more remarkable than a mark on the floor. "I'm going to put you to sleep. I'm not sure how long for, but it's easier this way. You won't feel anything."

Sebastian shrugged. He was about to say something else, some other denial perhaps, but I didn't give him the chance. My hand was in my pocket, around the Sien-Leoard Crystal, and Sebastian automatically lay down on the bed and dropped straight off to sleep; a sleep that would, until my intervention, last for one hundred hours —that ought to be more than enough time. I magically created a nice, comfortable chair for myself, as the cell didn't have one, and sat down in it, facing the bed and the person lying on it. I closed my eyes and separated my mind from my body, sending it out towards Sebastian, whose head, in my mind's eye, was slightly transparent, meaning that his thoughts and memories would be accessible to me.

I floated forward and into his head, placing myself in the darkness of his dreamless sleep and settling myself there. Then I floated downwards, though in my mind, it felt more like moving backwards, backwards through time, as Sebastian's memories zoomed past me in reverse. I kept stopping and starting, landing on all matter of scenarios. What I was looking for was a memory close to the day of the first school battle, for I had a feeling that if

Sebastian had been behind the escape of the Hammersons, as Stella suspected he had been, then his decision to turn traitor would have been between the school battle and the time the Hammersons went missing the following day.

I eventually found the battle itself and the aftermath of it, in which Sebastian had been invited by Mr. Woodward to speak in front of the whole congregation about how he had helped many of the Chopville staff to safety. It wasn't exactly what I was after, but hearing his thoughts, analysing his behaviour, even at that stage, I was starting to see why Sebastian would be attracted to working for the Hammersons, and I could have hit myself for not noticing it before. Sebastian was very proud, and very jealous.

Sure enough, I found the memory I was after. Sebastian was in his bedroom, lying on his bed, considering everything that had happened that day. It was late, about half past eleven in the evening (at which point I would have been losing, or had just lost, my virginity to Tulip), and he was pretty tired. He wanted to sleep, but his mind was buzzing with most unpleasant thoughts. He thought he had done a good job that day, most particularly of keeping a happy face on. But he was not happy, not happy at all. He was angry. He was mad. His mind was a mess of bitter thoughts and jealous grudges.

Most of all, it was people like Amelia who got on his nerves—Amelia and Natalie—Marc too, to a certain extent, although he had improved slightly. They were all so determined to bring him down, to make him feel pathetic, lousy, insignificant, when he knew otherwise. He had made a real difference that day, had perhaps saved several lives. Yes, he knew that Marc and John had been the real heroes in that battle, but surely he had come third. He had certainly been more influential during the fighting than the Woodwards, and even big Freddy knew it; hadn't he asked him to speak of what he did in front of them all? He certainly hadn't asked Marc and John to talk about what they did, and yet all those big-shots still refused to acknowledge how well he had performed that day, how quick thinking and responsible he had been.

Wouldn't he just love to show them. Somehow, wouldn't he just love to make them see for themselves just how good he really was, how significant, how important. He knew he would get his chance, of course; there would be other battles like that one. But would those chances be good enough? Would there really be another chance to make a major difference, to make them see? He was still struggling to believe they still hadn't accepted. Oh, but it was just because they didn't want to believe it—they didn't want to see it—it was just so much easier that way, wasn't it? Come to think of it, why did he even care what they thought? Why should he care what a bunch of self-absorbed Sorcerers and their loyal sheep thought of him?

And then a new idea occurred to him. Maybe it would be better for him, mean more to him, to be appreciated by people who didn't hold a grudge against him. There was another way to make a difference. In fact, weren't there just seven such people downstairs waiting for someone like him to come along and make a difference? Those people were fairly self-absorbed themselves, he wasn't about to kid himself otherwise, but they could—no, they *would* reward the person who got them out of what must look to them like a hopeless situation. Yes, of course they would. Maybe they wouldn't be particularly nice, but they would appreciate him, and that was something that the Woodwards and Fletchers and those who rallied around them simply wouldn't do. He turned over, feeling a little easier in his mind. Tomorrow, he would hang about the prison block, and he would find a way to get them out without anyone knowing.

With this decision made, I felt sleep begin to take him, so I zoomed forward in his memories, looking for the following afternoon. I found it very quickly; Sebastian, invisible and with an extender case over his shoulder, was examining an empty cell, testing the red line and, I knew by his thoughts, looking for a surveillance camera. He couldn't find one, but that didn't necessarily mean there wasn't one. He would have to stay invisible and hope that the Hammersons would understand.

He had decided earlier in the day that he would only take Arnold and Dorothy; it would be too risky to take the whole lot at once, especially with Stella out of her cell. He had then gone back to the beginning of the row and opened the door of each cell, closing it again when he saw Lucien, 3K17, and Cornish in the first three, not caring what they each thought. Tankom was in the fourth; she looked around at the apparently empty doorway as Sebastian stepped into it and shut the door behind him with some curiosity. At least that was what Sebastian thought it looked like.

"Who is there?" she asked in a level voice.

"You don't need to know who I am," said Sebastian, stopping just short of the red line exactly as I had just done in his cell, "just in case there's an invisible microphone in here somewhere. You only need to know what I'm here for."

"Which is what?" asked Tankom, still levelly.

"I'm offering a way out," he said, "for you and your son, if you wish to take it."

"Indeed," she said, scrutinising a spot just to the left of Sebastian's head closely—he felt great amusement at this. "Who has told you to offer us freedom?"

"Nobody," said Sebastian, realising quite suddenly that getting them to trust him might be a little harder than he had expected. "I'm not representing the Sorcerers or anyone in their ranks, if that's what you're thinking. I'm just representing—myself, I guess. I've got a plan. I dunno how successful it'll be, and if it fails, I'll be in one of these cells just like you, but I'm prepared to have a go if—if you think it's worth it."

He had to be careful. He didn't want her to realise that his reasons for helping were almost entirely selfish. He would gain no appreciation if she realised that unpleasant truth.

"Really?" said Tankom, and she looked and sounded more interested, and Sebastian's heart leapt. "What is your plan? Perhaps I can tweak it, make it more effective."

"I expect you could make it loads more effective," said Sebastian, feeling that this flattery would be a good step to take with her, "but I really shouldn't say, for the same reason that I shouldn't say my name. If you agree, though, I have a bag here that I need you to get in, one of yours I think; it expands on the inside."

"Ah, I see," she said appreciatively, and Sebastian's pride began to inflate. "It is invisible too, I take it?"

"Yeah, it is," he said, hoping that none of his distain could be heard. Of course the bag is invisible, he was actually thinking, because you would be able to see it if it wasn't. "So what do you say? Are you up for it?"

"What payment are you looking for?" she asked suddenly. "I am familiar with people like you. You will do us this favour, and then you will ask for something in return. What are you wanting from us?"

Sebastian had to think quickly; saying nothing would sound like a lie, because it would be a lie, and that would do no good at all. Finally he said, "I guess, if the plan works and you and your son get out of here, all I'd ask is that you stick up for me if the Sorcerers find out and come down on me."

"Yet that favour makes no sense if you don't help us at all," she said briskly. "What are you after? You must have a reason for wanting to assist us."

Sebastian considered again, then decided that he might as well tell the truth—or part of it. "I'd just like to make a difference," he said simply, "and—well—I really don't like these people."

"Ah," she said, considering. A silence followed, in which Sebastian stared at her and she stared at her wrinkled hands, thinking, contemplating. Finally she said, "Very well. I will go along with your plan because I can tell you're playing it straight with me, and yes, Arnold and I will use our forces to protect you should the need arise."

"Thank you, thank you very much," said Sebastian, making sure his tone was as grateful as he could manufacture without sounding snivelling.

He moved sideways to the button that controlled the line on the floor and pushed it. He then crossed the line and placed the bag at the foot of Tankom's bed before stepping back. Tankom, knowing what he was doing, felt for it, found it, and crawled into it. Once she was out of sight, Sebastian moved forward, felt for the bag, gathered it up, and retreated, pushing the button again to reset the line.

"Er, if it's okay," Sebastian said tentatively, his hand on the door handle, an unpleasant thought just occurring to him, "would you be prepared to speak to your son as well? Um, just to prove I'm being fair dinkum?"

"Yes," came Tankom's muffled voice from behind him. "That might actually be for the best."

I didn't hang around to watch the exchange between Sebastian and Hammerson; I'd seen enough to guess everything that had followed on that day. I remembered him coming looking for Amelia and finding me and Stella, who had been allowed out of her cell for a few hours that afternoon. He'd had a bag over his shoulder, which I now knew had contained the two former Sorcerers, and he had asked to be let out of the base so that he could spend the night at home with his family—and according to him, he hadn't even wanted to go. And when Amelia had turned up and he had told her this story, she had gone ahead and let him out, bag and all. Either Sebastian had been very good at controlling his thoughts so that she could only pick up what he'd wanted her to know, or she'd been too distracted to pay the proper amount of attention. Either way, getting the Hammersons out had been as simple as that.

There were a few things I wanted to see in Sebastian's memories that would come much later, most notably if he'd had a hand in Nicole's death (I'd have a hard time not killing him myself if he had), but firstly, I wanted to see what he had done the following day to free the rest of the prisoners from their cells. The corridor outside the prison block had been full of people that day; how had he managed to get in there and take them all?

In the end, I found, without having to watch the whole lot, that there had been no trick to it at all. There had simply been so many distractions around that nobody noticed the door to the prison block open and close—twice. Sebastian, who had just had his offer to do the Woodward army's shopping accepted, hurried away before he was to leave in order to go to the toilet. At least that was what he told them, but what he had really done was made himself invisible, taken the bag they had given him for the shopping (not the same one he had used the previous day) back down to the prison block, and, in fashion similar to the way he had freed the Hammersons and Cornish the second time around, knocked out and loaded the rest of the prisoners into the bag while remaining invisible himself. That explained why Stella had known nothing about how she had suddenly found herself inside the Hammerheart base with no memory of being transported.

I moved forward in Sebastian's memories, not wishing to see it all. His thoughts, his ideas, and his fantasies were all so horrible and disgusting. What made it worse was unlike the previous times I had done this, in Serena, Natalie and Rebecca's minds, Sebastian's thoughts were babbling inside my head much more loudly than they should have been. Normally, I should only have had to feel the greater emotions, enough to get the general picture of what was going on in his head, and tune out the other thoughts like they were a radio in the background. The two most sickening things I had to contend with in his mind were how much he came to despise us (me, Amelia, Natalie, Marc, and Tommy) gradually over the weeks, and the way he thought about girls. Several times, I found him putting in a great effort not to walk straight up to a girl (most commonly Natalie, Lena and Katie), and his only motivation for putting in such efforts was because he did not want himself seen in that light, with no care at all about how it would affect them.

More importantly, for the sake of being in Sebastian's mind in the first place, I was coming to learn just how much Sebastian had been doing behind our backs, or rather, right under our noses, without us even being aware. He, of course, was the one who had sent the Hammersons that fateful text message that had enabled them to prepare the ambush that cost Tulip her life. It was he who had informed the Hammersons of Stella's treachery and brought about her exile by doing so. He had also texted them on the sixth to let them know about the job Mr. Woodward had given David, Liam, and Craig; on the eighth when the three boys had left the Woodward base, letting them know to be ready; and again the following day, this time letting them know that Justin was a spy. In less than two weeks, he had orchestrated the deaths of four people I had known, not to mention setting the ambush that, if not for a huge amount of luck, would have killed me as well.

The Hammersons were, by this stage, paying Sebastian most handsomely for the work he was doing for them. He hadn't got the respect he was after when he had helped them all escape to freedom, but the text messages he had sent since from within Woodward headquarters had put him high on Hammerson and Tankom's popularity list. His name was top-secret around Hammerheart headquarters so that people like Justin couldn't give him away. Two days after Justin was killed, Tankom had told him personally that she hadn't forgotten his original request, that they would protect him should the need arise, and Sebastian had been most comforted by that. He was, by this stage, a level-three-ranked Hammerheart, but he had access to all the areas of the bases that the level-two-ranked Hammerhearts had. This was another way for the Hammersons to show him that they appreciated him, that he was important, and Sebastian's pride had been expanding with every passing day, making him even more determined to do right by them, to be the best Hammerheart they had, to rise up in their ranks, perhaps all the way to their level. This might be possible now that the Hammersons were no longer Sorcerers, and they had no heir since they had disowned Stella.

Unfortunately, however, lack of opportunities over the following days halted his progress, and he actually considered attempting to orchestrate some himself. He had felt quite sure that the Woodwards were still wise to the Hammersons' moves, but because Javelyn hadn't been public knowledge, he hadn't been able to work out who the new spy was. That hadn't stopped him from trying, though; on March 19, in the afternoon after school, he managed to follow Amelia into the Woodward living quarters without being detected. Amelia, he thought—and I agreed when I saw her—had looked a little distracted (probably by me, as that had been the day we had almost kissed), and it had consequently done Sebastian a huge favour. He had gone exploring around the living quarters, locating a couple of hiding places but not removing anything from them.

That had come on the twenty-fifth; he had once again followed Amelia into the living quarters, gone back to one of the hiding places he had found on his previous wandering, and taken the Darkness Crystal. Due to lack of opportunities to get away without being detected, he hadn't been able to hand it over to them until two days later. It didn't matter, though, because the Hammersons had rewarded him greatly: He had been given a new office, a better one; he had been given the authority to enlist other level-three and level-four-ranked Hammerhearts if he needed them to help him in a job against the Woodwards; and, on top of that, he had been given a whole load of money. When he had enquired about a promotion, Hammerson had told him that a level-two rank wouldn't suit the sort of work he was doing for them. Sebastian had felt slightly indignant but not enough to make him want to change anything.

Days later, Sebastian proved his worth to them yet again. Upon hearing that the Woodwards were awake to the Hammersons moves against the Australian and American authorities, he had sent them another text message, and the Hammersons had responded to it by using the Darkness Crystal for the first time. When Sebastian texted them again two days later letting them know that the Woodwards had finally discovered the Darkness Crystal was missing, they had gone and used it a second time. I was extremely pleased to note that Sebastian had been unaware of Marc, who had in that time gone into the Hammerson base in an attempt to get the crystal back.

Sebastian's next activity had been two days later, and this time, I was positively furious with myself for not working it out. There was absolutely no mystery as to how Sebastian had learnt that I was taking Serena on a date the following night, because he had been right there, watching us arguing about it, texting away on his phone, texting to Arnold Hammerson, reporting what was happening right in front of him. It wasn't what I had expected, though, because the plan the Hammersons had constructed on Sebastian's information had been pretty pathetic by their usual standards. Now, knowing that they had actually had time to prepare something better, I was at a loss to understand why they had gone about it the way they had. Unless… perhaps there had been another factor in that plan; perhaps Stella had found a way to make the plan less effective, without being discovered. That, however, wasn't information I could get from Sebastian's mind, so I didn't bother worrying too much about it just now.

Then I found a memory a few days later, on April 8, that I stopped on, for this would be worth watching. Sebastian decided to try something new: By telling Mr. Woodward that he wasn't being proactive enough, he hoped that the Woodwards might go ahead and do something foolish, something that, with a bit of luck, they would inform him of, in gratitude for leading them to that course of action. Given that Mr. Woodward had let him speak in front of them all about the school battle, then let him do the shopping, Sebastian believed there would be a realistic chance of this.

So that morning before school, he had gone to find Mr. Woodward. Unable to enter the Woodward living quarters on his own, he had been forced to wait outside them for Amelia, who came back at around eight o'clock after having breakfast with the rest of us to get ready for school.

"What are you doing here?" she said, stopping dead at the sight of Sebastian by the door and looking startled and a little disapproving. Sebastian noticed this and decided he didn't give two shits what she thought.

"I wanted a word with your dad," he said brusquely. "He's in there, right?"

"Well, yeah," she said slowly, "but—why?"

"That—" He broke off, trying to think how best to say what he was thinking. What he really wanted to say was, "None of your business," but that wasn't likely to get him through the door, now was it. "I just wanted to talk to him about something."

"About—" she started, but then, with a great sigh, she gave up and approached the door. Sebastian was relieved, and he never stopped to question what had changed Amelia's mind, but I thought I knew. This would have been back in the early days of her mental breakdown, and apparently arguing with Sebastian wasn't something she felt up to.

She opened the door to the living quarters and stepped through it ahead of him. He shut it behind them both and then, not wanting to look as though he was too familiar with this place, moved towards the nearest door, Mr. Woodward's office, and looked inside. Predictably, Mr. Woodward was in there, busy reading something and not looking at Sebastian. In fact, I had a feeling that he didn't even realise Sebastian was there; perhaps he was too busy doing whatever he was doing to notice that two people had walked through the door.

"Excuse me, sir," Sebastian said, slightly nervously.

He had good reason to be nervous, of course; quite apart from this being the first time he had spoken directly to Mr. Woodward face-to-face for several weeks, this would have to be the very first time he had done it completely alone. More importantly, he had to be careful how he went about this. If Mr. Woodward read his mind and realised that his intention was to trick the Woodwards into a trap, all would be lost. Mr. Woodward looked up in some surprise.

"Oh, good morning, Sebastian," he said, smiling slightly. "What brings you to this neck of the woods?"

"I was hoping for a word," said Sebastian, moving slightly forward into the office and glancing back at Amelia. She nodded and continued down the corridor. "Just quickly before I head off to school."

"Certainly," he said, putting his papers down on the desk and gesturing to a seat in front of the desk, one that I had sat in a few times myself, "but it will have to be quick—there's a lot to be done, you know."

"Yeah, I know," said Sebastian, taking the seat and glancing briefly at the contents of the desk before looking back at the Sorcerer, "and actually, that's sort of why I'm here."

Mr. Woodward raised his eyebrows questioningly, and Sebastian added quickly, "I'm not meaning to be impertinent or anything; I was just a little curious about the way things are being done."

"I see," said Mr. Woodward slowly. "Of course, there's nothing wrong with asking questions, but I hope you'll understand that there may be things I can't tell you, for the sake of security."

"Yeah, I know," Sebastian repeated. "That's okay, 'cause I wasn't going to ask those sorts of questions. What I want to know is—" He swallowed. "Okay, maybe you've done some stuff that you haven't made public knowledge, but it just seems to me that since what happened to David and Craig, you haven't really attacked the Hammersons at all. It's just been like trying to work out what they're doing and blocking them at every turn. At least that's how it looks."

"I see," Mr. Woodward repeated slowly, "and you'd be quite right, of course. Due to circumstances I'd rather not discuss, we have to tread particularly carefully, more so than we did in the early days. There's no reason to send any more people to their deaths for no good reason."

"I understand that," said Sebastian, "but—okay, again, I'm not being impertinent, but is that the right way to go about things? I mean to say, I really thought after we pretty much won that fight at school, the first one I mean, and we had the Hammersons locked up, I thought we'd won this war. But since they got away, we don't seem to have tried very hard at all to get back in that position, and I was just thinking maybe we could end this thing more quickly if we do that."

"I see," Mr. Woodward said for the third time, and Sebastian had to suppress a smirk; this was going rather well so far. "You think we're not being productive enough, is that what you're saying?"

"If you wanna put it like that," said Sebastian. "I'm just worried that, if they do something big really soon, and we can't stop before they do it—like those earthquakes. for example—well, we can only blame ourselves because we haven't done anything to prevent it. And surely the way to prevent all these things would be to capture the Hammersons again?"

Mr. Woodward considered this carefully. He looked as though Sebastian had given him serious food for thought. Sebastian found the sight highly satisfying; I found the sight highly ominous.

"You may have some good ideas," said Mr. Woodward finally. "I must admit I'm still predisposed not to put any more lives in danger, particularly those of teenagers like those who have died for our cause in recent times, but I agree with what you're saying, Sebastian. Trouble is, I also know that attempting things like that can sometimes do more harm than good."

Sebastian shrugged, now feeling more relaxed. He supposed that Mr. Woodward, who had been through this business many years ago, probably knew better than him what he was talking about. "Thanks," he said. "That's all I really wanted. I should go—gotta get ready for school."

Mr. Woodward didn't call Sebastian back; it was the end of the meeting. That had been a big win for Sebastian. I had felt the way he was carefully controlling his thoughts, careful not to think about the spy, in case that was enough to make the Sorcerer realise the spy was right in front of him, and careful not to think about stuff he wasn't supposed to know. He had done what he wanted, and to his delight, he had achieved what he wanted. Four days later, despite his predisposition not to directly involve the Young Army too much with the Hammerhearts, Mr. Woodward called on Jane, Darcy, and Sebastian for a job to abduct the Hammersons when he gave the all-clear. Apparently, since all three agreed to the job, Mr. Woodward felt little or no guilt about going back on his word. Of course, Sebastian texted this information to the Hammersons as soon as he got back to his bedroom.

I skipped forward a few more days; now I was close enough to the date of Nicole's death to make me feel very nervous indeed. After a bit of jumping around, I found his memories of being let out of the Woodward base by Natalie; he had asked to go home that night as soon as he found out and reported to the Hammersons that I would be out and unprotected. Of course, he had no idea that Mr. Woodward had organised to have the Hammerheart base infiltrated that evening. Once Natalie disappeared back into the base, Sebastian made himself invisible again, and then I suddenly learnt exactly how he had coordinated the attack against us on the stairs. Through some sort of experimentation, he had discovered that the goggles Marc had created on camp, which we had used to see Moran's ghosts, could also see objects that had been made invisible, and at some stage while he had been a Hammerheart, on one of his few trips down to the Chopville base, Sebastian had duplicated them a dozen times over.

So once Sebastian was satisfied with his invisibility and the fact that he would see us if we came out of the base invisibly, he settled himself against the wall opposite the study door, out of range of the magic that would detect his presence there, and began the wait. I fast-forwarded through the memory a few hours, until I found the spot where Amelia, Nicole, and I emerged from the wall—back in Sebastian's cell in the prison block, my stomach lurched at the sight of my sister—just hours before her number would be up. Amelia retreated back through the wall, and Nicole and I made ourselves invisible where we stood. Through Sebastian's goggles, we became transparent, making us look exactly like the ghosts had on camp, and an odd thought occurred to me: Did becoming invisible alter a person's life form? Or was this simply a quirk of the goggles that Marc hadn't intended?

Nicole and I linked arms and set off, Sebastian creeping along a good distance behind us but close enough that he could still see us in the dimming light; it was half past seven in the evening. I got from his mind as he walked that his job tonight, his only job, was to report my address to the Hammersons. He would not be involved in the attack, but that didn't make me feel too much better; he had no care at all what became of the two people ahead of him, of whom I was one. All he cared about was getting praised by someone and never mind what it was for. So when Nicole and I slipped through the door of 16 Lopher Lane, where Dad knowingly left the door open for us while he had a smoke in the yard, the address resounded in his head until he could get back to the Chopville base. For some reason, he did not want to text this information, but deliver it in person.

However, since he hadn't eaten at the Woodwards', he decided the information wasn't so urgent that he wouldn't have time for a bite to eat first. The dining hall would be just about empty, of course, dinner being over, but Sebastian happened to know that he would be allowed to personally request meals at any time of the day; yet another perk he had earned in his services to the Hammersons. When he stepped out of the lift onto the fifth floor where the dining and worship halls were, however, he saw something else that distracted him completely and caused him to duck behind a pair of enormous security guards.

Squinting between them, he had to be sure what he was seeing before he reported it or he would be in big trouble. I, however, knew he was seeing what he thought he was seeing, even before he had become sure of it himself: By the far wall, Lucien was deep in conversation with Javelyn. Sebastian didn't know Javelyn personally, but he had seen her enough times around the Woodward base to recognise her. They were probably talking about the whereabouts of the Hammersons, since Javelyn would have been preparing for the infiltration later that evening, but Sebastian wasn't thinking about that. His mind was racing with ideas, possibilities. If his suspicions were right, if she was the spy and he was the one who caught her out…just imagine the rewards. But he couldn't let her see him, not while she still had time to contact the Woodwards and break his cover, just as he was about to break hers.

Forgetting about dinner, he skirted the wall back to the lifts and ducked into the stairwell. Up to the first floor he went and along the corridor, looking at the markings on the wall and counting them. His new office was one of these restricted rooms, I got from his mind, but he wasn't going to his office. He stopped in front of a room I had been in a few times already and knocked on the wall just to the left of the marking. He waited, but when nobody answered, he set off along the corridor again, through the wall right at the end (he swelled with pride as he remembered that he was the only level-three-ranked Hammerheart who could get through that wall) and up the stairs to the Hammerson living quarters.

There were voices coming from the den, so Sebastian went that way, around the corner, and again he knocked on the wall beside the open door. Three people were in there—Tankom, Hammerson, and Cornish. None of them had heard him coming, and they all looked up at the sound of the knock.

"Ah, good, 3W41," said Cornish approvingly.

"Come sit down, Sebastian," said Tankom, gesturing to a seat beside Cornish, the only free seat at the table, and Sebastian was reminded forcefully of how Mr. Woodward had gestured him to sit down just the same a week earlier. "You have it?"

"Yes," he said. "Sixteen Lopher Lane; they both went in there about an hour ago, and I've found out something else."

"Sixteen Lopher Lane," repeated Tankom, glancing at her son, then at Cornish.

Hammerson shook his head, but Cornish said, "It rings a bell. Hang on, I'll get the map."

"What else did you find out?" Hammerson asked.

"I think I've just seen the spy," said Sebastian, "the one who's been reporting all the information about what you've been doing with the authorities."

"Where?" asked Tankom sharply, just as Hammerson said, at the same moment, "Who?"

"Just outside the dining hall," he said. "4R88. I've seen her loads of times around the Woodwards, but this is the first time I've seen her here. She was talking to 3M78 about something, but I couldn't hear what. I didn't want her to see me in case she reports me back to the Woodwards."

"Do you think she did see you?" asked Tankom.

"I don't know for sure, but I don't think so," he said. "I didn't hang around after I recognised her."

"Very good," said Tankom, glancing at her son again. "What should we do?"

"Well, I am going to begin organising a little surprise for the residents of 16 Lopher Lane," said Hammerson smugly, and Sebastian registered, a split-second before I did, that Arnold Hammerson was far more interested in attacking me than flushing out the spy. "Hank, you have it?"

"Right here, sir," said Cornish, laying a map of Chopville on the table before them and marking Lopher Lane with his pen. "How far down, 3W41?"

"About there," said Sebastian, indicating a spot on the curve, just after the intersection with Napoleon Road. "It's a double-storey house, er, fairly small front yard. Couldn't see much more than that."

"Very good, very good," said Hammerson. "Are you planning to spend the night at the Woodwards, 3W41?"

"No, I asked that I could go home," said Sebastian, "so that I could get the address and stuff."

He had been about to mention Darcy and Jane and the job he had got out of doing at this point, to warn them to leave the base in the next couple of hours, but Tankom broke in before he could get a word out.

"Arnold, 4R88," she said sharply. "What should we do?"

"Oh," he said, thinking, "er, Hank, could you go down to the fifth floor and see who's on guard duty there? We'll need to organise a trap for this 4R88. Can't let her return to the Woodwards. She has seen the open air for the last time, I think."

He and Cornish laughed while Tankom smiled amusedly. Sebastian did nothing; he felt hollow, aware that he had just orchestrated yet another death. Quite suddenly, pleased that he had done so well that night, he wanted to get out of the Chopville base, wanted to get back home so he could pull himself together. Fortunately, Tankom seemed to notice this and told him that he was free to go if he wished. Sebastian decided, as he slowly descended through the base towards the Hammerheart Highway, that he quite liked Tankom. She certainly thought more highly of him than the others. She was the only one who called him by his name rather than his code, for a start. Hammerson had been good enough to him, but he hadn't been friendly. Tankom had managed to, though. He was so lost in these thoughts that he didn't notice, although I certainly did, that on his way across the bridge over the tracks of the Hammerheart Highway, he walked straight past Javelyn, and her jaw had dropped in astonishment as she recognised him.

There was nothing else to see in this memory; Sebastian was leaving the base through a door I had never known about at the far end of the bridge, what I supposed must be the visitors' entrance (which was accessible on the surface by walking through an enchanted tree in Hamster's Stretch Reserve, quite close to the spot they had used as the entrance to Stella's birthday party) and heading on home. I therefore skipped forward a day in Sebastian's memories, landing on one at lunchtime on the seventeenth. Sebastian had made himself invisible yet again and was hanging around the door to the prison block, examining it. He knew that the Woodwards had put cameras in the cells since last time he had done this, but he thought that if he went about it the same way he got Cornish and the rest out, they wouldn't be any the wiser as to who was behind it. The problem would be getting in there at all; they had put an electronic (or magical, rather) lock on the door, and he wasn't brave enough to try his own key in the slot, just in case the locks recorded which keys tried to open them. He did, however, memorise the tiny number on the lock, a number I had never even noticed until now.

I only had to skip forward a few hours to find another noteworthy memory. Early in the morning on the eighteenth, Sebastian had followed me and Marc into the Woodward living quarters again. Frank Luivic would have been there as well, also invisible, but by some miracle, the two invisible people hadn't bumped elbows. Just as fortunately, Sebastian quickly and silently scooted off once he was through the door, not hanging around to overhear any words that passed between us and Mr. Woodward. He knew where the key-creating device was since his previous wanderings around here, though he had never used it. He went straight to it and began experimenting, giving himself access to a load of rooms he wouldn't otherwise be able to get into, but not his own bedroom—that was essential to the plan, as he would not give himself away that easily in case the Woodwards had a way of checking.

Then, the following afternoon, he had separated from the rest of us to go to the toilet, made himself invisible, gathered up his bag again, gone across to the prison block, and tried out his new key. It had worked, of course, and he had gone into the three occupied cells and used stunning and drawing devices (it was something that made the objects it pointed at fly towards the person using it) to quickly remove them from the cells. He had then retreated and gone up to the level-two room he had given himself access to and used the door within it to drop the invisible bag off at a hidden location in the park. He knew he didn't have much time, and he just had to hope that nobody would stumble across the invisible bag.

The following night, Sebastian had leapt into action again. Apparently he had been very uncomfortable spending the entire day in the Woodward base, forced to bide his time, as it was too dangerous and too soon to ask to leave. With his new key confiscated, he had followed Amelia into the Woodward living quarters again, gone straight to the key creator, and created a new key, just like the first one. He had then gone to investigate some of the hideouts he had given himself access to, finding many valuable and dangerous items but not knowing what many of them were. In the end, the only thing he took was, to my horror and his surprise, the Darkness Crystal; he hadn't known until that point that the crystal was back in the Woodwards' possession. He had then gone up to the same second-floor room he had previously used and gone back through the door, back into Hamster's Stretch Reserve. He had collected the invisible bag, released the Hammersons and Cornish into the night, given them the Darkness Crystal, and told them he would be in touch. He had then gone back through the door into the base, being sure to take the magic door away from the park in case the Woodwards determined which door had been used. Of course, I already knew that the Woodwards had done just that.

I skipped quickly over the following memories, looking for anything important. I had seen pretty much everything I had needed to see, but just in case there was anything else worth knowing…

On the twenty-fourth, Tankom gave Sebastian an order to capture Tommy if it was possible to do so without being found out. Sebastian had followed Tommy around that day and deduced that it would not be possible just yet. On the twenty-fifth, he had become aware that I was no longer around the base; he had asked Harry and Simon if they knew where I was, which of course they didn't. He had assumed that the Woodwards were hiding me and reported this information to the Hammersons. Also that day, he'd had a look at the new wall guarding the prisoners, but he hadn't been able to think of a way to get through it without asking one of the Woodwards, which would give him away. On the twenty-seventh, he had sent the Hammersons two separate messages, the first describing the drama that had taken place at school that day and that Natalie and Amelia seemed to have vanished, though he privately thought they would already know this, and the second letting them know that Hammerhearts were being converted to the Woodwards' side by way of the influential charm. It was close enough to the truth for government work, he supposed. Then, in the evening, he had volunteered to do some of the converting himself, only when he had entered the prison block, he had used a Hammerheart device instead of a Woodward one. He had done the same to other people around the base the following day, once the Sorcerers were all gone, which explained how he had gathered up that little army to use against us on the stairs. Finally, on the twenty-ninth, today, Sebastian received the order from Hammerson to bring H2, H3, and H4 in, along with their crystals, and it didn't matter if he was seen as long as he was successful, because they wouldn't need him for spy duty after today.

I had clearly seen all there was to see, so I withdrew from his mind and re-joined my body. Then I just sat there for a few minutes, staring straight ahead of me at the cell wall, unsure what to do. The whole experience had taken just under three hours, and it was now approaching midnight. Sebastian lay asleep on the bed before me, and I honestly didn't know what to do with him. Leaving him here would have been the kindest thing to do, though he certainly deserved much worse. Yes, so he had felt slightly guilty about sending Javelyn to her death, but was that enough? Why didn't he feel guilty for sending hundreds, perhaps thousands by now, of other people to their deaths, as all these worldwide coups could never have happened if he hadn't joined the Hammersons? Oh, but the answer to that was simple: He had made a difference, hadn't he? He had gained the appreciation of people who, he sincerely believed, would be running the world in a few months' time. He didn't care which side he was on as long as the people on that side appreciated and looked after him.

Bastard, I thought. Low, selfish, cowardly bastard.

I stood up and stared down at him, the Sien-Leoard Crystal in my hand, and I found it extremely difficult not to do something to him right now. What? What would I do, though? Kill him? It was tempting, but no. I would not stoop to that level. But it was all because of him: Tulip, dead, and I had blamed myself so much for that; Nicole, my own sister, dead just because she was my sister— my adoptive sister, moreover, a bit like my mother; and all these things because of him, because of Sebastian, and he was happy with that because he had made a difference—he had made himself noticed. I had intended to bring him around when I was done browsing his memories, but now that the time had come, I couldn't talk to him again. I just couldn't, not tonight. I therefore squeezed the crystal and, as I left the cell, Sebastian would wake up in exactly sixty seconds.

Chapter 12: Wake-up Call

To my surprise, several people had waited up for me: Marc, Tommy, Peter, James, and Serena. I had the impression that they had all expected the interrogation to be considerably shorter than it had been, but of course I hadn't told them exactly what that interrogation would involve. I planned not to, either, just in case I met some sort of moral objection against what I had done. They would need to know what I had found out, though.

"He was tough, huh?" said Peter when I sat down in the lounge room beside him.

"Not really," I said, looking around at the five of them. "I was just really thorough. Where's Amelia? I thought she would be waiting to hear—"

"Her place," said Marc bitterly, and I thought I understood the subtext in his tone.

"She did say she wanted to hear about it," said James reprovingly. "I guess she just wanted to have this time to herself, or maybe she's gone to bed, I dunno."

I felt disappointment threaten to take me. I had really hoped Amelia would wait up so I would be able to talk to her tonight, then perhaps go out of the base with her tonight.

"She'll need to hear about it," I said darkly. "Well, I suppose you've all guessed it, but he was the spy. He's been sending text messages to them for two months now. He let them out of here both times, he stole the Darkness Crystal both times, and he was the one who tipped them off every time we sent someone down there. Tulip, Craig, David, Justin, Javelyn, Nicole—we can blame all their deaths on him."

A shocked silence followed my little speech. Every face looked stunned and angry, and I knew that Sebastian would be lucky not to feel any sort of physical pain by the morning. Peter was the first one to confirm this idea.

"He killed Nicole?" he said in a hushed voice. "Was it him?"

"Well, he didn't do that," I said. "He just told them our address so that they could do it."

"I'll kill him," he said quietly, his fists clenched and a very ugly look on his face. "I swear to God, I'm gonna kill him."

I shrugged. Trying to talk Peter out of his rage might do more harm than good at this point. "I didn't do anything to him," I told them. "I just left him there. In fact, he won't even remember what I did to him to get the information out. I just reckon we should wait 'til one of the Sorcerers can make a decision on him."

"How'd you manage not to hurt him?" asked James, who looked almost as angry as Peter.

"With enormous difficulty," I told him, "but if I can do it, you can too."

Both of them glared at me, and Peter looked like he wanted to shout, but Marc swiftly intervened.

"So what about tonight, then? Was he supposed to bring us all in?"

"Yeah," I said heavily. "Hammerson told him it didn't matter if he was found out as long as he succeeded, 'cause they won't need a spy in here anymore. By the way, Marc, those goggles—"

"Hey, yeah," said Tommy suddenly. "Why were they wearing the ghost goggles?"

"'Cause they can see invisible things," I told them. "Was that intentional, Marc? Well, anyway, that's how they knew what each other were doing; they could see each other."

"Holy crap," whispered Marc. "The goggles—the goggles can do that? I hadn't meant that to happen, but then I never meant not to, either. The crystal must have needed to do that to make us see ghosts."

"If that's the case," said James slowly, looking from Marc to me, "then technically John should be able to see invisible people too, since he can see ghosts."

My mouth fell open. "I certainly can't, or I would have definitely mentioned it by now."

"So how did it happen, then?" asked James, looking back at Marc.

He shook his head. "I have no idea, but I suppose it doesn't matter. It's useful to know, though. Being invisible ain't quite as good as it used to be, if there's a chance our enemies can still see us."

There was another silence, this time broken by Tommy yawning. "If it's all right with you guys, I think I might head up to bed. Did he say anything else worth knowing, John?"

"I can't think of anything else," I said. "Well, those are certainly the important points."

"How did he steal the Darkness Crystal?" asked James. "You never said how he did that."

"He just followed Amelia through the door a couple of times," I said, "invisible and really quiet, and he followed us in one time as well. Then, once he was in there, he just had a look around, made that key that they took off him, and found the hiding places Mr. Woodward stores a lot of stuff in, though he only took the Darkness Crystal 'cause he didn't recognise the other things. He made a second key too, but if that disarming thing worked the way it's supposed to, he shouldn't have it anymore."

"We have another problem, guys," said Marc quietly, and everyone turned to look at him, Tommy spinning right around as he was on his way out the door.

"Yeah, like we really need another problem," said Peter sarcastically.

"The people who Sebastian used the influential charm on," said Marc. "They're in cells now, and they'll need to be converted back to our side, but I'm nervous about doing that after what James said earlier. Even worse, though, there might be more people around the base affected by it that weren't used in the ambush tonight. Did Sebastian say anything about that, John?"

"Er, not specifically," I said, remembering how I had only skipped over some of that time, not interested in seeing it all. "I suppose we can go back and ask him."

"Oh, let me do it," said Peter at once, clenching his fists again.

"Maybe I'd better do it," said Marc firmly. "I'm not sure I trust any of you guys not to knock his teeth out if you're alone with him."

"And what's wrong with that, exactly?" Peter enquired.

Marc sighed. "Let's try to be the good guys here, can we?"

"According to Sebastian, being the 'good guys' is exactly what got the Woodwards into the mess they're in now," I told them, "but in saying that, I agree. I suggest we leave it up to Mr. Woodward, assuming he can get back here sometime soon."

"Yeah, that's probably best," sighed James. "But I hate it. I really do. If Mr. Woodward goes soft on him, I dunno about you guys, but I'll be taking matters into my own hands."

"Yeah, and I'll be right beside you," said Peter at once.

"Me too," I said, standing up also. "So what now? We all going to bed?"

"Everyone except you," said Marc, grinning slightly.

Serena, who up until now had been silent, caught my arm as I left the room with Peter.

"Are you still going to see Amelia tonight?" she asked quietly.

I considered, then said, "I might try, but my hopes of her being awake aren't very high."

"Can we spend some time together if she's asleep?" she asked.

"Oh," I said, my insides jerking guiltily. "Um, I wish I could. Actually, maybe I can. How tired are you?"

"A bit," she said, grinning at me, "but I think I still have some energy to spare."

I sighed. "It's not what you're thinking. There's something I want to do tonight, and I was hoping Amelia would come out with me to do it, but if she doesn't, or even if she does, you can come too, if you like."

"You're going out?" James enquired, looking back at me from the stairs, and Peter ducked his head back out to listen too. Marc and Tommy were too far up the stairs to hear.

"Yeah, I will be," I told them. "Don't worry, it's only local business; I'm not gonna be fighting."

"How do you know you won't be fighting locally?" asked Peter. "Honestly, after tonight, I'd believe that's very possible."

"I guess it is," I agreed, "but I'll have the crystal, and maybe some goggles might be useful too. Do you still have yours?"

"No, but you probably do," said Peter. "The ones they were wearing tonight?"

"Oh yeah," I said. They had disappeared when I had done the disarming charm, so they should have reappeared in my room too.

"So what are you going out for?" asked James.

"Just to check on a few people, and bring them in here, for protection and stuff," I told them.

"Oh, okay," said Peter. "I'd come along, but"—he yawned—"you know."

"Yeah, both of you go get some sleep," I told them. "If you're up to it, I wanna try the life assistant tomorrow. I dunno if we can wait for Nat to come back."

"She won't be happy if we do it without her," said James, amused. "I reckon we'll leave you to deal with her when she gets back. Night."

"Night."

"What were they on about?" asked Serena when they were heading up the stairs again.

"What I was away for," I said. Then, on the spur of the moment, I added, "Maybe you can see it too—I don't see why not—but it's kind of difficult to explain just now. So what do you say to coming out tonight?"

"It'll last most of the night, won't it?"

"Probably. Actually, yeah, it would."

She sighed. "Promise me you'll keep yourself awake with magic tomorrow? Then we can spend at least a bit of time together? I've really missed you."

"I've missed you too," I told her, with some degree of truth. I really had missed her with all that had been going on. "And yeah, I think I'll do that."

"Promise me."

"Okay, I promise."

"Good." She hugged me, kissed me, and said, "Guess I'll see you in the morning, then."

"Yeah, sleep well."

"Good luck."

"Thanks."

I watched her out of sight, and then, feeling slightly nervous, not knowing what to expect, I set off through the door, along the main corridor down to the end, and through the door into the Woodward living quarters, the crystal paving my way as usual. Amelia was asleep, I knew it as soon as I stepped into the place, for the only sound I could hear was the ticking of a clock in their living room. I proceeded further in anyway, glancing into Mr. Woodward's empty office in some dismay. Of course I knew he was out and about, but the sight of the empty office seemed to drive the fact home like nothing else had.

I walked quietly through the place, looking in the living room, dining room, kitchen, and down the hallway where the bedrooms were. To my slight surprise, Amelia's bedroom, which was the first door along the corridor, was open. Did she think that with the place so completely deserted, it wouldn't matter if she kept it open or closed if she slept? Or did she always keep it open when she slept? Either way, it meant that I could look in there and see for myself if she was awake or not. But, as it turned out, she wasn't even in her bedroom.

Now feeling slightly anxious, I looked into the other two bedrooms, Lillian's and the one belonging to Mr. Woodward and his wife. They were both empty too, so unless Amelia was hiding in one of the hiding places Mr. Woodward normally reserved for his most precious and most dangerous items, she must be somewhere else in the base. My insides curled up at the idea that she could be in Marc's bedroom right now, entertaining him while I was wandering around here, trying to find her so that I could help her get back to her normal self. That was not a pleasant thought; it made me angry in a very selfish way, and I tried to drag my mind back to what I was doing.

I was definitely starting to feel worried now. Where was she? Was she, in fact, somewhere else in the base? Had something happened to her? Had someone done something to her? Had she done something to herself? There were only two other rooms I hadn't checked in this corridor, but as they were the bathroom and toilet and they both stood open and I couldn't hear a sound from either, they didn't seem like good candidates for her location. I supposed I'd better give them a glance, though, and wondered, as I moved forward, if I should just use the crystal again to track her down. Save myself some time and effort.

And of course, the moment I had made that decision, I found her. Amelia was standing in the bathroom, her back about three or four inches from the towel rack, staring blankly at the opposite tiled wall, not moving a muscle. She looked exactly as she had the previous evening when I had found her in Marc's hidden quarters. She didn't seem to have sensed me at all, perhaps wouldn't have heard me even if I had called out to her. She did not glance to her right and spot me in the doorway, nor did she glance to her left and spot my reflection in the mirror over the basin. Her eyes were wide, and it seemed that whatever was going on behind them was demanding absolutely all of her mental energy and attention.

I quickly and quietly moved backward, away from the bathroom. This did not seem like the best time to talk to her. It looked as though, before she had become lost in her thoughts, she had been either getting into or out of the shower, because apart from the towel draped over her shoulders, she was completely naked. I'd seen everything there was to see, and it had taken a couple of seconds to tear my eyes away from her body once I had registered her nudity, but that wasn't the problem. What worried me most was how she might react if I made her aware of my presence. The two most likely possibilities I could come up with, her screaming at me and her crying on me (without bothering to dress herself), surely wouldn't have desirable consequences, unless the latter resulting in my getting much closer to Amelia than would be proper could be called desirable.

I didn't want to leave her the way she was, but I honestly couldn't see a way of getting out of this situation without embarrassing her—something that would not at all help her while she was like this. I therefore did the only thing I could think of: I turned and walked down the hallway, away from the bathroom. I would go out alone tonight; I would seek those I wanted to bring to safety alone. Then, upon my return, I would come back here and see Amelia. If she was still standing naked in the bathroom, I would have to do something. I wondered briefly if I ought to tell Marc to intervene in that situation, then decided against it. If he knew I had seen Amelia naked...

So, feeling disappointed, I slipped out of the Woodward living quarters and proceeded back up to Room 2-94, the second-floor room Sebastian had used. Through it I went, straight into the Woodward study as though I'd gone through the official entrance point. Sebastian had brought it back to this point because he must have worked out that unless they had been moved somewhere else, all the second-floor rooms would come out in this study. It was well past midnight now, and the town was just as dark and silent as it had been the previous night. This didn't frighten me at all; on the contrary, it made me feel considerably safer, I supposed because any sound I heard out here these days wasn't likely to be friendly. I hadn't seen any natural daylight since I had returned from England, but now it didn't look as though it would be safe to see it again any time soon.

What the late hour did mean, though, was that the people I was looking for would probably be asleep and not too happy about me waking them in the middle of the night and trying to get them to come out. I would have to do it, though; there would be no other opportunity. I took maybe ten steps forward before swearing under my breath and teleporting myself to the front of the house on Lopher Lane.

Predictably, the house was completely dark and completely silent, just like the rest of Chopville. I squeezed the crystal and sent my mind out, into the house. Mum and Hilda (my grandmother on my mother's side) were in there, which probably meant that Marge and Violet were in the other house. Also unsurprisingly, Hilda was awake, lying in her bed in the study upstairs opposite our bedroom, listening to some talkback radio station (I'd not realised that a station was still on the air; who knew what crap it was broadcasting). I sent my mind out to Mum and, acting on a sudden stroke of inspiration, used the crystal to wake her up. She was thirsty and would have to come downstairs for a drink, maybe or maybe not checking on her mother on the way down.

And, of course, that was exactly what happened. I kept watching her via the crystal until she was in the kitchen, then quickly withdrew, approached the house, and tapped softly on the window. That was just proof of how inexperienced I was in this game. I realised how stupid I had been a second later when I heard the clear sound of something smashing from inside the house. I grinned in spite of myself—I would be okay, I'd be able to sort this out, but I might get a hair-raising telling-off when I did.

I sent my mind back into the house; neither Marge nor Violet had been raised, but Hilda was at the top of the stairs, preparing herself for the laborious task of hobbling down them, while Mum was frozen in the kitchen, listening as hard as she could for any sound of the enemy outside the house. I reached out and, grinning more broadly, tapped on the glass again. I heard Hilda call something out to Mum, completely unaware that someone was outside the house. Mum, meanwhile, had begun to creep out of the kitchen, bringing with her a long knife, into the hallway.

This time, I decided to ring the doorbell. Would that make her think I was friendly? Or would it make her think I was a particularly crafty Hammerheart trying to lure her into a false sense of security? I wasn't sure about Mum, but it certainly threw Hilda, quite literally; she toppled down the rest of the stairs, landing on the floor with a crack. She was hurt, badly. This would have to end quickly. Hammerson will be furious, I thought, 'cause he won't get a chance to kill me if this goes the way it's looking like it's going, and I had to fight down a laugh. It was a very bad time for laughing.

Mum, it seemed, was completely torn. She wanted to attack me, and she wanted to rush to her mother and care for her. She could not call anyone because the hospital had shut up shop. What was she to do? I tried to make her mind up for her by ringing the bell again, realising that I was really going to be in trouble when I got in there. There was nothing funny about the situation anymore.

"Open the bloody door," I called through it at her. "Mum, it's me! Open the door!"

Why didn't I just teleport through it? The idea hadn't actually occurred to me until then. That would have given them both a fright, of course, but not nearly as bad as the fright they were in now. Fortunately, most fortunately indeed, Mum heard me, and although she seemed not to have recognised me yet, she did at least realise that I was not dangerous—to her anyway. She moved right up to the door now and peeked through the eyehole at me, but due to the almost complete darkness out here, she still couldn't make me out.

"Who is it?" she whispered. "If that's you, Chester, I'll kill you."

"No, it's John. For Christ's sake, let me in."

"John?" she gasped, her mouth falling open in surprise. She opened the front door and stared at me through the screen door, and I stood there, waiting for the explosion, but it didn't come—yet. "What are you doing here?" she asked.

"Come to check on you lot," I said. "Er, can I come in?"

She sighed and opened the door for me, saying, "Why didn't you just ring first?"

I stared at her, astonished. Why on earth hadn't I thought of that?

"I was trying to be quiet about it," I said. "I was going to just teleport in here. Well, anyway—"

Once in, I hurried past her to where Hilda was moaning at the foot of the stairs. The crystal was out, and I was thinking just fix it. Whatever she hurt when she fell down the stairs, just make it how it was ten minutes ago. It didn't work immediately, but thankfully, it didn't take long before Hilda was in considerably less pain.

"I'm sorry," I told her. "That was my fault. I'm hopeless at being stealthy, by the look of it."

"That's one way of putting it," said Mum, very disapprovingly.

"Can you go and wake Marge and Violet?" I asked her. "I need you all in here, but maybe it's best I stay here and not go over there like I came in here."

Mum looked as though she would have quite liked to stay here and continue reprimanding me, but for the first time in my life, I managed to stare her down, and a moment later, she was ducking into the cupboard under the stairs and heading on over next door. I continued to work on Hilda with the crystal, removing the aches and pains that had resulted from her fall; the bones had healed right away. Finally, I was able to help her to her feet and assist her into the lounge room. She was watching me through the darkness with slight fear in her face.

"It's all right," I told her. "Didn't they tell you I've got one of the crystals?"

"Oh, yes," she said in a quivery voice. "You know, you really shouldn't be dropping in on us at this hour; we really feared the worst."

"I know, it's not great," I admitted, "but I can't do it in daylight, not now that the whole country wants me behind bars."

Noises from the direction of the stairs told me that Mum had brought the other two through to this house. By the sound of it, Marge was helping Mum with getting Violet through the tunnel, and she didn't sound all that happy about it. If she had been asleep when Mum came in, I didn't blame her. A few moments later, all three of them were in the lounge room, switching the light on and just about blinding all five of us.

"You'd better do something so this isn't visible from the outside, John," said Mum sternly to me, and I obliged at once. A moment later, the windows all over the house were enchanted so that from the outside, absolutely nothing whatsoever of the house's interior could be seen.

"John," said Marge, plonking herself down on the couch beside the spot in which they had deposited Violet. "What's this about? What's happened?"

"Well, plenty's happened," I said, "but you probably get the general idea already. What I came here for—and this was my decision, no one else's—was to firstly make sure you're okay, that the Hammerhearts haven't come here, and looks like they haven't.

Secondly, to give you all a chance to come into the Woodward base. I'm doing that with a few people tonight since nobody can get in or out now with all the Sorcerers all over the place. You guys interested in coming into hiding?"

A silence followed, in which they all stared at me, and I stared seriously around at them all in turn. I hoped they were really considering this. I could just imagine how they might feel that I was dragging them away from the home they loved, the homes they had lived in for more than fifteen years. Of course, there was much more to it than that; the Hammerhearts could turn up here, now that they knew my address, and they could either attack, believing I might be here, or hurt all that live here in an indirect attack against me, or they could take them all hostage. There were many possibilities, none of them good.

"I had thought of that," said Marge suddenly, glancing at Mum. "I don't like it, but these last two days have been bad."

"I will go with you," said Hilda at once. "This house doesn't feel the same anymore, not with you all living out, and after the fire."

There was a murmur of agreement.

"Surely it makes you all nervous, being in this place," I said, "with all us gone, and Dad and Charlie out there somewhere."

"Yes, it is," said Mum sharply, and I looked away. Mum and Marge both looked on the verge of getting emotional, and that wasn't something I needed to see.

"So, do you all wanna come?"

They exchanged looks, and then Mum said, "Yes, I think we probably should."

"Good," I said, standing up. "Can you all pack what you wanna bring, then? I have other people I need to see, but I'll be back before dawn."

They all got up as well and began bustling around the two houses, gathering up the essentials and packing them into a large bag with four internally extending compartments that I magically created for the occasion. I wasn't trying to be fancy; I just didn't think Hilda and Violet would be up to carrying their own bags, not that they would have packed very much, and Mum and Marge didn't need to carry two bags each. I left them to it.

It was just after one o'clock when I teleported out of the Playman house and onto the Maivises' front lawn, and just like the Playman house, it was dark and silent. With both sets of twins safely locked away, it was only their grandparents whom I would need to deal with. They would be enough, though; in fact, waking them up at this hour was a very scary idea indeed. Thinking of what Mum said, though, I decided to call them first.

Of course, the phone rang out, three times in a row. I assumed that they just didn't want to get up and answer the thing and not that something more sinister was going on. I therefore moved forward and rang the bell, sending my mind out from my body again to check for live beings in the area. Of course they were in there, lying in bed, awake and unanimously swearing at the rude, inconsiderate person who would think of calling them at this ungodly hour. At the sound of the doorbell, however, they both leapt out of bed and began staggering through the house.

The woman was heading for the phone, the man for the door—towards me. I took advantage of the positioning of the pair of them by recalling their number and letting it ring just as the woman reached the phone.

"Wait," she called to her husband, and she picked up the phone. "Who are you? If you're outside our house right now, I demand you get off our property or we will attack."

"Hang on, don't attack," I said quickly. "I'm not a Hammerheart. I'm a friend of Harry and Simon."

"How do you know about Harry and Simon?" she asked suddenly and sharply. "What's happened to the boys? What have you done to them? I swear, if you've touched a hair on either of their—"

"No, they're fine," I said hurriedly. "They're at the Woodwards. I only wanted to offer—"

"You know that? Are you saying you've got into the Woodward base?"

"Yes, I've just come from there."

Big mistake. The woman screamed at the top of her lungs. "Cyril! The Hammerhearts have got into the Woodward base and taken the boys!" Then to me she spat, "What about Misty and Michelle, what have you done with them, hey?"

"Nothing," I said loudly. "I told you, I'm a friend of theirs. You know me, I'm John Playman; I've been around here loads of times."

"You know about him too, do you?" she said. "You've taken the whole damn lot of them, haven't you? Where are Misty and Michelle?"

"They're probably fast asleep," I almost shouted, uncomfortably aware of the racket I was making in the silent night. "Look, can you just let me in? Before I wake up half the neighbourhood?"

"Oh, but of course you wouldn't want anyone to know what's going on," she spat. "The police are out of town, aren't they? Highly convenient, highly convenient. So all you have to worry about are the neighbours, and you think that if you come to us in the middle of the night—"

"Would it be simpler if I just came in there anyway?" I asked her.

"If you dare set foot in—" She was scared now, hardly able to get the words out properly.

She was thrust aside by her husband, who had decided to give up the idea of bursting out the door at me. "Who are you? What do you want with us?"

"I want to offer you protection," I said slowly and deliberately. "I am John Playman. You know me; I've been around here before. I know the Woodwards are out of town, but their base is still one of the most secure places around. You can be with both sets of twins and you can be safe. Do you want to come?"

"You know a lot, young man," he stammered. "If this is a trap —"

"For crying out loud! It is not a trap," I snarled, really annoyed now. "Look, I won't make you come; you can stay here if you like, but I would have thought you'd want to be brought into hiding in this time of trouble."

"Oh, you can try to lure us out there by telling us we're not bound by anything," he said more forcefully, "but if you want to do anything to us, you'll have to come in here and get us yourself, and if you've done anything at all to our children—"

"Geez, I give up," I said. "I suppose if I came in there and showed myself to you, you'd still think I was a Hammerheart in disguise or something. Tell me, what would you do if I could bring Harry and Simon to you tomorrow? Perhaps Misty and Michelle too? Would you think they were Hammerhearts in disguise, too?"

"You do that," he said. "You bring them to us tomorrow, and then we'll decide, but if you come in here tonight, you'd better bring at least a dozen of your mates with you—you'll need them."

"I doubt that," I said, annoyed beyond tact now, "but since I'm not up for fighting just now and I've got other people I need to check on, I'll be going. See you sometime tomorrow, Mr. Maivis."

I cancelled the call and, not wanting to stand there any longer, teleported about half a mile to the southwest. Predictably, Greenly Street was just as dark and silent as the rest of Chopville. It had a slightly different feel to it, though; the south side of the street was lined with large houses, slightly farther spaced apart than the houses in all the rest of town, while the north side was lined with large business buildings, all standing close to the street—the southern edge of the town central. It gave the street a cut-off feeling, making this stretch, up to the point where the street turned back into the town central, feel like a different place altogether. More importantly, in this situation, the buildings so close made me feel as though I was in much closer proximity to unfriendly humans than I had been at any other point that night.

I was standing on Natalie's large front lawn, about halfway between the street and the front porch, just out of the shadow of the house. It was double-storey like mine, but the ceilings of both floors were rather higher than my house; at least they were in some parts of the house. In the daylight, the house looked spectacular, as did every other house in the street, but at night, it had a dark feel to it, especially with no lights on. The same held for the rest of the front yard, with its large garden and fountain, although the fountain had been out of action for several years now due to the water restrictions.

I moved up towards the house and took shelter on the porch behind a hedge row, wondering what was the best way to approach this situation. Natalie's mother was nice, much easier to deal with than Harry and Simon's grandparents had been, but I was worried that I might really scare her, and if that happened, she would be most likely to hide somewhere in this big house and not come out, no matter how long I stayed around trying to persuade her I was friendly. In the end, I supposed calling her would be the safest way to go.

I wished I knew her mobile number because when the phone inside the house started ringing, it was loud enough for me to hear from the porch. It echoed all through the house, and the silence of the night made it seem like it could probably be heard from the houses on either side. Even worse, it rang for a very long time, and I was just thinking that I ought to cancel the call for my own safety as much as hers when she finally picked it up.

"Hello?" she squeaked. She had a cute little voice, and being so terrified only made her sound cuter. I had to grin into the hedge.

"Hi, Mrs. Fletcher?"

"Who is that?" she asked hesitantly.

"It's John Playman, Natalie's friend," I told her softly. Quite apart from not wanting to speak too loudly into the night as I had at the Maivises', I had to make her believe I wasn't dangerous.

"John?" she repeated in some surprise, but I was encouraged; that was already better than what I'd got from the Maivises, and I thought maybe it was because she had been waiting desperately to hear from someone affiliated with the Woodwards. "Oh, yes. What are you doing?"

"Just checking up on you," I told her. "Are you okay? Are you in your house?"

"Er, yes, I am," she said. She had been on the point of saying no, I felt sure, but of course, she had just answered the home phone—not a very good story. A pretty stupid question, too, I suddenly realised, since I'd just called the home phone.

"Good," I said. "Do you mind if I come in? Just so we can see each other?"

I heard her make a terrified noise, holding her mouth away from the phone slightly. "What for?" she asked. "Why you come in?"

"Well," I said slowly, thinking what I ought to say now, then deciding I might as well tell her what I was there for, "if you'd like to come back into the Woodward headquarters, I can help you get in. I've not long come from there, see."

"You have? Oh, have you?" she asked, and I could hear the enormous relief in her voice. "Yes, I want to be back in there. Can you get in there?"

"Yeah, I can take you in," I said. "I'm just out the front of the house. Do you wanna let me in or should I just let myself in?"

"I—um—you come in here," she said hesitantly.

So I cancelled the call and teleported into the house, finding her in the cavernous kitchen where the main phone, or one of the main phones, was. She was quite a young woman, about fifteen years younger than her husband and about eighteen older than Natalie, short and thin just like both her daughters, of Asian descent, and had clearly been in a state of terror for quite some time. I ended up getting her story anyway, since now that she was no longer alone, she couldn't stop talking. It turned out that she had returned to the Woodwards' house after work on Wednesday afternoon only to find that there was no one to let her in. She had called Mr. Fletcher on his mobile phone and got no response. Scared and with nowhere else to go, she had come back here and seen the early stages of the coup on the television. For more than twenty-four hours, she had hidden here in the house, trying to make it look as though there was nobody in it, terrified that the Hammerhearts would attack it, knowing how the Fletchers were Sorcerers. She had honestly believed that the Sorcerers weren't coming back, and she would be completely on her own from now on.

She hadn't slept for more than a few hours the last two nights, so I decided I'd better take her straight back to the Woodwards'. She didn't need to pack, of course, as all that had been managed several weeks ago when the Fletchers' living quarters had been established. I teleported her to the door in the Woodward study and led her through it. I took her all the way through the base to her living quarters; she knew the way around in here, of course, but she didn't seem to want to be left alone just yet. I ended up staying with her for about ten minutes, until being back here in the warm comfort of the living quarters had calmed her down somewhat. I left her when we were joined by Rebecca, who had been woken by the unexpected noise just outside her bedroom door.

I spent the next few hours teleporting all over Chopville, rounding up as many families of the Young Army who I knew as I could find. There were Lisa's mother and brother, both of whom came and went from the Woodward base but had been outside it when the coup began; Katie's mum and dad; Sophie's parents and a couple of aunts; Serena's parents; Kylie's parents and two younger sisters; Erica's parents; and Liam's father and the woman he was sleeping with, plus a younger brother. By the time I was done, it was five o'clock and not long 'til dawn.

The next job was getting them all to the Woodwards', starting with my own family, so I teleported back to 16 Lopher Lane, where Mum, Marge, Hilda, and Violet were ready and waiting for me with the magical bag I had created for them.

"That took a little longer than we had expected," Marge told me, frowning slightly.

"Tricky job," I said. "Well, are we ready?"

They were ready, so without giving them a chance to prepare for the sensation, I teleported us all into the Woodwards' study. Marge screamed and Hilda shrieked, but otherwise there were no problems. I ushered them through the door and told them to make themselves comfortable in the room and that I would come back when I had everyone else and help them find rooms. I didn't think I would need Mr. Woodward's permission to use the key creator, now that I knew how to work it myself. Of course, I came back several times before then, for each and every person I brought back into the base.

It was nearly six o'clock when I had them all in the second-floor room and vanished the door. I was getting pretty tired by now, but the job still wasn't done. There was barely room to swing a grasshopper in 2-94, and all these people looked just as tired, if not more so, than I was. I would have to find them all rooms tonight.

"Listen, folks," I said to them all. "I know a few of you already have rooms here, so if you do, you don't have to stay. In fact, it would make it easier for me if you didn't. For the rest of you, I'm gonna take you all down to the lounge room—you should be more comfortable there—'til I can get keys for you all and give you all rooms."

I was pleased that they all followed my instructions, even if there was some grumbling at the idea of going down to the lounge room for who knew how long. Of course, some of them had never even set foot in this place before now, so who knew what they were thinking they'd have to do. The Ponts left us to it while the rest of them followed me down to the deserted lounge room. I told them all to stay there or to go next door to the dining room if they wanted breakfast (as I could hear it getting underway through the wall). Then, after counting heads, I left them to it.

I was slightly nervous about going back into the Woodward living quarters again, but with the job still to be done, I pushed Amelia from my mind for the time being; I would have time for her later. I went straight for the device Sebastian had used to create his master key and created twenty-one new keys for rooms all up on the fifth floor. I knew it to be completely deserted, and I was unsure which rooms on the second, third, and fourth floors were free, and I didn't feel right about loading them into rooms on the first floor, although I supposed that might happen at some stage, now that we had almost entire families in hiding. I kept my ears open the whole time I was working on the keys, but I never heard a sound. I hoped that meant Amelia was asleep and not that she was still standing naked in the bathroom.

I returned to find that nobody had gone for breakfast, and that several of them were dozing on the lounges, their bags at their feet. I had some difficulty getting them all up, but once they were all ready to go, I took them all up to level five and began giving each of them a key and ushering them into each room, trying to put people from the same families next to each other. This job turned out to be the easiest thing I had done all evening, as they were all eager to get into their rooms and settle down. Once I was alone again, I went back down to my room, jumped in the shower, gave myself the first of what would be many energy boosters that day by squeezing the crystal and making it wake me up, then went down to ground level for breakfast just as others in the rooms around me were doing the same.

Chapter 13: Day Trip

I didn't take much time over breakfast, feeling anxious to go and find out what had become of Amelia since the last time I had seen her. Perhaps, on some subconscious level, I wanted to get to her before Marc did so that I could speak to her alone. In any case, most of the time I was in the dining room I spent filling people in on what I had done during the night—those like Peter and James, who had known, and those who hadn't, like Marc and Tommy. The only mention of Amelia came when Serena asked if I had taken her along, to which I responded that I hadn't. I wasn't sure she believed me, though, perhaps because she could detect that I was avoiding mentioning something about Amelia.

Unfortunately, to my irritation, Marc finished his breakfast at the same time I did, and since he had already decided to go and see Amelia before I could even mention that I hadn't spoken to her already, there was no chance of talking him out of it. I intended to go along with him anyway, though; it would have been most irresponsible of me as a friend not to, after the state I had seen her in last night. To his irritation, though, Peter entered into the discussion with a suggestion that made me enormously grateful that he was my adoptive brother; he still felt more like my brother than Marc did, even if he and I were growing closer with every passing week.

"Did you see—that guy again?" he asked.

"Er, no," I said, knowing who he was talking about. "Didn't get around to it."

"Good," he said, cracking his knuckles. "Listen, I don't mind doing it. Don't worry, I'll give him a chance to answer the question before I rearrange his face."

"You can't even get in there, Peter," said Kylie sweetly, taking one of his hands tenderly in hers. "Just calm down, okay? No need to get—"

"No need? No need?" he repeated, glowering at her.

"There certainly is a need to ask him if there's anyone else in here that needs to be put away," said James firmly, "but I tend to think it would need to be done by someone with some sort of magic; otherwise, we won't know whether or not to believe him. Even in there, he could still put one over us. I guess they would all need to be fed and watered too; maybe you should do that too, Marc, as you know the order of things in there."

Marc opened his mouth, clearly not happy that this job had been delegated to him, but after all, James's logic made sense, as it always did. He nodded stiffly.

So while he did that, I went back into the Woodward living quarters alone, nervous about what I might find in there. What I found was not at all what I expected. I didn't even get a chance to go and look for Amelia down the hallway, because her grandmother, Lillian Woodward, was in the kitchen, eating breakfast by the look of it.

"What's happened?" I asked, completely thrown by the idea that the Woodwards could afford to rest.

"What hasn't happened?" she asked bitterly, her words seemingly an echo of Peter's from the afternoon before.

"How come you're back here?" I asked, sitting down opposite her. "We've been watching with the crystals, and we didn't expect you to be able to come back for ages."

"Frederic's idea," she said thickly. "We have been using magic to keep ourselves energised for forty-eight hours, but he believes, as do the rest of us, that we would be more effective if we rested in intervals. I will be here until sometime early this afternoon, and then I'll have to go back out there so that Alice can come and take her rest."

"Does he actually want to win this war?" I asked, speaking the words I had thought over several times now.

"Of course he does," she said sternly. "Going out all guns blazing often leads to more trouble, as we learnt the hard way in the seventies. As it is, we've decided not to continue fighting them; it has become impossible to make a difference that way. Our aim now is to protect as many lives as possible while the fighting is happening. Then, once the situation settles down, we can begin to attack their strongholds again."

"That sounds extremely dodgy," I said uneasily.

"It's not ideal," she agreed, "but it's the best thing to do in the meantime. We will never be beaten as long as we have our magic and the crystals, as the Hammersons know, so protecting them is the most important job for now."

Reactive, I thought. Even with the disaster that the last two days had been, Mr. Woodward was still being reactive. Then, I had to remind myself, the Woodwards had won the first war, and that had been against three Sorcerers who had been in a similar position to the one the Hammersons were in now; I knew they had been because according to the research I had done a couple of years ago, no crystal chip had changed hands. Of course, I hadn't known about the crystals back then, but there had been no hint anywhere that at any point during the war, any of the Sorcerers had lost their powers.

How? What had they done to actually end it and cause the Hammersons to accept the treaty that had bound them for just over twenty-eight years? I couldn't remember reading anything about the final attack, the one the Woodwards must have launched in the final months of the war to weaken the Hammerhearts.

As much to change the subject as anything else, I asked her, "Did Natalie use that thing on you to protect your magic?"

"Ah, yes," she said approvingly. "That was a very good idea, John. There weren't many opportunities when our magic came under threat, but the few times armed Hammerhearts became suspicious of our presence, they certainly followed orders to neutralise our magic, so what you did certainly made a difference. How's Amelia? You still haven't sent her out?"

"Actually, that's what I came in here for," I told her. "She hasn't been great, but since I didn't see what she was like when Moran had her and Natalie didn't have time to tell me, I'm not sure if she's getting better or worse. Nobody's really had a chance to get her to talk yet, so I'm not sure how she's doing."

The only fact that made part of that statement false was that I knew perfectly well she wasn't doing well, based on what I'd seen last night, but Lillian didn't need to know about that.

"She's asleep at the moment," Lillian told me. "I looked in on her half an hour ago when I first got in; her door was open. I will be going to bed shortly too. You can wake her if you like, but be prepared for a bad mood—she doesn't normally like being woken up, especially by someone she's not expecting to see in her room."

I could have kicked something, but the fact of the matter was impossible to deny, so I spoke it. "I guess maybe Marc should wake her, then, although she's probably wanting to sleep all day. I have no idea what she was doing last night after we said good night. While I remember…"

I told her about the incident on the stairs and the answers I'd got out of Sebastian afterwards. Her face darkened as I spoke.

"Thank you," she said finally when I was done. "Thank you for sorting that out, John. That boy could have done so much more damage if he'd been allowed to run free much longer. I'm sure Frederic will be most relieved when I pass this news on to him."

"I expect so," I said, getting up and feeling disgruntled at the mention of Mr. Woodward, "and when you tell him about it, remind him that Sebastian had him just as fooled as everyone else."

I left before she could respond.

* * *

The day was cool, windy, and overcast at around one in the afternoon when I stepped through the back door of 2-94 and into the Woodwards' study. Harry, Simon, Misty, Michelle, and, just for the hell of it, Peter were right behind me. Everyone but Peter was completely visible; he was the backup, armed with as many magical devices as he could handle and wearing ghost goggles to look out for other invisible people. The rest of us had to remain visible; not doing so would have made it just about impossible to deal with the Maivises' crazy grandparents.

I was expecting the day to be about as quiet and lifeless as the night had been, but I was surprised. Some places were lifeless, such as the high school, hospital, police station, and court building, but otherwise the town central was just as active as it always had been. I thought I understood why: The local radio station, 3CV, was back on the air, as was one TV station (though the latter was being run by the Hammerhearts), and both were claiming that, for the time being, the fighting in Australia had ceased, at least on an official scale.

This was true too; all the fighting was now being done overseas, and no other countries were bothering to attack Australia now because the Hammerhearts were operating the worldwide takeover predominantly out of the United States. Moreover, as more and more countries in Asia came under quiet attack, it was impossible to know just how many countries had changed hands. The Hammerhearts' first tactic in every case was to use their bogglers and avoid spilling blood wherever possible. It was only the countries who became aware of the danger they were in and put up a struggle who were subjected to worse. The job had become extremely easy because many so far untouched countries were tearing themselves apart in anticipation, trying to determine if there were traitors in their midst. All we could gather about their progress was that they seemed to be gradually moving west across Asia—they would probably be in Europe by the end of the day, if they weren't already.

Meanwhile, on our own soil, there were still vigilante groups around, either taking advantage of the lack of control in the area or attempting to prevent the Hammerhearts from establishing their principles as law. But apparently as long as there was no mass fighting, civilians felt reasonably comfortable coming out in the open and doing their business as usual. This was both a comfort and a discomfort to me. It meant that it would be safer for us to walk around in the open—probably, but it might also mean that we were all in greater danger than we knew. Then again, if anyone in Chopville believed the story that I was a criminal, I might be in greater danger either way.

Flint Street was just like the rest of Chopville. Most houses appeared to be empty, but a few had televisions or stereos playing inside them, and one man was mowing his front lawn. There was an alley between a couple of houses on the south side of the street that led into the grounds of Chopville Primary, and as we passed it, I could see at least a dozen children making use of the basketball courts and play equipment, despite the fact that the school itself was closed.

The Maivises' house was around the corner (like Lopher Lane, Flint Street had a bend in it) and was one of the houses that appeared deserted. Considering how scared they had been the night before, though, and considering they were both retired, I doubted very much that it was. That became perfectly clear when either Misty or Michelle (I couldn't tell them apart as I could their younger brothers) unlocked the door and we all walked inside.

"Cyril!" a terrified shriek sounded from a room I couldn't see, though I expected it was the kitchen. If she believed we were enemies, yelling at the top of her voice was just the perfect way to hide herself, make it difficult to find her, and drag her away. "Cyril! Come quick!"

Harry and Simon swapped amused grins, while Misty and Michelle appeared rather disconcerted by the sound of their grandmother's voice.

"Don't worry, Mrs. Maivis," I called in the direction of the voice. "It's only me, the bloke who called last night."

"Mistake," all four twins muttered in unison, just as the woman let out an ear-splitting, hair-raising scream. I had described the phone episode to them a few hours earlier.

"*What!*" roared the man of the family from the other end of the house, and even over the din, we heard him clearly, thundering down the hallway towards his wife.

"Do you two wanna go in their first or should we?" Harry asked the two girls.

"You all wait here," I told them quietly. "Go sit in the lounge room or something while I go in there; they might attack you the way they're going. Peter, wherever you are, just keep a lookout."

"Sure," I heard him say from the front door.

"But if they might attack us, then they'll definitely attack you," hissed either Misty or Michelle.

"Yeah, probably, but I've got the crystal," I muttered back.

Too late. Before any of us could move, Mr. Maivis burst into the hallway, holding a cricket bat across his body, ready to swing.

"Hello," said Simon cheerfully. "Heard you gave John here a hard time last night. Didn't we ever tell you how some of our friends find it perfectly normal to land on the doorstep at two in the morning?"

"Course not," one of their sisters answered him. "You couldn't tell them that, or it would make them wonder about what you were doing at two in the morning. As if you'd do anything other than sleep at that hour."

"Sleep? Them?" said the other sister. "Two in the morning? Well, that's not what Katie and Sophie say, but I suppose they could be just talking."

"If Katie and Sophie were ever just talking," said Harry, "then they would only be selling our performances short. It would be impossible for anyone to overestimate what we do at two in the morning."

I had to gape at the four of them. I certainly wouldn't have been this comfortable discussing such personal matters so openly in front of Hilda or Violet, or even William and Carl when they'd been alive. Hell, I hardly would have said things like that in front of anyone other than Peter or James and the twins themselves. I wasn't completely surprised that Harry and Simon had no issues with it; it went with everything else I knew about their characters, and it would explain why their grandparents had always tried to make it so difficult for them to do the sort of things they talked about. What did surprise me was that Misty and Michelle seemed quite as comfortable with it as their brothers, although I wondered if the same could be said if they were the subjects and not Harry and Simon. Most importantly in this situation, though, the way they were talking seemed to convince their grandfather, as nothing else could have, that these four were his grandchildren for real. Their terrified grandmother, who had come in halfway during the exchange, was looking just as convinced as her husband.

"Harry, Simon, Michelle, Misty," she said firmly, "I want all four of you in the lounge room right now. Go on, get in there. You're never going back to that madhouse again."

"I was under the impression that I had just stepped *into* a madhouse," said Simon, raising his eyebrows.

"No cheek from you," she snapped at him, "or any of the rest of you. Move!"

"Er, maybe I should step outside for a while," I said hesitantly.

"No, you'd better stay," said one of the sisters (it was so annoying not to be able to tell them apart), "or they might murder the lot of us."

"You!" she howled, pointing dramatically at me, her eyes popping. *"You! Do—you—have—any—idea—how—much—stress—you've—caused—us? Get—out—of—our—house—or—I'll—call—the—police!"*

"If he's who he says he is," said her husband, his voice not raised but nevertheless full of anger, "then apparently the police are already after him. Of course, it doesn't surprise me that the boys would take to criminals, even if that boy hadn't been a criminal when they met."

"If you believe that crap, then you two must be Hammerhearts in waiting," said Harry boldly. "You should know they've taken over the media, and you're still prepared to swallow it? Besides, the police aren't even in town anymore."

"Actually, as I told you both last night," I said, my voice as calm as I could make it, even though my insides were boiling at the accusation, and it cost an effort not to touch the Sien-Leoard Crystal and make them regret ever saying such a thing, "we want to bring you both into protection, where the Hammerhearts can't get to you. I told you these four were safe, and now you can see that for yourselves. What else do I have to do to convince you I'm an honest person?"

"Forget it, John," said Simon quietly.

"Get out of our house," said Mr. Maivis, just as calmly as before. "I don't ever want to see you near our grandchildren again. I don't want you bringing trouble down on us like you did my son and his wife. We are grateful that you brought them back to us unharmed, though, so we won't call the police, but if you don't get off our property right now, we will."

"What do you want me to do?" I asked the four teenagers.

"They don't say, *I* say," said Mr. Maivis, a little more sharply, lifting his cricket bat ever so slightly, the implication clear. "Go now, before I change my mind."

I ignored him and focussed on the teenagers, Harry and Simon in particular. In unison, they both shook their heads, and I understood that to be my dismissal, but I also understood that they were not abandoning me or the Woodwards. They would be in touch, one way or another.

"Okay, see you, then," I said and, feeling unaccountably saddened, turned and walked back out of the door, hesitating a moment before shutting it, just in case Peter needed a moment to get out of the house. It wasn't until I was a few steps down the garden path that I realised: That could well be the last time I ever see any of them. The Hammerhearts knew about the Maivises—what if leaving here was tantamount to signing their death certificates?

"Geez," Peter muttered beside me as we reached the street. "I know you said they were difficult last night, but I wasn't expecting it to go like that."

"I should have just used the crystal," I said, furious with myself. "I should have just done what Amelia did to them when she was sorting them all out for Stella's party. They're even crazier than our family."

"We can come back for them," said Peter. "They'll have to let someone come back or let them come back to us, as most of their stuff is still in the Woodward base. We could take it back to them and get them out at the same time, always assuming Katie and Sophie don't kill us first—they're gonna be furious when they find out about this. Anyway, gotta stop talking now, or you'll look like a madman."

"True," I muttered, and I set off down Flint Street back towards the main road, ignoring Peter's sniggers all the way.

By the time we turned right onto Main Street, Peter had gone completely silent. Then, as we passed Grillion's canteen, the closed sign on the door making it one of the sorriest sights I'd clapped eyes on since coming out that day, I felt him move up beside me.

"Keep moving," he hissed at me, "over the bridge, away from the Woodwards."

My stomach fell in slowly dawning horror. What was going on? Not wanting to look as though anything had just happened, I straightened my posture and walked past the entrance into the park and onto the Main Street Bridge. I kept walking, waiting for Peter to whisper something else to me, and about halfway across the bridge, he did.

"Put a shield around us. They've got guns as well as magical stuff."

Now my head was spinning in panic. Who were they? And would they react to me putting my hand in my pocket, around the crystal? It seemed likely, if they had any idea about exactly how armed and dangerous I was, but that may or may not be the case, given that these people could just as easily be regular cops sent out here by Hall as Hammerhearts sent by the Hammersons themselves. Not until later would I consider that if they were regular Hammerhearts, their orders would be to bring me in alive so that Hammerson could deal with me in person. However, on balance, not acting now would be far more dangerous whenever they decided to attack. So I put my hand as casually in my pocket as I could, trying to look as though it was something I did absentmindedly while I walked, and formed the thought in my mind that would put such an invisible shield around me and Peter as he had suggested. I felt it work, and to my very temporary relief, nothing happened.

"Keep moving," Peter moaned, and now I could feel him right beside me, forced to walk close to me by the shield.

"How many?" I hissed out of the very corner of my mouth.

"Not sure—maybe twenty or so. Can't we just teleport out of here?"

I didn't dare to respond, but my greatest worry about that was the possibility that they might have others waiting for us at the Woodwards' house—surely, they must know that I would be heading back there. We would go back there, of course, but only after I had found a way to throw off all pursuit. How was I to go about making that happen?

We walked off the bridge on the other side and continued along the road. Now I began to worry about where on earth we were supposed to be going. It was important that I look like I know where I'm going, but where was I supposed to go now? Doubling back wasn't an option, especially as, judging by Peter's movement, my invisible pursuers were back there. So where could I go in this direction? I only had to give it a second's thought: The Playman house on Lopher Lane was the only suitable option. Marc's and Tommy's houses were also up here, but not good options; I had no reason to go to Tommy's, and Marc's house would be far too dangerous today—they could call for reinforcements who could come at me through the Hammerheart Highway and trap me inside. So it was towards Lopher Lane I directed my steps.

"They're encircling us," hissed Peter, a block from Lopher Lane.

My hand was still in my pocket, and I kept thinking thoughts that would continue to keep the shield around us as strong as magic could possibly make it. I wondered briefly if I should just give myself the ability to see them, whether by making them visible or making myself see invisible people, as the goggles could, but that would do no good. If I could see them, they would quite likely notice the difference in my eyes. I just had to trust that, when they attacked, the shield would protect us for as long as it took to knock them all out.

Now I could…not hear them, but sense them, moving around me. Some were still behind us, but there were some on the road beside us, moving around to cut off the footpath ahead, while others already in front of us seemed to be preparing to cut off access to the houses to my right. It was extremely unnerving, knowing they were there and trying to look as though I knew nothing at all. I kept walking, my head spinning in such panic that I almost felt as though

I was gliding along the footpath. They were going to attack very soon, yet I still hadn't decided how I would deal with them when they did.

I was about twenty feet from the corner of Main Street and Lopher Lane when the first gunshot split the air. I saw a flash of light as the bullet, aimed for my head, deflected off the shield and disappeared. I stopped dead and stood as still as I could, looking around me, hoping against hope that the shield was still working and that nobody in the houses around us would come out and put themselves in the line of fire. As it turned out, most people who had heard the gunshot were already pretending not to exist.

Six or seven seconds of silence, in which the attackers may have been deciding what next to do now that they had exposed themselves to me (not visibly, but I couldn't possibly not know that they were there), and then a thunder of shots. They seemed to cancel all other sounds, make them non-existent. The rattle of automatic fire roared on and on as bullets rained all around us, demolishing fences and letterboxes, exploding the tires of cars and smashing their windows, cutting through trees and causing branches and in some cases entire trunks to fall on top of nearby houses, ripping through front doors and smashing the windows of houses, clanging loudly off garage doors and ricocheting at angles. They whistled all around us, but although they were all being aimed directly at me from all angles, they all seemed to veer away as they came into contact with the invisible shield around me.

The firing suddenly stopped, leaving a ringing silence in its wake. The distant sounds of hustle and bustle that had echoed across the river from the town central before the attack seemed to have ceased. In the past, there might have been a distant siren approaching, excepting the attack on Tommy, at which time the police had been otherwise distracted. No such luck this time, because the police were the ones doing the attacking in the first place. I had no idea if any of them had survived the firing; it would have made sense for some of them to have been shot by their fellows' rogue bullets, but if any of them were gravely injured now, they were keeping their silence.

I was still standing, and completely unhurt. I felt sure that the attackers around me were stunned that I could have survived such an attack, were perhaps wondering now just what sort of magic I possessed that could have protected me, and understanding why the Hammerhearts wanted rogues like me out of the way. Peter was still beside me, just as invisible as they were and just as unharmed as I was. I probably could have continued to stand there, let them continue trying to attack me and failing every time, but then I thought of Mr. Woodward and how much trouble had been caused by waiting, and I immediately changed my mind.

I firstly thought of the twenty of them, assuming Peter had the number right, and flushed them all into visibility. They popped into sight all around me, and I saw that, though they had positioned themselves carefully so that they wouldn't hit each other—incredibly, seeing as none of them were wearing goggles like Peter—they hadn't banked on bullets ricocheting off me at angles. About a third of them were on the ground, at least three of them dead and the others gravely wounded. The ones that were still on their feet were completely stunned to find they could suddenly see each other, and within seconds, they had all dropped their weapons and raised their arms in surrender. I felt sure that they had been warned to do that if I showed signs of having magical power.

"Don't attack, sir," one man called out from my left; he looked like the leader, so I turned slowly to face him. "Come quietly and there will be no trouble."

Odd, I thought. I didn't give it a second thought. A moment later, he was unconscious on the ground. One by one, I knocked them all out, making it so that they would come back to life exactly an hour from now; that ought not to cause too much trouble. When the last officer had fallen, a complete silence ensued. Peter and I now stood in the middle of a ring of bodies, and the sensation was not a comfortable one. There were people watching through the smashed windows of houses, while more were creeping up the sides of the street, some taking video footage on their phones and digital cameras, all the better to get a look at what had happened, and I knew exactly how it must look to them: I was clearly every bit as dangerous as the Hammerhearts were claiming. Nothing could have lowered my spirits more than to see the looks of fear on their faces, especially as many of them were faces I had known by sight all my life.

Unable to face it any longer, I gripped the crystal again and made myself invisible. They only needed to know that I was gone, not that Peter and I were still wandering among them, still protected by the shield around us.

"Can't you just teleport us back to the Woodwards'?" Peter moaned as I walked us both past a row of unconscious police officers and onto someone's front lawn.

"No, we've gotta try to fix some of this up," I muttered back.

Peter groaned, but I ignored him. Whatever he said, I felt a large responsibility for what had happened here. These people had damaged property—their houses, their cars, their fences—and all because I had come walking down this way. I therefore spent the next three quarters of an hour using magic to, firstly, heal those officers who had been shot and were still alive (I didn't think they were Hammerhearts, so they didn't deserve to die on my watch), and after that was done, repair as much as I could, all the while keeping the shield around us both, as those who witnessed my work were terrified by the possibility that an invisible person was nearby. I couldn't get it all done in that time, but by three o'clock, it seemed a good idea to get out of there, before the cops came around. Peter sighed dramatically when we appeared in the Woodwards' silent study, which was blessedly deserted.

"They're not watching the house," he breathed. "Thank God. I was worried that they might have sent someone to head us off down here once they knew you were out."

I didn't bother replying until the pair of us were back through the door into the second-floor room we had used to get out. The door had been there the whole time, and anyone who had bothered to feel along the wall would have found it, but I could only hope the magical camouflage I had put around it before leaving had been sufficient protection.

"I'd thought of that too," I said finally, once we were safely secured inside the base. "What I wanna know is, now that we know they've got people around town waiting for me and the others, why didn't they just park themselves outside the Woodward house? They know that's where I'd most likely come out."

"I guess they assumed you'd just teleport to wherever you're going," said Peter, "and come to think of it, we should have just done that."

I sighed. The day had been a complete waste. What had we achieved? Apart from losing both sets of twins for as long as it took them to escape the clutches of their lunatic grandparents? Absolutely nothing, unless getting three police officers killed just for doing their job, however off that job was, counted for something.

"We'd better go and tell everyone what's happened," said Peter. "Oi, make me visible again, would ya?"

I obliged, and we both descended two floors to the lounge room, where I was unsurprised to find Marc and Tommy, working their crystals as they had been doing the previous day. What was surprising was that they were the only people in the room.

"Not much of a crowd," said Peter observantly, sitting down just inside the doorway.

"Yeah," said Tommy, looking up at us. "Dunno where everyone else is; a few in the library, but most of them are probably upstairs."

I sat down beside Peter and, feeling suddenly more tired than I had for a long time, hurriedly put my hand in my pocket and used the crystal to give myself another energy booster.

"You seen Amelia yet, Marc?" I asked him.

He shook his head. "Went in there a few times, but she's been sleeping the whole time. I'm starting to think she's used magic to put herself into some sort of enchanted sleep, and I'm scared to try to wake her up. I might have to soon, though; this is getting really disturbing, what's going on with her. How did it go at the Maivises'?"

"Terrible," said Peter at once. "Not only did we fail to bring them in here, we lost both sets of twins in the process. I think we'll be able to get them back eventually, but I'm worried about what might happen before then."

"What do you mean?"

We described the episode that had taken place in the Maivises' hallway. Marc and Tommy, neither of whom had ever met the twins' grandparents, were astonished and horrified by what had happened.

"We'll go back and get them in the night," said Marc. "Harry and Simon have never had trouble sneaking out at night. I can't see how they could struggle this time. Even if they do, I reckon our crystals can get around whatever their grandparents are gonna do to keep them under."

"What if they move away from Chopville before the night?" asked Tommy.

A brief silence followed that ominous thought. Then Marc said, "I guess we just teleport to wherever they are and bring them in that way. We can track them down wherever they go, I expect."

"There's something else too," said Peter. "When we were coming back, I was invisible but John wasn't, and he was attacked."

We did our best to describe the attack that had taken place. Surprisingly, however, neither Marc nor Tommy was as disturbed by it as I was. They should have been, seeing as they were in exactly the same sort of danger I was.

"Guess that settles it," said Marc. "You were way too casual out there. Even if the fighting's settling down, it'll never be quite so easy for us. We'll have to teleport everywhere we go from now on, I reckon, and be invisible when we can't."

More or less what Peter had said, and I supposed it would have to be the case. I hated that I would have to be so careful whenever I went out from now on, but until the Woodwards turned things more in our favour in this country, that would be a way of life.

"Well, on a lighter note," said Tommy loudly. "Marc, why don't you fill them in on the latest developments in the war."

"Aw, geez," muttered Peter. "What now?"

"Well, they've got complete control of every country in North and Central America," Marc told us, "and good amounts of control in most parts of Asia. They had to set off a few bombs, though, in China, India, and Russia, 'cause there was too much resistance, even with the bogglers. They weren't nuclear bombs, though, just—well, relatively small ones. So far, the only country who've been able to stand up well under the attack is Japan, but it's only a matter of time before they go under too; there's too much coming in on them from all sides. They've started in Europe too, from the east and working their way across."

"One of the bombs, though," said Tommy. "Natalie was right in the middle of the blast."

It was as though my world had ended. Natalie? In a bomb blast? But then my reason caught up with my frantic senses; Sorcerers can't die, no matter what harm comes to their bodies. That was a slight comfort, but that didn't change the fact that Natalie would have suffered beyond anything a person is meant to suffer, what would have killed anyone else instantly. Shades of Nicole, I thought, except that Nicole didn't have the protection of the crystal chip like Natalie did. I wondered vaguely what sort of magic Natalie would have needed to do to regenerate her body and wished, more than ever, that it was she who would be returning to base rather than her grandmother. Perhaps she would, if she was so badly shaken up.

Then, without warning, the mental image of Natalie in a bomb blast changed; I was once again drawn back to that image of a body, smothered in blackness and bursts of flame, obscured by smoke. I tried to put Natalie's body in place of the one I had always seen there and found that I couldn't; the image was unchangeable. It was nevertheless a relief to know that, if that vision meant anything, it wasn't anything to do with Natalie. After a short struggle, I pushed it away.

"Is she okay?" Peter asked.

"She is now," said Marc. "She's already fighting them again, but it wasn't good. Can you just imagine it?"

"Apparently it destroyed her body," said Tommy in a low voice. "She would have felt it for a moment, but mostly she was unconscious. Had to wait for Mr. Woodward to come and perform the magic to regenerate her body around the chip."

Nobody spoke for a long time after that. Finally, when my watch said twenty to four, I remembered that I still had another job to do that day, and my stomach lurched.

"Marc, have they done anything in England?"

"Huh?" he looked up, startled. "No, not yet, but I think they will really soon. They definitely have people over there, and at least one bomb that hasn't gone off yet, but the way they're working their way across, the UK should be safe for at least a few more hours."

"I've gotta go over there," I said.

"What?" they all exclaimed, and Marc added, "How come?"

"Underwood," I reminded them. "He works in the government over there. He'll be right in the line of fire when they try to take over Britain."

Marc groaned. "Are you saying we have to bring him into protection too? What for?"

"It's because of us that he doesn't have any protection," I reminded him. "I suppose it's not very fair to bring him in and nobody else, but I think we have a responsibility to him now."

"He's right," said Tommy, "but maybe we should keep him away from Lena while he's here; he'll recognise her and likely give her a hard time."

"Yeah, and Amelia too," I added. "Geez, how are we gonna manage all that?"

"You could keep Lena locked up in your bedroom," said Peter, grinning slyly at me. "As for Amelia, well, she doesn't wanna come out here these days anyway."

"We can work out something," sighed Marc. "I'm not gonna enjoy having him here, though, and he won't enjoy it either. He's gonna know we organised to get his life assistant; he might try to get it back off us while he's here. That's assuming he agrees to come—he certainly wasn't keen on coming in a month ago."

"Actually, you know, he should, whether he likes it or not," said Tommy sharply. "If the Hammerhearts get hold of him, if they somehow realise he's related to Smiley—and I guess it's possible, even if they haven't worked it out all this time—they might go hunting after him all over again."

"I thought they *were* hunting—" Marc began, but Tommy shook his head.

"It's just a feeling I've got," he said. "I just think that if they find out about Underwood, about the life assistant, they might redouble their efforts to get at him. Does anyone know where he is, anyway?"

"Somewhere safe, hopefully," said Marc. "So, John, are you going to England now?"

"The sooner, the better," I said. "What time do you reckon it is over there?"

"You tell us. You've been there most recently," said Tommy.

"It's nearly four here," said Marc, "so it's probably early morning over there; seven or so. Yeah, I agree, the sooner, the better. Today's almost certainly the day they'll go for Britain. Did you want to do it alone?"

I considered, then shook my head. Having Peter with me had been an advantage today, so maybe having someone with me in England would serve an advantage too. Whatever I had just decided, I would need to be visible while dealing with Underwood, so having someone invisible with me could turn out quite useful.

"I'll come with you," said Marc, reading my thoughts on my face.

"Me too," said Peter, getting to his feet.

I had misgivings about bringing them both along, but as the three of us reached the second floor, I realised I wanted the company after all. I did not want to do this job alone.

Chapter 14: Misfire

Returning to England was as simple as walking through a couple of doors. The room I had used last time was still set in the apartment I had briefly lived in during my stay, and that apartment would still be mine; I had paid for two weeks and most conveniently not told anyone when I had left, so desperate was I to get as far away from Underwood as quickly as possible. After all, it wasn't as though they could track me here. Now, it meant that we could just walk straight into it and not have to worry about finding a convenient location to set the door down.

On the other side, the first thing I noticed was the sky outside. It looked as though Marc had been quite right—seven in the morning looked a likely time out there. The second thing I noticed was how quiet it was; the apartments were all small and the walls thin, which meant that sound normally travelled fairly easily. It had been easy to listen on conversations next door and possible to make things out from apartments two or three doors down. This morning, however, the only sound was the wind battering against the building outside, and I didn't put the lack of noise down to the hour because a few days ago, I could quite clearly hear people getting up around me at this time of the day. The silence was ominous. I couldn't help feeling that even though the Hammerhearts hadn't launched an attack here yet, the locals were fearful that it would come anytime now. Standing in my old apartment, I understood exactly how they felt.

Peter was invisible and goggled once again. Once I had camouflaged the door again, he followed Marc and me out of the apartment and up to the next floor to where Underwood lived. I was feeling very nervous by the time we reached the top of the flight of stairs and turned into the dusty hallway. How would Underwood react to seeing me and Marc again, particularly so soon after losing his life assistant? I couldn't imagine it being anything pleasant, but it was most certainly necessary. As we reached Underwood's door, however, Marc stopped dead, and I saw that he was casting his mind outward.

"He's not home," he said softly.

"He's not?" I repeated, stunned. In all my contemplation, I hadn't considered that possibility. I had assumed that he would be smart enough, given the gravity of the war and the absence of his life assistant, to only leave his home when it was absolutely necessary.

"Shit," breathed Peter, whose mind had wandered down a different path from mine. "You don't reckon they've dragged him off?"

"It's possible," said Marc. "If so, we might be able to tell from having a look in there."

"Should have just waited 'til now to nick the damn life assistant," grumbled Peter.

"Shut up, man. You're supposed to be pretending not to be here," hissed Marc, concentrating on the door before us.

It clicked and swung open, and the three of us went inside. Marc's hopes were dashed at once, because there was no sign whatsoever of a struggle. Peter shut the door behind us (that looked eerie), and the three of us just stood in the small lounge room, looking around, listening to the silence.

"Okay, so what are the options?" asked Peter, trying to sound robust. "Could he have stayed out drinking all night?"

"Possibly, but given that it's Friday morning here—"

"What time does he start work? Does anyone know?"

"I'm certain he doesn't do night shift," I said. "I don't know if people in his job even have a night shift."

"Marc, are you absolutely sure they haven't taken anyone in the government hostage?"

"They hadn't," said Marc. "No, unless they came here for him, they couldn't have got him. It would have had to happen yesterday, and nothing had happened as recently as an hour ago."

"Maybe he's done a runner, then," said Peter. "You know, soon as he's realised he has no protection, and the coups have started everywhere, he probably thinks his best bet is to distance himself from the rest of his life as much as possible."

Marc and I stared at each other, both considering Peter's words. Now that they were spoken, they seemed like the most likely option. Good, I thought. If that was how it was, then perhaps Underwood would be more persuadable to join us. I supposed that would depend on exactly where he was now and exactly how tough he was doing it.

"Well, let's find out," I said, and I gripped the Sien-Leoard Crystal and sent my mind outward, searching for Underwood as I had once sought Rebecca Fletcher. On that occasion, I had known she was on the floor above me but not which room she was in, so I had asked the crystal to take my mind straight to her.

Now, I tried to do something similar to Underwood, and the crystal sent me away from the apartment building and out over early morning London. I zoomed along for some time until I was forced downward. A moment later, I was looking into a small stone house where Underwood appeared to be taking refuge. I was disgusted to see that he was lying, fast asleep, beside yet another woman. No, not a woman—a girl. She could have been as young as Natalie, probably even younger, yet it was immediately clear that they had interacted just as intimately, probably more so, than he and I had done. The crystal told me several things in quick succession about this scene: He was not supposed to be here, and the girl would be in a load of trouble with her parents if they found out she was sleeping with a man so much older than her. She, it seemed, was actually his regular girlfriend—at least, she thought so. After everything, he'd been seeing someone else all along. I wondered what that girl would say if she knew what I (Lena) had done, or what Stella had done.

I withdrew and after some more time found myself back in my body, staring at Marc. He was staring back, waiting impatiently, and I wondered why he didn't just follow me; he was perfectly capable of doing so, or perhaps he didn't realise he could just ask the crystal to take him there instead of getting there himself.

"We can just teleport there," I told them both. "He's sleeping with some other girl—his girlfriend, apparently—but we can just go there and get him, no problems."

"Good, so he's not in any danger?" asked Peter.

"The only danger he would be in is if her parents catch him," I said, smirking. I wanted that to happen, very much.

"Fantastic," said Marc, clapping his hands. "So we just go there, ask to see the girl, the parents go in and find the girl in bed with him, they kick him out of the house, and we can do whatever we want with him. Sounds like a plan."

"Geez, you came up with that one pretty quickly," said Peter, impressed.

"What if they don't get her?" I asked. It seemed all too likely. After all, we were complete strangers to them, and around the right age that the parents would more than likely think we were after the girl for exactly what Underwood wanted her for. Perhaps they knew their daughter well enough to think that we were boyfriends they didn't know about. If they had any idea what sort of guys she went for, this would seem quite likely.

"Well, we can use the crystals if we have to," said Marc.

"We can pretend we're boyfriends of hers," I said, wanting to bring them inside my imagination. "This could go badly, but if she's the sort of girl I think she is, and her parents know that, they'll probably believe us. They'll go dragging her out of bed, find Underwood in there—like you said, Marc—and then it'll be on for young and old."

"How much assault are we likely to come in for?" Marc asked nervously.

"I'm not sure," I conceded. "A bit, most likely, but we knew that before we came here, right?"

"I like the plan," said Peter. "Just one thing first: Did you see if her parents are out of bed yet?"

"No," I said. "All I saw of the parents, all the crystal told me, was that they were both there, because Underwood was scared of being discovered by both of them."

"Is he awake now?" asked Marc.

"No, he and the girl were asleep."

"What's the girl's name?" asked Peter. "Obviously you'll need to know that if you're gonna convince anyone. Imagine if they have another daughter."

"Geez, I didn't think of that," I muttered. "Blimey, what're we gonna do about that?"

"We can grab that out of their minds when we get there," said Marc, "and we can use the crystals to wake up her parents if we need to. Right, anything else?"

"What's the excuse for both of you being there?" asked Peter. "I don't imagine that two partners calling on the same girl at the same time would be too chummy with each other."

"Um, maybe John could be the partner, and I could be his mate?" suggested Marc, shrugging.

"No, I reckon we have a fight over her," I said. "That'll be more convincing; it gives us an excuse to come calling on her at this hour to start with. We can pretend we're both drunk and we've just discovered that we're sleeping with the same girl, and we both wanna confront her. The parents will more likely throw us both out than let us see her in that state, but they'll still be mad enough with her to go and wake her up and hopefully bust Underwood."

"Here's a suggestion," said Peter suddenly. "If you're gonna use magic, why don't you just use it to drag Underwood out of the house? It'd be much simpler than what you're trying to do."

"I wanna do this," I said. "I wanna ruin this as much as I can for him—a way of paying him back for what he's done to Amelia, and just for the jerk he is."

I knew better than the other two because of all the additional time I had spent around him. It had taken me, even in Lena's body, five full days to work him into the perfect position to snatch the life assistant, but through all that time, if my objective had been to get Underwood to have sex with me, I could have achieved it at pretty much any moment of my choosing. He had been physically attracted to Lena from the moment he had seen her and, now I knew, would have had no qualms about cheating on his real girlfriend on the spot.

The only reason I had taken so long to visit his apartment at night-time was to minimise the possibility of having to have sex with him without ruining my chances of getting the life assistant. Unfortunately, even though she had only tried to help, Stella's interference had only made him more cautious.

"Me too," said Marc fervently. "So, if we're gonna be drunk, we'll need to look and sound it without actually mucking with our minds, and if we've been fighting, we'll need bruises—"

We spent the next few minutes altering our bodies accordingly. By the time we were done, we both looked pretty stonkered indeed. We might have gone a little over the top with the bruises. They didn't hurt at all, but I was having trouble seeing out of my blackened right eye, and Marc was quickly becoming irritated by the amount of blood that kept dripping from his nose; though again, there was no pain at all.

"Geez, that's pretty spectacular," said Peter admiringly.

"You bet," I said, nodding, enunciating each word heavily. I was actually quite startled by what had just happened because I'd actually tried to say "yeah," but it had come out completely differently. Apparently, the charm did more than just make my voice sound drunk—it made me speak as though I were drunk too.

"We gonna do this thing or what?" Marc asked, speaking in the same sort of voice as I had just done.

"Yeah, man, let's go kick some arse."

"Are you two sure you can teleport like this?" asked Peter.

"Hey, come on, man, I'm not really drunk," said Marc indignantly, and anyone who'd heard that and not been aware of the charm we'd put on ourselves would have burst out laughing. "Fuckin' 'ell, man, this is weird, eh?"

"Yeah. Hey, yeah!" I said, and for reasons I couldn't understand even at the time, I collapsed to the floor, unable to control the fit of laughter that had just taken hold of me.

"Right," said Peter uneasily from above me. "Well, as long as you don't forget to teleport me along with you. Now, remember what you're supposed to be—"

"Hey, man, give it a rest," said Marc. "We know what weh doin', o'right? Jus' trust us."

"Okay, I'm ready," I said, staggering to my feet. It was much more difficult to move now than it had been five minutes ago.

I felt for my crystal, almost dropped it, got a hold of it again, and concentrated on the house in which I had seen Underwood and his girlfriend. A moment later, the three of us (two, as it looked) were standing on the front lawn of that very house. Still holding the crystal, I sent my mind inside the house in order to get a better idea of what was actually going on in there. The house was quite small, but the family was bigger than I had originally anticipated. Mum and Dad were having breakfast together, and by the look of it, he was only a few minutes from leaving the house for work. There was also an old man, one of their fathers, quite likely. In addition to them, there were two brothers; they were both maybe less than ten, shared a room, and were presently fast asleep. Most importantly, Underwood and his girlfriend were still asleep, and I had to think that he'd be lucky to get out of this one, even if we didn't interfere. The scene was as good as it would ever be.

"Her name's Siobhan," I told them both, a little more loudly than I'd intended, and I clapped my hand to my mouth quickly to stop myself babbling anything else.

"Cool," said Marc. "So, should we do this thing, then?"

"Yeah, let's go for it."

"Try to look like you hate each other," Peter said nervously. "Er, what do you want me to do?"

"Rugby tackle Underwood if he tries to do a runner," I said. Once again, I was seized by a fit of laughter, and I had to work very hard not to make too much noise. I had half a reason this time, though; Peter was small and skinny, the last person in the world who would ever be capable of laying a rugby tackle.

"Remind me never to get you drunk," muttered Peter. "Okay, I'll stay outside, then. Good luck."

Marc and I turned and staggered up the path to the front door, bumping shoulders a couple of times and almost falling over sideways. When we reached the door, Marc thumped on it with the palm of his hand, tried to shout Siobhan's name, and was interrupted halfway through the word by an enormous hiccup.

"Get out of it!" I snapped at him and, elbowing him out of the way, banged on the hard, wooden door with my fists. "Siobhan! Siobhan! You in there? Who do you think you are, you dirty slut! How dare you—"

The door flew open, as I'd been waiting for it to—I wasn't sure how long I could shout insults at a girl I'd never met. Unfortunately, Marc was back in action, and what was meant to be a hard knock on the door turned into a blow to the midriff of the family father. He grunted and staggered back a step, his face red with rage.

"Who the devil are you?" he whispered. "What the ruddy hell are you doing, coming here at this—"

He stopped dead, staring at us, and I felt quite sure it was the combination of our youth, our apparent injuries, and our obvious binge drinking that had completely thrown him off his game.

"Mr.—um, Siobhan's old man," I said, wishing I'd bothered to check what their surname was, "where's that dirty daughter o' yours?"

"Get off my property," he hissed, making to shut the door in our faces.

"*No!*" Marc and I roared in unison, hurling ourselves through it and knocking the man to the floor as he tried to back out of the way.

"Stanley?" called a woman's voice from the kitchen. "Stanley? I'm calling the police."

"*Siobhan!*" Marc bellowed at the top of his voice, and I joined him. "Siobhan! Get out here right now!"

"Oh," I added, seeing that I was still on top of Siobhan's father, and I scrambled off him. "Um—sorry, man. I was only wantin' to see Siobhan, and see if it's true what this fuck-arse said."

"What'd you call me?" Marc asked, getting up and clenching his fists. I had to admit to myself, whatever mess we were digging ourselves into, we were playing our roles magnificently. I just hoped Marc would stop before actually hitting me; he looked ready to.

"You 'eard me. I never wanna see your face again."

"Fuck you," he spat. "Siobhan? Where is she?"

"Get out! Get out!" roared Siobhan's father. He was back on his feet now and looked ready to force us back out the front door. "If I ever see you near my daughter again—"

"What?" I said indignantly. "Come on, man, didn't she tell you I'm the guy she's been seeing the last few months?"

"She's been seeing me!" roared Marc.

The man looked from one of us to the other, and I thought I saw, to my slight surprise, comprehension dawning on his pudgy face.

"Out, both of you," he said gruffly, grabbing my arm and swinging me back out the door with such force that I felt like my arm could have easily broken.

"*Oi!*" I yelped. "Man, that hurt. What you doin'?"

"Go and get that girl," I heard him say to his wife as he ejected Marc in the same fashion.

"She's got a window," I said loudly to Marc, except it was the father I was really speaking to. "I know, I used it to get out o' the house before I could get caught."

"I know, I used it too."

"*Siobhan!*" her father roared, our words having exactly the effect we'd been hoping for. "Get out here right—"

We both heard a shriek from the other end of the house that sounded like the man's wife, and I knew that Underwood hadn't got out the window in time.

"Change back," I said to Marc. "Time to make ourselves normal again—we done enough. Now we just gotta get Underwood before he gets away."

"Yeah, yeah."

We both dipped our hands to our crystals, and about five seconds later, our bodies had returned to their normal state. The door was shut by this stage, so we both hurried around the side of the house, looking into the windows as we went for the one I had just described. We caught sight of the two young boys, both of whom were wide awake and watching through the glass with interest as we passed. Siobhan's window was the next one along, and when we reached it, we saw a most satisfying sight indeed. The room was full of people: Mum and Dad, both standing over Siobhan, who was still lying in bed, caught red-handed. Underwood, meanwhile, was standing right beside the window. Judging by its half-up position, he'd been on the point of attempting escape through it when the door flew open. To add insult to injury, he was buck naked.

"What is this, Siobhan?" her mother asked. It was easy with the window half-open to hear every word.

"Um—well—I was going to tell you," she said nervously.

"Don't you go anywhere, young man," her father said threateningly to Underwood. He couldn't have gotten away anyway, not without getting uncomfortably close to Siobhan's father on his way out the bedroom door. "Siobhan, what is going on? Who is this man? And who are those two piss-pot boys who claim to have your interest?"

"Um—what?" asked Siobhan, raising her head slightly.

Her father gestured to the window, where Marc and I were now perfectly visible. They all looked around at us at the same time, and it was one of the funniest things I'd seen in a long time. Where the old boy in there had been thrown by the less than impressive state Marc and I had been in before, now he was thrown by the complete opposite. Siobhan's eyes were as round as coins as she stared at us, and the look on her face, if either of her parents had seen it, would have convinced them that she'd never seen us before in her life. Her mother only gave us a cursory glance; not having seen us in our apparently intoxicated state, her gaze had quickly shifted back to Underwood—she looked reproving, but she couldn't seem to stop her eyes lingering on his impressive biceps. He, meanwhile, was gawping at the pair of us through the window. He mustn't have been too worried about whatever Siobhan's parents had in store for him, because his colour had only drained when he had recognised the two of us.

"You," he whispered, his jaw hanging open.

"Jacob?" said Siobhan uncertainly, her eyes shifting onto him. "Jacob? Do you know them?"

"Jacob, is it?" her father said forcefully. "Well, Mr. Jacob, you're coming into the kitchen with me now, and we're going to—*come back here!*"

Too late. Underwood had turned and pushed roughly past him, and never mind the undesirable contact. The man turned and hurried after him. Siobhan made to follow (fortunately for her, she was at least wearing something), but she was stopped by her mother. The woman picked up Underwood's long since discarded clothes, threw them out the window at me and Marc (we leapt backward to avoid contact with them), and stared at us hard enough to drill holes in our faces.

"Who are you?" she asked coldly. "Where do you know our daughter?"

"I don't know them," said Siobhan weakly. She sounded afraid to speak. "I've never seen them before in my life."

Marc and I swapped amused looks. Neither of us cared one way or the other what Siobhan or her parents made of this situation. Now that we had sufficiently stuffed up Underwood's forbidden and probably illegal relationship, our goal was to grab him and take him back to our apartment, preferably out of sight of the family; they didn't need to associate us with magic.

And speaking of Underwood: The man himself suddenly appeared around the corner of the house, still naked, still furious, running straight at me and Marc. He was rather larger than both of us (only a little taller than Marc but considerably broader), and suddenly it looked like we might have to use magic after all. Before either of us could lay a finger on our crystals, however, Underwood was unexpectedly rugby tackled by an invisible someone who had been lurking quietly by the house. Despite his size, the surprise was enough to make him stagger; they both went tumbling to the ground just a few feet short of me and Marc. I couldn't see Peter, obviously, but I could just imagine him struggling to cause the naked man as much trouble (without actually hurting him too badly) as he could. To cap the scene, Siobhan's father appeared at the end of the wall at that moment, and for the third time that morning, he stood stock-still, staring at the struggling man on the ground before him in complete astonishment.

The excitement of the morning was too much for Marc; he collapsed to the ground, howling with laughter. I was tempted to join him, but I could see a number of potential problems that kept my head on straight. Underwood was quickly working out what was happening to him, and it was only a matter of time before he would have Peter on the ground. The longer Siobhan's father stood there, the greater the chance that he would also get involved in the struggle. Through the window, Siobhan was doing all she could to make her mother let her come outside, never mind the fact that she was only wearing a nightdress. Worst of all, the police that Siobhan's mother had called earlier were pulling up on the street out the front of the house at that very moment.

It was extremely difficult to decide what to do first and how to go about doing it. In the time it took me to make up my mind, the two police officers were halfway onto the lawn and Siobhan's father had turned away to meet them. It seemed clear enough that the most important thing to do was prevent the cops from taking Underwood, but unless he put some clothes on in a hurry, that was going to be very difficult indeed.

"Marc, help me here," I said as, gripping the crystal in my pocket, I caused Underwood's clothes to teleport off the lawn near the window and onto Underwood's body as though he had done it himself. The act achieved the dual purposes of covering those parts of Underwood that nobody but Siobhan really wanted to see and giving Underwood such an enormous shock that he accidentally let Peter go—at least that was what it looked like, though it was hard to tell without seeing Peter.

Marc regained his feet admirably quickly. He used his crystal to drag Underwood to his feet and back him against the wall. He and I moved forward together, and as we drew level with Underwood, Marc muttered, "Shut up your face, you're on our side now."

"Fuck you," spat Underwood.

"No thanks, I'm not the one around here wanting to do that," laughed Marc, glancing over his shoulder at Siobhan's window. "Oh, shit."

I looked quickly over my shoulder, and my stomach fell. Siobhan's mother must have hurried to join her husband, because Siobhan had dressed quickly and was now scrambling out of her window to join us.

"No," I moaned. "No, go back in, go back."

"Teleport," said Peter's voice—he had also regained his feet now and was somewhere on Marc's right, "quickly, while we still can."

"I'm not sure we can," murmured Marc, watching Siobhan jump down from the window and turn to face the three of us whom she could see.

"Who are you?" she asked fiercely. "What are you doing here?"

"We just wanted a quick word with this bloke," said Marc, waving his hand at Underwood, "but when we checked his place, he wasn't home, so we had to come here. Sorry to drag you out of bed and all."

Her lips tightened; for a moment, I thought she would scream at him loudly enough to wake all the neighbours, if any of them were still in bed. Underwood still looked angry, but it was clear that he was just as keen to keep Siobhan out of this as we were. He intervened swiftly.

"Go back inside, Shiv," he said, moving slightly toward her. Marc tightened his hand over the crystal, still hidden in his pocket. "It's okay, I've got this."

"You know them?"

"Sort of, unfortunately," he said, glaring sideways at us. "Just go back inside. I'll be in in a bit."

"But—"

She was staring past me and Marc. I made to turn, but before I could get all the way around, a hand fell hard and heavy on my shoulder. Too late to teleport now, I thought, as I squinted up into the face of the police officer holding me. The other one had seized Marc while Siobhan's father, perhaps having received permission from the officers, had grabbed Underwood by the arm and was attempting to drag him back towards the front of the house. This time, there was no one to stop Siobhan from screaming at the top of her lungs.

"Dad! Let him go!"

"Get in the house!" he bellowed over his shoulder at her. "Not one more word out of you, young lady! In the house—*now!*"

"Names, you two?" said the officer with such a tight grip on Marc's shoulder in what could only be described as a business-like tone.

"Marc Moran, John Playman," said Marc automatically.

"No," moaned Peter very quietly.

I opened my mouth; to cover the awkward moment, I was going to say, "we're not from here," but I never even got started. Neither officer seemed to have heard Peter at all. At the sound of our names, they both leapt back in horror. For maybe two seconds, they stared at us in disbelief. Then, to my complete surprise, they both yelled, turned, and sprinted back to their patrol car, clearly as fast as they could. They jumped in and took off immediately, forgetting their seat belts and, in the case of the one on the far side, to close his door.

"What happened there?" asked Marc blankly. "Did you do that?"

"No, I thought you did."

"They must have believed the story," said Peter, "about how you two are armed and extremely dangerous. Can't be very good cops to run like that, though."

We were recalled to our surroundings at that point by the almighty racket Siobhan was making. Her mother had joined the fray and was trying to shepherd Siobhan into the house. Underwood had, surprisingly, allowed himself to be led back into the house by Siobhan's father. Marc, Peter, and I took off, back around the front of the house and through the front door, to see Underwood backed against a wall, Siobhan's father holding both his shoulders.

"What have you been doing to my daughter?" he snarled.

"Noth—"

"*Don't you 'nothing' me!*" he roared, shaking Underwood so hard that his head bounced off the wall behind him.

Crystal time, I thought and, gripping it, caused the man to leap backwards, waving his arms in the air as though they had been burnt. I moved quickly over the threshold and advanced on the man, feeling disgusted with myself; what on earth was I turning into lately? Marc, meanwhile, had taken Underwood by the arm.

"You're coming with us, dude."

"To hell I am!"

"You okay, man?" I asked Siobhan's father kindly, making to help him regain his feet, but the man hurriedly scurried away from me across the floor, looking so crab-like that I had trouble keeping a straight face.

"What's all this noise?" asked a very croaky voice indeed, and an old man entered the room, leaning heavily on a walking stick. "What are you doing, Stanley? You should have left for work ten minutes ago."

Siobhan and her mother entered through the front door.

"Don't touch them," squeaked Siobhan's father as his wife made to grab Marc's arm. "They're not normal people."

"Sure we are," I said. They didn't need to know a thing. "Er, we'll just be going now. Come on, Marc—bring him along."

Underwood tried to jerk away from him, but Marc grabbed him by the arm. His other hand was in his pocket, so he had no trouble dragging Underwood across the floor to the front door. Underwood's feet seemed to slide along the floor as he struggled. Siobhan's parents seemed all for letting the three of us out of the house, but

Siobhan herself wasn't having a bar of it. She wrenched herself free of her mother and stood to block the doorway.

"I want to know who you are, both of you."

She looked aggressive, and I wished devoutly that we could just teleport out of here and never mind who was looking. After the reactions of the police officers, however, I had a very nasty feeling about doing that. Before either Marc or I could say something, however, she screamed and dived forward into the house, almost knocking Underwood over as she tried to hold on to him. I glanced sideways at Marc, about to ask if he'd done that, but before I could get a word out, I heard Peter say very quietly from outside the door, "Finger in the back gets 'em every time."

"I want to know who this is," said Siobhan's mother, taking her daughter's hand again and dragging her away from Underwood. "What were you doing with this man, Siobhan?"

"I told you I would," she snapped. "If you'd just said yes, I wouldn't have had to sneak around."

"*What did you say?*" her father thundered ominously.

"Time to go," I muttered to Marc, and we dragged Underwood out of the house.

A few steps past the front porch, however, our progress was impeded again. Siobhan's father had grabbed Underwood's free arm and was attempting to drag him back into the house. Underwood, it seemed, had little preference about where he wanted to be at the moment; he didn't try to pull in either direction but allowed himself to be pulled in both directions at once. Siobhan was screaming at her father to let him go, but he took no notice. I took care of the situation by moving around in front of Marc and facing the two men—the older of the two screamed and jumped back, letting Underwood go, and that was without me needing to do any magic at all.

"We've got company," said Peter's voice from about where I had been before.

I wheeled around to stare at the street, and terror froze me where I stood. The officers that had jumped and run upon learning our names had apparently called for reinforcements, but the people pulling up out the front and jumping out of the cars (there had to be at least twenty, probably more) were hooded, masked, and carrying the sort of weapons that shouldn't have been available to police officers of a country not being controlled by the Hammerhearts, though some of them were armed with guns just like the ones I'd faced only hours earlier. I immediately put my hand in my pocket and sprung up an invisible shield around Marc, Peter, Underwood, and myself, dragging the four of us very close together. I completely forgot to do anything for Siobhan's family—a colossal mistake.

"What the hell are you doing?" snapped Underwood, struggling against the invisible shield.

"Stay still!" bellowed Marc.

The four of us froze where we stood as a line of Hammerhearts spread out along the footpath and, without wasting a second, opened fire. Bullets shattered the windows and cracked the walls. They flew at our shield and, as they had not so long ago on the other side of the planet, shot off at angles, splintering the fences on both sides of the house. Jets of light flew around us from solid-outliners and agonators. Blunt flashes of purple light indicated the reflections the bludginators caused when they were deflected. Ropes shot from still more devices and, just like the bullets, ricocheted from us at angles.

"*Oi!*" roared Siobhan's father, waving his arm to get the attention of the attackers; his shout couldn't possibly have been heard over the constant automatic fire. "This is my—"

A jet of golden light connected with his unprotected hand and he dropped to the ground, writhing and screaming. Now his body was completely unprotected by the four of us and, a few seconds later, several bullets ploughed into him, ripping him apart. From behind me, I could just hear Siobhan and her mother screaming.

These Hammerhearts seemed much more accomplished at this sort of task than the central Victorian cops had earlier. They all moved quickly forward, careful to stay in a perfectly straight line, never letting up on their attack. The noise around us was thunderous, and the house behind us sounded like it was falling apart. As they drew close, I realised that we would have to attack them; if they reached the shield, they might know a way to remove it. I gripped my crystal and began making the weapons in their hands disappear. As each was disarmed, he or she would drop back and follow behind the rest of the armed Hammerhearts. When Marc joined me in the attack, however, the unarmed quickly outnumbered the armed, and those with nothing to do but watch quickly constructed a new plan of attack.

"Stop them!" Peter cried, as several of them skirted around the four of us on the garden path and shot straight into the house, but it was too late for that.

Five…four…three…two…one…zero. With them all disarmed, I felt it would be safe enough to remove the shield, but no sooner had I done that than ten of them jumped on us. Peter managed to slip away somehow, but the three of us were besieged, and the intention couldn't have been any clearer: get the crystals. I clamped my hand over mine and managed to use it to throw four of them off me before they could grab both my arms.

I then managed to get completely free for three seconds, and that was enough to do something I'd meant to do ages ago: immobilise Underwood and teleport him back to our apartment. I had to immobilise him because I knew perfectly well that he would be long gone by the time we got there if I didn't. With him out of the way, that would greatly simplify things here. I wasn't too worried about Peter; he was invisible, and now that the firing had stopped, he could stay safe just by keeping a good distance from the Hammerhearts. Now it was Siobhan's family I had to worry about; it was our fault (well, partly Underwood's fault but more directly ours) that they were in this mess at all.

It was Marc's turn to do magic. It took him only five seconds to knock out the five Hammerhearts wrestling with him. Together we were able to do the same to the four who'd given me such a hard time a moment earlier.

"That wasn't all of them," gasped Marc, bending over and clutching his stomach. "What—"

His voice was cut off by an almighty bang. I spun around again, just catching sight of a streak of blood out of the corner of my eye. Three of the previously disarmed Hammerhearts had, at some point, gone back to the cars and gathered up new arms; they were now running straight at me and Marc, and I did the only thing I had time for: dive. More bangs. I felt the whoosh of the bullets passing above me. Knock them out, knock them out—and all three of them collapsed just feet from me. I straightened up and looked around me quickly for signs of more Hammerhearts, and what I saw made me feel ill.

Several of the Hammerhearts that had run into the house had come back out. They had been chasing Siobhan's mother, by the look of it. What they'd wanted with her was anyone's guess, but it had been the three with the guns who'd got her; the bullets that should have hit me hit her instead as she'd run out of the house. Her bloody remains had fallen very close to those of her husband. Four more Hammerhearts were on the ground, having fallen over her as she'd fallen in front of them. I quickly dealt with them before they could regain their footing.

"John!" Peter called, and I could now hear him running towards me. "Oh my God—John!"

I had no idea what to say to that, so I said nothing at all. Instead, I turned my attention to Marc, who was on the ground beside me. He was definitely alive; the bullet looked as though it had gone straight into his thigh, only missing his manhood by a few inches. I looked at the wound. It didn't look good, and I didn't believe I could fix it quickly. But I couldn't leave him here. He'd be a sitting duck if any more Hammerhearts turned up. I knocked him out as I had the Hammerhearts, then put a thick, invisible shield around him.

"John—on your right!" Peter bellowed from behind me.

I looked around and, seeing what was coming, dived right over the top of Marc's shield, landing hard on my stomach on the other side, temporarily knocking the wind out of myself. Five more Hammerhearts had come out of the house; the last of them, I felt fairly sure. They were armed with knives they'd most likely stolen from the kitchen. I knocked two of them out with the crystal before being forced to move. Scrambling back to my feet and backing away from the house, I found myself beset upon by the remaining three, who had their knives raised. I had time to knock the one on the right out before the other two decided they didn't have time to continue advancing, and they charged me. I ducked out of the way of one, and Peter, displaying perfect timing for the umpteenth time that day, tackled the other one to the ground and nicked his knife. It was a pretty big achievement for him to have done that to both Underwood and another man, as he was so much smaller than both of them.

I scrambled around on all fours, the crystal still clenched tightly in one of my fists, and knocked the last two out. Then I just crouched there on my knees, hardly able to believe the struggles I'd faced that day. A wave of exhaustion suddenly crashed over me with the force of a tidal wave, and again, I drew much needed energy from the crystal. Slowly, very slowly, I pulled myself to my feet and looked around me. All was still and very horrible.

"Where are you, Pete?" I asked, hoping more than ever that he wasn't hurt. Apart from being my brother, he'd paid his way today more than I could ever have believed.

"Here," he said. He was only four or five feet away, and it sounded like he was just getting to his feet too. "John, there were other people in that house—Siobhan and those two boys, and that old man."

My stomach lurched; I'd forgotten about the rest of them in the wake of the two deaths I'd already witnessed. I turned back to the house and cast my mind out towards it, wandering through the rooms, examining the devastation the Hammerhearts had managed to cause inside it. The old man was on the floor almost exactly where he had been when we'd left the house, a knife protruding from his chest, a trickle of blood running down the side of his face from his mouth. The two boys had taken shelter in their bedroom; they were both hanging over the side of their beds, their throats slit. Siobhan was the only one still alive; she had slid under the sofa at some point before the Hammerhearts had entered the house. They hadn't found her, and it looked as though she intended to stay there for several hours—or forever.

"Blimey," I said. It was all I could have said.

"Well?" Peter enquired. "What's happened in there?"

"Siobhan's the only one still alive," I said hollowly, and Peter swore. "Listen, I'm gonna go in there and try to get her out. She'll freak out even more if she's approached by an invisible man. You stay here and keep a lookout."

"Sure," he said, "but John? Is Marc gonna be okay?"

"I don't know," I said truthfully, my stomach twisting. If those bullets were the same as the sort that had killed William and Carl, we were in a world of trouble. It would be even worse this time because I felt sure that the bullet was still in Marc's leg. The Hammerhearts would be in trouble too, of course, as surely the Hammersons still wanted to bring him in alive, but that would mean very little to us if Marc died. "Maybe—maybe you should keep an eye on him too, in case he gets worse before we can get him back."

I trudged toward the house, weaving around the bodies on the ground, walking straight past Marc with only a sideways glance. As I drew level with Siobhan's parents, however, I paused. Siobhan had already seen the destruction of her father, but she didn't need to see the way they were now. I used magic to separate their bodies (it was much easier than working out whose remains were whose), then levitated them into two magically created coffins, as I had seen Mr. Woodward do in the wake of Lisa's death. I then proceeded into the house, stepping over the bodies in the doorway.

Siobhan hadn't moved a muscle since I had mentally investigated the house. When I crouched down on the floor to peer under the sofa, she cringed away from me.

"You've gotta come out now."

"Get away from me, you!"

"No," I said, after a moment's hesitation. I could understand it from her perspective; her life had been fine before Marc and I had turned up, and now look what had happened. At the end of the day, however, she was the only one left, and she couldn't stay here alone. I didn't know what other family she had, but as far as I could see, the only person left for her now was Jacob Underwood. It was on the heels of that thought that I realised, and I could have groaned: She would have to come back to the Woodwards' too. "The fight's over— you need to come out."

"Go away!" she screamed. "Get away from me!"

"No," I said firmly, using the crystal to tip the sofa onto its back so that she was completely revealed. I took her arm and pulled her to her feet, staring into her face all the while, trying to convince her that I wasn't going to hurt her. She looked back at me, her eyes full of tears, her face tight with anxiety. She didn't trust me one bit, I could see that, but she seemed to recognise the truth of the situation.

"Where are they?" she asked, and I didn't know if she was talking about the Hammerhearts or her family.

"Come outside," I said, leading her back into the hall and out into the body-littered front yard. Her eyes fell on the two coffins a few feet from the door, and she let out a wail of despair.

"Wait here," I told her loudly, hoping Peter understood that it would be his job to make sure she did as she was told. "I'll be back in a minute."

I went back into the house, feeling extremely hollow inside. All I'd intended to do was find Underwood and bring him, perhaps kicking and screaming, back to the Woodward base. I certainly hadn't intend to wreck an entire family. Yet here I was, wandering through their house, rounding up their dead bodies. I removed the knife from the chest of the old man and put him in a coffin like the other two. The two boys took a little longer to find, as I hadn't been in that part of the house before, but I had, of course, seen where they were only minutes earlier. I levitated them into coffins, then, crystal held before me, levitated the three coffins out into the yard. Siobhan had apparently been far more interested in the fate of her family than the Hammerhearts, because when she saw the three coffins floating towards the first two, she broke down completely. I wished I'd left Underwood here after all—I wasn't qualified to provide comfort to someone who wanted nothing to do with me.

"What do you want to do for them?" I asked, approaching where she knelt.

She didn't answer right away; she was clearly too preoccupied. I waited impatiently, my mind straying to Marc and back every few seconds. Every minute I spent sorting this mess out could be ticking away any chance of saving Marc's life.

"Bury them here," said Peter from right beside me, making me jump (Siobhan appeared not to notice). "We don't have time to do much. We can bring her back here later if she wants to do more for them."

He was right; Siobhan didn't look like she'd be able to think straight for several hours at the very least. I had to remind myself she was probably not much older than me, and how it would be for me to lose Mum, Dad, Hilda, Nicole, and Peter all at the same time, bearing in mind that I would have been more used to the idea of death than someone like Siobhan, who wouldn't have been touched by the war until now. I moved onto the lawn, onto the largest patch of grass I could find, shifted the unconscious bodies off it, and then used the crystal to lift an enormous section of earth into the air. Down went the coffins, landing in a neat row on the bottom of the pit, a good ten feet below the ground, and then down went the earth, covering them up completely, the grassy lawn appearing exactly as it had moments earlier. That would have to do for now.

"Time to get out of here."

"What about these guys?" Peter asked. "What're we gonna do?"

"Nothing. They'll come around in twenty-four hours and no harm done. I couldn't give a damn what the Hammerhearts make of me and Marc being here. Come on."

I went back to the porch and removed the shield around Marc. Then, concentrating hard on the apartment many miles away, I teleported the four of us away from the battle field. The first sign that I'd done it right was the sound of Underwood's furious voice. "Let me the fuck out of—Shiv?"

I looked around me. Marc lay on my left, Siobhan knelt on my right, Peter was somewhere around me, and Underwood stood, still as a statue, in front of me and slightly to my right.

"Let me go, man!" Underwood snapped at me. "What the hell do you want me for, anyway?"

"Bringing you into protection, whether you like it or not," I snapped right back. I'd been through too much to want to argue with him now.

"Why do you care?" he asked. "You already got what you want out of me. Where's the life assistant, eh? What did those bitches you sent do with it?"

My stomach dropped, but I ignored him. The door back to the base was only feet in front of me; I levitated Marc into the air, removed the camouflage (Underwood swore loudly at the sight of the door), and guided him through it. I took him right through and lay him on the bed in the room before returning for the other two. Underwood couldn't move, and Siobhan wouldn't move—so it seemed anyway.

"Pete, wherever you are, help me here," I said, gesturing at Siobhan while I moved toward Underwood.

"Who are you talking to?" snapped Underwood, and for a moment I feared I'd left Peter behind at the house.

"Make me visible and I will," he said from behind me.

I obliged, watching Underwood's jaw drop in astonishment as the boy appeared out of thin air in front of him.

"Come on, then," I said, and without bothering to mobilise him, I used the crystal to drag him through the door, through the control room, and into the second-floor room. I turned back for Siobhan, but Peter was already leading her through; she still wasn't exactly calm, but Peter seemed to have at least temporarily gained some of her trust, probably because she hadn't seen him in the fight. I closed both doors, cutting off any means of escape either of them might have considered, locking us all in the room. Now, it was Marc who demanded my attention.

Chapter 15: Confusion

"Where are we?" Underwood snapped at me. "And who the bloody hell are you?" he added to Peter, glaring at the way it was he whom Siobhan was leaning on. I briefly considered remobilising him, then remembered Marc and decided against it.

"Never you mind," said Peter, frowning at him. "John, what are we gonna do?"

I looked at the door, trying to think straight through the panic threatening to overwhelm me. How could I be sure that Marc had been poisoned by the bullets that had taken William and Carl's lives? I still had the Sien-Leoard Crystal, but if I tried to check what was in Marc's body, the bullet might respond too quickly for me to stop it, as had happened last time. The longer I stood here, the less chance Marc would have of surviving. In the meantime, Underwood was stuck in this room, with nowhere else to go and no knowledge of what was around him. I would have to bring Amelia up here (there was no other choice), but what would the consequences of that be?

"You guys stay," I said. "Pete, make sure they don't go anywhere. I'll be back."

"Righto," said Peter, depositing Siobhan in a seat at the table and pulling one out for himself. Underwood stood like a noisy statue in the middle of the circle of couches at the back of the room, watching and glowering.

I left the room and hurried to the stairs, noticing that the living quarters were very quiet indeed (they had been all day, it seemed). I checked my watch as I went; it was just after six o'clock. Dinner would be starting soon. There were a few voices coming from the lounge room, though, I noticed as I descended the last flight of stairs (Katie, Sophie, Kylie, Serena, and Erica by the sound of it). And there was Tommy, waiting for me at the bottom of the stairs.

"John," he said in a quiet voice. "How'd it go?"

"Marc's hurt," I said hurriedly. "They shot him. We don't know if it's the same as what happened to you or not. You know where Amelia is?"

He looked horrified but said quickly, "No, but I think she's probably in her living quarters. Where is he?"

"Room 2-85," I said. "Peter's with him now, and Underwood— and Underwood's underage girlfriend."

"Aw, man," he said, and without another word, he took off up the stairs.

I hurried out into the corridor before the girls in the lounge room could wake up to my presence and went down it to the end. The

Woodward living quarters were closed, as always, and quiet, as was normal these days. Mr. Woodward's study was empty, of course, as was the lounge room, dining room, and just about every other room I passed. Lillian Woodward must have left by now, I supposed, because her room was empty as well. Unfortunately, Amelia's room was empty too, and that gave me a very ominous feeling. I was just thinking that I'd have to check the bathroom again and find a way to sort her out if she was in there like last night when she suddenly stuck her head around the side of the door to glance down the hallway at me. She had indeed been in the bathroom, though clearly in a more observant state than she had been the previous night. A good sign, I thought.

"John?"

"Amelia!"

I covered the distance between us in about six steps. Amelia stepped out into the corridor just as I reached her so that we could embrace. Too close, I thought almost immediately, as she rested her head on my shoulder and I gently patted her back. I could feel her very close against me, warm, vibrant, and thankfully not naked. She was certainly in a better state than she had been the previous night, probably the best state she'd been in since returning to the base.

I pushed her back slightly, though not letting go of her, so that I could get a look at her face. She looked simultaneously happy, relieved, and nervous. I could still sense an undercurrent of emotional turmoil, but at the moment, she seemed to be on a high, and I hated that I was about to bring her crashing down again.

"How are you?" I asked her.

"Okay," she said. "Been better but—" She sighed and rested her head on my shoulder again. "Nan told me what you told her this morning."

"Oh?" I said, trying to remember what Lillian and I had actually discussed while she had been eating breakfast, then assumed Amelia was referring to my recount of Sebastian's traitorous deeds. "Yeah. Well, it's what you expected, isn't it? After what happened last night on the stairs?"

"Yeah," she said, her voice muffled by my shoulder. "I dunno how we missed it, come to think of it. It's terrible."

"I know," I said. "Listen, do you wanna—you know—talk about things at all any time soon?"

I registered dimly that I didn't feel at all awkward saying those words. The only care I had to take (so it seemed) was in picking the right words to make sure that she understood she could confide in me. All the same, though, Amelia stiffened slightly in my arms.

"Yes," she said, not looking up. "Can I?"

"Do you think you can?"

"Maybe. I'm not sure. I'm not good at talking about things."

"If you could try, then that will really help."

"Yeah," she sighed. "If it's just you, though, not Marc."

"Why not?" I asked, my insides churning for more reasons than one. "He wouldn't be too happy about you only talking to me and not him, I don't think."

"He gets angry," she said in a small voice. "I know he doesn't blame me, but he doesn't make it—easy."

"Okay, then," I said. "Maybe we can talk tomorrow; I'm really tired tonight, been up since three o'clock yesterday afternoon. I need you to do something now, though."

"Sure," she said, straightening up and looking at me. "What do you need?"

It was my turn to stiffen; there was far too much subtext in that for my comfort, especially since she sounded almost exactly like Lena when she had said that. She didn't really look like Lena, though; she only looked like a sixteen-year-old girl who was extremely relieved to have someone she could trust. Both the look and the tone of her voice had made another part of me stiffen in a more excitable fashion, but I pushed it from my mind. This was no time to get carried away.

"Marc's hurt," I told her, "shot by Hammerhearts, and we don't know if the bullets are like what they used on William, Carl, and Tommy or not. Can you come and fix him up? 'Cause I'm not brave enough to try it again."

That wiped the smile off her face, as I had known it would.

"Shot?" she said, startled. "How? Where is he?"

"Upstairs," I said, taking her by the hand and practically dragging her down the corridor. "Did Lillian tell you I went out and brought a bunch of people into protection last night? Family members of Young Army people?"

"No."

"Maybe I forgot to tell her. Well, anyway, I did. I lost the Maivises, though, because their grandparents don't trust anyone. Anyway, we went to get Underwood as well, because we don't want the Hammerhearts to use him to track down Smiley all over again."

"You've brought him here?" she asked, her voice suddenly becoming little more than a squeak, but to her credit, she kept moving. We had just started up the stairs now, and behind me, I could hear the five year-nine girls following us up; they'd clearly heard my dialog from the lounge room.

"Yeah, just now," I said. "He was with his underage girlfriend when we busted him, but Hammerhearts caught up with us because the father called the police, and Marc got shot in the struggle. We had to bring her in too because her family—"

"Where is he?"

"Room 2-85. I just put him on the bed there."

"No, I mean Underwood."

"Um," I said, and the shifty tone in my voice was enough to make her stop dead. I stopped with her, and in those crucial seconds, the girls caught up with us.

"Is he in there?" she asked, her eyes blazing. "Is he in the same room as Marc?"

"Yeah," I said, feeling guilty and wishing I'd taken him somewhere else before fetching Amelia. "Come on, you gotta do this. For Marc."

"John," said Serena, tapping me on the shoulder. "What's going on?"

"We've got a situation," I said. "I'll explain in a minute. Come on, Amelia; we need you to do this. I'll take him away if that's what you need."

She had gone very pale indeed, and I couldn't blame her. Facing Underwood now would be almost as bad as facing Hignat and Wilwog. Behind me, the five girls were watching Amelia with concern, but Amelia had eyes only for me. She seemed rooted to the spot, and I could think of only one thing to do. I slipped my free hand in my pocket, closed my fingers around the Sien-Leoard Crystal, and used it to fill Amelia's head with serenity. It seemed to work—for now.

"Okay," she said, "but make sure he doesn't say anything to me. I don't even want to look at him."

"I'll keep him well out of your way," I said, knowing full well that Underwood would be in her direct line of sight the moment I opened the door.

"Who are you talking about, John?" asked Erica. "And do you know where James is?"

"I have no idea where James is," I said as we turned the corner and went deeper into the rows of rooms. "I assumed he'd be with you. As for who we're talking about, you'll see if you keep following us."

About a minute later, we reached the room. I could hear no noise coming from it as we approached, which was a good thing; I would have to use the crystal if an argument broke out between Underwood and the rest of us. I pushed the door open and backed into the room, doing my best to block Underwood from Amelia's vision. I took her to where Marc lay on the bed and left her with him before turning to look at what was happening in the rest of the room, and not until I saw it did I register that the silence was thick enough to cut with a knife. Underwood remained where he was, of course, being unable to move an inch—a statue of rage glaring over the top of the couches at those around the table. Siobhan and Peter also remained where they had been before, and now Tommy was sitting with them. Siobhan had her face in her hands and seemed to be ignoring everyone. Tommy's eyes were fixed on Marc and Amelia; he looked very worried. Peter, meanwhile, had turned his attention to the girls clustered in the doorway.

"You might as well come in, you lot," he said, "see if you can give this one a bit of cheering, since she won't listen to the rest of us."

"What the…" said Kylie slowly, entering ahead of the rest of the girls and pulling up a seat beside Peter.

"Very long story," he said, shrugging. "Er, Siobhan? Siobhan? Earth to Siobhan? Come in, Siobhan."

Siobhan lowered her hands slowly and raised her eyes at Peter. She appeared to have cried herself out of tears.

"What is all this?" she said weakly. "Where am I? I wanna go back home."

"They won't let you go anywhere, Shiv," said Underwood, scowling most particularly at me and Tommy.

"Actually," I said coldly, "I'll be happy enough to take her back home so she can get some things from there—invisible, of course."

"Oh really," he said, his voice sagging with disbelief. "You wouldn't dare do the same for me, though, would you?"

"Only 'cause we know you'll skedaddle," said Tommy, glaring at him.

"I wasn't talking to you, blacky," snapped Underwood.

"I might take you back as well," I said, "though I'll be using a lot of magic to make sure you can't escape. We won't put up with any crap from you, you understand?"

"Oh, really," he said again. "What the hell do you want with me, anyway?"

"We wanna protect you, you ungrateful bastard," snapped Tommy. "You work in the government over there—you'll be a sitting duck when the Hammerhearts attempt a coup, and we cannot afford for them to work out who you are."

"Yeah, that last part's all you care about, isn't it?"

"Shut up," I snapped. My attention had returned to Amelia, and while she was still bending over Marc, while she appeared to have already performed the most important life-saving magic, she was still far too stiff for my liking, unable to completely ignore Underwood's voice.

I felt a hand touch my shoulder again and jumped. Turning, I saw that it was Serena. She still looked confused, but she also looked worried. "John, what happened to Marc?"

"He got shot," I told her. "We got assaulted by Hammerhearts when we were trying to bring—that guy in."

"He'll be okay," Amelia said quietly. "It was those horrible bullets, but I've got the worst of it out of him. I can bring him around soon."

"Okay," said Katie, who was still standing with Sophie fairly close to the door, "and who is he?"

"I'm a complete stranger to you all, guilty of nothing more than being a descendent of a guy who used to work with that magic lot," said Underwood coldly.

"You're guilty of a lot more than that," said Tommy, just as coldly.

"And who are you?" Katie now addressed Siobhan.

"I'm no one anymore," she said, her voice cracking.

"She's his girlfriend, so it would seem," said Tommy, jerking his thumb in Underwood's direction, "although I dunno if she will be much longer if she finds out what he's like. Or, I dunno, maybe she likes guys like that."

"Shut up, you wanker," snapped Underwood.

"Don't cause trouble, Tommy," I said quietly, though I shot him a grin as I spoke. "This is gonna be ugly enough as it is."

"Yeah, it will," said Peter, getting to his feet, "so let's try to get some things organised while we wait for Marc. Anyone got the time?"

"Twenty-five past six," Kylie told him.

"Almost dinnertime," he said, thinking. "Er, Siobhan, maybe you should—"

"Dinnertime?" said Underwood loudly. "Where the hell are we?"

"Woodward headquarters," said Serena, "in Australia."

"Not surprising you'd be slightly jetlagged," laughed Peter. "Anyway, I was thinking you could both go down and have dinner, or breakfast, if that's how you wanna think of it, but, er, what are we gonna do about Lena, John?"

"Oh yeah," I said, thinking. I doubted that Underwood would say anything to Lena in front of Siobhan, not if he wanted to keep his affair a secret from her, but how could I be sure? "Maybe…Tommy, can you go and find Lena now and bring her up here?"

"All right," he said, getting to his feet, "but maybe I'll keep her out of the way until you've sent these two downstairs."

"Right," I said, turning back to Peter. "Anything else we need to do?"

"I guess they'll need rooms," he said, thinking. "Maybe up on level five, where you put the ones you got last night. I guess we will have to open that door again and let them back to get some of their stuff, though."

"I can do that after dinner," I said, and sighed. "Damn. I was really hoping I'd be able to sleep after dinner."

"Can I come with you, John?" asked Serena suddenly.

I glanced at Peter, eyebrows raised. If she could do the job as well as he'd done it today, then I had no issue with her coming.

"Yeah, I guess so," I said, "but you'll have to be invisible and wearing ghost goggles."

"If you say so," she said, looking relieved and partly surprised.

"How's he doing, Amelia?" Peter asked.

Amelia ignored him. She was still bending over Marc, now stroking his cheek. There was enough affection in that gesture for me to feel a pang of jealousy. Why hadn't I just enjoyed her more fully back in the hallway like I could have? Like she probably wanted me to? One glance sideways at Serena was enough to answer that question, and I felt disgusted with myself. No, John, you don't have to be the kind of opportunistic bastard who would cheat on his girlfriend and allow his biological brother to die a slow and terrible death just because he wanted a bit of pussy.

"Amelia?" Peter repeated loudly. "Earth to Amelia?"

She continued to ignore him. In fact, she appeared not to have heard him at all. I thought I knew what was going on and dipped my hand to the crystal. Sure enough, Amelia had erected a soundproof barrier around herself, much the best way to block Underwood out of her thoughts while she concentrated on Marc. I moved forward and tapped her lightly on the shoulder, making her jump. She quickly put the barrier down and looked around at me indignantly.

"What?"

"How's he doing?"

"He'll be fine," she said. "He's sleeping now."

"Okay," said Peter. "Let us know when you're ready to wake him up. Maybe you girls should all go down to dinner."

"All right," said Erica, "but I'm still very confused about all this."

"It's complicated," I said, "and it's pretty confidential, anyway. I'm not sure how much you're allowed to know about it."

"Nothing yet," said Amelia, "but perhaps you'll know more in time."

"Right," said Kylie, getting to her feet. "Are you coming down, Pety?"

"Soon," he said, his upper lip curling in distaste at the nickname. "I'm just gonna stay up here with Amelia for a bit. John, can you take them down to dinner?" He gestured at Siobhan and Underwood.

"Sure," I said, putting my hand in my pocket and around my crystal as I approached Siobhan and touched her shoulder with my free hand. "Do you wanna go down to dinner?"

I'd expected her to say no, in which case I would have taken her to make a key for her room instead. She surprised me, though. "Yeah, can I have something to eat?"

"Of course," I said, helping her to her feet and moving around the table towards where Underwood still stood. "What about you?"

"Do I have a choice?"

"Yeah, I suppose you do," I said coldly, "but I'm rather hoping you'll do the right thing and keep your girlfriend here company."

That got through to him. He scowled at me, but Siobhan met his gaze, and she was frowning. It looked as though she had got over her initial mistrust of the rest of us. I hoped, anyway.

"Fine," he said, "but you gotta take this bleedin' curse off me first."

I obliged, and moments later, the two of them were following along behind me out of the room. The halls were still empty, as was the main hall when we reached the rail overlooking the great expanse below us. I could hear noise from inside the dining room, though; it echoed up to us from two floors below. We descended through those two floors and went into the dining room, which was full with what looked like everyone still living in the base—although it only really packed about a quarter of the place. Underwood glowered sourly around at everyone, but Siobhan looked rather impressed. In fact, her expression looked similar to the one I'd probably worn when I first arrived here.

"You can work out what to do?" I asked them both.

"The food's up there, right?" Siobhan enquired, pointing at the conveyer belt.

"Yeah," I said, "and most of it looks like it's out already. I guess it would be a little weird since it would still feel like breakfast for you two, but just do your best. If you want something that's not already there, just speak to the conveyer belt and imagine what you wanna eat and it'll create it for you. Can you do me a favour and stay in here 'til I get back, though? That way I won't have to go looking for you to give you keys to your rooms later."

"Guess so," she said. Underwood made no response.

"And try to talk to people. They're all nice and friendly, and most of them around your age," I said, speaking more to Siobhan now. "I'm sure *they'll* keep you company," I said, pointing to where Serena, Kylie, and Erica shared a table that had three empty seats.

"Thanks," she said, and she smiled at me before taking Underwood by the hand and leading him farther into the dining room.

Siobhan will be okay, I thought as I backtracked out of the dining room and out into the corridor, heading back towards the Woodward living quarters. She seemed to have accepted her surroundings now. She was doing it tough after what had happened to her family, and she would probably break down again later on, but she'll be okay. Underwood, though, he was determined not to cooperate. I wasn't surprised, but I was disappointed. He clearly had no inkling of how much danger he had been in before. Why on earth hadn't Smiley clued him into how tenuous his position had been all this time? Maybe because he knew Underwood would never understand it. That certainly made sense to me.

I let myself into the Woodward living quarters, made the keys for Rooms 22 and 23 up on the fifth floor, and retreated back up to the second floor. I wanted to check on the progress with Marc before going back down to the dining room. My stomach rumbled unhappily and exhaustion threatened to take me again, but I pushed them both away for the time being. There were only five people in 2-85 when I opened the door—Marc, Amelia, Peter, Tommy, and Lena. Marc was still asleep on the bed, while the other four were seated around the table.

"Is it okay, John?" Peter asked.

"Looks like it," I said, shutting the door and pulling up a seat beside Tommy. "Underwood's still a sourpuss, of course, but Siobhan's doing okay. She'll keep him in line, I hope."

"What's going on, John?" asked Lena. "Have you brought him in here now?"

"Yeah, he's down having dinner now, and not happy with anything. You can understand why you're up here, though, can't you?"

"You don't want him to recognise me?"

"Exactly, but I don't think he's likely to give you too much trouble even if he does. Turns out he had a girlfriend all along, and she's with him now, so I doubt he'll wanna be seen with you in front of her. All I want from you is to leave them both alone. Stay out of their way if you can."

"That suits me fine," she said, smiling weakly.

"Geez, what a mess," moaned Peter. "We've got a guy who doesn't wanna be here now, on top of everything else. How do we know he won't do a Sebastian while he's here? Really take advantage of the place?"

"You really think the Hammersons would let him do that?" asked Tommy.

"Maybe not," sighed Peter. "Damn, I dunno. I'm exhausted."

"Me too," I said, "and I've still gotta go back out there."

"Is that really necessary?" asked Tommy. "We have loads of magic in here. Can't we just use that to get them what they need?"

"We can do that for Underwood," said Peter. "After all, he deserves no better. As for Siobhan, she probably wouldn't care."

"Actually, I do want to take Siobhan back," I said. "You saw what she was like when we teleported her away from her house—not up to anything. She deserves a proper chance to say good-bye to her family."

"Good point," said Peter, "but be careful, John; there's still a whole load of Hammerhearts lying around that house. Don't you reckon that would have attracted attention by now?"

"Yeah, probably," I admitted. "Don't worry, I'll use magic to make sure they don't know we're there. As much as I need to."

"Okay," said Peter, getting to his feet. "Amelia, maybe you should check on Marc now."

"Yeah, okay," she said, sliding out of her seat and approaching the bed again.

"I tell you what, though," said Peter. "I think I might go down to dinner. Getting hungry, you know. Been a long day. Lena, Tommy, maybe you two should come with me. Should I tell Underwood and Siobhan to come back up here when they're done eating, John?"

"Yeah," I said. "I told them not to leave until I got there, so yeah, just tell them to meet me back up here. That'll be the easiest way to organise tonight's stuff, I suppose. Also, tell Serena to come back up with them—she said she wanted to come along. And tell them to wait here for me, if I'm not here when they get here."

"Where would you be?"

"Well, I am hungry too, you know."

"Oh, yeah, okay, then," he said, and the three of them left the room, leaving me and Amelia staring at each other, both standing beside Marc's bed.

"You wanna wake him up?" I asked her.

"I guess so," she said, though she looked reluctant. "But—but are we gonna get any more privacy tonight?"

"Yeah," I said, "we can send Marc down to get something to eat when he's up to it."

She frowned, clearly unconvinced, but I stared her down, and eventually she nodded and turned her attention to Marc on the bed.

"He's okay," she said. "I think I can wake him up now."

We both pulled seats up beside Marc's bed and sat down. Amelia waved her hand at him, and he suddenly stirred to life, opening his eyes blearily.

"Hey, man," I said, grinning at him. "Welcome back."

"Hey," he said, trying to sit up, then deciding against it. "What's—am I—you got me out of there okay, then?"

"Yeah," I said, still grinning. "How much do you remember?"

"Um, not sure," he said, his eyes flickering to Amelia now. He looked relieved to see her by his side, and I felt another pang of jealousy. "I remember getting shot, and I remember you teleporting Underwood out of there. Is he here?"

"Yeah, he's fine," I said. "Siobhan's here too, though; her whole family was killed in all that. They're downstairs at the moment."

"Peter?"

"He's having dinner as well. He's fine; they never laid a hand on him."

"The Hammerhearts?"

"All unconscious. We just left them there."

"And what about you?"

"I'm fine," I said, still grinning. "Couple of close calls, but I got out okay."

Marc sighed. He looked very relieved. Weak, perhaps, but in no pain. "How are you, Amelia?"

"I'm fine," she said. "Just glad you're okay. Dinner's happening downstairs at the moment, so when you feel up to it, you can go down and grab something to eat."

"Yeah," he said, sounding unconvinced. "I am a little hungry, I guess. Mouth's a little dry. Er, not sure I'm up to walking, though."

"Oh," said Amelia, sounding disappointed. She waved her hand and a glass of fresh water appeared from nowhere. I helped prop Marc up against the wall while he drank from it.

"I'm sure we can give you some strength, though," I said. "I've been giving myself energy boosters from my crystal all day. In fact, you can probably do it yourself. You still have the Hero Crystal, don't you?"

"Yeah," he said, after checking his pockets. "Thank God, or we'd have to go back there."

"I'm going back, anyway," I told him. "Gotta give Siobhan a chance to get some of her stuff. Underwood too, perhaps, if he behaves himself."

"Geez, think I might sit this one out," he said with another great sigh.

"That's okay," I said. "You and Tommy stay back here and do what you've been doing. I'm going with Serena tonight, and I'm really hoping it won't take long. I'm due for a long sleep."

"I'll bet," he said, leaning his head back against the wall and closing his eyes. "Well, anyway, thanks for getting me out of there. I thought I was a goner. And you too for helping, Amelia. You did help, didn't you?"

"Yeah, once you got back here," she said, rather expressionlessly, I thought.

Now that Marc was okay, she seemed to want to get rid of him as quickly as possible. I felt no pang of jealousy this time, although I did feel a little nervous and more than a little guilty. I only wanted to talk to her and make sure she was okay, so why couldn't I shake the feeling that I was going behind Marc's back? I decided I might as well get things moving. I put my hand in my pocket and used the crystal to give Marc the same sort of energy booster that I'd been giving myself all day. I gave myself another one too just for the hell of it.

"Oi, I felt that," he said, sitting up straighter and looking at me. "That was you, wasn't it?"

"Yeah. You feel better?"

"Yeah, thanks a lot," he said. "You might as well make room, you two."

Amelia and I pushed our chairs back and Marc stood up before us, putting his weight carefully on his previously injured leg. It held him up fine, of course, and he jumped on the spot a few times before whooping.

"Thanks a lot, both of you. You coming down too?"

I glanced quickly at Amelia. This was the hairy point, I thought. Amelia saved me. "I don't think I will. I'm not very hungry, and I don't really feel like being down there with all those people."

"Ah," he said, sobering up at once. "That's okay, I get it." He moved forward and gave her a quick hug, a hug that would have been far more intimate if I hadn't been present, I felt sure. He looked at her and said more quietly, "You sure you're gonna be okay?"

"I usually end up being okay," she said, grinning at me over Marc's shoulder.

"Well, all right, then," he said. "I'll come and see you later on, okay?"

"Yeah, sure," she said.

He kissed her (I looked away at that point) and turned back to me. "Come on, man, or we won't be able to get a decent table."

"I'm not going down either," I said, nervous all over again. "I've —er—gotta sort out rooms for Underwood and Siobhan." He didn't need to know I had already done it. Hopefully he wouldn't mention that last to one of the few who knew that I had already done it.

"Oh yeah, good point," he said. "See you down there, then."

He left the room, and for the sake of authenticity, I followed close behind him, with Amelia bringing up the rear, leaving the door open so that Serena, Siobhan, and Underwood could get back in. We descended down to the bottom level, and while Marc headed for the dining room, which was still echoing with mostly happy chatter, Amelia and I went out into the corridor and headed for the Woodward living quarters once again.

"Sorry," she said quietly as we turned into the short stretch of hallway that led to the entrance to the Woodward living quarters. She was still behind me, so I had to look over my shoulder at her. I was alarmed by how disgusted she looked with herself.

"What? What's wrong?"

"What's wrong?" she repeated sarcastically. "Oh, I dunno. How about everything?"

"What are you apologising for?"

"You lied for me back there," she said, taking half a step closer to me. We were very close now; she was all I could see. "I hate it. I hate that I'm making things harder for you than they need to be. It's so goddamned messy!"

"Come in here," I said, taking her hand and walking her up the short stretch to the door and using the crystal to make it open for us. "Come on, come and sit down."

It didn't take long. By the time I'd taken Amelia into her bedroom and sat her down on her bed, she was well and truly in tears. I sat down beside her, put an arm around her, and let her cry her heart out on my shoulder, feeling a mixture of guilt that I was doing something Marc should have been doing, guilt when I thought of Serena somewhere else in the base, and relief that Amelia was finally able to let her emotions go, that whatever had been stuck inside her for two days was finally coming out. She leaned against me, put her arms around me, and just stayed that way, sobbing against me, and I wasn't sure what to do for the best. I put my arms around her and held her close to me, but beyond that, I wasn't sure what to do. I'd never been in a situation like this before. Should I just stay this way? Should I wait for her to finish crying so that she could talk? Should I try to get her to talk? Should I make soothing noises? I wasn't sure, but for now, my instincts told me to stay still and silent, just rub her back gently and wait for her to make the next move.

Eventually, she did, after a good few minutes of just staying in that position. She looked up at me, her face tear-streaked, and squeaked, "I'm sorry."

"Don't be," I said quietly. "Don't be sorry. None of this is your fault."

"I can't believe what I'm doing," she gasped, gulping for air. "What I've done. I'm pathetic. Why you guys even bother with me —"

"Because we care about you."

"I don't deserve that."

"None of this is your fault," I repeated firmly, putting a hand under her chin and making her look at me. "You can't help the way things are turning out."

"I'm making things worse," she whimpered, "what with you and Marc and all."

"Oh," I said, my stomach falling. Could this be the first time I'd have to discuss whatever was going on between Amelia and I? Well, the second, if you counted the day we had almost kissed. "Well, you can't help that either, you know. You said yourself that Marc doesn't make it easy for you to talk about this stuff with him."

"I know, but—" She sighed dramatically and hid her face again. "I dunno. He'd be angry with me if he knew what was going on in my head. You should be, too. You should be disgusted with me for doing this to you."

"Not really," I said, shrugging. "I tend to make things complicated for myself. Nothing you did."

"What am I doing?" she moaned. "Screwing around. I'm such a bitch. Underwood was so right about me."

"You're not," I said firmly, making her look at me again. "You're only making yourself feel worse by thinking like that. Look, why don't you start by telling me what it is you think will make Marc angry if you tell him?"

I had a feeling I already knew what it could be, but I wasn't prepared to let my mind get carried away with me. Better let Amelia come out and say it, if she could. She tried to lower her head, cast her eyes downward, but I had my hand firmly under her chin again, and I wouldn't let her look away. This would probably make it more painful for her, but she needed it.

"We don't work," she almost whispered. "This wasn't how it was supposed to go. We were supposed to be really good together."

"In what way don't you work?" I pushed her.

"We just—I dunno," she squeaked. "It's been like it right from the start, since they got us in the Basement. We've never been the same since, and I don't know why."

"You still like him, though, right?"

"Yeah, of course, but not like I used to," she said. "I used to be practically obsessed with him, and when I got him that night at Stella's party, it was like—like the best night of my life. No, it *was* the best night of my life. He seemed so perfect and understanding, even if he was a little shy, but then I suppose I never really had anything wrong with me back then. Since the Basement, though, he's been hard to talk to. I can't tell him any of what went on in there because he gets angry too easily."

"Ah," I said, remembering the day I had told him about Hignat and Wilwog. "Yeah, but, see, the thing is, he's not angry with you. He's angry because he cares about you and he doesn't wanna see you hurt. And mostly he's angry with himself because he can't do anything to make you better."

"I know that, and that makes me feel even worse, but it doesn't make it any easier."

"Have you explained this to him?"

Amelia whimpered, and I didn't need an answer.

"Okay, but—" I sighed. "What do you wanna do?"

"I don't know what I want anymore."

"Do you still want things to work with Marc?"

"I don't know anymore," she repeated, and I had to suppress my exasperation with some effort.

"Well, remember back to how you used to feel about him. Do you wanna get back to that? Think carefully."

Amelia leaned against me again and rested her head on my shoulder. She closed her eyes and went silent and still for some time, and I just waited for her response, no longer exasperated but just pleased that she was prepared to help me sort her problems out. Finally, I felt her shift against me.

"You think I should try to talk to him about this?" she mumbled.

"If it's what you want," I said. "I mean, if you want to sort this out, and for the sake of maintaining some sort of friendship with Marc, you probably should. I mean, what other alternatives do you have? You could break up with him, but you'll still have to spend a lot of time around him. Wouldn't that be a little awkward if Marc never understands what's going on?"

"Maybe," she said, "but would it be any better if he does know? What if we end up like Natalie and Tommy are now?"

"Natalie's happier now," I reminded her. "She's happier now since she's been on her own. Yeah, maybe a little awkward, but isn't that better than this?"

"But you think I should try to sort it out first?"

"Yeah, I do," I said, and this was completely honest. However I felt about Amelia now, I had enough sense to remember that nothing could happen between us, even if she ended up single, because I still wasn't. I felt pleased with myself that I could sit here with her and give her the advice a good friend would, the advice that really would be best for her and not something coated with bias to fit my vested interest. "You might as well try it. If you can sort it out, you can get back on track. If not, you can move on. Either way, it'll be better than what you're going through now."

"I guess," she said heavily. "I just feel so pathetic now. I used to be strong, but—the things they did to me, just—I just—"

I wasn't sure if she was referring to what the Hammersons did to her, what Hignat and Wilwog did to her, or both. Either way, I didn't want to hear it. I knew exactly what the problem was now, though— the way they had overcome her, the way they had taken advantage of her, had given her a feeling of great weakness, and the things that Hignat and Wilwog, in particular, had done to her—what they had reduced her to—had made her feel worthless. Underwood must have compounded that feeling by making her feel as though she was loose, a feeling that was clearly validated by the problems she was having with Marc and (although she hadn't said it outright) the feelings that she had for me as well. I thought I was probably right, though. Sorting this business out with Marc would be the first step to recovery. I could only hope that Marc would be prepared to help her, that he too wouldn't see her as weak, and most importantly would forgive her for having feelings for me. That last one was a big if, though.

Taking a leaf out of Amelia's own book from several weeks ago, I touched a finger lightly to her lips to stop her speaking before she could hurt herself further. "No need to think about that," I said firmly.

"You really make it easier," she moaned. "I dunno what I'd do if you weren't here."

She raised her head, and suddenly we were very close again, as close as we had been that fateful day back in my bedroom. In fact, we were even closer because we were sitting beside each other, our legs against each other, one of hers in fact crossed over mine, and on top of that, our arms were still around each other. Our noses were a mere inch apart, I could see the tears still in her eyes, and I suddenly felt very nervous indeed. Wanting to gloss over the moment, or perhaps ruin it, depending on how you looked at it, I said, "I'm fairly sure you would have battled on, as we all tend to do."

"I'd be lost," she said very quietly. "I mean—I guess I am lost, confused, but I think—I kind of like some of that confusion."

"What do you mean?"

For answer, she tightened her arms around me, leaned in that extra couple of inches, and kissed me firmly on the lips. I could have had a heart attack on the spot. My pulse quickened, my head spun in a combination of panic and pleasure, but my body had taken the initiative. Without meaning to, even though I'd tried so hard not to for weeks despite the fact that I wanted it more than almost anything else, I was kissing her back. It held for maybe twenty seconds before we broke apart, gasping for breath. We looked at each other, and in her face I saw the same emotions I was feeling—a mixture of pleasure and guilt—and it was all I could do not to kiss her again, or more. I had really enjoyed that. Lord help me.

Chapter 16: Returning

I didn't get out of Amelia's living quarters until almost eight o'clock, not because she and I got up to anything particularly interesting after the kiss, but because we had dinner together. I'd seen the Woodward's dining room a few times but never their kitchen, nor had I seen the Woodwards actually preparing their meals. What they had set up for themselves (and I supposed it was more for Amelia's mother than the Sorcerers) was a system similar to the conveyer belt in the main dining room, except in this case, instead of speaking to the device, you would touch it with your fingertip and clearly imagine what it is you wish to eat for dinner. I wondered if they'd got the idea from the Hero Crystal but never bothered to ask.

When she and I re-entered the main living quarters, it was to find a group of people clustered around the bottom of the stairs, as had been the case less than twenty-four hours earlier, in the moments before Sebastian's attack. Marc and Tommy were there, unsurprisingly, and they were accompanied by Peter, James, Kylie, and Erica. All six stared at me and Amelia in some suspicion as we joined them.

"Does it take an hour and a half to make a couple of keys?" Marc enquired, his eyes narrowed.

"I had dinner in there as well," I said. Might as well be honest, I thought. Can't get caught out lying that way. I had already told more lies than I should have.

"Sure, okay," said Marc, though he still looked suspicious. "Anyway, I've just sorted out the prisoners for their dinner. So what's happening now, then?"

"Underwood's upstairs, John," said Peter, "with Serena and Siobhan. I've given Serena my goggles; this was about half an hour ago, mind you, so they'll probably be sick of waiting for you by now."

"Cheers," I said, and the thought of the job that still awaited me upstairs caused another wave of exhaustion to wash over me, and I quickly dipped my hand to the crystal again.

"I was just saying before you turned up," Tommy said, "nothing's happened in Germany yet, but I'm worried it will, so what I wanna do is spend a good twelve hours or so over there tonight. If I can, anyway. So, James, do you think you can handle the Light Crystal tonight?"

"I think so," he said, a little uncertainly.

"You just make wishes with it, and it goes warm if it works," Tommy told him. "You'll work it out quickly enough. John, you should probably do the same thing if you wanna go to bed early tonight."

"Good point," I said thoughtfully. Who ought I give the Sien-Leoard Crystal to? Peter seemed the obvious answer, just standing right there, and he'd certainly proved himself deserving today, but surely he would want to sleep tonight after the day he'd had too. "I'll worry about that later, though. I need it for now."

"Right," said Marc. "So what's the plan? I guess I'm going up with James—er, where?"

"Your room, I guess," said James indifferently. "Doesn't matter much."

"You wanna join us, Amelia?" asked Marc hopefully.

"Yeah, think I will," she said, and Marc looked surprised for a moment before an enormous grin spread across his face.

We split up after that. Tommy gave James the Light Crystal and departed for bed, while Peter and Kylie went upstairs to enjoy each other's company for a while, I supposed. Peter had only done so after having a good look around the hall first, and I thought I knew why. We would all have to be careful of how we behaved with the opposite gender now that so many parents were living in the base. Marc, Amelia, James, and Erica went up to Marc's room, while I set off alone for Room 2-85 and yet another trip through a magic door.

"Geez, I was about to come looking for you," Serena said when I opened the door. "What took you so long?"

"Had a couple of things to sort out," I said vaguely.

All three of them were seated around the table, and although I couldn't be sure of it, I had a feeling none of them had spoken a word to each other since they had entered the room. They all got up as I closed the door.

"So what are we doing?" Serena asked me.

"Um," I said, thinking hard. I hadn't actually gone over the plan for this procedure yet, but it only took a few seconds to work out how I wanted to do it. I put my hand in my pocket, and a moment later, Serena disappeared into invisibility.

"Oi, what?" said Siobhan, staring blankly at the spot where Serena had been.

"I'm here," she said. "Er, John—"

Something waved through the air, and a moment later, I realised what had happened: Serena had just put the ghost goggles on, and it looked as though they were floating in mid-air. I dipped my hand again, and a moment later, they had vanished as well.

"No good," said Serena. "I can't see them anymore, either. How did you do it with Peter?"

I swore. What was going on? Now that she said it, I wondered what I'd done last time. Peter had seen the invisible attackers earlier that day, but if Serena was right, she wouldn't be able to see anything because the effect of the goggles had been made invisible just like the goggles themselves.

"What are you doing?" Underwood asked sharply. "What the bloody hell is this all about?"

"Be quiet, I'm trying to think," I snapped.

It didn't take long to work out what I'd done differently. Once I had made both Serena and the goggles visible and invisible again at the same time, Serena could see through them just fine.

"All right, here's what we're gonna do," I said to them all. "You," I jerked my thumb at Underwood, "will come through first. We'll go to your apartment and you can collect the stuff you wanna bring back here. Don't try anything silly, though; both Serena and I will be on the lookout, and I don't mind using magic to keep you in line if I have to. Incidentally, do we have an extender case anywhere?"

"Don't think so," said Serena. "Should have mentioned it earlier. You can create one, though, can't you?"

"Yeah," I said, and a couple of spells later, a bag identical to just about every other of its kind I'd ever seen fell into my hand, and I chucked it at Underwood.

"You just wait for us here," I said to Siobhan. "If your friend here behaves himself, we shouldn't take too long."

"Okay," she said. She looked nervous, and I couldn't blame her. How would she be returning to that house that had almost been destroyed? That house where the life she had always known had been destroyed?

The three of us (me, Underwood and the invisible Serena) went through the door at the back of the room and emerged into the empty apartment a floor beneath Underwood's. Being back in a place similar to the one in which he lived seemed to make Underwood turn a little more subdued, at least for the time being. He kept his mouth shut as we left the apartment and headed upstairs to a place that would have most definitely been familiar to him.

"You have a key, right?" I asked him quietly.

"Course I do. What do you think I am?"

"Just checking."

He let us into the very familiar apartment and immediately went about gathering up his things. Serena stood behind me in the doorway while I stood slightly off to the side, so that anyone passing in the corridor outside wouldn't see me. I just stood, my hand on my crystal, watching Underwood for any sign of trouble. He, meanwhile, was sparing nothing at all, trying to cram absolutely everything into the bag, including all his furniture. A couple of times, I was forced to help widen the bag to fit the enormous objects through the opening.

"You know you'll be able to carry all this back," I said, "but just remember, some things might get broken if you keep piling couches and beds on top of them."

"That's it for the furniture," he said, straightening up and wiping sweat off his face after the effort of sliding his queen-size bed into the bag. "Besides, I'm sure you and your magic pals can fix them up if they do get broken."

"We can," I said, "but that doesn't mean we will. Don't take it for granted."

Underwood scowled, but I didn't relent. That was just something he would have to come to terms with.

Five minutes later, the apartment was stripped bare. Underwood stood in the middle of it, looking around himself. I was struck dumb by the look of intense emotion on his face. Perhaps there was an ounce of decency in him somewhere after all, and only a sentimental moment like this could bring it out of him.

"Ready to go back?" I asked him.

"Guess so," he said. "I hope you realise how you're ruining my life by doing this."

"Hope you realise how we're saving it, actually," I said, moving back towards the door. "You'll get chances to live later on. What are you complaining about, anyway? You've got a much sweeter deal than your girlfriend."

"That's the worst part," he said, scowling even more heavily. "Why'd you have to drag her into this?"

"We never planned to," I admitted, "but you saw what happened back there."

None of us spoke again as we left that apartment for the last time and returned to the one with the magic door still in it. Back in 2-85, Siobhan was lying on the bed where Marc had been earlier and appeared to be dozing. She stirred when the three of us re-entered the room.

"Is it my turn?" she asked blearily.

"Yeah, in a minute," I said. "Now listen," I said, turning back to Underwood, who still stood just inside the room with his bag over his shoulder, "do you think you can find Room 22 up on level five?"

"I can try," he said doubtfully.

"You can," I said, thinking that he would have seen the way it was set up when he was out in the main hall. I handed him the key to Room 5-22 and sent him on his way.

"That wasn't too bad," said Serena, looking relieved. "I was expecting a Hammerheart attack or something."

"I knew that would be the easier part," I said. "That's why I wanted to get it out of the way first. This time, we're going back to where we were attacked earlier, and then—er, Siobhan?"

"Yeah," she said, sitting up and staring at me.

"You do wanna stay here, don't you?" I asked. There might be a much simpler way to sort her out if she still had family over there.

"I can't go back home," she said, lowering her head again and sounding close to tears.

"I know, but do you have any other family or anything?"

"None I can live with." She sniffed.

"What are you thinking, John?" asked Serena.

"All right, then," I said, "but I suppose if there are still others over there, they'll need to know what happened. So even if you don't wanna live with them, you'll still have to see someone and tell them."

"No, I don't think so," she said, looking up at me, and to my surprise, she looked angry. "You can do the explaining. This is all because of you and that Marc guy, anyway."

"It is not!" snapped Serena. "They only wanted that Underwood guy. You wouldn't have even known about any of this if he didn't have a fetish for underage sex."

Siobhan bristled at that, and it was an effort for me not to laugh. That was the second time in my memory that Serena had hit the mail on the head so quickly without knowing all the details. The previous time, she had guessed exactly what was happening between Natalie, Tommy, and Rebecca simply based on the abridged story Rebecca had given her and what she already knew about Tommy and Natalie's relationship.

"I doubt they'd listen to me," I said, wanting to smooth the situation over quickly. "They don't know me, and in case you haven't realised, I'm only a teenager. Besides, I wanna stay invisible the whole time; otherwise, we might have to tangle with the Hammerhearts again."

"We can see my uncle," Siobhan said quietly. She still looked very angry and kept shooting glances at the spot where she thought Serena must be. "He can sort it all out."

"Okay, fine," I said, checking my watch. It was half past eight, and I wanted to get this out of the way quickly now. If my judgement was right, it would be closing in on noon in England. "Brace yourself now, Siobhan."

I dipped my hand to the crystal again, and a moment later, Siobhan vanished from sight.

"What?" she said, not realising what had happened.

I made myself invisible as well and said, "Come on, you two, let's go."

Both doors were still open, and the three of us went straight through them, colliding with each other several times in the process, although Serena did best at staying out of the way, as she was the only one who could see anything. Once we were all in the empty apartment on the other side and I had camouflaged the magic door, I put a spell on the three of us so that we could see each other as mere outlines. It would probably be useless in broad daylight, but I just felt a bit odd having nothing to go by at all.

"Just stay still a minute, you two," I said quietly. The building was still eerily silent, even though it was the middle of the day now. "I'm just gonna check how things are back at the house."

Neither girl moved or responded, so I gripped the crystal in my pocket and sent my mind out away from them, across the city to the small block of land where all the trouble had occurred a few hours earlier. The crystal took me there within a few seconds, quicker than it had the first time, no doubt because I knew exactly where to look. What I saw of the house was the very worst thing for us: The block of land had been taped off, and police officers were cleaning it all up. The bodies of the Hammerhearts were being loaded into a truck parked on the side of the street to be taken God only knew where. Other officers were in the house itself, examining the damage inside.

The bodies of the family had all vanished beneath the ground, of course, but it seemed they had a fair idea of what had happened anyway. The looks of fear and resignation on the faces of the officers was enough to prove that. I supposed they had been told of the assault that had taken place there, and I knew they had seen blood on the floor (mainly that of the grandfather but also the two boys, none of which I had gone to pains to clean up). But I also knew there was more to it, for outside, three masked Hammerhearts were supervising the operation closely. They were all armed with agonators, and their presence was no secret.

"We've got a problem," I said when I had returned to the apartment, and I explained what I had seen around the house. "So, any ideas? Do you still wanna do this, Siobhan?"

"We can't do it all today, can we?" she asked solemnly. "They won't leave the place alone for ages."

"Probably not," I admitted, "but if we wait, there mightn't be much left whenever we come back. It might be worth the risk."

"So what's your plan, John?" asked Serena. "Do we go as we are and just try to stay out of their way? Any invisible magical shields or anything?"

"Not sure," I said, trying to think. "What do you think, Siobhan? How important is it to get your stuff?"

"Most of it I can live without or replace," she admitted, "but there are a few things I'd just die if they took away. Did you see if they were around the back?"

"Back of the house? No, only out the front and inside it."

At least, I thought that. I hadn't actually looked around the back, but now that Siobhan mentioned it, that seemed a logical spot to teleport to. It was hard to work out any sort of plan from here, though, so I dipped my hand to my crystal and created an invisible shield around the three of us, pushing us together.

"What the—John?" Serena said nervously as the three of us tried to put a few inches between us.

"Don't worry, it's just the shield," I told them. "I'm teleporting us on three…two…one."

We went through the sensation and seconds later were on the lawn behind Siobhan's little white house, standing before a neat little garden hedge. There was nobody close to where we stood, but only ten feet away, just around the corner, a single police officer was examining Siobhan's window, apparently having detected something unusual about it. Perhaps he'd been told of how Siobhan had climbed through it earlier, assuming the two officers had seen it at the time.

Siobhan let out a little moan. "The window. I was thinking the—what do we do?"

"We get a little closer," I hissed back. "Everyone quiet, and let's try to coordinate our footsteps."

I was more worried about the three of us ending up on the ground than our footsteps being overheard, but I supposed both were possibilities. We crept forward to within a few feet of the police officer, stopping just past the corner of the house.

"Now what?" hissed Serena.

"You just look out for invisible people," I hissed back, but not quietly enough. Before us, the officer's head snapped up and he looked nervously all around himself, his hand slipping down to the butt of the gun at his hip.

In a similar motion, my hand was back on the crystal, and a moment later, I was attempting to perform some of the most complicated magic I had ever done. Before our eyes, the gaze of the police officer suddenly fell out of focus. He tried to give his head a little shake but had lost all his will to resist only a moment later. Slowly, very slowly, he crouched down before Siobhan's window and recommenced running hands along it. To any officers who came around the corner, or to those in the little boys' room (I could see them moving through the next window), he would appear to be busy at work.

"Come on," I muttered, "let's get behind him so we can see through the window."

We got into position a few feet behind the officer this time and peered into Siobhan's room. It looked exactly as it had the last time I had seen it, except that it was empty of people. The door was still wide open from when Underwood and Siobhan's parents had bolted through it, and beyond it, the hallway and a cupboard door directly opposite Siobhan's door. What we could see of the hallway was also empty, but I knew there to be people walking the house, looking for evidence. If the focus was on the living room and the young boys' room where the deaths had occurred, we might be in luck.

Teleporting us into the room was the next obvious step, but it presented another complication: Where was the best place to put Serena? I supposed if this police officer continued to study the window, placing Serena in Siobhan's doorway would be the best option. Then again, if we just carefully closed Siobhan's door, it was reasonable to think no one but this officer would notice the difference, and if I kept him preoccupied, then we should be okay. I hoped.

"Hold on," I hissed, and made the tiny teleportation through the wall before us.

Once inside, I vanished the shield around us and quickly created three separate shields. The two spells in quick succession caused the three of us to jerk away from each other slightly.

"Thank God," muttered Siobhan.

"Here," I hissed, magically creating another internally extending bag and handing it to Siobhan. "Pack what you want in this. Is everything you want in here?"

"Yeah."

"Good. Serena, close the door, then just keep an eye on it and through the window. I'm gonna make sure this guy behaves himself. Siobhan, just let us know when you're done."

It didn't take her long. Serena had closed the door and positioned herself beside it, directly opposite the window. I stood beside the window, hand on crystal, repeatedly performing spells to keep the police officer's mind vague. Siobhan flittered around the room, putting various objects into her bag. It was mostly books, CDs, clothes, a few stuffed toys, and some other assorted stuff that would have been worthless to anyone else that vanished into thin air around the room. Within five minutes, she hissed, "I'm done."

"Good," I said. "I'll fix this guy up, and then I'll teleport us straight back to the apart—"

With the worst timing possible, Siobhan's bedroom door flew open, freezing the three of us on the spot and almost causing me to choke. The officer in the doorway, however, was turning his head away even as he pushed the door open.

"If I've told you once, I've told you a million times—you don't tamper with the evidence!"

"I haven't done anything," an indignant voice yelled from somewhere else in the house.

"This door was open—I marked it down when we first got here —and doors don't normally close by themselves on windless days."

"Maybe it's all the wind coming out of your mouth that blew it shut," the voice called back as the officer turned fully away from us and headed back up the hallway towards the lounge room.

I didn't waste any more time. Turning to the officer at the window, I performed what I hoped was a normalising charm and, to my relief, saw the officer's eyes return to sharp focus. He straightened up with a jolt and looked all around him, clearly suspicious of what had just happened to him. Before he could look back into the room, however, I had teleported us out of his reach.

"Is that what you'll have to do every time you go somewhere, John?" asked Serena when we landed back in the apartment. "I mean, to avoid a scene like what happened to Marc earlier?"

"Looks like it," I said. My whole body was filling with giddy relief; it felt like being filled up with warm water. "That's the first time I've been so close to Hammerhearts and not been caught since this thing started, thank God."

"Hang on, we're not done yet," said Siobhan. "I still need to tell someone in the family what happened."

"Oh yeah," I said, touching my crystal and quickly giving myself yet another energy boost, "but leave your bag here for that. You decided who you wanna see?"

"Yeah, my uncle," she said quietly. "He and I—well, we're okay, but I only need to tell him what happened and that I'm going away."

"Do you feel okay?" I asked her anxiously. She had done okay so far, but she was bound to become emotional again soon after what she'd been through.

"Yeah, at the moment," she said. "Let's just do this. Er, how do we get there, though? You don't know where he lives, and if I give you the address, will you be able to find it?"

"Probably not," I conceded. Could there possibly be a way to use Siobhan's thoughts to teleport us to the right location without giving her the crystal? "You concentrate on your uncle. Concentrate really hard on him."

"Er, okay."

I took a firm hold of the crystal and carefully separated myself from my body, floating up and into Siobhan's mind. I could see clearly the man she was concentrating on and, with one squeeze of the crystal and a thought of my own, teleported us straight to him. I wished I'd thought to ask Siobhan where he was likely to be at this time or that I'd thought to mentally check on him first, as I had checked on her house before teleporting, because we couldn't have landed in a more dangerous place if we tried.

Siobhan's uncle was a doctor in a hospital of some sort. The size of it couldn't be determined from the inside where we had teleported. He was currently in an operating room with another doctor and several nurses, not to mention a single patient on a bed. The complication was the trio of masked men lining them up along the wall at agonator point, the looks on their faces suggesting that one of them had already learnt of its use. The patient, who was unconscious, was being completely ignored by everyone in the room thus far.

"Straight line," one of the Hammerhearts said sharply. "Straight! This medical centre is being shut down. We are taking you all away to have you examined. You all stay in a straight line. No talking."

"Examined?" one of the nurses, a middle-aged woman, asked nervously.

"No *talking!*" roared the same Hammerheart, striding towards her and jabbing her hard in the chest with the agonator.

"To see if you are good enough to be Hammerheart medical staff," another Hammerheart answered more calmly. "Once the new Hammerheart hospital is in operation, only the finest will be permitted to operate, just like only the finest may be operated on."

"Now, you all just stay still," the third Hammerheart said warningly. "You will feel something in a moment. It won't feel nice, but it won't hurt you either, so just stay perfectly still and don't struggle against it."

He pulled a solid-outliner from his pocket, and I knew what was coming. The only thoughts I had were of Siobhan's uncle and how impossible it would be to tell him anything once he was taken into Hammerheart custody. I didn't consider the ramifications of preventing the Hammerhearts taking their hostages, didn't have any idea that stopping them now would only cause the deaths of everyone else in the room later on. I didn't even stop to realise that the Hammerhearts' takeover of the United Kingdom was well underway now.

I squeezed the crystal and thought only of making that solid-outliner disappear. The Hammerheart clenched his fist suddenly before looking down at it in some confusion. I didn't give him or either of the others time to work out what had happened. The next thing they knew, an invisible force was wrapping around them and shunting them toward the door that led (judging by what I could see through the glass) into a ward. They all yelled in fright, twisting and turning and trying to get a look at the entire room, apparently trying to locate the source of the pressure. The one who had been holding the agonator was squeezing it and shooting jets of golden light all over the room, though thankfully the few that hit those along the wall only lasted a split-second.

"What the hell are you doing?" Serena hissed in my ear under cover of all the hubbub. "If they work out there are magic people in here—"

"What choice did I have?" I retorted, squeezing the crystal again and making the door to the ward open to admit the Hammerhearts, rather like the mouth of a monster opening to admit its unfortunate dinner. "We only have to tell him, and then we can get the hell out of here."

Once the door had shut behind the Hammerhearts, I separated from Siobhan and Serena and moved forward to where the medical staff still stood stationary along the wall, clearly in shock and unable to move. I moved close to Siobhan's uncle and said, very quietly, though knowing there was no point trying to hide my presence from the others, "You're very lucky we came when we did."

Though privately I thought he was unlucky that I had come at all, as I felt sure he'd rather I hadn't come if it meant his family were still alive.

"Who's that?" asked the other doctor, while two of the nurses let out little whimpers and fell to their knees.

"Never mind who I am," I said firmly. "I only came to see you." I jabbed Siobhan's uncle in the chest, and he started. "You—I dunno your name, but you need to know something."

"Sounds like an Aussie," said one of the nurses still on their feet.

"How do you know me?" asked Siobhan's uncle shakily. "Who are you?"

"I don't know you, and you don't need to know me," I said, starting to lose patience. This place was making me edgy. "All you need to know is that some of your family was killed this morning by Hammerhearts."

I felt so merciless having to tell him in this way, but I really couldn't think of any other way to do it. I wished Siobhan would get her butt over here and help me out, but looking over my shoulder, I saw that Serena was in fact restraining Siobhan, who looked ready to scream in terror, judging by the little I could see of them anyway.

"Killed?" he said weakly, while a few of the others in the room let out gasps of horror and disbelief. "Who?"

"I don't know them, either," I said hurriedly. "I only know your niece, Siobhan, survived. Everyone else living with her didn't."

The man went very pale indeed, and if not for the two on either side of him, he might have fallen to his knees.

"Sorry to have to tell you like this," I said. "You also need to know that Siobhan has chosen to stay with us, for her own protection. I can assure you that she'll come back when all this stuff has settled down, assuming there are no other disasters that we can't imagine."

"Where is she now?" he asked.

"Safe," I said, glancing over my shoulder again. Siobhan made no sound, so I assumed I was going about this the right way. "That's all you need to know. Now, I suggest you try to make a break for it while you have the chance."

"No, they shouldn't," said Serena sharply. "They'll be killed if they get caught running. Better they stay here and make like they tried to do the right thing."

True enough, I supposed. "Okay, stay here and you should hopefully be fine. Just do what they say. That's the best thing."

I hated giving such advice, but surely it was the right advice?

I moved back across the room to where Serena and Siobhan still stood. Once beside them, I dipped my hand back to the crystal in my pocket, thinking of the apartment we'd come from. My hand never even reached my pocket. The door through which I had ejected the three Hammerhearts burst open with an almighty bang that left a small crater in the wall beside it. Five Hammerhearts entered in a flurry, three of them probably the same ones that had been here earlier, but it was hard to tell, as they had all looked so similar and none of them had codes on their chests. Perhaps these people had only been recently recruited and hadn't been given codes yet.

The first Hammerheart raked the room with a solid-outliner before the rest of his group had even come in behind him, aiming not at those along the wall but at the empty air around them. None of them were wearing ghost goggles (apparently that technique hadn't made it this far across the world yet), but they were nevertheless attempting to bring us in, or more specifically me, since I'd been the one to use magic. Most alarmingly, it nearly worked. One jet hit Serena's hand right at the point where she was gripping Siobhan's upper arm, and white stuff began to spread over both of them, marking their position to the Hammerhearts.

I didn't have time to perform any magic this time. I could only drop to the floor and roll away from the girls so that I wouldn't get caught too. The second Hammerheart drew level with the first and performed the same action with a bludginator; the third did the same with an agonator; the fourth used a device that shot out ropes (I didn't know the name of it, but I had seen it used once before); and the fifth used a gun. Siobhan and Serena, who had also dropped to the floor together, had been lucky to avoid the wave of attacks as they flew over their heads, but their outline was now clearly visible to the Hammerhearts.

The others in the room weren't so lucky. A few of them had been firstly joined together by the solid-outliners; several of them were ripped apart by the bludginators, though not to the point of death; the agonators' jets of light knocked all those still on their feet to the floor; and the ropes caught all those not already trapped by thicky prison and a couple who were, so that the white stuff spread along the ropes and started to wrap around those within them. The gun, of course, did the most damage, firstly killing the patient on the bed (if he wasn't already dead) and then ploughing into each and every person stuck along the wall, the reports deafening in the confined space.

"One more round," the leading Hammerheart bellowed in the wake of the shots, raising his solid-outliner again. They were now lined up along the wall directly across from the now departed medical staff, only the wreckage of an operating room between them.

It took me several seconds to determine that none of the doctors or nurses had survived, by which time the third Hammerheart was already shooting his jets of golden light around the room again, and again they were all flying over our heads. Once I had, however, the only course of action occurred to me, the only option left to us: We had to get out of here right now, and never mind what became of the dead here. It was a cold thought, and briefly made me wonder if this war was beginning to turn me heartless, but there was no time to contemplate that now. I reached carefully for the Sien-Leoard Crystal, located it, and teleported the three of us away from that hospital and onto the floor of the apartment that was starting to feel like a bit of a refuge to me.

Times when I needed to use my own solid-outliner were few and far between, but I was nevertheless glad, when they did, that I still carried mine with me inside the pouch. It always sat in my pocket these days, the one not containing the crystal. I withdrew it now, extracted the solid-outliner from the top, and turned on the two girls, who were now completely immobile. A single click later had them both rolling on the floor away from each other, breathing heavily and somehow struggling to control their extremities.

"Oh my God," panted Siobhan. "Oh my God. Oh my God. Now what? There's no one left. Who am I supposed to tell now?"

"No one," snapped Serena, struggling to her feet and grabbing onto my shoulder for support. "We've done what we can, Siobhan. You'll just have to be content with staying here and knowing that you're safe."

Siobhan, who had managed to get to her knees, bit her lip, her eyes filling with tears.

"I'm sorry," I said, crouching down beside her and touching her shoulder lightly, sure that she would push me away just as she had only hours earlier, "but Serena's right. We really have done all we can."

"I know," she sobbed. "I know you have."

"Come on, let's get back through that door and get rid of it," said Serena, picking up Siobhan's bag, which had been left on the floor near to where she now stood. "Looks like the Hammerhearts are in control here now, or close enough to it."

Siobhan and I got up and followed Serena through the door into 2-85, me with the job of closing both doors behind us. Serena, who had waited just behind the door for me, now stepped forward and threw her arms around me. In my ear she whispered, "Don't you think you should make us all visible now?"

I dipped my hand to my crystal, did as I was told, and then for some time just stood there with Serena, our arms around each other, leaning on each other, enjoying the feel of each other. It was easily the most intimate moment between us for some time, even though there was nothing whatsoever sexual about it. After a few minutes like that, we finally parted. An enormous wave of exhaustion crashed over me and, once again, I had to use the crystal to give myself an energy boost. I looked around for Siobhan and spotted her sitting on the bed, where she had her head in her hands. I moved over to her and tapped her lightly on the shoulder, withdrawing the key I had made for her from my pocket.

"Are you okay?" I asked her.

"What do you think?" She wept, and I grimaced. I supposed that had been a rather stupid question.

"Do you wanna go to your room?" I asked her. "Do you wanna see Underwood?"

"His name is Jacob," she snapped.

"Here," I said, ignoring her comment and handing her the key. "Room 23 on level five. Do you think you can find it?"

"Yeah, probably," she said, getting up off the bed.

That look was definitely there now. She wanted nothing more than to get away from the two of us. Serena handed the bag over, and moments later, the door of 2-85 was swinging shut behind her.

"Poor thing," said Serena, taking my hand. "What a day she's having. What about you? How are you feeling?"

"Okay, I guess," I said doubtfully.

What I was struggling with was the realisation that my life had really been turned upside down. That had been the third time in something like seven hours that I had been attacked by Hammerhearts, and all in three different locations. Would I ever be able to go out again without putting myself, as well as everyone around me, in mortal danger? Somehow, I doubted it.

The overwhelming feeling at that stage, however, was weariness, not just physical but mental as well. I had done far too much without having been allowed to rest. I checked my watch and saw that it was now just after half past nine.

"How many hours you been up for?" Serena asked, seeing what I was doing.

"Er, thirty, I think," I said uncertainly. In truth, I couldn't do that simple calculation in my head anymore.

"Come on, then," she said, wrapping an arm around my waist and leading me forward. "Upstairs with you."

"You didn't wanna spend more time with me tonight?" I enquired, slightly surprised and a little bit hurt. Was she going off me?

"You look too tired," she said, "and I'm not, so maybe tomorrow. Is that okay?"

"Yeah, I guess," I said heavily. The thought of my bed upstairs was distracting me from everything else.

"In any case, I'm so pleased you made the effort to get your sleeping patterns right again," she said and gave me a quick kiss on the cheek. "That will really help us, so long as there are no more trips across the world in store any time soon."

"I'm pretty sure that's the last one to England," I said, "though I have no idea what's around the corner anymore."

We walked in silence until we reached the top of the stairs on level three. Marc's bedroom door was here, and it was here that Serena stopped.

"Did you want an update from in here?" she asked me.

"Not really," I said. "Will get one tomorrow."

"Okay," she said and made to move on, but then another thought occurred to me.

"Wait, hang on. I said I was gonna give them my crystal for the night."

"Really? What for?"

"So they can use it, since I'll be asleep."

She gave this a moment of thought, then seemed to realise what I meant. She backtracked a step and knocked on Marc's door.

"Come in if you're good-looking," James called out, and Marc and Erica laughed.

"Damn," Serena called back. "Does that mean that John can come in and I have to wait here?"

"John?" Marc called back. "Nah, I'm fairly sure he doesn't fit the bill."

James and Erica laughed loudly at that, but my mind was elsewhere. Amelia was the one I had considered giving the Sien-Leoard Crystal to, always assuming she consented to take it, but what if she wasn't even in there anymore? Who else could I give it to? Erica and Serena were the only two available for the job, and I didn't feel that Erica would take such a responsibility seriously enough, not that I knew her well enough to make that judgement. It was just a feeling I had.

"Open the door," I grumbled at Serena, forgetting in my sleep deprived state that she had no way of opening the door without the right key. Fortunately, a moment later, Erica opened it from the inside.

My worry had been pointless, I saw, for Amelia was indeed there, sitting on Marc's bed and leaning back against the wall beside it. Marc was also on the bed, sitting before one of the pillows, while James was in a seat at the table. The pulled out seat beside him was surely Erica's.

"Hello," Erica said, smiling at me and clapping Serena on the shoulder. "How did it go with you two?"

"More trouble," said Serena. "We got some more people killed, but Underwood and Siobhan are okay. They got their stuff and are upstairs now."

"More trouble?" repeated Marc. "What sort of trouble?"

"Hammerhearts," said Serena obviously. "What else? They're taking England, so they were sort of unavoidable."

"We know that bit," he said. "What about you, John?"

"What about me?" I repeated. "I'm going to bed. So stuffed. I only wanted to give you guys the crystal."

"Oh yeah," he said, glancing at my fist full of thin air as I pulled the crystal from my pocket.

"Who's gonna use it?" said James. "I'd do it, but I'm kind of busy with one crystal already."

"I can do it," said Erica eagerly.

"Amelia?" I enquired.

"Yeah, I can do it," she said evenly, and my insides relaxed.

I moved across the room and handed the crystal to her, feeling as though a huge weight had come off my shoulders as I did so but also feeling like I was handing part of myself over to her in the process.

"Thanks," she said, turning it over in her hands. "I'll give it back tomorrow morning."

"You don't wanna keep it?" I asked. Of course I wanted it back, but it seemed appropriate to ask. After all, by right, it wasn't really mine to own.

"No, I'll only use it tonight because you can't," she said. "You do well with it."

"You sure you don't wanna tell us what happened out there?" Marc asked, staring from me to Serena and back again.

"No thanks," I said heavily. "It wasn't much different from what you and I went through, but I don't wanna relive it. I've had enough of that stuff for a while."

"But it might be important."

"He doesn't have to talk about it," said Serena harshly, glaring at Marc. "I'll come back and tell you about it in a minute if you like, but you don't need to hassle John over it."

"Okay, okay," said Marc hurriedly, looking a little scared. I would have been amused by it if I hadn't been so tired, but right now I could only feel enormous gratitude toward Serena, who seemed to be doing more for me than I deserved, given what I had done to her.

"You're dead on your feet, John," James observed. "You go to bed. We'll see you in the morning."

"See ya," I said weakly.

Now that the crystal was out of my possession, I had no way to give myself the energy I needed to keep going, and knowing this fact only seemed to sap the little energy I still had. Serena assisted me to my bedroom and pretty much fussed over me until I was lying in bed. Only then did she leave the room, and I knew very little after that. Wonderful, blissful sleep rolled over me, and I allowed myself to fall into it.

Part 3: Calculation

Chapter 17: Renovated

Once again, when I had been counting on a most restful sleep to recover from a hell of a lot of mental exhaustion, other factors intervened. This time, it was yet another detour from normal sleep into Stella's mind. That made the third time in less than a week. By this stage, I was getting heartily sick of my sleep being interrupted by these visions. Normal dreams, even those involving me and Stella on Rock Haulter, were preferable to these. Some of the visions I'd had of Stella were rather alarming. This one, in particular, could only be classed as a nightmare.

Stella had been tied uncomfortably tightly to a thick, metal poll, a pillar supporting the ceiling above. She was outdoors, under cover of some sort of building. A large building, so Stella believed. It was dark, but she herself was cast in a circle of light coming from a bulb not far in front of her. She was trembling all over, trembling and aching, having already endured two rounds of torture by way of the agonator. Hall was standing feet away from her. He and she were roughly the same height, but her eyes were continually drawn to the agonator in his hand, as he was the one putting her through this pain. Her father, however, the one ordering Hall to use the weapon, was a farther few feet behind him, leaning against another pillar and watching Stella with a mixture of cruel enjoyment and frustration. After all, he still hadn't achieved all he wanted from this meeting.

"The deal is as good as it could possibly be, Stella," he said, appearing calm on the surface, though Stella knew him better. "All of this, everything in the world, could be yours. It will be yours, as after all, neither your grandmother nor I can live forever, now can we? Unless, of course, we get our Sorcerous powers back, but that is no guarantee, is it? Wouldn't you like to have all this power? Don't you think you could put it to great use? Don't you believe that you could make the world a better place than even we could?"

Privately, Stella did believe that, but she was resolute in her decision: She would not join forces with her family, not now.

"All you need to do for us," Hall continued in her father's place, "is tell us what became of the two with whom you were travelling. You have no fondness for either of them, we know, so do not play us for fools."

"I don't know where they are," she snapped, and this was the complete truth. Moran and Lucien, when the three of them had been busted, had teleported away by way of the Villain Crystal. She believed they would have taken her with them if not for the fact that one of the Hammerhearts had already taken her with a solid-outliner. She actually trusted that they would have taken her with them, because wouldn't that have made her father more mad than ever?

"You want this, Stella," said Hammerson softly, moving forward a few paces, then a few more, past Hall and very close, within arm's reach. "You can deny it as much as you like, but you know you want it. You know that you'd prefer you had it than us, that much you can admit to yourself, but there is more to it than that, and we all know it. You have the noble Hammerson blood in your veins, after all. Think of the power, Stella. Think of what you could do, what you could make of the world—what the world could make of you."

In spite of herself, her father's words were putting images into Stella's mind. She couldn't deny it to herself—it was all true, every bit of it. The pull of power was very strong indeed. She didn't have to be a killer; she didn't have to be anything like her father, grandmother, and great-grandfather. She only had to be herself. After all, she was a good person with a good heart and good intentions. She could stop all this fighting and restore some order around the world. But then what? Restore things to how they had been before? Is that what she wanted? Surely, if you took the fighting out of the equation, her family's plans were better for the world in general. Wouldn't it mean that there was less division in the world?

"Yes, of course," her father said, even more softly, reaching out and placing the cool tip of one finger lightly on her forehead. She tried to jerk away from the touch but was impeded by her binds. "You do want it. You want it very much."

"No!" she gasped, still trying to evade her father's touch. "No! I don't!"

But she did. The more she thought about it, the more it appealed to her.

I jerked awake at this point, not needing to think about what had just happened. The vividness of that dream made it all too clear that it hadn't been a dream, and its contents were extremely unnerving. Stella was caught. Would she go over to their side for proper, at last? Would she be given a choice in the end, or would they use a boggler to sort her out? I scrambled out of bed, retrieved the paper on which I had written notes of Stella two days earlier, scribbled as much as I could remember, then promptly dropped off to sleep again.

I returned to them when I woke a few hours later, reading them carefully and trying to remember if I'd missed anything, but all I could remember was what I'd written. With a sigh, I jumped in the shower before heading down to breakfast.

Plenty of people were waiting for me in the dining room when I entered. Most irregularly, Serena was not one of them. She turned up about ten minutes after me, but after bidding me a quick good morning, she went to sit with Erica, Kylie, Katie, and Sophie, as there was no room at my table. Marc, Amelia, Tommy, Peter, and James had saved a spot for me at their table, and they all waved me over as soon as they saw me.

"Good sleep?" Peter asked when I pulled out the seat between him and Amelia.

"Yeah," I said. "Only one problem with it."

I told them of everything I'd written. All of them looked disquieted by it.

"What I was always worried about," sighed James. "She's got a good heart, but she's been around that lot for way too long. I really hope she can resist them."

One look around the table was enough to work out the state of all the others. Marc and James were by far the most exhausted out of the five, and I suspected both of them would be straight off to bed, if not after breakfast, then not too long after it. Amelia also looked tired, though not as tired as the boys, probably because the boys had been up for something like twenty-four hours now compared to her fifteen or sixteen most likely. Peter and Tommy looked refreshed enough, as anyone would in the morning.

"Let's hope not," Tommy now said, "but I suppose there's not much we can do if she does take their offer. So are you gonna tell me what you guys were up to last night?" he now addressed Marc and Amelia.

"Well, what can you tell us about what you saw over there?" Marc asked him.

Tommy shrugged. "It started while I was there, though I think we all expected that after the Underwood business yesterday. Nobody was surprised by it like they were here, so basically the message to civilians was to keep our heads down and stay out of the action. There's a lot of fighting going on over there, but from what you guys are saying, it's just the Hammerhearts letting the Germans fight each other, like the only weapon they need is the fear factor."

"Yeah, we figured that," said James. "That's how it is everywhere the Hammerhearts are going now, and a lot of places they haven't even touched yet. So you and your parents just stayed in the house, then?"

"More or less," said Tommy. "My father went out in the morning for something, but only for a couple of hours. He was there when I woke up around midday."

"Midday?" repeated Peter. "But you went over there early."

"Yeah, that is early for me. I don't usually wake up over there until early evening, sometimes after dinner already."

"Geez, I just assumed you went to bed in the evening here and woke up in the morning over there," said Peter. "Shows how well I'm doing."

It wasn't until after breakfast that any plans for the day were laid out. The time had finally come to use the life assistant, which would be done inside Amelia's living quarters. That was James's idea for additional security. The complication was working out who should be present at this event. Marc, Amelia, Peter, James, Tommy, and I were in by default, but that was where the arguments started. This particular debate took place in quiet whispers around the foot of the stairs, and by that stage, Serena had caught up with me again. I remembered that I had said she could possibly be involved in this, and apparently she remembered as such too. Most of the others had no problem with her being involved, all except James, who for some reason didn't trust her. Fortunately, he was overruled in this debate.

Natalie was another complication. We knew she had returned to base at some stage in the night because although Rebecca hadn't seen her herself, her mother had and had told her. Rebecca had spread the news all over the dining room at breakfast, but nobody seemed to know where she was. According to Rebecca, she had checked in Natalie's room this morning, but it had been empty. The only solution we could come up with was to keep an eye out for her and bring her along if we saw her.

I also wanted to bring Lena along. After all, didn't she deserve it after the assistance she had given, the sacrifice she'd made? Though of course they didn't need to know the benefit she had already received for her help. In a bizarre twist, however, quite a few of the others thought we should include Underwood instead of her.

"If he's coming, then you can catch me up later," said Amelia flatly.

"Surely that's more trouble than it's worth," I said.

"Don't you think he has a right to be there?" James persisted. "I mean, it is his grandfather we're talking to. What if he wants to talk to him as well?"

"He's had ages, more time than he would have given us," Marc retorted. "I don't reckon he has a right to be involved."

"How's this for an idea," suggested Serena. "We don't get him involved now, but if you can find out where this old dude lives, you can drop him and leave him with him."

A silence followed this. There were a lot of unknowns in the idea, I supposed, but perhaps Serena was onto something.

"That's a good idea," said Peter. "Okay, leave him out of it for the meantime. Oh, now, what perfect timing."

He was one of the few facing into the hall; many of us had to turn to see what he was looking at. Underwood and Siobhan (the former of whom seemed determined to pretend the world around him was imaginary) had just emerged from the dining room and were heading towards us. Well, more specifically towards the stairs. Underwood skirted around us and shot up the stairs without a backward glance, but Siobhan lingered close by us.

"What's up?" Marc asked her.

"You two," she said, addressing me and Marc. "Jacob needs a favour from one of you. He's just too proud to ask."

"Does he now?" Marc enquired, raising his eyebrows. "I guess me risking my life trying to save his counts for nothing to him, but go on. What does he want?"

She pursed her lips but ignored the jab, and I could understand why. She didn't need to be reminded of what had happened at her house the previous day. "Well, he's having trouble unpacking his bag —"

I snorted before I could stop myself, and beside me, Serena burst out laughing. That, I thought, was poetic justice if ever I heard it.

"So can one of you two help him?" she continued.

"You can take this one, John," said Marc, not seeing the joke and apparently unwilling to be around Underwood at all. "I have business to take care of with our friends across the corridor. We all meet up in Amelia's place at nine, then?"

So that was the plan. Amelia gave me back the Sien-Leoard Crystal (it felt so wonderful to have it back in my possession again), and I followed Siobhan up five flights of stairs, being followed by Peter, James, and Serena for three of them. Underwood was leaning against the rail opposite the door of 5-22, looking grumpy and surly and not at all deserving of any assistance in any form in my opinion, but who was I to decide that?

"You're a coward," I said when Siobhan and I were a door away from him, "but a lucky coward. I'm only helping you this once."

"Cheers," he said, looking unwillingly relieved and trying hard not to show it.

"I'm only doing it for her," I said, nodding at Siobhan. "At least she was smart about what she packed."

Siobhan grinned at that. As I had expected, she had settled in here far more easily than he had. Underwood unlocked his room, and the two of us followed him inside. Level five rooms were smaller than those two levels below. They were, in fact, identical to those on level four. They had only a wardrobe and bathroom, like level three rooms, a reasonably sized bed, a bedside table, and a writing desk in the corner. I wasn't sure what I had expected, but it wasn't what I saw. Underwood had dumped his bag on his bed, but apart from that, the room appeared not to have been used at all. Even the rest of the bed looked untouched. I supposed he must have spent the night in Siobhan's room, and though she probably needed the comfort, the thought made my blood boil. He really was a prick.

"So how do you wanna do this?" I enquired.

"Just take everything out of it," he said. "I can handle the moving."

"I'm fairly sure you won't fit everything in here," I said, remembering how he had packed all the furniture in his little apartment—the tables, lounges, and that great big bed.

"Sure we will. You can just make it bigger," he said simply.

"No, I can't," I snapped. "I've never done anything like that before."

"You did with the bag," he retorted. "How's this any different?"

"If I muck it up, I could bring the whole bloody building down!"

"Fine! Let's just see how we go, then."

It turned out not to be too bad in the end, after I had shrunk the existing furniture to the point of oblivion. It was very cramped, but everything fit. As I had predicted, some of his possessions had been ruined by having such heavy furniture on top of them for such a long time—plates and glasses mostly—and I had been forced to create some new ones for him, even though I told him several times that he wouldn't need them. Siobhan stood by the door through all this, just watching in amusement. I knew she still didn't entirely trust me, but I also thought she knew her boyfriend was going a bit over the top in taking advantage of us.

"Is that all?" I enquired in a very sarcastic tone some twenty minutes later.

"Yes, that is all," he replied in exactly the same tone.

"What about you, Siobhan?"

"I don't need anything," she said, moving away from the door so that I could leave. "Thanks for helping out, John."

There was a slight hesitation before she spoke my name, and I only realised then that it was the first time she had addressed any of us by name. A good sign, I thought, but not one I intended to worry about now.

"Sure," I said, opening the door and backing out. "Have fun, you two."

"What are we supposed to do in this place, anyway?" he asked.

"Whatever you like," I said simply. "If your key opens a door, then you're allowed to go through it. Just don't smash anything, that's all."

It sounded like the strangest advice I'd ever given, but once again, I didn't care. Surely all either of them would want to do now was sleep, if their sleeping patterns were still in British time. I left the room and descended two levels, my mind turning to Natalie. I felt a pang of guilt at the idea of not waiting for her to use the life assistant, especially if she was still in the base somewhere, but I supposed if she didn't want to be found, then she could hardly feel bad about not being included. In my room, I withdrew the life assistant from my top drawer before turning back and heading for Amelia's living quarters.

* * *

The atmosphere inside the lounge room of Amelia's living quarters was rather tense when I entered it some five minutes later. Most of them were already there; Amelia, Tommy, Peter, James, Serena, and, to my slight surprise, Lena. Apparently they had decided, while I had been away, that she did have a right to be present after all. It was these last two who provided the tension in the room: They sat on adjacent couches, very carefully looking anywhere but at each other. The other four sat around them, clearly trying to ignore the pair of them, and one look told me that Amelia and James were the two succeeding in that matter. James looked just about ready to drop off to sleep while Amelia appeared to be deeply lost in her own little world. I felt a stirring of unease when I thought that Amelia's own little world could, in fact, be reading either Lena or Serena's minds, both of which were unprotected, and if those two were thinking about each other…

"Here he is, one half of the dynamic duo," said Peter mockingly as I sat down between him and Serena.

"Give it a rest," I muttered. I knew what he was trying to do, but I definitely preferred to handle a situation like this best in silence.

"You got it, John?" Tommy asked.

"If you mean the life assistant, yeah, I've got it."

"Did it go okay with Doctor Perve up there?" Peter asked.

"Peter," I groaned. Amelia had jerked convulsively at his words. "Yes, it was fine in the end."

Marc entered the room just after nine o'clock, by which time the rest of us were well and truly ready to get this business underway. Unfortunately, however, the expression on Marc's face distracted us all almost immediately.

"They haven't broken out again, have they?" asked James.

"No," he said, sitting down beside Amelia and throwing his head back into the couch. "Well, one of them has, I suppose you could say. We've got a bit of a problem, guys."

We all waited for him to elaborate, and when he didn't, Peter prompted, "So what's the problem?"

"Well, we need to do something about them soon," he said. "I dunno what Mr. Woodward's plans were—well, I sort of do, you know, with the conversions and all that—but as for the others…" He sighed. "Well, anyway, two of them are going on hunger strikes as of this morning, and another one of them committed suicide, by diving off his bed head down, by the look of it."

"Oh man," breathed Tommy.

A silence followed this, and then Marc said, "Well, any suggestions?"

"Yes, perhaps," said James, sitting up straighter in his seat. "We have to decide what it is we wish to achieve by keeping them here. Are we wanting to punish them for being Hammerhearts, or are we wanting to prevent them from re-joining the Hammersons' ranks?"

"Mr. Woodward would say the latter, I think," said Tommy. "You think so, Amelia?"

"Yeah, he probably would," she said, "and I suppose we really should make it so that they don't wanna die in there, but we can't make it too nice for them either."

"I tell you what," said Peter. "Maybe I'm just too easy-going, but I don't have a problem with making it nice for them, just so long as we cut off any possible access to the outside world. I reckon if that were me, the isolation would be punishment enough."

"That's what I'm thinking as well," said James. "I guess it varies depending on the person, like most of them are only here just for being Hammerhearts and not because they've done anything particularly wrong. For the ones that have, like Hignat and Wilwog, and Sebastian—(his face darkened)—they shouldn't receive any special treatment."

"Special treatment?" repeated several people.

"You know what I mean." He shrugged. "Thing is, though, I really don't know how we can change things in there."

"Design a whole new prison for them," I suggested. "Basically provide everything the prisoners need to survive in there and make it impossible for them to leave, and make it a reasonably nice environment, something they might enjoy."

"What would they do in there?" Marc asked.

"I dunno," I sighed. "Whatever, I suppose. It's not like they do anything in there now. Maybe give them the same sort of stuff we have—a library, some games, a gym, you get the idea."

"But no Internet," Peter added.

"Well, duh. Can't give them any communication with the outside world."

"Right," said Marc. "We can probably manage to create something like that for them. The other problem is the conversions. It really hurts to see people like Liam still locked up in there, especially after all he's done for our side already. We really need to think of a solution for those types, not to mention people like Candice Young, who seem completely screwed in the head."

"But she's the only one still here," said James. "All the others went out with the Woodward soldiers. The only reason she didn't go with them is 'cause she's too young. Pardon the pun."

"One problem at a time, Marc," I said. I privately thought I had a solution to both problems, but I wasn't about to get publicly carried away with myself.

"Okay, then," he said. "You wanna do the prison stuff, John?"

"Yeah, I reckon I could," I said.

"So what about the life assistant? What are we gonna do about that?"

"Put it off a little longer?" I suggested, grinning slightly. "Let's say we meet back here at one o'clock."

That would give Natalie plenty of time to get herself ready to be involved, unless she wanted to be out by then, in which case she would just have to miss out.

"So what about all of us?" Tommy asked.

Everyone looked around at each other, clearly waiting for someone to take charge and start giving orders. After some fifteen seconds like this, I couldn't stand it any longer and took the initiative.

"Marc, James, you two go to bed," I said. "You both look dead on your feet. Only, Marc, you'll have to—oh, wait." I paused, thinking. If Marc was the only one who could use the Hero Crystal, then either he would have to stay up around the clock day after day to use it, or there would have to be periods where the Hero Crystal was not in use. I decided that the latter was probably better. "Never mind. You're off the hook. Guess that means you're on your own, Tommy."

"What am I doing?" he asked.

"Using the Light Crystal," I said. "Just see what you can do with it. Now, Amelia—"

I stopped again, trying to think. There were two other things that had to be done, but both of them involved someone leaving the base, and surely both of them would require magic. Amelia could do one or the other, I hoped, but neither if she was too tired. She raised her eyes to my face when I spoke her name but didn't say anything.

"You up for a bit of work?" I asked her.

"What sort of work?" she asked.

"I guess you've got two choices," I said, "and I guess you go with whichever you think you can do better. I'm sure Peter will be happy to help out."

I shot him a sideways look that was supposed to say 'you'd damn well better help her out.'

"What are the choices?" he asked flatly. His tone suggested he wanted a day off, but I doubted anyone would be getting a day off around here any time soon.

"Retrieve the Maivises," I said. "If they're still in Chopville, then it'll be easy. If not, then I guess that's where the magic comes into it. The other option is to look into the location of the Darkness Crystal. We really need that back in our hands before they decide to do more with it."

"We'll do that," said Amelia, clearly using magic to give herself some additional energy. "Use magic to see where it is. If it's too dangerous for us to take it back on our own, we'll go after the Maivises. Is that okay?" she asked Peter.

"Yeah, that's fine," he said.

"Do either of you two wanna help them?" I asked Serena and Lena now, neither of whom had spoken the whole time I'd been there. I had the feeling that neither of them felt they were truly a part of this group yet. Both of them seemed surprised to be addressed with an option, but they both looked unwilling.

"I was hoping to keep you company," said Serena, gazing at me imploringly.

"Later on," I said, patting her arm lightly. "I'd rather do this on my own."

I felt another pang of guilt. The only reason why I didn't want Serena with me was because she would likely make it difficult to concentrate on what I was doing.

"Can I go with you two?" Lena asked Amelia.

"I guess so," she replied, looking surprised.

"Guess that leaves me with what?" Serena asked, looking around at us all.

We all looked around at each other again. When nobody offered a suggestion, I said, "Guess it means you've got the morning off."

Serena didn't look at all happy by that, and I was pleased to see it. It was certainly a good sign that she really wanted to help us.

* * *

Up in my room, sitting on my bed with the Sien-Leoard Crystal in hand, I turned my attention to the task ahead. I had only ever seen magic like this performed once. On that occasion, Stella had constructed a bathroom for us in a box about the size of the average shoebox. My idea was to copy her design, and I had a feeling I could probably do it and probably without spending nearly as long on it as she had. Although, given that this would be considerably more complex than that bathroom had been, I probably would end up spending longer than she had.

So I set to work, firstly creating a box about the size of an ice cream container. The next bit of magic I had to perform was the door into the place, and the complications started there. I wanted it to be a normal door that people could pass through, that prisoners could get into but, once recognised as prisoners, they could not get out of it until they were no longer recognised as prisoners, and that only certain people could get through to start with. I didn't want to allow for a situation such as the one Sebastian had created; it would mean not using the electronic keys. It was a lot to remember, so in the end, I decided just to create a normal door. At least, a tiny door proportionate to the size of the container.

The next step was to create everything inside the container, but that seemed to me to be done a lot more easily if I could be inside the container. That way I would know exactly how things would look to the prisoners. So I got up off the bed, placed the prison on my bedside drawers, and created a magic door an inch away from the wall beside them. The door would open directly into the prison, shrinking all that passed through it so that they would also be proportionate to the container. Stella had called this spell a "transgation charm."

The inside of the prison was eerie. Apart from the door, it was endless space to three sides of me, and endless darkness. I knew there were four walls, a floor, and a ceiling, but they were all lost in darkness. The first spell I cast, and one of the most complicated I had ever done in my life, was to make the ceiling of the container reflect the sky outside above Chopville. My initial intention had been to provide windows like those in the infirmary that reflected what could be seen through the windows of the house the Woodwards owned on the side of the Jade River, but this seemed like a better idea. There would be buildings in here, but at least, to the prisoners, it would feel as though they could come outside during the day if they wanted fresh air.

The spell worked, and for a few moments, I had to slit my eyes against the brightness of it. The sky was overcast but not raining. That thought was the inspiration of the second spell: don't allow rain to fall inside the container. The third spell was to keep the air in here fresh, so that it would feel even more like being outdoors than just by looks. I then turned my attention to the floor and walls, making the walls look like tall fences and the floor covered in grass. I even erected a few trees some distance away from the door.

I spent the next half hour or so walking around the container, constructing a nice looking yard for the prisoners. I knew the questions would come from the others. Why was I giving them all this? The fact was I didn't know. I just had this feeling that it was the right thing to do for them. It was a way for them to live, not a full life but a life all the same. They were all Hammerhearts, so it seemed unlikely that they would hurt each other, like they probably would in a normal prison. The yard basically consisted of a garden with paths winding through it, benches for people to sit down under trees (it would be nice in the summer), and a swimming pool in the middle. I covered it up for the time being, though; it wouldn't be needed for six months yet, and a heated indoor swimming pool felt too good for these people.

Once that was done, I turned my attention to the edges of the yard. In my mind, I could imagine the building surrounding the garden, but I hadn't exactly decided on how the building should be designed. In the end I went with a very basic configuration. The building in which the prisoners would live stretched around three edges of the container. I wanted the door into the place to enter through an administration building, which I would get to last, a place where the prisoners would not be able to go.

The prisoner building had five storeys. The building was accessible through four doors at the two ends and the two inner corners. With each door came a staircase to access the upper levels of the building. There was a single dining hall in the very centre of the connecting stretch along the back wall of the container. The food in the dining hall would be supplied the same way the conveyer belt in the Woodward dining room operated. I hadn't tested it, but I had made the crystal copy its design, so that should have been enough.

Each storey had two communal bathrooms, obviously one for the ladies and one for the gents. They were located at the inner corners of each storey. True to my word, I had also created a games room, which also served as a lounge room, and a gym, located on either side of the dining hall.

The rest of the building was taken up with rooms. They weren't really cells as such because I hadn't bothered putting any bars in them, and the locks on the doors were on the inside. The rooms were small and only contained a wardrobe, bed (fairly small), desk, and window that looked out into the prison yard. All the rooms pointed into the prison yard, the walls that faced the fences around the edges of the container were only the corridor, and there were no windows there.

It was a good design, I thought. Simple, but good enough. The most important thing was that it served its purpose, and if any new purposes came up in time, we could deal with them then. I was making the assumption that these prisoners would be civilised with each other at least, even if they couldn't be civilised with the rest of us.

I was almost done. All that remained was to ensure the security of this place—the most important thing of all, in other words. I'd had some vague thoughts about the sort of security that I could use to protect this place. The most effective way to keep an eye on the prisoners was not by way of security cameras, but something far more direct. Stella had once told me about a thing called comprehensive memory, which recorded everything that passed through a person's mind, everything they heard, saw, felt (both physically and emotionally), smelt, tasted, and thought. Initially it went against my inclination to do this, remembering the few times I had been inside other people's minds and the moral regret I had felt afterwards (that hadn't been present in Sebastian's case, though), but my final decision was based on the theory that most of these people had waived their right to privacy, and those who were under an influential charm really had nothing to fear if they had nothing to hide. Recording the comprehensive memory of each and every prisoner in the container was a lot to keep track of, but I felt sure that it could be done.

I therefore went about creating a small building around the entrance door. The building contained a small passage that led directly from the door to another door into the prison yard, plus two other doors to the sides. One of them led to the area where comprehensive memory could be examined. The other led to an interrogation room. At least, it was a place where people such as Mr.

Woodward could talk to individual prisoners or small groups of them separately.

I did the complicated magic after that. It took some time because I had to do it slowly to make sure I got it right. The only way I knew I could get it secure was to make it assume that every single person who entered the prison yard was a prisoner, excepting certain people who it would identify by scanning their brains. I would have to make it recognise those people later, as I would need them with me to do it. Everyone who was a prisoner would have their memory recorded and stored in the administration room, and if we needed to scan their memories, a device that I had created would allow us to sink into the stored memory the same way I had sunk into Sebastian's memories two days earlier.

By default, no prisoners could pass through the door to the administration building unless they were accompanied by an authorised person. Even if they were accompanied, they could only go into the interrogation room. They could not leave the container unless they were no longer recognised as prisoners. Nobody at all apart from authorised people could enter the administration room. The invisible lines on the floor would prevent people going through doors they weren't supposed to. There was one thing it always assumed, though—any changes to who was authorised and who was a prisoner would require magic, which basically came to the same security that Mr. Woodward's prison had. It was the only way to make absolutely sure that no loophole could be exploited. I hoped perhaps I could come up with something better down the track, but for now I would have to be satisfied with this.

The job was done. It had taken just under two hours in the end, which I supposed had been a pretty good achievement given how much magic I had performed with the crystal. I left the container and emerged back into my bedroom, feeling satisfied with my morning's work, though already pretty tired and ready for a rest. There wouldn't be any rest, though, not when I still had an hour before lunch and could use the time to move the prisoners from their cells into their new home and do the necessary magic to seal them in.

So I vanished the door, scooped up the container, and left my room, descending three levels into the hall, already thinking about how would be the best way to do this. The easiest thing to do seemed to be to just create a magical door that would move along to each cell so that each prisoner could enter straight into the container. Would the prisoners work out what to do? Would they be able to go and get their own rooms? I had to hope so because organising each and every one of them promised to be yet another few hours of work at least.

I used the crystal to pass through Mr. Woodward's protective wall into the prison block, where the first thing I did was use magic to stick the container to the roof, in the corner just above the door that looked like a wall. That was another idea I had gotten from Stella. It would be untouchable and well out of the way there. The next thing I did was recreate the door I had vanished up in my room and put a spell on it that would make it follow behind me as I moved from cell to cell. That taken care of, it was time to meet the prisoners.

It took some forty-five minutes to take care of them all, and the delays for the most part were caused by many of them being unwilling to move at all. I had to use the crystal to force a few of them through the door and into the yard. I was having serious doubts now about them. It was a good design, it would be better for them than these cells had been, it would be a million times better than if they had been imprisoned by the Hammerhearts (and I wondered if any of them had thought of that), but the general attitude suggested that it still wouldn't be enough. They would have to be satisfied with it, though, because as far as I was concerned, it was the absolute stretch of generosity and, since they were Hammerhearts at the end of the day, many of them having made that choice consciously, they deserved no better.

The work finally done, I took the door back outside the prison block and placed it over the top of Mr. Woodward's enchanted wall, making it look like that door was always part of the building. I then used magic on the knob so that only authorised people could turn it. Of course, it would validate such authorised people by scanning their brains, much more reliable than fingerprints. I was the only authorised person so far, so I opened it, stepped through into the administration building and then into the yard, having a look around. A few of the prisoners were standing around the yard, looking positively dumbstruck by what had happened. None of them were quite stupid enough to assume they had been freed, though this knowledge only seemed to add to their confusion. Most of them seemed to have gone into the building, for which I was grateful. I supposed I would have to do an inspection of it later on to make sure they were doing things properly in there, but that was later. For now, I left them to it, closing both doors behind me and isolating them inside that little container.

After all that, it was time to eat. I went straight into the dining room and was joined quickly by a highly disgruntled Tommy.

Apparently he'd hardly been able to do anything that morning since the Light Crystal had no way of letting him know what was happening in the world around him. He'd used it for about half an hour, doing as much as he could think of for our side, before giving up and doing his own thing for the rest of the time. Lena also joined us during his recount. I knew it was because of what had happened that morning, but I had to wonder now just how much she was going to involve herself with us or, more specifically, how much she would involve herself with me. She looked good enough to eat, but for whatever reason, I wasn't fetched this time.

Serena wasn't too far behind her, though, and Peter not too far behind them. The two of them (Peter more so than Lena) recounted their adventures of the morning to us. They had been successful in locating the Darkness Crystal; it was being held in a highly secure chamber in a Hammerheart base located in, of all places, the middle of the Pacific Ocean. Unsurprisingly, they had been unable to get inside it. What they knew had been learnt by eavesdropping on some off-duty officials discussing Arnold Hammerson's plan to use the crystal as a bargaining technique. Well, that was how they put it. It was more like blackmail, though, for it would be something along the lines of, "Hand over the Hero Crystal or this tornado is gonna wipe out this city and this many lives. Okay, that's done, now let's try again. Hand over the Hero Crystal or this earthquake will strike approximately here, killing this many people," and so on. It was an alarming prospect and only emphasised the fact that we needed to get that crystal back as soon as possible.

As for tracking down Harry and Simon, they had once again been successful. In fact, it couldn't have been easier, for the four Maivis twins had been moved by their grandparents to relatives living in Echuca. Peter had knocked on the door. The grandfather had opened it, recognised Peter, and promptly slammed it in his face. Peter had gone around to the back door and done the same, for the same result. He had then knocked on the lounge room window, causing both grandparents to go nuts at him and a middle-aged man, the owner of the property I supposed, to threaten to call the police. That would have been devastating for them because apparently the first thing Hank Cornish had done that morning was order the police in Victoria and New South Wales to return to work, since they had finished the screening process for those two states. The fortunate thing about the window episode is that Harry and Simon saw Peter and promptly fetched Misty and Michelle from one of the bedrooms and engineered a quick escape through a side window. All four twins, plus their grandparents, who had seen part of the escape through another window and made to follow, outraged, were now safely inside the Woodward base. The two grandparents had finally accepted it once they'd seen the place, although they were certainly very pissed off with the whole situation.

I also heard snatches about the progress of the war from people around us who had been following it on television, taking in all the Hammerheart propaganda and attempting to read between the lines to work out what was really going on. From what I gathered, the fighting in this part of the world was temporarily over, as so many countries had gone under completely and were now only dealing with guerrilla combat. Indeed, Australia was already starting to come out the other end, what with Cornish and those around him working very hard to restore some order in the place, albeit the wrong sort of order. The same held true for most other countries in the Pacific region, although none of them were making progression as quickly.

Meanwhile, most countries in Asia were either in contention (for lack of a better word to describe the sort of fighting that was going on) or taken over completely. Those that had been taken over were still enduring plenty of internal fighting, not to mention occasional attacks from other countries that were still relatively free of the Hammerheart influence. Most of Europe was in a similar state, though since they weren't as far along, most countries (particularly western countries) weren't yet in Hammerheart control. Only in southwest Asia, particularly the Subcontinent and the Middle East, did the Hammerhearts themselves need to get violent, though given the political state of many of those countries prior to this business, I doubted they would have any sort of control of that part of the world for a long time yet. No African or South American countries had been attacked as yet, but that hadn't left them unaffected by what was going on by any stretch of the imagination. If this wasn't a world war, I didn't know what was.

Chapter 18: Through the Flames

By one o'clock, the six of us were back in the Woodward lounge room. Marc and James didn't join us; they were clearly still asleep, and we didn't want to disturb them after the good work they'd done the night before. Natalie was there, though. It appeared that she had come in here at some point over lunch and Amelia had spent the time catching her up on everything that had been happening around here. When Peter asked her where she had been all morning, she had told us that she'd made herself invisible while she slept so that she wouldn't be disturbed. She had no memory of Rebecca entering her room, though. As I sat down between Peter and Serena once again, her eyes found mine, and I thought I saw something in them that hadn't been there before. It looked like newly discovered knowledge or a newly discovered feeling, no doubt brought on by her experiences of the last few days. The moment seemed to make us both uncomfortable, though, because we both looked away quickly.

"How did it go with the prisoners, anyway, John?" Peter asked. "I forgot to ask earlier."

"Well, they're somewhere nice now," I told them. "You guys can see it later if you like. I'm not completely sure about the security, but I did put spells on it that ought to seal them in. Only authorised people can get in and out, though, so I'll have to authorise anyone who wants to check it out."

The others looked—well, not so much impressed, but perhaps just pleased.

"Right," he said. "That settled, should we get on with it?"

I pulled the life assistant out and stared at it, remembering all Underwood had told me about how it worked, which wasn't very much. The most important thing I knew I had actually learnt from Stella, from the second most recent dream I'd had about her. When Underwood had let her use it, she had communicated with the old man by touching the most sensitive spot on the life assistant. That sensitive spot surely had to be the small pad, about the size of my fingertip, located in the very centre of the topside of the object.

"I'll have a go and see if anything happens," I said. "If I remember rightly, Underwood had to check that Smiley was there and ready to talk before he could do any chatting."

They all fell still and watched with interest as I touched my fingertip lightly to the pad. I held it there, waiting, anticipating, but nothing at all happened. I pressed down on the pad a little harder, then a little harder again, knowing that it wasn't about to work. Stella had only touched it lightly, and the thought had been planted in her head from afar almost straight away. So why wasn't it working for me?

"Anything?" asked Lena in a hushed voice.

"No," I said. "It didn't do a thing."

"What's it supposed to do?" asked Serena.

"Mental communication," I told her. "Smiley's supposed to put thoughts in my head through this."

"Smiley?" Serena repeated, sounding amused.

"You just said you had to check if he's there before you can communicate," Peter reminded me. "That probably means you have to project a thought into it, rather than waiting for one to come out of it."

That sounded right. In fact, it sounded obvious. Stella wouldn't have needed to do that herself, not if Underwood had done it for her, so the question now was how was I supposed to do it? I touched my fingertip lightly to the pad again and tried to think at it, tried to call Smiley's name inside my own head, hoping that would be enough to send the thought down my finger, into the pad, and to wherever Smiley was now, and whatever similar device he used for this long-distance telepathy. For a few seconds, nothing happened, but then I felt an external thought push itself into my head. I was no stranger to the sensation, having had external thoughts from the Sien-Leoard Crystal before, not to mention the ones Amelia had sent to me. These felt the same as those had. What I got wasn't words of any kind, but a simple idea that my brain interpreted easily—recognition. Smiley recognised me.

"I've got him," I said, removing my finger from the pad so that Smiley wouldn't pick up on my relaying of messages. I supposed it wouldn't matter much if he did, but why confuse the issue.

"Ask him where he is and if we can come and see him," Peter told me.

I put my fingertip back to the pad, but before I could form another thought to send to him, another of his pushed its way into my head. It was a mental image of a young man: Jacob Underwood. Where is he? Is he okay? Smiley was asking after Underwood, so I answered his enquiry before making any of my own. Better to let him dictate the terms of this conversation for now. I visualised Underwood and Siobhan together in the room Underwood had upstairs, including all of Underwood's furniture cluttering the place. It served to show Smiley that Underwood was safe inside the Woodward base.

"So where is he?" Tommy asked in a hushed voice.

I didn't answer. In fact, I barely heard him, my whole attention focussed on the telepathy going on. Two thoughts came through in rapid succession. The first was approval of what I had shown him; the second was a visualisation of his own. It was me, when I was a baby. Smiley was holding me and telling Mr. Woodward, who stood before him and looked a little younger than he did now, that I was in danger and needed to be protected. I responded with an affirmative —yes, that was me—and then I followed it up with a question of my own. I already knew that Moran and the ghost woman were my real parents, but there seemed no harm in making sure, so I visualised the two of them together, remembering the time I had seen them both together, just before I had turned and left them in the room that had guarded the Sien-Leoard Crystal. His response was quick, and it was an affirmative: Yes, they had been the parents who had given me to him.

"You all just be quiet and wait," I heard Peter hiss at the others. "Wait 'til he's ready to talk."

Do you know what sort of danger I was in? I sent the thought into the device and got a cagy response back that I could make neither here nor there of. It seemed that he had suspicions about what the danger was, or perhaps he knew more than he was letting on. Either way, he didn't want to share. That didn't sit too well with me, so I asked the question the others were waiting for me to ask: Where are you?

Instead of answering the question, however, he sent another mental image to me. I knew what it was immediately: A vision of standing in the open doorway, facing into the main hall on Rock Haulter, which, as it had always been in my dreams and had never been in real life, was completely empty, only this time, Stella wasn't there either. That tag attached to that image told me that it—that image, those dreams—were much more significant than I had given them credit for. Why? That was my next question, and the response came in two parts. The first was the beginning, which suggested that all that had happened to me began there, on Rock Haulter, in the main hall.

An interesting thought, but not one I had time to dwell on, because another thought was coming through. It was another mental image, and the moment I recognised it, I tried very hard to push it from my mind. He was showing me, in much greater clarity than I had seen yet, my disturbing vision, the one that had plagued me ever since I had met Graham that day. Dark, smoky, glowing flames, and in the centre of it all, a body lying prone, burning. It was clearer now because it was fresh; the images I'd had before now were mere flashbacks to the one I'd had in Graham's room, and that itself had only been a memory, based loosely on what I'd seen on television. This was much more, though. This was as vivid as if I were seeing it before me at that very moment. I shuddered involuntarily and felt Serena, who was sitting beside me, slip an arm around me. Apparently she'd felt it.

I wanted to ask what it meant but decided to ask again: Where are you? This time, he answered the question properly, showing me a towering mass of rock I knew all too well.

"He's on Rock Haulter," I told the others exuberantly, removing my finger from the life assistant again.

"Rock Haulter?" Peter repeated. "Fantastic. I've been looking forward to getting back there again."

"Of course," sighed Tommy. "Of course, it's so obvious now. That would be the perfect hiding place for him. He must have gone on the boat with us, and that's why he hasn't seen me since before camp."

"How are we supposed to get to Rock Haulter, though?" Natalie asked. "The portals only open once a year. Do we have to wait 'til next February?"

"There are other portals," said Serena. "Lisa told us, remember? I can't remember where they all are, except that one of them is definitely near South America."

"Looks like we're on another international holiday, then," said Peter in mock cheer, while I felt like groaning. Of course, if we wanted to get to Rock Haulter again, we would have to go through some other portal, whichever one opened next.

"But each portal only opens for like half an hour a year," Lena said. "Even if you can work out exactly where they are, you still have to work out exactly when they open, and how long do you have to wait for that to happen?"

"We can find all that out easily enough," said Amelia quietly. "My dad's probably got a lot of that stuff in his office somewhere, but even if he doesn't, we only need to know the details for one portal to work out the details for all the others. I know they're all on the same line of latitude and exactly ninety degrees of longitude apart. Since we went through our portal at around two o'clock, that probably means we have to go through the next portal at that same time—local time, of course. And to find the date, well, we just count from February ninth, when we went through."

A silence followed that unexpected speech. Then Peter said, "We can get James onto all that stuff. He's great at working things like that out. John, ask him if we can come and visit him? Actually, ask him if he could come to us too. I don't think he would, somehow, but it's worth a try."

I did as I was told, putting my fingertip back to the pad again and thinking about what Peter had just told me. Another two thoughts came through from Smiley's end. The first was a good one, the second not so good. The first was an affirmative; yes, we could come and visit him. The second thought (in fact, it was more of a condition, what we had to do for him if we were going to visit him) was bring Jacob Underwood with us. I groaned aloud, removing my finger once again.

"What's up?" asked Tommy. "He says no?"

"He says we have to bring Underwood with us if we go to see him," I told them.

"Oh, fantastic," said Peter sarcastically. "Well, actually, maybe it's not so bad. We can leave him there, like Serena suggested this morning."

"Okay," said Amelia, sitting up straighter. "I like that idea. John, tell him we'll be there as soon as we can."

I relayed the message back to Smiley, and his response was a quick, sharp okay. Good, I thought, removing my fingertip from the life assistant and putting the object back in my pocket. Smiley seemed to be a nice guy, sure, but the sooner we could get over there, see him, and come back, the better I would feel. It would also be a relief to get rid of Underwood, again, the sooner, the better. I just didn't enjoy the thought of him being inside the Woodward base. As for what became of Siobhan at that stage, whether she went with him and stayed with him or stayed here, we would have to work that out later.

"Thank God," said Tommy when he saw that the communication was done for now. "Now we're finally in touch with him, after two whole months of stuffing around looking for him."

"Looks like we're heading back to the Rock," said Peter. "That's our next job; between now and the next portal opening, we gotta work out where it is, when it opens, and how we're gonna get through it."

The meeting broke up not long after that, most of us breaking off in separate directions. I headed for my room, again without Serena and again for the same reason as before, but as I was about to ascend the stairs, I was called back, not by Serena, or Amelia, or even Lena, but Natalie.

"What's up?" I asked, retreating down the few steps I'd already climbed and approaching her where she stood just by the door into the corridor. "You not confused about anything that's going on around here?"

"No, Amelia told me everything," she said.

On closer inspection, I saw that she looked extremely nervous, constantly shifting her weight from foot to foot and flushing slightly, even though she hadn't really said anything yet. Her nervousness made me feel uncomfortable.

"So what's up?" I asked her.

"I just needed to tell you something," she said, and with an enormous physical effort, she took a step forward and put her arms around me. I was so utterly caught off guard that my arms rose to push her away. Instead I put them lightly around her before gently disengaging from her, keen to move on past this moment and all too aware that Serena was somewhere just around the corner.

"What's on your mind?" I asked, holding her by the shoulders at arm's length and forcing myself to stare right into her face, an action that made her blush like a tomato, and I could feel heat in my own face too.

"I guess…" She stammered and hitched before trying again. "Well, you know how much I've seen and done since Tuesday, and I guess—I guess it's just taught me a few things I should have known before."

"Yeah, it is one hell of an experience," I said, and I understood. Even though I had probably seen even more of it by way of the crystal, it wasn't the same as actually being out there in the thick of it. If anything, it was more like watching it on television and being able to influence the things that happen on the screen.

"Yeah, well, what I learnt was that I've taken way too much for granted for too long," she said, and I felt her small shoulders seem to lower under my hands, as though she wanted the floor to open up and swallow her. "I guess I just want you to know that."

"Er, okay," I said, now not having a clue what she meant. "So what are you saying?"

She searched the air around me, as though making sure nobody in the hall was eavesdropping. It sounded empty to me but for the quiet conversation in the lounge room, and the part of the corridor I could see through the open door was also empty. Natalie lowered her voice and said, in a tone that seemed to send a tingle right down my spine, "I just want you to know how I feel, 'cause maybe I haven't been open enough before, and I really don't wanna regret anything if something bad happens to either of us."

"Okay," I said slowly, my stomach lurching. Did she mean what I thought she meant? Was she saying that she wanted me to know how she was interested in me? Was she going to become as forward about her feelings as Amelia had been? Or worse, Lena?

"Thanks," she said, taking a step back and breaking the physical contact between us. She was blushing more than ever. "I've gotta head back out there now. See you tomorrow, hopefully."

* * *

Later that afternoon, I was back in my bedroom, sitting on my bed as I had been that morning, and once again alone, save for the Sien-Leoard Crystal, which was all the company I needed. By this time, Marc and James would probably be waking up, and soon be finding out what we had learnt that morning. If Underwood and Siobhan had slept through the day as I suspected they had, they would be waking too. Natalie, who had occupied my thoughts a hell of a lot since our conversation earlier, had returned to the war while her father had returned to base and was now resting in the Fletcher living quarters. The rest of them were doing their own thing, I supposed. No further jobs had been decided on after our meeting, so I could only suppose that we were waiting to catch Marc and James up before making other moves ourselves. I, however, had something of my own I wanted to try, which was the reason for my seeking solitude now.

The prison was as good as I knew I could make it, at least until flaws in its design were discovered, hopefully not resulting in any escapes, but that didn't mean I'd been all too comfortable loading the prisoners into it. I hadn't forgotten that some of them, perhaps many of them, weren't Hammerhearts by will, that they were mind-boggled into joining their ranks. It had hurt to force some of my classmates through the doorway, particularly Liam, after all he had previously done for our side. So now I was working on a device that would counter the magic done to them. Properly counter it, not like what Mr. Woodward had done. I doubted that Mr. Woodward could have foreseen the negative effect those devices, the rebogglers as they were, would have on people.

The magic I had so far performed on the device, which was physically identical to both the bogglers and rebogglers, although a different colour, would firstly determine if any mind-altering magic had been performed on a person at any point in their life, not by searching them for currently active spells, because the influential charm didn't leave any traces of magic, but actually going back in history and searching for any magic that may have touched the person in the past. If it had, it would firstly record all their memories of everything that had happened since the influential charm had been performed. Then it would wipe the person's memory of everything it had recorded before replacing the recorded memories back into their brain, only removing the person's wills and desires as it went. That way their wills ought to return to how they had been before they were boggled with only a memory of what happened in between. It was very difficult to know, sitting here in my room, if such magic would do what I wanted it to do. Theoretically it should, but that didn't mean I wouldn't do further unforeseen damage to the person's brain in the process. My intention was to test it out sooner rather than later, perhaps on Candice Young. She may have started out an innocent schoolgirl, but that didn't change what she had done since, nor did it change the fact that since she was already so messed up, there was little to lose by using her as a guinea pig.

Only half my mind was on the job I was doing, though, because it kept straying back to the things Smiley had shown me earlier that afternoon. The two visions—the one depicting the recurring dreams I'd been having since shortly before the Rock Haulter camp, and the fiery vision I'd been having for six weeks now—why had Smiley chosen to show those things to me? Was he implying that there was greater meaning in them both than I was giving them credit for? I supposed that was possible, but that didn't explain how Smiley could have known about those things in the first place. Then again, Smiley was no normal old man, I told myself. But what did it mean, then?

When he had shown me the vision of the main hall on Rock Haulter, I'd got a fleeting idea of a beginning. That hall had been the beginning of something for me. What did that mean? I vaguely remembered, the first time I had entered that hall at the very start of camp, having a feeling of déjà vu, though I had since decided that it must have been because of the dream I'd had about that hall two nights earlier. Was that all there was to it, though? What if I really had been there before, when I was a child, before I was a Playman? Since it kept showing me Stella there, or more specifically, me and Stella alone in there, did it have something to do with whatever was between us? Was she perhaps having the same dream I was? I'd never spoken to her about dreams—ventures into each other's minds, but not mere dreams. On top of all that, though, why was I only having these dreams now? Why hadn't I been having them all my life, like I had been entering Stella's mind all my life? It was all so confusing, and I could come up with nothing at all, no answers to the many questions racing around inside my head.

I also thought, rather reluctantly, of the other vision, the one that depicted nothing but death. At least that's what I thought, anyway. Death, darkness, or evil—one of the three, surely. Why had Smiley shown that one to me? I'd always thought it was just something that popped into my head every time I thought about people, fire, and the two coming together. Surely there was no significance in that, unless it was because the visions still gave me the creeps and Smiley knew a way to stop me from thinking about such things. If the vision was supposed to be retelling something from my past, like the recurring dreams, or telling me something I needed for the future, like I suspected of the recurring dreams (for now I felt sure they were telling me something I may need to do as well), I had no idea what it could be. I knew it had nothing to do with Natalie being blown up, because when I had placed her body in the shadows of my vision, it hadn't fit.

So it was, for the second or third time since it had happened two weeks earlier, Nicole's death I thought of. That seemed perhaps a little more likely, though in another way it seemed far less likely. The vision showed the body down in a horizontal position as it burnt—its shadow in a horizontal position, anyway—whereas given the way Nicole had died, you couldn't say she had been in any particular position at the point of death at all. The thing that made it more likely, though, was that the scene of the Playman house before Lillian Woodward and company had performed the magic to save it had been very similar to everything else in that vision—the glowing flames, the surrounding heavy smoke, the blackness (obviously it had been the middle of the night in real life), and of course the shadows.

I hadn't really understood much of what had happened that night at the time. I had known it was deliberately lit, of course, and when I had seen the man (the Fire Man, as I thought of him), I had known it was magical. I knew more now, of course, both from the investigation done afterwards and by what I had learnt from Sebastian's memories, so replaying the series of events in my mind was fairly easy to do. I'd tried very hard not to think about it much until this point, so maybe reliving it would be the final step required to finally get over it.

It had started regularly enough for me. It had only been the third time I had gone home to Lopher Lane for the night since first coming to the Woodward base way back in late February. The previous two occasions had been uneventful; on one of them I had been with Peter, the other I had been with James. Felicity and Jessica had also been home a couple of times, but it was only Nicole's first time since getting her room. She had always been quite happy living inside the Woodward living quarters. All six residents of the two linked houses had been aware of our arrival and the approximate time we would be coming so had carefully left the door open for us by way of Dad having a smoke in the front yard, quite at his ease.

Nobody had acknowledged our presence until we made ourselves visible, and that had only been once Dad had come back inside and shut and locked the door behind him. We didn't get to see our parents and grandparents much anymore, what with us all living inside Woodward headquarters and them still living here, although Dad and Charlie came into base on occasion to catch up with what the Woodwards were doing, so whenever we came home, we always spent a good hour or two catching up on news from both sides, all clustered around the large dining table in the Playman house, the place where we always used to eat our dinners and have many a family argument. The same had happened that night. Not an argument, I mean a good, long catch-up session.

I always enjoyed seeing the oldies these days. Even Hilda and Violet, who normally seemed like a pair of bitter old ladies to me, were nice to see these days. They still found ways to joke about their ill health, and they would never miss an opportunity to slag off Dad and Charlie, who were only too happy to return the favour. Mum and Marge asked mostly about school, whether we were keeping up with our assignments, concentrating more on them than the war outside, because the war was not for children. They still hadn't gotten the idea out of their head that we were an enormous part in the war, a greater part than Dad and Charlie by far.

We had been in the Easter holidays at that stage so had gone to bed fairly late, around midnight. I'd stayed up later than that plenty of times, but most of those times, I'd spent half the evening in my room. I had lain down, thinking to myself that, while the privacy was nice and I had become accustomed to privacy since having my own room at Woodward headquarters, it didn't feel right here. This room wasn't complete without Peter lying in his bed on the other side of it. I had fallen asleep and into some silly dream about Harry and Simon standing in front of me, slowly undressing themselves and beckoning to unseen women to come forward and enjoy their company.

Both twins had been naked but for their jocks when I had been rudely roused from the dream by a high-pitched noise coming from outside my room, further down the hall, at the top of the stairs. I had jerked awake roughly, sitting up and listening hard, taking a few seconds to recognise the sound for what it was: the smoke alarm. Our house had two smoke alarms, one upstairs and one downstairs. The one downstairs had gone off many times before but always because of something not necessarily gone according to plan in the kitchen. The smoke had never carried up the stairs though, for someone had always been quick to open the kitchen windows before it could happen, so I had never actually heard that one go off before. Now that it was—now that they both were—I had known something was very wrong.

I had clambered out of bed and staggered across the room to the door and opened it, sticking my head out into the hallway and sniffing the air. Sure enough, the smoke was strong, and getting stronger. The heat had been getting worse, and as I listened, the sound of glass blowing out from downstairs, followed by a roaring sound and a wave of hot air from the direction of the stairs, had told me all I needed to know. There had been other noises too, closer but small because of the continuing blowing from downstairs, but perhaps the scariest thing was the light I had seen at the end of the hallway. It had been shining up the stairs from the bottom level, and it was getting slowly brighter, as though the fire itself was creeping up the stairs towards the inhabitants of the house. We had to get out of here quick or we'd be in real trouble.

Marge, Charlie, and Violet had been next door, but the rest of us (the Playmans, in other words) had all been in this house. That hadn't meant the Thomases were exactly safe, especially if the fire spread through the tunnel, but they had been in a lot less danger than we were. Hilda, who had been roused just as I had, came staggering out of the study, staring at me in utter horror.

"John, what—"

"The house is on fire," I had shouted at her. "Quick, come through here."

I had reached instinctively for the Sien-Leoard Crystal, only to remember that I didn't have it with me. Mr. Woodward didn't want me to take the crystal with me when coming home for the night; he believed it put the crystal in danger of being stolen. Of course, he didn't have a problem with me taking it out of the base any other time, which made no sense to me, but such is the hypocrisy of life, I had supposed. What he had given me instead, which I had kept in my pyjama pocket, was a signaller much like the one I had taken into the Hammerheart base on the previous occasions I had infiltrated it, one that would call magic to my assistance in the form of one of the Sorcerers if I was under attack. I hadn't realised it was a Hammerheart attack at the time, but I had pushed the red button (the danger button) anyway as I took Hilda and assisted her into my bedroom.

There was only one safe way out of the house, one hopefully safe way, and that was the tree outside my window. We had just reached the window when Mum and Dad came hurrying into the room, both of them already having realised that this was the only way out of the house, mine being the only upstairs window close enough to a tree.

"Come on, Nicole," Dad had bellowed through the wall separating our bedrooms. "I banged on her door on my way past," he had added in a more normal volume. "She'll be coming."

Getting Hilda safely down the tree promised to be a very difficult task indeed, so Mum had gone out the window first, where she was able to assist Hilda from the front. I had been next, climbing onto the nearest branch and helping her balance Hilda, who was far too weak to support her own weight just by using her arms. Dad had climbed carefully onto the branch behind me and allowed himself to drop nimbly to the ground far more easily than I would have believed possible of him, but then he had been keeping pretty fit lately. From the ground, he had been ready to catch Hilda should the worst happen.

I had been about to drop to the ground myself when I had taken one last look through my bedroom window, expecting to see Nicole there, ready to climb down the tree as we had done. She hadn't been there, but someone else had been standing in my bedroom doorway, lighting the room and the hallway behind him in a terrible flickering light, his mere presence charring the doorframe on both sides. He had taken the shape of a man, though as he was made entirely of fire, there couldn't possibly be a physical form. He hadn't had a face that I could seen, but I had nevertheless sensed a clear and utterly evil consciousness about him. I had been gripped by a fear so strong that I slipped right off the branch and landed hard on my knees on the ground below, feeling a terrible pain in my back and hardly caring. It had been preferable to another second in view of the Fire Man, as he would now be in my mind.

From outside the house, I had been able to see quite clearly the damage that the fire was doing downstairs. It had been nothing short of horrendous. The brick walls themselves seemed to be glowing with the force of the blaze; the windows had all blown out and smoke was billowing through them, although suspiciously, the flames, which were licking at the edges of the frames, weren't shooting embers through the windows onto the ground; and through the window, I had seen, quite clearly, the contents of our kitchen and dining room, melting as the fire consumed them.

Hilda had managed to get one branch down before slipping. Mum had made to catch her and almost toppled out of the tree herself. Dad, ready, had caught her, both of them toppling to the ground. With the granny safely out of the way, she and Dad moving away from the house, and me crawling along behind them, Mum had been able to slide down the trunk of the tree and follow them well out of the way of danger.

"Where's Nicole?" Mum had shouted over the thunder of the burning house behind us.

"Wasn't she behind you?" Dad had asked, glancing up at the tree again.

I hadn't been looking up at the tree, though, or my window, through which my parents were waiting to see Nicole emerging. My gaze had been on the downstairs windows, horrified as I watched the destruction taking place in there. The home that I'd lived in all my life was falling apart before my eyes. As I watched, I'd heard an almighty crash from inside, and saw, through the smoke, part of the ceiling, or the upstairs floor, fall into the dining room. There goes the study, I had thought grimly.

"I didn't see her," I had told them, not wanting to mention the Fire Man. I had only seen it for a moment, and part of me still believed that it had been my imagination. "Maybe she didn't hear the —"

Maybe she didn't hear the smoke alarm, I had thought, and my insides had gone very cold. Nicole was a very heavy sleeper; one could walk around quite comfortably in her room while she were sleeping without being in any danger of her being woken by the noise. The noise of the smoke alarm, even though it was closer to her room than mine or the study where Hilda had been sleeping, may not have been enough to wake her. If that hadn't, and she had also managed to sleep through Dad pounding on her bedroom door, however, surely half the floor caving in would have roused her. But if half the floor was gone, and it looked like it included the part of the hallway Nicole would need to cross to get to my room, she might be trapped inside her room. If she woke up in time, her only option would be to jump from her own window.

"Nicole!" Mum had screamed at the top of her voice, directing it towards Nicole's window above us. It was dark, and there appeared to be no activity behind it. "Where are you?"

"How did this happen?" Dad had asked in a kind of whimper, staring at the house, the house he had owned for a third of his life.

"I don't know, but I've called for help from the Woodwards," I had said, and it was only as I said the words that I realised what had probably caused the fire. "Oh, this is probably the Hammerhearts doing. They must have worked out we live—"

I had been interrupted by another explosive bang. Looking around at the house again, we had all seen the top of the house before us, my room and the hallway behind it, fall into the dining room. The flames had consumed it all instantly, charring and then melting everything they touched, rising high into the night, the smoke cloud surely covering half the neighbourhood by now. Yet still the flames had not spread to outside the boundaries of the house. Most of Nicole's room had still been intact, though the wall between her room and mine had fallen away, and it was through this gap that we finally caught sight of her. She had been stepping from side to side, trying to avoid the floor as it crumbled beneath her feet, trying desperately to find a way out of the trap she was now stuck in. As we had watched, the floor had crumbled away beneath her desk, and it had fallen away, swallowed into the inferno. Perhaps not worse than that, though a lot more scary from where I was standing, had been the Fire Man. He was very real indeed, and he had, at that point, been moving slowly towards Nicole—stalking her.

"Nicole!" Mum had screamed again, terror clear in her voice as she too saw what was going on.

Nicole had heard her. Her terrified eyes had located the four of us in the middle of the back yard, and in that moment when her eyes had met all of ours, we knew the inevitable was moments away. Not for the first time in my life, I had been staring at a ghost. I had still been praying desperately that help would arrive before it could happen, but as the seconds lengthened, I had known it was no good. Sure enough, when there had been nowhere for Nicole to go but down, and just as she was bending her knees, perhaps about to try to jump all the way over the pit below and onto the lawn, the Fire Man reached out and caught her around the chest.

What had followed had been right up there with Tulip's death as the two worst things I had ever seen in my life. The Fire Man had been quite tall—more than six feet—and even though I still thought he didn't have a physical form (did he?), he was apparently quite strong too. Nicole was lifted cleanly off her feet, screaming in agony as her pyjamas burned away around her, screaming as the Fire Man wrapped her up in an embrace of death.

Everyone on the lawn had been screaming right along with her. I had been in too much of my own pain to do anything, but both Mum and Dad, just about out of their minds, had run back to the house and attempted to climb up the wall still holding Nicole's bedroom up, howling as their hands burned on the boiling brickwork. They had been quickly pulled back by Marge and Charlie, who, along with Violet, had arrived just in time to see the finale of the terrible event.

The floor beneath them had collapsed then, sinking into the inferno below and taking the back wall of the house with it. The Fire

Man had descended, looking as though he were levitating on the smoke itself. He was still holding Nicole, and Nicole had still been alive, which was a very bad thing indeed because although her human shape had still been discernible, most of her skin (and all of it above the waist) had blackened, and the flesh beneath was boiling. Her hair, too, had been burned away, but her face remained, still seeing and still screaming weakly.

All I and those around me had been able to do was watch as the Fire Man put his head against Nicole's face and opened his mouth— a mouth I hadn't even known was there. If he had been a real man, he would have been kissing Nicole all over her face—smooching, really, such was his passion. In actual fact, it had looked as though he were eating her, holding her higher and tilting her forward so that her head disappeared into his mouth, followed slowly by the rest of her body, burning away as it went, then disappearing. The Fire Man, now on the ground again, had looked over at us, and this time, I had seen something resembling a face. It had been smiling.

It had ended very quickly after that. The Fire Man had melted away to nothing, leaving no sign of Nicole's remains, while what had remained of the fire had quickly consumed the rest of the house before seeming to retreat inwardly, leaving nothing but charred ashes in front of us. As if it were suffocating (though oddly I could still breathe quite comfortably from where I stood), the fire had burned its way down rapidly towards the centre of what had been our house until finally, a single spark had shot up into the night. Then the fire had gone.

Help had arrived at that point in the form of Lillian Woodward, plus five more Woodward personnel, hurrying around the side of the ruined property toward us, but they had been too late. By the time the flames had sunk to the ground, now no more than glowing charcoal in the middle of the property, nothing remained of Nicole's body at all. It had been as though the Fire Man had taken her with him and was, even now, digesting her in his oven of a belly. All that had remained was those other fragments scattered around the property, fragments of who knew what had been before, what the fire had failed to melt entirely. It had been terrible to watch, but I couldn't even begin to imagine how Nicole must have felt in those final moments, waking up and finding herself in the nightmare to end all nightmares.

"What on earth?" the Sorcerer had gasped, stopping a few feet away from us and gazing in horror at the last of the fire. "What has happened here?"

"We don't know," Dad had said, moving forward to meet her, roughly pushing his emotions to the back of his mind. Charlie had come over to join them, but the others—Mum, Marge, Hilda, and Violet—had been too overcome with grief to participate, and I was with them.

"Looks like a pretty bad house fire," one of the soldiers had said, as though the rest of us couldn't have worked that part out for ourselves.

"John said it might be an attack," Dad had said, looking over at me, his brow furrowing as he noticed, for the first time, that I was hurt. "Maybe the Hammerhearts finally found out our address. Come on, we need to clean this up. I only know that it started downstairs, whatever it was."

They had set to work, Lillian performing the magic, firstly to heal me of whatever injury I'd been carrying, then investigating the remains of our house. The fire had gone out very quickly, but she still performed magic on the ruin in front of us to make sure it was safe to walk on. They had then gone about like investigators, using magic to separate the fragments, looking for a sign of what may have caused this disaster. They had also gathered up what had turned out to be human remains, using magic to determine which fragments had once made up Nicole's body and collecting them in a plastic bag.

It had only taken ten minutes for the initial investigation to wrap up. Two of the Woodward personnel had set down the remains of Nicole beside us. Mum had taken one look at the contents of the bag and wailed. When I had looked, my insides had seemed to melt just like most of the house had. All that had been left of Nicole was a thick liquid substance, some of it white, some of it brown, some of it red, some of it yellow, and all the rest of it combinations of those colours. Ashes were floating inside the bag, which seemed to provide the final proof of Nicole's demise. Lillian, meanwhile, had brought over the remains of something else to us.

"Chester, Charlie, have a look at this," she had said, holding it out in front of them.

Not wanting to look at Nicole any longer than I had to, I had come over to get a closer look at what Lillian was holding. This had been the only thing in the fire that hadn't been melted. It looked damaged, but not nearly as damaged as the rest of the house. I'd had no idea what it was, but even then, I had seemed to understand that this was the cause of the fire. It was a metal object that had been burnt black, a cube about the size of my hand, one side of it open. The other five sides had all had small holes in them. In her other hand, I had noticed that she held the sixth side of the cube, which was identical to the other five sides.

"I've never seen that before," Dad had said, looking at it over her shoulder.

"It is indeed a Hammerson device," she had said. "A portable fire, if I'm not mistaken, only I don't believe it is a normal fire. I'll need to take it back to base to be sure of that, though."

"It didn't look like a normal fire," I had told them. "It looked like it was only going for this house, nothing else. It didn't touch the one next door. Even this tree didn't get burnt at all. And—and it was alive. It wanted to kill us. It took a human shape."

"What?"

I nodded, and Dad said, "Yes. While the flames burned the house, a man—or something made out of fire that took the shape of a man—went for Nicole. I thought"—he had swallowed—"I thought the shape looked familiar."

"Oh," Lillian had said, her face falling. "That does sound familiar. I think I know what this is, and you're right, John; a Hammerheart fire wouldn't just destroy anything at random. Chester, we will begin restoring your property, but can you take this back to base and give it to Frederic?"

"Okay," he had said, rather weakly, as he took the remains of the portable fire with him. He had also taken Nicole with him as he walked around the edge of the property, heading back toward the street.

Charlie had taken control at that point. "John," he had said gently, "come on, mate, I need your help here."

He had been referring to the four women, all of whom still seemed unable to pull themselves together. As I watched, however, Marge had managed to get unsteadily back to her feet and begun helping Violet to do the same. Charlie assisted Mum, who had gone to pieces completely (it ached horribly to see it), but I stood firm.

"I don't wanna go anywhere," I had said. "I wanna help with this."

"No," Charlie had said just as firmly. "Leave this to Lillian and the others. You need to sleep. Come on, you can sleep in James's room. I'm sure he wouldn't mind under the circumstances. Could you help Hilda, please?"

I hadn't wanted to, not one bit. All I had wanted to do was help Lillian set this place to rights again, anything to take my mind off Nicole, but there was no shifting Charlie. I had sighed and helped Hilda to her feet and across the backyard toward the Thomas residence, which had been completely unharmed by the fire. I had glanced back once at what had been my home for all my life up until now, and the sight of the pit of ashes had caused my vision to blur with tears I had been able to hold off until now.

Chapter 19: Edumacation

James presented his findings to us two days after the communication with Smiley, by which time the general state of the world was beginning to stabilise, incredible as that may sound. The fighting overseas was beginning to ease in most places, apart from the Middle East, but there was nothing particularly new about that. By that stage, the Hammerhearts had taken control of two entire continents and had almost submerged two more. They still hadn't done anything overt in Africa or South America, but from what Mr. Woodward said, that was only because they believed they had done enough for the time being, and they wanted to stabilise what territory they had claimed already before finishing the job. Their main concern now was dealing with small groups of people in many countries putting up resistance against them, but now they had the full might of the authorities to back them up.

In Australia, things were starting to return to something resembling normality. The police were back on the job all over the country now, and even a small number of medical facilities had been granted special permission to operate in the interim. Schools were still out because nobody had had time to draw up the exact guidelines by which they were to operate. Hall, his teaching days well behind him, still had a special taskforce out looking for the five us most wanted criminals. It turned out that the cops who had attacked Peter and me days earlier had actually been those approved from all over the country, the most trusted ones Hall could find, apparently.

Mr. Woodward had returned to base on Friday evening and had since begun strategising a more careful way to bring the Hammerhearts down. The Sorcerers had since retreated into hiding, only coming out to cause minor disruptions in the Hammerhearts' efforts to rest complete control of Europe and Asia. I knew very little about his plans for the future, and I still hadn't had a chance to ask him, or anyone else, the thing I wanted to know most—what the Woodwards had done to win the previous war. The vague impression I had, however, was that the most important thing to do was protect the crystals, and the second most important was to deal with Arnold and Dorothy Hammerson directly, either by killing them or capturing them and putting them under spells that would prevent them causing any further trouble.

At about eleven o'clock on the morning of Monday, May 3, however, I found myself in one of the most unlikely places imaginable. I was standing with Marc, Peter, James, Tommy, Natalie, and Amelia, and we were out of the way of everyone else in one of the farthest corners of the Chopville High Transgators. Through an agreement done between Mr. Woodward and Mr. Hall (not the police chief but the nicer one who had taken over from him when he had been arrested), school had secretly reopened to restore some order in people's lives in Chopville. Students had nothing to do and were not learning anything, and parents were sick of the burden that this caused. Of course, the whole thing was top secret because the police would have come swarming in if they knew anything was happening. What this meant was that some parents couldn't be trusted with the knowledge, so their children missed out. What it also meant was that Marc, Tommy, and I, along with the two Sorcerers, could safely attend without fear of being taken into custody, for everyone involved knew of our innocence.

"I've got pretty much all the information we'll need to get through," James told the seven of us quietly. He was holding a sheet of printed paper, and now he smoothed it out so that he could read it. "The portal opens on the eleventh at two o'clock. At least it will be open at two o'clock and will close at about twenty past."

"That's local time, I assume?" Tommy enquired.

"Yeah. It would be eight o'clock our time," said James. "It's normally accessible from Durban in South Africa, although it's farther from their port than our portal is from Port Melbourne. A Russian institution will be going through the portal this year, but it will take them three days—sixty hours—to get from Durban to the portal."

"That sounds ominous," said Peter, shaking his head. "It means we have to be over there by the eighth, and then—"

"Don't be silly, Peter," said Natalie. "We don't need to go to South Africa; we only need to go straight to the coordinates of the portal and be there when the time comes. You do have the coordinates, don't you, James?"

"Yeah," he said. "I expect one of you could use magic to direct us to the exact location when the time comes. It wouldn't be hard for us to do if the navigators on the ship can do it."

"And that's more of what I was worried about," said Marc quietly. "Russia is mostly Hammerheart territory now. It certainly will be by the eleventh. You realise they'll probably send at least half a dozen Hammerhearts over there as well? That could really cause problems for us."

"I don't think they'd send too many," said James. "They usually only send their very best students, plus a few officials, because it costs a fortune to get down there—nothing like what we were able to do—and they stay there for a month compared to our few days. Besides, South Africa could turn around and tell them to get stuffed; they don't have to listen to the Hammerhearts."

"As usual, James, you go right off the topic," laughed Peter.

"I don't think South Africa would say no to them, though," Amelia pointed out. "They would probably want to, but don't forget, they'll be shit scared by now. They wouldn't wanna make things worse for themselves, 'cause we all know the Hammerhearts will get to them eventually. And even if they do have the balls to get in the way, the Hammerhearts could find a magical solution to get to the portal, same as we're going to do, or at the very least use a port in another country."

"Well, let's assume that there are going to be Hammerhearts on the Rock," said Peter. "Marc's probably right, but it shouldn't complicate things for us. All we have to do is make sure nobody sees us, and we should really do that even if there aren't any Hammerhearts there. There's no reason why we need to socialise with anyone else; we only need to see Smiley and maybe have a snoop around the caves for a bit of fun."

"And we can do that," I added, remembering the two keys I had hung on a hook just inside the tree house we had used as our campsite last time.

"That gives us eight days, more or less," said Amelia. "Eight days to work out how to get to the portal. Should be as easy as creating a water vessel for ourselves and teleporting it to a spot very close to the portal."

"Don't forget to make it invisible," Peter added, "just in case."

"One other thing to work out," said James seriously, "although we do have time to give it due consideration. Who should go?"

"All of us?" suggested Natalie, though she looked doubtful.

"We don't all need to go," said Marc, "and I can see your point, James. Some of us might be needed back here, depending on what plans Mr. Woodward has."

"Only these two, surely," said Tommy, gesturing at the two Sorcerers. "Come on, Marc, surely if the three of us take the crystals through, they'll be considered safer than ever, and there's no reason why Peter and James can't come."

"We have time to work that out," said James. "Personally, I don't mind if a reasonably large contingent of us goes along, just as long as we take precautions so that nobody is noticed. The only exception is you two, because of what Tommy just said."

"Yeah, you're right," said Amelia. "We do have time to think about that. I wanna go, though; I dunno what my dad wants from me, but I'd really like to see Smiley. I have no memory of him at all."

That was all we had time for. Peter, James, and I had to return to the space designated for Room 12 to begin period three, English, with Mr. Hall. I had attended only a handful of these English classes with this new Hall, and the only word I could use to describe them was…odd. I couldn't put my finger on exactly what was odd about them, though; this man was pleasant to all his students, he knew his English, and he was fairly good at teaching it. Yet there was something strange about it all the same. James believed it was merely because of his name, but Peter shared my feelings. The man was nice enough, sure, but he still made me uneasy.

"Right, let's get to it," said the teacher, sitting down at his desk and looking around at the lot of us. The class was the same as it had always been, except that Hignat and Wilwog weren't present, and neither was Matthew, whose father was apparently in some official capacity and couldn't be trusted with the information. "Lots to do, lots to catch up on. Firstly, though, I trust you all remember the words I gave you last week?"

There was a grumbling of ascent around the soundproof space. I glanced enquiringly at Peter, not having been present for whatever Mr. Hall was talking about. Peter had opened his book to a list of about fifteen words, all of them long enough to cover half the page.

"This is a closed book test, a *closed* book," he said, emphasising the point by snapping his own book shut. "I don't want to see anyone cheating, so everyone, close those books."

Peter grimaced at me and made to hide his book under the table without closing it.

"I saw that, Peter," said Mr. Hall sharply, and Peter grinned sheepishly back at him. "Keep an eye on him, James."

James glared at Peter until his book was closed and safely hidden under his pencil case. I looked at him, silently begging for help. How on earth was I supposed to do this test?

"Now, you all remember the rules, I assume," Mr. Hall went on, "but for those of you who don't, when I read out each word, you are to rewrite it, spelling it correctly, and provide a brief definition of it for me. One mark per correct spelling, two per correct definition, or one if the definition is partially correct. Please take out a blank piece of paper. Three minutes before we begin."

"I'm screwed," I muttered to Peter, "utterly screwed."

"So am I," Peter muttered back.

"Just do your best, John," James muttered back. "You have a good excuse for not studying. As for you, Peter, you deserve all that's coming to you."

"Your support is invaluable to me, James," Peter muttered, grinning again.

"Can't I just have a quick look at the words?" I pleaded with James.

He shook his head. "Can't let him see me showing you, or we'll both be in it."

"Okay, let's go," Mr. Hall said loudly, and silence fell. "First word: acquiescence. Thirty seconds."

Acquiescence—what the hell? I thought I'd heard the word maybe once or twice in my life. I glanced at Peter; he had managed to spell the word out, with a couple of crossings out, but was stuck on the definition. James had no trouble with either spelling or definition. He was already waiting expectantly for the next word by the time I put my own pen to paper and managed to scribble out a hasty and no doubt incorrect spelling. I had no time to come up with any sort of definition, though.

"Second word: belligerent. Thirty seconds."

Belligerent—now that sounded a little easier. Didn't that mean stubborn? Or something similar to stubborn? I quickly spelt it out (with only one L), then glanced sideways at James. His definition included the words "aggressive" and "hostile," so I just quickly wrote those with not a moment to spare.

"Third word: cataclysmic. Thirty seconds."

On and on it went. I struggled my way through, fumbling for spellings and positively lost for definitions for all but a few words, and even those definitions were either made up or excerpts from what I could make of James's work beside me. It eventually ended, by which time Peter was swearing fluently under his breath and many others around the room were moaning in despair. James was the only one who looked happy with himself.

"Please write your name at the top of the paper," Mr. Hall told us all. "I'll try to get them all back to you by the end of the lesson. In the meantime, I'm going to put a DVD on for you that I think you will all find interesting. I have some questions I want you to answer while you watch. Ellie, please collect everyone's tests. Harry, or Simon, or whichever one you are," he said to the closest twin, which was in fact Harry, "please hand these around to each student."

The rest of the lesson was fairly dull. The video, which was a documentary on the use of language in society, might have been interesting if it weren't for the questions we had to answer. Mr. Hall sat at his desk in front of us all, going through the various tests and setting aside the ones he had marked. When the video had finished, still leaving a little more than five minutes before the end of the period, he called Simon out and asked him to hand everyone's tests back.

"Well done to you all," he said, looking around at the class. "The average mark was around twenty out of forty-five, which, although it may be less than fifty percent, is still a pretty good effort given the disruption to classes over the last week. James, your score of forty-one was head and shoulders above the rest of the class and probably elevated the average by at least a couple of marks, so could you please join me out here in a moment. I would also like to see—" he glanced down at something on his desk, "Sophie, Harry, Simon, John, and Peter, please. The rest of you spend the next few minutes finalising your responses to the questions."

"He wants to see us?" Peter said, grinning at me. "He wants to see us with James? Wow, we must have done really well after all."

"Always the optimist, Pete," laughed James.

"I'm not an eye doctor," Peter said, grinning at him.

Simon passed in front of us, dropping our tests on our desks. I glanced left and right respectively before looking down at my own test. Peter had received a muscular twelve while James, of course, had been given a modest forty-one. I looked down at my own test and saw, to my horror, that I'd received a mark of two. Just two.

"Geez, John," said James, looking concerned as he looked at the number. "I know I said you had a good excuse, but that's really—disturbing."

"I'm surprised I got any marks at all," I said, glancing down my list of words to see where I had scored. By the look of it, a couple of the definitions (the ones I'd copied from James) had received partial marks.

"Well, let's see what he wants with us," said Peter, getting to his feet.

James and I followed Peter to the front where Mr. Hall was in conversation with Sophie. By the sound of it, he was displeased by the sarcastic definitions she had given him. Harry stood nearby too, and he grinned at us as we approached.

"You're in the shit bin too, then," he said to Peter and me, pretending James didn't exist.

"Looks like it," said Peter. "I'm not sure what I did wrong, apart from not get a lot of marks."

"I'm not sure what me and Simon did either—"

"Simon and I," James corrected harshly.

"I mean, we both got twenty, and if that's the average…"

He left his sentence hanging, still ignoring James.

"Just be warned for next week," Mr. Hall finished with Sophie. "If we have to have this discussion again, there will be a penalty. Now, you two," he said to Harry and Simon when the latter had arrived, "why are your answers exactly the same?"

"They are?" said the twins in unison, glancing at each other and wearing identical looks of surprise.

"Indeed, they are," he said. "Now I know you weren't copying because both your heads were down the entire time, so what's the explanation, boys? Were you perhaps copying from a sheet under the table that I could not see?"

"Course not," said Harry. "Just—coincidence. Ask any of our other teachers; we almost always do that."

"I see," he said, squinting at them both. "In any case, you both did fairly well. I hope you're telling the truth, boys. I'll be keeping an eye on you both next week, so be warned."

"Consider us warned," said Simon cheerfully, swapping an amused look with his brother.

"Right, now, as for you, Peter," said Mr. Hall, looking at my brother as the twins departed. "Have you got your test with you?"

"It's on my desk."

"Go and get it, please."

In the momentary absence of Peter, Mr. Hall turned to James. "Here, I think you might enjoy this."

He took something from his pocket and handed it to James. It looked like a small square with dots on one side.

"What is it?" James asked, turning it over in his hands.

"Something for you to work out in your own time, but I think you deserve it," he said easily. "Now, Peter," he added as Peter returned to us and handed over his test, "how do you explain this?"

He pointed at the word 'vernacular', which was the last word on the test. Peter had spelt it correctly, but rather than providing a definition for it, he had instead drawn a large and rather crude circular shape.

"What is that supposed to mean?" Mr. Hall asked him.

"Oh, yeah," said Peter, flushing slightly. "That's a piece of shit, 'cause by the time we got to the end of that test, it all felt like a load of shit to me."

Harry and Simon, who were sitting close enough to listen, burst out laughing. Mr. Hall stared at Peter in astonishment for a few seconds before breaking into laughter himself.

"That is very crude," he said, "very crude. No more of that in the future, Peter, or I'll have to penalise you. As it is, I can't give you any marks for that because a piece of excrement doesn't—"

"You mean shit, sir," said Peter politely.

"—doesn't define vernacular," he finished. "Other than no mark, there will be no punishment for you."

"Thank you, sir," said Peter, polite as ever (though I was familiar enough with him to recognise the mocking).

"Hey, you know, even shit is a pretty boring word these days," Harry told Mr. Hall and sighed like an old man. "If only you'd seen the display Simon and I put on for the class back in March."

"The less I know, the happier I'll be, Harry," said Mr. Hall, grinning at the twins. "Now, John," he said seriously, turning his attention to me, "it is not your poor mark that concerns me, but rather the manner in which you went about achieving it."

"I'm not sure what you mean," I said, "but I really did what I could. I wasn't here last week, so I had no idea I was supposed to study for this."

"That may be so, but it doesn't give you an excuse to peek at your neighbour's work."

I stared at him, my mouth very dry. Now I understood why I was in trouble.

"Not acceptable behaviour," he said, opening his folder and beginning to slip his notes into it. "The penalty for plagiarism is extreme, but since this is your first time, I'll let you escape with a single detention this afternoon. Meet me in Room 12—the real Room 12—at half past three this afternoon, please."

"Fine," I said dispiritedly.

I trudged back to my seat as Mrs. Worlker was arriving to take our History lesson. Fortunately for me, I wasn't caught out by any of the material she presented to us. The rest of the day passed in much the same fashion. I spent lunchtime with Serena, seeking privacy by leaving the Transgators (though we weren't supposed to) and privately enjoying each other in our usual Maths classroom. Being intimate with a girl in a classroom wasn't something I'd ever expected to do in my life, but it was nevertheless exciting, especially with the additional thrill of possibly being discovered at any moment, though, fortunately for us, we weren't. The last two periods, which were normally physical education for us, were spent catching up on homework tasks we'd been given in the first four periods.

Soon enough, we were all released from school. The procedure for this took much longer than usual; students were only allowed to leave the gym, where all the Transgators were setup, in dribs and drabs, filtering very slowly through the locker bays and then out of the school. Fortunately, as I had been part of the Room 12 group, I had managed to get out before half past three. Mr. Hall, the good Hall as I thought of him, even though he had just given me a detention, was waiting for me inside the room I had become so familiar with this year.

"Come inside, John," he said, beckoning me through the door and following behind me. "I think you'll find the next half an hour to be both useful and interesting."

It turned out to be lines, though by comparison to the usual ridiculous lines the other Hall had always given me, it could be considered useful. I wrote and rewrote the fifteen words from the spelling test earlier, along with a short definition for each. Then, in the last five minutes, Mr. Hall rubbed them off the board, took what I had written, and verbally tested my memory. If that had been how I had performed in class that day, according to Mr. Hall, I would have received fifteen marks; apparently, I hadn't been paying enough attention to what I was copying.

It was definitely a relief to get back to the Woodward base not long after four o'clock. The school grounds were eerily deserted and, to add to my insecurities, I was without the protection of the Sien-Leoard Crystal. Mr. Woodward had made a firm point that no crystal was to leave the base during school hours, for none of them could be taken inside the Transgators and would therefore be left completely unprotected in the gym. I therefore made myself invisible with a standard invisibility toggle and kept a hand firmly on my solid-outliner as I walked through the grounds, down the short stretch of street, and through Hamster's Stretch Reserve.

"What happened to you?" Marc asked when I found him and several others in the lounge room—Peter, James, Amelia, Serena, Kylie, Erica, Harry, Simon, Katie, Sophie, Lena, Darcy, Jane, and Siobhan, who had been gradually spending more and more time with other people over the weekend and who had been accepted into year-ten at school that day.

"Like a trip down memory lane," I said, sitting down where Serena had saved me a spot. Natalie, who had helped me through the wall, sat on my other side. "He basically gave me the test again, but I swear it felt just like being in detention with that other nutter."

"I wouldn't be surprised if they're related," said Peter. "I know they don't really look alike, but let's face it, how many Halls can there be around here? And let's not forget how passionate they both are about the English language."

"Anything interesting been happening around here?" I asked.

"A couple of things," said Tommy. "Mr. Woodward seems to be finally getting his act together. There's a meeting on tomorrow evening to do with strategies from here on. As for us, we're gonna wait until after that before deciding any more of our plans."

"Okay," I said slowly, raising my eyebrows. There were a lot of people around us just now, and I wasn't sure how much they were allowed to know, but I assumed it was nothing.

"Then there's what's happening tonight," said Harry. "Something that I'm sure we will all find highly entertaining. Personally, I'll be struggling to keep down my dinner while I absorb the propagandistic crap being spouted, but that might be just me."

"What are you talking about?"

"There's a show on TV tonight," said Serena. "An hour-length special delivered by the Hammersons themselves and their closest Hammerhearts, talking about all their great plans for the future."

"I've got a feeling we'll be mentioned at some point," said Marc, "being their most wanted criminals."

"You really think so?" asked Katie. "I know they're still publishing articles about all your various crimes in the papers, but would they really start talking about magic in this show? Surely they know that most people in the general public are still on the side of the Woodwards by default. I can't imagine them wanting to appear too *belligerent*—(she italicised the word with her fingers)—towards the Woodwards."

"What time is it on?" I asked.

"Eight thirty," said Simon. "Prime time viewing, of course. Are you going to indulge in faecal matter with a side order of dog puke with us this evening?"

"Yeah, I guess so."

In the meantime, however, I had another job I wanted to do, or rather, continue with, for I had been slowly working on it over the weekend. My first opportunity to test the unboggler I had created hadn't come until Saturday evening, a few hours after I had created it. As I had planned, Candice Young was my test subject. It hadn't been difficult to get her to agree to it. I had located her in the gym, where she spent nearly all her time these days, working hard and talking to no one (the end result of such labour was one very sexy body indeed). When I had asked her to come with me, she had immediately stopped what she was doing and followed me out into the hall and up to my room.

"How have you been?" I had asked her.

"Fine," she had replied. It was a lie, but I hadn't pushed it.

"Enjoying things around here?"

"Yeah," she had said unconvincingly. "People don't really talk to me very much, though. I'll show them all. Who'll be laughing when the Woodwards go down?"

"You want the Woodwards to go down?" I had enquired.

She had considered this before slowly shaking her head. "That wouldn't be good."

I had grimaced. This back and forth state was the condition she had been in ever since I had returned to base.

"Maybe I can help you," I had said, gripping her shoulder with one hand and curling my fingers around the unboggler in my pocket with the other. "Do you want to be helped?"

"No, I'm good," she had said, shrugging. "The Woodwards are okay."

"What about the Hammersons?"

"Oh, yeah. They've got great plans for us all. It'll only be a matter of time now before they can really get stuck into them."

"You're looking forward to that?"

"Sure, it'll be great for everyone once they have control. Then they'll flush this place out and kill—oh wait," she faltered, only just realising that she were wishing death upon all those around her. Her expression was quite horrified.

"Just stay still now," I had told her. "I have something that might help you."

"I don't need—"

"Come on, Candice," I had said and, using the element of surprise, pulled her into a hug. At that point, I had only needed to raise one hand so that the reboggler was pointing at the back of her head and give it a single click. Candice had gone very still in my arms for several seconds. I had taken one look at her face and saw that she had been rendered unconscious by the device. I had straightened her up and held her from me at arm's length so that I could see her face as awareness slowly returned.

"Oh—what—oh—"

"Are you okay?" I had asked, directing her to my bed and sitting her down.

"I—oh—"

I had watched her in something close to panic. Her mouth had been slightly open and her eyes popping alarmingly. What had I done? Had I made a terrible mistake with the magic?

"Oh—my." She shook her head hard.

"Are you okay?" I had repeated slowly, attempting calm.

Her eyes had found my face, and she stared at me for several seconds, apparently unable to speak.

"Candice?" I had said, leaning closer to her.

"What have I done?" she had said in a hushed voice.

She had seemed fully aware of herself at that point. I had looked carefully at her face and thought the expression on it was something like horror.

"Do you feel okay?" I had asked. "Back to yourself again?"

She had nodded before bursting into tears. That, it seemed, was the unforeseen consequence of using the unboggler—terrible shame and guilt at the actions she had performed under the influential charm. Other than that, it seemed to have done the job perfectly. The magic seemed to have cleared Candice's mind, but in hindsight, I wondered if that had been such a good thing. She had been close to distraught all through Sunday, spending most of her time in solitude and only coming out at meal times and trying desperately to seek forgiveness, to atone for what she had done. I remembered how much I had despised her when we had first brought her into custody, but now I only pitied her.

I had managed to turn six more prisoners with the device in the time since Candice—Liam, George, and Robyn, who had all been part of the stairwell dozen, plus three adult Hammerhearts who Marc and I had brought in two weeks earlier. I'd also ruled out several other prisoners whose minds had never been enchanted by the influential charm. I now intended to spend the remaining hour and a half before dinner seeing who else I could bring back to the right side, three being my aim. Oddly, many prisoners tried to evade me when they learnt I was inside the prison yard. Like bugs running around in the bottom of a jar, I thought with some amusement. I always took the Sien-Leoard Crystal in with me to give myself a further advantage should they choose to get nasty, so I was able to locate them easily enough. By dinnertime, I had converted four more of the stairwell dozen, which, if my calculations were correct, only left a further four, as Sebastian didn't count.

* * *

At school the following day, the buzz of conversation mostly centred on the television special the Hammersons had put on the previous night. Katie's belief that the Hammersons would focus the episode on their plans for the future and be far more conservative in their denigration of the Sorcerers and those allied with them turned out to be grossly off the mark. All six Sorcerers had watched the special with us. It had been Mr. Woodward's belief that much of what was shown would either be false or slanted because surely the Hammersons would expect them to watch it, but he also believed that if they read between the lines, they could learn a bit more about what the Hammersons were planning and perhaps gain some ideas from their tactics.

The first five minutes of the program had been all about the Woodwards and Fletchers and their stubborn refusal to accept change. The Hammerhearts had gone to great pains to make sure that everyone understood the bad influence the Sorcerers were having on their progress. They had then got stuck into their plans for the future; people such as Hank Cornish and Nick Appleton (3A93, it turned out), who had been appointed his deputy, were shown on screen, speaking about the way the country would be run over the following three months, by which time it would be ready to join a much larger body of authority that would govern the entire world, top down. There was very little shown about the progress in the war overseas, as the program was produced only for Australians.

It was the last ten minutes of the program that provided the greatest talking points for those of us closest to the Woodwards. The three Hammersons came on screen and began talking about their own personal plans for the future. Stella had apparently consented to be shown, although she did no talking and refused to look at the camera directly. It was the first time I had seen her properly for a long time, and I couldn't help noticing that she had lost quite a lot of weight, and considering she had always been tall and slim, she had now become rather unpleasantly gaunt. The two older former Sorcerers spoke of how everyone in the world would become one; there would be no more divisions in society, no more opposing factions, no more conflicts. Laws would be tightened to an extreme point where, eventually, no person would dare commit any sort of crime, and if they did dare, they would never do so again. No person would ever seek more than they are entitled to. Rankings in society would be determined by loyalty to the Hammersons. Those most resentful would be bumped down to a level below the point of servitude while those most loyal, particularly those who had been Hammerhearts before the global revolution, would receive all the highest honours.

They then turned their attention to the Woodwards again. They made it quite clear that they intended to regain their magical powers, which, of course, would be essential in maintaining the empire they envisioned. Photos of the six Sorcerers were shown on the screen, and viewers were advised to stay clear of them at all times until they had been stripped of their power, after which point the Woodwards and Fletchers would become the lowest point in society. Arnold Hammerson then spoke of us—me, Marc, Tommy, Moran, and

Lucien—stating that we were still at large and Police Chief Hall had all the resources available to him, plus the might of the Hammersons themselves, necessary to find us. Tankom then spoke of Stella (Stella had closed her eyes at this point), stating that, eventually, years down the track, she would be the single ruler of the world, but in the meantime she would be given a special assignment. Tankom had said very little about what that assignment involved, but I knew what it was from the little she did expose: She intended to stand by her word to Sebastian, and it would be down to Stella to find a way to free him, just as he had supposedly freed her.

Our time table on Tuesdays was Maths, French, double IT, Health Studies, and Media, and most of that day was fairly boring. The Maths classes, which were normally divided into Elementary, Intermediate, and Advanced classes, had to be generalised to accommodate students from all three groups. The second language block was even worse. Unable to divide the class at all, Peter, James, and I had finished the Maths exercises we had been given. Periods three and four were information technology, and we had been provided with a laptop computer each so that we wouldn't have to leave the Transgators. The last two periods had been entirely theory based. All in all, I was very happy to leave the school grounds at the end of the day.

"There's definitely something going on with Hall," Marc said to me and Tommy as the three of us were passing through the school gates, a glaring target to any potential attackers, though thankfully there were none that day.

"Like what?" asked Tommy. "I thought everyone said he was all right compared to the other Hall."

"He is, but I still don't know about him," said Marc. "We had him for Science just now in period six, and he was—well, a bit weird."

"In what way?" I asked, wondering if he was eluding to the same sort of feelings I was having about him.

"I'm not sure," said Marc, shrugging. "I can't put my finger on it, but I asked Felicity and Jessica and they agree with me. It felt sort of like he wanted to get me alone somehow. You know, he was the one who organised this whole schooling thing; I can't help wondering if there's some sort of secret to it he's not letting on."

"I suppose it's possible," said Tommy. "Thank God we're still allowed to bring our little pouches of weapons with us or we'd all be screwed. Not as good as the crystals, but I suppose it's better than nothing."

"My feeling is that he is hoping we'll be caught," said Marc. "The whole school, I mean. I know we're using the Transgators, but it doesn't take a genius to work out something's going on. We're just as noticeable as ever when we're coming and going from the place."

"Isn't someone watching the school, though?" I asked. "Natalie's dad? I thought I heard that somewhere."

"I did too," said Marc, "which only adds to my feeling. If Mr. Woodward thinks it's necessary to station a Sorcerer to watch from the outside, then perhaps he's got a bad feeling about it as well. I know Natalie and Amelia do have their magic protected, but if there is some dodgy business going on, you never know what sort of situation they might need to get us out of."

Tommy muttered something indistinct, and when we both looked at him, he just said, "Let's just wait and see, shall we? We might as well make the most of it because once the school opens for proper, the three of us won't be allowed to go."

Chapter 20: Confidence

Mr. Woodward had been so busy since his return to base that, excepting the hour he had spent in the lounge room watching television with the rest of us, I had barely seen him at all. What it meant was that none of us had had a chance to fill him in on the latest developments in the Smiley hunt, and he had shown no interest in enquiring about the life assistant. Amelia and Natalie therefore approached him in the minutes preceding the tactics meeting, which was to begin at half past five that afternoon. The whole base was to attend, making it the first time we had used the enormous Meeting Hall since that fateful second last day in February.

The hall was just about full to capacity by the time the two Sorcerers returned to where Marc, Tommy, Peter, James, Lena, Serena, Underwood, Siobhan, and I sat in the front row on the left, the same seats we had used on the other occasions.

"We should be able to decide on the crew by tomorrow or the day after," Natalie told us. "He reckons either of us can go, but not both of us, and you three definitely have to go. Especially you," she said to Tommy, only giving him a cursory glance, "since you're the only one who'd recognise the old guy on sight."

"And I'm definitely coming, right?" Underwood enquired briskly.

He was still showing overt bitterness to just about everyone inside the Woodward base, but he hadn't been at all backward in his interest in finally meeting his grandfather. Unsure of the best way to deal with him, James had decided to tell him exactly what Smiley's condition was just so that he would leave us alone. It hadn't really worked, as the rest of us had expected, but apart from letting him sit with us in the front row, we were still refusing to let him in on what we were doing. The likelihood of Siobhan coming with us as well seemed fairly high, but none of us could be sure what would become of her after that, once we had left Underwood behind with his grandfather—that was still the plan, although we hadn't confided that part to Underwood yet.

"Yes, you're definitely coming," said Peter coldly. "Now just give it a rest."

The meeting got underway shortly after that. Mr. Woodward and Mr. Fletcher did most of the talking, the two older ladies sitting in the front row across the aisle from us most of the time. They spoke firstly of what they had achieved the previous week—what precious little they had achieved the previous week. A small amount of their effort had gone into jeopardising the Hammerheart movements, but mostly, they had concentrated on protecting innocent lives from the line of fire, wherever such a fire happened to strike. Mr. Fletcher likened the situation to a tsunami: organising civilians and moving them to high ground to avoid the wave would be more effective than attempting to push the wave back out to sea.

The death toll so far was estimated to be between eight and nine thousand worldwide, which, according to Mr. Woodward, was an enormous achievement for both sides given the magnitude of the fighting in some places. It was considered a win to both sides because, and this was just Mr. Woodward talking and not what I necessarily believed, the Hammerhearts would not want to wipe out tens of millions of people in their attempts to take over, although they wouldn't hesitate to fight with fire if it were necessary. That had been the result of the last Sorcerous war and could well be the result of this war too should the fighting spread to more countries and escalate, but the Hammersons would grudgingly accept the sacrifice if it was necessary to defeat the Woodwards. As for the Woodward soldiers, they had lost close to a hundred fighters during the three days of global mayhem, none of whom I had known, for which I was grateful. The Hammerheart casualty list was expected to be several times longer, but more because they had instigated much of the fighting than because the Woodwards had gone in for the kill.

They then moved on to plans for the future. Mr. Woodward firstly reiterated his belief that the Hammersons would wish to stabilise the territory they had already claimed before finishing the job in the two remaining continents. He said that the Hammersons would assume, no doubt correctly, that they already had the resources required to stave off any attacks launched against them from African or South American countries. Apparently, this could only be seen as a problem for the Woodwards. It was essential to begin reclaiming territory before the Hammerhearts could dismantle too much of the world's structure, yet their best chance to launch an attack of their own would be while the Hammerhearts were busy taking control in new areas.

Mr. Woodward's strategy for regaining control was fairly straightforward: cut off the snake's head and the snake dies. This meant that they firstly needed to either kill the Hammersons or capture them and put them under some sort of spell that would prevent them causing any more trouble. He said nothing about how they were to accomplish that, how they were to locate the Hammersons to start with, and how they were to penetrate whatever powerful protection they surrounded themselves with, nor did he specify which of the Hammersons he was talking about. He made no mention of Stella at all, which made me wonder—had Mr. Woodward assumed she was against us based on her involvement in the television production the previous night, despite the fact that I had given him almost conclusive evidence in her favour? I didn't know, but it made me wonder…it made me nervous…

He then spoke very briefly of what they would do once they had the Hammersons under control. It was his belief that the Hammerhearts would quickly lose direction once they lost their leaders, an assumption based on the aftermath of the first attempt to take Chopville High. In that situation, they had been able to carry out plans already made before the Hammersons' downfall but had not made any further plans of their own. Unfortunately, however, the Hammersons had already given their Hammerhearts enough directions in the meantime to keep them busy for quite a while, even if they were to be taken in. It would therefore be necessary to put the influential charm on people such as Cornish and Hall, as well as those many other important Hammerhearts who had been given positions of authority in other countries around the world, and get them to undo the damage already done before reinstating whatever governments each country had had prior to the coup. A simple plan, I thought, but one that would probably be much more difficult to carry out.

Given that they would have to wait for exactly the right moment to strike, however, Mr. Woodward also spoke of a few other plans that they could attempt to carry out in the meantime. The most important thing, as had been pointed out several times already, was to protect the Hero and Sien-Leoard Crystals. The Light Crystal was important as well, but the consequences of losing that wouldn't be as catastrophic as if we lost either of the other two. The Darkness Crystal also had to be reobtained (news of its theft had obviously been passed onto him), a plan for which was currently being constructed. My gut feeling was that either I, Marc, or both of us would somehow be involved in that plan. The other thing that had to be done was track down Moran and bring him, and more importantly the Villain Crystal, into custody to protect him and it from the Hammerhearts, to prevent the Hammerhearts from using him or it, and to prevent Moran himself doing a whole load of damage against our side. While he had been useful to us, he could just as easily be useful to them.

Predictably, when the meeting finished about ten minutes before dinner, Mr. Woodward called me, Amelia, Natalie, Marc, and Tommy to join him and the other Sorcerers out the front as everyone else filed out of the large hall.

"Let me guess," said Amelia when there was enough space between our group and the general crowd. "You want us to work on one of these extra plans of yours."

"I think you will have some time on your hands," said Mr. Woodward. "After all, we do need all hands on deck."

"But we've got school, and—you know—our other plans," Tommy protested.

"I'm aware of those things," said the Sorcerer, "but I still think you'll have time. From what I can gather, you have almost completed the organisation of your plans to return to Rock Haulter. The final plans I'm sure you can deal with on the weekend. As for school, I understand that you are given a number of free periods due to the way the new system is organised, so there's no reason why homework should keep you busy in the evenings."

"Great," muttered Marc.

"So what? Are you sending us out tonight?" Natalie asked.

"Not tonight, but tomorrow night," said Mr. Woodward. "Natalie, Amelia, obviously you two can't enter the Hammersons' bases, so it will be down to you two to try to bring the Morans in, preferably with as little fuss as possible. As for you three, I understand why you won't like the job I must give you, but someone needs to do it."

"Amelia did tell you where the Darkness Crystal is, didn't she?" I asked. "You know we'll not have the advantage we did last time of knowing our way around their base?"

"I'm fairly hopeful that you can work it out as you go," said Mr. Woodward. "And don't look at me like that, John. At least we know that the three of you can safely take your crystals into their base, so if there is a struggle, you will have a distinct advantage, especially if you prepare yourselves well before starting."

Marc swore under his breath.

"You do want to do your bit, don't you?" Mr. Fletcher asked sternly.

We all looked despondently at each other.

"I'll agree to do my bit on one condition," said Natalie, staring calmly at her father, then at Mr. Woodward.

"What's that?" asked Mr. Woodward, not looking particularly interested.

"Someone has to find Stella," said Natalie. "I know what it looked like last night, but I think we should give her the chance to come back to us. She was really good to me and Amelia last week, much better than Moran and Lucien treated us. I just feel like we owe her one, perhaps more than one, after all she's been doing for us all this time."

"What has she been doing?" Mr. Fletcher asked.

"Loads of stuff. She told me some of it herself, and I got other bits of it from her mind."

"I'm already aware of some of it myself from what John told me last week, but I'm afraid I can't allow it," said Mr. Woodward, shaking his head and looking regretful. "I believe Stella was working with us before, based on the evidence John gave me, but if she has been with her family since last Friday, we might be too late in bringing her across. I'm afraid I can't entirely trust her anymore."

"Well, it was nice doing business with ya." Natalie shrugged.

"Natalie!" snapped her father, and Natalie flinched. "Your magic is not a right. It is a privilege, and gives you a large responsibility. If we can't rely on you to pull your weight in this war, as you agreed to do before accepting this responsibility, we'll have to consider transferring your crystal chip to Rebecca."

Natalie flushed before her father had even finished his threat. I imagined that it wasn't the threat to strip her of her magic that humiliated her, but the accusation that she was being irresponsible. From what I knew about Natalie, that train of thought seemed more likely. She looked for a moment like she might argue, then shrugged and lowered her eyes, looking upset. I had an urge to put an arm around her, but the knowledge that Serena was waiting for me somewhere out there, not to mention the fact that her father was standing right there, made me think better of it.

"So, tomorrow evening," said Mr. Woodward, "when you arrive back here after school, you can do any preparations you feel you need for your respective tasks. You can set off after dinner, and be sure to keep in regular telepathic contact with us back here. Amelia, you know how to do that. As for you three boys—"

"I know how to do it," I told him. "I've done it before with Amelia."

"Good, that saves the girls showing you how," he said and sighed. "I really am sorry to have to involve you all. I know you'd rather not be given such weighty jobs, but like I said before, we need all hands on deck."

"We know," said Amelia grimly, "but you know it is important to us what we're already doing in tracking Smiley down."

"I know that too, and I agree that he may have some answers for you, even though you have already learnt the knowledge you were initially seeking from him."

"Not really," I said. "We know who my—my parents are, but we still don't know exactly what happened back then, or why Hammerson wanted me dead right from the start, and if it's got anything to do with me and Stella. I dunno if Smiley knows much about that, but…"

"It's quite likely that Smiley knows a lot more than you would expect," said Mr. Woodward. "He has a knack for—knowing things, wouldn't you say, Tommy?"

"Yeah, he always knew if I'd practised or not," said Tommy, grinning.

"Is he a mind reader?" Marc asked.

"No," said Tommy. "I dunno what he is, exactly. You'll see for yourself when you meet him."

"That sounds about right," said Mr. Woodward. "So you all know what to do? Good, then off you go. I believe dinner is just beginning in the dining room."

* * *

I had been extremely well behaved in the last few days, not having had any one-on-one moments with Amelia, Natalie, or Lena at all since the previous week. I had certainly given them all plenty of thought, though. Amelia appeared to be on the mend, and I knew from Marc's hints that they had been doing a lot of talking lately, though apparently the talking wasn't going the way Marc would have liked. Natalie hadn't followed up on our short conversation on Friday afternoon, but I had caught her watching me several times since, and although she blushed every time I did, she never tried to cover the moment. As for Lena, she hadn't changed in the slightest, often watching me but always keeping her distance, for which I was grateful.

It was Serena who I'd given most of my attention to over the last four days, as far as girls went, anyway. Her behaviour over the last week had been an enormous improvement over what she had given me throughout most of our relationship. Perhaps it was that which, on a subconscious level, renewed the affection I had felt for her in the first couple of weeks we had been dating. It was also perhaps guilt that contributed to my extra effort to hold my own in the relationship. There hadn't been any fights lately, and on top of that, Serena now had a much better idea of what I'd been facing behind her back over the last couple of months, having been in the line of fire once and witnessing the use of the life assistant. We got talking that night after tea, and later I would think of that moment as the one last chance I was giving our relationship of working out.

It started, appropriately enough, at the end of dinner, by me saying I would go and finish some homework, since I may not have much time over the next three days.

"Good for you," said Peter, winking at me. "Since I haven't been given any special assignments, I think I'll go and embark on my own private project with Kylie."

"Ooh, what are we doing?" Kylie asked, her eyes lighting up.

"Don't share it with the rest of us, please," muttered James, who was still finishing his second helping.

"May we, James?" Erica asked sweetly, tugging at his arm.

"Er, well, I was gonna do some reading—"

"Geez, James, you're such a nerd," laughed Peter. "Why don't you read Erica tonight instead of your books?"

Erica burst into giggles at that, while James scowled.

"Can I join you, John?" Serena asked, catching Natalie's eye. Natalie had been watching me from the next table a moment ago and had just opened her mouth, perhaps to ask the same thing (probably not, but I could imagine, right?).

"Sure, you'll be a nice distraction," I said, grinning at Serena and only feeling a slight pang for Natalie.

"See you all tomorrow," Serena called to the others as she proceeded to drag me out of the dining room before I could change my mind.

They all called their good-byes but nobody intercepted us all the way out of the room and up the stairs to the third floor. I sort of lost track of things at that point, almost as though I were only partially conscious over the following few minutes, and the thought of doing homework that night was long since left behind by the time the two of us were sitting together on my bed, some thirty-five minutes later.

"I'll never get sick of that," Serena panted, brushing hair out of her face. "There was a while there where I thought we weren't going to do that again."

"I know," I said, leaning back against the wall behind my bed and thinking that in a few minutes, I would want more of the same. "I guess it's sometimes hard to find time with everything else going on."

"Sure, but that—" She struggled to work out what she was trying to say for a moment. "That was just frustrating and all, but I understood what was happening, so yeah. It was a couple of weeks ago, though. I just thought maybe—I dunno. Things weren't— weren't great then."

My insides chilled. It was the first time either of us had spoken so directly of the events that had almost broken us up. The impending urges I'd felt seconds earlier seemed to shrivel and vanish.

"I guess not," I said awkwardly, trying to think what on earth to say for the best, "but it feels okay now, at least."

"It does," she agreed.

She was looking at me, and I forced myself to look right back at her, initially awkwardly, but as the moment prolonged, it seemed to become less so. She slowly drew back towards me and rested against me, and I took her weight again, waiting for her to speak, which she eventually did.

"This time next week, we'll be going through the portals again," she sighed.

"Yeah, how 'bout that."

I'd told Serena she was definitely coming since she'd witnessed the use of the life assistant. So far, the confirmed party was me, Marc, Tommy, one or both of Amelia or Natalie, Peter, James, Lena, Serena, and Underwood. More than likely that would be the entire party, although since it was Rock Haulter, a place so many of us had enjoyed not long ago, that number could increase by a few.

"This guy you're seeing, this Smiley," she said, smirking as she spoke his name, "who exactly is he? I mean I know he's Underwood's grandfather, but why do you wanna see him so badly?"

I hesitated for a moment. How could I answer that question without it leading to a recount of everything we had done over the last two months? It wasn't that I didn't want her to know, but it was a lot to talk about and some of it would be hard to speak of, particularly the subject of my adoption and the business with Moran and that ghost woman.

"He's an old friend of Mr. Woodward's," I said, trying to send my mind a few sentences ahead, to pave the way before I spoke. "A really old guy who was around in the last war. He's also Tommy's Maahoo teacher. We need to see him 'cause we think he might have information that'll help us work out why Hammerson wants to kill me."

"Really?" she said, her mouth open in surprise. "How would he know? Was he a Hammerheart at one stage or something?"

"No, he's just—well, he's got some special magical talent," I said. "Like how Tommy has two bodies, and Daniel was a Sorcerous Seer."

"And how you can see ghosts," she added.

"Yeah, that," I agreed. "Anyway, Smiley's talent has to do with ghosts and people coming back and such, like what happened to

Lisa, but more importantly, he was around at the time Hammerson started hunting me and had a hand in my going into hiding."

"You haven't been in hiding, have you?" she asked, raising her eyebrows. "You are now, but not the rest of the time."

"Er, yeah, I was," I said, hesitating some more. "Remember how Stella said ages ago that they didn't know it was me they were hunting until recently? A couple of months ago? That's 'cause they lost track of me after Smiley's assistance."

"Oh, okay," she said, shrugging, clearly still confused. "They know who you are now, though. Do you know how they caught up with you?"

"Yeah, we know that part," I said. "Something Hall gave me in detention that he passed onto the Hammersons confirmed I was the one. Perhaps they'd had an inkling it was me and wanted to be sure."

As I spoke the words, I suddenly realised exactly where that inkling had likely come from: As soon as Stella realised I was the one whose mind she was invading, Hammerson had probably picked up my identity from her mind. That seemed to increase the likelihood that he was hunting me for reasons to do with my connection to Stella.

"Okay," Serena said, nuzzling into me. "I still feel like I'm missing a lot, but I guess I'll catch up."

"Yeah, there's a lot of complicated stuff going on," I said, hugging her tighter and beginning to feel that urge returning. "Even I have trouble keeping tab of it all sometimes, but I'll try to tell you what I can."

It would have been a relief to have Serena completely in the picture. I found myself thinking that, since we had been together since the first of March and she would have only missed the very first meeting, it was pretty silly of me not to include her in everything we had been doing all along. Maybe that would have further complicated Lena's input into the theft of the life assistant, but who would know. All I knew was that, even now, hoping the guilt wouldn't drive me crazy, what I had done with Lena was the only thing I could not tell Serena. Oh, and what had happened between me and Amelia, of course, but that hardly counted as part of the story.

"All right," she said. "Start by telling me how you know Smiley was involved in—in whatever happened when Hammerson started after you."

I sighed. "Did you ever wonder why I don't look much like either of my parents?"

She raised her head and looked at me, her expression surprisingly unsurprised. "No, but I did think—maybe—"

She looked very awkward, so I just said it for her. "I was adopted."

"Ah." She leaned back against me again. "I didn't think of that, but I did wonder why your birthday is so close to Peter's. Only two months apart. I just figured there was something odd going on that there was a reasonable explanation for. Guess I was right. So—so you're saying that the Hammersons were after you before you were adopted, and you were adopted by the Playmans for protection?"

"Yeah," I said, impressed, not for the first time, by how quickly she had made the connection. "Smiley was the one who gave me to Mr. Woodward, who then passed me onto the Playmans."

"I see," she said. "So you must have had some sort of connection with the Hammersons before Smiley took you that was broken by the adoption. Are you sure Smiley wasn't a Hammerheart?"

"Trust me, he never was," I said. "At least, I'm fairly sure he wasn't. We thought at the start that my parents—my blood parents— must have been Hammerhearts, and that was one thing we wanted to find out from Smiley, because neither Mr. Woodward nor Mum and Dad know who they were. We've found out since, though."

"You did?"

"Yeah. This—you probably won't believe this."

I marshalled my thoughts, working out the best way to tell her that wouldn't result in her shrieking in surprise.

"Go on," she prompted.

"Well, you remember back on camp…"

I told her firstly about the three ghosts Moran had called back, and tried to describe how that woman had made me feel. Serena kept a closed expression as I spoke. I then told her about the returnamy and how Stella had suggested that the Hammersons had somehow identified me from her presence and how I had felt about her, and so discovering her identity was the first step in unravelling the mystery of why they were hunting me.

"I asked Marc and Lucien if they knew any young women he might call back who would help him," I said, "and they both mentioned their mother—you know how they always said he killed her—but that seemed unlikely. Turns out that it really was their mother, though. I saw her again in a picture in their house and asked Marc who she was."

"Okay," she said slowly, "but what's this got to do with you?"

"Well, I also asked Cornish who she was," I said, "that night me and Tulip got caught. I didn't expect him to answer, and Hammerson went nuts at him when he did, but he told me she was my mother—my real mother."

"Your mother—" she said, then stopped dead. I could see her thoughts ticking over in her eyes. Taking this connection took a little longer than some of the others, but sure enough, she got there. "So you and Marc are half—but you look—"

"Not *half*-brothers," I said, smirking awkwardly, and her mouth fell open in astonishment.

"You mean he was—they were—your real family?"

"Yep," I said, pulling her back against me so that I wouldn't have to see that look on her face any longer. "Moran must have found out I was in danger and passed me on to Smiley before the Hammersons could get at me. As punishment, Hammerson killed his wife and made him take the blame for it. We don't know that as fact, but we expect it went something like that. But it still doesn't explain why I'm in danger in the first place."

"My God," she mumbled. "My God, what a mess. Does it get more complicated than that?"

"Oh yeah, definitely," I said. "We do have a theory as to what it all has to do with."

"You mean why they want you?"

"Yeah," I said. "This is gonna be hard to explain, and you do realise that you can't repeat this to anyone at all."

"I assumed that from the start. Go on."

I told her of the connection between me and Stella. She raised her head again and listened in, not astonishment, but slight disbelief.

"Try to keep an open mind here," I told her. "We both know about it now. She knew before me, which is why she approached me way back before all this started. I only found out in the Basement when I saw her and knew it was real."

"I believe you," she said quietly, "but it's just—just—so incredible."

"Sure it is, but that's how it is. I've been using it to keep an eye on her since we disowned her. That's how I knew she was alive all this time."

Serena gave her head a little shake, not in disbelief but as though to clear it. "You think that Hammerson knows about this?"

"I don't know for sure, but it's a reasonable assumption. He could read her mind back then, and if she'd been thinking about it, he must have picked some of it up. That night he got me and Tulip, he tried to connect me and Stella to something called an undoer. It didn't work because Moran came and saved the day, but I'm guessing he wants to undo whatever magic is binding us together before he kills me."

"Okay," she said, nuzzling me again.

A short silence followed this, and I made no effort to break it. Serena needed a few moments to absorb everything I had told her. It was rather a lot all at once, I supposed.

"Okay," she said again. "Okay, I think I got all that. It's a lot, but —okay. So you've been hunting Smiley all this time? It took a while."

"Yeah, it did," I said. "We talked to Mr. Woodward, then went down into Marc's place to see if there were any clues there, then checked out the Hammerheart base, and all that gave us nothing. Then we went over to England with some references Mr. Woodward gave us—this is about a month ago now—and got in touch with some guys who eventually put us in touch with Underwood."

"Oh goody," she said sarcastically.

"Yeah," I said. "He didn't wanna cooperate, but he gave us enough before he worked out who we were for us to know he was in touch with his grandfather. He gave us a lot of trouble, though, especially Amelia. You know it was him who caused her to relapse the way she did?"

"Seriously?"

"Yep. Anyway, we didn't go back to him for a while. We knew the best way to get him to do what we wanted was to bait him with a good-looking girl who looked like she might be of age. That's where Lena came in, but she didn't wanna cooperate for a while either— thought it was a disgusting job and all, which I suppose it was—but eventually we convinced her there was enough good in it. Luckily for her, she didn't end up needing to sleep with him."

I kept my voice as even as I could as I spoke, and fortunately Serena wasn't looking at my face. Even more fortunately, she made no enquiry of how we had gone about convincing Lena to assist us.

"So you and her went over there to get the life assistant from him?" she said. "'Cause you were saying that's how you contact Smiley."

"Yep, that's what we did," I said. "Stella had been over there too, though; she almost got it off him before we had even got there. She left me a note over there that gave me—well, no new information, but I suppose confirmation of what we would have to do to him."

"You're so sure she's on our side, aren't you?"

"Yeah. Well, I do have a closer connection to her than anyone else."

Another silence followed, and once again I made no effort to break it. It seemed that Serena now had the general idea of what we had been up to all this time, without all the specifics. That suited me fine. Whatever else she needed to know, she would find out as we went along and surely ask plenty of questions in the process. I just leaned back against the wall behind the bed with Serena resting against me, head on my shoulder. It wasn't as comfortable as it might have been if we were sitting on one of the couches rather than the bed, but I wasn't complaining. Now that the talking seemed over for the time being, I was ready to get back into the more physical intimacy.

"John," she said after a while, and she sounded a little more hesitant than she had been so far, "can I ask you something?"

"Sure," I told her. "I know I probably haven't told you the whole story, so you ask whatever's still confusing you."

"It's not really part of the story," she admitted, looking very nervous indeed, and my curiosity rose, as did my own nerves. For the second time, I had to restrain my urges.

"Well, you can still ask," I invited, hoping it had nothing at all to do with Lena.

She bit her lip, then seemed to steel herself to say what she was thinking. "I guess it's been on my mind for a little while. Not bothering me, just curious, since even before we started dating."

"Go on," I prompted.

"Did you and Stella ever—do anything together?" she asked, going red in the face and pressing it into my chest so that I couldn't see. I saw enough, though, and I very nearly started.

"If you mean what I think you mean," I said carefully, "when would we have done something like that?"

"Well, you and her…" She cleared her throat and started again. "You brought her up here for like over an hour a couple of months ago."

"Oh, that," I laughed. "I know Peter was teasing me about doing God only knows what, but all she wanted with me was to tell me about the returnamy. We discussed our connection too. That was the first time we did. We only stayed up there as long as we did because she wanted to prolong leaving the base. And maybe she wanted to be with me too, I'm not sure. But no, nothing happened."

"So are you saying—" Her voice was muffled, but I could still make out her nervousness. "Are you saying that—that I'm the first?"

I blushed too this time and was immensely glad she couldn't see my face. "Do you mean my first girlfriend or my first—you know?"

She burst into giggles for about five seconds before answering. "You mean sexual partner? Yeah, I mean both."

"Aha," I said, grinning and thinking what was best to say. Only a moment of consideration brought me to the truth. Or rather, half of the truth, but how to say it? "Well, you're my first girlfriend, yeah, but my second sexual partner."

I wasn't sure what she had expected, but apparently it wasn't that. She raised her head and looked at me in considerable surprise. "Really? I'd have thought it would be the other way around. Are you saying it was casual?"

"Erm, kind of," I admitted grudgingly, "but probably not in the way you're thinking."

"In what way then?"

"It's hard to explain."

"Who was it? Anyone I know? Please don't tell me it was Lena."

Curse my treacherous face, damn it to hell.

"It was, wasn't it?" Serena pushed me. "When did it happen? Was it recently?"

"It was Tulip," I said, slowly and deliberately, lest my face give anything else away, "and I think you can guess when that would have been."

Serena froze, dumbstruck. "Tulip? Are you serious?"

"Yep, serious," I told her, wishing this topic hadn't come up.

"I forgot about her."

I felt a spike of anger pierce me at her words. "Forgot her? *Forgot her?*"

"I mean I forgot how you and her got close those couple of days," she said hurriedly. "I never forget she went with you that night."

I breathed deeply for a few seconds before managing to get myself under control again. Serena hadn't done anything wrong. No reason to let myself get irritated with her. "Tulip offered to help me with whatever I wanted in gratitude for saving her life in the school battle. I didn't want to at first because I thought I'd get her killed, which I did, but I eventually agreed because I realised I couldn't really stop her putting herself in danger if that's what she wanted. It was her offer that we do—that thing, and I accepted it because I needed the comfort that night after how I felt so guilty about William, Carl, and Lisa. That's all there was to it. The feelings were no deeper than that."

Although they could have been if I had allowed it. Tulip had said that if a girlfriend was what I wanted, she could be that as well. I hadn't wanted to commit to her because I had still been holding onto hope that Natalie could soon be mine. Now that I thought about it, maybe Serena wasn't the first girl I had treated badly, any more than she wasn't the first girl I'd had sex with. Did it matter that Tulip had been the one to offer? Had she, perhaps, wanted more than what I'd given her, but hadn't said so? This was *so* not the time to be having these thoughts.

"Oh, John."

"Don't tell me it's disgusting," I said, shaking my head and looking away from her, blocking the unpleasant thoughts before they could seriously distract me. "I've had time to work that out, but at the time it felt right, or at least reasonable."

"I wasn't going to say that," she said, sounding hurt. "I was just —sorry to make you think of all that again."

I shrugged again. "It's okay. I don't feel as bad about it now since I found out what Sebastian did, but still."

"I know, I know," she said, "and—forgive me for saying this—I think you must have had some sort of feelings for her that maybe you didn't realise. Not what you'd have with a girlfriend, like what— what—"

"What we have," I supplied her.

"Yeah," she said, apparently relieved to hear me say it. "But what I'm saying is what you did for her out there in the hall—that pendent thing—that can only have been heartfelt."

I shook my head. "That was out of guilt and respect, and because there was no funeral. That I'm aware of, anyway."

"I know," she said again, putting her arms around me and pulling me against her, so that now she was leaning against the wall and I was resting against her.

Another silence followed, but it was short, and this time I was the one to break it. "Serena?"

"Yeah?"

"Return the favour," I told her, grinning slightly.

"What favour? What do you mean?"

"Tell me," I said, still grinning in spite of myself, "am I your first?"

I already knew part of the answer to that. Serena had not been a virgin the first time we had been physically intimate, and I knew the difference firsthand in hindsight now that I had seen Lena. Just for the record, Tulip hadn't been a virgin either, but I had already guessed that based on the very little she'd told me about her previous partner. I had a moment to wonder if I knew anyone under the age of sixteen who was still a virgin. Well, Lena had been until very recently, and Natalie probably still was, and Stella probably was, and Nicole may have been.... Okay, there were a few, but they seemed to be the minority now.

"Oh, John," she protested, squirming against me.

"Come on, I told you," I told her.

"It's bad," she moaned. "God, it's bad. Worst thing I've ever done."

"Okay, I take that as a no," I said. "So how many, then?"

"Do you mean boyfriends or—or sexual partners?"

"Both."

"Only one, one for both. The same one," she said, extremely grudgingly.

"Aha," I said and left it at that, but now that the subject had been brought up, Serena didn't seem to need prompting.

"It only happened once, though," she said in a bit of a hurry, a bit like Stella trying to justify her behaviour those couple of times. "About three months before I came to Chopville. He was older than me, seventeen, and I was thirteen, and he really wanted it, really bad. I didn't want it yet, wanted to make sure he was the right one, and he sort of persuaded me that we were in for the long haul, and I—I just let him do it. It was good, I suppose, but it all fell apart like three days later, and that was all my fault, and I felt so bad for letting him in when it was such a waste for a first time."

I felt a little stunned but grateful that she had given me a line to comfort her. "It's not your fault, Serena. He must have been really persuasive, and I guess you believed at the time that it felt right."

"I know, but…" She sighed. "It was my fault how it all ended. I saw him with his arm around another girl—one his age—and I assumed the worst. I was wrong in the end, but he couldn't trust me after that, and I guess I didn't trust him either since I let it get like that."

"Do you trust me?" I asked before I could stop myself, and immediately felt my insides tense.

"Oh, John," she moaned again, holding me tighter to her. "Must we?"

"Yeah, I reckon we must," I said, forcing myself to crawl out of the tunnel I had entered. "I know it must be hard with chicks like Lena only a couple of doors down, but do you think she'd still be chasing me if I were really interested?"

"I wouldn't know," she said dispiritedly.

"You don't have to trust her, or anyone else," I said quietly, "but can you trust me? I trust you totally, but I can't see us working out too long if you can't do that."

Not that I deserved her trust one bit, I thought bitterly, despising my actions of the last month.

"I guess you're right," she said, shifting her position so that I had to raise myself off her for a moment. When I caught a glimpse of her face, I saw tears in her eyes and promptly changed direction, instead taking her in my own arms and holding her close.

It seemed that all the fears, worries, anxieties, and whatever else Serena had been holding onto over the last six weeks or so were now forcing their way out of her, and I knew I was required to be her rock at this point. So we just sat there for several minutes, Serena sobbing against my shoulder and me just holding her, rubbing her back, similar to how I had been with Amelia the previous week, only this time I felt a little more in my comfort zone, either because I'd done this before or because Serena was the one I was supposed to be comforting.

Eventually, she managed to pull herself together enough to speak. "I do trust you, John," she sobbed, "but I just—it's so hard to feel secure! I mean, I've seen so many other girls looking at you, and I just—I just worry that I won't be good enough to be your only one. Is it so unreasonable to expect a teenage guy's mind to stray?"

I held her tighter, trying to think what was the best way to respond to that and trying not to feel pleased about the way she had described 'so many girls' being interested in me. "Of course you are good enough," I said slowly, picking my words. "I mean—okay, all of us may be interested in several people at a time, but those of us who have morals won't act on those interests. Surely you can go out there and find a few other guys you might be interested in after me?"

God, I felt like such a hypocrite.

"Probably," she sighed, raising her head. I took the opportunity to wipe a tear away from her eye with my finger. "It's just hard. I didn't think of myself as insecure before, but I guess I must be."

"Maybe you just need time," I said, hoping I was right. "Surely long enough together with no dramas from other girls will help."

"I dunno. They're always gonna be around."

"We have to try," I insisted, thinking that if worst came to worst, I could find a way to get rid of the others. "Do you wanna try?"

"Yes," she said, leaning back against me. "I'll do whatever it takes to keep this thing going, John, and that's a promise."

"I promise the same thing."

I smiled. My guilt over what I had done with Lena was still enormous, but I still found myself able to smile. Why? Because my promise was completely genuine. I felt no urge whatsoever to do anything with any other girl. Not Lena, not Amelia, not even Natalie for the time being, and that was an enormous thing considering her apparent renewed interest in me. I also felt happier than I had in a while, because finally, I felt my own resolution. I knew I would be fine from here on. There would be no further interference in my relationship with Serena from anyone. The feeling was a great one, but of course, old feelings had a way of returning, as I found out a mere four days later.

Chapter 21: The Water Base

Little less than twenty-four hours later found me, Marc, and Tommy employing a tactic that had worked a few times and fatally failed a few times, so it only seemed sensible to try it again. The base Peter had told me about, the one in the middle of the Pacific Ocean where the Darkness Crystal was being kept, was completely new territory to all of us, such that we had no idea exactly where it was. The result of that was that we would have to use the Hammerheart carts to get there. We didn't even get that far before the problems began, though, for the entrance into the Hammerheart Highway we had always used up until now, the one in Marc's house, had finally been cut off from the highway.

"Okay," said Tommy as the three of us climbed back out of the fireplace into Marc's former living room. "So we can't go through there. Any other ways you know to get into the highway?"

"There's a guest entrance to the Chopville base in the Stretch," I told them, "but I couldn't tell you exactly where it is."

"What about Hignat's place?" Tommy asked. "Or Wilwog's? Do either of you know where they live?"

Marc shrugged. "I wouldn't know anything about them if it wasn't for their—er—"

"Jerkiness?" I supplied, grinning. "I vaguely remember Stella saying something about them living in one of these, like what you live in, Marc, and there are only a handful of houses like this one in town. I dunno where the others are exactly, but I'm sure an aerial view of the town will make them easy to find."

"Sure thing," said Marc. "I think there are some out in the far west of town, only a few blocks from here, but I'll have a look. You guys cover me for a moment."

Marc put his fingers around the crystal in his pocket and rolled his eyes up in his head. Tommy and I waited in the dark living room while he searched the town, looking around us nervously, though not really expecting any trouble. It only took about thirty seconds before Marc returned to himself.

"There are three," he said, "but I think only two of them are actual houses, and I was right. They're southwest of here, close to where the Jade River runs out of town."

Marc made us all invisible, as we had been on approach to his old house, and teleported us to the spot he had seen. The two houses before us, probably Hignat and Wilwog's, were almost identical. They were both the same shape and size as Marc's, but the lawn around them was very different indeed. Unlike the Morans, the

Hignats and Wilwogs clearly had pride in the appearance of their properties; they had gone about creating a lavish garden, complete with fish pond and birdbath. If it weren't for the two separate buildings and two letterboxes, nobody could have guessed that it wasn't a single property. This connection was much more obvious than the tunnel connecting the Playman and Thomas houses, yet it couldn't really be seen as illegal either.

"Nice place," Tommy muttered grudgingly.

"You reckon either of them are home?" I hissed at Marc.

"I didn't check, but I suppose it's probable they would be," he hissed back.

"Maybe they're at the police station, concocting some sort of scheme to get their sons back," muttered Tommy.

"Be serious, man," snapped Marc. "I'll have a look in there. Hang on."

We all went quiet again as Marc went still once again, reaching out with his mind to peek into the underground houses, only the entrances of which we could see. He returned to us in about a minute. "They're together, them and their wives, in that one." He apparently pointed at one of the houses before realising that neither of us could see which he was referring to. "Er, I mean the one on the left," he added sheepishly.

"So the one on the right is empty?"

"Exactly, and the entrance into the Hammerheart base is hidden in a cupboard in the laundry, so come on. Let's do this thing."

We moved forward onto the property, bumping into each other several times (Tommy almost ended up in the fish pond at one point, by the sound of it). Marc forced the front door open with his crystal and locked it behind him once we were all over the threshold. He then made us all visible once again and, hoping this was Wilwog's house, as he would probably be too stupid to set up surveillance cameras, we followed Marc down the stairs and through the house to the back where the laundry was. Opening the closet door, we saw that it was only a short slide down into the Hammerheart Highway.

"Hold on, you two," I said. "Those carts are only for two people, and there are three of us."

"No probs," said Marc calmly, and a moment later, he was holding a most familiar bag in his hands. "Here, Tommy, since you're probably the most defenceless out of the three of us—no offense, mate—you can climb in here."

"Right," he said grudgingly, and when he was safely in the bag, Marc made the now two of us, plus the bag, invisible once again before sliding down the slope into the Highway, me right behind him, pulling the door shut as I went.

The following few minutes were fairly routine. Marc pushed the button to call the cart; the cart came; the two of us climbed in and shut the door, cutting off the echoing sounds of carts around us; Marc rested the bag with Tommy inside it in his lap and strapped himself in tight; I took the seat in front of the controls, me being the one who had used them previously, and also strapped myself in tightly; and I searched for the base Peter had mentioned and eventually located it in the cart's on-board computer. I then pushed the go button and we immediately set off on a breakneck journey longer than any I had ever been on before. The force of it was such that Marc and I were pulled back in our seats, pinned in place and unable to move a muscle. I felt my own face contorted by the extreme g-force of the ride. It lasted for six entire seconds, which I supposed was incredible considering it had probably gone at least two or three thousand kilometres. I even had time to wonder, once it had pulled up sharply, why the force hadn't just crushed the pair of us, as our bodies surely weren't meant to withstand such speeds (even if we'd been normal-sized), but my wondering was only a moment.

We had arrived in a place that looked very much like the Chopville base, though a lot smaller in scale. The tracks we were on were the first in a set of just six lines for Hammerhearts to run on. That told me plenty about this place before we even got in there. It was clearly not used for much at all other than storage of precious items, which was understandable considering the Highway was the only means of accessing it. Who knew how deep under the ocean it was or the exact coordinates of it. I didn't expect it to be completely empty of people, though, considering the Darkness Crystal was being kept here. Fortunately for us, though, the place we were in was still and lifeless.

To my side of the cart was nothing but a wall, so we slid out the door on Marc's side, pushed a button on the virtual parking meter to send the cart speeding off to some other location around the globe, and headed up the stairs onto the bridge above the tracks.

"Over here," I hissed, grabbing Marc's invisible arm and leading him towards the only entrance into the building above or below or whichever way, just in case there was a visitor's entrance somewhere around here as well, although I doubted it. The place I had in mind was around where I had created the very first capsule back in the Hammerheart base more than two months earlier. "Just into this corner here. I'm fairly sure we'll have room here."

We had already worked out this part of the plan earlier that afternoon. Before anything else, though, Marc put the bag down and allowed Tommy to climb out of it. When he was on his feet, Tommy took his own capsule out of his pocket, newly created but almost identical to the one Tulip had used. He enlarged it in a clear space (it seemed it was just big enough to accommodate the capsule) and climbed into it. The capsule was already invisible and had been since we had left the Woodward base.

Marc and I waited together for perhaps thirty seconds before I heard Marc hiss, "That's it. My turn."

The signal was for Tommy, who would be able to see Marc through his window (such was an additional enchantment I'd put on it since learning of the goggles) to nudge him in the back by flying fast into a spot between Marc's shoulder blades. It wouldn't hurt either of them, so there was no worry, but it had to be done with enough force for Marc to feel anything. Marc also had an invisible capsule in his pocket, identical to Tommy's, and he now repeated the procedure Tommy had just done. I waited, feeling slight bursts of breeze occasionally from over the side of the bridge, presumably disturbances caused by rocketing Hammerheart carts nearby, although none of them came through the base. Fortunately, no one came through the door in front of me either.

About a minute later, I felt a blunt jab on the back of my neck and knew all too well what it meant. I took my capsule from my pocket, pressed the button, then, when it was the right size, climbed into it and pressed the button to put the roof over myself. Two more button pushes later and I was strapped in tightly and the capsule had shrunk to a microscopic size that would not cause any air disturbances noticeable by any Hammerhearts.

"Everyone all right?" I asked into the microphone. Like last time, the capsules had audio links between them.

"Yeah," they both answered, and Marc added, "All fine here. So how are we gonna do this?"

"Let's just get under that door and see how the place is laid out," I suggested, swerving my capsule down towards the insubstantial crack beneath the door.

The stairwell was considerably smaller than the one in the Chopville base. The Hammerheart Highway was on the very bottom level, and one quick look up the shaft revealed that there were only two levels above it. I zoomed the capsule between the flights and flew up to the second level, swinging around to look through the door into the corridor beyond, a procedure made impossible by the fact that the door was closed. I continued up to the third level only to see that it too was closed.

"Okay, how's this," I said into the microphone. "You two have a look around the third floor and I'll look around the second. Remember to be very careful flying over lines on the floor. Use your crystal to check first, Marc. I expect the third floor is likely to have more interesting stuff than the second, though, so when I'm done, I'll come and join you two. Got all that?"

"Sure," said Marc. "Where are you, Tommy?"

"Just going up to the top floor now," said Tommy. "Where are you?"

"Apparently the same spot as you," said Marc, clearly amused.

I tuned their conversation down to a distant background chatter while I turned my attention to my own exploration. Slipping under the door into the second floor corridor, I saw at once that I had been right in thinking that the top floor would be where the protected items were stored. Apparently the second level was the living quarters for those Hammerhearts whose job it was to guard the top security base. There were no Hammerhearts in sight on this level, but plenty of evidence that they had been here not long ago. Tuning back into Marc and Tommy's conversation, I realised that I was once again correct.

"Must be pretty damn important, then," Tommy was saying, "'cause normally it's down to the level-five Hammerhearts to guard things."

"What level are these?" I asked, guessing the answer.

"Three," said Marc, "and they definitely look like soldiers. There are three of them here where we can see, and they all have great big guns on their backs and quite a lot of smaller weapons strapped to their belts."

"What do you mean, 'where you can see'?" I asked as I zoomed around the level-two corridor, making sure to do the job properly before joining the other two.

"Well, we can't see the whole place yet," Marc told me. "It's not a long corridor, but it has those doors that look like walls, so you never know what's behind them."

"You do realise that you can fly through those walls, don't you?" I reminded them.

"Yeah, we know, but we're just assessing this place first," said Tommy. "Hey, Marc, I think I see a weakness in their defences. I know they're pretty heavily armed, but they don't look very alert."

"Of course they don't," said Marc. "I hardly blame them. They know no Sorcerers can get in here, so they probably think this is a waste of time."

"Their living quarters are down here," I told them, "so they must be stationed here for quite a while, perhaps in shifts of a week or so. Anyway, that's not important; if we have to make trouble with them, perhaps we can put them all out of action before they have a chance to call for backup, and you wouldn't expect anyone to come for a while."

"Unless there's a spell on this place to alert the Hammersons if the guards get attacked."

"Or perhaps a spell that detects any intruders at all who aren't Hammerhearts, or who come in the middle of a shift or something, in which case we're screwed."

"We can't worry about that," I told them quickly before they could let their panic carry them away. "Look, we've got more magic than a hundred of them if they do call for backup, and as long as we don't get normalised, we'll have an advantage over them. Marc, maybe you should fly your capsule through each of the walls while Tommy stays back and keeps a lookout. Use your crystal to make sure it doesn't detect you or do any magic on you, just in case there are extra spells on it."

"Anything interesting down there, John?" Tommy asked.

"No, nothing at all," I said. "Not unless you're interested in going through these guys' clothes. I'm on my way up now."

"Good," said Marc. "Let me know when you get here. I'll try the walls once you're here, so that you can defend me if something happens."

"How about if I do the wall," said Tommy, "and if anything happens to me, you two can both cover me. You can check the wall before I go through, Marc, and John, perhaps you can do some magic on these guards in here that'll distract them while we work without them knowing they've had magic done to them."

"So not knock them out, then?"

"Yeah, exactly."

I thought back to what I had done to the police officer examining Siobhan's window and supposed it was the best way to deal with the guards. I flew under the door of the second floor corridor, up between the flights of stairs and under the door into the third corridor. The scene was small and laid out clearly before me. The floor was stone, like most of the floors in the Chopville base. The second floor had been carpeted and made to feel more comfortable to its inhabitants. The lights were dim but clear enough to illuminate the three soldiers who had been granted guard duty. They were all level-three males, none of them recognisable. Tommy had been right when he said they weren't concentrating on their job; one of them was reading a newspaper, another was listening to an iPod, and the third was sending a text message to someone. They might have been a little distracted, but in my mind it didn't make them any less dangerous; they were all tall, fit and seemed to give off an aura of experience and competence, probably the reason why they had been given this job and the same reason why they didn't really appreciate its importance.

"Okay, Marc," I said, "I'm here. Have a look at the protection on the walls while I deal with the guards. Tommy, wait 'til we're both ready."

"Sure thing," said Tommy, sounding excited.

Silence filled all three capsules after that as Marc did whatever he had to do while I zoomed farther into the corridor towards the trio of Hammerhearts. None of them reacted in any way to the capsule's presence, which was entirely expected, of course. I took the Sien-Leoard Crystal from my pocket and rolled it around in my hands, but before I could perform any magic with it, I was struck by an odd thought. Previously, I had been under the impression that the crystals were too magically powerful to have spells placed upon them—the reason why they could not be taken into the Transgators, why the Light Crystal had not come with me into the returnamy, and why the note Stella had given me along with the Darkness Crystal had not remained attached. If all that was true, then why were we able to bring three out of the five crystals in here (not to mention the one we were seeking) when we knew all the Hammerheart bases to be shrunk, and additionally we ourselves were shrunken inside our microscopic capsules?

Such thoughts were not at all productive, and while I made a mental note to enquire about it later, I pushed it from my mind for now. I turned to face two of the three guards, the third being behind me. Then I changed my mind and turned another ninety degrees, backing away from the guards until I had all three of them in plain view. I thought back to the scene in Siobhan's bedroom, squeezed my crystal (a motion that was in fact unnecessary but seemed to give me reassurance that the magic would perform better), and before my eyes, the three guards were immediately overcome by dazed expressions. All three of them slumped back against the walls behind them and just sat there, breathing deeply. I could have let them continue what they were doing and be unmindful of anything else around them, as I had done with the officer, but I figured this time it was quite unnecessary.

"Good work, John," said Tommy, sounding impressed as I zoomed back towards the door to the corridor, for no particular reason other than I assumed the other two to be somewhere down there. "How about you, Marc?"

"All seems to be clear here," said Marc. "At least the doors themselves are no different from the ones in the Chopville base. I haven't checked behind them, though, so maybe you should use your own crystal to protect yourself before going through. If that doesn't work, then I guess either me or John will have to come with you."

"Which door did you try?"

"Actually, I've tried them all, but I guess we start with the first one on the right?"

"What do you want me to do?" I asked. "Stay back here and make sure these three behave themselves?"

"Yeah," said Marc, "but depending on what we find behind these doors, you might have to come and help out."

"Sure," I said, turning my capsule to face the door through which the other two would go first while always looking down the corridor towards the three guards.

It had only just occurred to me that based on the position of the guards, the Darkness Crystal would more likely be on the other side of them, but I didn't bother suggesting that. We came here to investigate, not to take action necessarily, and if we were only investigating, then we might as well do the thing thoroughly. I sat back into my capsule and, struck by an idea, gripped my crystal and sent my mind out to the door before me while using my physical eyes to keep an eye on the guards. It was the first time I had ever used both my inner and outer vision at the same time and it was extremely confusing, not to mention difficult to focus on either of the visions I was seeing, but I persisted, all the while listening to Marc and Tommy's dialog.

"I'll go first," Tommy was saying. "Then I'll tell you what I see. If I say nothing, then come straight in behind me. Got it?"

"Sure," said Marc, "but be ready to speak the moment you get through that door."

"Don't worry, mate. Okay, here I go."

Marc and I both held our breaths as Tommy zoomed on through the door. My mind flashed back alarmingly to the moment I had lost audio contact with Tulip, that terrible click of finality as she was normalised into a floating cage, bursting the bounds of her capsule. I closed my eyes to clear the memory and was suddenly on the other side of the door, looking at the inside of a small, dingy room, all four walls of which were lined, top to bottom, with filing cabinets. Drawer after drawer, row after row. This surely had to be an archive of just about everything the Hammerhearts had done since the 1960s.

"Looks like a storage room," said Tommy. "No people in here, that's for sure. I don't think the Darkness Crystal would be in here either, but I guess there's no way of knowing that for sure without searching every single drawer."

"That's okay," said Marc. "I've actually just had another idea. Get back out here, Tommy. I wanna try something."

"Try what?" Tommy asked, and I heard him pulling levers to steer himself around and back through the hidden door.

"Well, last week you said you could feel the Darkness Crystal being used in the Light Crystal."

"Yeah, that's right. That's how I knew we didn't have it."

"Well, maybe you could use the Light Crystal to at least point us in the direction of the Darkness Crystal."

A short silence followed this projection as Tommy and I considered Marc's words. I chipped in first. "That's not a bad idea, you know. Well, it's worth a try anyway. No harm, surely."

"Unless someone is using the Darkness Crystal right now," suggested Tommy darkly.

"If I know the Hammersons like I ought to, being around my dad and Lucien all my life, I don't think they'd let just anyone use a Magic Crystal. It would have to be someone who is both important enough and skilled enough not to muck it up. After all, the magic depends entirely on what's going through the person's mind, and with the Darkness Crystal, I expect a blunder could be extremely costly. I guess the point I'm trying to make is, if it was being used now, this place would probably be more heavily guarded than it is right now."

"That's true, perhaps," said Tommy, "unless the additional security is in the room where the Darkness Crystal is right now."

"Yeah, but you know what," I said, "even if they did feel the Light Crystal being used, the person might not understand what it is they're sensing. Then, even if they do, they probably wouldn't realise that they could use it to work out that it's in the same building as them. I'm not gonna get ahead of myself or anything, but surely we have enough reason to believe that we have a better understanding of the way the Magic Crystals work than most of the Hammerhearts."

"Probably," said Marc. "And anyway, Tommy, didn't you just use the Light Crystal? If they could sense our presence here, then they should have already come after us."

"Okay, you've convinced me," said Tommy, laughing slightly. "Let's see how this goes."

We all went silent again. In the intermission, I drew my mind back to my body, and, once I was looking through one set of eyes again, took the opportunity to contact Mr. Woodward telepathically, as we had agreed, and inform him that we were in the base, undetected, but hadn't located the crystal yet.

"It's very vague," said Tommy, "but I think its signal is coming from that door there."

"Well, that was the most intelligent thing you've said all evening," laughed Marc.

"The one between those two blokes."

It didn't take a genius to identify the door. Of the three guards, two of them were on either side of a door (a hidden door, of course, but we knew how to recognise them easily by now) while the other was directly opposite it. Now that Tommy had pointed it out, it seemed the most obvious door in the place to go.

"Okay," said Marc. "Same procedure again?"

"Yeah," said Tommy. "Be ready to back me up, and John, since we're so close to the guards, I guess you be even more ready than you were before."

"Sure thing," I said, curling my fingers loosely around the crystal again and deciding not to use it to send my mind outward again, because Tommy was probably right. It was so much more important to keep the guards in place this time.

We all went quiet again as Tommy went through the door, but the silence was only short-lived.

"Oh geez," he muttered. "Okay, nothing happened to me, but this has to be the place. There are two more people in here and they're not guards, not armed, but definitely up to something. You'd better get in here, Marc."

Curiosity was too much for me. I sent my mind outward and straight through the door just as Marc came through. The room was small and contained a very familiar box. The sight of it made my heart leap for a moment, before I realised that we would need to leave our capsules in order to take the crystal from it. Worse was the two men standing on either side of the box, talking in low voices. We all stopped to listen to their words. One of them was reading from a piece of paper while the other kept tapping his watch periodically.

"According to this, it will be young 1H4 who is given the honour," the one with the paper was saying.

"1H4," the other repeated, this one British judging by his accent, nodding. "Yeah, that makes sense. So what's the deal going to be?"

"Well, you know how we've been getting such a good amount of inside information about the comings and goings of the Woodward base for such a long time?" said the paper boy. "It's all been because of 3W41. He was very lucky that nobody thought to take his watch from him when they caught him, so he's been able to keep us up-to-date. Well, not very much, obviously, apart from the fact that the prisoners have been given a revamped prison yard. Well, anyway, according to this, 1H4 is to be the one to bring 3W41 back to Tankom, as she made a deal with him that she would stand up for him if he got into trouble."

"So she will use this crystal?" the watch man enquired.

"I believe she will make contact with Frederic Woodward first and inform him that she will use the crystal if the condition is not met."

"You really think 1H4 would do that? We all know how flaky her loyalty has been in recent times. I thought she was dead for a while there."

"Well, if the big boss thinks so, then we should take his word for it. I mean, who knows her better than him?"

"True. So does it say on that thing when this will be happening?"

"It only says that it depends on how long it takes her to make successful contact without being caught herself. Since this deal was struck on Saturday, I expect it's taking her a while to work out how to do it."

"Yeah, or she's stalling."

"It's not for us to know that," said the man, brandishing his piece of paper at his British fellow. "Look, that's all it has on here, and the way things are going, it's all looking up, even if 1H4 is still sitting on a fence with splinters in her bum."

"Sure, sure," said the other man, putting his arms down by his sides. "So what's the deal for us?"

"The deal for me at this point is to return to Canberra, where I will enjoy a nice long sleep. The deal for you is that you will buzz 2H9 every five minutes until six o'clock in the morning, at which point someone will arrive to take over, and you will return at six o'clock tomorrow evening. Agree?"

"Well, yes, as my life would be at stake if I didn't," said the Brit. "No problem. I can manage that, I believe. Do you know who'll be relieving me?"

"I believe it will be 3D77."

"Come on," said Marc quietly, as though the men might hear us if we spoke too loudly. "We'd better get out of here before that guy comes out and sees the guards all doped up."

My stomach lurched as I realised he was right. The paper boy, whose code was 3L29, I now saw, was preparing to take his leave. I zoomed backwards through the door and, barely thinking about it, returned the guards to a state of normality. There seemed a heart-stopping moment where they knew their minds had been screwed with, but it was brief. A moment later, they had returned to exactly what they had been doing moments ago.

"If he's leaving, then perhaps we should wait 'til he's gone before trying to leave ourselves," suggested Tommy.

"How do we know he's not just going down to their living quarters?" Marc asked.

"Because he said he was going to Canberra," replied Tommy. "And you're right, Marc. If he's contacting Hall every five minutes, then there's no way we could take him out without Hall working out that something's going on. We'll have to try to take him out first."

"You think?" I asked. "They'll definitely notice Hall's been put out."

"Course they will, but they won't suspect the real reason behind it. They'll just think we're attacking him because he's so important to them."

"And because we hate the wanker," I added coldly. "Look, I dunno what the time difference is here, but surely Hall would be sleeping in some of this time."

"We need to talk about this first," Marc said, "so let's just get back to base before working out anything new."

"Did you hear what he said about Sebastian?" I asked, my mind returning to one of the things that had made me start about their conversation. "I did wonder why Mr. Woodward always told us to take their watches when we put them in the prison block, and we did forget to take not just Sebastian's but everyone who'd been in the stairwell dozen."

"None of the others would have had watches, I expect," said Tommy. "Surely one of them would have told us by now, since they've all been brought back."

"We'll have to take Sebastian's, though," Marc said. "I know he can't spy from where he is, but that doesn't mean he can't strategise with the Hammerhearts from within our base."

* * *

"Well, that does explain a bit," whispered Peter.

It was the following morning, and I had just finished recounting the adventure in whispers to Peter and James through nearly all of home group.

"True," said James. "The watches—we've seen them tapping their watches before. Guess we now know what that means. Stella, too. That must be the mission they've given her to get her back on side, or whatever it is they're trying to do with her. If she's had five days to get in touch with Mr. Woodward, she's certainly taken her time. Guess that's a good thing for us."

"Doesn't change the problem, though," I muttered. "We need to get that crystal back before she can use it. You never know what sort of trouble they might cause with it, but if they're sending messages to Hall every five minutes, the only way to do it is to take Hall out of the equation first, like Tommy suggested."

"That's easy enough," said Peter. "Get Amelia and Natalie onto it while you three go back to the Pacific base and wield your magic."

"Bugger off," I muttered, grinning.

Period one was just getting underway. Mrs. Worlker, who had overseen home group, had just bustled off, and now Mr. Hall was arriving, waving for quiet before he'd even entered the Room 12 space.

"Thank you all," he said. "Now, we will be continuing with our essays today. Remember, this is your final essay for the semester, so if you haven't done particularly well on the two previous essays, you will need to work extra hard on this one. Before we get stuck into that, though, it is time for me to dictate to you a list of words that will be your spelling test next week. We'll make it next Thursday so that you have a full week to prepare for it."

"Oh joy," muttered Peter.

"John," Mr. Hall said sharply, his head snapping in my direction, and I started.

"Yes, sir?"

I glared sideways at Peter, sure his voice had gotten me in trouble for no reason.

"I need you to do something for me," he said. "Do you know where office four is?"

"Er—I think I could find it," I said. Actually, I knew full well where it was, having followed the other Hall, Hignat, and Wilwog into it once before.

"Well, I'm sure you know where the teachers' offices are," he said, "and you will be able to find office four once you get there. My desk is number twelve. I left a folder on my desk that contains a handout I wish to give to the class that should assist you all with your essays. Would you go back and collect it for me?"

"Okay, I guess," I said. "Will I miss anything?"

It seemed like a stupid question, but it also seemed strange that he would single me out for this job.

"You'll miss the dictation of the spelling words," Mr. Hall said calmly, "but I'm sure James will be happy to let you copy his when you get back, or at recess. I'm sure Peter would too, but at least James can give you greater assurance of accuracy."

"I'm sure he would," Peter agreed, grinning cheekily, but I knew the look in his eyes too well—he was in fact insulted.

"Okay, I can do that," I said.

"Try not to take too long, John," Mr. Hall added as I made to push the button. "You know the rules, after all. Just be as quick as you can."

"No problem," I said, and I pushed the button on my desk.

Seconds later, I was back in my seat in the gym, my head in the Transgator on the desk in front of me along with Thursday's books. I pulled my head out of the box, removing the earphones as I did, not bothering to move the books at all. I then straightened up, only to find myself surrounded. Hammerhearts—at least two or three dozen of them, encircling the Room 12 space of desks and Transgators, their various weapons pointing directly at me.

Chapter 22: Ambush

"Eureka," one of them said, his eyes on my face, the hand holding his agonator not moving at all. "That was a little too quick for my liking, but no matter, no matter."

I looked slowly around me, recognising a few familiar faces. None of these Hammerhearts were masked—such precautions were unnecessary in this age of Hammerheart authority. 3K17 was there, as were 3E57 and 3P69. The one who had spoken was coded 3H42.

"You, boy," he said, "have much coming to you, I'm in the way of thinking, but firstly, hand over the crystal."

My heart skipped a beat. I didn't have the crystal with me. In a way, that was a good thing, for the crystal, anyway. In another way, it was a very bad thing, because not only did it mean that I had little way to defend myself, but as soon as they realised I didn't have it, they would move in on me without any hesitation at all. I had to stall them.

"Where's Mr. Fletcher?" I asked the one who had spoken. "I thought he was watching the school."

"He was easy to deal with," said a female Hammerheart just outside my line of sight. "This little beauty can deal with Sorcerers as easily as anyone else."

My heart skipped another beat. It was surely impossible. How had they found a way to strip him of his magic after the protective work I had done a week ago? I risked a glance at her and saw that she was actually holding a solid-outliner. Now I understood. Mr. Woodward had had the same problem in the first school battle. Why was it so difficult for Sorcerers to combat thicky prison?

"Yes, he was," said 3H42. "Now, if you don't mind, Playman," he uttered the word as though it put a sour taste in his mouth, "hand over the crystal."

"Do I know you?" I asked him. "You look familiar somehow."

It was no bluff. I was sure I hadn't seen him before, yet something about him did seem familiar. I studied his face, trying to figure out what I was seeing.

"We have not," he said, colour flooding his face—anger, not a good sign. "And I hope we never do again."

"Remember to watch his hands," a voice said quietly from behind me, from outside the circle of Hammerhearts.

This voice was far too familiar to be ignored. I spun around, both of my hands, which had been on the point of entering my pockets, flying up to my chest. The Hammerhearts stiffened, but between them, I saw the owner of the voice, and cold fury began clouding my mind. Hall, the original Hall, had returned to the place where he had begun to build his reputation.

"You," I hissed, my gaze sharpening so that everything I was seeing seemed more defined than ever before.

"Turn back this way, if you please, Playman," 3H42 said coldly from behind me.

I seemed to lose myself in an instant. I moved slightly forward, only able to take a single step due to the desks in the row behind me, at which Serena, Kylie, and Erica were still crouched over their Transgators. In the same motion, I withdrew a bludginator from one pocket and a solid-outliner from the other. Both were in the air, but that was all I managed. A bludginator swipe from behind slashed across my back, stinging me horribly and causing me to stumble. The Hammerhearts standing behind the three girls raised their weapons, but none fired. Hall, standing farther back, made no move at all. I moved slowly to my feet, keeping my hands low so that none of the Hammerhearts, apart from those side-on to me, could see the devices still in them. I turned slowly back to face 3H42, noticing as I did that apart from my movements and the breathing of the Hammerhearts, the gym was completely silent. Everyone was inside the world of the Transgators, and there was no way for me to get back to them. What would these Hammerhearts do to my body if I tried?

"Good boy," said 3H42, smiling coldly. "Now, if you please, the crystal."

I stared at him, my mind whirling in panic. Somewhere below the surface, I knew Mr. Hall, the one inside the Transgators, had played a part in this, and I made a quick mental note never to refer to him by his title again, but it was definitely not at the top of my worry list. I was still searching 3H42's face, trying to identify what I was seeing, and more pressingly, I seriously needed a tactic here, some way I could get myself out of this mess.

"I think he needs persuading, Tom," said a bulky Hammerheart who was standing just behind the Transgator in which Harry crouched. "What you say, chief?"

"Yes, it does look that way," said Hall's voice. "3H42, perhaps you'd like to do the honours."

But my mind had fixed on the name—Tom. I now knew who he was, as though the name had sharpened the features even further so that I recognised them for what they were: Tom Hignat, Ather Hignat's father.

"Hold on," I said, carefully lowering one of my hands back into my pocket. Several Hammerhearts made to attack me but held their fire, at least for now. The items in that pocket were the bludginator in my hand, an invisibility toggle, and a signaller, the same one I had used to call for help when our house had been torched.

"Yes?" 3H42 urged, raising his eyebrows. "Are you ready to cooperate with us, boy?"

"What if I don't want to cooperate with you?" I asked him. "What if I can perform a simple spell to kill the whole lot of you? Just imagine what…I could do if…you attack me and I can still… perform magic with it? But if you don't attack me…I could spare you."

Only half my mind had been on what I was saying, though, as I was also busy uncurling my fingers from the bludginator, locating the two buttons on the signaller and pushing them both in. Hopefully the Woodwards would understand that to mean I was in such serious trouble that I couldn't be seen calling for help. Meanwhile, several of the Hammerhearts looked as though I had given them food for thought, but it was Hall who answered the question.

"We do not cut deals with known killers, Playman. 3H42, do what you will."

"Known killers?" I repeated, spinning around to face him again. "*Known killers?* The irony in that—"

Excruciating pain hit me from behind. I screamed, toppling over onto the floor, hitting my head on a desk on the way down and then again on the sprung wooden floor. In that state, I barely noticed. My hands flew out of my pockets and I was writhing and thrashing, my entire world consisting of nothing but blinding, white-hot agony. Yet somehow my brain was still working, and I tried with all my might to close my throat against the scream, to still my body and just cope with the pain as it was and couldn't be changed, but nothing worked. When the pain finally let up, I was quick to spring to my feet, the aches left over from the agonator felt but barely affecting my movement. Something spun out from beneath my left foot, and looking down, I saw, with complete horror, that the contents of both my pockets had flown out when I had wrenched my hands free. Worst of all, at least two of the Hammerhearts had noticed.

I dived for the invisibility toggle, the only device that would give me a hope in hell now, but one of the side-on Hammerhearts hit me with a terrifyingly accurate stunner before I could place a hand on any of them. I went completely rigid, falling to the floor, my knees hitting the surface with two extremely painful thuds, the pain only intensifying as I slid along the smooth wood. The other side-on Hammerheart hurried forward, scooping up all my weapons in his arms.

"Very nicely done," said 3H42 approvingly. "You can let him up now, Kristian."

I felt my body relax, and I once again sprang to my feet, only this time, my knees almost buckled and I had to grab the back of Peter's chair to steady myself. I suddenly realised that both he and James, the only two I could get to without passing through the circle of Hammerhearts, also had invisibility toggles in their pockets, but was it possible to get to them without the Hammerhearts being able to stop me? Highly unlikely. I moved slowly back in front of my own Transgator, my eyes now back on Hignat, my mind still working hard.

"Now," he said, the sneer in his voice not unlike his son's, "what else do you have to say for yourself?"

"I still wanna know what you'll do to me if I don't wanna give you the crystal," I said quickly, trying hard to keep my voice level and contemptuous.

"Well, we will continue with what we just did," said 3H42, "at least a few more times. If you still refuse, we will bring you into custody."

"I thought you'd do that anyway," I shot back at him. "Arnold Hammerson wants me alive. Surely your orders would have been to take both me and the crystal."

It was true, of course, yet the Hammerhearts were still surprised that I had understood the point so quickly. Several of them looked about to take half a step back from me, but Tom Hignat was unmoved.

"You're very clever, Playman," he said. "Okay, in that case, we'll have to work out a new deal. Chief?"

"Perhaps he would be more willing to cooperate if we were to advance on either Marc Moran or Tommy Blue?" Hall suggested from behind me.

"I also know that you'll take them anyway," I said loudly, not bothering to turn around this time. "Tankom wants Tommy for something, and you all want the Seventh Sorcerer. You think I'm stupid enough to think you'll let them go if I give you my crystal?"

Several of the Hammerhearts burst into laughter, and the female one who had spoken earlier jeered, "You hear that? He calls it *his* crystal now."

"I think young Playman has begun to take a few things for granted in his little oppressive world inside that Woodward base," sneered Hignat. "Now, young man, perhaps you will be more willing to respond if our good friend Eric teaches you a few things about manners."

"Who's Eric?" I asked, more curiously than anything else.

Hignat gestured to someone behind me and I turned to look. The Hammerhearts behind me were all poised to attack, but the one just to the right in front of me pointed at himself. He was a level three like the others, but his build was more along the lines of the level-five guards that had been so prominent around the Chopville base. My stomach lurched. What lesson was he going to teach me? And how much more of this was I able to take?

"Let him see what you're about," Hignat said from behind me.

Eric moved a fraction of a pace forward and reached out with one hand and into his pocket with the other. He drew a bludginator from his pocket while with the other hand he reached into the Transgator before him and pulled Kylie's head out. He pulled her back in her seat so that I could see her face. She was completely vacant, her eyes glazed, the earphones still attached to her ears, keeping her locked away and oblivious to what was happening to her physical body. He drew her head back farther so that she were looking up at the ceiling and placed the bludginator to her throat. My own throat went extremely dry.

"So what do you think, Playman?" Hignat asked, but I couldn't bring myself to turn and face him. "I would personally be tempted to order Eric to finish her off and threaten you with one of the others, just as payback for you and your forsaken friends holding my son hostage for so goddamned long, but I'm more professional than that. You hand the crystal over, and that little girl will be spared. You won't be spared, of course, but there's nothing any of us can do about that. So what do you say, boy?"

For the time being, I said nothing, not because I wanted to be smart but simply because I had to weigh the situation. I would not sacrifice Kylie for my own safety, as that was all it was. If it was a case of protecting the crystal, then that, perhaps, could possibly be different. As it was, however, Kylie would only die so that I could stay alive a little longer. Was that a worthy sacrifice? I didn't think so, not one bit in fact, but how could I stop them from doing it? I couldn't hand the thing over because I didn't have it. Meanwhile, how long could I prevent them from killing her without just giving myself up? If there was a chance the Sorcerers were still coming, then it may be worth the risk, but how could I know?

Eric seemed to think I was taking too long to answer Hignat's question. He pressed the blade of the bludginator into Kylie's throat. Blood oozed over it and down her throat, but he hadn't made to kill —yet.

"Wait, stop," I said, panicking and deciding, without really deciding, I had run out of time. "Don't kill her. I was playing you guys for fools. I don't even have the Sien-Leoard Crystal with me. Mr. Woodward wouldn't let us take the crystals out of base since they'd be unprotected in here."

"Is that so?" sneered Hignat. "See, Playman, I'd be tempted to believe you—"

"I, in fact, *do* believe him," said Hall silkily from ten feet in front of me. He was watching this entire scene with what looked like amusement. "It sounds like the sort of thing Frederic Woodward would do—value the crystals more than the lives of so many children."

"So what should we do in that case?" asked Hignat.

"Well, firstly, since he thought he could outplay us," said Hall, smiling nastily at me, and in a moment of terrible clarity, I knew what was coming, "Eric, do what you will."

Eric gripped Kylie's head in one of his enormous hands and raised it so that she was actually lifted slightly out of her seat, her neck extended to its fullest. He drew the bludginator back before, with a casual flick of his hand, he brought it forward hard, fast, and straight, slicing into Kylie's throat and right through her entire neck. It was the first time I'd ever seen a Hammerheart actually stab a person with a bludginator; they could do plenty of damage without needing to make physical contact with their target. Her body sagged forward against her desk, while Eric raised her head to chest height so that I could see it clearly.

I didn't look at it, though. I couldn't look at it. My eyes were on Hall, and as I had when I had first laid eyes on him, my mind was saturating again in cold fury, though this fury was ready to become hot fury at any moment. This man had just ordered the death of a girl he had taught less than two months earlier. It was nothing new, as he had delighted in torturing Tulip, but this was just one step too far. If it hadn't been personal between me and him, it certainly was now.

"Put that thing away, would ya," said the Hammerheart on Eric's left, stepping slightly away from the head. "It's making me sick."

"Yes, do so," Hignat agreed. "Now, I guess we just take him in?"

"Just guard him for a moment," said Hall. "I think it wise to take H2 and H4 now while they are still defenceless. If this boy doesn't have his crystal, then neither will the others."

"Does that mean we fail our mission?" one of the Hammerhearts asked.

"Not entirely," said Hignat. "You people," he said, looking sideways to the ones on his left, "go and fetch H2 and H4. Load them into bags. Bring their entire Transgators with you if you can't get them out. They can continue their schooling while we take them into custody. No reason for them to know a thing."

They set off, weaving through the rows of desks toward the space reserved for Room 23, which was about a third of the way across the gym from where I stood, stunned. Kylie—poor Kylie— what would have happened to her in the Transgator? Would she have popped out of existence? Would she have suffered at all as life left her physical body? Or—my insides chilled at the thought—was she in fact still alive inside the Transgator and now unable to return to a body? Trapped in there forever? Something Lisa had once told me came to mind. If that were true, Kylie could possibly steal someone else's body if she pushed the button on their desk before they could do so. In my heart, though, I didn't think Kylie could still be alive in there. This couldn't be the same as being trapped in between as Lisa now was. The only thing that held me together where I stood was terror. That and perhaps shock were the only things preventing the senses of grief, loss, and white-hot rage taking over me.

"How do you feel, Playman?" asked Hall silkily, his eyes fixing on mine, the delight far too evident. "Are you upset for your little friend? Perhaps feeling for your brother? Perhaps he could keep her head as a souvenir of the day he lost both his brother and his little girlfriend. Does that sound touching?"

A few of the Hammerhearts chortled, including Hignat, but most of them were stony faced, their arms still raised, poised to strike. I ignored them. It was as though nothing mattered in the world but me and Hall. The footsteps of the Hammerhearts approaching Marc and Tommy, Kylie's bloodstains all over just about everything in the row before me, Serena crouched defencelessly right in front of me, the fact that it could so easily have been her instead of Kylie—none of it mattered anymore. Even the fact that I would probably be meeting with Arnold Hammerson again in a few hours meant nothing. All that mattered was that evil man standing ten feet in front of me, smiling coldly at my situation. Even the slight revenge we would have taken on him in order to reclaim the Darkness Crystal didn't matter anymore. I knew I was completely disarmed, completely defenceless, and had no hope at all of reaching him, but I still wanted to dive over the desks and fly at him, cause him as much pain as I possibly could. The Hammerhearts seemed to know this, for they tightened the circle around me, still alert and ready to attack at the instant of trouble.

And that was when trouble really began, but it wasn't at all the trouble I or the Hammerhearts were expecting. It was also proof that

Kylie's death hadn't gone unnoticed by those in the Transgators. They were, in fact, extremely quick at working out the truth of the matter, as not even Hall could prevent them from getting involved. It was Harry and Simon who bounced into action first. Apparently having been listening to the situation for ten seconds, still as statues lest anyone noticed they'd returned to their bodies, they'd gauged exactly where the situation was and exactly where each of the Hammerhearts were. When they bounced out of their seats, they were both armed with solid-outliners and bludginators.

Simon managed to collect only two Hammerhearts with his jet of white light, as he had aimed at the section of the circle that had included the few that had been sent to get Marc and Tommy. Harry managed to take six before he was struck down by a jet of golden light, fired by Hignat at point-blank range. More activity burst around me as Peter, James, Katie, and Sophie all bounced into action. Knowing I was the only defenceless one in a battle zone now, I hit the floor, gasping for only a moment before Peter came down on top of me.

"Get up, man, get up," he panted. "Holy shit—what the hell is —"

"I don't have any weapons," I gasped. "Get off me, man."

"No weapons? But—"

"You got a toggle? Make me invisible."

"Subdue them!" Hall bellowed, his voice bouncing all over the gym, making him sound like a demon. "Don't let them overpower you!"

"Let's get out of here," Peter muttered.

He rolled off me and we both staggered to our knees, looking at the scene around us. Peter's idea of getting out of here was a good one, but I couldn't see any way to break through the circle of Hammerhearts, even with the battle going on. Erica and Serena were now out of their Transgators too, but unfortunately they, along with Sophie, had been too close to the Hammerhearts to get off any shots. Serena and Erica were in fact off their feet, suffocating in tight headlocks under each of Eric's arms. He appeared to be using his hands to manipulate the two girls into a position where he could get a good grip on their necks. This realisation flooded me with panic once again.

"Pete, you gotta stun him," I said. "Not the solid-outliner. Just make him let those two go before he breaks their necks."

I looked at my brother. He had caught sight of Kylie's head, which Eric had left in a place of pride sitting on top of her Transgator, but at my words, he forced his attention back to the urgent matter at hand. He withdrew two things from his pocket, but neither of them was a stunner. One was a bludginator, which he firstly slashed vertically so that a large gash appeared down the front of Eric's shirt, missing both girls and causing some of his own blood to join Kylie's on the floor. The other item was, to my surprise and perhaps horror, an agonator, the first time I had ever seen someone from the Young Army wield an agonator. A moment later, Eric was on the floor, Erica and Serena tumbling out of his arms and tripping up a couple of other Hammerhearts who'd been trying to get a shot at the twins.

"Get down, you two!" I heard James yell from behind me.

I spun around in time to see that, past James, the back doors of the gym were open and Hammerhearts were flooding through them. They'd clearly been the backup in case there'd been any trouble, and now they were ready to take charge. All three of us ducked again as at least a dozen jets of light in varying colours sawed over our heads, a few of them gashing some of the students on the other side of the Room 12 space, a few more of them collecting other Hammerhearts.

Their plan was to surely pack us into a tight circle before raining magic down on us from all sides until we were shattered on the gym floor. I would not let it happen, not now. I crawled under the desk Serena had been sitting at earlier, emerging into the space where Eric had been standing before and was now thrashing and screaming and making one almighty racket three feet to my left. Erica and Serena were back on their feet too, and I made for them, as much for my own protection as to make sure they were okay. Peter, who had followed me, was swiping his bludginator in every which direction at the oncoming Hammerhearts. Erica was doing much the same, her eyes flickering to me every second or two, but Serena had her back to me. Her eyes were on Hall, and she seemed to be sizing up her options.

"I wouldn't, Forgrey," said Hall in a soft voice, barely audible over the sounds bouncing around the gym.

He reached over his shoulder and swung a gun over it from his back, a firearm I hadn't even seen until now, astonishing in itself given the enormous size of the weapon. As Peter and I reached the two girls, the four of us made toward Hall slowly, not carelessly, not enough to force him into action.

"You're so dead," I hissed at him, knowing he wouldn't hear a word I said anyway.

"Why shouldn't I?" Serena asked, more loudly so that he would hear her.

She, like Peter, had her agonator in hand while Erica was sporting her solid-outliner and stunner. As we drew within five feet of him, he fired off a shot. The sound was explosive and made me cringe. He had deliberately aimed for the spot just between Erica and Serena's ankles, clearly to enjoy this moment as long as he could before killing, clearly wanting to make his point, assert his dominance in the standoff. The bullet hit the floor just behind us, causing splinters of wood to slash against the backs of our legs. Peter and I were fine, as we were wearing pants, but the splinters had drawn blood from the two girls.

"Not…another…step," he said very slowly, very firmly, levelling the gun directly between Serena's eyes. "Don't make me do it, Forgrey, because you know I will."

Erica made to level her solid-outliner at Hall, but with a casual flick, the gun was pointing at her instead. Peter, however, was too far to Serena's left to be seen in Hall's peripheral vision. A swipe of his bludginator later, Hall's forehead had turned the colour of red. He staggered, but the barrel of the gun never wavered.

Then something else happened, something none of us had anticipated. Hall yelled as something suddenly attached itself to his hand. It looked to me like a great big spider with at least fifty legs and about twice the size of a fifty-cent piece. He let the gun go, holding it in his other hand, pointing at Erica still, though far less steadily, while trying to shake the thing off the other hand. Then he yelled again as another of the things landed on his head and appeared to attach itself there. His other hand flew up to his head, letting go of the gun completely. It bounced off the floor, let off a single shot in the direction of the foyer, shattering one of its windows, and fell still.

It was a chance none of us were going to miss. Peter swiped his bludginator again, Serena shot her agonator (for only a few seconds admittedly), Erica shot her solid-outliner, and I snatched up the gun. Then, leaving Hall to struggle against the whiteness creeping over him, the four of us turned back to observe what was happening in the rest of the gym.

It was not good. The Hammerhearts had completely trapped Harry, Simon, James, and Katie, while another group of Hammerhearts had carried Sophie over to the other side of the gym to do God only knew what. Meanwhile, Marc and Tommy had also been seized, as had Natalie and Amelia, all four of their heads appearing square-shaped due to the Transgators.

"What on earth happened to him, though?" Erica asked, glancing over her shoulder at Hall again.

"That's what happened to him," said Peter, pointing towards the foyer.

We all looked, and my heart skipped a beat. There, in the glass doorway, making no effort to conceal himself whatsoever, stood none other than Bernard Moran. His expression was completely relaxed as he continued to work his Villain magic, though in this case it all seemed to be against the Hammerhearts. There was something else, though, something extremely odd about his appearance. There seemed to be a light around him, or at least around his shoulders, as though some sort of glow were being cast by the back of his head, bouncing off the windows and reflecting somehow into his face. A trick of the light, it had to be.

"We have to get the Woodwards," said Serena. "Anyone got a signaller?"

"I signalled earlier," I told her. "Pete, can you stop that already?"

I jerked my thumb over my shoulder at Eric, who was still in a world of pain, though he seemed to be barely conscious now. Peter obliged and, leaving the enormous Hammerheart twitching on the floor, we moved around the edge of the Room 12 space so we could aim at the pack of Hammerhearts trapping the others. It seemed incredible to me that so many students and teachers sat here, going about their schooling, completely oblivious to the battle raging all around them.

"God, we need serious help," moaned Erica.

"Solid-outliners, you guys," said Peter. "Erica, you go for the left side, Serena, the right. I'll go for the middle. John, perhaps you go after the guys who got the Sorcerers."

That would certainly be tough. I wished I'd snatched a few weapons off Hall besides the gun. There were about a dozen of them, not to mention any others that joined them before I could attack. I ducked and tore back the way we had come, around the Room 12 space and towards the back doors, for that was where the four in the Transgators were being taken. I slowed down, not daring to shoot at running speed, and fired a shot that caught one of the Hammerhearts in the knee. He buckled and went down, yelling, while the two he'd been working with to carry Natalie stumbled with her added weight.

"Oi, don't let H3 get away," one of them yelled, and all eleven remaining (at least I thought it was about eleven) dropped their prisoners and rounded on me. There were no desks in this area, no cover at all for me against the barrage of magic that would surely tear me apart in mere moments.

I fired off two shots, stepping back as I did so that I could keep hold of the gun. The first missed everybody while the second caught another Hammerheart in the shoulder. He staggered, clutching at it, but still daring to attempt a shot at me with his other hand. The jet of golden light missed by a few metres. I felt two bludginator swipes, one across the chest and another gashing both my thighs. A jet of white light connected with my right wrist and I quickly held it out from my body while firing again with the other hand, the weapon making my arm vibrate all the way to the shoulder. I had to aim high so that I wouldn't shoot the ones in the Transgators. I knew I was risking killing someone, but if these bullets were by Hammerheart standards, these guys were in for a long, painful stint anyway. Both of these shots were successful and two more Hammerhearts went down, yelling in pain.

The thicky prison on my right hand was spreading steadily from the spot, now covering my palm and working over my knuckles while progressing up my arm in the opposite direction. I knew it would eventually get me completely and I knew I had to be somewhere safe from the Hammerhearts when it did. I therefore steadied myself and shot from the hip, raking the pack of Hammerhearts with bullets, the noise deafening me, the gun wanting to jump out of my hand with every shot. I'd never taken such punishment in one hand as the backfires I was getting from this gun. I felt two more bludginator swipes from the pack, but that was all. The firing had been remarkably successful, and I couldn't work out why that should be so. All the Hammerhearts were now on the ground, two of them dead and the others either dying or seriously hurt. There you are, John, I thought savagely. You are officially a murderer. Are you happy with yourself? Will you be able to sleep at night? Especially if those two had been guilty of nothing but getting in the way of an evil influential charm?

I scrambled forward, toward one of the still living Hammerhearts, the closest one, knowing I had very little time. The thicky prison had reached my elbow and just frozen it in a ninety-degree angle. I put the gun down on the floor, far enough from his hands that he couldn't reach it, rested my white-gloved hand on his face so that he wouldn't give me any trouble, and searched him. His hands were open and empty, but a bludginator lay on the floor not too far from him. I reached into one of his pockets, found a few things there, and pulled them out. One of them was an agonator, but the other two were things I'd never seen before. I searched another pocket, this one on his other side, and found what I was looking for. I pulled the solid-outliner free, shot my right hand with it, and shot him again with it for good measure, before gathering up the gun and making for the back door again.

If I'd known a way to bring Natalie and Amelia back from the Transgators by force then I would have done it, but since I didn't, the only other thing I could do was find Mr. Fletcher and free him from his thicky prison. I had no idea why none of the other Sorcerers had turned up yet, or perhaps they had and were also trapped by thicky prison, who knew. I therefore sprinted for the back door, not wanting to think about how much time I had left, not wanting to consider the possibility that Kylie wasn't the only one we had lost today.

As I closed in on the back door, however, I saw a figure standing just inside it who made me freeze, sliding on the floor for a foot or two. If the Hammerhearts had coordinated this scene well, then Moran and Lucien had done pretty damn well for themselves too. My big brother was holding a gun, considerably smaller than my own but apparently a good shot all the same. I now understood why my shooting had been so good—it hadn't been just me firing. He seemed to take no notice of me at all as I stared at him, but continued to watch the battle between the Hammerhearts and Peter, Serena, and Erica. I dearly hoped those three were making a good show of things over there but didn't want to think about it too much.

I changed direction. I didn't think Lucien would kill me, but given that he was still affected by Tankom's influential charm, I didn't want to risk it. I instead ran back to Natalie and Amelia and crouched down beside them, examining the Transgators. The only button I knew of on this thing was the one inside the box they would have pushed to enter it. What would happen if I pushed it from the outside? Would it be the same as that person pushing their own button and returning to their body? I didn't know, and thought it might be too dangerous to try. I instead searched the outside of the box, looking for any buttons or panels that might reveal buttons. And, to my delight, I found such a thing. The small compartment contained only a few buttons and a dial that had many numbers around it. Natalie's was pointing at Room 23, which explained how the Transgators divided students into rooms. There was a power off button, but there was also a release button, and that was the one I tried for all four of them.

I knew it had worked before I'd even tried it with all of them. Natalie jerked spasmodically for a moment before seeming to roll out of her Transgator onto the floor. She sat up, looking like she'd just received a staggering blow and had no idea what had happened to her.

"What the hell," she said softly, before catching sight of me. "John, where am I? What—"

"Hammerhearts," I shouted at her. "Quick, get over there and help those guys."

I pointed at the large cluster of Hammerhearts. A satisfyingly large number of them were joined together by whiteness, but there was still too much activity over there for my liking. Natalie stared at this for a few moments before Amelia sat up, looking groggy and thoroughly disoriented.

"Amelia, come with me," Natalie said quietly, grabbing her wrist and jumping so that both of them seemed to fly into the air for a moment. I knew it was magic rather than strength that had enabled her to do that, as Natalie certainly wasn't much in the tough department. I didn't see their faces after that as Natalie led the counter-assault on the Hammerhearts. My attention was on Marc and Tommy as they too emerged from their Transgators.

"Where the hell am I?" asked Tommy, staring around. "John, Marc, what—why did we come back? And where are the desks? And who—"

He'd seen the Hammerhearts Lucien and I had gunned down. His jaw dropped.

"Geez," Marc muttered, scrambling to his feet. "Jesus Christ. We should have known the Hammerhearts were in on this whole school thing."

"You guys have weapons?" I asked them, and when they both nodded, I added, "And invisibility toggles?" When they nodded again, I said, "Make us all invisible, then. I lost all my weapons. Leave Natalie and Amelia to sort it out. We gotta make sure they can't catch us, since we're the ones they want."

Marc did the honours, whipping his toggle out and shooting it first at himself, then me and Tommy in turn.

"I thought Natalie's old man was watching this place," said Tommy as the three of us turned for the back doors.

"He was, but they got him with solid-outliners," I told them. "I signalled the Woodwards, but they haven't responded as far as I know. Come on, Marc, just ignore—"

Marc had slowed when he'd seen Lucien. I dragged him on, but before I could say anything else, explosions shattered the air as guns were fired. We all spun around, me still holding Marc's invisible wrist, and saw that now that Sorcerers were in on the act, the Hammerhearts had to resort to killing just about anyone. Blood flew into the air, shockingly red, and I didn't want to think whose it was.

"Come on, we have to go," moaned Tommy. "Come on, come on."

It was true. All we could do for sure was get ourselves caught up in the drama, perhaps getting ourselves killed. We made for the exit once again, slipped past Lucien (he either didn't notice or chose to ignore us), and emerged into the fresh autumn air.

Chapter 23: Parting

The battle (what turned out to be the third battle at Chopville High in as many months, surely the most dangerous school in Australia by now) ended fairly smartly in the following minutes. Mr. Fletcher had been based just outside the gym, difficult but not impossible to spot in his position. He was presently keeled over, pure white when the three of us found him. Tommy released him from his thicky prison. The Sorcerer struck out for a moment before jumping up and tearing into the gym foyer. I hoped, for his sake, that Moran had got out of the way before the Sorcerer caught him.

The three Sorcerers were able to bring the situation under control fairly quickly, although several Hammerhearts, including both Halls and Hignat's father, managed to flee the scene. Kylie was the only non-Hammerheart fatality. Harry, Simon, Katie, James, Serena, Erica, and Peter had all been hurt, critically in Simon's case, but they had all been treated at the scene. Sophie had been in fairly good shape, considering; the Hammerhearts that had taken her away had fled when Natalie came after them, leaving Sophie baring no physical injuries that anyone could find. That only made the rest of us more nervous, though, because Sophie was extremely shaken and wouldn't speak of what had happened to her. All the offending Hammerhearts, according to what both Natalie and I had seen of them, were male, which opened the door to a horrible possibility: Had Sophie suffered something similar to what Amelia had in the Chopville base? Only, in Sophie's case, it would have been a whole gang of them instead of just two. Thank God it could only have lasted a few minutes at most.

Natalie and Amelia had escorted the rest of us to base while Mr. Fletcher had entered the Transgators and announced to the rest of the school that the temporary schooling system they were running had been terminated. It must have been a shock to most classes, who would have had no idea whatsoever of the violence happening all around them. It was in this time that I was able to reflect on all that had happened that morning. That Hall, the one I had come to think of as the 'good' Hall (yeah, I know, what a laugh) had instigated this whole setup, I had no doubt. After all, he had helped organise this temporary school. Was the whole thing a trick to get me, Marc and Tommy? It seemed an incredible length to go to, but then it shouldn't have surprised me. The Hammersons had the might of half the world's power on their side now—no, more than half. They could go to any length they wanted, and taking us down, particularly the Seventh Sorcerer, would be high on their list of priorities.

Kylie—poor Kylie. She'd done nothing at all to deserve the end she had been given. What had she suffered at the point of death? I knew better than to ask the others. They would have seen if she'd suffered at all or just popped into nothingness, but it was way too soon for them to speak of what had happened. I felt my own kind of grief, guilt once again, as I had been unable to prevent them from killing her, fury and enormous animosity towards Hall—both of them, in fact—and complete and utter shock. By lunchtime, I had come up with a resolution: When we put him out of action in order to take the Darkness Crystal, it would be by way of death. I had murdered once, and now I was ready to do it again. I thought back to a week ago when, in England, I had wondered if I was becoming cold and heartless as a result of this war. I still knew not whether I had been then, but I knew I was now.

Natalie and Amelia, who had returned to school as soon as they'd dropped us off at base, returned at about two o'clock that afternoon, and they, along with almost everyone who'd been at school that day, sat around in the lounge room, ready to discuss the horrible events of the morning.

"So what's happened down there since?" James asked them.

"Well, everyone's been sent home," said Amelia wearily, "and the gym is being cleaned up, but not by us. We left that to the Hammerhearts to sort out. There's no chance of us being able to run that school anymore, so everyone will just have to wait 'til the new government can get its act together."

"Do we know how it all happened?" asked Erica. "Was our English teacher responsible for it?"

"Course he was," I said bitterly. "You saw him—he sent me back there when he could and probably would have tried to do the same to Marc and Tommy."

"We have no proof, though." Amelia shrugged. "And in any case, he got away, along with your old English teacher. It's enough to suppose that it was all a setup, though."

"Yet another blunder made by Mr. Woodward," scoffed Peter. "He really thought this new guy was more trustworthy than his loser brother or cousin or whatever they are."

"You can't blame my father for that," said Amelia defensively.

"Course we can," snapped Marc. "Amelia, he's supposed to be a mind reader. Why is it that so many people can fool him? Well, maybe not so many, but Sebastian could for a whole two months—at close range too—and now this."

"He's only trying to be the good guy here," Amelia retorted. "Are you saying that we have to descend to the level of the

Hammersons in order to beat them? 'Cause if you are, I'm surprised you're not on their side."

A shocked silence followed this before Marc spat, "Of course we have to descend to their level to beat them. Being good is what got us in this mess in the first place, and you think continuing to be good will make us come out the other end?"

"It did in the last war," she said quietly. "Neither my father nor my grandmother have ever descended to the level of the Hammersons before. If they could beat them once, they can do it again."

"Do you even know how they won the last war, Amelia?" Marc asked her mockingly.

Amelia flushed, and Natalie, sensing danger between two halves of an unsteady relationship, said quickly, "We know Mr. Woodward always does what he thinks is right, and of course he wouldn't kill unless he had to, but he knows we'll have to kill the Hammersons in the end. That's not descending to their level, but it should be enough."

"Never mind Mr. Woodward for now," said Harry loudly. "Look, I saw Marc's old man back there. Did you two catch him?"

"We saw him," said Amelia. She looked rather hurt but was at least making an effort to move on with the conversation. "But we couldn't catch him. He made a break for it when we saw him, and when we tried to follow, he just forced us back somehow, and then he was gone. We saw Lucien too, but only for a moment. Moran had already planned their escape, I think."

"How did they know there would be trouble?" asked Katie. "Come to think of it, how did they even know we were at school?"

"They knew when the last battle was happening too," said Natalie. "Well, Moran did anyway. Lucien wasn't with him then."

"Lucien's with Moran now?" enquired Jessica. "I thought he was still under the Hammersons' influential charm."

"He is, but he's abandoned them or something," said Amelia. "As to them knowing what's going on, we still suspect Moran to have the Villain Crystal, even though none of us have ever actually seen it. If he does have it, then it might be cluing him in as to where he can go to cause trouble."

"All right, okay," said Harry, sounding calculating. "Yeah, I guess that could be possible. Anyway, John, what actually happened to you? We didn't know anything was going on out there until Kylie —well, we knew we had to go back. Hall tried to stop us, and that's when we sort of suspected he might know what it was about, so we didn't let him. What actually happened?"

"Well, they were waiting for me," I said. "I'm not sure why, though. It would have been a lot easier to abduct me while I was in the Transgator, like they were going to try to do with Marc and Tommy. Well, anyway, they wanted me to hand over the Sien-Leoard Crystal, but I didn't want them to know I didn't have it because then they wouldn't hesitate at all with me. They tried to bargain with me with silly things that I knew they were only saying and didn't mean, like they would let me go if I handed the crystal over, or they'd let Marc and Tommy go if I handed it over but not me since they'd been given orders to take me in. That's when they realised they weren't fooling me, so Hignat introduced—"

"Hignat?" said several people, and Serena added, "I don't remember seeing him there."

"Tom Hignat," I told them. "Father of the shitbag we've got locked up in here."

"Geez," muttered Peter.

"What did he do?" asked Serena.

"Introduced me to Eric," I told them, unwilling to proceed with the next part of the tale.

"Who the hell is Eric?" asked Erica. "I'm insulted."

A few people chortled at that, but it was an odd sound in the present conditions.

"He was the guy who tried to break your neck," I told her, "who Peter rescued you from."

Peter's face darkened. He, at least, understood what I wasn't saying.

"What did Eric do then?" asked Liam. "And how do you know his name, anyway?"

"Hignat called him by name," I said, "and Hall too, and well, he —well—he used his bludginator to—to—"

"Don't say it," Peter cried out, looking more anguished than I'd ever seen him in my life. "For God's sake, John, don't say it!"

I couldn't have said it anyway, because the moment I had thought too closely about Kylie's beheading, my mind had fixed, firstly on the spray of blood that had drenched everything around her, and then, perhaps even worse, on the way her body had slumped forward against the desk as her head was lifted into the air, disconnected, by that brutal Hammerheart. Worst of all, though, was simply remembering the corpse itself. Without warning, the vision became the one I always seemed to see these days. Now it was Kylie, lying prone and headless, charred and burning, surrounded by bursts of fire, barely visible through smoke, cast into deathly shadows…

"John?" said Serena's voice distantly. "John, are you okay?"

"I—yeah, I'm fine," I said shakily, wrenching myself back to the lounge room and hurrying to get through the rest of the story. "Well, anyway, some of them went for Marc and Tommy while the rest of us waited, Hall tried to bait me a bit, and then you guys who noticed trouble turned up."

That was all I wanted to tell them. None of them needed to know I had actually killed at least two Hammerhearts that morning.

"What I wanna know," Serena now said, "is why Mr. Woodward didn't turn up? I know Mr. Fletcher was there, but John said he used his signaller."

"Do all the Sorcerers get the signals from the signallers?" asked James. "Because if they do, Mr. Woodward probably didn't respond because he assumed you two, or your father, Natalie, would have it under control."

"We didn't get any signals today," said Natalie, "but yeah, if we hadn't been in the Transgators, we all would have got it. I guess Mr. Woodward may have assumed my father had it under control, or else that there was enough magic around to make sure the situation didn't get out of hand. It's also likely that he and the other two were busy with something else, anyway."

"That figures," said Tommy darkly, though not as darkly as Marc had spoken earlier. "If we'd had the crystals with us, then they would have swarmed like flies, but since it was just us—oh no, they would have had it under control."

"It's not like that," Amelia protested. "My father doesn't want anyone in this room to be hurt, or anyone in that school, in fact, but it's down to him to protect the entire world from these people. You expect him to drop everything to come to your aid whenever there's trouble?"

"Oh, sure it is," said Marc dismissively. "Look, John says he was disarmed at least a few minutes before they attacked Kylie. That's ample time for Mr. Woodward to come and help out. Surely he must have realised that if the Hammerhearts had penetrated far enough into the school to put someone with a signaller in danger, it must mean they had found a way to deal with Mr. Fletcher. Why didn't anything like that occur to him? I'll tell you why: It's because he places far greater value on the crystals than any of our lives."

"He does not," snapped Amelia, flushing again, though angrily this time. "How can you say that? If he didn't care about any of us, then why is he working so hard to sort all this mess out? He wants you all to be able to live normal lives. Why can't you just give him a break? He may be magical, but he's still human. He's not God, for heaven's sake."

"He's not doing enough," said Marc stubbornly. "You'd think he'd learnt from last week, but he hasn't changed any of his tactics at all. He still wants to tiptoe around and keep the Hammersons guessing, and meanwhile they've realised that as long as the Sorcerers don't come after them, they can do whatever the hell they like."

"He's playing smart," snapped Amelia. "Rushing out there all blazing magic for the world to see is exactly what the Hammersons want. Fighting their way only does more harm than good. They learnt that last time and won't make the same mistakes."

"So you're saying that last time it was even worse than this?" Katie asked. She was sitting beside Sophie, her arm around her. Sophie was leaning partially against her, partially against Simon, not looking at anyone or saying a word.

"Well, it was different last time," said Amelia. "The difference was that they never went for the government in any country. Instead it was most parts of the world uniting with us to fight them, and it was all guns blazing from both sides. So many died because of that, but this time, the death toll has been much more modest, and we can thank my father for that."

"That might be so, Amelia," said Marc hotly, "but at the same time, the Hammersons have got closer to their ultimate goal this time than they ever did before. It's all well and good that they haven't killed as many people, but it'll amount to nothing in the end if they do take over the entire world. What happens if they do penetrate this place and steal the crystals? We'll all be regretting our side's conservativeness in the moments before we're all slaughtered. Your father planned it this way, so he has to take responsibility for all the consequences, and you can add Kylie's life to that list now."

"It is not his fault!" Amelia shouted, stiff in her seat, clearly restraining from jumping to her feet. "He wasn't there. You cannot blame him for anything that happened today just because John got caught in a trap! Just shut up about it, okay?"

"When are you gonna wake up to him, Amelia?" Marc asked, raising his voice too, but not quite to a shout. "I know he's your father, but you're still prepared to defend every little thing he does, even though we know of mistakes he's already made in this war. If he's really smart, he would go out guns blazing. Not carelessly, because he doesn't need to be, but if he plays it smart, he can shorten the war by years and save millions of lives. If that's what he's about, then he should have thought of that by now, but if you ask me, since he was only a teenager last time, he hasn't got the backbone to give the order himself."

"*No!*" Amelia screamed, and that was all she wrote. Leaping to her feet, Amelia swung around, her blond hair flying out from her body as she shot out of the lounge room like a bullet, leaving a stunned silence in her wake.

"Marc," said Natalie reprovingly, her voice sounding even quieter than usual after Amelia's scream.

"Sorry," he said, shrugging and looking mildly abashed, "but it's all true. It's not my fault she can't see her father's faults."

"But you shouldn't have said all that," said Natalie, still calmly but with an undercurrent of tension as well. "If you have a problem with the way Mr. Woodward goes about it, and I must admit I do see some of your points, you should talk to him about it, but don't blame. We have to stick together in this or the Hammerhearts will tear us apart, and blaming each other will only do that without the Hammerhearts needing to do anything."

"Guess that's true," he sighed, getting to his feet. "I'd better go talk to her."

"No, I don't think you should," said Natalie, getting hurriedly to her feet. "That might do more harm than good. Let me talk to her first."

She didn't stay to let Marc argue but turned and strode out of the room without a look back, leaving another stunned silence in her wake.

* * *

I had a meeting with Mr. Woodward only a couple of hours after that heated discussion. Marc and Tommy were supposed to be present, but Marc was busy trying to patch things up with Amelia, while Tommy suggested that since the Sorcerer would also want to know about the events of that morning in addition to what we had done in the Pacific Hammerheart base, I might as well handle the two things on my own. I didn't have a problem with it. I still had my own bitter feelings towards Mr. Woodward and his method of handling the war in recent times, but I thought I had a better chance than the other two at stopping the discussion turning into a blame game.

"Let's keep this quick, shall we," he said briskly, sitting down at his desk while I took the seat opposite, the same seat I'd sat in while telling him about so many other adventures. "We'll start with last night. What exactly did you do?"

I recounted everything Marc, Tommy, and I had seen and overheard in the water base, and the precious little we had planned to follow up that investigation. I also told him how, just prior to lunchtime, in order to take my mind off Kylie, I had entered the new prison yard, used the Sien-Leoard Crystal to track down and corner Sebastian, and force his watch off his wrist.

"That is very good progress," he said, smiling faintly. "I suggest the three of you attend to that, perhaps on Saturday. If you get it done in one shot, that will give you two full days to prepare for your trip to Rock Haulter. Make sure Amelia and Natalie are aware of all you know so that they can help you. So that you're in the picture, I spoke to Natalie this morning about how she and Amelia went, but unfortunately, since Moran has made himself untraceable, and since he has used his own magic to do the same to Lucien in order to make it more difficult for us, they were unable to make any progress at all. Now, as for this morning, what exactly did your English teacher do?"

"Well, he asked me to go get something from his office," I told him, "told me not to be too long, and then the Hammerhearts were waiting for me, so it was all organised."

"Yes, it does seem that way," he said thoughtfully. "So, go on, recount it all for me, please."

I didn't want to—I really didn't want to—but I found myself talking anyway, lowly, slowly, bitterly. Describing Kylie's death, even without the gruesome details, was extremely difficult, though. I'd already done this once when Tulip had died; why did I have to do it again?

"I get the idea," the Sorcerer said after several seconds of silence. "What happened after that?"

I continued the story, telling it to the end. I mentioned that I had shot some Hammerhearts in order to escape from them but made no mention of the fact that I knew at least two of them to have been killed. Another silence followed when I finished before Mr. Woodward spoke again.

"Thank you, John," he said. "I think you did very well in the conditions. Do you feel okay about it?"

"I guess," I said vaguely, not entirely truthfully. After all, how could I overlook the fact that I was, at least in part, responsible for Kylie's death? Marc's words kept returning to me too, but there was no way I was bringing that up with Mr. Woodward now.

"Let me know if you have any problems, won't you," he said, sitting up straighter in his chair. "Dear, this is one nasty mess we have to sort out. That's all for now, John. You can leave, unless there's anything else you wish to discuss."

"No, that's all," I said, getting up a little too quickly. Had he sensed something in my tone?

* * *

For the rest of that day, Kylie's death seemed to have brought the Young Army to a standstill in the sense that everyone close to her was incapable of doing more than sitting around in the lounge room in hushed silence or retiring alone to their upstairs rooms to do who knew what. It seemed slightly different from Nicole's death in some way, perhaps because more people had known Kylie closely than they had known Nicole. Kylie had been friendly with just about all the year-nines, whereas Nicole had only been close to us Playmans and Thomases, Harry, Simon, Natalie, Marc, and Tommy. In any case, it was Kylie's closest friends—Katie, Sophie, Serena, Erica, and, of course, Peter—who were most affected by her untimely demise.

James, who'd had a crush on Kylie prior to dating Erica, was also badly affected by the events of the day and held me up on the way into dinner so that he could speak to me without any of the others hearing. Serena, who had stuck with me all afternoon excepting the meeting with Mr. Woodward, partially for her own comfort but mostly, it seemed, to assure me that none of this was my fault, looked suspiciously over her shoulder at us but didn't hang back to listen.

"I just need to know something," he said. His face was stricken with grief, but there was a determination in it as well.

"Sure," I said, "just as long as I don't have to relive any of it."

"No, I don't wanna know the details," he said quickly. "I just need to know—Kylie was sitting next to Serena. Did you, by any chance, do something to make sure they went for someone other than your own girlfriend?"

I was stunned. I don't know what I had expected, but it certainly wasn't that. I managed to stammer, "Do you think they would take any notice of what I wanted?"

"Well, no," said James, "but Hall knows us. He must have known you were closer to Serena than Kylie. Why did he go for her instead of the one more likely to matter to you?"

"Are you saying Kylie doesn't matter to me?"

"Of course not," he snapped, "but you know what I mean."

"Look, he only went for her because he was standing right behind her. If they'd done the circle differently, it could have been Serena, or Erica, or any of the others in that row on the other side of the room. It's just bad luck that it was Kylie and not someone else."

"Bad luck?" he repeated. "Would you say it was good luck if it had been someone else?"

"What point are you trying to make?" I asked him, starting to feel annoyed.

"My point," said James, "is simply what I said before: It doesn't make sense that they would go for Kylie over Serena if they know Serena's your girlfriend."

"You think?" I said hotly. "Maybe you didn't see Hall point his gun at Serena later on, or maybe you've forgotten that Hall hates Peter just as much as me and might wanna get back at him too."

I thought I knew what he was getting at now. The accusation that I had somehow tricked them into thinking I'd be more affected by Kylie's death in order to save my own girlfriend's life, and never mind the person who had to suffer because of that, was positively outrageous, not least because it was coming from one of my best friends.

"I haven't forgotten that," said James coolly, "and I know full well that if Hall had had enough time, he would have preferred to do them both, and perhaps a few others as well, but it doesn't change things."

"I dunno what's got into you," I snapped at him, the strain too much for me now. "You should know me better than to think I'd not care if Kylie was killed."

"I didn't say you wouldn't care at all," he said firmly, a little anxiously perhaps. It did nothing to improve the situation. "I can see that you do care about it just by your face, but would you care the same if it had been Serena? Or perhaps if it had been—you know—someone else you like?"

I snapped. It was simply too much. I made no reply but turned around and stalked into the dining room, hardly looking where I was going and accidentally knocking a plate of food out of someone's hands (someone I either didn't know or didn't recognise). Once I had got my own dinner, I calmed down enough to look around for somewhere to sit. Serena and Peter were waving me over to a table where they were sitting with Erica. My stomach dissolved when I saw her, and particularly when I saw the empty seat beside her. I scanned farther. The twins were sitting with Katie and Sophie, the two girls still distraught; Tommy was sitting with Jessica, Felicity, and Lena (there were two empty seats there, but the idea of picking Lena over Serena gave me a swooping stomach). I would have liked to see Natalie or Amelia, or even Marc, but none of them seemed to be around. I looked back at the table I would have gone to automatically on any other day. Peter and Serena were talking together, and I again resisted the urge to go over there. James hadn't joined them yet (in fact, he didn't seem to have come in at all yet), but I knew he would eventually, and I couldn't face him again tonight.

Someone came up to the conveyer belt behind me and I turned to see who it was, more out of reflex than anything else, and because it didn't sound like it could be James. It was Siobhan. She may or may not have noticed me, I couldn't tell, but her head was down and she seemed to be concentrating on nothing but getting her dinner, and no doubt Underwood's too.

"Hi," I said flatly.

She looked up at me, and I was taken aback to see that she appeared to have been crying. The redness in her eyes suggested it at least. "What's up?" I asked her, resisting an urge to reach out and touch her shoulder. She still hadn't quite forgiven me and Marc for what had happened a week ago. She probably never would.

"Nothing," she said, just as flatly, "just getting dinner."

"Are you okay?" I persisted.

She looked over my shoulder, her lower lip trembling slightly. I looked back as well; Underwood was sitting at a table with three other guys, all from year twelve. Although I didn't know Siobhan very well, I had a feeling she would never have chosen to sit with those sort of people if it wasn't for her being with Underwood.

"I am okay," she said, a little jerkily.

You couldn't lie straight in bed, I thought dully. Aloud, I said, "Are you getting his dinner as well?"

"Yeah," she said, turning her attention back to the conveyer belt and picking up a plate.

"Why doesn't he get his own dinner?" I asked. "Too lazy?"

She stiffened. "He—he wants to save our spots."

I looked back at Underwood's table. There were two empty seats there now and nobody coming along with a desire to fill them.

"Why didn't he let you stay back there and save his seat?" I persisted further, knowing I was asking for trouble but no longer caring. The conversation with James had driven all caution out of my mind. "Surely any gentleman would go get his lady's dinner for her, and pay for it too, in normal circumstances, anyway."

"He likes to give me things to do, that's all," she said earnestly, picking up another plate, as she had already filled one with food. But before she could load anything onto this new plate, I caught her by the arm.

"You don't wanna go back there, do you?" I said, jerking my head back in the general direction of Underwood's table.

"Yeah, I do. Well—" She faltered, noticing that I wasn't believing any of her bluff. "What's your point?" she asked, and I was reminded so much of my conversation with James and how I seemed to have moved around to the other side of the table.

"I don't even know," I admitted. "All I can tell is that you're not particularly happy about something, and that, judging by how you looked over there just before, it's got something to do with him."

"Oh," she said, clearly taken aback, and I knew I had hit pretty close to the mark. "I'm happy enough, I guess. I guess he is a little annoying at the moment, all bitter about everything and controlling, not wanting me to get to know anyone here, but it's okay, really."

"So why go back there?" I asked her. "I'm sitting over there." I pointed to Peter's table; since James hadn't turned up, I figured I could risk it. "Let him get his own dinner for a change."

She stared at Peter's table for a few seconds before raising herself up somehow and saying, "Okay, I'll do that. See how he likes coming after me for a change."

"He'll love that," I said, almost laughing as I led her over to the table.

"John," said Serena, pulling a chair out beside her for me to sit down while Siobhan took the empty seat on Peter's other side, the one Kylie would have normally taken if Peter, James, and I had all sat together with our girlfriends. "What was that all about? I was starting to think you weren't coming to sit with us. Wasn't James with you?"

"He *was* with me," I said heavily. "He seems to think I managed the situation back at school so that the Hammerhearts would take someone other than you."

"He what?" she asked, looking confused. "That doesn't sound right. You couldn't have done anything like that."

"I know that, but he seems to think it's strange that they went for Kylie instead of you, especially since Hall knows about us."

"You gotta be joking," said Peter, putting his cutlery down in disgust. "I got a lot of respect for James and how he sees just about everything we don't, even if it is annoying sometimes, but that's just stupid."

"Maybe he's just jumping to absurd conclusions out of emotion," said Erica reasonably. "Where did he go? Do you know?"

"I don't know, and really don't care," I said, starting on my dinner. "He didn't follow me into the hall, but I expect he'll be along soon. He does get hungry, after all."

"How are you, Siobhan?" Serena asked.

My attention wavered from the conversation for a moment as, looking up, I spotted Marc entering the dining room. He was alone, which was rather interesting. I knew he'd spent a great deal of the afternoon with Amelia, trying to work things out after the blow-up in the lounge room. The fact that he was alone now made me wonder. I'd had the impression, even before today, that he and Amelia's progress in rebuilding their relationship over the last week hadn't been going the way they would have liked. I hadn't asked any questions of either of them about it in case he found more meaning in my interest than there was, what there might have been a week earlier, and I certainly didn't want to give Amelia false hope, in case she was still thinking about that kiss. His face also suggested that his afternoon hadn't been a fun one. He headed up to the conveyer belt before taking a seat at Tommy's table.

"I was under the impression that he just hates everyone in general," Erica was saying as I returned to the conversation.

"He doesn't like being here," Siobhan conceded, "but I don't think he hates everyone. Just Marc, John, and Tommy, apparently, but I think that's only 'cause they stole something from him."

"Stole?" Erica asked, looking at me with curiosity. "That doesn't sound like those three."

"We didn't steal anything from him," I retorted. It was only half true, of course, as Marc and Tommy hadn't actually done the stealing, and Underwood had no idea that I'd been there at all. "We do have something that was his, but since we're letting him come with us next week, he should consider himself lucky."

"He won't tell me anything about that either," Siobhan grumbled. "I don't even know if I'll be allowed to come. What did you take, anyway? He won't tell me."

"Really?" I asked, slightly surprised. He had told Lena and Stella about the life assistant, so why not Siobhan? Was it because, although she was pretty, she wasn't quite as attractive as Stella and barely in the same stratosphere as Lena? Was it because Underwood was only dating her while he looked for a taller, hotter chick to replace her? Was it the complete opposite of that, and he just preferred to share less about himself with the girl he liked the most?

"Well, I guess that's his business whether he wants to tell or not," said Serena fairly.

"I'm guessing he doesn't tell you a lot, huh," said Peter interestedly.

"He tells me some things," she said bemusedly. "At least, I'm not aware of too many things he doesn't tell me. He doesn't give me all the details about every little thing because I don't ask. I don't wanna seem nosy or anything."

"Well, you'd know him better than any of us, but he seems to me like the sort of guy you would need to be nosy with," said Erica. "Otherwise, you'd just never know what he's up to."

"Well, maybe," Siobhan admitted uncomfortably. "I mean, he's always been so nice to me, but I don't really understand his attitude about some things—especially here. I mean, I'd have thought I'd hate this place so much more than him after what you guys did, but he's just acting—" she shrugged, "and he won't tell me anything. He doesn't seem to want me to talk to you guys. He won't actually say that, but I can tell. It's like there's something going on with you and him that I'm not supposed to know about."

"Yeah, there is," said Peter. "Oh, well, maybe not. Hard to know."

"What are you on about, Peter?" Erica asked.

Peter swapped an uncomfortable look with me, and I knew what he was thinking. "Not now," I told him.

"What not now?" Siobhan asked, and she was suddenly looking as fierce as she had when Marc and I had chased Underwood from her house. "What do you two know about him that I don't?"

"Why not now?" Peter asked me.

"Wrong time and place," I told him. "Look, Siobhan, Underwood—"

"His name's Jacob!"

"I couldn't give a damn if his name is Tobias Nathaniel Wilfred Constantino Methuselah Gaylord Fuckleberry," I said dismissively, and Peter, Serena, and Erica burst out laughing. "The fact is he has more magical connections than he's prepared to admit to most people for his own safety. We've tried to get him to cooperate with us for about a month now, but he kept pushing us away, so we did the only thing we could."

"What's that? Break into his house and take whatever it is?"

"Didn't break in," I told her. "He let the person in willingly enough. Tommy and Marc had nothing at all to do with it, so I dunno what he's got against them. I was there, but he doesn't know that either. I know this doesn't make any sense, but you should be ready for the truth before you hear it. Maybe you should actually ask him where he was in the few days before we caught up with him at your place."

"He said he was really busy at work because of what the Hammerhearts were doing."

"He probably was, but that certainly wasn't all he was busy with," said Peter.

Siobhan didn't like the sound of that one bit. "Just tell me what he was doing before I go crazy here, will you?"

"Just as long as you understand that we went ahead with our plan without knowing that you existed," I told her.

"Way to beat around the bush, John," muttered Serena. "I'd tell you straight out, Siobhan, if I actually knew myself. All I know is that it had something to do with Lena."

Siobhan considered this, her expression darkening. "So you're saying that another girl was involved," she said, looking at Serena, "and you're saying that you did it without knowing I was around," she added to me. "Sounds like you got this Lena person to be friendly with him."

"She's good," Peter remarked. "Siobhan, you see that girl over there? The blond one?"

"Yeah," she said, her expression even darker as she took in Lena's extravagant beauty. "What did she do?"

"Well, in one respect, she didn't do much," I told her. "Lena didn't have entire control over what she was doing because I was sort of—well, controlling her myself, so you can't blame her for anything that happened. Believe me, she was disgusted by it all."

"If you're saying she didn't know about me, then I guess you'd be right. What did she do?"

"Well, like I said—"

"*John*," she said sternly, "what did she do?"

"Apparently she didn't have to do a lot," said Peter, looking over at Underwood, and an expression of malice crossed his face. I knew he was about to finish what we had started a week earlier, to completely decimate Underwood's relationship with his girlfriend, and that was exactly what he did, describing what Underwood would have done with Lena if he'd had the chance in such a way that Serena and I were grimacing reluctantly, Erica was looking scandalised, and I had to shove him hard so that he almost fell in Siobhan's lap to shut him up. Siobhan's face had fallen further and further the longer it went on. She may have suspected as much, but that didn't seem to soften the blow. Way to go, Peter.

"He didn't do anything like that," I told her, "because she took it without needing to give him that. But he would have done, so I guess for you it means the same thing."

"Dunno why you trusted him at all, really," Peter said, steadying himself in his seat, the malice gone. "I mean, Lena wasn't the only one. There was someone else who tried to steal from him but was unsuccessful, and who knows how far she went with him—probably not all the way though, you'd think."

"Give it a rest, Peter," muttered Erica, glaring at him. "We're sorry you had to find out like this, Siobhan. If Underwood was a smart guy, he would have told you himself. You were bound to find out eventually, living so close to all of us now."

"You're right," she said tearfully, "both of you—all of you. I guess I must have known and just chose not to believe, but I really did—really—oh God, why do I always pick the jerks?"

She couldn't seem to finish the sentence. She slumped forward over her apparently forgotten dinner and wept. Peter and Erica each put an arm around her, but she seemed not to take any notice. Serena and I swapped miserable looks. It really was unpleasant witnessing this sort of thing. Not wanting to watch, I looked around the hall. Natalie had entered at some point without my notice and taken a seat beside Marc at his table, but James and Amelia were still no-shows. I didn't care too much about James—if he didn't want to see me, then that was his problem—but I was starting to feel anxious about Amelia. She'd done so well over the last week or so, but if this set her back to how she had been back then, I would surely be having a few stern words with Marc before too long. I hoped it wouldn't be necessary. Amelia falling apart again might rekindle the feelings for her that I had suppressed since the half-accidental kiss, and that was something I definitely did not want now that I had begun to straighten up my sorry act.

Chapter 24: Mentality

Friday was a day off now that school had been shut down, but according to the latest news, it mightn't be shut down for long. Cornish had appointed another Victorian Hammerheart, whose name was unfamiliar, as the education minister for all primary and secondary schools in Australia, a job that was sure to be enormous but apparently one he felt could be done by a single person. Since each school was to have all the same content taught, I supposed the only main job would be making sure each and every school was ready to teach Hammerheart-approved content. This would be done for all schools in Victoria and New South Wales by the end of the following week and for the rest of the country by May 21.

Straight after breakfast, I gathered Marc, Tommy, and Peter together (only those three because I couldn't be bothered tracking the others down) to tell them something important. For the first time since a week ago, my dreams had turned into a living wander into Stella's mind. On this occasion, she had been very tired but also very scared. Her family knew that she was stalling, so she needed to make it look like she was making some progress. She had entered the Woodward's house and, staying away from the study lest her presence be detected by the Woodwards' beeping watches, searched for a safe place to leave a message for Mr. Woodward. The note she had written under the supervision of her father, and bearing his signature for authenticity, was in her pocket, along with a much smaller note that nobody else knew about, explaining her *real* predicament and requesting assistance. The tricky thing about the situation was that she wasn't alone; 3K17, who had been one of the lucky Hammerhearts to escape the battle of the day before, had been ordered to supervise the leaving of the message in case Stella chose to jump into the study, reveal herself to the Woodwards, and allow herself to be taken in. Stella liked 3K17 but only a little bit. She seemed to see her as one who might be prepared to go against an order of Hammerson's if she saw it as being unfair, but Stella didn't trust her with the knowledge of the secret note.

"Did you see where she left it?" Tommy asked me.

"No, I woke up before they were done," I said. "So maybe we should get out there and have a look."

We were lucky; Natalie's father had been on his way out to do whatever it was that the Sorcerers were now doing, and he agreed to hitch us a ride through the wall. It was actually he who spotted the note Stella had left. He took it down from the spot on the mantelpiece where it stood proud but, for a moment, wasn't prepared to let any of us read it.

"It might be dangerous," he insisted. "It could have magical spells on it that might do unseemly things to the person who reads it. Better let us handle it."

"It's only from Stella," I told him. "She doesn't have that sort of magic anymore. Trust me, it's fine. Is there another note there?"

He looked slightly confused. "No, there is only one note here."

He opened it and read aloud, without anything magical happening, "Frederic Woodward, I request, on behalf of my father, that you release Sebastian Williams from your prison. The consequence of not meeting this request will be the use of the Darkness Crystal directly against you and yours. Please respond in a manner you see fit by twenty o'clock Australian Eastern Standard Time on the evening of Friday, May 7, or action will be taken. Signed, Stella Hammerson, and approved by Arnold Hammerson."

"She was forced to write that," I told him, "and she left another note around here somewhere that was supposed to explain that she was being forced."

"Well, I can't see it," he said, tucking the note into his pocket, "but I'll bear that in mind, John. Ultimately, it's up to Frederic to decide what action is to be taken, but I highly doubt he will bend to such blackmail. Is that all you wanted to come out here for?"

"Yeah," said Tommy, "but while we're here, we might as well look for that other note."

"Very well," he said. "Just go back into the study when you want to be let back in. You know the drill. And remember, boys, you aren't exactly safe here, so be ready to use your crystals at any time."

"We will, sir," said Peter. "Or at least, they will. Thanks for helping."

"That's tonight," Marc said as Mr. Fletcher left through the back door. "They're gonna use it at eight o'clock tonight. What are we gonna do? We need to plan how to get it back, but we don't have enough time to do it by tonight."

"They might not use it tonight," Tommy said, trying to be reasonable. "They only want a response by tonight. They might not actually use it until tomorrow or something. We still have time."

"Maybe so," I said doubtfully, "but either way, we've gotta get down and planning today or we'll be in big trouble."

We began searching the house, Marc and I using our crystals to allow our minds to wander more freely.

"Hey, John, I've been meaning to ask you," Tommy said to me as he looked around the lounge room. I was standing in the next room while using the crystal to search in the bathroom. "What happened with you and Siobhan last night? What was the crying about?"

"Oh, we told her about what a lying, cheating bastard her now ex-boyfriend is," I told him, "and Peter might have gone a little hard on the bluntness. I didn't really want to there and then, but she wouldn't let it drop once she realised we knew something."

"Wow," said Tommy. "Wow. So Underwood has nobody here now. No friends."

"Well, apart from the older guys he was sitting with," I said. "They might all be bastards, for all I know, but then they did all agree to come here when we gave them the option, so we shouldn't be too hard on them. As for Siobhan, she's probably gonna get chummy with Serena and Erica now."

"Geez," he muttered. "Well, not a happy night for relationships all round, then. Did Marc tell you what happened with him and Amelia?"

Marc was searching the unoccupied bedrooms with Peter so couldn't hear the conversation.

"No, I haven't heard," I said, my stomach beginning to churn, "but I saw him come in to dinner alone last night. Are they okay?"

"Broken up," he said quietly. "According to Marc, she just doesn't have the passion anymore, and they just can't agree on things like they used to. He said he really wanted to help her through the hard time she's had lately, but she wouldn't let him. I haven't seen Amelia since, but I know Marc's pretty devastated by it all."

"I thought he looked a little down," I admitted truthfully.

"Maybe you should go find Amelia," Tommy said suddenly. "You and her are pretty tight, aren't you?"

"Well, sort of," I said uncomfortably. "I sort of had to help her out because I understood some things better than Marc, only 'cause I was there with her through that Basement stuff. I guess I'd better go find her later on and see if she's okay."

None of us could find the note Stella had intended to leave with her main one, and I had to suppose that a circumstance I hadn't seen had made it impossible for her to leave it with the other note. We therefore re-entered the base with the help of Natalie, and after hurriedly explaining what we'd been doing, I took off down the corridor for the Woodward living quarters. As I passed the door into our living quarters, however, a voice pulled me up short.

"John! Hey, John, come in here a minute."

I groaned and turned into the living quarters. That had been James's voice. He was standing by the foot of the stairs and looking just as uncomfortable as I felt. It was the first time I'd seen him since the spat of the day before, but we both knew ours was a bridge that had to be rebuilt, as much for the sake of the Young Army and the Smiley mission as for the fact that we were practically brothers.

"What's up?" I asked flatly. Behind me, I sensed Marc, Tommy, Peter, and Natalie watching the exchange with curiosity.

"Listen," he said awkwardly, "I just wanted to apologise for what I said yesterday. I wasn't fair on you and not like me at all. I guess I was just—you know—upset and all."

"We were all upset yesterday, James," said Peter. "Don't you think I have as much reason as anyone to be upset? But you don't hear me saying stupid things to anyone."

"You said something pretty stupid to Siobhan," I muttered, unable to suppress a grin, and Peter winked at me.

"It's a little different, Pete," said James coolly. "You know how I felt a few months ago. Well, anyway, John, yeah, that's pretty much all. It was wrong of me to have a go at you like that. I know you wouldn't do something like that."

"Yeah, thanks," I said, not altogether mollified. It was all well and good to say it was wrong to have said those things, but I still had a feeling James felt them deep down.

"What on earth did you say to him, James?" Natalie asked, a little sharply.

I knew she was ready to jump to my defence a little too late, and I hastened to shut her down. "It's okay, Nat, it doesn't matter anymore."

"Yeah, don't bother yourself with it, Natalie," James agreed. "It's between us two, and I think we've sorted it out now."

"Okay," she said, but she gave me a look that I thought was supposed to say "you'd better tell me if he gives you any trouble." I smiled in spite of myself and turned back out of the living quarters, Amelia's state of being back on my mind. I felt Marc's eyes on my back as I left him and the others farther behind.

* * *

The five of us were ready to go with our plan by two o'clock the following day, but unfortunately, as we had feared, we had been too late. Whether it had been Stella or someone else who had used the Darkness Crystal, none of us knew, but either way, they had delivered on their promise. We (Marc, Tommy, all the Sorcerers, plus Amelia's mother, Natalie's mother, Rebecca, and I) had all sat around the Woodward lounge room, watching the television and talking about things in general, waiting for a sign of anything disastrous out there. Mr. Woodward had insisted that, while it was a possibility the

Hammersons would act swiftly, it wasn't necessarily a certainty. If only he'd been right.

We had all been worried that we wouldn't see anything about it on the television until the following day, or perhaps never at all. We were right to think that, but most unfortunately, we had seen the magic for ourselves—not on the television but right there in the lounge room.

That night, at about twenty past eight, Amelia's mother had had an enormous heart attack. It had been completely sudden and, for a woman of near perfect health in her early forties, completely unexpected, or, at least, should have been unexpected. Lillian Woodward, the Sorcerer most experienced in combining magic and medicine, had leapt into action, but there had been no hope from the start. The severity of the attack had been such that it had killed her almost instantly, and once that moment had passed, no magic (not even Tommy's quick attempt to repel the dark magic with the Light Crystal) could have revived her. Mr. Woodward had sent a message, by way of magic, to Arnold Hammerson, informing him that such tricks would not be tolerated, that he would be held directly accountable for his wife's death if the time for cost counting came any time soon, and that the matter between them was now personal, as personal as it was between him and Tankom (that sparked my interest, but none of the Woodwards were up to answering questions). It mentioned nothing at all about when Sebastian would be released from the Woodward base.

Now, the following day, all of us who had witnessed the fatality were in shock and, in Amelia's case, desperate mourning. In my mind, it only highlighted the urgency of the situation. Stella would probably leave another note for Mr. Woodward in his house tonight, and none of us wanted to know what disaster they might try for Sunday night. Marc, Tommy, Amelia, Natalie, and I left the base just after lunchtime to get stuck into the plan.

The first part was quite simple, or at least should have been simple. It involved the five of us simply getting into position. Marc, Tommy, and I headed down into the Hammerheart Highway, then to the Pacific Ocean base the same way we had done three days earlier, while the two Sorcerers located Hall. If they couldn't get to him inside one of the bases, the plan was for them to wait until he left the underground. They would also have to find a way to get him on his own so that they could put him out of action in private. The idea being that, although the Hammerhearts would eventually work out what happened to him, the more time we had before that happened, the better it would be for us. Amelia and I would be the link between the two groups, us having already performed telepathy together before. When they gave the signal and we also confirmed that we were ready to jump into action, they would knock Hall unconscious, and we would knock whoever was standing by the Darkness Crystal unconscious. That was all the plan included. The rest would be down to improvisation.

Both Hignat's and Wilwog's houses were empty on this day, which made getting into the Hammerheart Highway a breeze. Tommy had crawled into a bag again while Marc and I had taken the breakneck ride eastward for several seconds before pulling up in that familiar parking bay for Hammerheart carts. We had gone about getting into our capsules exactly as we had the previous time, then ascended to the upper levels of the base. Although it wasn't strictly necessary, I had gone into the second-floor corridor, just to make sure it was as it had been last time, and thankfully it was. The top floor was also as it had been the last time, although the three guards had changed from last time. That hardly mattered, though, because they all looked just as disinterested in the reason why they were here as the others had. These three were in the middle of what looked like a game of Uno on the corridor floor when we arrived on their level.

"Should we wait here or go in there?" Tommy asked, obviously referring to the door we all knew the Darkness Crystal to be hidden behind.

"I guess one of us should wait here," Marc said. "I tell you what, John, you wait here like you did last time, but let us know if anything changes out here. I doubt it will. Then, when it's time, you can put those guards out there into fairyland for a while, while we do what we have to do. Tommy and I will go in there and let you know what's happening in case you have to relay any messages about it to the others. How does that sound?"

"Sounds fine," I agreed, and I positioned myself in the top corner above the door to the stairs, exactly where a security camera would be if the Hammersons had believed it was necessary to put a camera in this base. From where I was, I had a view of the entire corridor, plus I was out of the way of anyone who might decide to come through the door.

They went into the room, and a moment later, Marc said, "First observation, the room contains only one person, and it's not the same one who was given guard duty last time."

"Second observation," Tommy added, "everything else about the room is exactly the same as it was last time."

"That's useful to know," I said sarcastically.

"Third observation," said Marc sharply, "the clock on the wall in this room—which I don't even remember seeing last time—says the time is just after twenty past seven in the evening. Our watches are five hours behind that, so at least we now know what local time they use here."

"Fourth observation," said Tommy, "I dunno why they care. It's not like any sunlight gets in this place. They could use Australian time, American time, British time, Antarctica time, or even bloody Mars time and it wouldn't make a difference."

"Fifth observation," I cut in, "I think it matters very much. At least we can work out when they change shifts here based on the local time. Do you think they work in six-, eight-, or twelve-hour intervals?"

"Probably not twelve," said Marc. "Eight or six would be my guess. They'd want whoever is doing it to be fully alert the whole time, and a twelve-hour stint in this place is bound to make anyone sleepy."

"A twelve-minute stint in this place wouldn't be much better," Tommy muttered.

"John, perhaps you'd better make contact with the others," Marc said. "Just let them know that we're in the base and ready when they are. At least, there's no trouble yet."

"Okay," I agreed.

I squeezed the Sien-Leoard Crystal and sent my thoughts out to Amelia. Not knowing where she was or even which direction, I could only think of Amelia herself, Amelia as I had seen her last. This concentration on Amelia surprised me completely into thinking about her in a way I was strictly trying not to. I remembered all those feelings I'd tried so hard to control for over a month; I remembered those few dreams I'd had to clean up after; I remembered how she had been there to support me on those few occasions I had needed it; I remembered how I had been there for her when she had needed it; I remembered the kiss, the feeling of it, the guilt mingling with the pleasure, the desire, and the realisation that, if I could, I would gladly do it again. I shuddered with self-disgust. What on earth was wrong with me? Four days and two deaths after my resolution of commitment to Serena, here I was, once again desiring another girl.

The worst thing about all that was, far from letting Amelia know where we were and what condition the Pacific base was in, I had just confided a whole load of hidden emotions in her. When her telepathic response came, it had an air that suggested that, if she had to speak her mind, her voice would be trembling. She wanted me to concentrate on what we were doing and, if I wanted to, we could actually talk about things later. I had spoken to her about Marc the previous day after Tommy had told me about their breakup, but in that meeting, Amelia had said very little about her feelings and had seemed rather distant with me. I therefore hadn't stayed long, slightly disappointed that she didn't want to really confide in me, but now that I felt her undercurrent of emotion, I understood why she hadn't. Her desire for me was as strong as it had been the day we had kissed, perhaps even stronger now that she was alone and clearly felt lonely. She did still want me—very much, in fact—but didn't believe it could happen, didn't believe that I would let it happen. That was nice of her to think that, but now I wasn't so sure.

"Anything, John?" Tommy asked.

I started. "Not yet," I lied. "I'm just concentrating on the right things to think about. It's tougher than you'd expect."

No, it wouldn't happen, not if I wanted to be a good guy again. I sent this thought to her by the crystal, then clambered to add to it. I needed her to understand firstly that what I'd accidentally sent her had been brought on by my needing to concentrate on her to send the message. Thank God I hadn't sent that to Natalie, I thought, but let go of the crystal at that point. I then needed her to understand that it was all true, but unfortunately for us, I was set on making it work with Serena. If things between us went the way her and Marc had, then we could talk about it.

Her response came very quickly this time, clearly distance not being a factor. It was difficult to understand exactly what she was trying to tell me this time, though. It was either that she would wait for me as long as she needed to because I was the only one who really understood her, or that if I went to her and made her mine, she would never go to anyone else because I was the only one who understood her, properly. Either way, it was not a comforting thought. I didn't intend to be with her any time soon, as much as I desired her, and the idea of her waiting around for me, as I feared Natalie was also doing, not to mention Lena still, was not a good one to entertain. She deserved to be with someone who could give her his all and not, like me, have other girls to deal with.

The next message I sent her was more concentrated than ever because I used the crystal's magic to filter my thoughts. I only wanted her to receive an emotionless message, which would only contain information about what we were doing and nothing about our feelings. The sooner we got past that, the better. Her response came again and it appeared that she was now employing the same technique. She and Natalie had located both Hall's home in Chopville as well as the apartment he had been given by Hank

Cornish in Canberra. He was present at neither, though, so they were instead following Cornish as he moved from department to department in Parliament House, giving orders—they had clearly reorganised the running of things since they had taken over the building eleven days earlier—the idea being to hope that he would either make direct contact with Hall or someone else would mention a likely location where he might presently be. The fact that they couldn't directly locate him with magic suggested that he was probably in one of the Hammerheart bases, though, so I relayed that information back to the boys.

"Okay, then," said Tommy. "Looks like we're playing the waiting game, doesn't it."

"I might be able to help out a bit," said Marc. "This guy hasn't contacted Hall yet, but when he does, maybe I can find a way to tap into the message. I know I can't try to stop it from getting there. If Hall doesn't get it, then obviously he's gonna know there's trouble, but maybe his return message will help me get a bearing on where he is. It's worth a try, don't you think?"

"Anything's worth a try," I said, "as long as you do whatever you have to, to make sure they don't pick up you're eavesdropping."

"No problem," he grunted.

We all fell silent, me now watching and listening to the Uno game happening on the floor fifteen feet away from me. It was about a minute later when I heard Tommy whisper, "Here we go—watch tapping time."

Silence once again, only this time we knew Marc to be working whatever magic he needed to. Tommy and I waited, me holding my breath in anticipation, still trying to push Amelia from my mind. Eventually, Marc said, "Well, it worked. Kind of."

"Yeah? You know where he is?" Tommy asked.

"Here's something we didn't anticipate," said Marc, a little airily. "We should have, though: It's not Hall he's sending messages to."

"It's not?" Tommy said, surprised. "But then—why not? It's daytime over there. Surely it'd be more sensible."

"Maybe Hall only does night shifts," I suggested, "when he's knocked off work. Say, if it is an eight-hour shift, it'd be five p.m. 'til one a.m. our time. Who did he send a message to this time?"

"2L11," Marc replied. "I think I know who he is—"

"Yeah, I do too," I said quickly. "Prominent around Chopville, he is."

"Wasn't he the one who worked at the Melbourne base?" Tommy asked.

"I'm not sure if we ever found out where he worked, except that it was a city larger than Chopville," I said. "Did you see where he is, Marc?"

"No, unfortunately not," said Marc. "I think the message is telepathic, the way it's sent. He taps a certain spot on his watch and thinks to send, and when the person on the other end hears the beep from their watch, they tap it themselves and get the message put into their head. I got 2L11's message, which was basically just a 'good, keep working,' but it didn't have anything about where he is."

"I'll let the girls know to change their target," I muttered, pulling the crystal from my pocket again and feeling disappointed that we wouldn't be able to exact vengeance on Hall as part of this plan.

I focussed my mind hard before sending the message. I knew I had to concentrate on Amelia again when I tried to send it, though, so I focussed on her first. Unfortunately, it was far more difficult than I would have liked. My mind wanted to imagine the two of us together. It wanted to imagine us holding and kissing each other. I raised my free hand and hit myself hard in the head. Stars popped in front of my eyes and pain struck, taking my mind off Amelia and back to where it was meant to be.

"What was that?" Marc asked. "That thud noise?"

"Sorry," I muttered, abashed that they'd actually heard the sound through my microphone. "I just—er—dropped the crystal. My bad."

"Righto," Marc muttered. "Let us know when you get a response from them."

"Sure," I muttered back, rubbing my head and frowning.

How was I supposed to do this? Not only was my mind getting carried away when I let it, but it was leading my body on a merry dance as well. I had felt a definite stirring below my waistline before I had hit myself, and it still hadn't quite subsided. I squeezed the crystal again and concentrated, not on Amelia this time because I knew that to be a terrible mind trap, but on 2L11. I concentrated on the fact that it was he who was in contact with the crystal guarder back here, then basically asked the crystal with my mind to send that thought to Amelia. It worked, but even that had been close, for as soon as I had allowed myself to think of Amelia, all those thoughts had come seeping back into my mind. This time, I really did drop the crystal so that hopefully none of them would be sent through along with the intended message.

I had to focus my mind before I could pick up the crystal, and when I did, I was sure that I had probably missed her response. In fact, I had missed it, but fortunately not all was lost—the crystal returned it to me without any problem. She and Natalie were on the job and would report back when they either found 2L11 or found that they couldn't get to him. Once again, I relayed the message to the boys.

"Okay," said Tommy. "So we're playing the waiting game for real now?"

"Looks like it," said Marc. "Well, we're sort of doing exactly what these guards are doing, without the card game."

"Yeah, the waiting game," said Tommy, apparently grinning judging by the tone of his voice.

Silence once again as I waited for a message from Amelia, and the boys waited for a message from me from Amelia. It was impossible not to let my mind stray in that time. I tried desperately to keep it in check by thinking of Serena, reliving some of the more enjoyable moments we had shared over the last two and a bit months. It should have worked, and in a way it did work, but as soon as I thought I'd done enough, thoughts of Amelia seeped back into my mind, somehow over-powering any thoughts I had of my girlfriend.

This was absolutely terrible. What on earth was wrong with me? Why couldn't I keep my mind on Serena like I was supposed to? It would have been bad enough if it had been Natalie I couldn't stop thinking about, certainly as I'd imagined myself with her for a very long time, since before I'd even had a sex drive. That wouldn't have necessarily been acceptable, but at least it would have been understandable, but this? My feelings for Amelia, and surely hers for me too, had sprouted from nothing but the sharing of rather extraordinary experiences. That didn't mean we had to come together in this way, did it?

I really wished I could talk to someone about it, but I wasn't entirely sure if I had anyone I could really confide in anymore. Marc was most certainly off limits; he'd kill me if he thought this business was somehow a factor in Amelia's decision to end their relationship. Peter was still struggling after Kylie's death, not to mention his own vested interest in Serena. He had suppressed that without any trouble while I had been with her, no sign of jealousy at all, but that might change now that he was on his own and no doubt feeling very lonely. James…well, something had come up between us since Thursday, and I wasn't sure I could trust him to see things from my point of view anymore. Who else was there? No one I could think of.

Except there was someone else, someone I had almost forgotten about. The thought of going back and seeing him again put a definite smile on my face. He'd told me to go for Natalie last time. What would he say this time, now that Amelia was single and it was she who I couldn't seem to get my mind off? I also remembered how, back then, most of my thoughts about Amelia had been clean, whereas now—now—

"Do you guys want me to keep tapping their communications, just in case?" Marc asked us after a few minutes.

"Yeah, couldn't hurt," Tommy replied.

Amelia's next contact came about ten minutes later. 2L11, it transpired, was the new education minister in Australia. He was presently in Sydney's western suburbs, moving from school to school with a team of about two dozen Hammerhearts, evaluating each school and all staff members employed by that school. The details of the procedure weren't included in her message. What sort of magic had they tapped that was enabling them to race through a job that huge? I had no idea. She would let me know when they had managed to get him alone and were about to jump into action. I relayed the message to the boys.

"Good stuff," said Marc. "Blessing in disguise since Hall was harder to get at."

"Kind of disappointing, though," I admitted. "I owe Hall several. I'll have to get back at him later."

Our watches said nearly three o'clock before Amelia made contact again. She and Natalie had given 2L11 a case of what they were calling "apocalyptic diarrhea." He'd already had a nasty accident in the passenger's seat of the transport vehicle he and his fellows were using, but it promised to be ever so much worse if he didn't stop and drop. They had stopped outside a McDonald's and he had hurried into their toilets just in time to let loose a torrent of— well, I was treated with far too much detail in the telepathic message as to exactly what came out of the poor guy. Two Hammerhearts were waiting outside the men's room for him to return, but nobody had actually gone in with him and nobody else was occupying the stalls or urinal. It was the perfect time, and they were acting as soon as the message was sent.

"That explains it," Marc said when I told him and Tommy it was time. "His last message back seemed strangely distracted."

"You go first, John," said Tommy, "then let us know so Marc can deal with this guy. We both have to be ready to get out and have a look."

"I'll see if I can't use the crystal to break it open first," Marc said. "If it doesn't work, then, Tommy, you'll have to use your tools when you get out. John, you just take care of those guys out there first— absorb them in their little game."

"Sure thing."

I took the crystal out again and stared at the three guards, thinking back to the police officer outside Siobhan's window. All three of them quickly lost their focus for a few moments, slumping slightly, their heads drooping and their eyes closed. Make them see nothing except each other and the game they're playing, I thought at the crystal, and the three guards returned to their play immediately, with renewed vigour it seemed, slamming their cards onto the pile one after another. The job was complete without any fuss.

"Okay, knock him out at your discretion, Marc," I said into the microphone.

"Okay, here we go," said Marc. "Tommy, you stay put for a moment, okay?"

"Whatever you say," said Tommy uninterestedly.

I decided that I had to see this, so I squeezed the crystal and sent my mind outward, through the wall and into the room I knew the box containing the Darkness Crystal to be stored. I was just in time to see the guy who'd been given the duty of guarding the box topple. His back hit the wall behind him and he tumbled over sideways, sprawling in the space between the bench with the box on it and the door.

"Nice one," said Tommy. "Now what?"

"Let's see if I can get it open," Marc replied.

We fell silent and waited, watching. Several seconds passed, then several more. Finally, Marc swore under his breath.

"No luck?" I asked. I'd expected that. The Hammersons had designed that box so that only their secret method would be capable of opening it, and magic specifically designed to open it wouldn't work.

"Nothing," he said. "Tommy, guess you're up, and make it quick."

I'd described to the two of them before coming what I knew about the box and how it could be opened. As we hadn't known before we'd come who would be given the opening duties, I had duplicated my invisibility balls and master keys so that we all had one of each.

We fell silent as Tommy first landed, then pressed a series of buttons that enlarged the capsule, opened the roof, and unstrapped him. Tommy didn't bother making himself or the capsule visible, but we were able to follow his progress anyway. A hole quickly appeared in the side of the box, moulding itself to the shape of a key. Seconds later, the hole filled again as the top of the box swung open. I never saw the crystal as Tommy took it in his hands and bolted for his capsule again. We heard him enter it only seconds later.

"Okay, done," he panted. "Got the crystal in my pocket, the other one from the other crystal. Light on one side of my body, darkness on the other. I must remember to write a song about that sometime. Marc, you'd better clean this joint up quickly. How long did you put that guy out for, anyway?"

"Should stay out for fifteen more minutes," he replied, "which is plenty of time for us to get out of here. By then, we should be well and truly back in Chopville."

"That sounds fine," I said, "but I'd better make sure the girls keep 2L11 occupied for that long as well; otherwise, he'll know something's up before fifteen minutes."

I didn't have to concentrate as much on Amelia this time. Perhaps because my mind was buzzing with what we had just done, it was easier not to get sucked in by desire. I informed her that the guard here would be unconscious for another fifteen minutes and enquired to exactly what they had done to 2L11. Her reply came almost immediately: They had caused him to faint, as far as he knew because of the extraordinary amount of liquid love leaving his body through the back door. They could bring him around at any time, but now that they knew, they would keep him there for fifteen more minutes, no matter if anyone came in to see if he was okay or not. Yet again, I relayed the message to the boys.

"Good stuff," said Marc. "Tommy, are you in the air yet?"

"Shrunk," he muttered. "About to take off now."

"Okay," said Marc, and he set to work returning the box to the state it had been in prior to our interference, though obviously without a crystal inside it now. "John, be ready to fix those guys out there up so that we can hightail it out of here as quickly as possible."

I retreated my mind back to my body and watched the intense Uno match while waiting for the boys. I could hear Tommy breathing into his microphone and knew him to be filled with adrenalin for what he had just done. Marc was ready in about thirty seconds. A moment later, he said, "Okay Tommy, let's hit the road. John, do your thing."

I squeezed the crystal and thought, simply, return their minds to their normal state. Then, not bothering to see if the spell worked (it hardly mattered now that we'd already got the crystal), I turned my capsule and dived for the crack under the door to the stairs.

* * *

The mission had been a complete success. None of us had any trouble returning to base, no alerts were issued to shut down any part of the Hammerheart Highway, no word returned that anyone knew the crystal was missing, and nobody suspected that what happened to 2L11 was foul play by any of the Sorcerers. He had come back to consciousness leaning back against the wall behind his toilet ball, feeling more wet around the rear than he'd probably ever felt in his life, but by then, the flow had stopped. He must have been astounded when he looked in the toilet and seen how much crap had come out of him, but for the sake of his pride, he mentioned nothing of it to any of his fellow Hammerhearts. He was back on the streets of Sydney causing trouble only minutes later, and Natalie and Amelia had already teleported back to Chopville by then.

Frank Luivic, the spy Marc and I had brought over from the United States, had become part of a standard taskforce of Hammerhearts, doorknocking in each and every street in each and every suburb of each and every city and country town in Australia, whose mission it was to round up every single person in the country and evaluate their standing in society. The word was that none of them were being converted as yet, but some of them were being imprisoned while others were promoted to Hammerheart status based on either their interest or their qualifications. These people were to have their minds boggled at a date to be determined. Mr. Woodward informed him of the theft of the Darkness Crystal and requested that he let him know when the Hammersons found out about it, assuming of course that they would tell their followers.

We had given the Darkness Crystal to Mr. Woodward upon our return, only to have it given back to us. Mr. Woodward seemed to have decided that we could provide greater security for it than he could.

"I don't care what you do with it," he said, "as long as you don't use it and you don't allow a situation to come about where any Hammerhearts can steal it back."

With our duties to Mr. Woodward completed, we were now able to turn our attention fully to our trip to Rock Haulter, agreeing to have one final meeting to work out the details on the following evening. Throughout the rest of the day, Amelia occupied my thoughts, but due to Serena's determination to monopolise my time, I didn't get a chance to catch up with her and have a much needed air-clearing talk until the following morning. I did my best to enjoy Serena's company, but despite my best efforts, I couldn't help imagining that it was Amelia with whom I was spending the night. Thank God I didn't actually say her name instead of Serena's.

Chapter 25: Decision

I woke up early the next morning, around five o'clock. Serena wasn't in my room. I'd been more tired than her before I'd gone to sleep, so she'd done me the favour of going back to her own room and letting me rest, perhaps thinking that it was the success of the job we'd done that had made me tired. For all I knew, that had been part of it. It was perfect for what I wanted now.

I took the invisible Sien-Leoard Crystal from my bedside drawers and sent my mind outward to find Amelia. It zoomed me along to where I knew her to be anyway, in her bedroom in her living quarters. I wasn't trying to spy or anything but merely determining if it would be okay for me to go and see her now or leave it until later. I expected her to be asleep like just about everyone else would be, but to my surprise, she was awake, sitting up in bed (well, leaning against her headboard, actually), her hands across her belly, and appeared to be in deep thought. I wondered if she was thinking about me, brooding on what had taken place and imagining herself with me, wishing she could have me and knowing she couldn't. I shook my head hard. That may or may not be true, but that was an arrogant way of thinking.

Since I couldn't be sure exactly what she was thinking of (thanks to her mind being blocked) and since she was awake, as I had been checking for, I supposed I ought to try and see what reaction I got. I retreated back to my body so that at least that part wouldn't be sent to her (she didn't need to know I'd just seen her) and concentrated on sending her another telepathic message. This time, all those thoughts I'd struggled to contain the previous day came flooding back to me again and I did nothing to resist them. Instead, I gloried in them, knowing it was wrong and yet knowing I might as well enjoy it now because it would be the last time. After today, Amelia and I would be set. We would be friends, perhaps very close friends, and that would be all.

I concentrated on the message that I wanted to send her—that I was awake and that I wanted to know if she was awake and if she wanted to see me now before breakfast. I knew the message had sent immediately and wished I could see Amelia's reaction to it. She responded to it about five seconds later, a slight delay compared to what I had expected and compared to the immediacy of a couple of her communications the previous afternoon. Her message was a short, sharp, excited affirmative. It didn't contain anything else whatsoever, but there had been enough excitement in there (all be it nervous excitement) to make me believe that either she had been thinking about me after all or she'd been thinking about something else and merely looking forward to seeing me later on.

I squeezed the crystal again, sending my mind back to her to check on her, this time to check how she was preparing for my arrival. I only thought to do this because at the moment I'd been about to get out of bed and hurry to her, I remembered that I was only wearing pyjamas. It didn't seem like a big deal, but I couldn't be sure how important she would see this meeting, if she'd bother to get herself properly dressed so that it would be a little less casual. When I saw her, she was still leaning back against the headboard of her bed and looking, perhaps, even more relaxed than she had earlier, more content somehow. I could only suppose from that that my contact had come as a relief to her. Perhaps she'd been thinking that I wouldn't want to see her, to speak to her about it, perhaps even to be alone with her at all. She was making no move to get up and do anything, so I retreated back to my body, jumped out of bed, and tore across the room for the door, making myself invisible as I went, just for the sake of it.

It only took me perhaps three or four minutes to get down the stairs, out into the corridor, down to the Woodward living quarters, and past the door I wasn't supposed to be able to open. Amelia had sent another telepathic message to me as I had been descending the stairs, telling me that she was in her bedroom and to just come in when I got to her living quarters. Excited as I was, however, awkwardness was also a prominent feeling. I felt it more and more as I approached her living quarters, and positively in droves as I approached her bedroom, creeping so that I wouldn't wake either of the other Sorcerers. Perhaps the other thing that added to the feeling was the fact that I couldn't see any light coming from her room, which meant that she was sitting in the dark, which meant—what? What did that mean as far as she and I went? Anything?

"Close the door," she said quietly when I took a few steps into her dark bedroom.

I obliged, throwing the room into almost complete blackness. I thought of turning on the light switch, surely a very standard move, then decided against it. It would probably give her the fright of her life if I did that. I had a pretty good idea of where I was in relation to her bed, though, having been in this room a few times now, so I made my way blindly towards it. When my knee made contact with her mattress, she assisted me by making her hand glow dimly, identifying her position and lighting her face. She had been crying, something I hadn't noticed on either of my mind trips down here.

"How are you?" I asked, sitting on the very edge of her bed near the head so that I could be next to her. There was room for her to shift over a bit, but I wasn't about to push her aside.

"I miss my mum," she said sadly.

I remembered what had happened the last time I had comforted Amelia while she was upset, but I couldn't stop myself from doing it again. That might have made me a lousy boyfriend, but I supposed it made me a lousy friend to do the opposite. I reached out to her and put my arms around her. She leaned against me and sobbed quietly, putting her own arms around me so that the light from her glowing right hand no longer illuminated her face.

"I'm really sorry," I told her. "We could have saved her if we'd only insisted on taking the crystal on Friday instead of Saturday, and we probably could have done it."

She shook her head. "This is my dad's fault, you know. He wanted it done on Saturday. He wanted to see what they'd do. I know he said he thought it was unlikely that they'd act, but I'm sure he didn't really believe that. He actually thought we could prevent it on the spot if we had Tommy using the Light Crystal at the same time. He deserved this, he really did."

"Amelia," I said gently, "isn't that a little harsh?"

"No, not this time," she sobbed. "I'll support him to the end, but this is one he has to take responsibility for. I think he knows that too, since he wanted us to dispose of the Darkness Crystal instead of doing it himself."

I sighed. "You're probably right about that, but like I said, don't be too harsh on him. He'll be hurting from this too."

"I know he will," she said. "I've been thinking about that a bit this morning. I've been awake since about two."

"You need to sleep."

"I'm okay, really. I got enough hours, I'll be fine. Listen, I've decided not to go to Rock Haulter."

That caught me by surprise. "What? Why?"

She sighed again. "It's just—the right thing to do, I can feel it. I wish I could have met Smiley, but I guess I can live without it, as long as I get to know everything you guys find out from him. I just think I'm needed more back here, you know, since I've got more magical experience than Natalie and might be more useful around here in whatever work my dad wants us to do, and well—he and I sort of need each other. It's just us now. I mean, well, we do have Nan, but it's not the same. We copped the loss more than she did since she was only her daughter-in-law. Then—well—maybe it'd be better not to be there."

"Of course it would," I told her quickly. "You know we all value your input."

"I know," she said, and sighed again. "But maybe it'd just be better if I'm not there, you know, 'cause of—well—"

"Because of us," I said flatly. Now I knew what she meant and knew she was right. "You think it'd be better for us if we have some time apart."

"What do you think?" she asked.

This whole conversation had taken place with us holding each other, not seeing each other's faces, but now we drew back from each other so that the light from her hand lit both our faces. She looked very intent, and something else. Hopeful? Yes, that's what it looked like. She was hopeful. What was she hopeful for? For me telling her that she and I could, in fact, have something more than just friendship? Or was she perhaps hopeful for the complete opposite?

"It probably is true," I said, "even though I wish it didn't have to be that way."

"I know," she said, and managed a weak smile. "You know, after what happened last week, I sort of knew that no matter what happened with me and Marc, I'd never get what I really wanted. I could just tell."

I nodded. "I've already been a terrible boyfriend to Serena, and I'm trying to change my ways, I really am. What happened yesterday was sort of like an overload. You know how sometimes, if you hold your anger in, it eventually explodes out of you." It took a lot of courage to get that far but now that I had started, I wanted to take full advantage of it. "I've tried so hard not to think too much about you—about anyone other than Serena—and I guess yesterday when I had to think about you so that I could talk to you, it just happened. It wasn't meant to, and I certainly didn't want you to have to see it."

"I'm glad I did," she said, smiling again. "I was confused about you. You know, not knowing exactly what you really wanted or where I fitted in. I guess I am still a bit confused but maybe a little less now that I know it's not me you want."

I considered this, then said, very carefully, "If it wasn't for my resolution to Serena, or being with Serena, I guess—I guess things would be different."

She stared at me for a few seconds (during which I could have been lost in her blue-eyed gaze) before saying, "I hope we can still be friends, because I think I need you now. Not many people know what I've been through lately like you do. I'd be lost without you, John, and if I have to have you as only a friend, then I'll take it. I'll never give up hoping, though."

I smiled miserably. That was more or less what I'd wanted, yet it somehow filled me with sadness. "That's good, just as long as you don't knock others back if they try to get close to you too. You don't need to be lonely while you watch me with Serena. Besides, you'll probably be better off that way."

"That's very gracious of you," she said, "but I don't think I'm ready to jump into a relationship with someone new yet. If it was you, then maybe it would be different since we already know each other so well, but someone else? No, I need time to recover from this. I still care about Marc, see. I can't just forget him that quickly."

"Good," I said. "That wouldn't be right if you were—you know —on with someone else the next night, and I'm fairly sure Marc feels the same."

Her smile faded slightly. "I did take your advice. I really did try to explain how I felt to him, to make him understand, but it just didn't work. He intimidated me into making it impossible to tell him some things—like about you, for instance. Then, the other day, I guess it was too much. It would have been living a lie to stay with him any longer."

"Living a lie," I repeated. "Yeah, guess so."

I wondered if I was also living a lie. Perhaps several lies.

"I really wish I didn't complicate things for you," she said sadly, "but I can't just not feel like I do."

"Don't blame yourself. I have a way of making things more complicated for myself. I've got no intention of leaving Serena for another girl but I guess—maybe—if I feel like I'm—living a lie—"

"Then you should," she said, "'cause it wouldn't be fair, not just on yourself but Serena too, and—and on whoever it is you really want."

I'd been about to say "you" before I remembered Natalie. Natalie was the one I wanted the most, had wanted more than anyone else. What would happen if I was with her? Would I still find myself thinking about Amelia? I thought I probably would, and I hated the idea, but what to do about it? Then again, I would most definitely think about Natalie if I was with Amelia, or anyone at all. I knew what I needed was to put this attraction aside somehow and simply take Amelia as my closest female friend, but how on earth could I make myself do that?

"Guess you're right," I said, "and maybe I'll know one way or the other soon enough. I guess—I guess I won't give up hoping either, but not so much that anything will happen any time soon."

"Okay," she said. "But John, where do I fit in?"

"I don't even know," I admitted, hating myself.

She didn't smile at that. "I wish you did. I just know that me and Serena aren't the only ones you think about."

"You do?"

She smiled vaguely. "Trust me, I don't judge anyone. I've been reading too many minds for way too long to judge someone for having multiple interests, or even for acting on multiple interests, even if I wouldn't necessarily do those things myself."

"Well, trust me, I'll grow up some day, and maybe then I'll be more trustworthy."

"You'll be fine," she said. "You just need to make the right decision this time and not have it made for you."

"Like Serena did," I said. "Well, that was sort of both of us."

"You really believe that?" she asked, raising her eyebrows. "I saw how she was the week before you and she started, the pressure she was putting on you, what with everything all up in the air as it was, and then she got you when you were most vulnerable, straight after Tulip. I bet just about anyone could have got your interest then if they'd played it smart enough."

I considered this. It was perhaps more blunt than it had been in reality, but essentially true. Serena had initiated most of what had gone on that night, and it was mainly my own loneliness that made me submit to her. Did that make it right? Did it make her the one I wanted?

"It's starting to feel like things get more and more complicated whenever I speak about my relationship," I said feebly. "Look, I just wanna make sure you'll be okay."

"I will be," she said, "just as long as you're around. And try to make the right decision soon, whatever that is. I know what's going on in Serena and Lena's minds, and while I'm sure their feelings for you are genuine, it doesn't mean they're the right ones for you to be with, whether for two months or one night."

"You know a hell of a lot," I said, impressed against my will.

She smiled vaguely again. "I wish I didn't. It sucks to know the absolute truth about everyone's thoughts. It's so much more unpleasant than you'd expect."

I nodded. "You know what they say about eavesdroppers, but I guess in your case it's involuntary."

I took her face in my hands and kissed her lightly on the cheek. "Thanks for understanding, Amelia. You really know how to be objective."

"Thanks for supporting me and just being here for me," she said. "I guess a kiss on the cheek is all I'm gonna get?"

"Do you want more than that?" I asked, interested to see what she'd say and wishing—part of me wishing, anyway—that I could do more. She wasn't wearing a bra, I saw. What else wasn't she wearing?

"Maybe, but I wouldn't let you do any more," she replied. "I care about you and want you to do right by yourself."

I smiled. "I guess I need someone like you to keep me in line. See you in a couple of hours?"

"Sure," she said. "And remember, you were never here."

"Got ya."

* * *

I had scoured the dining room at breakfast that morning to see if Graham was out and about. I knew he was still around the base as recently as Thursday night, as I had spotted him while standing by the conveyer belt trying to decide where to sit. I had seen him in a far corner table with Rob, Bob, and Grillion, all four of them relatively sober given that it was still so early in the day. I had then kept an eye on him all through breakfast, and then, when he had got up from his table and left the dining room, I had followed at a distance. When I saw him on the second level, crossing the line of doors towards his room nine, I decided that he must surely be planning to spend the morning in there, doing his reading or whatever it was he did up there. Rob, Bob, and Grillion had gone off in different directions, so I had to assume he had cut from them.

Now that I knew where he was and determined that he was probably available for a drinking session, I entered the lounge room, where I found a number of familiar people congregated: Felicity, Jessica, Harry, Simon, Katie, Sophie, Rebecca, Jason (Lisa's younger brother), Candice Young, and several others, all below the age of twenty. Part of my urge to speak to Graham had been blunted by the resolution I had reached with Amelia earlier on, but I still felt I needed some advice. If I was going to make the right decision, a bit of impartial advice couldn't hurt. As a slight twist, however, to add a bit of interest to the experience (and because I had the crystal, which I could use to make sure they didn't repeat anything, not that I expected they would, anyway), I wanted to use the opportunity to introduce Graham to Harry and Simon.

"Roll out the red carpet, folks, Mr. Playman has arrived," Harry announced loudly, raising a hand and tipping me a salute. "Ladies and gentlemen, if you please, lower yourselves to your knees and bow before him, for he is our saviour, and shall guide us—"

"Knock it off, Maivis," I snapped, his bluff making me feel distinctly uncomfortable.

"My liege, I prostrate myself before you," he said, bowing deeply and winking roguishly at me. "Please forgive me, for I have sinned grievously. My sleep shall never be left undisturbed as I ponder, oh great one, over the offence that I have caused—"

"Just punch him on the nose, John," Jessica called out.

"Get his brother while you're at it," added Felicity.

"You two," I said to Harry and Simon. "If you didn't have any plans for this morning, I've got something I'd like you to—er—accompany me with."

That wiped that silly smirk off Harry's face. He straightened up and said, "You've got another job? And you want us?"

"It's not a job," I said quickly. "Nothing dangerous. Actually, you should enjoy it. At least I think you would, if we can do it. You interested?"

"Based on the very little you have told us, how could we not be," said Simon, standing up to join his brother.

"Quite agree, old chap," said Harry, slapping his brother on the back. "Now why is it that John doesn't want these lovely, most trustworthy people here to know what we're about to be doing?"

"Maybe it's something that Katie and Sophie wouldn't want you doing if they knew," suggested Rebecca, smiling sweetly at me.

Harry and Simon whistled. "Maybe it is, young Rebecca, daughter of the light, spirit of the Sorcerers."

The twins exchanged another look, then looked back over their shoulders at Katie and Sophie. The two girls were watching on suspiciously.

"Daughter of the light?" Rebecca repeated, startled. "Spirit of the Sorcerers? What's *wrong* with you two?"

"How long have you got?" Jessica asked drily.

"Nothing suspicious, promise," I said, directing my words to Katie and Sophie. "If anything, it's my own arse I'm covering up, not these two."

"If you say so," said Harry as he and Simon approached the door and stood with me, staring back into the lounge room. "But for the record, I always assumed Serena had your arse well and truly covered."

I turned and headed for the stairs, taking large strides that Harry and Simon, with their longer legs, kept pace with without any trouble at all. Not until we were two floors up and had turned off the stairs did I say, without looking back at them, "She doesn't have it covered enough, which is the reason why we're coming along here."

"Now that wasn't what I expected," said Harry. "What's up with you, John? If this has something to do with Serena, then what do you need us for?"

"I don't strictly need you," I said, stopping just short of Graham's door, "but I thought it might be an idea. Look, I met this guy here a couple of months ago when I tried to open the wrong door, and I reckon you'd really like him. The reason why I wanna talk to him now is—well—I'm having a few issues."

"With Serena?"

"Er, sort of," I said hesitantly. "Let's just say, having Serena hasn't really solved my female problems."

"Amen to that," said Simon. "You know, as much as I have enjoyed being so steady with Sophie for some three months now, I must concede my envy of you a few weeks ago. Serena, Lena, Amelia, and Natalie—that's not a bad quartet to have going for ya."

"What?" I said, completely taken aback. How had they known about all four of them?

"Yeah," Harry agreed. "I was the same. I mean, I guess I wouldn't have liked the complication, but I might have tried my luck with all four of them as much as I could. Well, I know Amelia was still with Marc then, but judging by how she got so defensive, I wouldn't be surprised if she has a spot for ya, mate, and we know you and her have gotten pretty close lately. Maybe she'll show more interest now that she's single again."

"I still don't—"

"Trust me, mate, if you could have seen that girl fight that night, you'd agree with us totally," said Simon confidentially.

"Oh," I said flatly, understanding where their knowledge had come from. Struck by a sudden thought, I asked them, "What happened with that, anyway? I've heard all sorts of stories, but they all seem exaggerated. You two were there when it started, weren't you?"

"The boy asks deep questions," Simon said to his brother.

"Indeed he does, old chap," Harry remarked. "We were holding down the fort, as we tend to do, and Serena was across the room from us, talking to Kylie and Erica, about what I have no idea. Lena came into the room, alone, and sat down to a chat with Jane and Darcy. This was before they went off to snag a couple of Hammersons, you understand."

"Sure, sure," I said, nodding that they should continue.

"Well anyway, they weren't sitting next to each other but they were close enough that Lena heard something Serena said that caught her attention. We didn't hear it, mark our words, nor did we hear whatever Lena said in response, but we did hear Serena when she said something along the lines of, 'he's more interested in commitment than girls who advertise their bodies like prostitutes.'"

I swore under my breath. I knew Serena must have said something pretty hurtful to get Lena's back up, since Lena was normally not the argumentative type (so far as I knew), but I hadn't imagined it would be something along those lines. "What did she say?" I asked.

"Nothing at first," said Harry. "She just gave her head a little shake, as though to say, without saying aloud, that Serena had a lot of growing up to do. It probably would have ended there had Serena not persisted. She'd only been looking for more of a reaction, I'm in the way of thinking, but naturally she bit off more than she could chew in the end. Of course, a body like Lena's—plenty there to bite, I reckon."

"Ahuh," I said dully, having heard enough about it now. "Well, for the record, a lot more stuff's been happening than you guys know about, with all four of them. Apparently I've got a decision to make, and I'd like to talk to Graham about it. You guys are welcome to voice your opinions over a few drinks if you like, but just remember —what happens in this room *stays* in this room."

"Understood," said the twins in unison. Harry added, "You know, if this guy's such a stud muffin and so knowledgeable about women, we should make coming up to this room a weekly ritual. You said his name is Graham?"

"Yeah. He's a bit like Rob and Bob, so you get an idea. I hope he doesn't mind a chat. Let's find out."

I was about to knock on the door, then changed my mind. Taking my key from my pocket, I inserted it into the slot and attempted to open the door. Of course, nothing happened.

"Er, John?" said Harry, hiding a smirk.

"No, no, let's see how long it takes him," Simon muttered to his brother.

I heard noises from inside the room, not exactly the same as last time but close enough. I at least knew that he had put down whatever he was doing before and had just got up from the couches at the back of his room where he had been sitting. He was now trooping across the room to the door. Just for the sake of déjà vu, I swung around and looked down over the rail into the hall below.

"And now he sees we're only on the second floor," Simon announced brightly, just as the door behind me opened.

"You okay, boy?" he asked, and then as I turned, "Oh, it's you again. Ya old dog, taking the same old road. I'd ask if ya skippin' school again if it wasn' Sund'y."

He boomed laughter and clapped a hand to his broad chest. "So what's doin', kiddo?"

"Just thought of dropping by for a catch up," I said. "You know, it was pretty fun last time and I haven't come by since—well, then. Hey, these two wankers here are Harry and Simon. I think I mentioned them last time."

"No wonder my ears were burning," said Harry, "and here was me thinking it had something to do with the match Katie was using to clean my ears out."

"You two'd be Bruce's boys," he said, scrutinising the twins. "Yep, I can see 'im in ya faces. Well, you three might as well come in an' take a seat. I 'aven't even started drinkin' yet. Was plannin' on holdin' it off 'til ten or so but hey, while we're young."

He turned and trooped back into his room, the three of us behind him, swapping amused looks.

"So what's been happenin' in your little world, boy?" Graham asked me as he approached the panel along his back wall I knew to contain his drink supply.

"The same as most other people around here," I said, a little flatly. I really didn't want this discussion to be a serious one, but how else was I supposed to answer that question.

"Yep, I bet it is," he said, returning to the table and sitting down opposite us with the same two bottles of beer as last time. Harry and Simon had already pulled out seats to my left, and Graham poured each of us a glass of light beer before filling his own glass with his preferred custom combo. "How's good old Chester? Still fearin' for his life?"

Harry and Simon swapped startled looks, but this time, I knew what Graham was alluding to. "Yeah, even more now than ever before. Mum doesn't want him to go out. She's afraid he'll get killed out there, but I don't think she realises that the more he stays in the house, the more likely she'll end up killing him herself."

Graham boomed laughter. "Bottoms up, boys, to good fortunes and good times for all."

"Hear, hear," said the twins in unison, and the four of us drank.

"So what's your story, you two?" Graham asked. "I used to know ya old man back in the olden days, along with this boy's old man, too. We used to drink together. How's he doin' these days, anyway?"

I started. I knew that Graham was particularly jolly, but surely he knew that Bruce Maivis had been dead for thirteen years or so. Harry and Simon, however, barely raised an eyebrow between them.

"He's doing really well," said Harry. "Really proud of us and all. It seems he thought we were gonna turn out a pair of players."

"Not what I heard," said Simon. "He told me he was disappointed we hadn't turned into players. 'Wait until you're at least twenty-five years old before settling into a proper relationship. The experience you gain as a youngster will set you up perfectly,' he said. 'And the more partners you have in that time, whether they be sexual or not, the more variety of experiences you'll have under your belt.'"

"And the more you have under your belt," Harry went on, "the better off you'll be in the—*long* run."

We all roared with laughter at that one and took a few more sips from our drinks. Graham, his sipping days well behind him, took several swigs.

"You got that right, boys," Graham boomed jovially. "I was jus' sayin' the same to ya mate here last time, seemed so worried about every little step 'e 'adn't taken yet."

"That sounds like John," said Harry. "In fact, we even made up a name for that sort of behaviour; he's been 'doing a Playman'. He's got a lot of chicks running after him and he's too scared to turn around and face them, aren't ya, Johnny boy?"

"Yeah, I guess I am," I said. This hadn't started on my terms, and now I had no idea how it was going to go. Nevertheless, I was after advice from these guys, and even if it came in the form of gentle barbs, it may still be useful.

"How's ya little girl goin', boy?" Graham asked me. "I forget 'er name, sorry. Must 'ave 'ad too much that day."

"Serena," I told him, "and she's doing okay. We're doing okay, actually. Had a rough period for a bit there, but she became more understanding after a few days apart, and we've had a good talk since then."

"Not to mention good…other stuff," Simon added, winking at me.

"The other stuff helps, too," said Harry, grinning broadly. "I mean, talking's all well and good, but when it comes down to it, it's —how does that song go—'more than words'?"

The twins laughed loudly and high-fived each other.

"Good ta hear," said Graham. He took a long draught from his drink, almost draining it, watching me. He put the glass down and said, "So you an' 'er settled, then?"

"Er—no, not really," I said uncomfortably. "I mean, there are three other girls who might have feelings for me still, and I have feelings for them still."

"Here we go," said Harry, swapping another look with his brother. "You know what, Johnny boy, if you're so sure that Nat likes you, then I dunno why you didn't just take her as soon as you found out, before players like Tommy could get their dirty hands on her crystal-clean body."

"It's not that simple," I said bitterly. "I don't wanna hurt Serena."

"John, John, John," sighed Simon, wiggling his finger at me. "How do you expect to get out of this without hurting Serena? If you still like Natalie, or Lena, or even Amelia, heaven forbid, you won't be happy with Serena, and it'll end up in tears anyway."

"Lordly though you may be, my dear lad, everyone gets hurt playing this game we call love," Harry pointed out, flicking the air between us as though to tap me on the nose (I stuck my middle finger up at him). "You may be careful, you may be considerate, but you cannot prevent other players from getting hurt. Like you, they must each take care of themselves."

"Tha's what I was sayin' last time, I reckon," said Graham. "Go on, boy, work it out. Ya sure they still want ya. Okay, so which one do ya want most?"

I didn't answer right away. This was the hairy question, I knew. It was definitely not Lena; if it was, I would have taken her when she offered herself to me months ago and definitely would have kept her after the night I had tainted myself. Lena was not the sort of girl you let go unless you had a damn good reason not to keep her. Aloud, I said, "Well, it's not Lena. She's really nice and she does want me—"

"And she'd be great in the sack, don't forget that," Harry added, grinning.

"Yeah, I know she is," I said, shivering in spite of myself, "but that's not really the—"

The twins whistled again. "You know that? You mean you've actually been there, done that, and you're trouser kazoo is still in one piece? Wow, I'd have thought a hot, sexy goddess body like hers would have sucked it right in and never let you have it again, or if so, you'd never be capable of having another erection."

I shrugged. "Worst thing I ever did, but not a mistake in the scheme of things. Trust me, I did the wrong thing for the right reason."

Harry and Simon swapped another look, but it was Graham who spoke. "You mean ya actually got in 'er? Well done, boyo. You're learnin' well."

"What?" I said, startled.

"Yep, well done," he said, grinning. "Cheatin' ain't good, obviously, and ya wanna get that outa ya system now before ya lose someone ya really care about, but at least ya loosenin' up a bit."

"I guess," I said, though I didn't think much of his supposed wisdom.

"I tell you what, John," said Harry seriously. "A lot of this problem is caused, I reckon, by you being unable to stop yourself looking at her. I'd be the same. Hell, I am the same, and I know Katie hates that, but at least she knows Lena's got bugger all interest in me. Anyway, the point is, if you can act like she doesn't exist, she might stop being interested in you too."

"Of course, you need another guy to come along and take her away before you can *really* get rid of her," said Simon, "but as long as she won't stop looking at you, other guys are gonna struggle."

"Maybe get Tommy to try," suggested Harry. "We know how he likes 'em, and she'd probably put out for him. She's not as prudish as Nat, for lack of a better word."

I shrugged. "I can deal with Lena. At least she's been the easiest to deal with for as long as I've known her. I'm not sure why. I mean, I know she's so tantalising and all that, but she just never really grabbed me."

"What about in your fantasies?" Simon asked. "I bet she popped up and grabbed you quite firmly there. Grabbed you and held you, ran her fingers up and down you, lowered her—"

"Don't even go on with that," I said, squirming uncomfortably. "Look, maybe in fantasies she is great, but that's where it ends. As far as relationships go, I'm really not interested in Lena, and at this stage, I think we can rule her out."

"At this stage, sure, mate," said Harry. "Okay, what about Amelia? Where does she fit in?"

"Ahead of Serena," I muttered, and no sooner were the words out than I knew they were entirely true.

"Ya sayin'," said Graham, who had been drinking nearly the whole time the twins had been talking. He was on his third drink while us three were still halfway through our first, "that out o' four girls, ya girlfriend is only third preference?"

"Yeah," I said heavily, "but look, there's a lot of stuff between me and Amelia that nobody else knows about. Starting with the Basement experience—that's a deep thing to go through together."

"You went through that with Serena too," Harry pointed out.

"And by that logic, you should be panting after me and Harry too," Simon added.

"It's different. Me and Amelia shared a cell nearly that whole time," I said, "and she went through something in there that I really shouldn't talk about but was really bad. We sort of had to nurse each other through a lot of it, and remember, like you guys would have thought, we thought Stella had killed three of our friends."

"True enough," said Harry. "So go on, then. You're saying you and Amelia have been really good friends since. That's okay, but why the attraction now?"

"It's been there for a while," I said, "since the day I made that pendant out there for Tulip. It just happened that day, and after that, I couldn't stop thinking about her a lot of the time. There was a day that we nearly kissed, just after Serena and I had argued, and then when she was having her psychological breakdown, we just seemed to get even closer. Then, last week, the day Marc got shot, I managed to get her to talk to me and—and—we really *did* kiss."

Both twins were silent this time. The only sound in the room was Graham topping up a fourth glass, finishing the bottle in the process.

"Okay," Harry said finally. "So—you're as bad as each other this time. Maybe Marc and Serena should hook up some day."

"Nah, kiddo," said Graham. "She probably needed it if 'er boyfriend didn' understand 'er, but ya can't know she's really interested in ya as well jus' based on that."

"She is," I said heavily. "Look, I made a resolution a week ago, to myself this is, that I would never kiss or do anything else with Amelia, Lena, or Natalie while I was with Serena; it would be just her. I screwed up yesterday, though, 'cause when I had to send a telepathic message to Amelia, I accidentally imagined all sorts of the wrong things, and she received that instead of what I really wanted to send her. We sort of had to talk about it. I know she does want me, but she won't take me. She doesn't want me to leave Serena for her."

"Don't blame her," said Simon. "She's worried that you might leave her for someone else—Natalie, most likely."

I shrugged. "We sort of agreed not to do anything, but that doesn't change the fact that I think about her way too much for someone who's not my girlfriend."

"What about Nat, then?" Harry asked. "How much do you think about her?"

I thought about that carefully. I thought I knew the answer; the question was how to explain it. Finally, I said, "I think about her often, but it's a consistent thing. I want her as much as I've ever wanted her, but I'm not as obsessed with her as I am with Amelia."

"There ya go, boyo," said Graham, putting his glass down and spilling a dribble of drink. "An obsession ain't true. You get with

Amelia now and ya find it ain't what ya expected, or the feelin' won' las' long. With Natalie, it might be better."

"Or might not," Harry added. "But John, he might be right about one thing: The way you've said it, it sounds like Serena was obsessed with you just like you're obsessed with Amelia. Look how it's going now, all fun and games, right? Well, we know you've liked Natalie for longer than you've had teenage hormones to inspire you, and we have it from James, completely confidentially of course, that she has a certain interest in you as well. Seems to me like both of you have had this interest for quite a while, but it has never dominated either of you. Maybe that's a recipe for success. I don't know. I can't talk since I only knew I liked Katie after a single dream, but we're doing fine."

I weighed all this up. What they were saying sort of made sense, but once again it didn't change the fact that I kept thinking about Amelia. If I did end up with Natalie, how did I know that these thoughts about Amelia would be in my control? More pressingly, though, it didn't make it any easier to decide how to deal with Serena. I could think of only one solution: I simply had to stop having these thoughts about Amelia. It was the only way.

"Okay," I said slowly. "So you're saying that if I go for Amelia, I have to be prepared for it not to be how I imagine it to be now, and if I go for Natalie, you think, without knowing, that just because of the way we think about each other, we should be able to keep it going."

"That's what you made of our advice," said Simon, shrugging. "It's not what we think that matters, John. If that's how you interpret what we say, then perhaps that's the line you'll take. If you ask me, I think you should go for Nat while you still can, but it's up to you on that score."

"What about Serena, then?" I asked heavily. "Obviously I have to break up with her first, but don't you think the consequences of me dumping her and jumping across to someone else would be bad?"

"Well, they wouldn't be good, not if you care about Serena's feelings," Harry said, "or if Serena plans revenge against you."

"Yeah, but what about the person who I end up with? You just said Amelia would be worried I'd do the same to her."

"Yeah, she might. I might too, but come on, if that's how you do, then you deal with that when it comes up. Sure, it's playing around, but if that's how you work, then that's how you work. These decisions are all yours; you can't let someone else make them for you. At the same time, you gotta be ready for the consequences, whatever they are. You also gotta be ready to be on the other end. You might end up with someone who cheats on you or dumps you for someone else. If it hurts, then maybe you'll know better what to do for yourself next time."

"How do you know all this?" I asked him, far too impressed.

"Wake up, John, I'm tipsy," he said, holding up his empty glass.

He and Simon laughed loudly and clanked their empty glasses together.

We stayed there for another couple of hours. The session ended the same as the last one had, when Graham had stood up and, without looking at or speaking to any of us, trooped off to the bathroom to let loose. I used the Sien-Leoard Crystal to clear all our minds before the three of us departed the room and descended back towards the lounge room. By that stage, I had made a temporary decision, and it was not really a decision at all: I would not act yet. I would wait until we had returned from Rock Haulter, after I'd had some time away from Amelia, with Serena, and with Natalie not too far away. Hopefully, after that time had passed, I would know better what was to be done. I would only act sooner if something happened that gave me an obvious solution, a solution I honestly believed in.

In a way, having that plan gave me comfort, but in another way, it made me feel like a coward. Here you go again, John, staying on the back foot and just waiting to see what happens. A bit like Mr. Woodward's approach to the war, I thought bitterly. Isn't that how you got to where you are? And you expect it will solve your problems for you? Not quite. I knew I'd have to make a tough decision eventually. Even if Natalie and Amelia both got themselves boyfriends soon, it wouldn't change my feelings for them. Yet it was Serena that I was most concerned about. What to do about her. I still wanted to believe in my resolution, and as long as I was in a relationship with Serena, then I wouldn't do anything else with other girls, but it did, unfortunately, mean that I still had to think about them. It was the best I could do, though, and I dearly hoped it would be enough.

Interlude: Beginnings

"Well, here we are," said Peter, shutting my bedroom door and heading for the table where he pulled up a seat. "Moran's still at large with the Villain Crystal, but we'll need a good, long plan to get that back."

We were all seated around the table: me, Marc, Tommy, Peter, James, Amelia, Natalie, and Serena. It was Sunday night, less than forty-eight hours before we would set off on one of the most important ventures of our lives. Certainly one of the most important of mine, anyway.

"Yeah, but we will need to do that," said Tommy, "and not just because Mr. Woodward wants us to. I know he was all good and useful the other day, but the problem still exists that if the Hammersons get that crystal he's got, we'll all be in it."

"Yeah, and I wouldn't mind seeing Lucien again," said Marc. "I've missed him a bit lately, and now that we know those things John made actually work, it'd be nice to bring him back to our side where he belongs."

"What about Stella?" Natalie asked. "I'm still sure she's on our side, whether she killed Amelia's mother or not."

"I'm not so sure I'd wanna see her again if she actually had been the one to use that crystal," Amelia mumbled.

"Same," Natalie agreed. "I would be, too, and I'm really scared it might have been my mum next if they'd got a chance, or my sister. But I still think she's on our side, and I think we owe her after the things she's tried to do for us."

"Natalie, I'll acknowledge that Stella had done some useful things for us," said James cautiously.

"Here we go," yawned Peter. "You think she was acting so that we would take her back?"

"She may have been," said James, "but I think it more likely that she really had been on our side—*then*. Now, though, we can't be sure, especially after that dream John had last week. Didn't you say she was tempted by what her father was saying, John?"

"She was," I said. "Well, at least, she was interested in the idea of ruling the world, kind of like what you said back on camp, James. The only difference was she wasn't interested in killing to make it happen. She seriously believed she could do a better job than her family were doing."

James shook his head. "This world isn't meant to be ruled as such, and Stella's crazy if she honestly believes she can do it without killing. Most people don't want to be ruled by any one person, except perhaps for those like the Hammerhearts who actually support a single ruler for reasons we can only guess at. Most people, though, enjoy their lives the way they are, and the only way that anyone can actually rule over those sort of people is to kill all those who get in the way. That's more or less what the Hammersons are about, and it's the only way to accomplish what it is they want. If Stella tried to rule without killing anyone, she'd need everyone boggled to make it work; otherwise, she'd probably end up murdered by the end of the week."

"Thanks a lot, James," said Natalie, shrugging. "But look, if we bring her in here, then she won't have to rule, and we won't give her a chance to."

"What if she betrays us again?" he asked.

"She never betrayed us in the first place," Natalie reminded him. "Sebastian was behind all that. We know that now, and Stella wasn't given a choice except to go along with it."

"So you're prepared to take the risk on her?" he asked. "Well, Mr. Woodward said he wasn't sure, but I guess I'm prepared to reserve judgement. Maybe Stella would be harmless as long as there was always someone to keep a close eye on her."

"Can we talk about Rock Haulter now?" Peter asked. "Are we all ready to go?"

"Yeah, we're ready," said Amelia. "We just have to decide who's coming and work out what sort of water vessel we'll use to get to the portal. I've already told some of you, but just so that everyone's clear, I've decided to stay behind to help my dad after—after what happened."

"Fair enough," said James kindly. "As for the rest of us, I don't see why we can't all go. I would like to bring Erica with me as well, if it's okay with you guys, not because I want her to be involved in what we're doing but just because I don't know how long we'll be there for and I'll miss her too much before too long."

"How sweet," said Peter mockingly, and the envy was obvious.

"Can we do that without making it necessary that she be involved in everything that we're doing?" Marc asked.

"Sure we can," said James. "If we arm her well enough, she can stay back at wherever it is we choose to sleep and guard the place from any Hammerhearts or rogue Russians."

"What about Lena?" asked Tommy. "She had a bit to do with getting the life assistant after all, and she was there when we spoke to Smiley."

"She doesn't need to come, does she?" Serena asked bitterly.

"She doesn't need to," I said, thinking that it would be a lot easier for me if Lena remained behind, but if I were to be a good guy, I had to be fair. "But maybe she should be allowed to decide. Siobhan knows what she and Underwood did now, so it might be that with Underwood going as well, Lena won't want to."

"What about Siobhan?" Peter asked. "She's only here because of Underwood, and now they're broken up."

"Maybe we let her decide too," said Amelia, "but I suggest that those three—Lena, Erica, and Siobhan—if they come, that they not be too much involved in what you guys do with Smiley. I say the same for Underwood too; once he's met his grandfather, he can go jump off the jetty, for all I care."

"Let Smiley decide that," said Marc firmly. "The old man's supposed to be smart, so I expect he'll find something for Underwood to do while we sort out our business with him."

"Okay," said James, clapping his hands once to emphasise the point. "We've got all day tomorrow to make that decision. What time on Tuesday do we leave, bearing in mind that the portal is open at eight o'clock our time."

"Well, you have the exact coordinates of the portal," said Peter, "and I'm guessing we have enough magic to teleport the vessel—whatever it is—to those coordinates or close enough to them. Perhaps we need to be there an hour early so that we won't accidentally miss the portal."

"That might be more precaution than you need," said Amelia, "but I agree. It shouldn't hurt. We do have that magic available, but you'll need to be by the water when you create it, just to be safe. Maybe you should teleport to a secluded beach somewhere earlier in the afternoon. How does that sound?"

There was a murmur of ascent as everyone in the room mumbled agreement.

"One more thing," I said. "The Darkness Crystal—should we take it along and hide it there on Rock Haulter?"

"That's not such a bad idea," said Tommy, "but we'll have to do a damn good job of it since we won't be around to guard it in the future."

"That's a really good idea, John," said James. "I know we got the Sien-Leoard Crystal, but that was only because it was meant for the right hands. We can make it so that this crystal is meant for *no* hands. How does that sound?"

We all agreed with that idea too. A few ideas were tossed around regarding how we could be sure nobody could ever access the crystal once we had hidden it, and eventually it was decided that we would pull something together when we got to the Rock. With those details settled, we got to discussing some of the lighter details, such as sleeping arrangements. Because there were eleven of us, it meant that we would need at least two of the three campsites we had created last time.

"We won't get to see Group E's," said Peter, "'cause the only one who knew the password at the end was Kylie. Also, that rod they used to open the outer door—well, Kylie had it, but I have no idea how to get it. Her family could have done anything with it by now."

"I doubt we couldn't work out what the password is," said Marc. "As for the rod, well, I made that thing originally, so I don't see why I couldn't make another one."

"Okay, so two groups of four and one of three," said Serena, counting around. "I don't see a problem with that, just as long as couples can have privacy somehow."

"Well, since there are only two couples here," said Tommy, "why don't you each have a campsite to yourselves, and the rest of us will take the third one."

"Ridiculous," scoffed Marc. "Look, me, John, and Natalie should all go separately so that each group has magic in it, but as far as who goes in what group, we can work that out later."

I felt slightly disappointed that I wouldn't get to be close to Natalie, but I shelved it for now. Surely, it would be better for me and my flimsy commitment to Serena if Natalie weren't too close by. On the other hand, being able to resist thinking of her when she is around could be even better for me and Serena in the long run. That was my head talking—my mind, my brain, my want to be a good person—but if I allowed my heart to open its mouth and give its opinion, it would want Natalie a lot closer than Serena.

We also discussed the water vessel we would use to get to the portal. It would be down to me and Marc to create it when we had teleported to the west coast of Australia. I hoped Marc had given its physique some consideration because I certainly hadn't, but beyond that, we didn't bother discussing it because it would probably be a work in progress from the moment we started. A feeling of nervous excitement was pulsing around the room. We were only two days away from being back there on Rock Haulter, ready for the next big phase of our discovery, of learning crucial information both about the Hammersons and about ourselves.

Interlude: Endings

Tuesday, May 11, was set to be a very long day, and that would have been without the six additional hours we would gain from travelling to a time zone comparable to Dubai. A solemn event had to be negotiated before we could embark on our adventure, though. Kylie's funeral was not to be a pleasant experience, and given the circumstances surrounding her death, she would not be allowed a dignified funeral by the Hammerhearts, who were just as much in control in this area as any other. Mr. Woodward had therefore created, for cases such as Kylie, a funeral parlour and burial ground right inside the Woodward base, employing magic similar to what I had done in the prison yard. Kylie would be the first person to be buried there while Amelia's mother, whose funeral would follow Kylie's, would be the second.

Neither funeral was a fun experience, as all the funerals I'd ever been to hadn't been (and Tommy's attempt to lighten proceedings —"you can't spell 'funeral' without 'fun'"—was flimsy at best), but they were at least dignified services, something they would not have been if we had done the thing officially. For me personally, Kylie's funeral had been much harder to bear, just because I had known her more personally than Mrs. Woodward. I spent much of that time with my arms around Serena, giving as much support as I was receiving. Peter was on my other side, and I turned my attention to him regularly. He was really struggling, but to my immense gratification, Siobhan, who was sitting on his other side, was giving him all the comfort I could not—a big thing for her considering her own personal losses recently. Given that she, Lena, and Erica had all agreed to come along with us to the Rock, I began to wonder if Siobhan would slip snugly into the void in Peter's heart that Kylie had just vacated. It would certainly be a better fit for her than Underwood had been.

The second funeral had been a little easier to bear. I had again been with Peter and Serena, sitting in the second row, but Amelia had been sitting directly in front of me. She and the other two Woodwards (the only three remaining Woodwards) were the only ones sitting on that bench on this side of the parlour. The Fletchers sat on the first row of the other side. What it meant was that there was a lot of space on Amelia's left, and after I'd watched Amelia sobbing uncontrollably for several minutes and receiving negligible comfort from her father and grandmother, who most of the time were either comforting each other or out of their seats, I got out of my own seat, squeezed Serena's hand reassuringly, and, crouched low, scooted along the rest of the row to the left, swinging around the front bench and sitting down beside Amelia. She barely looked at me but allowed me to take her in my arms and cry out against me. On any other day it would have been nice to hold her, but at that moment it made me feel thoroughly miserable, and I looked over my shoulder at Serena to show her it was so.

It was an enormous relief when the services concluded. The two bodies were buried in the graveyard, but no service took place around them. Instead, everyone proceeded to the wake, which was held in the same room where a few birthday parties had been held since I had been here. I stuck by Serena through most of that time, no longer required to be Amelia's rock since so many others were giving her their condolences. I would have been more concerned about Peter's well-being if it wasn't for Siobhan. She never laid a hand on him as far as I saw, but she never left his side either. Natalie kept sidling up to me throughout the wake too, tearful the whole time, though I thought it was more a result of the funeral services themselves than the actual losses.

Once the wake was over and people began drifting off in their own directions around the base, it was time for us to collect our bags, which we had packed the previous night, and say a last good-bye to those who knew we were leaving—the Woodwards, Fletchers, and, of course, our parents. Dad and Charlie, who seemed to be extremely proud of us at that moment, even though we hadn't actually done anything worth being proud of, slapped us over the back and told us to use the trip to Rock Haulter for all it was worth. Mum and Marge saw us off gracefully enough, even though they weren't particularly happy that we were going away again without adult supervision (in a veritable orgasm of idiocy, James pointed out that Underwood was legally an adult, resulting in several parents telling him to keep a close eye on the rest of us). Then, on our way out of the base, we stopped by the graveyard to see Kylie's grave. It was a beautiful headstone, engraved with a message from each of her family members and, most honourably, embossed with a logo, the Woodward logo, which I'd seen on the graves (both the first and second graves) of William and Carl. It symbolised that the person had died as a fighter for the Woodwards, a fighter for life, and, during the first Sorcerous war, it had been the greatest honour to be associated with that logo, dead or alive.

Part 4: Discovery

Chapter 26: Journey's Commencement

It was about three o'clock in the afternoon when we finally got around to teleporting to the west coast of Australia. It hardly mattered where along the coast we landed since the vessel would be teleporting way out into the Indian Ocean, as long as it was in a place where we most likely wouldn't be seen. It wouldn't be feasible to make all eleven of us invisible since we needed to work together, and certainly wouldn't have been at all sensible to make the vessel invisible while we were working on it. That would be done when it was ready to set sea.

We had quite a lot of magic with us (four of the Magic Crystals plus one Sorcerer surely qualified as a lot of magic), but it was down to me and Marc to perform the magic to create the vessel. While we worked, Natalie took the rest of the group a few hundred metres inland and performed a newly discovered piece of magic while they waited. It had been Natalie's discovery, in fact, which would put her in the record books forever. At least, all three Woodwards said it was something they had never heard of before. Serena, an avid fan of the Harry Potter books, liked to refer to it as the ever-popular 'invisibility cloak', but Natalie, the only Sorcerer capable of performing it properly at this early stage, said it was more like an invisibility veil, which wrapped itself around a group of people or objects. Those outside the veil couldn't see a thing hidden under it, but those under the veil could see each other as though there were no spell cast over them at all. It was a clever piece of magic.

"You got a shape in mind?" I asked Marc.

"Maybe, not that it matters," he muttered. "Why don't we just make it the shape of a normal boat?"

"Sure. How big?"

We set to work, with me doing most of the work, so it seemed. I was able to create the outside frame of the ship with only a single spell. A second spell created a hatch that would give us access to the hollow interior of the frame. A third spell made the entire outside of the vessel waterproof so that no water could enter the crack between the frame and the hatch, or if the hatch somehow gave way. The water would just sit on top, no matter how great the pressure pushing inward was. We then teleported ourselves onto the top of the ship, and then, with another spell, I lifted the entire frame into the air, moved it far enough out to sea that it could be submerged in the water, but rather than sinking, it floated on the surface, bobbing around in the waves, Marc and I struggling to keep our balance.

"You'd better make a spell that can make it automatically resist water currents," Marc told me, falling to his hands and knees and attempting to grip the far too smooth surface of the vessel.

I obliged, and a moment later, though we could feel the waves hitting the frame, the vessel didn't move at all. It simply sat in the water, most of its body under the water but enough of the top still free that Marc and I remained dry.

"Okay," said Marc, getting back to his feet. "That's better. What else do we have to do?"

"I think the rest of the magic has to be done on the inside," I said, imagining banks of control panels that would control the visibility of the ship, its ability to teleport, and other steering capabilities.

Marc strode over to the hatch and lifted it up, saying, "First thing we need is a floor in there; second thing is a ladder to get down there from here; and third thing is a button on both the inside and outside to open this hatch."

"Agree," I said, moving up beside him and staring down into the blackness inside the vessel. "And a light wouldn't be a bad idea either."

The height of the vessel seemed to me to be sufficient to provide two separate levels of rooms on the inside, so I used the crystal to create two floors. One was on the very bottom of the ship, which really was nothing more than a base upon the bottom of the frame, making it a smoother surface to walk on. The second level was exactly halfway up. It had no hole in it yet to access the bottom level, but that would come later. The next thing I did was create a ladder that stretched all the way down from the hatch to the floor below.

"Good work," said Marc, crouching down and staring into the hole. "Looks high enough for us all to stand up. Should we climb in?"

"Yeah, sure," I said and stood back to let him go first.

When I reached the bottom, I saw that Marc had created walls around the sides of the frame, making it feel more like a dark room of some kind. The point at the front of the ship had now become some sort of squarish area that, to me, looked perfect for a control room. I moved over to it and, squeezing the crystal, created a wall there to separate it from the rest of the ship, then another spell put a door in that wall. Marc, who had been on the other side of that wall, opened the door and said, "Nice one. You know, I reckon you can do just about all of this by yourself."

"I know, but we'll get done quicker if you can do one part and I do another," I said. I wasn't going to let him get away with slacking off just because I was more experienced at creating this stuff than he was. "Look, there's another level below this one. I'm not sure what we'll do with each of them."

"Well, how's this," Marc said. "This level can be a dining room, with a conveyer belt like at the Woodwards, 'cause we're probably gonna be here long enough to get hungry. I know you can do it 'cause you made one for the prisoners. We can keep the luggage up here, too. Down there can be more comfortable—you know, lounges, beds perhaps, and a couple of bathrooms."

"Now you're talking," I said, grinning. "Can you start on the bottom level, then? Oh, and as far as the bathrooms go, crap from the toilets can be pumped out of the vessel into the water. It won't matter if there's a hole for it since the outside of the ship is waterproof."

"Okay, sounds good," he said. "I'll see you in a bit."

I turned my back on him and, after I had created a light for the control room, began concentrating on what controls this vessel might need. The first thing (and one of the most basic) was a window. No, two windows—one to see directly out the front of the ship and the other to see what was in front of the ship at surface level, or in other words, on the surface of the water. It seemed more sensible to create the first as a window and the second as a display screen in the control panel. I therefore squeezed the crystal, and the entire front part of the room became a large window, the glass extremely thick—not that it mattered since the outside of it was waterproof. There was very little to see through it, though, so I made a mental note to create headlights out the front once the control panel was ready.

The next step, of course, was to create the control panel, along with—how many seats? I considered this and decided that three was a good number. I had no idea how many people this vessel would need to make it controllable, but I supposed three was a good number. At least the driver could have company while he or she worked. I squeezed the crystal again and a panel, stretching the width of the window, appeared there. It was grey and featureless now, but it wouldn't be for long.

A few more squeezes of the Sien-Leoard Crystal, along with a few carefully controlled thoughts, caused two display screens to pop into being. The first was a standard view of the surface of the sea at exactly the point of the window, while the second was linked with a camera that I had just created. This particular device was my only idea for looking out for other water vessels or, more importantly, Hammerhearts. I had already made the camera itself invisible and intended to create no control that could change that. The camera was also designed, automatically, to move when the vessel moved, and would only divert if ordered to by the controls in the control panel. What I thought I probably did need, though, was a place to store the camera while the vessel was not being used, for once we reached Rock Haulter, it had to go somewhere. I therefore created a slot on the outside of the vessel, to the left of the window, which the camera could slip into when it was recalled.

I quickly made the camera waterproof, then set to work on its controls, setting them up beside the screen I had just created for it. Right now it was showing an eagle-eye view of the vessel, sitting there on the water with the hatch wide open. The camera controls consisted of a single button, which would call the camera to its slot or release it from the slot when pushed, and five levers. There were two horizontal—one that moved the camera from side to side, and the other that turned it left or right—and three vertical—one that moved it up and down, one that moved it backwards and forwards, and one that would tilt it upwards or downwards.

The camera sorted, I pushed the button, returning it to its slot. The screen went dark when I did that, even though I hadn't asked it to, but this seemed reasonable enough. I heard a click against the wall and knew it to mean the camera was safely locked away in the slot. That done, I turned my attention to the rest of the controls for the vessel. I created two buttons, one that controlled headlights outside the window (although like the capsules, these headlights would only be visible from the inside of the vessel) and the other to toggle the invisibility of the ship. I tested the headlights and was satisfied that they worked. They still gave me little to look at, but I supposed, out here in the sea and as close to the surface as we were, there wouldn't be that much anyway. As for the invisibility, I had done enough of those sort of spells that I had to hope it had worked.

I stopped for a moment, thinking. What else did the vessel need? The only three other things I could think of were, firstly, three chairs; secondly, standard controls to move the vessel; and thirdly, teleportation. I looked behind me and, using the crystal, created three comfortable chairs around the control panel. I sat down in the centre seat, where the panel before me was bare. It was just to the right of the surface display and just to the left of the camera display. It seemed that the camera would most easily be controlled by the person sitting on the far right, while the steering of the vessel would be done by the person in the centre. If things kept going the way they looked like, the person on the left would be responsible for controlling the teleportation.

The controls I created for steering the ship were similar to those of the camera, but a little more basic—two horizontal levers with two vertical levers on either side. The only lever I had left out this time was the tilt, and only because it probably wasn't safe if the vessel tilted forward or backward too extremely. I doubted tilting would be necessary, anyway. The lever to move the vessel backwards and forwards was probably the most important one because it also controlled speed. I had completely forgotten to test the speed of the camera's forward motion, so I quickly cast a spell that would allow it to go at two hundred kilometres per hour and no faster. I cast the same spell on the vessel's controls so that it, too, had a maximum speed through the water of two hundred kilometres per hour. To cap that part of the job off, I cast another spell that would make the outside frame strong enough to withstand such speeds under the water.

Now it was time for the last bit: the teleportation. I remembered that James had the exact coordinates of the portal we would be entering, so I decided that all this panel would need was a way of entering these coordinates, plus a button to activate the teleportation. An unpleasant thought occurred to me: What if the space we were teleporting into was filled with something? This wasn't a problem when it was just people teleporting to a certain location, because we didn't have to land at an exact point, only near enough. I could make it so that water would shift aside automatically as the vessel reformed in the new location, but what about other objects? The best I could do was cast a spell that made it impossible for the teleportation to work if the vessel wasn't completely under water and if there was no landmass in the desired location to teleport to. Any other objects in that space (sea creatures, submarines, whatever) would be teleported to the location the vessel had just left. It was a little odd, but it seemed the only way.

Now, to enter the coordinates. I thought about this for a few minutes before beginning the magic. Hoping that this would be easiest for whoever this job fell to, I created a panel with thirteen buttons—ten digits, a plus sign, a minus sign, and a decimal point. I then created a large button below it and put the necessary spell on it to perform the teleportation to the coordinates just entered on the panel. The buttons accepted decimal values representing the latitude and longitude coordinates. I didn't understand exactly what that meant, but the crystal was letting me know that it was the easiest way. The times I had seen latitude and longitude coordinates, they had been shown in degrees, minutes, and seconds, so I had to hope that James would understand how to turn them into decimal values. As for altitude, it would teleport at the same altitude as the one it had just left.

I looked around the control panel, fairly proud of what I had managed to do. I couldn't think of anything else to put into it, so I turned and left the room, shutting the door behind me. Marc was still busy on the bottom level, by the look of it. I could see where he had created a hole in the floor, just beside the ladder to the hatch, and there appeared to be another ladder leading down to the bottom level, sticking out of the top of the hole. I walked over to the ladder, daylight hitting my eyes as I passed under the hatch, and created walls around them, separating them from the bulk of the ship but for a single opening. A door probably wasn't necessary here.

The rest of the top level was fairly simple. I created a room between the hatch and the control room. It now looked as though the control room was a door at the end of a hallway, with the hatch being an opening off to the side of the hallway. At least it would be a hallway if there was a wall on its other side. I put a door in the new room and created a bunch of large lockers that could be used to store all our luggage. I used the space to the other side of the hatch to create the conveyer belt, simply duplicating the model used by the Woodwards' and reshaping it to fit the space. The rest of the level was quite spacious. I fitted it with a large dining table, permanently attached to the floor, and about a dozen seats, which would accommodate everyone nicely. The one final thing I did was create three rows of lights in the roof. Again, these would be eternally on and would have no controlling switch.

My part of the job appeared to be done, so I strode over to the hatch and peered down into the hole Marc had made. There was light down there, and I could hear him walking around, so at least he appeared to be doing his job.

"Marc," I called down to him, "how's it going down there?"

"Pretty well," he called back. "You can come down if you like. I'm nearly done."

I lowered myself into the hole and climbed down the ladder into the lower level of the vessel. The bottom of the level was very similar to the top; it looked like an alcove in the side of a hallway, only in this case it really was a hallway. The bottom level was fairly cluttered, perhaps uncomfortably so once all the others joined us, but maybe it wouldn't matter if we spread out enough.

The back of the vessel appeared to be made up of small rooms, each containing two or three armchairs, some of them recliners, and a desk. Three rooms to my left looked like studies, each with a writing desk and computer. The three largest rooms, which stretched down the opposite side of the vessel from the ladder, were bedrooms. They each had a pair of armchairs and a bed. The beds were singles but they were fairly sized singles, so if two people wanted to lie together, it might be a tight fit but it would definitely be possible. There were also two bathrooms right at the front, below the control panel (obviously one for the ladies and one for the gents).

"Did you go okay with the toilets?" I asked Marc, who was putting the final touches on the computer rooms.

"Yeah, they'll be fine," he said. "And since the place didn't flood when I created the holes for the stuff to go out of, I don't think we'll have a problem with them when we get going."

"Good, 'cause I need to go now," I said, noticing the hotness in my bladder for the first time. "I tell you what, this place is probably good enough to bring the others along, so you go back and get them while I guard it."

"Er, okay," he said, "but—but how am I gonna find them? They're all under Natalie's invisibility veil and I'm on the outside of it. Even if I teleport right in the middle of them, I still won't see them."

I shrugged. "Don't see why that would be a problem. Just make the crystal push you under the veil, or maybe one of them will be nice enough to say something to you."

Marc shrugged likewise. "You reckon that'd work?"

"Don't see why it wouldn't," I said. "See you in a bit."

I went to the toilet while Marc was away, testing everything in there (the flusher, the basin taps, the shower and bath taps), and they all seemed to work fine, and if the men's room was okay, then the ladies' room surely would be too. Once that was done, I climbed up the ladder to the first level and stared up at the hatch. I had forgotten to create an easy way of opening and closing it from the inside and out. I climbed the ladder to just below the roof and created a button on the wall that would open and close it, then climbed out of the hatch, settled myself on the top of the vessel, and created another button on the top of the hatch to make it open from the outside, along with a spell to make it impossible to open the hatch by force. Why do that when there was an easy button there to use.

I stood up, marvelling in how the waves kept hitting the vessel yet hardly moving it at all. I turned in a slow circle, looking around me. It was a good view of the waves, all of them quite large but none splashing over the top of the vessel. I could still see the Australian coast in the distance but couldn't see too much beyond it. I just stood there, the Sien-Leoard Crystal in my hand, waiting for the others to return. I kept trying to think of more magic I could perform on this great black water vehicle but came up empty-handed. I supposed, if anything else was necessary while we were out there, I could use the crystal then. I checked my watch and saw that the time had progressed by seventy-five minutes since we had arrived at the coast. That meant that we had about three and a half hours before the portal would open. That was ample time considering we were going to teleport to it. I felt glad that Marc had created all that luxury on the bottom level. Three hours standing around in there with not much to do, well, at least we would be comfortable.

Marc and the others, with all their luggage, teleported onto the top of the vessel a few minutes later. A few of them staggered slightly, perhaps thrown by the teleportation itself rather than anything about the vessel, but none fell.

"Wow, this is pretty cool," said Tommy, looking around in awe. "You two have done a good job."

"Hold your applause until you've seen its interior," said Marc proudly. "Okay, John, how do you wanna do this? People first or luggage?"

"Maybe get the people down first," I suggested. "I can use magic to bring the bags down and store them in the luggage room."

"Sounds good to me," he agreed. "Okay, folks, I'm sure you can all see the hatch, so you all line up and follow me down."

Marc approached the hatch and lowered himself into it. Peter followed closely behind him, then Natalie, James, Siobhan, Erica, Tommy, Lena, Serena, and Underwood last. I knew he wasn't enjoying the company too much, but he did look rather excited by this part of the adventure, or perhaps it was just knowing that he would very soon be meeting his long-lost grandfather.

I now stood alone on the surface of the vessel, trying to think what was the best way to get all these bags down. I knew I couldn't climb down that ladder and hang onto them. I wished I'd created some sort of dumbwaiter to lower them in but a bit too late for that. Instead, I used the crystal to levitate them into a line, stretching from the hatch across the deck. I then climbed down the ladder, using the crystal to make the bags follow me, still in a line, floating slowly downward after me. The babble of excited chatter filled the top level. I looked around briefly and saw that all of them had taken seats around the dining table and were clearly waiting to be told what they could and couldn't do. I went into the luggage room and began snatching the bags out of the air and storing them in the lockers. Once I'd got all the bags that had followed me down, I climbed back up the ladder just to take one last look at the surface. Once I had confirmed it bare, I retreated back down the ladder, pushing the button to close the hatch as I went.

"Okay, guys," I said loudly, calling them to attention. "I know this isn't exactly comfortable and probably not ideal no matter how you look at it. I'm open to hearing any suggestions for improvements, but before you give me anything, you might wanna take a look at the bottom level."

There was an interested murmur at this point. Marc beamed, clearly proud that he had been the one to perform that particular magic.

"Also," I said loudly, "I may need someone to volunteer to steer this thing. I don't mind doing it, but if anyone else wants to and thinks they can handle it—er, James, we sort of need you up there, though, you and your coordinates."

"That's fine," he said. "You know, I don't mind doing all of it, if you reckon a single person can do it."

"You probably could do it alone," I said. "If not, I expect Erica would be happy to help you out. There are three seats in there, but you definitely won't need three people the whole time."

"Sure, I'll sit with you, James," said Erica eagerly.

"What's on the bottom level, John?" asked Lena.

"You can go down and have a look," I told them all. "Marc did all the work down there while I was creating the controls for this thing. I will say, though, that it looks pretty comfortable down there."

I gestured to James and Erica, and they followed me into the control room, which looked just as it had when I had left it.

"Wow," said Erica, stopping short in the doorway. "This looks like some pretty serious stuff."

"You can sit there," I said, tapping the seat on the right, "and control the camera—security provision, you know. James, you'll need to enter your coordinates on this. See if you can make us come in from the north side of the portal so that we'll be in familiar territory on the other side."

James observed the panel with the buttons to enter the coordinates. "How do I do this?"

"Just enter them," I said, unsure exactly what he was asking. "I wasn't exactly sure how to make that part easy, so I just did what the crystal suggested. It has to be done in decimal values, though, so I hope you know how to do that."

"Oh, crap," he sighed, taking a slip of paper from his back pocket and reading it. "No, I'll have to convert these."

"You can do that?" Erica asked.

"I reckon so. I understand how it's supposed to be done, anyway."

He sat down in the seat before the teleportation device while Erica took a seat before the camera controls. "So, John, show me how to use this thing," she said.

We spent the next few minutes fiddling with the camera. Once Erica had the hang of the controls, she had fun zooming it around the coast, exploring the surroundings. It was only when I spotted our vessel in the water again on the display screen that I remembered our visibility and felt a touch of disquiet. The Hammerhearts almost certainly had access to satellites up there somewhere. I quickly pushed the invisibility button and was satisfied to see the vessel vanish from the display screen, leaving nothing behind but an unusual-looking disturbance in the water.

"What happened?" Erica asked sharply.

"This button makes us invisible," I said, pointing at it. "James will have that control when he's ready, not that we'll need it again until we get there."

"How big is this camera, anyway?"

"About the size of your hand. Just try to stay near the ship. If you lose yourself, just push that button to call it back."

"It's no use," said James, frustrated. "I can't think like this."

I leaned back against the doorframe, trying to think. "We really need you to be able to make that conversion in the next few hours."

"He'll get it by then, John," snapped Erica.

"I should," said James unsurely, "but—I just need to concentrate."

"Maybe go downstairs," I suggested. "Find a room alone and get comfortable so you can work it out, or come to think of it, use one of the computers down there."

James's face lit up. "There are computers down there?"

"Yeah. Of course, Marc created those, so I dunno—"

"No, they'll be perfect," he said, jumping to his feet. "He created Harry and Simon's computer before he even knew what he was doing, so these should work fine."

"Harry and Simon?" I repeated, surprised. I couldn't remember ever hearing about that.

James didn't hang around to clarify what he said but instead bustled out of the room and headed for the ladder. I glanced at Erica, who shrugged indifferently.

"So what are the rest of these controls, John?" she asked.

I spent a few more minutes showing her the steering controls and headlights. I was pleased that, when she moved the vessel around, apart from a slight vibration, I felt no sense of movement at all. I knew it was moving though because of the displays (both of them), not to mention the window in front of us.

"I did think of something you could add to this, though," said Erica, sitting back in her seat and looking at me. "This camera's all good and useful, but if we really do run into Hammerhearts, even being invisible, we have no way to deal with them. Don't you think we need weapons of some kind?"

I considered this, surprised that I hadn't thought of it. Of course we needed weapons. We would be just as helpless as David and Craig had been if we didn't. I therefore turned my attention to the bare spot on the panel to the far left, beside the teleportation device. I then spent about a minute performing spell after spell, arming the vessel with five different weapons, giving it twenty different ports on the outside, five on each side. On the control panel, the controls were set out in a square. The square itself was a screen with a cross in the centre that the person in this seat would use to take aim, and it had five buttons around each side of the screen, colour-coded according to what they did. There were also various controls that resembled joysticks that would aim the weapons.

"I guess with this you really will need a third person," I said, looking back at Erica.

"Not if you also give me some sort of public address system," she said. "Then I can just call for help if James and I spot any trouble."

Yet another good idea. I moved across to where she sat and created a microphone and slot for it on the panel to the right of the camera controls. The microphone came with a switch on the panel just below the slot to turn it on and off. Another spell later and every room on the vessel, apart from this one, had a speaker connected to the microphone.

"Thanks," she said, smiling sweetly. "So I guess I just sit here and keep an eye on these screens until James gets back?"

"Could you?" I said gratefully. "That'd be great. I should go check on the others."

It looked as though everyone had moved downstairs because the top level was completely deserted. I wasn't too surprised. They had a long few hours ahead of them, which was plenty of time to get comfortable. I climbed down the ladder to the bottom level, feeling as though I was descending into darkness, but in fact there was just as much light here, perhaps more, than there had been on the floor above. I looked at the large light bulbs Marc had attached to the roof and was struck by an idea. One thing the vessel was missing that would have given it a feeling of comfort was carpet, so I squeezed the crystal and the entire bottom level, apart from the bathrooms, was suddenly covered in nice soft carpet.

"I felt that," I heard a voice call from somewhere to my left.

That had been Serena's voice. I turned and, looking into the first room, whose door stood open, found her sitting there, presently alone. She stood up when she saw me and threw herself into my arms, and I held her, slightly amused.

"This is a really nice place," she said quietly. "It would probably get a little bothersome after several hours, but it'll be good for the wait before we can go through the portal."

"That's all it's for, after all," I said, disengaging from her and looking around.

From where I stood, I couldn't see into any other rooms, so I stepped back into the hallway, Serena following me, and looked into a few more of the doors. Most people, it seemed, were alone at the moment. The only exception was Marc and Tommy, who were standing on opposite sides of one of the small rooms and talking quietly. Two of the three computer rooms were occupied; Underwood appeared to be checking his Facebook page while James had a spreadsheet open with several cells containing numeric values. I wondered vaguely how Underwood was using the Internet—what sort of connection?—then decided the modems were obviously magic, so who bloody well knew what they were doing. Meanwhile, Natalie and Lena were laying back in recliners in separate rooms at the opposite end of the vessel and looking quite at their ease. I couldn't see where Peter or Siobhan were, but I did notice that one of the bedroom doors was shut. Did I dare go in there? I decided I didn't.

I ended up sitting back in the room where I had found Serena, with her beside me, and after about ten minutes, we were joined by Marc, who said that Tommy apparently wanted some alone time. That's where I was for a little while, until I spotted James pass in front of us and I got up to follow him.

"You got the decimal values?"

"Yeah," he said, shrugging. "I'm not sure what's wrong with me today. I just couldn't seem to get my head around them. I ended up using a spreadsheet to work them out. I'll put us about fifty miles north of the portal so that we can approach it properly and from a distance, which means we'll need to allow—how fast can this thing go?"

"Two hundred K," I told him.

He did a bit of math, then said, "Well, twenty to twenty-five minutes would be more than sufficient. You wanna come upstairs with me so we can do the teleportation?"

The time was just after five o'clock by my watch, which was still on Chopville time. That gave us about two and a half hours before we had to set off. Fifteen minutes after that, the portal would be wide open and accepting traffic. Marc, Serena, and I followed James up the ladder and back to the control room to perform the teleportation.

"You got the coordinates, James?" Erica asked as he seated himself in front of the teleportation controls.

"Yeah, the decimal coordinates," he replied. "John, what are these?"

He tapped the square, around which lay the buttons for the defences.

"Just some stuff I did while you were away," I told him, "but you'll be in the middle seat most of the time, so you don't really need to know how to use it."

"What sort of defences?" asked Marc.

"Well," I said, "that square—the ones on top shoot from the front, the bottom ones from the back, and the side ones—well, you get the idea. The white buttons shoot thicky prison, the red ones shoot lasers, the grey ones shoot bullets, the black ones shoot torpedos, and the blue ones shoot nets. That should fair us well against any Hammerhearts, especially as the frame of this thing would be strong enough to withstand most things they can throw at us. Except perhaps bombs."

"Wow," said Erica, stunned. "What's the likelihood of them having bombs?"

"Very unlikely," said Marc, "considering our location. The Hammersons might suspect the Woodwards to attempt entering the portal, or to send someone, like us, but they probably expect they'd have enough in their arson that they won't need to use a bomb."

"Hope you're right," said James. "Okay, I've entered the coordinates the way this thing wants me to. Are we ready to give this thing a try?"

"How do we know if it works?" asked Serena. "These screens might not change at all."

I thought about this. In a way, Serena was right. So much depended on our navigation being pinpoint precise, and right now, there was no way to know exactly where we were in relation to the portal. After all, the portal was invisible. What I supposed we needed was another display screen—not a square screen like the two already installed, but more like a single line that would show the coordinates of the vessel, which the navigator (James) could use to steer us towards the coordinates of the portal. There was room on the panel above the teleportation device, but the more logical place to put it was right in the centre, directly above the steering controls. I gripped the crystal in my pocket and imagined the screen being there, filled left to right with digital numbers as well as little plus and minus signs. A moment later, what I had imagined was there, with a pair of coordinates marking our current position.

"That's helpful," James remarked, looking over at it. "Can you move this thing forward so I can see if the numbers change at all?"

I took hold of the controls and did as James said, powering the vessel forward, heading west, farther out into the Indian Ocean. I watched the numbers on the screen: They were changing, both of them, albeit slowly. I supposed, since both of them were changing, it probably meant we weren't pointing exactly west, but judging by the way the longitude was changing quicker than the latitude, it wasn't hard to work out that it was more west than north or south.

"I think I get it," said Erica, who was also watching the numbers. "So these numbers will change to the coordinates James enters after we've teleported to them? Is that how we'll know?"

"That's the idea," I said, sitting back in my seat. "So, James, you ready to give it a try?"

He nodded slowly, and we all went still, holding our breaths as James first braced himself, then pushed the teleport button. I had teleported plenty of times before and had become so used to it that now it just felt like being lifted up into a cloud and then placed gently down in a new location with nothing perceptible in between. In actual fact, what it really felt like if you hadn't become used to the sensation, was a sense of flying through a whirl of colour and sound as your body was sucked into a state of nothingness so that your essence could be transported to a new location and your body reformed there. I'd had plenty of time to think about teleportation, and although I had no proof that that was how it worked, I supposed it had to be something along those lines.

This time, it was slightly different. Since it was the vessel that was teleporting and not just the people inside it, none of us actually felt like being sucked into nothingness. Instead, everything in the control room (the window and all the display screens) went completely dark. The lights stayed on, though, which meant that we were still able to see each other, although none of us could move a muscle or make a sound. We couldn't even breathe, but it was in no way uncomfortable. As we had all become nothing, it wasn't necessary for us to breathe. Instead of floating, it felt as though we had become weightless. Maybe that amounted to the same thing, but it didn't feel quite the same. It only lasted for perhaps six or seven seconds, though; everything came back all at once when the teleportation was complete. The window filled with a view of water again, the display screens came back to life, and we were all able to move again.

"Success," James said after a moment, and he pointed to the coordinates on the newly created navigational screen. They were now the exact values he had entered into the control panel.

"Well done," I said, an enormous weight coming off my shoulders. Perhaps one of the hardest parts of the mission had been completed without a hitch. "Now, we just have to wait 'til our watches say, let's say, twenty to eight. That'd be a safe time to head off to the portal."

"Agree," said James, getting out of his seat and standing in the narrow gap between the seat and the control panel. "Now, John, since you're in my seat, would you care to move?"

I scrambled out between my seat and Erica's and allowed James to seat himself beside his girlfriend.

"So what now?" Marc asked. "We just wait for the next—more than two hours?"

"Yep," I said. "Let's go downstairs and find something to do down there. Oh, and Erica, make an announcement to all the others that dinner will be happening in the dining room at six o'clock by our watches."

* * *

The following two hours were, generally speaking, fairly pleasant. Serena, Marc, and I had descended to the second level only to find Tommy and Natalie waiting for us at the bottom of the ladder, ready to enquire about what had just happened to the vessel. They had both been suitably satisfied when Marc told them we had teleported to a spot some fifty miles north of the portal.

"Is everyone else down here happy with that?" Marc asked.

"I think so," Natalie replied. "Actually, Peter's asleep, so he probably didn't notice a thing. Siobhan is sitting by his bed. Dunno what she's actually doing in there, but clearly she didn't wanna get up and risk waking him. Lena asked me to let her know what happened, and Underwood…well, I guess he's just letting us take care of it whichever way."

"Good," said Marc. "Well, since we've still got forty minutes before dinner, I think I'll jump on one of the spare computers."

"You wanna come sit with me for a while, Nat?" Tommy asked casually.

All four of us looked at him in some surprise. Natalie and Tommy had generally got over most of the unpleasantness of a couple of weeks ago, but they still hadn't gone out of their way to be alone together, and Natalie had always been rather cool with him when she had to speak to him directly. That was the case now as she said, "Why do you want me to sit with you? Why don't you go hang out with Marc like you were earlier?"

Tommy shrugged and looked at Marc, who also shrugged. "It doesn't matter to me," he said.

"Doesn't matter to me, either," said Tommy, looking back at Natalie. "Does it matter to you? 'Cause if it doesn't, you might as well come with us."

"If it doesn't matter to you," said Natalie, cool as ever, "then why don't you go and sit with Lena or Underwood? There's only one seat in those rooms, but like I said, if it really doesn't matter to you, you won't mind."

"If it doesn't matter to him," Serena chipped in, "he'll go and sit with Marc, because at least then he won't have to sit on the floor."

"Or have someone sit on his lap," Marc added, grinning slyly at Natalie. She glared sharply back at him.

"Come on," I muttered to Serena, taking her by the hand and leading her away from the other three.

Let them sort themselves out, but I didn't want to be around to see it. I knew what was happening here: Tommy still had the hots for Natalie, and he seemed to believe he had given her enough time to cool down after their first failed relationship. He was ready to try again. I felt very annoyed about it because once again, I seemed on the verge of missing another opportunity to be with her. On the other hand, wasn't that what I wanted? If Natalie went off the market again, it only left Amelia to worry about, and if I was set on not leaving Serena for Amelia, then it meant that Serena and I would survive after all. It was all so confusing, but I knew one thing for sure: I did *not* want to see Tommy and Natalie back together.

Serena and I took one of the remaining bedrooms so that we could cuddle together more comfortably. We didn't get up to too much in that little room. Quite apart from not having a lot of time, there were the additional worries of either being overheard through the walls or being interrupted. Nobody did bother us, though, and the next time we saw another living soul was at dinnertime. Through the whole time, though, I found myself unable to really appreciate Serena's company as I had wanted to, what with the lingering worry about what was happening elsewhere in the vessel, and the recurring doubt that after all my efforts (both successful and not) to do the right thing, I was about to make an enormous mistake.

There were ten of us present at dinner. Erica was the only one who hadn't come at six o'clock (ironic, since she had made the announcement) and she had closed the door so that we wouldn't disturb her while she patrolled the waters, but James said he would eat quickly so that he could relieve her and she could come out for a quick dinner while some of us were still here. Curious to see how things had progressed between the others, I looked carefully around the room as I ate. Peter was sitting on my right, and although he hadn't said very much, he appeared to have found some inner peace since this morning. Siobhan, who was sitting on his other side and also rather quiet, may have been the cause of this.

In fact, it wasn't just those two who were quiet. Everyone was quiet. The atmosphere seemed tense from all corners. Underwood sat at one end of the table, Serena to one side and James to the other; apparently none of the others wanted to sit near him, and he certainly didn't want to be anywhere near Marc, Tommy, or me. Lena seemed determined not to make eye contact with any of Underwood, Serena, or Siobhan; that gave her barely anywhere to look, considering she was sitting directly opposite Peter. To my displeasure, at the other end of the table, to Lena's left and directly in front of the hatch, Tommy was sitting next to Natalie; they weren't talking, but the fact that she had consented to sit beside him was more than I would have liked.

I wasn't in a very good mood by the time dinner came to a close. Get used to it, John. These people will be your only company for a while yet. For now, though, I'd had enough of them, so I decided to go into the control room and sit with James and Erica for a while, in the left seat. That would make me the vessel's defender, I supposed. It made the following hour more pleasant than most of the time in the vessel had been. It even felt a little more relaxing than the time I'd spent with Serena.

At last, our watches had ticked to seven forty in the evening back at home. The surface display showed that where we were, it was early afternoon. It was time to go.

Chapter 27: Through the Portal 2.0

Now that the time had come to move the vessel towards the portal, we unanimously decided that everyone should come up from the bottom level and gather in the dining room again, so that they would be immediately aware if there was any trouble. There were no ships heading our way, but according to James, the Russians would be coming towards this portal from the northwest as opposed to our straight north, so they would probably miss us, unless we were unlucky to be going through the portal at exactly the same time as them.

"I tell you what, Erica," I suggested, "raise the camera up nice and high and just keep turning it in circles so that you can see in all directions. Don't actually move it; that way it'll stay directly above us while we're moving. James, just go for it, but try to time it so that we reach the portal and go through it at eight o'clock."

"Don't worry, I've got that under control," he said. "Just in case we do get there at around the same time as another ship, what should I do? Try to beat them in?"

"Nah, just wait for them to go through and then follow."

"And what if they've sent other ships to wait for us?" Erica asked. "I don't mean ones that will be going through, but ones that are just here to stop people like us from entering?"

"Then…we attack," I said solemnly. "We've got weapons to use against them, and if they don't do the job, I'll just give them a taste of Sien and Leoard's wrath."

"Sounds like a plan," said James, and he pushed forward on one of the vertical levers.

We all felt the vibration as the vessel began powering through the water, getting faster and faster. Through the window, the water churned around us. I could only imagine the disturbance the vessel was causing, moving under the surface of the ocean at such a great speed. Behind me, I could hear the rest of our crew climbing the ladder and gathering around the seats closest to the control room so that they could listen in on what was going on.

"Hey, James, I forgot to ask you," I said, remembering something from earlier. "You said Marc made a computer for Harry and Simon. When did he do that?"

James looked surprised. "I thought everyone knew that."

I shook my head. "He never said anything about it to me, nor did the twins. How did you know?"

"I just guessed," said James smugly. "I did notice that Harry and Simon were putting an effort to keep it a secret, but for the record, that was more likely for Marc's benefit than their own. Remember that computer he made back when we first found out he was the Seventh Sorcerer? He gave that to Harry and Simon 'cause they asked for it. Lisa also got a new laptop out of the deal, but she just went by and took that from him when she was ready. It was a bigger deal for the Maivises because they had to get Lucien to drive it around for them, 'cause obviously their grandparents weren't too interested in helping them out. They were pretty badly grounded back then."

"Aren't they always grounded, those two?" Erica asked amusedly.

"Most of the time," James agreed, grinning. "Well, anyway, they did let out a few hints about it, most accidentally, but for me, it was Harry suggesting 'Pentium' as our password on camp that confirmed it."

"I see," I said, reflecting back on the twins' behaviour. They had been most interested in sewerage around then, but I couldn't remember too much talk about new computers.

The minutes continued to tick by and the vessel continued to approach the portal. James had his slip of paper on his lap and he kept glancing between it and the coordinates display as he held the forward motion lever steady. Erica had taken my advice and was turning the camera in 360-degree circles a hundred feet above the water, allowing it to move directly above the vessel. I was continuing to watch the other displays (the surface display and the weapon aimer), but both revealed nothing. No sign of trouble so far.

We came to within two miles of the portal by exactly 7:53 by our watches. According to James, the research he'd done over a week ago had revealed that the portal would have been open for exactly seven minutes already and would stay open for another twenty-seven. That gave us plenty of time, so long as there wasn't any trouble.

"Full steam ahead," I said enthusiastically. "Erica, keep an eye on things."

Good advice, for a mere twelve seconds later, Erica cried out, "Ships ahead!"

We all started. James slowed our forward momentum and glanced down at the surface display. I could see them too, off in the distance. They couldn't have been more than a few hundred metres away from the portal. They were set in a large ring around it, about eight of them, and clearly their intention was to guard it, to control who entered it. I supposed that any authorised vessels would have some sort of signature that would be recognised, but as for us, their orders would be to take us down at all costs.

And it was worse—much worse, in fact. Someway beyond the ships and slightly off to the east was another water vessel of some kind—something much larger than any of the other ships. Not waiting for Erica, I dipped my hand to the crystal and sent my mind out to investigate. It was an aircraft carrier, a monumental one, loaded with more planes than I could count. One was taking off as I watched, and several more were already in the air, circling. And as if that weren't enough, there was a submarine off to the west of the portal, not presently in motion, but I understood what this all meant. The Hammerhearts were sparing no expense to control the portal, and they were defending it on all three levels—above the sea, on the sea, and below the sea.

"Aw, Jesus," James moaned.

"Holy cow," Erica said as she and the camera caught up with everything I had already witnessed.

"Remember, they can't see us," I reminded them, "and if they are wearing ghost goggles, they might not know what to make of our vessel. We have the advantage of doing this on our terms."

"But there's so many of them," James said, his eyes wide and frightened, but to his credit, he didn't slow us down. Not yet, anyway.

"We still have to get past them, though," said Erica. "How deep under the water does the portal go, James? Do you know?"

"If you're suggesting we try and go under them, I wouldn't even risk it," said James. "You can see how they've spaced themselves apart there, enough space there for a few ships across, and the little I do know is that the three dimensions of the portal are all equal in size."

"Probably not enough, then," I said and sighed. "Could we pretend to be an authorised ship?"

"Doubt it," said James flatly. "Even if we could use magic to get the right signature or whatever they use to validate, they might still know the difference. They might know to expect only one or two ships, but one extra and the alarm will go up."

"So? Make them kick one of the other ones out instead of us," Erica said eagerly.

James shook his head. "Too much risk in that."

"So what's your idea, James?" I asked, but I knew what it was. There was only one option left.

"We have to attack them," he said solemnly. "Even if the Russians do turn up while we're working on them, I doubt they'll have enough firepower to get involved. We don't need to stop them coming through."

"What if there are Hammerhearts on their ship too?" I asked. "And let's face it, like we were saying the other day, there probably will be. They'll wanna take as much advantage of the island as they can now that they have so much control."

"We deal with them on the ground," said James, "which we can do, with all the magic we have on our side. So, John, how are we gonna do this?"

I mentally scrambled, trying to think of every possible way we could do this. I had never been in or even seen a battle like what we were about to face. I knew nothing whatsoever about maritime warfare strategy. I also had a feeling that the weapons I had installed probably weren't going to be enough to get past the Hammerhearts. What worried me even more, though, was that the vessel mightn't be strong enough to cope with their retaliation, because there would most definitely be one. It was meant to be, but would it hold up?

I looked over my shoulder and said, "Marc, you'd better get in here. Natalie, put a shield around everyone back there. Make sure it's resistant to anything solid, water, and any kind of shock."

"John, what the hell?" I heard Serena call, sounding terrified.

"We're gonna be fine," I said, hoping I sounded more confident than I felt, "but we can never be too careful."

"What's going on?" Marc asked, appearing in the doorway.

"Take a look," said Erica, indicating the screen before her and zooming the camera around so that Marc could have a good look at all the obstacles ahead of us. As he did, James began slowing down at last, leaving maybe five hundred metres between us and the nearest ships.

"Aw, man," he moaned. "We need to get in there quickly before they get all those planes in the air."

"You're responsible for protecting us," I told him. "I'll be responsible for attacking them, however much we need to."

"Good plan," said James. "So how do we do this?"

"Give me a minute," I said, trying to think my way through the battle ahead.

"Okay, but hurry up. We can't afford to wait too long."

"I know that," I snapped at James, and the control room fell silent.

So, what to do…what to do…

My mind flicked involuntarily to the gym battle just days earlier, and the fact that I had been forced to kill in order to survive. There was a high probability that something like that might happen again. I didn't want that on my conscience, and I didn't think the others would either. So, how to minimise the chances… I cast my mind around for an idea, any way that we could avert most (if not all) of the trouble, and to my surprise, I came up with something that might actually work. The key was to get as close to the portal as we could without them detecting our presence. We were invisible, of course, but the water still churned around us as we moved, and the closer we got, the easier it would be for the Hammerhearts to spot the disturbance. I couldn't think of any way to avoid that altogether, but there may be a way to give them as little reaction time as possible.

"Erica, are those ships facing away from the portal?" I asked.

"They seem to be," she said, moving the camera around to look, "but they can probably shoot from their rear and broadsides as well."

That was disappointing but not surprising. I dipped my hand to the crystal again, sending my mind back out to examine the scene ahead of us. There were more planes in the air now, but with a bit of luck, we wouldn't need to worry about them. I tried to get the crystal to indicate to me exactly where the invisible portal was, but it wouldn't work for me. I sighed. It was still the best option.

"I'm going to teleport us into the circle," I told the other three. "Not right into the portal, but right behind those ships."

"But the coordinates—"

"I'm using the crystal to do it, not the thing you used before, James."

"But won't they notice the water?" Erica asked.

"They might," I said. "That's why we have to be ready as soon as we get there. Are you, Marc?"

"Whenever you are."

"What the hell is that?" said James sharply, pointing out something on his own screen, which was still showing the surface of the ocean above the vessel.

I looked at the screen and gaped for several seconds before it slammed home what must be going on and what was about to happen. It looked like a narrow band of rain was fast approaching us from the direction of the portal, despite the fact that there were hardly any clouds in sight. The source of the so-called rain was clearly visible on Erica's screen, and a moment later, it became apparent to everyone else as the bullets began slamming into the top of the vessel. It was one of the loudest things I had ever heard in my life, and the vibrations that rolled through the structure almost toppled me out of my seat. Marc, who was responsible for protecting us from the assault, was knocked clean off his feet back into the room outside, and looking over my shoulder, I saw that he had almost fallen down the ladder. Thankfully, everyone else out there seemed to be safe, thanks to Natalie's shield. I tried to make my mind focus, to perform the magic to make us resistant to the current assault, but the concussions were too intense.

"Move us!" I bellowed at James, my voice sounding strange in my own ears.

He too had been knocked back in his seat, but with a massive effort, he pulled himself forward and pushed on the forward lever. We moved out of the line of fire, and silence fell. I used the crystal, firstly to clear my head (which thankfully worked) and then to do the same for Marc, James and Erica's heads as well.

But in the short time that we had been under attack, the Hammerhearts had been taking further initiatives. I could see some of it on Erica's screen and some on James's, but I sent my mind out again to get a clearer picture. Two of the planes that had most recently taken off were flying higher and higher, much higher than the many others, which were zooming around at maybe two or three thousand feet. A few of them had Hammerhearts leaning out of the side of them and shooting jets of light down towards the water, some of which looked suspiciously like thicky prison. If any of those hit us, they would all be able to see exactly where we were, invisible or not. The submarine was on the move too, descending into the water and moving forward in our general direction. I had no idea what their intention was, but as long as they didn't know our exact position, they probably couldn't do much to hurt us.

The ships guarding the portal hadn't moved, but something seemed to be going on over there all the same. Hatches seemed to have opened in the sides of three out of the eight ships, and from them were streaming smaller vessels, each of them perhaps big enough to seat three or four people, although whether or not they were manned was impossible to tell. They weren't normal vessels, though; some of them had dipped below the surface of the ocean while some moved across it, and yet others seemed to be flying into the air. None of them were as yet approaching us, but they were spreading out from each other, and strange lines—almost completely invisible to the naked eye—seemed to be connecting them (I wouldn't have picked up on that last detail if I hadn't been using the crystal). I thought back to something Frederic Woodward had said to me months earlier: "W37 and 38. W stands for weapon. Not agonators or bludginators—those are devices with the letter D in their code. No, these weapons are designed to cause all sorts of trouble for anyone who comes across their path." Mass terror and destruction, he had described it, and it didn't surprise me in the least that they would resort to that to protect the portal.

"Sorry," Marc panted, finally reappearing in the doorway. "That one's on me. I'm gonna—"

But whatever he was gonna do, he never got a chance. Another Hammerheart attack descended upon us, shells this time, sending all of us reeling for a second time. Marc was knocked off his feet again, and the Sien-Leoard Crystal slipped out of my hand. I heard it go bouncing across the floor, ricochet off the wall beside me, then, thanks to the vibrations, go rolling out of the control room. It may have gone bouncing down the stairs after that, but thanks to the noise, I didn't hear it.

"Move us again!" I bellowed at James, desperate to recover myself before they could try anything else.

He obliged, but before we could get out of range of the firing, something slammed into the vessel from directly in front of us, hard enough to force us backwards away from the portal. I looked through James's screen, then Erica's, and saw the probable cause. Those line-connected vessels weren't just for show, and those lines were clearly more substantial than they looked, because they were somehow moving us backward. Further to that, they had moved around to either side of us and were attempting to close the gap. There was still some room to move since they hadn't got our exact shape and size yet, but there wouldn't be for long. We were really only left with one option.

"We have to go down," Erica said, reading my mind.

James took the controls again and began moving us down, and I just had time enough to think we might be okay when something monstrous slammed into us from below, forcing the vessel to rise hard enough that we actually left the water for a moment before we splashed back down. The impact was so hard that I actually felt the g-force push me vertically downwards, hard enough that several muscles in my neck and back strained in protest. It was immediately followed by a brief moment of weightlessness as the three of us lifted out of our seats before slamming down on our backsides.

And none of that was the worst thing. From outside the room, even over the thunder of the fire and well and truly over the top of a cry of pain from Marc (now he really did sound like he'd fallen down the ladder), I heard three clear sounds: a loud snap as something broke, an almighty blast as a wall somewhere downstairs shattered, and the clear sound of water entering the vessel. Either the force of the blow was powerful enough to break through all our protection, or more likely whatever they had fired at us had some sort of pre-performed magical enchantment designed to counter exactly our type of protection.

I was torn in several directions at once, and rationalising my way through them was not easy with the attack now hitting us from five out of six three-dimensional directions. My head pounding, the vessel feeling like it could disintegrate at any moment, I nudged James and, when I had his attention, shouted, "Reverse!" Then, without waiting to see if he did it, I looked over my shoulder and shouted through the door, "Natalie, go downstairs and help Marc! And find my crystal while you're at it!" If Marc had also lost hold of his crystal, then Natalie was now our best chance of survival and so much of the next five minutes would depend on her magical skill.

And meanwhile, all I could do was sit and watch the screens as outside, the battle unfolded. Thanks to the small line-connected vessels, which had now isolated our position in three directions, the Hammerhearts knew exactly where we were. Overhead, the planes continued to circle and fire down at us—some with bullets, some with shells—and the concussions when those hit were extraordinary. I was glad that half the group was protected by Natalie's shield, but meanwhile, James, Erica, and I, not to mention Marc, could be in serious danger even if they didn't break through in more locations.

I resorted to the weapons I had created earlier, weapons which I now realised were far outclassed by those of the Hammerhearts. I supposed part of me hadn't really expected that we would need them, or I was subconsciously counting on the Sien-Leoard Crystal to protect us if we got into an actual battle. The torpedoes were too slow to have any effect; they slipped beneath the lines and just kept going, unaffected by whatever magic was keeping us locked in. The nets were even more useless, and although I was able to hit one of the vessels with a laser, it didn't do any damage. I did take one down with a single bullet, though; the thing exploded in the air, allowing me to see that it was indeed unmanned, but the gap that had been created as it broke apart in the water was instantly re-joined by lines from two vessels on either side of it. Yes, I could fight this way, but I had no chance of winning, and meanwhile the screens showed that the Hammerhearts had finally blocked off our retreat as well.

"Teleport!" James yelled at me.

I didn't get his meaning at first—how could I teleport us now without the Sien-Leoard Crystal—but then I got it as he nodded at the teleportation panel I had created for the vessel. The coordinates James had entered earlier were still on the screen, so all I had to do to return to them was push the button. But when I did, something strange happened. For a moment, it felt like we were about to teleport, but then in almost the same instant, we were in the same position, still surrounded by invisible bonds. I tried it again but the same thing happened, and I had to resign myself to yet another failure: The Hammerhearts had made this trap anti-teleportation as well, as though anticipating that they may need to trap Sorcerers at sea.

I'd had enough of this helplessness. Since I couldn't be any use here, and it was only a matter of time before the Hammerhearts pulled a new trigger (if they could do this much with their pre-performed magic, they probably had a way to kill us all), I decided to see what state Marc and Natalie were in.

"Stay here," I yelled at James and Erica, getting up and lurching out of the control room.

But James's idea of "stay here" turned out to be to try to move us in every direction save upwards, and I kept getting almost knocked off my feet as the vessel kept bouncing off the sides of our trap. At least he didn't try going downward. I might have been knocked out if he'd tried that again. Holding on to the wall, I entered the dining room to see Peter, Serena, Tommy, Lena, Siobhan and Underwood around the dining table, all on their feet and all totally unhurt. Thank heavens for small favours, I thought, and even more so when the Hammerheart attack finally subsided and I was able to hear myself think.

I could hear what was finally happening around us now, and it was not good. The bottom level was flooding, and Marc and Natalie's panicked shouts were coming from down there. I hurried to the ladder, looked down into the gap to see if it would be safe to jump (no time for climbing), and then James hit the side of our trap again, causing me to lose my balance and fall down anyway. I managed to grab onto a rung about halfway up as I was falling, twinging both shoulders and causing me to fall up against the ladder, the blow of my ankles on the floor somewhat cushioned by the ice-cold floodwaters at its foot. Marc was standing right beside the ladder, holding onto it to keep from being swept to the back of the vessel along with the water.

"Geez, John," he said, not looking too thrilled to see me. "As if it weren't complicated enough already."

"What's going on?" I asked, looking around. The water was flooding in quickly, but not too quickly—we may have at least ten minutes before the water was up to our chests. It seemed to be coming from the toilets and sweeping towards the back of the vessel, and as I watched, Natalie came hurrying towards us from that direction, taking large, exaggerated steps to move her feet above the tide as she ran in order to accelerate her speed. She looked business-like in that moment, and even in our dire situation, I couldn't help finding her attractive.

"Feel up to a swim?" she asked me and, without needing to hold anything to balance herself, grabbed one of my arms and forced something into my hand. I felt my eyes widen as I recognised the object—she had found and returned the Sien-Leoard Crystal. My spirits lifted with hope, which was immediately dampened as I recalled the words she had just spoken.

"A swim? What—"

"The Hero Crystal fell out of the vessel when James did one of those—"

Right on cue, James tried to move the vessel again, causing Marc and I to stagger against the ladder. Grimacing, Natalie pushed on. "I need to go out there and look for it, and now that you have magic, you can come out with me and get us out of this trap."

That wasn't at all inviting. It was a war zone out there, and even though I had magic to protect myself, it was an incredibly scary environment to knowingly walk into. Easy enough for Natalie, after all she'd been through. But then again, it was a war zone in here too, and this had to be done before the Hammerhearts did whatever it was they meant to do next.

Natalie hadn't waited for me but had hurried over to the toilets. I said to Marc, "Go up there and make sure James doesn't do anything stupid," and hurried after her.

We found the hole in the floor of the men's room. It wasn't very big on the inside (it must have done much more damage on the outside, judging by the noise I'd heard earlier), but it would be big enough for Natalie and I to get through if we went one at a time. As I watched, Natalie took a deep breath and, with skill that must have come from her magic, dived down into the hole, looking almost as fluid as the water heading in the opposite direction. I hesitated for a moment, trying to think if there was anything I ought to do before leaving the ship. As long as the hole is here, we would be able to get back in, but as long as the hole stayed here, the vessel would continue to flood. I therefore reinforced the waterproof spell over the hole, causing the flood to instantly stop without making the hole disappear. Another spell later, all the floodwaters on the bottom level disappeared, and after a bit more thought, a third spell placed a shield around the outside of the vessel that only Natalie and I could pass through. That ought to protect Marc, James, and Erica from any more of the same sort of Hammerheart attacks.

It was time to go. I quickly cast an invisibility spell upon myself, then jumped into the hole, sinking into the freezing cold water like a stone. Natalie must have been thinking much more clearly than I had been if she'd already performed whatever magic necessary to cope in these conditions. The first spell protected me from the cold, the second one allowed me to breathe as if there were a constant supply of oxygen around my head, the third allowed me to swim more smoothly, and the fourth allowed me to see and hear more clearly underwater.

I was now free of the vessel and could clearly see what was going on around me. Even at this depth, there was activity. The unmanned vessels I'd seen sealing us in were completing the final phase of the trap beneath the vessel. Natalie had slipped through before they'd had a chance to close the gap entirely, but I would have to somehow reopen the trap if I were to escape. I could also see the submarine, but with its work done, it was in retreat. I considered attacking it, almost decided not to, then, thinking that it might come back if given a chance, focussed my mind on it. A moment later, it was placed within an invisible shield of my design, a shield that would remain immobile in the water, would be impassable in both directions, would be impervious to all magic except if it were performed directly by me (I'd been sure to include that exactly in the spell), and would be incapable of any communication with the outside world. They ought to be sufficiently neutralised until I could deal with them later, I thought, although truthfully I only intended to set them free as soon as we were safely through the portal.

Speaking of which, it wouldn't stay open forever, so if we were gonna get through at all, I had to hurry. I placed a shield around myself—something I probably should have done before jumping in the hole—then tentatively drifted downward against the bottom of the trap. I bounced back and felt that a great amount of force had gone into the shield I had just created. I was protected from it, but I had a clear sense that if I'd touched it, I would have been killed instantly, crystal or no crystal. Remember, John, you're not immortal, even while you're holding the crystal, if you forget to use the right magic to protect yourself.

So how to get out? Teleporting probably wouldn't work, but it would be negligent of me not to give it a go anyway. Somehow the same thing happened; I reappeared a fraction of an instant right where I'd been before, only with the same sense that my shield had absorbed a lot of energy from the trap, as though I had touched it again. For all I knew about teleportation, maybe I had. I tried to use magic to push the barrier back. No luck. I tried to create a hole in the barrier. No luck. Frustrated, I tried to blast it. Nothing.

Tick…tick…tick…

I was close to panic now, knowing that if I didn't hurry, we would be out of time, and it would be entirely on Natalie to get us out if we were to survive at all, let alone get through the portal. Trying to stay calm, I wracked my brains. If this thing was created by the Hammersons to be used by their supporters and not themselves, as it seemed to be, and it was designed to trap experienced Sorcerers, then it would have to be clever enough to prevent anything Frederic Woodward might think to try to escape. That didn't give me a lot of hope, but there was one thing that did: In order for the Hammerhearts to use it and not lose control of it, it had to have a weakness somewhere, a weakness that could only be…

Eureka! I knew what sort of magic I needed to try. I had a moment of doubt (surely Arnold Hammerson would have thought a Woodward would try this), and then I pushed it away. I gripped the crystal and focussed on the area of water on the other side of the barrier. A light appeared over there, confirming that I was right. I made the light drift forward, growing and expanding until it surrounded me on all sides. One spell later, the light had retracted back to its original point, taking me with it. To make sure it worked, I attempted to teleport again, and this time, it worked. A moment later, I was bobbing invisibly on the surface of the ocean between the trap and the ships surrounding the portal.

Of course, I thought, the trap had worked the same as the lines that had secured the prisoners in the Woodwards' Prison Block. I couldn't have passed out if I'd been inside when the trap had been set, but anything on the outside could pass through without any trouble. Except that without a button to control the magic, it meant that Hammerhearts could remove prisoners from the trap just by hanging onto them as they passed through the barrier. So, by creating a piece of magic on the outside of the trap and then using that magic to bring me through, I had quite easily fooled the system.

Tick…tick…tick…

Now to business, but what to do first? Move the ships out of the way, stop the planes from attacking the vessel, free the vessel from the trap—all that had to be done and quickly, but looking up, I saw something else even more urgent. Earlier in the battle, two planes had separated from the swarm and had circled higher and higher over the battlefield. Those two planes were now at least thirty thousand feet above the water, and as I watched, something small but bright was falling from them, fast. The planes below had left an opening directly over the vessel, and you didn't have to be a genius to figure out where that thing—whatever it was—was going to hit. I asked the crystal, and the response I got was chilling: When that thing hit the trap that the Hammerhearts had set up, everything inside would be vanished—turned into a complete vacuum. The only exceptions being any Magic Crystals or crystal chips still inside. In other words, all my friends bar Natalie had less than thirty seconds to live.

Fortunately, I only had to perform my own vanishing spell to solve the problem. Then, even as the vacuum maker was glinting out of existence high in the air, my attention had turned to the two planes responsible for the near miss. A moment later, before they had time to fire another vacuum—before they would even have registered that the first one had failed—they were trapped just the same as the submarine below.

The other Hammerhearts didn't immediately realise that something was wrong, but it didn't take them long. Some of them, both in the planes and the boats, had been following the progress of the vacuum with their eyes as it fell, no doubt wanting to see the moment when all the defences around four of the five Magic Crystals—including the Seventh Sorcerer—were eliminated. They saw it vanish, and looking up, they saw that the two planes—while still intact and still airborne—were frozen in place. They may have tried to communicate with the pilots, I'm not sure, but they knew that only magic could have done that.

Everything the Hammerhearts had done up until this point had been with military precision, but this new development was more than they could handle. Knowing they didn't have time to work out a strategy, or even communicate quickly enough to everyone that there was a problem, some of them in the planes took matters into their own hands. They went on the offensive, flying around without any organisation and shooting bullets and shells wildly into the water below. Plenty of bullets hit my shield and ricocheted into the water at angles, but I didn't see any sign that the Hammerhearts had noticed. One shell hit one of the ships guarding the portal, but I didn't see what effect it ended up having. Two planes collided some distance to my right; both of them burst into flames, but fortunately one Hammerheart ejected from each of them. I hoped those two had been the only ones aboard.

Tick…tick…tick…

Most of the Hammerhearts were smart enough to send their attacks towards the vessel whose location was known. Even though it was still invisible, it was the only known source from which the repel could have come. Unfortunately for them, even while they had been working out what was happening, my attention had been on my friends. It only took me two spells to vanish the Hammerheart trap, unmanned vessels and all. The first spell, a simple vanishing spell, hadn't even worked, but it had worked fine on my second attempt when I had specified to the crystal that it should just copy whatever the Hammerhearts would do to make the trap vanish. I quickly checked where Natalie was, found that she was using magic to guide herself back to the vessel, having collected the Hero Crystal, then, for my own peace of mind, reformatted the shield around the vessel that would repel both magic and physical attacks, which only she and I could pass through, and which only I could remove. It wasn't much different than the one I had already put there, but somehow it felt stronger. By the time the Hammerheart attack hit them, they were already protected.

Several things were happening now, all of which I would have to deal with in some way, and crucially, after checking with the crystal, I had less than five minutes in which to do it if any of us were going to get through the portal. I sent a telepathic message to Natalie (I'd almost sent one to Marc before remembering that without the crystal, he had no way of hearing), telling her that the trap was gone, the vessel was shielded, that there were just four minutes and forty-three seconds to spare before the portal would close, and that if I couldn't get back on board in the next three minutes, that they should just go through without me. I would hate that, knowing who was on the other side of that portal (and the idea of leaving Tommy alone with Natalie for an unknown amount of time, not to mention being away from my *actual* girlfriend), but I had no intention of getting left behind if I could help it.

Tick...tick...tick...

The ships between me and the portal hadn't moved, but those around the other side had moved towards the aircraft carrier, and one had moved below the two parachuting Hammerhearts as though to catch them. Beyond the portal, I could see a new ship approaching, this one looking like a small cruise ship rather than a battleship/cruiser/destroyer/whatever these other ships were. It had to be the Russians, also cutting it fine, perhaps advised by the Hammerhearts to go around the battle and approach the portal from the other direction for their own safety. I considered stopping them but didn't; if there were Hammerhearts on there, we could deal with them later, but the Russians were innocent and didn't deserve to miss out just because of the idiots controlling them.

Tick...tick...tick...

For my next move, I considered the planes buzzing around over my head, still trying to cover every square metre of the ocean's surface with their attack. It felt like I should deal with them somehow, but what for? They couldn't hurt the vessel anymore, I supposed, so did that mean that they could do nothing to hurt us? I tried a blanket spell that would do to all of them what I had done to the two at thirty thousand feet, but typically in these situations, it didn't work. I sent another telepathic message to Natalie to deal with them if she could once she was safely on board and to get Marc to help her, before I turned my attention to the final obstacle: the ships.

Tick…tick…tick… Four minutes to go.

Those ships were big, and they would be tough to attack. That meant that just moving them out of the way would be best, but how to do that? I thought about it as quickly as I could, during which time the Russians' ship vanished into thin air as it passed through the portal. The solution I came up with seemed appropriately poetic, and I felt myself grinning like a kid at the irony. Before I began performing the magic, though, for my own safety, I teleported myself out of the water and atop the vessel, safely beneath its shield in addition to my own. I had a moment of vertigo as I found myself standing on what appeared to be thin air, but I quickly shook it off and focussed on the job at hand.

Tick…tick…tick… Three minutes and fifteen seconds to go.

I began placing a shield around the ships guarding the portal, extending it so far that it included the aircraft carrier and the ships that had gone to protect it. I extended it to my right so that it included the ship that had gone to catch the parachuters. I extended it upwards so that it included all of the planes above, and finally, I extended it downward so that it included the submarine below. This raised two complications: Firstly, the vessel itself was now within the shield; and secondly, the portal was within the shield, although I doubted that last would be affected by what I was about to do. All the same, just to make sure nothing disastrous happened, I very carefully performed two spells that would extract the portal and the vessel from inside the shield, even though they were in the same space.

Tick…tick…tick… Two minutes and forty seconds to go.

I had a moment in which I considered the power of my position. Those Hammerhearts had fully intended to kill all of us. Not just kill us, but vanish us entirely, leaving behind no body and, quite possibly, no soul. That was pure evil, and now, I could do the very same to all of them in a single instant—all thousand of them, or however many there were out here. Except, of course, I wasn't evil, and so far, apart from the possible deaths in the plane crash, we had succeeded in not killing a single Hammerheart. I therefore gripped the crystal and cast a spell, teleporting everything within the shield a hundred kilometres to the north. A moment later, they were all gone, seemingly leaving me alone in the Indian Ocean.

Tick…tick…tick… Two minutes and twenty seconds to go.

Let's go, I thought. I sent a telepathic message to Marc and Natalie both, whether he could receive it or not, telling them to move now. The vessel began moving at once, making me think that James had made the decision to go without waiting for my say-so. Good man, I thought, although I wondered if he'd thought about how I would get through. I staggered atop the vessel as it built up acceleration in the water, even though it wasn't affected by the waves and swells of the ocean. I looked down for something to hold onto, remembered that the vessel was invisible, and quickly cast a spell to make my feet stick to the surface.

The last thing I did was cast my mind to the Hammerhearts and, with a single spell, removed all the shields I had placed around them, including those specifically for the submarine and the two high-fliers. They were far enough from us now that there was no need for the shields anymore. I then removed my own shield and the one around the vessel—also unnecessary now—and a moment later, we passed through the portal. There was no significant change in the surroundings—the ocean had been relatively calm on the outside, and it was relatively calm on the inside—but I had a sense that we were through, and when I enquired of the crystal, it confirmed the best news of the day. I breathed out a sigh of relief. We made it.

Chapter 28: Private Investigation

I took a moment to enjoy our victory before unsticking my feet from the vessel and then teleporting inside it, appearing at the foot of the ladder to the hatch. Everyone was there waiting for me, except for James and Erica, who were still piloting us. Marc and Natalie were standing in the doorway to the control room and beaming, while the rest of them were still on their feet around the dining table.

"Nicely done, John," said Peter, grinning at me. "Say, did you know you're presently dripping all over the floor?"

Oh, I'd forgotten how wet I was. I quickly cast a spell to dry myself, then looked around. I took a moment to grin at Peter and Serena—and Lena, who seemed to want something from me—before hurrying to the control room, Marc and Natalie getting out of my way so that I could enter. Within, I found James and Erica, who were also grinning.

"Good work, John," James said, slapping me on the shoulder as I sat down in my earlier vacated seat. "I'll be interested to know how you did all of that."

"Sure, I'll fill all you guys in when we get to our camp. Er, not that I mind, since I'm here, but were you gonna leave me behind?"

James looked surprised, then understood. "Nah, I knew you'd want us to get through as quickly as possible, and you could get through on your own just fine if you didn't come through at the same time as us."

I thought about this for a few seconds before deciding that I was satisfied. He was probably right, after all.

"Okay, cool. Erica, use the camera to find the Russian ship—"

"Er, John," she said, sounding nervous. "The camera—I don't think it came through. It's still showing outside the portal. It must have been too high."

"Oh," I said, slightly surprised. "Well, no drama, just press the button, call it back. It should come straight through. There's still time —well, barely."

"Oh, okay."

"As I was saying, locate the Russian ship while James gets us to the jetty, see if you can work out where they might land and let us know if we have enough time to get out before they get near us. I'm gonna see if I can figure out what the Hammerhearts on the outside are doing. We can't have them following us through. Just announce when you've got us up beside the jetty."

"We couldn't just teleport from here to the island?" Erica asked.

I thought about this. Now that I did, it seemed the most obvious thing to do. However, when I gripped the crystal, it gave me resistance. Why was it doing that?

"I don't think we can," I said, wonderingly.

"No surprise," said James. "Amelia and Stella couldn't teleport us around here last time. Even Fewul couldn't help us out there."

"They could make those doorways," Erica started.

"That won't work from here," I told her, "even if one of us did know how to do it. You guys," I called over my shoulder, addressing Marc and Natalie, "can you make sure the bottom level is cleaned up before we get to the island? There's probably still a hole in the floor down there."

"On it," Natalie called back, and I immediately focussed on the next job at hand.

Only forty seconds remained before the portal closed, so to prevent myself getting chopped off at the mind, I cast a spell to reel my mind back to my body automatically before the portal could close. I then sent my mind out, back through the portal and out to where the Hammerhearts were. To my relief and slight surprise, the Hammerhearts had given up the fight—they weren't following us. Even now, the planes were landing, they were counting the cost of their defeat, and, most importantly as far as they were concerned, they were trying to figure out how to explain all of this to Arnold Hammerson. They knew what had happened to them, and they knew where they were, but there just wasn't enough time for them to get back to the portal, let alone stop us from going through. Satisfied, I quickly returned my mind to my body.

"It's all good," I told James, Erica, and anyone who was listening. "The Hammerhearts will know that someone unauthorised and with magic is on the island, but they won't be able to send anyone new after us. The best they can do is make the Russians keep an eye out for us. We've definitely got the upper hand for the time we'll be here."

"Good." James sighed. "We should get to the jetty pretty soon. I'm not sure how long it'll take, but I'd guess it wouldn't be too much more than twenty or thirty minutes at the speed we'll be travelling at."

"Should we just wait around for it?" Peter asked, looking through the doorway.

"Er, well, if you've left anything downstairs, then you should use this time to get it," I said. "Otherwise, yeah, just sit around here and wait."

"If we've left anything downstairs, it's probably screwed." Peter grinned. "But okay."

I decided that after all I'd done in the last half hour or so, I deserved a rest, so I left the control room and took a seat at the table beside Serena and looked around at everyone. Marc was sitting beside Tommy, and Natalie, to my displeasure, returned to her seat on Tommy's other side when she climbed back up the ladder. She seemed to look more comfortable next to him than she had at dinner, and that was a very bad sign. At the other end of the table, Peter was sitting beside Siobhan, and Lena was on Peter's other side. The former two were just looking straight ahead, shooting glances at each other occasionally, but Lena had eyes only for me, and I tried very hard to avoid them. The trouble with Lena was that she knew that all she needed to do was put herself where I could see her and make occasional eye contact—her super tight body and my groin would do the rest of the work for her. Underwood sat on Serena's other side and he, like Peter and Siobhan, was looking in no particular direction, except for the occasional glances he spared for Lena. I knew what those glances were and was a little surprised: he still desired her. On top of everything else, he still desired her. Would he still desire her as much after he'd observed her real personality for a while, instead of my acting personality in her body? I supposed it was probable with a guy like him.

It only took about fifteen minutes before we had reached the jetty, but another five before James and Erica were able to line the vessel up beside it. From what I heard, none of James's displays gave him a good enough view of exactly where the side of the vessel was in comparison to the jetty, so Erica had to bring the camera around the island to let him know if he was close enough. Apparently, the Russians were still far enough away for this to be safe. When the time came and James had made the vessel visible again, everyone lined up by the ladder, Marc at the front, and once the hatch was up and we were seeing natural daylight again, they began climbing out and congregating on top of the vessel.

I was the last one out, so it was down to me to handle the luggage. I did what I'd done at the start, setting them in a floating line behind me as I climbed up the ladder and out of the hatch. By the time I was on the surface and the hatch was closed again, everyone else was already waiting for me on the jetty. Marc had created a set of steps leading from the roof of the vessel down to the level of the jetty, so I hurried down them, the luggage still floating along behind me.

"So what do we do about the vessel?" Natalie asked.

"Make it invisible again and leave it somewhere?" suggested Serena.

"Shrink it and bring it with us?" suggested Tommy.

I had to admit, Tommy's suggestion was considerably better than Serena's, so I squeezed the crystal and watched as the ship shrank and shrank until it was the size of the Sien-Leoard Crystal and floating way below us on the surface of the water. I drew it up to my hand, caught it, and stuffed it into my pocket, turning to the others and saying, "Problem solved."

"Good," said Peter. "Now let's get up to the tree house before the Hammerhearts get around here."

* * *

Our watches said it was just after nine o'clock by the time we reached the tree house, although judging by the position of the sun in the sky, I knew we would all need to change our watches pretty soon. Most of us found the ascent fairly easy given that we had done it all before and recently enough that we remembered where each and every branch was. Siobhan and Underwood struggled on the way up, but with both Marc and Natalie behind them, they were never in serious danger of falling.

"We're not doing this every bloody time, are we?" Underwood barked, panting as he finally crawled onto the balcony of the tree house.

"Some of the time," I replied, approaching the door. "We have two other campsites. Maybe you can sleep in one of them if you don't wanna come up here as often, but we'll still have to have meetings and stuff. Let's face it, it's one of the safest places around here. Is everyone here? 'Electroencephalograph.'"

"What the hell?" Peter said, stunned, as the tree house door slid open in response to the password I had set before leaving this place the last time. "John, how the hell are we gonna remember that?"

"Easy, just think EEG," said James, following me into the tree house.

"Easy for you to say, elephant head," Peter muttered darkly.

The interior of the tree house was just as empty as it had been the last time we had been here. Even the outside of it hadn't changed very much. The control panel was still beside the open doorway, the large clock face still hung in pride of place on the wall to the right of the doorway, the only window was still opposite it, and directly opposite the doorway were two more doors, the one on the left leading to the bathrooms and the one on the right being the storage room Stella had created before we had left. Seeing those two doors there and remembering how they had been created took me by surprise. Quite suddenly, I missed Stella very much. I wished we had tried to abduct her from her family before we had left for the Rock. To focus my mind on something else, I gripped my crystal and began placing our luggage in a line below the window.

"Okay," said Marc, the last in line, once he had crawled over the threshold. He repeated the password to close the door before turning back to the rest of us. "So now we're all here. What's the plan?"

"I reckon we should wait until tomorrow morning before we go and find Smiley," said Tommy, who had been looking around himself in awe the entire time he'd been here but now turned his attention fully to us. "John, did you bring the life assistant? We might need him to let us know exactly where to go."

Underwood scowled very heavily at the mention of the life assistant but made no comment.

"Yeah, I've got it," I replied. "I'll make contact with him a little later on. I think we've gotta sort out the rest of today first. Who's sleeping where?"

"Actually, I've been doing some thinking about that," said Natalie, a little shyly, and whenever I heard that coy tone in her voice, I always wondered what it was she was thinking that made her so nervous. It had been the case the day she had told me she, apparently, wasn't taking anything for granted anymore, and it was the case now. "I think," she went on, "that maybe we shouldn't split up. It mightn't be the most efficient way to go."

"I did think of that too," Erica chipped in, "but surely, if we have you in one campsite, John in one, and Marc in the last, you three can use magic to keep in touch and stuff."

"That's what I assumed we'd be doing too," said Marc.

Natalie shrugged. "We could, but the only way to make that properly efficient would be to make a link between the three campsites, and that'd be a real security flaw if one of them is discovered."

I thought I could see where she was coming from. Last time, we had done a hell of walking around in order to continually meet up after activities. There was no reason why we couldn't just walk to a specified campsite each morning, but we could probably save a considerable amount of time if we didn't have to.

"The security is a good point," said James. "Well, I like your theory, Nat, but there's a slight hitch. I don't think any of the campsites is big enough for eleven beds. Well, maybe ours would be if we got rid of some of the couches, but—"

"I reckon I could fix that," I put in. "I could make a block of bedrooms for us all or something, and maybe make that accessible by all three campsites."

"Wouldn't that pose the same security threat?" James enquired.

"Not if what I've got in mind works," I said, grinning.

I wasn't going to try to explain it to them yet, but my idea was based on the portal we had just come through to get here. Lisa had once said that the portals remembered who you were so that when you left them, you would come out the same portal you entered through. I couldn't see a reason why I couldn't put a similar spell on the door to the set of rooms I was thinking of creating. The difficult part would be creating a door in each campsite that opened onto the same door in a single location, but I was willing to give it a try.

"So what? John's gonna make our rooms?" Erica asked. "Is that what's happening?"

"Looks like it," said Marc, shrugging. "So what about in here, then? Should we have couches or something?"

"How about a round table," suggested Serena, "where we can eat dinner and stuff, with nice, comfortable chairs we can sit in so that we can also have meetings there. As for the other campsites, they should already have enough furniture in them, don't you think?"

"They would," said James. "We never got rid of any of the stuff in ours."

"Okay," said Marc, getting to his feet. "I like the idea of a table in here, so everyone back against the walls while I sort it out. John, your password is pretty good, but I reckon I agree with Peter—quite a few of us are gonna struggle to remember it, so maybe you ought to change it to something a little easier."

"Guess so," I said, shrugging and approaching the control panel. "You guys all hit me with suggestions."

I opened the control panel and the first thing I spotted were the two keys hanging on a hook just behind the door, one with a tiny letter S on it and the other with a tiny letter L. I unhooked and pocketed them both before resetting the password from the previous one. It had initially been Daniel's suggestion, so clearing it was something of a pang, but I supposed Marc had a reasonable point.

"'Simpleton,'" suggested Peter. "That describes most of us Chopville faithfuls, don't you reckon?"

"'Long live the Woodwards,'" said Tommy.

"'Fucktard,'" suggested Underwood.

"'Hammerheart hunters,'" said Serena.

"If we could have just a single word, that'd be great," I said. "Er, not 'fucktard,' though."

"'Single'?" suggested Peter.

"How about 'liberation'?" said Natalie.

The suggestions dried up at that point. Liberation—that was a pretty good one, not just because of the word itself but also because of the meaning behind it. We all looked at each other for a moment before James said, "Well, John, we all seem agreed on that one, so go right ahead."

"'Liberation,'" I spoke to the control panel, before saving the password and shutting the door on the controls. "Now, as for that," I said, pointing up at the enormous clock, staring down at us like a face with a lot of numbers on it, "I don't think we wanna be screeching our presence to the whole island."

"Totally agree," said James. "Besides, once we're in your bedrooms, we mightn't even hear it. Better we all have our own alarms."

The table was in the middle of the room by now, large and round, just as Serena had described. Marc was going around it, duplicating the comfortable-looking armchairs he had already created. A few moments later and he was done. There would have been perhaps more than eleven seats there, but that wouldn't have mattered too much. There was still enough room in the tree house to move around, after all.

"Okay," he said, "you can all sit down now. So what's next?"

"Everyone change your watches," said James. "I know we'll probably all be tired in a couple of hours, but the fact is we've still got at least another five or six hours before we should sleep."

"I can help you guys out there," said Natalie. "I kept myself going for sixty-seven hours a couple of weeks ago. I can handle keeping you guys up for five, I think."

"I'll let you know when I start yawning, then," said Peter amusedly. "Wow, sixty-seven hours."

"I tell you what," said James. "For the meantime, this is what we should do. John, you get started on our bedrooms. Marc, see if you can locate our Russian friends with your crystal. Keep an eye on them and see if you can work out if there are any Hammerhearts in their number. As for the rest of us, er—any ideas?"

I didn't bother listening to the rest of their conversation but set to work on my idea right away. I created something a bit like a shoebox (like what Stella had done last time), and soon after, it contained a hallway with six bedrooms on either side. Each room had a large bed, identical to the ones on the vessel, a set of drawers, a closet, and a desk. Each room also had a speaker that would play an alarm when it was time to get up. The time of the alarm could be controlled by a panel beside where the door into the hallway would be when it was done. I also wanted a bathroom in there, though, so I vanished the bathroom door from the tree house back wall and placed it inside my box, at the far end of the hallway. The near end also had a door, and this was where the hard part began. I created a door against the back wall of the tree house exactly where the bathroom door had been. That was the start of it, but in order to complete it, I would have to go to the other two campsites. Then, just to complete the procedure, I vanished the storeroom. That cost another pang for Stella, but the fact was, we really didn't need it anymore.

"Is that it, John?" Erica asked.

"That's it," I told them. "The inside of it's done, so you can take your bags in there and get settled. Guys in the rooms on the left, girls on the right. It probably doesn't matter too much, but we might as well keep some order about the place."

"Good stuff," said Serena, getting to her feet and heading for the bags by the window.

"Marc, how's it going?" I asked him.

"Okay," he said vaguely. "They've landed on the jetty and are bringing all their stuff in. There are eighteen Russian students and it looks like they'll be sleeping in the upstairs rooms of the main hall along with their managers. There are twenty-five Hammerhearts with them, but I don't know if they'll stay with them."

"Probably not," I said, thinking. It wasn't great, but not unexpected either. "Well, you guys, before you all go in there, I have to go to the other two campsites to give them access to our bedrooms. Anyone wanna come with me?"

"You're saying you need an escort?" sneered Underwood.

"Someone really should, just in case," Natalie said. "Any volunteers?"

I wished Natalie had volunteered herself but forced the disappointment away. Once again, John, you ought to be grateful for a chance to make your life less complicated. True, that, so why did I feel so flat?

"I think I should," said James. "I know the password to Group F's campsite. You'll have to sort yourself out with Group E's, though."

"Oh, yeah. Marc, the rod."

"Oh right."

He drew his mind away from whatever he had been watching and a moment later was holding something long and metallic in his hand, which he handed across the table to me. I used the crystal to create two new doors against nothing, linked them to the inside of the bedroom box (which incidentally was up in the top corner of the room alongside the bathroom, as the prison yard had been), and made it so that they would follow behind me. Just to be sure it had worked, I opened one of them and looked inside to make sure it led into the bedrooms. We all loaded our luggage into our rooms before leaving. For the record, mine was the first on the left, next to Peter's and opposite Erica's.

* * *

James and I returned from our thoroughly uneventful venture up to the mountain at around five o'clock. The shadows were getting longer, making it probably the most difficult time of the day to climb up to the tree house. Thank God for the Sien-Leoard Crystal, I thought, as I narrowly prevented myself from slipping twenty feet down a branch that turned out to be more slippery than I had anticipated. The doors had been set into the backs of the houses Groups E and F had used, replacing their bathrooms since neither of them were necessary anymore. They both worked—I knew so by performing an experiment in the Group F campsite.

"Tell me what you see through that door," I told Peter as we stood together in the hallway between the doors of our bedrooms.

"I see the tree house," he said, "and Marc looking like he's stoned. Why you ask?"

"Good," I said, satisfied, because what I could see was in fact the inside of Group F's campsite—exactly what I'd wanted.

By the time we were all back in the tree house, everyone was back sitting around the table and watching Marc. He was sitting exactly where he had been when James and I had set off, his crystal still in hand, his eyes closed, his expression rather vacant. We knew what he was doing but still wished he'd at least give us a bit of commentary. It cost a great effort not to risk breaking his concentration by speaking to him.

"John," Serena whispered, "perhaps you should take a look as well."

"Not just yet," I muttered back.

I felt sure that Marc would return to us soon and it would be better just to wait. If it turned out that we needed to watch two places at once, then I supposed I would help out, or at least create a television screen we could use to watch without having to use magic around the clock. Sure enough, only a few minutes later, Marc looked up at us.

"So what's the deal?" Tommy asked.

"Well, they know about us being here," he said, still a little vaguely but apparently beginning to come back to himself now. "They all saw the business just outside the portal and had it confirmed by the ones who survived. You guys should be glad to know that only two people died out there—that's good 'cause I was hoping we wouldn't have to kill the whole lot of them. Well, anyway, the Hammersons will probably know soon if they don't already."

My heart sank. So there had been a couple more people in those planes. Was that it, or had a couple more died as a result of something else I had done? It was a haunting thought.

"Where are they staying?" asked Lena.

"Well, the Russians are all staying in the main hall," he said. "They're here to explore and study as much magic as they can, but they've been told not to tangle with us. They're supposed to call for the Hammerhearts if they spot any of us, but the thing is none of them, not the Hammerhearts or the Russians or anyone, knows exactly who we are, how many of us we are, and so on. They probably suspect me, John, and Tommy are involved, though, and that's bad enough. As for the Hammerhearts, they're sleeping in a chamber inside the mountain. Not a very secure one, though. So if we wanted to pick a fight with them, it'd be really easy. Their job is to tap into as much magic here as they can and bring as much of it as they can back to the Hammersons. I think they'll also be looking for us, though. Not picking a fight but just quietly looking around so that maybe they can get the drop on us. Can't see that happening, though."

"You reckon Sebastian could have had time to tell them about our campsites?" asked James.

"It's possible," said Marc. "They don't seem to know at the moment, but if he did tell anyone, there's a chance the news could be passed along to these guys. All we can do is be ready for them at all times."

That didn't sit well with too many people.

"Isn't there any way we can increase our security?" asked Natalie.

"We could make an alarm or something," suggested Lena. "I noticed the speakers in our rooms. Perhaps make an alarm that goes off if anyone enters one of our campsites."

"If we can turn it on and off like the electric stuff around Group E's campsite," said Peter, "then it'd probably work. Well, if we're in bed. What if they burst in on us like they did that time back at Marc's house and we have no warning at all?"

Marc considered this for a while before saying, slowly, "Then I guess me, John, and Natalie will really have our abilities tested."

"How about we just have someone watch us all the time?" suggested Erica. "The human factor, you know? I was under the impression that Lena, Siobhan and I had only really been brought along for that purpose anyway."

"That could work," Lena agreed. "If we do eight-hour intervals, then we'll all have plenty of time for eating, sleeping and bathing too."

Siobhan looked very nervous by this. "I've seen the things you guys use, the weird knives and those things that shoot that white stuff, but I've never used any of them before. How can I defend myself if I get in a tangle with Hammerhearts?"

"She makes a good point," said Serena. "Perhaps we'll have to give her plenty of practise before she can actually stand guard around here."

"Do we need a guard for all three sites or just the one we're using?" Peter asked. "If we can get into the bedrooms from all three sites…"

That put a dampener on the sentry idea. The easiest way to get past the sentry would be to enter the bedrooms by using one of the unguarded campsites, unless we had Erica, Lena, and Siobhan watching a separate site each, but how could they possibly do that around the clock? I found myself wishing we had brought a few more people. Harry, Simon, Katie, Sophie, Jessica, and Felicity— with those six on site, we could have had all three sites covered for twenty-four hours a day. Too late now, though. The portal had long since closed and wouldn't be opening for another three months. By then, our business would be well and truly done here.

"Anyone got any other ideas?" said Serena flatly.

"I have a possible idea," said Marc quietly. "Let me just see something."

He held the Hero Crystal up before his eyes, staring into it and clearly feeding on some mental energy from it. We all waited curiously to see what he was trying to do. Finally, he looked back up at us, his expression relieved.

"I wanted to do this a few weeks ago," he told us, "but the crystal was sending me bad vibes about it. I don't really understand why. Perhaps there was too much magic being used in too many places all at the one time. In any case, it seems to have settled down just enough that I can do it without any unexpected consequences."

His words sounded familiar. I knew where I had heard them and thought I understood what his idea was. "You're thinking of calling Fewul?"

There was a collective gasp around the tree house. "Fewul?"

"Yeah, that was my idea," Marc replied. "I'm well aware that we could do a lot more with the Beast of Magic than guard us while we sleep or while we're away from the campsites, but I really do think it's all we'll need it for. It doesn't exactly have its own life, see, which means it can probably split itself into three so it can guard each site. It certainly wouldn't need to sleep, and if we want it to guard us as we walk around the island as well, it could probably find a way to do that too. Finally, if Hammerhearts do come calling, it has the power to deal with them without being damaged in any way itself."

A short silence followed this speech. I always felt nervous when I thought too deeply about the Beast of Magic. My first impression of it wasn't a good one, after all. If Marc was right, though, it would be useful now, and if we didn't call it back, it could be even more useful when we got back home. It had been fine the last time we had used it, with the exception of it causing William, Carl, and Lisa to be eternally damned. I supposed if we were to take any of its advice this time, we should remember to ask all questions first.

"You're sure it's not dangerous?" Natalie asked.

"Pretty sure," said Marc, grinning. "So should we step outside and see what happens?"

"*Pretty* sure?" James repeated. "That doesn't sound too comforting. Is that how you work before taking potentially life threatening risks, Marc?"

"Okay, I'm absolutely, completely, unutterably sure," said Marc exasperatedly. "Trust me, I've got this."

There was still plenty of tension around the room, but Marc seemed not about to be swayed. He got to his feet and headed for the door, muttering the password as he went.

"Marc, hang on," said Erica frantically. "Shouldn't we talk about this first?"

"It's fine," he repeated. "Trust me, I know what I'm doing, or at least—(he waved his fist full of crystal at us)—the Hero Crystal knows what I'm doing."

"You sure the crystal couldn't be leading you on?" Natalie asked.

"I don't think it would be," I said, also getting to my feet. "I've had the feeling that the Sien-Leoard Crystal has led me on before, but that's understandable 'cause it has the power of the Villain and Darkness Crystals in it as well. Marc's is just the Hero Crystal, so do you think it would lead him on?"

There was a general grumbling at this, but a few more people were on their feet now. Outside the door, Marc was already summoning magic from the air and drawing it towards himself and the crystal in his hand. The process had already begun—too late for anyone to stop it now. The crystal in Marc's hand was glowing, shooting jets of white light into the air. Grey smoke was pouring from it, forming into a large shape in front of Marc.

"What form do you guys want it to take?" Marc asked. "Actually, what three forms?"

"How about Amelia?" suggested Natalie. "Make Hammerhearts think she's come with us if they see Fewul."

"And Marc's dad and Lucien could be the other two," added Peter. "I would have suggested Stella, but that might be a bit of a giveaway if they know she's with her family at the same time."

"Or if her family thinks she's up to no good," added Natalie.

Marc, most of his attention on what he was doing, nodded and gave the order to the beast before him just as it had become a solid shape—that great, black teddy bear its natural form seemed to resemble. The beast split into three and each form shrank and reformed. Moments later, Marc's dad appeared to be standing directly in front of him, with Lucien at his left hand and Amelia (my heart stopped at the sight of her) at his right. I knew it wasn't the real Amelia, yet I couldn't prevent the wave of desire crashing over me. There was something seriously disturbing about desiring the Beast of Magic, even in this form.

"Good God," I heard Underwood roar behind me.

"I've seen her before," said Siobhan, "but who are those two?"

"Everyone back in the tree house," Marc called, "nothing to see here. Fewul, you come too, but from now on I'll be calling each of your forms by the name of the person you're imitating."

Amelia, Moran, and Lucien all nodded in unison (it was an extremely odd sight), and they all followed Marc back into the tree house, the rest of us scuttling out of their way. Marc muttered the password again to close the door and took his seat, the Beast of Magic in its three forms standing behind him.

"So one of them will guard up here," mused Tommy. "Who's going where?"

"My dad up here," said Marc. "Lucien down in Group F's site and Amelia in Group E's. Is that okay with everyone else? I don't think it would make much of a difference, to be honest, but we might as well do it that way."

Nobody had any objections, so Marc sent the beast on its way. Moran could soon be sitting on the balcony outside the tree house while Lucien and Amelia had set off for the ground and their respective spots to guard.

"Marc," I said quietly, unable to deal with the nagging feeling any longer. "I just—I have to know. Those two Hammerhearts you said died, did they—like—was it something I did?"

They all noticed my tone and knew what it meant. A few looked troubled, most looked sympathetic, but Marc didn't seem too concerned. "It was a plane crash, John. They collided with each other. The passengers both ejected, but there was no time for either of the pilots. That's not your fault. If anything, it's their fault for getting in our way."

I wasn't sure I agreed with that entirely, but at least it wasn't a direct result of my magic. It was really more a result of their own disorganisation that had caused the mix-up that had cost those two Hammerhearts—hopefully evil and not under an influential charm— their lives. I did feel a bit better about that, and I reckoned it wouldn't keep me up at night. Compared to what I'd done in the gym, it certainly wouldn't.

And that was pretty much it for the rest of the day. Marc created a telephone and used it to let the Woodwards know that we had arrived safely at Rock Haulter, but not without trouble, and that the Hammerhearts knew someone against them was here. We all tried our mobile phones first, but unsurprisingly, there was no signal here. We then had dinner at around half past six (another dinner) and split up for the night, the atmosphere being generally two awkward for us all to have a relaxing conversation. I had spent the rest of the evening in my room with Serena, but my mind strayed to Tommy and Natalie at regular intervals, and what might be going through each of their minds at that very moment.

* * *

It was two o'clock in the morning and I was wide awake. In the dream, I had crept up to the main hall in the dark, as quietly as possible lest any of the Hammerhearts notice me. There had been something inside that hall, something behind those doors that I had to see—needed to see. I had edged the door open and slipped through it, not bothering to close it behind me. The sooner I could get this over with, the better. Yet as I took a few steps farther into the gloom, a gust of wind suddenly blew the door shut behind me.

The thud wasn't very loud, yet it had seemed to resound. That had been when I realised that I wasn't alone in that hall, a fact I hadn't been aware of until then. I knew who was with me, and sure enough, as I had turned slightly to my right, there she was, standing only ten feet from me. She was waiting for me to approach her, waiting and ready to take off, ready to goad me into giving chase as she seemed to enjoy doing. I approached slowly, closing the distance very gradually—it seemed to take forever.

Eventually, though, I had found myself in front of her, closer than I'd ever managed to get. She raised her arms slightly, as though inviting me to come between them. Slowly, not wanting to frighten her away, I moved in, raising my own arms as I went. For the first time, I was touching Stella in my dreams. The moment had held for perhaps one second, or just about any amount of time given the way dreams usually worked. It was cut short when the world around us erupted into a great burst of fire. It illuminated everything, danced over both our faces, seared both our bodies, yet all I could see through my eyes was Stella—and all I could see was myself through Stella's eyes.

I had woken and found myself sitting up in bed, covered in sweat and my bed covers wrapped so tightly around me that I could barely move. For a few seconds, however, I didn't even try, for the vision of the flames was still flickering behind my eyes and, predictably, it quickly changed to my vision that had become just as regular as the recurring dreams. Blackness—smoky—red, hot, fiery —and in the middle of it all, Stella, just as she had been looking at me in the dream, her bright blue eyes her only easily discernible feature. I shook my head hard and struggled out of the doona that seemed to want to squeeze me to death.

I didn't understand what it meant, why it had come up now just after I'd arrived on Rock Haulter, as it had the last time I'd been here, or what the fire was supposed to resemble. I knew nothing for certain in that quarter, but what I suspected was that if the main hall was somehow involved in my history, and what had happened at the very end of the dream suggested it certainly had been, I was in the right place to work out what was going on. I didn't have to wait for Smiley. What was the harm in having a quick look for myself?

I got out of bed and dressed hastily. The air would be pretty chilly out there, so I rugged up, gathered the Sien-Leoard Crystal, and crept out into the empty tree house. There, I sent my mind outward, first checking that my fellow travellers were asleep (they all were) and then the surrounding area for Hammerhearts (there were none). The only conscious being in the vicinity was Fewul, in the form of Moran, sitting on the side of the balcony. Would he say anything to me as I passed him? That would be weird on two levels —talking to Moran now that I knew who he really was, and then knowing it wasn't really Moran at all.

As it turned out, however, he only watched me as I passed. I waved at him once and he seemed to take it to mean I was no harm. I hoped he would react the same when I returned. I climbed easily and rather effortlessly down to the ground and fought my way through the trees to the path. By that stage, I was wide awake and ready for just about anything, despite the fact that I'd gotten no more than four hours sleep after a very long day. I had no idea what to expect. In fact, what I expected was nothing at all, but I had to try this, anyway, for my own peace of mind if nothing else.

The trees opened up suddenly and there it was, a dark shadow just a hundred feet away from me. I approached it at a jog, one hand on the Sien-Leoard Crystal but not yet performing any magic. I was well aware of the possible danger yet didn't feel a need to make myself invisible or give myself any extra protection. I closed the little remaining distance to the closed doors of the hall in very little time and stopped in front of them. I had a vivid memory of the vice principal telling us all that we were not permitted to enter the hall while the doors were closed. Old demons were hard to shake off, it seemed. I pulled down on one of the handles. It was locked, so I squeezed the crystal. The handle came down easily. I edged the door open a fraction, just as I had in the dream and slipped inside, but this time, I pulled it shut behind me.

The hall looked very different from the last time I had physically been here. It appeared that the Russians had a different purpose for it than what we had done with it. That made perfect sense given their numbers. I supposed that it would be set up properly during the following day, but for now it contained nothing more exciting than boxes stacked on top of more boxes. A few of them had been unloaded, it seemed, for at the far end of the room where the stage area had been last time, a row of desks had been set up. There was nothing on them yet.

I moved farther into the room, listening hard for any sound above or to either side of me. Marc had said that they were sleeping in the rooms above the hall. Where the teachers had slept last time, in other words. It wouldn't have cost me too much if my footsteps were heard from up there, but it would have been an inconvenience if I had to flee in a hurry. I couldn't think of anything else to do but continue walking and hope that the fact that I was alone in here would help me in some way.

The good thing was that it did feel different now from how it had on camp for the obvious reason that it wasn't full of a chattering buzz of students. It meant that I could concentrate on—on what? I didn't know. Maybe the idea was not to concentrate at all but instead allow my mind to relax completely and go wherever it willed. I stopped walking, surrounded by towering rows of boxes, and just stood there, breathing deeply and reflecting on one simple fact: I was back in the place I had dreamt of so often over the last three months. Not just that. I was back in the place where it had all begun. That was what Smiley had said. Where what began? What exactly did this place mean to me? Why did I feel, the first time I had set foot in this place in February, that I had been here before?

My state of relaxation had become so complete that I was in danger of toppling over backwards against the boxes, but that never happened. Instead, something much more bizarre happened: I felt as though I had moved somehow, but in no particular direction that I could identify. The atmosphere seemed to have changed too. It was as though it had become thinner, more flaky. I reached out to steady myself against the nearest row of boxes, and while I felt my hand touch the cardboard, it never actually made contact but instead sank right into the box (I discovered that it contained books of some kind). That wasn't the most alarming thing, though. The feeling also came accompanied by voices, a quiet but positive babble of them. The loudest of them were speaking Russian but there were others too, more distant voices that were speaking English, and I recognised one of them as the vice principal's, ordering students to hand all their quizzes in and head back to their campsites to pack up.

I could have jumped with shock at the recognition, and the moment I realised this, the world as I had always known it suddenly returned. My hands hadn't touched anything in reality (whatever reality was—who could be sure), but now I really did stagger and reach out for the nearest box. Thankfully, I was able to grip it without any problem. Even more thankfully, the column didn't topple. All I could do was stand there and wonder. What on earth had just happened to me? The scariest thing about that was I hadn't even been touching the Sien-Leoard Crystal when that had happened. If it wasn't the crystal's doing, then how could I have suddenly heard voices from the past? Not just ones I'd heard before but more recent ones that I only knew about?

I stood there for a few more minutes, wanting the sensation to return so that I could examine it more properly, but the longer I tried, the more I came to realise that it wasn't going to work tonight. Apparently, I needed to be completely relaxed to allow it, and I simply couldn't calm down after what had just happened. I gave up and began trying to find my way back to the door. It turned out to be trickier than I had expected, but by using the crystal to give myself a light, I managed it in only a few extra minutes.

472

I headed back to the tree house, now wondering in the cool air of the morning if I hadn't just imagined the whole thing. I didn't believe I had just imagined it, but then how could it have happened if it wasn't just my imagination? I knew full well that the whole group wouldn't have believed me if I dared to tell them, so I didn't even entertain the idea. What about Smiley, though? He was the man behind so much of this, after all. Could he provide some sort of explanation for what had happened? I had no idea, but I knew that if anyone could, it would be him.

Chapter 29: The Old Man

The first thing I did when I woke up the following morning was contact Smiley with the life assistant and let him know that we had arrived on the island. The second thing I did was apologise to him in case I had woken him up, but to my surprise, he said he'd been awake for hours already. He informed me of the location of the chamber in which he resided but told us we would need to make another stop-off somewhere else before we could get to it. I highly doubted it would be necessary, what with four of the five Magic Crystals and a Sorcerer with us, but most of us agreed that the best thing to do would be to just take his advice.

"It just seems a little silly to me," said Serena irritably, not cheered by the prospect of a whole load of extra walking.

"Trust me, it'd be worth it," said Tommy firmly. "He must know that we have magic with us. Whatever he's got in mind will make things easier for us somehow, I'm sure of it."

So at around ten o'clock, we left Moran (Fewul) guarding the tree house and descended through the trees back towards the path. For a layer of security, Natalie wrapped another invisibility veil around us as we walked, just in case. She also put a soundproof barrier around us, but unlike the one Amelia used to protect herself against Underwood, this one only worked one way—sound from the outside came in, but any noise we made on the inside wouldn't go back out. The only way we could be discovered now would be if one of us accidentally smacked into a Hammerheart. The initial intention of Siobhan, Erica, and Lena not really being involved in our business with Smiley seemed to have faded slightly, for now that we had Fewul doing the job we had planned for them, there was nothing else for them to do but keep us company. I didn't mind too much for now, but I hoped we could find another use for them soon. Particularly Lena, who would soon, if this trend continued, learn a lot more about me than she already knew.

We approached the rock and made our way west around it, passing the opening that led to the Group F campsite and the path that led up to the Group E campsite. Neither form of Fewul was visible from outside the rock. We passed the place where we had done rock climbing on camp and even the slope that led up to where Moran (the real Moran) had hidden. It was around now that I suddenly remembered the woman—the ghost woman—my mother. Could she possibly still be here on Rock Haulter somewhere? Was it possible that I might get to meet her? Perhaps even speak to her? There was something distinctly awkward about speaking to Moran as my father, but those feelings didn't exist at all when it came to my mother. I could never see her as anything other than peaceful, something that I could definitely not say for my father. I supposed I still didn't know for certain what she'd been in life (perhaps she too had been a Hammerheart), but something, perhaps my own prejudice, made it nearly impossible to believe she had been. But then, why had she put up with him being a Hammerheart? It was all so confusing, but I couldn't bring myself to think ill of my deceased mother.

Sunlight came back to us as we continued to round the rock, now reaching the south side of the island. There were many caves around here, most of them well up the rock face but a few of them close to ground level. I had to start concentrating on these caves now. Smiley had said it was somewhere around here that we would need to start climbing. It would be distinctive by a cave opening the shape of a smiley (surely that had to be a coincidence), but it was not the smiley cave we would be entering. A track passed just directly above it, and once we reached that track, we just had to follow it up for about two hundred metres. According to Smiley, it ended in a hole, and if we fell in that hole, we'd have a lot of trouble getting back out, but there was a cave just to the left of that hole and it was in here that we had to go.

"How much farther to go?" James groaned.

"Say that again and I'll spare you the trouble of walking by levitating you ten feet in the air hanging upside-down," said Natalie irritably. "I'm sure you've done more walking than this, James, or have you just not been keeping fit lately?"

"Probably haven't been," he panted. "I mean, we're not allowed out so much anymore. We're not all so lucky to get out every day to protect the lives of the—"

"Don't get snippy," snapped Tommy. "Once we get to wherever Smiley is, you can relax all you like. Just hang in there, mate."

"There it is," I said suddenly, pointing. The smiley on the rock face was a little jagged, but that had to be it, all right, and there was the track right above it. All we had to do to get to the track was climb up a few ledges.

"That thing looks ready to eat us," Marc remarked.

"We're not going in there," I told him. "Follow me. Natalie, make sure you've got James's back in case he lets go."

"Your support is invaluable to me, John," James panted, attempting to exchange a wicked glance with Peter that the latter seemed to miss.

I led them up those few ledges until we were able to climb up onto the track in question. The smiley mouth was about ten feet farther up the track from here, and as long as nobody accidentally fell into it, we would be okay for now. I set off down the track, Marc, Peter, and Tommy close behind me. James and Natalie were bringing up the rear, but Underwood, who was in front of James, was certainly taking this part of his adventure reluctantly, almost as reluctantly as he'd been back at Siobhan's house. Erica, Serena, Lena, and Siobhan were in the middle of the pack and they were just being generally quiet, perhaps not sure what to expect. That was totally understandable, as none but Serena had any inkling of what Smiley was about.

There was the hole ahead of us. It had been easy to see from farther down the track but seemed to become more disguised the closer we got to it. What made this part of the adventure more difficult was that there were quite a few caves up here. We needed the one just to the left of the hole—that was what Smiley had said. Did he mean that cave there? Or did he mean the hole just in front of that cave that made it almost impossible to get into?

"Er," I said, coming to a stop. Thank God I did when I did, for as I looked down, I realised I'd almost fallen straight into the hole at the end of the track.

I looked left at the cave. That had to be it, surely, but could Smiley have been referring to that hole as a cave? I edged over to it and glanced down. Its interior was completely black and ominous. I bent, scooped a few loose rocks off the ground, and tossed them into the hole, listening hard to hear them land. Several seconds later, I heard the tiniest of splashes.

"If there's water in there, then it's probably not it," said Tommy. "At least, I hope it's not it."

"I think that's it," I said, pointing to the cave now directly ahead of us. "Hang on."

There was no easy way to get to that cave without using magic, so I gripped the crystal and a moment later, a narrow bridge crossed the hole to the cave.

"That thing doesn't look very strong," Peter said hesitantly.

"One at a time, then," I said, and without looking back, I took the bridge at a brisk walk.

It rocked from side to side as I walked but never gave. I reached the entrance to the cave without any difficulty. The others all crossed more hesitantly than I had, but apart from Erica almost losing her balance and grabbing the rope rails for support, none of them had any trouble. Soon enough, we were all on the other side.

Remembering that we'd have to come back this way, I decided not to get rid of the bridge for now.

"So what now?" Marc asked. "We just go into this cave?"

"Reckon so," I said. "Smiley didn't give me any further advice, so the rest of it must be pretty straightforward. The only other stuff he told me was how to find him after we've done this."

"I still think we're wasting our time up here." Serena sniffed.

"Too late to turn back now," said Tommy, shrugging. "You ready to lead us on, John? Maybe make a light or something first, though."

I obliged, but it turned out not to be necessary for long. The cave turned out not to be very deep. There was a door set into the back of it with an L keyhole beside it. I had brought both keys with me when we'd left about an hour ago now and I took the L-key out now, inserted it into the hole, and turned it. The door opened inwards and the others preceded me inside. I took the key from the lock, but the door didn't close as I had expected it to, so, assuming that it would do so automatically after a certain amount of time as the ones guarding the Sien-Leoard Crystal had, I hurried through it.

The new room must have had magical motion sensors installed because it lit up when we had entered. Our eyes hadn't quite adjusted to the dark, so the new brightness didn't bother us too much. It was a long, narrow room that stretched off into the distance. I couldn't even see the far wall. The wall to our right was bare, but to our left, it was a different story. Waist-high rails stretched out from the walls about halfway across the room, dividing the floor into what looked rather like parking spaces. In fact, that was what they were, for parked between each set of rails was an odd-looking contraption I had never seen before. This had to be the reason why Smiley had sent us up this way. He wanted us to use these things.

"What are those?" asked Lena.

"They look a bit like dodgem cars," Serena remarked.

Underwood snorted. "He made us come up here for dodgem cars? Are you telling me that I came all this way to meet my grandfather only to find he's got dementia?"

"Does it matter? He's still your grandfather," said Siobhan, her voice cold enough to create icicles.

"Guys," said Marc in a hushed voice. He had his fingers around the Hero Crystal and his face was transported. "Guys, these are hovercars."

Hovercars? Really? A few of us moved forward cautiously to examine the nearest few. Each car seemed to vary from the one next to it. For one thing, they were all different colours, mostly bright colours apart from the shiny blacks and greys. Mostly they were oval shapes, but some of them were higher than others, some longer than others, and some less rounded than others, but the interior of them appeared the same. They were all one-seater and roofless. If these really were hovercars, then it would probably explain why Smiley had sent us up here. Having access to these really would make things easier for us as far as getting around the mountain went.

"Well, we might as well test them out," said Natalie. "Maybe I should go first, since nothing really bad could possibly happen to me."

She picked out a small, pink hovercar and jumped in. She started it up by pushing a button. The noise it made was odd, nothing more than a quiet humming that would probably increase in volume as she drove it forward. As we watched, the car rose slowly into the air until it was hovering three feet off the floor. Natalie was sitting back in her seat and looking perfectly relaxed.

"Guys, you might as well pick your cars and get moving," she called. "These things are super easy to operate."

She put her foot down and the car shot forward, not very fast but certainly enough in the confined space. The car came to within a few feet of the wall and seemed to hover there, knowing it couldn't approach any farther. She turned it back the other way and tore at the row of hovercars. Her car rose farther into the air in the few feet between them and hovered right over the top of them, before shooting right over all our heads (we felt a great gust of air push down on us so that we were all forced into a temporary crouch) and out the door.

"Hey, wait up," Peter called.

The rest of us quickly jumped in random cars and tried to work out how to get them moving. Mine was one of the longer ones, a bright red colour. There was a single button that was to turn it on and off, a steering wheel, two pedals on the floor, a seat belt and shoulder straps, and that was it. I strapped myself in, started it up, waited for it to rise three feet into the air, and turned it for the door. The others were ready to go now too. After they had all shot past me, Underwood bringing up the rear in a big, black thing, I left the room in their wake, hoping Natalie hadn't gone too far.

Firstly, though, I turned my car back to the door and looked at the keyhole. The L-key was back in my pocket, and now I took it out and tried to get close enough to turn the lock back. If that didn't close this door, then nothing would. The car didn't want to get close enough to the wall, however, so I had to jump out and down to the ground to manage it. Once the door was closed (thank God it worked), I leapt back up into the car, fastened my seat belt and shoulder straps again, and tore out of the cave.

The others were all zooming around the rock face above and below the cave I was in. I scanned them and was pleased to note that there were ten of them. The cars seemed able to fly over just about anything the mountain could throw at them. In the time I watched, I saw Siobhan's pale blue car take an eighty-degree slope without so much as a cough. The only thing I thought might cause the cars difficulty was if they fell in a hole like the one directly in front of me. Ninety degrees or higher was probably beyond them, and if water got in the way, then—well I didn't want to think about that. Those were only minor drawbacks, though. These hovercars would really be useful.

On the heels of this thought came a more dismaying one: If the Hammerhearts got hold of these, then it would make their lives a lot easier too. I therefore scanned for Marc, spotted him in a shiny bronze-coloured hovercar a little way down the track, and began hovering my car over the rickety bridge I'd created earlier to get to him. Once I got back on the track, I vanished the bridge with the crystal before attempting to work my way through the cars zooming around ahead of me. I nearly collided with three different hovercars. On one occasion, my car jumped over theirs, while the other times it was they who jumped over me. Eventually, though, I managed to hover up beside Marc.

"We need to put a defence here," I told him. "If the Hammerhearts get hold of these—"

"I thought of that before," Marc replied. "I'll get Fewul onto it when we get back to the campsite, whichever one. You reckon I should make the form up here resemble one of the other Woodwards?"

"I was thinking one of the twins," I told him, "or Katie or Sophie or—well, any of them. You get the idea. Don't you think we should go find Smiley now?"

"Agree," he said and began calling to the others around us to gather in close so that we could conference. They all came reluctantly, clearly wanting to have a bit more fun with their hovercars.

"Listen, Nat," Peter called across to her, "could you do your invisibility thing again? I know we're probably still invisible, but these cars might not be under the veil."

"I expect you're right about that," she agreed, and performed a binding spell by raising her arms over her head and circling them.

"Okay, good," I called to them all. "Now listen, I've got a pretty good idea where Smiley's cave is, and these things will make it a lot easier to get to it. All you guys need to do is follow me and make sure no one gets lost."

I turned and guided the car down the track, right down to the smiley and over the ledges. The car hovered easily back down to the ground. I probably could have kept up on the rock face, but apart from being dangerous, what with all those holes and caves up there, it was much easier to keep my bearings down here. I looked over my shoulder once to make sure the others were following me and, satisfied that they were, took off eastward.

Smiley's place of residence was in a cave around the eastern side of the mountain, not too far from the one the Hammerhearts were using, incidentally, but much farther up and much more secure. In fact, we wouldn't be able to get in at all unless he chose to let us in—which, of course, he would, since we had Underwood with us. He never went into any of the details about the sort of security we would be confronted with when we got there. All he had told me was that it was in a cave approximately eight hundred feet above the ground on the eastern side of the mountain and that it was distinctive by the golden rocks glittering just above it.

We just kept driving, farther and farther east, all the while keeping an eye out for Hammerhearts. The rock began shielding the sun from us at around one o'clock as we gradually turned towards the north. It was about ten minutes later that I decided we had better start climbing the mountain. We had so far done well at not being noticed by anyone, but we were surely starting to cut it fine. I turned to the left and began climbing the car up the slope, a fifty-degree slope at this particular spot. Eight hundred feet was a fair way up so I just kept on going, dodging the various caves and holes and continually looking back over my shoulder to see the others snaking along behind me.

I decided, when I was probably about halfway up, to use the crystal to assist in the navigation. It began urging me towards the left, meaning that I had gone too far north on the ground earlier. I veered in that direction, still dodging the caves, many of them no more than little holes that contained nothing but were inconveniences, until I finally saw it, far off to the left—a set of bright gold rocks, very distinct from the various shades of brown, grey, and black of the rest of the rock face. Below the golden rocks was a cave, a rather small cave. Getting the hovercars in there would be a challenge, but again, I reminded myself, Smiley wouldn't have asked us to get them if he didn't think we could park them somewhere.

"Follow me this way!" I bellowed over my shoulder at them, and began turning left and heading that way, my car hovering on a forty-degree sideways angle.

To my surprise, I had been wrong about the cave. It may have been small but the hovercar fit into it just perfectly, and once it was in and heading down a narrow slope, the going was easy. The new passage twisted and turned in just about every direction—left, right, up, down—but the hovercar took care of everything. It was completely dark, but that didn't even matter. The car would veer when it came too close to a wall and tilt up or down when it came to slopes, and all I had to do was keep the acceleration steady and not too fast.

Finally, after several minutes of this, with nothing but the noise of the car and the echoes of the other cars behind me, the passage opened out into a much larger area, dimly lit by an unidentifiable source. There were no parking spots, as there had been where we had picked up the cars, yet there was definitely enough room for them. There was already a small, shiny, silver hovercar parked in here— Smiley's, I supposed. Opposite me was a small, grey door with a keyhole next to it. I drove up to it and parked within a few feet of it. I pushed the button to turn the car off and heard the fans below it gradually easing up so that it slowly lowered itself back to the floor. The others began piling in beside me and turning their own cars off.

"This is it," Peter said quietly, sounding rather awed. I couldn't blame him. Smiley had definitely found a nice place to set up residence. Had he somehow created this? I doubted it. This mountain would have been full of mysteries like this just waiting to be utilised by someone.

I got out of my car and approached the door, thinking of the security Smiley had set around himself. When I saw the letter above the keyhole, however, I was surprised again. Apparently the first layer of security was one we could deal with easily enough. I heard the others gathering behind me as I stared at the keyhole.

"You gonna open it, John?" James asked.

"Sure," I said, and withdrawing the L-key again, I inserted it into the lock and turned it.

The door swung inwards again, revealing another room beyond it, this one very different from anywhere we had so far seen inside the mountain. It was softly carpeted in a natural, grassy substance, but below that substance was the same rocky surface as anywhere else. The walls were tiled and the roof was lit up with long, pleasantly glowing lights. Several armchairs and couches were placed around a low coffee table that presently had nothing on it. Directly opposite the door was another door, also closed, but instead of a keyhole, it had an intercom next to it. Other than that, the room was empty.

"Is that his admirable security?" James asked, staring at the intercom. "Well, maybe there's a camera in there that I can't see, but you'd hope that door there is pretty damn strong."

The others all gathered in behind us, looking around. Several of them took seats and waited for someone else to do something. Natalie took the opportunity to lift the invisibility veil and soundproof barrier off us. At least Smiley would be able to communicate with us now. After about two minutes, the door swung shut of its own accord.

"Oh great," said Underwood. "So does that mean we're all stuck in here now?"

"No, we will not be stuck in here," said Marc. "I could probably use the crystal to get us out if Smiley doesn't know a better way. Where is he, anyway?"

"In there, probably," said James. "Who wants to call him?"

Tommy and I were the only two on our feet. I made the decision for him by scooting across the room and falling into a seat beside Serena.

"Okay," he said, "let's see how we go." He pressed down on the button and said, "Sir, I dunno if you know we're here, but—er—we're here."

"Clever," muttered Underwood. Marc, who was sitting next to him, elbowed him to make him be quiet.

"Hello to you, young Tommy," said a jittery, British-speaking old voice from the speaker that nevertheless carried all around the room. The sound of it seemed to make Underwood shiver. "Now, what have I told you about forgetting to say hello when you commence a conversation?"

"Sorry, sir," said Tommy sheepishly.

"I am very pleased to hear your voice again," the voice said. "I will join you in the sitting room in a few minutes. Please wait quietly."

"Will do, sir," said Tommy, and he left the intercom and took a seat beside Lena.

Silence followed, the anticipation palpable. Most of them were surely unsure what to expect. Tommy knew exactly what to expect and was merely looking forward to seeing his mentor again. For me and Underwood, the moment was more significant. In both of our cases, this old man was at least partially responsible for us being alive today. I felt Serena's small hand creep into my own and I gripped it tightly. It was a small gesture, but definitely one I appreciated.

At just before half past one, the door beside the intercom creaked and swung open. From the other side of it, a voice called out, "Welcome to all of you."

Rafael Smiley entered the room, pulling the door shut behind him. He was holding a remote control of some sort in his other hand, but I had barely a thought to spare for it.

"*Holy crap!*" I burst out before I could stop myself.

I knew I was being disrespectful, but I simply couldn't prevent the words from exploding out of me. If the Transgators at school, Marc's hidden quarters, the Light and Darkness Crystals, and the infrastructure the Hammersons had built were the strangest things I'd ever seen in my life, they had all suddenly lost their place.

"John!" several voices protested in alarm.

"It is okay, my friends, it is okay," said Smiley reassuringly. He took a seat on Tommy's other side and turned to face him. "How are you, young Tommy? Been practicing like I asked you, I suppose?"

Tommy shrugged guiltily. "A little bit, but not as much as I used to. I guess not having lessons has taken some of the regular wind out of my sales, but I still practise Leoard's Lament. You know, just in case we need it."

"Very good, very good. Not perfect but still very good," he cried out. "Now, who is this beautiful young lady sitting beside you?"

The conversation went on from there with Smiley working his way around the group and, either for his own amusement or because he actually believed it, kept assuming special connections between every person sitting beside every other person. Lena was firstly Tommy's lover, and then she became Peter's lover. Then Peter became Siobhan's lover (Peter kept a straight face at this point, but Siobhan appeared to squirm under the pressure). Siobhan and Natalie were special friends, perhaps with benefits, and then Natalie was Marc's girlfriend.

Only at this point did the conversation get a little more serious, but through all of it, I couldn't take my eyes off the man's appearance. He was definitely alive. That is to say, he was not a ghost, yet he appeared not to be completely solid either. I couldn't see the back of his seat through his form, yet at times I thought I could see through him, at least around the edges. The phenomenon seemed to give him a shimmering quality, but if the others' lack of reaction was anything to go by, I was the only one who could see it. Why?

"The Seventh Sorcerer," Smiley cried out, pointing at Marc. "Now I've been looking forward to meeting you, young man. A very special place in magical history you will now hold, don't you agree?"

"Well, if you wanna believe the prophecy and think I'm the only one who'll ever use magic," said Marc shiftily, "then you may be right."

"But he's too modest to actually agree with you outright," added Lena, grinning at Marc. Marc tried very hard to hide his reaction to that grin, but I knew what that squirm meant all too well. If I hadn't been in public, I would have grinned and rubbed my hands together in satisfaction.

"Believe the prophecy," Smiley cried out, pointing at him again. "Did it lead you wrong last time? Of course it did not. Question Sien and Leoard's prophecies at your own peril, young man. Now—"

His gaze moved to Underwood, who had been looking extremely awkward the whole time, but who now raised his eyes and met Smiley's unflinchingly.

"Good to see you, at last, Jacob," said the old man, much more solemnly than he had spoken since he had entered the room.

"You too, Pop," said Underwood, his voice hitching slightly on the last word. To most people's intense embarrassment, especially given what we all thought of his character, there were tears deep in his eyes, but he held them back for now.

Smiley continued around the circle, speaking to but not spending long on James, Erica, and Serena, before finally reaching me. We met each other's eyes for a few seconds before, unable to stand it a moment longer, I simply said, "Hi."

"Hello, young John," Smiley cried out, pointing at me just as he had done to several people already. "Good to see you again, and in much less trying circumstances."

"I suppose so," I said uneasily.

Smiley didn't spend any more time on that topic for now but instead turned to the group at large and said, "I am very pleased to see you all. I knew you would be coming eventually."

"That's good," said Natalie, a little edgily, "but you could have made it a little easier to find you. It took us two whole months."

"Ah, but what is the good in simply knowing where to go, young Natalie?" Smiley asked, turning his odd gaze on her. "Wouldn't you agree that the true discovery is in the journey rather than the destination?"

Natalie looked stumped by that. James took over. "I would agree with that, sir, for we did actually learn a few interesting things along the way, like about John's parents and coming across—*him*—(he jerked his head at Underwood)—but you have to understand, the search did take a toll on us. How do we know that lives weren't lost because of the delay?"

"How can you know that more lives wouldn't have been lost if there had been little or no delay?" Smiley retorted.

James now looked flustered too, but he didn't let down his stand. "We obviously have no way of knowing how things would be different now if a different course had been taken months ago, but it's enough to suppose, given the way the Hammersons have been playing their cards in recent weeks, that if we could have prevented them from coming this far, it is most probable that they could never have done the sort of damage they have."

Leave it to James to spearhead our attack in such an intellectual debate, I thought, and the irritation I'd had with James since last Thursday was gone in a stroke.

"My dear boy," said Smiley solemnly, "your argument is entirely predicated on the assumption that the information I can give you can have a drastic influence on the Hammersons' momentum."

That wrong footed James completely. He opened his mouth, closed it, opened it again, and said, rather weakly, "I was under the impression that it could."

"No, we weren't," said Marc quickly. "Look, Mr. Smiley—"

"My dear boy," Smiley cried out, pointing dramatically at Marc. I had a vivid mental image of Smiley in a court of law, pointing up at the judge, the lawyers, and each member of the jury each time he addressed them. I had to fight down a laugh. "You may refer to me as Rafael, if you too will permit me to call you Marc."

"Okay, er, Rafael," said Marc, smiling slightly. "We knew you couldn't give us information that would really change things; otherwise, you would have given it all to Mr. Woodward and we wouldn't have had to come here at all. We understand that, but what James is trying to say, I think, is that the sooner we could have had this information, the sooner we could have acted on it, and perhaps that could have been more beneficial to our side. Anyway, that doesn't matter. We're here now, and I guess it's time we had a long discussion about everything."

"You, Marc," Smiley cried out, pointing at him again, "you have already proven yourself a worthy Seventh Sorcerer. Not only do you accept the way things have turned, which is, of course, essential if you wish to have any positive impact on the situation, but you understand that dwelling on hypothetical scenarios of the past is negative, unproductive, and will lead you nowhere at all. You, James, you could benefit from young Marc's wisdom here."

James went pink and sank back into his seat. Still a little weakly, he said, "That was only my point, Rafael. I do understand that there's no point dwelling on hypothetical scenarios—"

"Again, boy, you have missed the boat," Smiley cried out, pointing at James now. "Hypothetical scenarios may be extremely useful if you are looking ahead. *Ahead, boy, ahead.* What is the use of looking back and saying, 'If we did this, that may have happened.' It is completely pointless, but looking forward, now that is a different story, my friend."

James shrugged again but made no reply.

"My young friends, all of you," the old man said, spreading his arms wide, "I am in the way of believing that none of you are precisely unintelligent, yet you must understand and accept certain things before I can impart to you the knowledge and wisdom I believe you have come to seek from me. That, right there—(he pointed at Marc again)—is the most basic of truths to accept—everything that has happened, and will happen, must be accepted for what it is. We do, of course, have the power within us to change certain aspects of the future by way of our choices, but you must always remember that a decision cannot be undecided, that all actions will be reacted to, and that all the consequences that arise from our actions, as well as the reactions to those actions, rest upon each of our shoulders. I am both fortunate and unfortunate to have been given a certain talent that has gifted me with more knowledge than we, as humans, have a right to know. That is not to say that I know and understand all the mysteries of life, however. What I know has taught me that lesson in a big way—that what happens, has happened, and must be accepted for what it is."

Nobody spoke. Nobody wanted to interrupt his monologue. Everyone, however, each and every person in the room, was listening to him with rapt attention. So far, I was managing to understand him, but I had a feeling that the more philosophical he got, the more trouble I would have keeping up with him.

"So," the old man said, more quietly now, lowering his arms and resting them in his lap, "we have all come here to share knowledge and wisdom. You might ask why it had to be now, and why it had to be here. I had reasons for both. As recently as three months ago, and young Tommy here can verify this, I was not at all indisposed. I have been instead residing in various places, but all the time in what I call my 'shadow'. I would only leave my shadow when it became necessary to interact with humans. This measure was for my own safety for, as I'm sure you have all guessed, the Hammersons have had a high price on my head for a very long time. Unfortunately, at my age, I am no longer fit to run from them as I once was. That is why it was necessary to come here to Rock Haulter. I was on board your boat on the day of February the ninth, hiding in my shadow so that nobody would become aware of my presence. It was necessary that nobody, not even Frederic Woodward, know that I had finally come to this place where, I am in the way of knowing, understanding and accepting, that I will rest for the final time."

"What?" Underwood burst out at this point, unable to stop himself. "Are you saying that you're dying?"

"You look surprised, young Jacob," said Smiley quietly. "Yes, I am dying, as we all must. I have seen the length of my lifeline, and I'm afraid it does not stretch much further than this day. The actual reason for this is based on the simple fact that for a very long time, I have feared drawing any sort of attention to myself by visiting any kind of medical practitioner. This, however, is unimportant in the scheme of things. If I had cared for my health, I may have been killed by the Hammersons at the same time of the same day, or else had an unfortunate accident at that time. That, right there, is another lesson that you all must learn: Once we reach the end of our lifeline, or time span if that term is easier for you to comprehend, we must accept our drawing to the afterlife and go quietly, or else reap terrible consequences."

Eternal damnation, I thought, and shuddered as I remembered that William, Carl, Lisa, Hal and Pol Maivis, and, of course, my mother had been victims of those terrible consequences.

"So you're saying that there's no harm in being careless?" asked Peter.

"Young Peter," sighed Smiley, "if you are naturally careless with your life, then it will not matter if you attempt to be careless or not."

"Rafael," said Marc quietly, "you said there was a reason why it had to be now that we talked. Why?"

"Because, young Marc, you could not have come here until this day regardless of when you learnt of my location," said Smiley reasonably. "The timing of our meeting would always be dictated by the opening of the portals, but that is not the only reason. Each and every one of you was lacking in certain experience that I needed you to have before you could be ready for this wisdom you are seeking. Through tracking me down, you were able to learn so much more about yourselves. It was a most productive way to utilise your time. You all became most particularly resourceful, something that you will need in spades after I have finished with you. I have no answers for you, my young friends, but what I do have are certain understandings that are, in themselves, completely unrelated to the Hammersons or to the war. Once we have finished our imparting, you will go away and apply your newly found understanding to your current situation. I can only hope, very much, that it will be useful to you."

Chapter 30: Knowledge and Wisdom

"Where do we even start?" asked Natalie. "There's so much to talk about."

"The best place to begin, young Natalie, is always the first place your mind goes," said Smiley. "So, young lady, tell us what is on your mind."

Natalie blushed pink at that but determinedly held Smiley's gaze. "Okay," she said. "Well, I'm curious about how much you know about death and—well, what happened to Lisa."

"I am sorry to tell you that I know nothing at all about the mysteries of death," said Smiley solemnly. "All of us must die, of course, and it is only when that time comes that we are blessed with the knowledge and wisdom of the afterlife. Of course, by that stage, it is impossible for us to return and impart such information to those who are not ready for it, and it is right that it should be so."

"That's all true," said Peter, "but what Natalie was referring to was those who are called back as ghosts, or actually as living people."

"Ah," said Smiley, even more solemnly. "Yes, of course. Remember, once a person reaches the end of their lifeline, they must go quietly or be subjected to terrible consequences. At the point of death, and this is only a theory I have with regard to the subject, I believe that each of us is scanned by a great power that is imperceptible to us. It may be a God or gods of some kind, or it could be a natural force that has no awareness of its own. Either way, the point is that it must know, at any stage in the future, if that soul will be seen again in this dimension. If this is so, a small part of the soul in question must remain behind, in a place between dimensions where neither time nor space exist. It is in this dimension that the knowing of the future exists, but not for those poor partial souls trapped within it. They are only capable of knowing within their time span, and by time span I mean the time between their natural birth and their final death. If the person is only called back as a ghost, of course, there will be no final death; they will continue to exist until such time as they are given a second, temporary life."

"So what happens to the soul after its final death?" asked Marc. "Oh, and by final death, I assume you're referring to the second death."

"Yes, the second death," said Smiley, "but that implies that the person actually dies twice. In fact, a person who does not pass into the afterlife does not die at all. Their body dies, of course, but as you know, a body can be regenerated from the point of death a single time. When that temporary body ceases to exist, that is known as the final death. After that, the person will exist only as a partial soul, incapable of leaving the in-between in which it is trapped. They will not be able to move into the afterlife, nor will they be able to come back here, not even as a ghost. Moreover, they only exist within a certain time frame in that space. If the time of their final death has already passed, the only way to access them will be to return to the time frame in which they were between their natural life and their second life."

That didn't sound good at all. William, Carl, and Lisa had been dealt the worst hand possible, and not even by their own choosing.

"What about ghosts, then?" asked James. "Where do they fit into all of this?"

"Ghosts, too, are partial souls," said Smiley. "Souls which have, by our actions in life, prevented them from being able to pass on to the afterlife, but they can never have had their body regenerated. They instead exist as a form that is partially in and partially out of the in-between. It is where I like to spend much of my time, but I shall explain that part of my story later."

"What exactly is the 'in-between'?" asked Tommy.

Smiley considered this carefully before answering. "The world each of you see, I'm sure you will agree, is in three dimensions. You are capable of seeing two of these dimensions at any one time. We have the 'up and down'—" he leaned back in his seat and ran his hand up and down the wall behind him, "we have the 'left and right'—" he bent over and ran his hand along the floor, parallel to the couch he was sitting on, "and we have the dimension of depth, or backwards and forwards if you prefer that terminology—" he ran his hand outward from the base of the couch. "That is all well and good, but to understand the in-between, you must attempt to conceive of something more.

"Try to imagine in your minds, whether by visualisation or some other technique that works for you, a fourth dimension—a fourth direction one can move along in addition to the three I just pointed out to you."

"The fourth dimension?" James repeated, looking confused. "But isn't that time? Are you saying that you move back and forth in time in this new direction you're talking about?"

"Not at all, young James," said Smiley firmly. "The time axis—I prefer not to think of it as a dimension, although I suppose technically it is—can only be accessed in a place where it does not run. Here, in this spot along the fourth dimension, time runs ever forward, with no speeding up or slowing down. The time axis cannot be accessed if it is constantly in motion, but if you enter the in-between, where time does not exist, you suddenly have an extra option open to you: You can move along the time axis to a desired point, any desired point that is within your time span."

"I'm confused," said Natalie vaguely.

"And I'm incredulous," said James, and I smiled in spite of myself—typical James. "All the best scientists of today are sure that time doesn't always run at the same speed—"

"Ah, young James, you're not telling me anything I didn't already know," Smiley cut in. "I made a point of researching all I could about relative physics and what is believed of the space-time continuum. However, while the dimension of time may be combined with the three observable spacial dimensions, the existing theories as they stand do not allow for additional spacial dimensions. Put your existing knowledge aside for the moment; otherwise, you will have an impossible time imagining what I am trying to describe."

"I'm one step ahead of you," said Peter dully.

"If you cannot conceive of the time axis now, do not fret," said Smiley gently. "As I was saying, try to imagine a fourth direction that exists in addition to the three I demonstrated to you before. *You* cannot move along it, of course, as you are all three-dimensional beings, but that doesn't mean it does not exist. Such an important part of this is being able to understand and conceive of things that you cannot see with your eyes, hear with your ears, feel with your bodies, or perceive in any physical way. This world, the world we live in, exists at a point along the fourth dimension, as do other worlds in either direction, but there is space between these worlds, and it is in these spaces where time does not exist. As none of the three previous dimensions are accessible in these spaces either, you can also say that space does not exist."

"How do you know all this?" asked Peter. "You said something about a talent earlier—what is this talent?"

"My talent, young Peter," said Smiley, pointing at him again, "is the ability to move along the fourth dimension, become something less than a physical self so that I can leave time and space behind me. Try to imagine our world as a bowling alley: Each and every person is located at exactly the one point along the fourth dimension, which in this case would be a line straight down the centre of the lane. The in-between spaces would be the gutters, and the edges of the bowling lane between the centre and the gutters are other points along the dimension where substance is partial. It is here that ghosts exist when they are called, and it is also here where I retreat to when I hide in my shadow."

"Mr. Smiley," I said before I could stop myself.

"Rafael, young John," Smiley cried, pointing dramatically at me. "I am Rafael to you, my young friend. Proceed."

"I can see ghosts," I told him. "Not just that, but I can hear them when they speak too. What exactly does that mean for me?"

"It means that you have perception of the fourth dimension, my dear friend," Smiley cried out, pointing at me again. "It does not mean that you can access it. Do not make the mistake of confusing the two abilities. Such an ability is extremely rare, however, and I'm afraid that apart from that limited explanation, I have little knowledge of how much a person who can see ghosts in a physical sense can do."

I felt slightly disappointed but nodded anyway. He had said that so much of this was about accepting what is, so I had to accept this now.

"Rafael," said Erica hesitantly, "you said something about there being other worlds along the fourth dimension. What did you mean by that exactly?"

"Ah yes, that there are," said Smiley. "You can use the bowling alley example again to visualise them, with each lane being a new world and all three-dimensional beings in each world being exactly in the middle of their respective lanes. I have visited only one of these worlds before, to one side of our world. I never went in the other direction, and if there is another world on the other side of the one I entered, I was unable to reach it. I only visited that other world once, and I was very lucky to return from it alive. Interdimensional travel isn't always safe, as we cannot know what is likely to confront us until we try it. The magic of our own world is daunting enough without the possibility of dealing with things that sit well outside the scope of our imaginations. That is why I prefer only to edge to either side of the centre of our bowling lane but not enter the gutter area."

"What was it like?" asked Serena curiously.

"That, I think, I can explain to you later on," said Smiley gently. "You came here to learn about things I know that may assist you in your war against the Hammersons and their minions. Last year, before the Hammersons set their plans in motion, I utilised my talent to its full potential for what I was sure would be the last time. I moved into the in-between and along the time axis to various points within my time span. Fortunately, I have been alive since the enmity between the two Sorcerous lines began way back in the early sixties. I collected a great deal of knowledge and understanding of various events leading to further events by hiding in my shadow and observing the goings-on of many things the Sorcerers did in their time."

"Really?" said several people.

"How much can you tell us?" asked Marc.

"I could tell you many things, young Marc," said Smiley, smiling, "but I would prefer to show you many of them. When I arrived here on Rock Haulter and had an extraordinary amount of concentrated magic at my hands, or at least that within the caves I was physically capable of accessing, I was able to record many of my memories to a format that you will be able to take with you and relive at your leisure."

"Comprehensive memory?" I enquired, remembering Stella's explanation of it months earlier.

"Indeed, comprehensive memory," Smiley agreed, "and when I send you on your way, I can give you directions to a certain cave that contains the magical devices required to play back such memories."

"Can you give us a few examples?" asked Peter.

"I will let you know what they are before you leave, young Peter," said Smiley, "but right now, before I continue to provide you with further information—I understand that you, young Tommy, have things you'd like to clear up with me, perhaps a bone to pick, and you too, young John. I will get to you two very shortly, but right now, I want you all to explain to me the progress in the war. I would like to know as much as you can tell me."

It was our turn to talk, so Marc took the lead, talking all about how the Woodwards, Fletchers, and Hammersons had been going about things over the last two and a half months. Peter, James, and Natalie chipped in regularly, but I felt little interest in this passing of information. Smiley would occasionally throw another piece of philosophical wisdom at us as they spoke, but mostly he just listened and asked for clarifications. Lena, Erica, Serena, and Siobhan were listening to this discussion about as raptly as Smiley was, clearly catching up things they themselves hadn't known either, but Tommy and Underwood looked the same as I felt—slightly bored and just wanting to get to a new part of the conversation.

"I can understand your feelings, young Marc," said Smiley wisely, "but I feel it necessary to inform you that Frederic's decision not to launch a full and immediate assault on the Hammersons now is based on a sound tactic. Yes, of course the Hammersons have the upper hand as we speak, but before we criticise the Woodwards for their handling of the current situation, we must understand and accept that the Hammersons, who could have done this at any point since the end of the previous war, chose to wait twenty-eight years before having another go. Now what did the Hammersons do with themselves for twenty-eight years? They were preparing, strengthening their magical power and protection, recruiting, but most importantly, they were strategising. The Woodwards did not make the most of this time, and you can criticise them for that, but their decision not to was based on the treaty they drew up with the Hammersons at the end of the war, and their belief—perhaps their delusion—that the Hammersons would abide by the conditions it outlined."

"Well, there's the lesson for ya." Peter grinned. "Never trust evil people."

"Indeed," Smiley agreed. "It is the drawback of being on the side of good; you must sometimes trust where trust is not necessarily deserved. The point I am trying to make, however, is that in order for the Woodwards to have any chance of resting control from the Hammersons, they must strategise equally as effectively as the Hammersons did for all that time. Additionally, they must do it with a lot more pressure upon their shoulders than the Hammersons ever had, because apart from worrying about the assault that must eventually come, they must attempt to prevent the situation developing too far for them to act at all. Such planning and strategising cannot be done overnight, but knowing Lillian and Frederic as I have, I feel sure that they will be working well beyond the point of exhaustion in order to save the situation. Launching an assault without a developed plan would only result in much more death and destruction than is necessary, young Marc, and that is the reason why the Woodwards have not taken that approach."

"It makes sense," said James, "but I dunno. I'd still like to see them be a bit more proactive."

"Did they not attempt to bring the Hammersons into custody?" Smiley reminded us. "Did they not attempt to bring the Villain Crystal into custody? Did they not succeed in bringing the Darkness Crystal into custody? The Woodwards *are* being proactive, as proactive as they can be, but they still cannot do too much. The Hammersons would only have half an eye on the Woodwards' activities at the moment, and I believe that is how the Woodwards would like it. And do not forget: They are right when they say that as long as the Hammersons don't have the Magic Crystals, they can never be invincible."

"That doesn't change the fact that the longer we have to wait for them to be ready to act, the more damage they'll have to undo," said Natalie dully.

"That, unfortunately, is a fact that we must accept," said Smiley solemnly. "The situation has fallen this way, and whichever way we choose to deal with it, there will be difficulties and there will be loss. The Woodwards appear to be taking a line that in the short term may appear worse but in the long run will be more beneficial for all."

"Rafael," said Marc, "the last war—I know that it must have been bad, and the death toll was massive, but the Woodwards still won it. What did they do to win it? Was it like what they are doing this time?"

"Ah," said Smiley, "now, Marc, my young friend, surely even you must have realised that this is a very different situation from the one thirty years ago. The Hammersons were Sorcerers and thus had to be dealt with in a very different manner. Back then, as nothing like a Sorcerous war had ever been experienced before, the Woodwards attacked from the off, which resulted in a great loss of life, a loss of control of many parts of the world, and almost resulted in the Woodwards losing their magical powers. If that had happened, none of us would be sitting here today.

"It appears that the Woodwards have learnt their lesson. They now understand that attacking is not the only way to win a war and that sometimes a good defence is the best offense. To answer your question, young Marc, the war ended in a way that, excepting the case of a miracle, cannot be repeated. Back in the month of October, 1981, the Hammersons had destabilised many countries around the world. They had not managed to establish any of their own rule, but they had achieved much of their goal. The world feared them, and the Woodwards, the protectors, had been driven into hiding.

"In order to explain to you exactly what happened, I will need to recount one of my own adventures to you. Back in the year of 2000, when my talent was still underdeveloped and I was still attempting to learn all I could about what had happened to me, I had moved along the fourth dimension into a new world. If you would like to use the bowling alley example, I crossed the gutter into the next lane parallel to our own. I had only been there for perhaps three or four seconds before I was seized by one of the beings that inhabit that world— three-dimensional beings like all of us, yet evolved in a very different way."

All of us were silent, barely moving a muscle, transfixed already by the old man's story.

"These creatures call themselves Honnies, which could translate to just about anything in English, and, of course, refer to us as humans. Their society is run very differently from ours, but much of their operation is concentrated on their minds. In order to illustrate how their minds work, you must try to imagine your own mind as a ball. All your thoughts, memories, and emotions are contained inside that ball. Now, if you can imagine the ball of your mind being about the size of a tennis ball, a fully developed Honnie would have a mind the size of a beach ball. Do not make the mistake of believing that this necessarily makes them smarter, however, because they usually only use a small percentage of their own mind on knowledge. Their great gift is to contain other minds within their own. They can open the ball of their mind and swallow smaller minds within it. They have total control over any minds contained within their own. They can influence thoughts, memories, and emotions; they can control actions; and—this is the fate of many a weak mind in their world—they can dissolve the smaller mind, making their own mind even stronger and thereby destroying the smaller mind.

"Now, the important part of this is that as soon as I entered this world, my mind was taken by a Honnie. I suddenly lost the ability to move back along the fourth dimension because the Honnie would not immediately let me. I was extremely fortunate, however, because the Honnie who caught me was most understanding. Honnies have their own language, but they can communicate with humans by placing thoughts into our heads and reading the reactions to those thoughts. That was what he and I did, sharing a great deal of knowledge and wisdom between us before he allowed me to return home. If he hadn't been interested in the sharing of knowledge and wisdom, then he would probably not have let me return, because the natural instinct of Honnies is to dispose of humans. Their breed of being is developed to prey on humans. They dissolve our minds and, either because of our nutritious value or because they can think of nothing better, feed on our bodies. They are roughly the same size as us, and in many ways, they look a lot like us, but they are many times stronger physically and many times more powerful in the mind.

"I understood well enough at the time what was happening to me, however, because it was not the first I had ever heard of Honnies. Of course, I had known very little about them prior to the experience of 2000, but I had at least been aware of their existence. This is because of a regular occurrence in our world that humans are generally unaware of. Honnies like to have a supply of humans in their world for them to feed on. They breed their own but do not bother to educate them. When they need a fresh supply of intelligent humans, they have an ability to open holes between their world and ours—a gateway in the fourth dimension, if you will. I believe science fiction represents such gateways as 'vortexes.' They do not use magic to do this but, so far as I can gather, some sort of mathematical formula that only the most important Honnies in their world have access to and only skilled 'collectors' are allowed to use. They come here, gather a small selection of humans into their mind, and return to their world with those humans. They never take very many because they like to remain discreet."

Several people were shifting uncomfortably. I didn't blame them. The idea that there was a breed of being out there even more thirsty for human blood than humans themselves was positively disturbing.

"Now, the reason their system works is because, unlike humans, Honnies do not have a great sense of self, ambition, or hunger for individual power," he went on. "Each and every one of them understands and accepts his or her position in society based on their level of mind power and aims no higher. Only once in recent history has a single Honnie risen up and decided that he wanted more in life than his current position offered him. Quite likely, he was inspired by the minds of those humans he had consumed, for he certainly wouldn't have gotten the idea from anything else in their world. He was one such collector I spoke of before, whose job it was to come here and acquire humans. However, when he was granted the honour of coming here in the month of October, 1981, he decided to act upon a different plan, his own plan. It involved planting himself somewhere safe in our world and collecting humans and absorbing them, collecting them and absorbing them. It is possible for them to do this over great distances, so his plan would have worked perfectly. He would eventually have had control of the entire world, and with such an enormous supply of humans for him to feed upon, by the time any more Honnies came to investigate, he would have been stronger and more powerful than any of them.

"Fortunately for us, he never got started, for the place the gateway opened up to landed him in a situation he had not expected. He found himself smack-bang in the middle of a pro-Hammerheart gathering in a public park, at which Lester and Dorothy Hammerson were both present, and once he witnessed Tankom's magic used directly against him, he fled for his life. Honnies had never known that humans could possess such power, and he was quite understandably shaken up by it. A spy within the Hammerhearts' ranks reported the unusual event to Lillian Woodward and, although she had no understanding of what this creature was capable of, she took it upon herself to track him down and offer him protection. When she did, and did so in a manner that did not threaten the Honnie, he agreed to use his mind power to assist the Woodwards.

"Between the two of them, Lillian and the Honnie constructed a plan that involved locating and capturing at least ten thousand of the Hammersons' soldiers. The Hammersons had already lost about ninety percent of their army over the war, but there were still many thousands of Hammerhearts around, and they understood that, if they could make the Hammersons believe they were capable of wiping out their entire army and leaving them with nothing at all, the Hammersons would finally concede defeat and agree to a treaty. The plan was to capture a good many Hammerhearts and once he had them in his mind—he said he was able to control all ten thousand of them, but I personally suspect he may have killed some of them to make his lot easier and his mind stronger—the Woodwards would contact the Hammersons and inform them that they had hold of a large number of their soldiers and would kill them all and begin to take more if the Hammersons did not cease their operation.

"This part of the plan never eventuated, however, because the Honnie, perhaps deciding that this world was too messed up to be saved, or that he'd acquired enough humans already, or perhaps that our world was more dangerous than he had known, broke his deal with Lillian and took all these soldiers back through a gateway to his own world. The Woodwards were still able to use the experience, however, telling the Hammersons that they had already killed ten thousand of their soldiers and would kill more if the Hammersons did not cease their operations. So much of it was in the Hammersons believing that the Woodwards actually could repeat the experience, and luckily, after a few weeks of contemplation, Tankom decided that they couldn't afford to take the chance. They agreed to sign the treaty, and thus sank into a state of silent seething."

Well, I thought with bitter amusement, it's nice to know that a simple question can still inspire a lengthy answer. I didn't really feel amused, though; I felt extremely shaken up. I thought I now understood why the Woodwards were behaving the way they were. Smiley was right. We couldn't just hope that another Honnie would come and sort things out for us this time. Yet clearly the Woodwards did understand that eventually, if they were to defeat the Hammersons, there would have to be a great final slaughter, only this time, the Hammersons themselves would most likely be part of that slaughter. Peter was right—you couldn't trust evil people. A treaty would not work again, because it had never really worked the first time.

"Wow," said Peter finally.

"How much do the Woodwards understand about what happened?" James asked.

"They understand the very basics," said Smiley, "or at least Lillian does. Frederic, who was a young man at the time, was only gifted with the story the Woodwards fed to the Hammersons, and young Amelia, I believe, knows nothing at all about that final apocalyptic slaughter. At least she never did as a child. All Lillian Woodward knows is that the Honnie is a being from another place, a distant planet, I believe she thought, and was capable of doing great things with his mind. None of us understood about the fourth dimension in those days, so we had no way of knowing that while they live in a different world, it is still on the same planet."

"Planets have more than three dimensions?" James enquired.

"Indeed, they can," said Smiley, "or at least, this one seems to. I cannot verify much on that topic, though, because Honnies have no interest whatsoever in anything above the level of a skyscraper. Oh yes, they do have buildings in their world. Space exploration, however, is not something they contemplate in their society. The idea of life on distant planets, or even distant planets themselves, isn't even entertained, as are many other areas of science which would inspire curiosity in a human. So, for all I know, their world could be a different planet from ours. Perhaps if I'd tried to move further along the fourth dimension, I might have come to another point where there is a world with no planet. That is, I may have ended up floating in space. Or perhaps, given that the planet is round, I may have gone through numerous worlds before ending up in this one again. I do not know."

"And it's probably not important anyway," said James. "I was just curious. So—so you're saying that the Woodwards probably couldn't have won the war last time without the Honnie?"

"I am saying no such thing, young James," Smiley cried out, pointing at him, and I couldn't help feeling amusement at how Smiley was consistently disagreeing with James. "Hypothetical claptrap all over again. We have no way of knowing what might or might not have happened in 1981 if there had not been interdimensional intervention. If, by your statement, you are implying that the Woodwards cannot win this war without the assistance of a Honnie, you are jumping to a terrible conclusion whose evidence is deeply flawed. As I told young Marc here, this situation is very different from the last and must be dealt with in a different manner. Could a Honnie's assistance be beneficial to the Woodwards? If it were possible to get a Honnie to agree to help, then yes, it probably would, but it is foolish to believe that the Woodwards are incapable of dealing with the Hammersons as they are, as it is also foolish to think that a Honnie alone could solve all our problems."

"Okay, okay," said James quickly, "but do you think it would possibly be a good idea to at least attempt to get help from a Honnie?"

"How do you propose to do that, young James?" Smiley asked seriously. "Other than what has happened to me, Sorcerers have never been able to move any further along the fourth dimension than the in-between. The only way you could access the world of the Honnies is by asking me to go there and attempt to persuade them to send someone back here, and I can tell you now, without any form of hesitation, that I would never agree to do such a suicidal thing as that. Death may be calling to me as it is, but I rather think I am entitled to some dignity after the long life I have lived. Honnies have rigid conventions that they choose to live by, and no Honnie would be willing to assist in events in our world, break out of their regular routine, for no benefit to their society. Remember, they have no sense of self, so it wouldn't be possible to trade them anything they would consider valuable. As for the Honnie who came here in 1981, I wouldn't be surprised if he had been killed upon returning to his own civilisation, assuming there were another Honnie powerful enough to do so. In short, young James, your chances of securing a Honnie's assistance are as good as naught."

A silence followed this. None of us could think of anything to add to that and James, perhaps feeling that he had been humiliated enough, decided not to continue the conversation. Smiley noticed this and instead turned his attention to Marc.

"You, young Marc, as the Seventh Sorcerer, I believe it will be your intervention that makes the critical difference in this war," he said seriously, "and you also, young John. You have both been dealt greater hands from the moments of your births that any teenager is capable of comprehending, but I hope, very much, that you two boys are up to it. As for defeating the Hammersons and restoring the world as we knew it to be, it will be down to you, young Natalie, and your fellow Sorcerers, to wield your magic for the power of good."

"Do you think we should use the Beast of Magic?" asked Marc.

"To deal with the Hammersons?" Smiley enquired. "That, I think, is up to you, young Marc. I don't believe that you will really need to use the beast. Doing so may deal with the situation more quickly, but not necessarily for the best, but as I said, that is up to you. You must use the best judgement of yours and those around you to make such decisions as that."

"What about Tommy?" asked Erica. "Does he fit into this anywhere?"

"Young Erica," said Smiley solemnly, "you all fit into this. All of you have a role to play, however great or small. Young Tommy here has already proven his worth by way of his Maahoo and, according to your story, guarding the Light Crystal for an extended period of time. That, I believe, is no small feat."

"All of us?" repeated Natalie. "Even—*him?*"

"You wouldn't even be here if it wasn't for me," snapped Underwood.

"That is very true," Smiley agreed. "The device young Jacob has used to keep in contact with me, and the similar device I have used, were created by Frederic Woodward some twelve years ago when I was forced to flee for my life. Through Gerald Fick, it fell into Jacob's hands, thereby making him my only connection to the outside world, except, of course, for you, young Tommy. I think, through this, it is fair to say that Jacob has already played a very large role in the events leading to this meeting."

"Why did you want him here anyway, though?" Peter asked, and the moment the words were out of his mouth, he clapped his hands to it, knowing he'd been both insensitive and impertinent.

"Yeah, like I don't know you'd rather I not be here," said Underwood bitterly. "All of you."

"He is my grandson, young Peter," said Smiley. "My grandson whom I have had regular contact with for a long time but had not seen since he was only a child. I am aware that all of you would have experienced a loss of some kind in your life, but Jacob and I have lost our entire family. We are the only two left, and I feel it is right that we should be together. I also think it would not be fair on him if we hadn't met at least one more time before I passed on. I would be honoured, Jacob, if you would remain here with me after your friends return to Australia."

"Really?" said Underwood, his mouth open in astonishment. "You sure?"

"Very sure," said Smiley, smiling pleasantly at him. "It would be a great comfort to me to have someone with me. It would also be useful to have a fit, young man with me to do some of the things I cannot. As for you, being here should ensure your safety, both now and after I have moved on."

"I—well—thank you," he said, his face transported. "I'm honoured."

"You are very welcome," Smiley replied. "To begin, young Jacob, I have a little task for you."

"Already?" said Peter, grinning wickedly at Underwood.

"Indeed, already," said Smiley.

He took something out of his pocket—the remote control I had seen him holding earlier. I had completely forgotten about it what with all the discussion that had taken place since. He pointed it at the door through which we had entered and pressed one of the buttons— the door swung open.

"There you go," said Peter, grinning again at Underwood. "Less than a minute and he's already showing you the door."

"Snap out of it, kid," snapped Underwood. "What do you want me to do?" he added to Smiley.

"I would like you to return to the place where you set up camp with your friends," said Smiley. "I would like you to take your vehicle there, and be as careful as you possibly can. I would like you to gather up all your belongings and return here. Can you do that without drawing unwanted attention to yourself, young Jacob?"

"I think so," said Underwood, "if one of them—and they're certainly not my friends—would make me and the hovercar I'm using invisible."

"No worries," said Marc, getting to his feet. "Come on."

They both left the room, Marc in the lead. Nobody spoke while they were gone. We just sat still, looking at each other and listening to the sounds from outside the door. It swung shut before Marc could return, but Smiley pushed the button on his remote control when Marc knocked on it. As he sat down, through the open door, we listened to the sound of Underwood's hovercar lifting off the ground. Nobody spoke until the sound had faded away completely.

"And now that young Jacob has departed," said Smiley solemnly, "let us turn our attention to other, more personal matters."

Chapter 31: Knowns and Unknowns

"Rafael," said Marc, in that respectful tone he'd used while speaking Smiley's first name several times already, "one of the reasons why we set off on this mission in the beginning was because of the mystery of John's past. We know you know something about it because Mr. Woodward said you were involved, and because you said he'd been dealt a big hand of some sort earlier."

"Indeed," said Smiley solemnly, turning his gaze on me now. "I do know some things. Not all, I'm afraid, but perhaps enough to give you a grounding. You, young John—you know who your biological parents are, yes?"

"I do now," I told him. "I didn't in the beginning, though. I only knew my mother was dead and that Moran had called her back as a ghost. It wasn't until I saw her in a portrait on his wall and Marc told me who she was that I worked it out. I still don't understand what happened back then, though."

"Sadly, my young friend, I do not understand it all either," sighed Smiley. "However, I will tell you the little I know. Firstly, young John, you must know that you were given to me at a very trying time. Your entire family was in terrible danger from the Hammersons and the whole exchange had to be done without their knowledge. They were not to know that anything had happened to you until you were already safely tucked away where they could not find you. Bernard Moran came to me, knowing that I was close to the Woodwards—he did not dare approach them directly—and offered you to me and practically begged me to find a safe place to hide you. All he told me was that Arnold Hammerson wanted you dead, and he would stop at nothing to get his hands on you. He also said that he, Cindy, and Lucien were risking their own lives by performing this exchange. I was suspicious, I admit, but I could also see the fear in his face, and I agreed to take you. I handed you to Frederic and, for your safety, did not enquire as to where you ended up. I only discovered you were a Playman three months ago."

"You saw him on the boat with us?" Peter enquired.

"Not at all," Smiley cried out, turning quickly and pointing a withered old finger at Peter. "If I had, young Peter, he probably would have seen me in my shadow, what with his extremely rare ability. No, the information came to me by way of Bernard Moran himself, who also happened to be on that boat and who had recognised John as his son a week earlier. He didn't see me on the boat, but he acquired the services of two ghosts shortly after he arrived on the island, and they informed him of my presence. That first night, he sought me. He found me attempting to climb the mountain and it was by his assistance that I was able to reach this place."

"He helped you?" said Serena, stunned. "He certainly didn't try to help us."

"Indeed, he helped me," said Smiley. "He believed he owed me a great service and was prepared to repay his debt in any way he could. He could not be seen to be helping you or he would have been killed upon his return to Chopville. Indeed, he will be killed if the Hammersons ever get hold of him. He told me what he had been sent to Rock Haulter to do, and although he never assisted you in any obvious way, I did get him to agree to do three things in your favour."

"He did?" asked Natalie. "Was appearing to be an idiot one of them?"

"If it was, it wasn't a condition I imposed upon him," the old man replied. "No, I asked him to do three more important things. The first, and most important thing, which I think he may have done regardless, is that he was not to kill any of you. I am most glad that he didn't. The second thing was not to use the Villain Crystal against you, which I am also in the way of believing that he did not do. I don't think he would have done that anyway, though; if he could not secure the Sien-Leoard Crystal, then he would need the Villain Crystal in his possession to give himself any small chance of surviving after you had left him. The third thing I asked him to do was leave the Light Crystal somewhere where you could find and take it. He believed that as soon as you became aware of his presence on the island, you would raid his hiding place and take anything you could from it. He made sure to announce himself to you so that he could be sure this would happen. If it had not, he may have been forced to leave it somewhere more obvious for you to pick up."

I listened to this in astonishment. Moran had been doing all these things without our notice. He had appeared so thoroughly against us, and all along, he had actually been helping us. It was unthinkable.

"What about the ghost of his mother?" asked Tommy. "We know he called her back, but according to John, Fewul didn't get rid of her when he got rid of Hal and Pol Maivis. Do you know where she is now?"

"I'm afraid not," said Smiley. "I did not see Moran again after our meeting on that first night. I know from my observations, however, that he was able to use the Villain Crystal to firstly give himself the medical attention he needed, and secondly to scour the mountain for a while and equip himself accordingly before he returned to Australia. His wife accompanied him in this time, and I believe, since I have not seen a sign of her since, that he either called her back, but more likely took her with him when he left. She may still be with him now, acting as a sort of guardian angel to him."

"Yeah, I think so," I said, remembering a couple of startling things. "Stella ran into him at one stage and got in a battle. Moran won with his Villain Crystal but only because Stella had been really scared of him. It might have been her doing that, because ghosts can mess with feelings and emotions in that way. Also, I think I might have—have seen her myself."

"You have?" said Peter, stunned. "When?"

"At school," I told him and the others. "Last week when—well, you know. The first time I saw him, I thought I saw something shimmering around him, or behind him or whatever. I didn't recognise it as a ghost, but now that I think about it, it might have been her, standing behind him, protecting him."

"Wow," said Tommy. "Er, Rafael, do you know anything about her—before she died?"

"Hey, come on," said Marc, grinning at his friend. "You could have asked me that."

"Maybe, but what I really meant was, how much was she—you know—like him?" Tommy asked, shrugging and looking slightly embarrassed.

"If you are asking whether or not she was a Hammerheart, young Tommy, I am quite sure that she was not," said Smiley. "From the very little I knew about them before my direct dealings with Bernard, she was a good woman with a devotion to her love so great that she would accept anything and everything about him. She may not have approved of his dealings with the Hammersons, but she would not try to stop him. In fact, she couldn't have done, because anyone who turns their back on the Hammersons is promptly reeled in and either killed or held hostage.

"I do believe that she helped him to be a better man, however. When they started a family, he became less interested in his Hammerheart duties and more interested in raising his young son, Lucien. I believe the destruction of his family broke his spirit in a way that he could never recover from. He became unpleasant again, but unlike before, he harboured a deep grudge against Arnold Hammerson. His attempt to rest power from the Hammersons was, he considered, payback for what they had done to him. He only took the Woodwards' magic as well because of the lingering hatred against them since the war, and also for the obvious reasons you youngsters would have worked out at the time."

"Do you know what happened after John was taken away?" asked James.

"The Morans were punished, of course," said Smiley sadly. "Moran lost his wife and, of course, was not able to have any relationship with his youngest son. Young Marc here was always safe because he is the Seventh Sorcerer, and of course, as soon as the Hammersons realised they had the Seventh Sorcerer among them, they were keen to protect him and, of course, hide him from the Woodwards and their influence. There was, however, one other thing they did, and it regarded young Lucien. I don't know exactly what it is, but Arnold Hammerson made him a victim of one of the rarest magical spells that has ever existed."

"Lucien?" repeated Marc. "What's that? He was always so normal until Tankom got him with her influential charm. Does it have something to do with that?"

"I don't know for sure, but I think not," said Smiley. "Not if Tankom actually had to perform the spell herself. The spell I speak of is one that Arnold Hammerson is only the second Sorcerer in history to be capable of performing, and the only other one was Mary Sien. It involves planting what you might call a time bomb on that person—a curse of any kind will be activated a certain time or be triggered by a certain event. Nobody except Arnold Hammerson knows what that curse is or when it will be triggered. I doubt that young Lucien would even be aware that he is cursed, but eventually, he will succumb to whatever dark magic Arnold Hammerson has forced upon him."

Nobody said anything to this. Smiley's matter-of-fact tone was very disturbing indeed. What on earth was wrong with Lucien? What would eventually happen to him, and when would it happen? Questions that nobody had any answers to, but the pity for Lucien was clearly evident among the group.

"Can I just change the subject," said Erica a little hesitantly after a while. "Mr.—er, Rafael, I mean"—she grinned and blushed—"you said something earlier about the Hammersons wanting Marc on their side because he's the Seventh Sorcerer, and to protect him and hide him and all that. What I don't understand is how did they even know that he was the Seventh Sorcerer? Did they work it out the same way we did with that prophecy or what?"

"Ah, yes," said Smiley, his eyes fading. "Now you listen to this, young John, for I believe it concerns you as deeply as young Marc here. For as long as educational institutions around the world have been given rights to access Rock Haulter for ten years at a time, both Sorcerous lines have also had direct access to the island. The Hammersons lost that right in the treaty of 1981, but they found a loophole by forcing one of the schools each year to allow them to bring some of their own people on the same ship. There was nothing the Woodwards could do to prevent it, as the treaty did not include direct dealings between the Hammersons and schools.

"Now, a procedure that the Hammersons have been conducting for a very long time is performing tests on the children of Hammerhearts. It is both a test of purity, determining if that person can be trusted in the future, and also a way of detecting any special talents. They came here to do it each year, and it was by this way that they discovered both of your talents."

"You mean that Marc's the Seventh Sorcerer and that John can see ghosts," Serena said, clearly for verification.

"Indeed," said Smiley. "But as for you, young John, they have discovered more than just that. What it is they discovered, I do not know, but I believe it was here that your troubles began. It was from Rock Haulter that Bernard Moran was forced to flee, separately from the Hammersons so that they could not corner him and take you from him."

"Did they do these tests in the main hall?" I asked casually, knowing Smiley would pick up on the subtext. He should, since he had shown the hall to me himself.

"I believe the tests are done in various places around the mountain, young John," said Smiley. "My suspicions with regard to you do involve that hall, however. Your friends mentioned the dream you had many weeks ago now that revealed the truth about young Marc being the Seventh Sorcerer. I also picked up from your mind a lurking worry about other recurring dreams you were having. I do not know what this ability is or if it is somehow connected with your ability to see ghosts, but I can say that it is almost certainly magical. Its potential, I do not know. The Hammersons' interest in it, I don't know either. However, it seems likely that since you keep seeing the main hall in your mind, it may have played a part in your history."

I considered mentioning what had happened to me in the main hall last night, then changed my mind. If Smiley didn't know any more than he had just said, then he probably couldn't explain what had happened in there. Instead, I said, "Are you aware of the thing between me and Stella?"

"I know no more about that than you and her do, my dear boy," said Smiley sadly. "I only learnt of that when I felt young Stella's mind three weeks ago, and sadly, her knowledge on the subject was extremely limited. It would seem a likely reason why Arnold Hammerson wants you dead, but I have no idea how it could have happened. You and young Stella would have needed to be in the same place for something to have happened to you, perhaps for a piece of dormant magic to be activated."

"The main hall?" I suggested. "I mean, all those dreams have Stella in them."

"You never said anything about these dreams before, John," said Peter accusingly. "Only the times you actually see into her mind."

"I did once," I retorted. "Once you found me on the floor after one of them, but that was only the very first one. Look, Rafael, if me and Stella were together in the main hall back then, do you think it would have been before or after they tested me for weird abilities?"

"Well, that depends," said Smiley. "Do you think they are aware of what is between you and young Stella?"

I considered this, but before I could answer, Marc cut in. "They probably are. Remember what we were talking about ages ago? It would explain why they were always so horrible to her, knowing what was inside her. Plus they wanted to undo something about you and her first before they killed you; it surely had to be the connection. If killing you outright wouldn't work, they would need to remove the connection to make sure there was nothing binding you to life."

"Yeah, I agree with that," I said, "but it doesn't mean they knew back then. There could have been some other reason for them wanting me dead. Let's just say they only found out about this thing with Stella from her own mind. As soon as she found out who I was, they would have seen it in her mind, and in order to prove it, they made Hall give me the returnamy. Once they saw that I could see ghosts, and that my ghost mother turned up in it, that would have been all the evidence they needed."

"That all sounds possible, John," said Marc, "but it assumes that there's something else going on with you. What other reason could the Hammersons have for wanting you dead? And I mean the initial reason for them wanting you dead way back in those days."

I shrugged. "I have no idea, I really don't. It could be something to do with ghosts, possibly."

"That, I think, is a fact that we must accept we do not know," Smiley interrupted. "It may be possible to find out, but sitting here speculating will not give us the answer. For you, young John, it will be a case of you learning the truth in due course. Your search for knowledge has led you to me, but I'm afraid that it is not yet complete. I'm also afraid that none of the memories I have to show you will necessarily give you even a clue as to the answer, but that is for you to determine."

I shrugged again. "Cheers. Well, since you can't tell me anything else, do you have any suggestions for me to keep looking?"

"We all know that Arnold Hammerson is the only person who knows the full story behind all of this," Smiley pointed out to me. "That is, so far, the only clue we have. We do not know if it is to do with your connection with Stella or how that connection came about. You could treat the two issues as separate investigations or as one. The choice is yours, but I'm afraid I can offer you no more assistance than that."

"One other thing," said Marc quickly, "and I promise after this, we'll get onto Tommy's business. Mr. Woodward said a while ago that when you got your talent from that plane crash, the people who the Hammersons were after, the Maivises, were trying to report something about Stella. Do you know what it was? Did they fill you in on the secret in the terminal or something?"

Smiley shook his head. "I am aware that the information they were delivering to Frederic concerned Stella, but I do not know what it was, nor does anyone else alive today. I enquired as to why my plane had been brought down, but of course nobody knew. The information died with the Maivises, making that particular operation of the Hammersons' a success. Or, at least, it would have been a success, if not for the aftermath."

"What aftermath?" asked Tommy.

"What happened to me," Smiley replied, "and what happened to you, young Tommy. We have no way of knowing exactly what our talents mean to the Hammersons, but it is safe enough to assume they mean something. If not, they would just let us go; they would have no interest in hunting us. Yet they have been hunting us both for thirteen years now."

"How much do you know about that plane crash, anyway?" asked Peter.

"I know that it was brought down by magic," said Smiley. "The aviation investigation that followed the incident revealed that the reverse thrust on one of the engines had deployed in mid-flight, but they were never able to determine why it happened. I suspect, as does Frederic, that it was loose magic floating around after the crash that settled into me and young Tommy here, the only two survivors. That in itself is a mystery. We should never have survived at all, but that is yet another fact that we must accept we may never know. It may have been no more than sheer luck.

"I have theories about exactly how we landed with our particular talents, however. For instance, an investigation done by an assistant to the Woodwards revealed that one of the fatalities of the incident was a Hammerheart, a Hammerheart who had been killed many years earlier and brought back to being by the Hammersons, perhaps in relation to whatever information the Maivises were delivering. Again, we cannot know for sure. It seems possible to me that his transference to the in-between, combined with the loose magic, may have settled into my body, thereby giving me my particular talent.

"As for you, young Tommy, we are less certain. This body—(he reached up slowly and touched Tommy's arm)—was either created by the loose magic or had belonged to someone else prior to the incident and the loose magic transferred some of your life force into it at the moment of its previous occupant's death. We don't know, and we are unsure that any of the Hammersons know, which of those occurred, or if it was something else entirely. The loose magic itself, obviously it would have been necessary for the Sorcerer in question —and we believe it to be Tankom, although we have no way of knowing for sure—to have been far from the plane at the time the magic cast upon the left engine was activated. It is perhaps possible that because of this distance, and also because Tankom is not capable of performing the time bomb curse I spoke of earlier, that some of her magic was misguided and was not used to bring the plane down. Exactly what that magic was, we cannot know, but since it gave us both a certain rare trait, the ability to play the Maahoo, we can suppose it had something to do with that. But once again, we must accept that we don't know."

"Sir," said James tensely, "if you're so sure that Tankom couldn't do the time bomb curse, then how can you be sure it was she who brought the plane down? Wouldn't it make more sense for Hammerson to have done that, since he is more capable of it?"

"Because Tankom is the one who knows of our abilities," Smiley replied. "Arnold Hammerson knows who I am from the war, of course, but I don't believe that Tankom ever explained to him about my talent. I am also given to understand that, like Arnold Hammerson knowing the full story behind young John, Tankom is the only one who knows the entire reason why they are hunting young Tommy. Then, of course, there is the fact that the magic didn't go quite according to plan. If it had, young Tommy and I would have both been killed in that crash and given no extra talents at all. If Arnold Hammerson had used his time bomb curse to bring that plane down, nobody would have had a chance."

510

"Mr. Woodward said that they couldn't be completely sure that it was really Tommy," I pointed out.

"Perhaps Frederic is keeping an open mind about it," said Smiley, "but I personally believe that it was Tommy. For one thing, I recognised you immediately when I laid eyes on you some two years ago now in Sydney; your facial features had not changed very much from when you were an infant. For another thing, you exhibited all the signs I had expected to see of your unusual talent, especially when I first put a Maahoo in your hand and observed your reaction to it. I cannot see how that divided boy could possibly be anyone other than you, young Tommy."

"What exactly happened anyway?" Tommy asked. "Mr. Woodward said that you took me and then lost me or something. My earliest memory of the whole thing is wandering around the outback somewhere until I was eventually found."

"Indeed, I did take you," Smiley agreed. "I became aware that I had changed almost immediately, and when the investigators were unable to identify you—"

"They couldn't identify him?" said James sharply. "Wouldn't that mean that this body must have been created? How could it possibly have belonged to someone else if they couldn't identify it?"

"Not just that, but I'm fairly sure Tommy once said something about his two bodies sharing DNA," Natalie added.

"Yeah, they do," said Tommy, "but I can see where he's coming from. If this body really had belonged to someone else, then maybe my life essence, or whatever you wanna call it, changed it somehow, made it unrecognisable from what it had been before, and scrambled my DNA in the process. It's possible, don't you think?"

"It is possible," Smiley agreed, "which is why I have kept an open mind to the possibility. However, it is yet another unknown fact that we must accept. What we do know, and can accept that we know for certain, is that the investigators were unable to identify you. Your German self, your original self, was identified, so that you were sent back to Germany as an orphan. This you would have no doubt followed, but sensing that something odd and magical was going on, I took you and fled from the authorities. Hammerhearts were beginning to get involved behind the scenes, and I couldn't help noticing their interest in you. I had no specific instructions to take you; it was merely a whim upon which I acted."

"But they caught up with you eventually?" said Tommy.

"Yes, they did," said Smiley solemnly. "I was in Australia by then. The Woodwards had moved to Australia from Great Britain a few months earlier upon the revelation that the Hammersons had picked out a small rural town called Chopville to be their centre of operations and residence. I had been cautious about entering the country, knowing that Hammerhearts were watching and waiting for me to appear. I couldn't risk contacting the Woodwards directly for assistance, for I feared that would give my position away to any watching Hammerhearts. It took a few weeks, but eventually, I managed to get through the Sydney airport and out of the city before they could catch me, but unfortunately, I didn't get any farther than that. They nabbed me on the railroad, and I was lucky to survive at all. I managed a quick escape but was unable to take you with me—a regret that haunted me for many, many years until I found you safe and well again. I don't know how it came to pass that the Hammerhearts lost you; that is no doubt something that only those directly involved fully know about."

"Why did the Hammersons come to Chopville?" asked Natalie. "Seems like a long way to come just to settle down in the middle of nowhere."

"My evidence suggests that it was because of young Marc's family," Smiley said, "who had resided in Chopville since long ago. Whether to keep an eye on Moran after his treachery or to watch over the Seventh Sorcerer as he grew, I'm not entirely sure. That young John was also living in Chopville may or may not have been a suspicion of theirs, but I tend to think it was a stroke of luck on their part that they landed so close. The Woodwards, of course, believed that it was John they were coming after, having known nothing about Marc being the Seventh Sorcerer, so they had hastened to follow, only knowing that if it were important enough to the Hammersons to cause them to relocate, it was probably worth the same amount of trouble to stop them."

"Okay," said Tommy, a little shakily, "all right, okay, but sir," he looked imploringly at Smiley, "you've known me for more than two years now. How come you didn't tell me any of this? I mean, I've always grown up wondering what was wrong with me and never understanding. Even got depressed over it. You seemed to understand me better than my own parents did. They knew, of course, but—well, you know."

He looked desperately around at the rest of us for help. Smiley gazed at him steadily for several seconds before replying.

"Young Tommy, you only needed to understand and accept that you were living two lives at the same time. You understood that, I know, but you may not have learnt to accept it. The knowledge of how it had come about and, more importantly, that there were dangerous Sorcerers still hunting you, was not something any child should have to live with. When I first met you in Sydney, you were a thirteen-year-old boy, quiet, polite, and hungry for understanding of the unusual. Now, you are an able-bodied sixteen-year-old, no longer lost and confused, and ready to shoulder a grown man's responsibility in a troubled time.

"I could not gift you with the knowledge you always desired because at that tender age, it would have distracted you and may have sent you on a path detrimental to your future. I had to wait until you had grown and matured. I was able to speed up the process by persuading your parents to move closer to the proximity of the Woodwards, despite the enormous risk of placing you so close to the Hammersons at the same time, but ultimately it was up to you to prepare yourself. When I came to you one evening for a routine Maahoo lesson and you immediately enquired about Leoard's Lament, I knew, from that very moment, that the time had finally arrived. I knew I had nothing left to teach you, that my own time was running out anyway, and that it was now time for me to leave you to your own devices for the next leg of your journey of personal discovery.

"You can have no idea, young Tommy, how it fills me with pride to see how much you have grown since I met you two years ago, how you have grown since three months ago, even. In the short time I knew you, you became to me like the son I never had. I like to believe I assisted you to become the young man you are now, as repayment for almost losing you to the Hammerhearts."

It seemed to be an emotional moment. Tommy and Smiley were staring intently into each other's eyes. Then, slowly, they reached out to each other and embraced.

That was the end of the sharing of knowledge and wisdom, as Smiley had put it. It seemed that there was no more to be discussed. The conversation lifted and became lighter. Smiley may have been an old man and may have talked himself into exhaustion, but that didn't make him any less interested in our lives. We sat around for a while later, just talking and exchanging tales. We told him how things were and had been for us in Chopville, and he told us stories from his life. When a knock sounded on the door, Smiley opened it with his remote control and there stood nobody, a bag I knew to belong to Jacob Underwood floating in mid-air.

"Oh yeah," said Marc, whipping his crystal out and making Underwood visible again. "Hang on, I'll go fix up your car."

Marc got up and passed Underwood as he left the room.

"Thank you, young Jacob," Smiley cried out, pointing first at him, then at the door through which he had entered the room earlier.

He pressed another button on his remote control and it swung open. "In there, if you please. There is a spare bedroom. Load your stuff in there and make yourself comfortable. Before you unpack, however, there is a box on the coffee table in my living room. Could you get it and bring it to me, please?"

Underwood nodded and set off, passing Smiley and disappearing through that door. Smiley pressed another button on his remote control that was clearly meant to hold the door open because it did not swing shut behind him. Nobody moved for a few moments after that until Marc returned, and just in the nick of time. The moment he was over the threshold, the door swung shut behind him.

"Just a quick question," Marc said, crossing the room to his vacated seat and plonking himself down, "purely trivial you know. Why is that clock there—(he pointed up to a large clock face on the wall opposite him)—six hours ahead of our watches? For us, it's nearly four o'clock, but that clock says it's nearly ten."

Four o'clock? I glanced down at my watch and saw that he was quite right. We had been in here for ages. No wonder my stomach was rumbling so angrily.

"For me, young Marc, it is nearly ten o'clock," Smiley replied. "Remember, I came through the Australasian portal, whereas you came through the Indian portal. If you went outside now, you would see a late afternoon sun. At least you would if you moved far enough around the mountain. If I went out there, however, I would see darkness, perhaps a half moon in the sky."

"What?"

"Oh," said James, his expression clearing. "That does sort of make sense. Guys, just think about it."

"I'm thinking about it," moaned Peter. "If I rupture something in my brain, don't be alarmed."

"I think I get it too," I said. The understanding was barely there, but I knew if I could only grab hold of it... "You guys remember what Lisa said ages ago? Pete, Nat, Serena, you were all there. She said that Rock Haulter isn't really a place on Earth, so you wouldn't expect it to have a moon. We did see a moon, though, through our window that night. Pete, you contradicted her by pointing out that there was a sun, but what if there isn't really a sun? What if both the sun and the moon are generated by our own minds based on what we would expect to see? If it goes like that, then obviously day and night would reflect the time zone of the portal we came through. It seems to make sense."

"Yes, it does," James agreed. "Well done, John. That's fairly advanced thinking for you, but you've made me proud."

I stuck my middle finger up at him.

Underwood returned at that point, carrying a small, square, nondescript box in his hands. Smiley held his arms out for it and Underwood lowered it gently into them.

"I have had a wonderful time with you youngsters," Smiley told us, "but I'm afraid the time has come for us to part company. I have here a box containing several of my memories, incidents I have taken the time to go back and witness for myself. I am passing them on to you in the hopes that you will use the knowledge you gain from them wisely, but I have nothing else I can share with you. If, at any time during the remainder of your time here on Rock Haulter, you feel an urge to come up here and discuss anything with me, you are more than welcome. All I can do now is sit back and wait for the inevitable drawing. Good luck, my friends. Just remember, you have the power at your fingertips—it is how you choose to use it that will determine your success or failure in this war."

He looked slowly around the room, fixing on each and every face for a moment before moving to the next. "Each and every one of you," he told us, "has a part to play in the course of events to come. I have no doubt that each and every one of you will perform admirably and courageously."

* * *

"Well, there you go," said Peter half an hour later. "That's what we've been working towards for the last two months. I know it wasn't a complete success—we didn't find out everything—but at least we know where we're heading now."

We had taken Smiley's box of memories and ridden our hovercars anticlockwise around the mountain until we reached the farthest northwest point. We had then gone down the mountain and parked the cars along the base of the mountain, right by Group F's cave. We were now in the house they had built there, sitting around the various couches and contemplating all that had happened that afternoon. Natalie was the only person not present; she had been delegated the duty of finding a convenient cave in the mountain and placing various spells on it to make it easy for us to park our hovercars in there. It had to be impossible for people to enter in and out of the cave unless they were using hovercars, and those cars were wrapped in Natalie's invisibility veil; she had cast the veil again upon all of us and our hovercars immediately after leaving Smiley's cave. Once she had done that, I would go up there and create a door from that cave to the three campsites. It wouldn't be a security risk if

Natalie's protective enchantments around the entrance to the cave held.

"He certainly does know a lot," said James, "but some of what he said just didn't sit with me."

"That figures," snorted Peter. "Anyone who disagrees with our great Lord James *must* be off his rocker."

"Don't be silly, Peter," said James, flushing slightly. "Okay, I'll give you an example. I can accept what he said about people belonging with the dead once they die and that they don't die properly if they're brought back. What he said about a person only having a certain amount of time before they die, though—that's just nonsense. No way can his talent, if you can call it a talent, prove that our lifelines are only a certain length from the moment of our birth. I'm sorry, but that just doesn't sit with me."

"I actually agree with James on that one," Erica chipped in, and I hid my grin behind my hand. Erica was quite intelligent in her own right and probably an independent thinker most of the time, but I still found it unsurprising that she would agree with James, especially if his way of thinking had rubbed off on her in all the time they had spent together. "It would be like saying, for example, if I were to leave this camp in a few minutes and be gunned down by Hammerhearts, if I chose not to leave the campsite, I might suffer a brain aneurysm or heart attack, or else Hammerhearts would burst in here and kill me while the rest of you miraculously survive. It's like saying that our choices mean nothing because the consequences would be the same, yet he also tells us that our choices mean everything."

I was only half listening. Most of my thoughts were stuck on all Smiley had told me about my situation. Arnold Hammerson wanted me dead. Tankom also wanted me dead, but more because of my recent interferences than anything else. Why did Hammerson want me dead? How long had he known about the connection between me and Stella? How exactly had that connection happened, anyway? And how on earth did the main hall here on Rock Haulter fit into all of this? I knew I'd forgotten to bring up two things I'd meant to ask Smiley (the glitch in the invisibility goggles and the startling vision of fire and smoke I kept seeing), but perhaps the discussion had given me an acceptance that those were things I would learn in due course; or if not, I would not be meant to know.

"I disagree," said Lena, another independent thinker. "It's not a question of whether we determine fate or fate determines us. I tend to think we and fate determine each other at the same time. To use your example, Erica, if you chose to step out there and there were

Hammerhearts waiting for you, your time of death may well be at that point, but if that were so, it would be determined by that choice. The knowing you would make that choice, if I've got it right, is well beyond our making the choice, if that makes sense. If you had not made that choice, your time of death would be at a later date because, again, fate knows you would make that choice. In other words, our lifelines constantly change by our choices, and those made by other people. It's only people like Smiley who have fixed lifelines because they found a way to perceive it."

"I need a pill," moaned Serena, and several people burst out laughing.

James was considering Lena's words. Very slowly, he nodded. "That is possible, Lena, but if you've got it right, then a person's time of death is not something that anyone is supposed to know. The knowing that—the idea of that information being available to anyone other than fate itself, would change the course of events. I guess that's what I was thinking of earlier but perhaps you're right. It's like Smiley said several times, though: It's not something we can know for certain, so there's no point worrying about it."

"Of course we're not supposed to know when our time of death is," said Marc. "It's against the laws of magic to know that. You saw what happened to Daniel; he saw someone's time of death in his reading, and it cost him his life. I bet that if he hadn't run for it that day, if he'd told us what he'd seen, we all would have died along with him."

"Never mind that," said Peter. "Those memories in that box, what do we do with those?"

"I guess we find that cave Smiley told us about so we can watch them," said Marc. "We can do that tomorrow. For tonight, though, after we've had dinner and Natalie gets back in here, I've got something else I want to take care of."

Chapter 32: The Corridor Paradigm

The sun had gone down; since it was now nearly winter in the southern hemisphere, it was to be expected that the sun would set earlier than it had when we had been here in February. We had had our dinner and now, at just after half past eight, Marc and I had left the others behind and set off on a mission of our own. For them, it was a night off; for us, it was, for what we hoped would be the only time during our stay on the Rock, an encounter with the Hammerhearts. It was slow going because neither of us had brought our hovercars. This was a mission Marc wanted to do on foot.

We had spent some time using our crystals to spy both on the Hammerhearts and the Russians, just in case they had the potential to cause trouble as well. They had sent their students around to the west side of the mountain (not too far from Group E and F's campsites) to study the rock itself. Apparently they were trying to determine if Sien and Leoard had made this a normal rock or given it special properties. Their mentors had stayed back in the main hall, unpacking all their equipment and transforming the hall into a study.

As for the Hammerhearts, they had started searching each and every cave on the eastern side. With access to both the S- and L-keys, they were able to get into many different chambers and explore the magical secrets within them. Unfortunately, they had been able to create and concentrate a number of weapons from Sien's caves as well as create a number of useful devices to not only assist them in battle but create creature comforts as well. They were on their way back to their campsite where they intended to load these devices into a number of extender cases (the official name the Hammerhearts gave to the bags that made themselves larger on the inside to accommodate any volume and weight).

Marc and I had sprinted from our campsite, clockwise around the mountain, with the intention of getting to the Hammerhearts' campsite before they got there. We were still under Natalie's invisibility veil and soundproof barrier, so we hadn't bothered to go to any trouble to conceal ourselves. I was all too aware of the loud thumping of our feet as we ran, and I had to keep reminding myself that no matter how loud it sounded to us, nobody else would hear it. We hadn't decided exactly what we would do with the Hammerhearts, though. Neither of us wanted to kill them, yet we had to make it so that they would eventually return to the Hammersons, exactly when they were expected, but with none of the magical items they were expected to return with. It was essential that no outside Hammerhearts know that anything is going on, so all contact between these Hammerhearts and the outside world had to go ahead as usual. We knew that these poor Hammerhearts would no doubt be punished upon failure, but we had to hope that that punishment wouldn't be by way of death. We could only do so much for them. We couldn't protect them from their choice to be Hammerhearts.

I was using the crystal to navigate us towards the campsite. We knew what it looked like, but you could never be too safe. We were both totally out of breath by the time we recognised the cave they were using, only six feet above ground level. Above the entrance was a ledge, fairly narrow but enough for Marc and I to plant our feet. It would be disastrous if we toppled over forwards and landed on or right in front of the Hammerhearts, though, so when we had managed to get up there, Marc used his crystal to glue our feet to the ground (a weird feeling but a success all the same).

"They're—just—up—there," panted Marc, who was still struggling to catch his breath.

He pointed off to our right—south. I squinted off in that direction, listening hard for footsteps. "Are you sure?" I hissed back at him.

"Yeah, positive," he hissed back. "I'm watching them. Less than a hundred metres."

Damn, if only it weren't so dark. I squeezed the crystal and considered all sorts of spells that might make it easier to see and rejected them one by one. There was just too much risk. I had to settle for hoping we would see them clearly when they were directly below us.

"I've got an idea," hissed Marc. "Let most of them go in, and then we get the two at the back of their pack. Make them come out here and wait, and when the others start coming out, we get them as well. Once we've got them all, we can probably control all of them at the same time with a single spell."

"That'll take hours," I hissed back.

"Not if we drive them out," Marc replied, and he sounded like he was smirking broadly.

I wondered what hair-brain scheme he had in mind, but it was too late to ask. In the distance, I could now see a dim light approaching. The Hammerheart at the front of the pack was carrying a flare of some sort which he/she was holding high above his/her head to light as much of the ground and rock base as possible. The others were following behind, whether in single or double file I didn't know yet. Seconds later we could see them more clearly; they were all armed with large guns and carrying small bags over their shoulders. The bags would surely hinder their speed at drawing those weapons. They also no doubt had a number of existing Hammerheart devices around their waists, but it was too dark to make them out.

"Remember, get the last two and make them wait down there by the mountain base," hissed Marc.

I nodded and turned my attention to the nearest Hammerhearts, little more than ten feet away and closing rapidly now. Seconds later, they were right below us and passing into the chamber above which we stood. I turned my gaze to the back of the line; there were two of them there and they looked possibly the most alert of the group, turning their heads around and around to keep the group's back covered. I kept my eyes on them and was sure Marc was doing the same. We waited, our nerves jangling. Their number had shrank to eight—then six—then four—and then—

I squeezed my crystal, centring on the one on the right (since I was standing on Marc's right), and he stopped dead, as did the one beside him. They changed their trajectory, moving off to our left and parking themselves side by side in front of the place Marc and I had used to climb up to this ledge, thereby providing a barrier against any Hammerhearts who tried to come up here—not that they would have, of course. They could much more easily shoot us down from the ground. The two Hammerhearts were now under a domination charm each.

"We'll have to wipe all of this from their memories once we're done," Marc hissed. "Okay, what I'm gonna do is pump gas into their chamber."

"Gas?" I repeated, alarmed. "I thought we agreed not to—"

"It won't kill them," Marc assured me, "just make them desperate for fresh air. Trust me. I know it'll go right in to the back since this cave doesn't actually have a protective wall in it they can hide behind."

I nodded and waited. Marc focussed his attention on the entrance to the cave below us and gas began forming in a concentrated cloud. The cloud moved into the entrance of the cave and began spreading into it. As it drifted upward, however, I caught a whiff of the stench. My eyes watered and I covered my face in disgust. It could have been the unhealthiest smelling fart a human was capable of pushing, smelling strongly of rotten eggs, curry, alcohol, and something else I couldn't put my finger on.

"Geez," I gasped.

"Be ready," Marc hissed sideways at me, his own mouth and nose covered with his free hand.

I cast a spell over both of us so that we couldn't smell that terrible—terrible—oh hell, it was beyond description. Now we were able to lower our hands and squint at the ground below us. The cloud was no longer visible. It had dispersed to a mist and spread entirely into the cave. We could hear people coughing and spluttering and choking on it from below and behind us. If they'd been planning on having dinner, I thought amusedly, they would surely have lost their appetites by now.

Moments later, Hammerhearts came bursting out of the chamber, reeling and barely able to stand upright. Marc and I were on them immediately, hitting them with domination charms and stopping them dead in their tracks. Unfortunately, the plan, which had so far gone off without a hitch, began taking a turn for the worst at this point. Yet more Hammerhearts burst through the opening, six of them in fact. We got the two at the back of the pack (that made six under the charm now), but the ones at the front crashed into the two just cursed, and all four of them, plus the two they'd run into, ended up on the ground. I scrambled to perform the domination charm several times over, hissing at Marc out of the side of my mouth, "Let me do the spell. You just make the cursed ones move out of the way."

More of them were spilling from the entrance now. One of them tumbled off to the right and retched, bringing up a puddle of who knew or cared what. I gave him a moment of grace, concentrating on those who had come with him. There were four of them, and one by one they went under. Them, plus the sick one, made eleven.

No, only ten, for one of the ones I thought I'd got earlier when the scrum had gone down was still fully conscious. He was on his feet now, staring around himself in horror. I turned on him, but in the instant before he went under, he opened his mouth and bellowed, *"Sorcerers!"*

We knew we were in trouble now. With eleven down, that left fourteen more Hammerhearts, and the next ones that came out were ready for us. They seemed to know what we were doing but not where we were, for when they came, a pack of seven burst out at exactly the same time, and they had all unslung their guns. Marc and I took down one each but were forced to duck as, fanning off in different directions, they opened fire. Bullets flew right over our heads, chipping the rock behind us. They flew off into the trees, snapping branches and frightening small animals. They had aimed away from the cursed Hammerhearts, but two of them whom Marc had not had time to move into position weren't so lucky.

There were seven out here now, which left seven inside the cave, suffocating on the putrid gas but knowing it was necessary to do so for now. Still ducking, Marc and I took care of the ones shooting closest to where we were. As they went down, more Hammerhearts spilled out of the chamber to take their place. We were forced to enchant them as they came, making the three who'd come out earlier aware of roughly where we were. As the last of the final seven was struck dumb by Marc's domination charm, they turned and aimed at the rock.

They opened fire, and this time we were even luckier. We ducked lower and bullets missed our heads by inches while others ploughed into the rock to Marc's left, sending up chips of stone that rained down around us but never seemed to hit us. It was extremely difficult to concentrate on performing magic with bullets raining all around us, but we did our best. One of the Hammerhearts immediately stopped firing—the centre one. The other two changed their tactic, knowing it was down to them to flush the person or people responsible for this out. They switched to automatic fire and sprayed the rock face behind us. Chips of rock fell on and all around us and we had to hope that, in the darkness, they would not see floating chips of rock in the air, marking our positions. As they were both aiming high, we were able to perform our spells simultaneously. They both stopped firing, and a deathly silence followed.

Marc moved those two into position with the rest of the cursed Hammerhearts—the twenty-three of them. The two who had been killed by the hail of bullets were beyond moving, and we decided we would deal with them as soon as we were finished tinkering with the survivors. I wasn't very happy about how that had gone. The Russians couldn't have not heard the fire of bullets and would perhaps come and investigate. We would have to get someone from this group to contact them and let them know that, while they hadn't caught anyone magical, they hadn't suffered any casualties. Let them learn about these two later.

I unglued our feet from the ledge and we edged our way off it, down towards the group of stunned Hammerhearts. I wasn't sure about Marc, but I was scanning the group for any renegades—men or women who were strong enough to throw it off as I had done. What would we do with them if there were any? I supposed the influential charm would be the only way. Fortunately, there didn't seem to be any.

We set to work, performing several spells to close any loopholes by which anyone could discover the truth about what had happened out here. These Hammerhearts would be seen to travel around the mountain but collect nothing and remember nothing of what they saw. One of them would contact the Russians when the Russians expected to be contacted; the same applied to whoever was monitoring the situation from outside the portal. Then they would set about digging graves for the two who they had killed with their fire, and nobody would learn about that until they were leaving the island. Finally, most importantly, they would be aware of our presence here on the island and appear, to anyone else, to care very much about catching us, but they would make no effort to do so. That done, Marc flushed the gas out of their chamber and forced them to enter it, the four at the back of the pack carrying their departed fellows on their shoulders.

* * *

"We really were considering coming after you guys," Tommy told us. "What on earth went wrong?"

"I guess we just didn't plan it well enough," I told them. "But it worked in the end. They won't give us any more trouble, and apart from the gunfire, nobody else will know anything unusual happened to them."

I could tell by their faces that several of them weren't convinced. Neither was I, really, but apart from having one of us with them at all times, monitoring them, I couldn't see any way we could ensure that they would be on their best behaviour. When I voiced this, James said, quite matter-of-factly, "Send Fewul to do that. It's not like we need all our campsites guarded anymore."

"Geez, why didn't I think of that," Marc muttered, and swore. "I guess the Russians could still find us, but I suppose the odds of them getting to the other two campsites are pretty long, and the odds that they'll be able to open this one… Do you guys know if there's any word in the Russian language that sounds like 'gynaecologist'?"

The door slid open at his last word but closed again as he repeated it impatiently.

"Dunno why you picked that password anyway," Peter muttered to James.

"Okay, how's this," said Marc. "New plan: We'll make Fewul only one form who stays with us at all times and acts as protector if there's any more trouble—though I doubt there would be—and it can watch all our campsites, plus the Hammerhearts, from wherever it is. Just use a magical eye or something. It can let us know if there's any trouble at any of those sites and can act on my orders without us needing to do anything ourselves."

"You can make it do all that?" asked Tommy.

"Should do," he replied, shrugging.

He muttered the password yet again and walked out into the cave where Fewul, in the form of Lucien, was standing sentinel. A minute later, they both returned and the door slid shut again behind them.

"You guys okay with Lucien being his form?"

"Sounds pretty familiar," said Peter. "I gotta admit, it was weird walking past your dad this morning."

It was half past nine by my watch and I was feeling pretty tired after not having slept properly the previous night. I was seriously considering heading off to bed at any moment, not just because I was so tired or because I wanted to get up in the night again and go back to the main hall, but there was a situation taking place within the group that was putting me in a bad mood. Over the last nearly two weeks now, since Natalie had blushingly approached me, she and I had shared a lot of curious looks. I would often catch her looking at me, and while she would blush, she would make no attempt to hide her gaze. She was still as shy as ever, clearly, but she seemed determined that, before anything unpleasant should happen to us, I should understand her feelings towards me. I wished she could just come out and say it, but then what would that have meant for Serena? That was a different issue, but right now, it hardly mattered.

Since we had arrived on Rock Haulter, however, there had been not a single glance to catch. The looks I had come to expect of Natalie were now being spared for Tommy—all for Tommy. It hadn't happened so much while we had been with Smiley, but the rest of the time... He had caught her out several times, and while she had quickly looked away, clearly not as comfortable with it then, she had still blushed, perhaps deeper than she ever had with me. I had also seen her squirming a few times, far too self-conscious when Tommy turned his attention on her than I would have liked. And, most unfortunately, Tommy knew it and was giving her more and more attention. What did this mean? My sense of suspicion told me that somehow, Tommy had done something that had caused her interest in him to be rekindled. If anything, she was more interested now than she had been when they were dating, and certainly more than she had ever been in me. Why, though? Natalie knew what he'd done to her. Why did it suddenly look as though she desired nothing more than to wrap herself around him?

It shouldn't have bothered me, not while I was with Serena, but it did. I told myself fiercely that if Natalie wanted to get back with Tommy, it was entirely her prerogative, and I should not resent either of them for it. I also told myself over and over that my feelings of resentment were caused by a protective instinct, that Tommy had betrayed her once and might do it again. Yet Tommy had grown since then. As far as I knew, he hadn't been with another girl since the one Natalie had caught him with. I couldn't lie to myself: The reason why I didn't want to see Natalie and Tommy together again was because I still wanted her for myself. If they got back together, not only would they probably do a whole lot more than they had last time and not only would I miss out on probably being Natalie's first (for I thought she was probably still a virgin), but on top of all that, they would probably be in it for the long haul this time. You snooze, you lose, Johnny boy. Just remember that next time.

It was a lot to worry about, and I just wasn't up to it, so at a quarter to ten, I stood up and told the others I was having an early night. They were disappointed, most particularly Serena (surprise, surprise), but also, and this really was a surprise, James was disappointed. I would have liked Natalie to show some sort of disappointment too, but none came. She barely turned her head as she bid me good night.

Lena was still staring at me as avidly as ever as I left them in the sitting area of Group F's campsite, but that sort of attention was definitely not what I wanted. It was difficult not to feel at least a bit resentful towards Lena for her continuing interest. When was she going to take the hint? I sighed as I shut my bedroom door. If Lena kept doing that to me, and I became as self-destructive as I had been the night I'd found my way into her, there could possibly be a repeat occurrence. I didn't think Lena would settle for that, though, not after she'd had a taste and decided that she was still interested.

Why on earth hadn't I just asked Natalie out when I'd had the chance? I could have avoided all of this—all of it. That afternoon when I'd listened, by way of the hidden microphone in Felicity and Jessica's room, we had both been single, and Serena and Amelia hadn't even been factors. Stella hadn't been a serious consideration either, whether she had been interested or not. So, it had been Lena —only Lena, and I could only suppose that while not wanting to hurt her had been part of it, and uncontrollable nervousness at the thought of finally confessing my feelings to Natalie another, I had been holding onto a fantasy—a wet dream, really—of being the guy who could have his way with Lena.

How could I have been so stupid? How could I have allowed such things to get in the way of the one thing I really wanted? Was it because I was too cowardly to be with Natalie and effectively procrastinated our relationship? Was it because I wanted to get a bit more experience—more than the naught I'd had at the time—before starting anything with her? Was it because I was a total douchebag who, if honest with himself, wanted to play around with all of them? Was it because I had no fucking idea what I wanted at all?

You're fourteen, I had to keep reminding myself. You're allowed to make mistakes, so long as you learn from them when you do. So many people had given me advice on how to handle this, and a lot of it had been along the lines of "do what's best for you. Don't hold yourself responsible for the emotions of others." That basically meant that if I had to trample a few hearts to protect my own, I should do it. They had also told me that this was okay because they were young too and wouldn't take long to get over it. I tended to believe that, but that didn't make it any easier.

"Never mind your heart for the time being, John." That was James's voice speaking inside my head, and I opened my ears to it immediately. "You don't have to do anything at this very moment, but consider your situation with nothing but logic and see where you end up. Shall we work through it together?" Damn straight, we should. I hadn't a hope in hell of doing that without James, even an imaginary James.

"Okay, start by asking yourself why you're attracted to each of these girls, and work from there. In Amelia's case, it's pretty obvious; it's a connection that, in a happier world, wouldn't have come about. Your proposed solution was that she be your best female friend, and I'd say that's logical, given that the one thing the two of you have in common is too painful to even think about. What kind of relationship would that be? Not a happy one, would be my suggestion. As for Serena, I'd suggest that the main attraction to her is her own attraction to you. Is that a good reason for being in a relationship, do you think?"

No. It's one of the lousiest reasons to be in a relationship that I could think of, and lying there in bed, I actually groaned aloud and had to cover my mouth in surprise of the sound. James was right, of course—about both of them, in fact. Perhaps it would still be possible to have a relationship with Serena in spite of that—after all, there had been plenty of times when my affection for her had been true—but perhaps it wasn't enough. It was clear that my heart lay elsewhere, so now that I knew that, I had to work out exactly where it was. My automatic thought was Natalie, of course, and that brought the resentment toward Tommy flooding back.

After a while, when I realised that these thoughts were achieving nothing but keeping me awake, I turned my attention back to the main hall where I intended to be heading again in a few hours' time, resolving to revisit this mental struggle tomorrow. I dwelled on it for some time, thinking of Stella and thinking of what had happened there last night, hoping I could make it happen again. I knew it required relaxation to the point of unconsciousness. No easy state of mind to achieve, especially if I kept thinking about human beings of the female variety, but I just had to hope.

I had been lying there for some time and was starting to feel drowsy when a possibility occurred to me, and I sat up, my eyes opening wide. Something Smiley had said had suddenly connected in my mind with the unusual event that had happened in that hall last night. Could it be? Could it? I lay back down again, feeling more excited now. If I could make it happen again, I might find out if I was on the right track. That was all, for the instant of excitement had been enough to push me over the edge and into dreamland, or rather, into Stella's mind once again.

"*You—are—not—trying—hard—enough!*" bellowed Hammerson.

"*I am!*" Stella screamed back.

Hammerson drew his hand back and slapped her hard across the face. Her head rocked back and hit the stone pillar behind her, to which she was tightly tied once again. The blow to her head ached immediately, blurring her vision, which had already been fairly blurred with tears anyway, and her cheek stung where Hammerson's hand had made contact with it. Behind him stood three Hammerhearts; Brendon Lawson (2L11), Hall (that's Chief Hall to you, sir), and Tom Hignat. They were all holding bludginators at the ready. It was very dark and, I deduced after I'd woken up, probably two or three hours before sunrise, if they were in Chopville's time zone anyway.

"I want no more excuses from you, young lady!" Hammerson spat at her through clenched teeth. He looked positively insane with rage. "It is not a difficult assignment. You are merely stalling."

"I am *not* stalling!" Stella shouted back. "But if you still don't believe me, then why not get someone else to do it? Then you'll see I'm not the fucking problem."

"Do not raise your voice to me!"

"Why the hell shouldn't I? Let me go, for the love of God."

Hammerson slapped her again, throwing his entire weight behind the force of his hand. Little stars popped in Stella's eyes. She had only occasionally felt this miserable in her life.

"One more time, Stella," he said, more quietly now. "One more time, one more chance. You will do whatever it takes to get inside their base. You will do whatever it takes to retrieve the Darkness Crystal. You will do whatever it takes to bring 3W41 out with you.

You will do whatever else you can while you are in there. If you fail again, young lady, your punishment will be most unpleasant."

"Get stuffed," she replied in a voice of cold distain. "Okay, I'll try again, but you don't scare me. The only thing you've got left to do to me is kill me, and how bad could that be?"

Hammerson looked over his shoulder at the other Hammerhearts, clearly surprised by that response. When he looked back at Stella, he was furious beyond imagining. He whipped his agonator out and thrust it on Stella. She screamed as the pain hit her, and I withdrew from her mind, snapping up in bed and almost toppling sideways onto the floor. Far back in my mind, I could still feel the agonator working on Stella, but it was surely my imagination. I was safely back in my room on Rock Haulter.

I straightened myself up and checked my watch. Only eleven o'clock. I lay down, shivering slightly. I could hear quiet voices around me. The others must have been getting ready for bed. I just lay there and listened to them, thinking of Stella—poor Stella. They were asking her to do the practically impossible and torturing her for failing. It was the last thing she deserved, yet as long as Mr. Woodward was uncertain about her, there was nothing at all that we could do to help.

I had more trouble falling back to sleep now, my mind on Stella (nothing remotely sexual about these thoughts), but eventually I managed it. When I woke up again, it was the dead of night. Well, not quite. My watch told me it was half past five. My heart stopped. I had overslept. I scrambled out of bed, got dressed hastily, and hurried from my room. Fewul, in the form of Lucien, was sitting motionless in the sitting room, but he did not stop me as I crossed the room to the door to Natalie's car park. I jumped in my shiny red hovercar, of which I was becoming fond, and started it up. Once its lower fans had lifted it off the floor, I steered it out of the car park, up the short corridor that almost served as a sort of runway, and out of the magically created hole in the mountain.

Down the hill I went, dodging the caves and enjoying the wind blowing my hair. Soon the ground levelled out and I took off down the slope that led past the tree house and towards the main hall. By the time the trees opened and the hall swam into view, ahead of me, to the east, the sky had the tiniest tinge of light just above the horizon. I parked the car close to some nearby bushes, knowing it would be safe under the invisibility veil, turned it off, and jumped from it without waiting for it to lower all the way back to the ground. I hurried to the doors, dipping my hand to the crystal and knowing that, now that I was so close to other people, I had to tread more carefully. I had no idea what time the Russians rose in the morning, but I hoped they'd wait until at least half past six before coming down into the hall.

The door opened on the command of the crystal and, as I had yesterday morning, I edged inside and slid the door carefully shut behind me. The inside of the hall had changed considerably in twenty-four hours, as I had known from my spying with the crystal. There were now rows and rows of desks, many with computers, many with devices I'd never seen before, and many with nothing at all but pads of paper. It was empty as far as other people went, but that didn't change the fact that I had to do this quickly. I would have a lot more trouble relaxing if someone came in while I was here.

I moved slowly away from the door, thinking. Where would be the best place to put myself? The middle of the hall seemed a good place, so I headed down an aisle between the rows of desks, found a spot that was close enough to the middle of the room, pulled out a seat, and sat down. The silence around me was complete but not heavy. It was as though the slightest breath of air would be perfectly audible in the room, if there were a breath of air to be felt. I sat back in the chair and considered what I was about to attempt to do.

I was entertaining the idea that, yesterday morning, I had somehow heard echoes from the past in this very room, the most recent people to occupy it. Smiley had said I had a perception of the fourth dimension. He had also said the time axis could only be accessed from the in-between. In other words, one had to be able to move along the fourth dimension far enough to leave the first three dimensions behind. Yet he had also said I could not do that. My perception was no more than an awareness of the dimension, rather than an ability to move along it. I wasn't about to make the mistake of confusing the two. The way Smiley had said it, if I really had moved along the fourth dimension, I would have felt it far more physically.

My idea, however, was simply based on perception. In my mind, I saw the time axis as a corridor, and points along it were rooms branching off the side of it. To enter in and out of these rooms, one would have to move along the fourth dimension, but that meant that if the doors were open, a person with a perception of the fourth dimension might be able to hear voices from those rooms closest to him. It was a possibility, wasn't it? I wished I could discuss it with James (after all, who would be the quickest person to pick up on where I was coming from with this), but what were the chances of him taking me seriously? This investigation was one I had to make on my own.

There was one thing I didn't get, though. I took Smiley's word for it that I couldn't move into the fourth dimension. If I could, he probably would have seen that shimmering quality around me just as I had around him. Yet last night I had put my hand through a cardboard box, right through it. I could still remember the feel of the books inside it. If I hadn't moved at least partially into the fourth dimension, gone into a shadow like Smiley did regularly, then what had that been all about? Had it been my mind playing tricks on me? I didn't think so. No, the only possible theory I could come up with to explain that one, other than Smiley being wrong, was that my mind had somehow detached from my body. If that were true, then perhaps it would be possible to use my mind to move along the fourth dimension and leave my body behind.

This train of thought was getting me nowhere. How could my mind relax if I kept exploring these possibilities? I would think later. Now, it was time to relax. I sank more heavily into my chair, putting my head back into its cushion, hoping dearly that this would relax me enough without actually putting me to sleep. I tried to clear my mind, and only when I stopped trying did I actually succeed. I merely sat there, the silent hall around me, Russians sleeping above me, and that was all. Nothing happened.

I sat up after a while, my body feeling heavy and sleepy. I checked my watch. A quarter past six. I couldn't hear any movement above me yet, but felt sure that they would probably be waking up, showering, or whatever their order of things was by this time. Back at the campsite, they may already be stirring. The alarm was set for half past six, but it wouldn't be surprising if one or two got up earlier so that they could get the first shower. I stood up, disappointment flooding my mind, and left the hall.

The fresh morning air was nice on my face as I slid the door shut and used the crystal to lock it behind me. I took a moment to enjoy it, leaning back against the wall beside the door, my body feeling extraordinarily heavy, apparently not quite recovered from the almost-doze I had sunk into back in the hall. I rested my head back against the brick and barely felt it. Something seemed to keep me there, something that mingled with the disappointment that bound me to the spot, making the idea of heading back to the campsite now unappealing. I stood there, leaning against the wall, the fresh morning air incredibly relaxing…

It happened, taking me by surprise but not enough to break the trance immediately. I felt a slight movement in no particular direction. I heard sounds, echoing sounds that I could identify but not understand. A jumble of confusion and panic—Russian students, returning to the hall and clearly anxious to get in quickly. This had to be the previous evening, after they had heard the gunfire. I made myself focus on what I was hearing, tried to sharpen the sounds, to pick out individual voices. It seemed to work, but the more I concentrated on what I was hearing, the less of my current surroundings I was able to perceive. As I was barely noticing anything else now anyway, this made no impression on me.

I was drifting backwards, a sensation I recognised all too well. It was how moving backwards inside a person's memories had felt. The sounds sharpened to the point that I might have been standing right there with them: Panicky young females, jabbering away in Russian; male voices behind them, trying to hurry them up; a more official voice, most likely trying to organise his students as they attempted to enter the hall. That wasn't all, though. I could feel their panic like an aura around me; I could sense the evening air, not to mention the various fragrances on the students; but most important of all, I began to see them, actually see them in my mind.

It was as though I were standing a short distance into a cave, looking out at people moving around in the light outside. The images were nowhere near as clearly defined as the sounds, but I now understood that if I wanted to move closer, I would be able to, at least a little bit. There weren't very many of them, as I had already deduced (both by the sounds and the previously acquired knowledge), but they were carrying a lot of heavy looking equipment in their arms. A chubby man was standing so close to me that he was obscured slightly by the darkness out of which I was watching. He was clearly the one trying to get the students into the hall in an orderly fashion. Another man (a much younger one, perhaps only a few years older than me) hurried around the side of the pack, directly at me.

My instinct to move out of his way was automatic, and the moment I moved a muscle with my physical body, the spell broke. I was once again standing beside the door of the main hall in the dawn, no longer leaning against the wall but slightly to the right of where I had been due to the movement I had just made. I stood there for several seconds before giving my head a slight shake and moving towards the bushes where I had parked my hovercar.

That had been far more than I had expected, and I wasted no time on my way back to the campsite reflecting on what had just happened. It seemed to confirm my theory that my mind had left my body, that it had firstly moved along the fourth dimension, then along the time access, then could have moved back along the fourth dimension again if I'd wanted it to. Judging by the cardboard box incident, it could also move along the three physical dimensions I was accustomed to, but without actually moving my body, that would be very difficult to do. As far as the mind went, I had moved out of my room, along the corridor to the previous room, and had stood in the doorway, watching the progress inside it. Apparently, I had gone in far enough that I was no longer affected by the time axis, that I had returned to the progress of time and could observe the progression of events.

How long could I have stood there, watching and listening? Probably all night, until my mind caught up with my body again. I didn't know, but it opened up a possibility to me, one that hadn't taken long to occur to me. If I could use this talent to observe the past, depending on how far back I could go, I could watch everything that happened in the main hall when I had been an infant, to perhaps identify what event had taken place in there that had concerned me and Stella. As I approached Natalie's car park, I now understood what the next phase of my personal journey was: I would use this ability to its full potential.

Part 5: Memories

Chapter 33: Rift

We found the cave Smiley had told us about at around ten o'clock in the morning of May 13. He had told us it was on the northeast side of the mountain about six hundred feet above ground level. We had taken our hovercars around to the general area and, using the Sien-Leoard and Hero Crystals, had navigated our way around the various holes in the rock until we reached the one that was, according to the crystals, the one we wanted. Unlike Smiley's cave, however, it was not built with enough space to park ten hovercars. Two of us had been able to park in the entrance, but the others had to place their cars carefully on the rock around it.

"This looks pretty dodgy," James observed. "I know the Hammerhearts won't give us any trouble anymore, but what about the Russians? They come along here and trip over an invisible car—there's gonna be hell to pay."

"That's why Lucien's here," said Marc. "Fewul, you stand here and make sure no one comes along. If anyone does, then use magic to send them off in another direction without them realising. Also make sure nothing happens to any of our cars. Got it?"

"Yes, master," said Fewul in Lucien's voice.

"Are we allowed to come in and watch?" asked Siobhan.

She, Lena, and Erica were becoming increasingly aware by now that the job they had been brought along for had been made redundant by the Beast of Magic. None of them were entirely sure just how far into this business they were allowed to get. My initial feeling was that we should have just left them at the campsite or else out here on the rock with Fewul, but it didn't really seem fair on them to have brought them all this way and then leave them standing around doing nothing. The general unspoken consensus seem to be that after they had been witness to our discussion with Smiley, they were now as much a part of this as Peter, James, and Serena.

"I guess they can come in," said Natalie, not all that happily.

Marc led the way into the cave, carrying the box of memories Smiley had given us. The door before us had yet another L keyhole in it, and once I had applied the right key, the ten of us entered the room beyond. It was a very strange place, perfectly square and very dark and with a very empty feel to it. The walls, floor, and ceiling were all made of dark, grey stone. There was nothing in it except a small device by the door set into the stone.

"Any ideas?" Tommy asked quietly as the door swung shut automatically behind us. His voice echoed a great deal in the stone room.

"Here," said Marc, who was holding his Hero Crystal again.

He approached the device by the door and set the box down beside it. He opened it and pulled out a small object. None of us had actually examined the form of the memories until this point. They were small enough to hold in one hand but too large to wrap your fingers all the way around. They were black with a white flap that looked like it lifted up and revealed something beneath. Each of them was numbered. The numbers had been attached by tape, making it clear that this was an edition Smiley had added himself, probably identifying the order in which we were to view the memories.

"Just give me a moment here," Marc told us. "I'm fairly sure the memory goes in here. How we're supposed to watch it, I'm not sure, but I guess we'll find out."

He sorted through the memories until he had located the first one. He examined the device for a moment before lifting a lid and placing the memory inside it, lifting the flap up and sliding it into a slot so that the device could access the inside of the object. Closing the lid, he examined the device for a few more moments before pushing a button, the only button on the thing, by the look of it.

"That did it," said Tommy at once.

"Holy crap—" Serena started. That was all she had time for.

It was working, all right, but not at all how I had expected. I had imagined one, or perhaps all the walls turning into screens through which we would watch the memory, the sounds being generated around us (magical surround sound or something of the sort). Instead, my surroundings dimmed—then faded—then everything was gone. For a moment or two, I was nothing at all, before my body returned and my senses became focussed once more. I had a remarkable sense of déjà vu, standing in what looked like the entrance of a cave, looking out at people in the open. I knew at once what was going on. What I was seeing, what I was feeling in my body, what I was thinking, all added up to one thing. I was inside Smiley's mind, viewing his memories in exactly the same way I had entered Sebastian's mind and viewed his memories two weeks earlier.

I also understood what I was seeing, and not just because I was also getting Smiley's thoughts babbling away inside my own head. He was standing in his shadow, as he had described it, and I recognised it from when I had done the same thing that morning. The remarkable difference between what I had done and what Smiley was doing, however, was that Smiley's body had come with him; he was more than just a body in one location, sending his mind back through the time axis. I wanted to look around for the others, to gauge their reaction to what would be entirely new for them, but I had been totally taken away from my surroundings and had no control whatsoever over Smiley's movements.

I turned my attention to what Smiley was watching, the events that were taking place outside our shadow. Presently there was all of nothing to see, merely three people sitting on one side of a table—an elderly man, a woman who might have been in her early thirties, and, in her arms, a small baby boy. On the other side of the table were two empty chairs. The room appeared to be a study of some kind, though a fairly old-fashioned one—certainly no computer to speak of. A desk behind the room's occupants was covered in papers and, around the walls, various filing cabinets stood, one of them open. A clock directly opposite Smiley showed that the time was just after three o'clock. It was an analogue display, but Smiley's thoughts indicated that it was the afternoon.

I looked at the people in the room and just as I recognised one of them, Smiley's thoughts confirmed their identities. The middle-aged woman was none other than Dorothy Hammerson, Tankom herself, most likely before she had earned that nickname. The infant in her arms was surely a baby Arnold Hammerson, the baby who would grow up to murder so many, including my own mother, and was still trying to kill me. It was an incredible thought. The elderly man beside Tankom was her father, Lester Hammerson, the cruel instigator behind the first Sorcerous war. I had never seen him before, not in a photo or old video or anything, but with an enormous jolt of what would have been my stomach if I'd still been in my own body, I recognised him. I had never seen his face, but he and I had crossed paths once, on a mild, terrifying night in April. Even though he was years in his grave, he was still killing.

I still wasn't sure what was going on here, and Smiley wasn't speculating on what the point of this visit back in time was, but before I had much time to wonder, there was a knock on the door and Lester got to his feet. "At last," he said. "I was beginning to wonder if we had had an unfortunate miscommunication."

He stepped around the table, strode towards the door, and opened it.

"Good day, Roger," he said pleasantly, holding his hand out to the man in the doorway. "I really do appreciate you taking time out from your busy schedule to come over here to meet with us. We have much to discuss."

The man to whom he was speaking was not quite as old as Lester but certainly on his way there, mid-fifties at least. There was a woman behind him, and though she was younger and far more attractive than I'd ever seen her in life, I recognised her facial features at once as Lillian Woodward's. The man with her must surely be her father. Roger, Lester had called him, although if Lillian had taken the Woodward name from her husband, Roger would go by some other name. I didn't know, and once again, Smiley wasn't speculating on it.

"It is nice to see you again, Lester," said Roger, inclining his head a fraction before looking up at Lester. The Hammerson Sorcerer was the taller of the two by several inches. "You know I am always prepared to come and meet with you, or to invite you to see me on my side of the Atlantic, but I must admit, your most recent letter was slightly disconcerting."

This seemed to take Lester by surprise. "Come in and take a seat, both of you, and let us palaver," he said, sweeping the two of them ahead of him and closing the door softly behind them. "I don't know what about my letter could have given you that notion, so let us sit and clear it all up. I'm sure that, once any misunderstandings have been dealt with, you will have no ill feelings towards our proposition."

"I hope that is so," said Roger, taking the seat opposite the one Lester had not long vacated. "How are you, Dorothy?"

"Doing well, thank you, Roger," she replied politely. "How are you? And you, Lillian?"

Lillian and Lester were taking their seats at the table by this stage.

"Very well, thank you," replied Lillian.

"You didn't bring Frederic with you," said Lester, sounding disappointed. "I was looking forward to meeting him. You will have to return sometime soon, Lillian, so that I can meet the budding young Sorcerer I have heard so much about."

"I'll be sure to do that next time," she replied, "but he has been on the sick side lately and I thought it might be best to leave him with Peter this time. How is Ian?" she added to Dorothy.

"He is fine," Dorothy replied. "He had to work today, but he sends his regards."

The poor bastard would be pushing up daisies by now, Smiley thought before he could stop himself. Up until that point, Smiley had turned himself into the perfect listening machine, keeping his mind as blank as possible so that he could take in all that was being said and done without interference from his own mind. That one thought had slipped before he could stop it, and I now felt him scramble to clear his mind again.

"Send him our best, won't you," Roger told her. "So, Lester, shall we get down to business?"

"At your discretion," said Lester, nodding. "Dorothy, could you please provide our guests with refreshments?"

"Tea for both of us," Roger replied when Dorothy looked at him questioningly.

She used her magic to create the cups of tea, which she pushed carefully across the table to Roger and Lillian. Baby Arnold in her lap made a grab for one of them, but Dorothy expertly prevented his hand from getting too close to the hot liquid. She then provided a drink (an alcoholic beverage, by the look of it) for her father and a coffee for herself before sitting back in her seat and taking her son in her arms once again.

"Now, Lester," said Roger formally, "your letter of two weeks ago implied a rather ambitious undertone on your part. I am interested to understand exactly what you have in mind for the future with regard to 'using magic to its full potential.'"

"Indeed," said Lester, just as formally. "Do note at once that I am not speaking of pushing the magical laws to their boundaries. No one in this room has any interest in providing a means to evade death, travel in time, or any of those other things that our noble ancestors Mary Sien and John Leoard weren't able to tap in their time. My goals are far more modest. We already have certain abilities that, for as long as our families have had the honour of possessing magic, have not been utilised for all the good they could for mankind."

"Continue," Roger invited and took a sip of his tea.

"As we all know, throughout history, magic has been seen by many as a dark art," Lester went on, "and in that time, it made perfect sense for real Sorcerers such as our ancestors to keep low profiles. Now that western society has moved toward a school of thought based primarily on rationality rather than superstition, many people are turning an open mind to the idea of magic being a part of their lives."

"I'm not sure you've thought this through," said Roger, but Lester held up a hand.

"Do let me finish, please," he said respectfully. "If I gave the impression that my idea was to provide all citizens of this great nation with a direct means of accessing magic, I apologise. Such an idea would, of course, be at best impractical. It seems to me, however, that magic has been far too underutilised for a very long time. When I was growing up just after the turn of the century, my mother was ashamed of being a Sorcerer, and my father persuaded her not to use magic, to pretend it didn't exist, if it would make her feel better. As a consequence, I was forced to find my own way.

"The point I am trying to make here, Roger, is that I believe the time has come for us to step out into the world and use our magic to intervene in this turbulent society we live in."

"Are you suggesting that we take up a role as social superheros?" Roger enquired incredulously.

Lester inclined his head respectfully and replied, "I'm not quite sure what you mean by that, but I'm not talking about inconsequential matters here, Roger. Using our powers to resolve a dispute between two neighbours over the cost of building a fence between their properties, for example, would be like mankind discovering electricity and deciding that its most practical use would be to make one's hair stand on end. There are far greater tensions in the world today that, I'm sure you would agree, our magic could bring to a smooth and speedy conclusion."

"Are you referring to the political difficulties in Europe and Asia?" Roger asked. "Because if you are, again, I'm not sure you've thought this through. Call this the age of rationality all you like, but very few governments around the world will appreciate having their authority to make certain decisions taken away from them by folks such as us."

"Perhaps the authorities wouldn't," Lester agreed, "but remember, we also have powers to make them nice and agreeable to our cause. Remember also what a single government of a single country desires is not necessarily for the good of mankind; many governments operate for the good of the government. It is never possible to make everybody happy, of course, but I'm sure you'll agree that the general population and its good is more important than a single government, or the politicians within it."

"Once again, Lester, your vision is remarkably short-sighted," said Roger. "You need to understand that people do not like being told what they can and can't do—"

"Roger, my friend, it is impossible to run any society without telling people what they can and can't do," Lester interrupted. "The difference between the way society is run now and the way it could be run if we could use our powers to influence—"

"Hold on," said Roger, more sharply now, some of the respectful tone he had maintained so far falling away. "Are you suggesting that we use our magic to overthrow the government and set up our own rule?"

"I'm sure it does not need to come to that, Roger," said Lester, though I noticed, as did Smiley, that he clenched his fists as he spoke, "but I'm sure you would agree that, if we did actually run things, we could solve many more problems in society than any government could."

"How grand are you imagining this to be?" Roger asked. "Are you thinking of applying this only to America, or are you thinking on a global scale?"

"That depends on how far we wish to stretch our magic," Lester replied. "Certainly taking over a single country would not solve any international relations, nor would it deal with the many problems faced by overseas nations. In the end, however, I believe it would be most beneficial for the world if we could establish a rule over all countries, unite them as one, and provide them all with a structure where our magic can be used to ensure the best for all."

"So this is your idea of using magic to its full potential," said Roger, looking both angry and disgusted now. "Rise up against every authority in the world, one by one, use magic to overthrow them all, and install a single oligarchy with us six Sorcerers as the rulers over all. Tell me, Lester, how did you intend to do this without spilling any blood?"

"Roger, Roger," Lester cried, losing patience now, "why should any blood be spilt in a revolution when we have magic at our disposal? We wouldn't need to kill, or even hurt, anyone. We would only need to tamper with certain minds and then sit back and pull the strings."

"Isn't that a bit immoral?" said Lillian, chipping in for the first time. I had almost forgotten about her, Tankom, and baby Hammerson.

"It would only need to be done where opposition is met," Lester replied. "We will have greater issues at hand once that is done. Establishing the right structure for all will be a challenge, I do not deny that, and we will have to deal with troublemakers harshly, I regret to say, but these are all necessaries we will need to face for the good of mankind."

"Where opposition is met," Roger repeated, and now he stared Lester down. The elder Hammerson looked suddenly anxious.

"Come now, Roger. The plan is a good one, but it surely will not work unless all six of us work together."

"You use that as your only excuse," said Roger coldly. "That it will all be for the good of mankind. That single reason, or variations of it, have been behind many of the world's greatest blunders over the years. Too many wars have been started because those in power believed their idea was the right one for their people. I'm sorry, Lester, but I cannot believe that your intention is for the good of the people of the world. I think it more likely that once you have established your desired rule, it will be for the good of us—or more specifically, yourself."

That did the trick. Both men were angry now.

"I am very disappointed by your attitude," said Lester, getting to his feet. Beside him, Dorothy did the same, the baby still nestled in her arms. "I respect your opinion, but I'm afraid you and I cannot see eye to eye on this issue."

"I will never, nor will anyone in my family, agree to using magic to rule over common folk," said Roger, standing up also.

"Then you and I have nothing left to say to each other," said Lester coldly.

"Nothing at all," Roger agreed.

He turned and, his daughter right behind him, looking nervous, walked to the door, opened it, and left without a word. The two Hammersons exchanged dismayed looks. The baby let out a wail.

The scene faded very quickly, and moments later, the stone room we had been in at the start had returned. The feeling created a sudden and momentary feeling of vertigo that caused me to stagger slightly, but perhaps my experience in these matters prevented me from falling. Around me, however, several people let out involuntary yells and there were several thuds and gasps of pain. Looking around, I saw that Marc was the only other person still on his feet and only because he had quickly grabbed hold of the device in which he had put the memory. Everyone else was on the floor or attempting to pick themselves back up.

"I think I broke my tailbone," grunted Peter.

"I think I broke my sense of reality," said James loudly.

"That was—just—wow," said Erica, unable to articulate anything else.

"So that's what it's like to watch someone's memories," said Tommy interestedly, leaning against the wall behind him. "You actually become the person whose mind you're in. Guess it makes sense. Well, no mystery as to what we just saw, I suppose."

"That's how it all started," said Marc. "That must have been nearly fifty years ago now, if Hammerson was a baby."

"Smiley did say it started in the early sixties," said Natalie.

"Can I offer a suggestion?" said Peter. "Next time we watch a memory, everyone sit down."

Several people laughed at that, and quite a few followed his suggestion, me included. Marc had just removed the first memory from the playback device and was now searching the box for the second one.

"I tell you what," he said to the group at large, "and this is only a suggestion, so feel free to disagree with me. We can watch another memory now, and then we'll call it a morning and head back to the campsite. Have lunch, have the afternoon off, and then we can have an early dinner at—let's say five, then come back here after tea for an evening session. How's that sound?"

A short silence followed before Tommy said, "I don't mind that."

There was a general muttering of ascent around the room.

"Okay, cool," said Marc. Having finally located the memory with the number two taped to it, he straightened up and began fitting it into the playback device. "Everyone ready to see what else Smiley's got for us?"

We were ready and we all sat, waiting expectantly for him to push the button. Marc took a firm hold of the playback device in one hand, hesitated for a moment, then pushed the button. A few moments of nothing before our surroundings faded once again and we sank back into Smiley's recent past.

The first thing I noticed was that it was Christmastime in this memory. The radio in the corner was playing a Christmas carol, not to mention the tall Christmas tree in the other corner. The second thing I noticed was that where the previous memory had been in the home or base of the Hammersons, this memory was clearly in the home of the Woodwards. Lillian Woodward was sitting in an armchair and knitting something, in a completely non-magical fashion. She was the only one in the room. The rest of what had to be the Woodwards' sitting room was deserted. She appeared quite relaxed, but something, perhaps nothing more than Smiley's imagination, gave the place an air of tension.

A doorbell rang from somewhere in the house. Lillian made to get out of her seat but a young male voice called from another room, "I've got it—oh my!"

"Who is it?" Lillian called back.

The voice didn't answer. Lillian waited, listening, her knitting temporarily forgotten. Smiley also listened, as did I. We heard the door open, followed by an exchange of voices. After about a minute, I heard the door shut again, and then footsteps approaching the room we were in—two pairs of footsteps. Moments later, two people entered the room through the door beside the Christmas tree. The one in front was a teenager I recognised at once as Frederic Woodward (his visage reminded me vividly of James, despite the fact that their physical appearances were nothing alike). Following closely behind him was a woman I also recognised: Tankom. Judging by the looks of the three Sorcerers and their approximate ages, this had to be the mid to late seventies.

"Dorothy!" Lillian cried in complete astonishment. Her knitting fell to the floor, and she barely noticed it. "This is—wow—what a surprise. What brings you here?"

"I've come on the behalf of my father," Tankom replied. "He has a matter he wishes to address with—well, I think he's more interested in the message getting to you, now. How is Roger these days?"

"He has been ill lately but is making a nice recovery. Do sit down. It's been far too long."

"I know," Tankom replied, sitting down in the seat beside Lillian, who took up the one she had been in earlier. Frederic, clearly unsure what his current position was in the company of one of the Hammersons, stood hesitantly beside the Christmas tree, watching Tankom nervously. "It has been too long. Sixteen years of silence has been too unfortunate."

"I couldn't agree more," said Lillian enthusiastically. "I can't tell you how pleased I am that your father is prepared to make an attempt to bridge the gap after all this time."

"Actually, he is not in much of a mood for putting past differences behind us, I regret to say," said Tankom, a little heavily. "In fact, that is why he sent me instead of coming here himself. I'm sure you remember our last meeting as well as I do?"

"Yes, I do," said Lillian, warily now. "Not one of my more pleasant memories, but not one I can discard just anytime."

"I agree," said Tankom. "Tell me, Lil, what do you think your father went away from that encounter thinking?"

Lillian stared at Tankom for several moments, apparently trying to decide if this was a trick question. Finally, she said, "Well, he was angry, and I think he was very nervous. He and I never discussed it, but I believe he spent many years watching movements all over the world, waiting for a sign that Lester would put his plans into action."

Tankom mulled this response over for a few moments herself before replying. "If you're saying that your father noticed nothing, then that is probably what my father would want to hear. You see, Lil, while neither I nor my father have made any moves against any form of authority since our last meeting, something we would have been happy to do immediately if we'd had your support, we have been working underground."

Teenage Frederic Woodward started at this and began slowly backing away from Tankom.

"What do you mean by that?" Lillian asked. "What exactly have you been doing?"

"Well, when I said underground, I meant it literally as well as figuratively," said Tankom, smiling slightly. "We have been setting up a secret structure that, when put to use, will maximise our ability to seize power when the time comes. We have also spent the last ten years recruiting an army who will assist us, our new structure making it possible for them to do so effectively."

"Hold on," said Lillian, straightening up in her chair and not looking remotely relaxed anymore. "Are you saying that you are putting this crazy plan of yours into effect immediately as of now?"

"Not quite immediately, but very soon," Tankom replied. "My father wished to gauge your reaction to the idea, and to offer you and your family one last chance to join us. It would really complicate things for us if we had three Sorcerers—equals to us—opposing us, but we would be prepared to put the effort into finding ways to minimise your potential impact on our plans should you choose to meddle."

Lillian stared at Tankom in disgust before saying coldly, "I'd like you to leave my house immediately."

"Very well," said Tankom, getting to her feet. "But do us a favour and let your father know of what has transpired here as soon as you can. We have no specific dates in mind, but we will be on the lookout for an overt sign of your discontent in the meantime."

"If you do anything to anyone, Dorothy, if anyone in your family uses their powers against any form of authority, you can expect an immediate response from us."

Tankom bowed. "I'm sorry it had to go this way, Lillian. I look forward to seeing you again in the near future, hopefully in more pleasant circumstances."

Tankom turned and found herself facing a startled Frederic Woodward. He was still standing in the doorway and looking very nervous, but as Tankom made to leave, he stood his ground.

"You're gonna go down, you are," he said aggressively, pumping the air between them with a couple of punches. "You and your family are gonna be kissing the dust at your feet—"

"Stop that at once, Frederic!" Lillian snapped at her son. "Let the woman leave."

He frowned deeply at his mother but moved aside anyway. Tankom swept by him with distain. As Tankom's footsteps retreated down the corridor in the direction from which they had come, the two remaining Sorcerers stared at each other anxiously.

The memory faded, and moments later, reality had returned once again. There was no sound of staggering people this time. The sense of vertigo was the same but sitting down helped. I made a mental note to create comfortable armchairs to relax in while we watched for next time.

"Interesting," said Peter in a tone that suggested otherwise.

"It *is* interesting," said Tommy, more seriously. "I mean, it's not stuff we really need to know, but how many people in the world would have seen what we just saw?"

"Easy enough to count," said James. "Them three, Smiley, and us ten—that makes fourteen."

"It was a rhetorical question." Tommy shrugged. "The point is, we're being treated here. I think we all agreed the best way to work out what's going on now is to work out what went on in the past. Now we're getting to see bits of that."

"Let's hope we get to see something more relevant to our problems, though," said Peter.

"Well, there are still a bunch of memories left to see," said Marc, looking into the box. "How about we head back for lunch and come back here this evening?"

* * *

We split up after our lunch. Three o'clock found Marc in the tree house talking to Amelia on the phone there. Lena was also in the tree house, reading quietly. James and Erica had gone into Group F's campsite and were presently in there alone, doing who knew what. I supposed they would retire to one of their bedrooms if things got going too much. Fewul, still in Lucien's form, was standing guard outside Group F's campsite, as it was the easiest to get to and the only one whose inhabitants couldn't see outside. The rest of us had spent the time since our lunch in the Group E campsite, just sitting around and talking about stuff unrelated to our Rock Haulter mission.

At around three o'clock, I decided to get up and move. Perhaps it was a good thing that Lena hadn't deliberately put herself in my line of sight again, but I was getting extremely disheartened as I watched whatever was going on between Tommy and Natalie. They certainly weren't back together and didn't look as though they had discussed anything between them—yet, but they certainly snuck glances at each other quite a lot. Mostly, it was Natalie doing the sneaking, because Tommy didn't seem to mind if he was caught. He was quite comfortable with the way things were playing out. As for Natalie, I had no idea at all what she was thinking. What could she be thinking? How could she justify being attracted to him all over again after what he did to her last time? Girls are so strange, I thought unhappily.

In order to get away from it all, I decided to ask Peter for a private word. It wasn't such a bad idea. After all, I had brought Harry and Simon up to speed on my own events and not told Peter or James anything. James didn't seem all that interested anymore, as far as I could tell, and I had always been nervous discussing Serena with Peter, knowing he had been attracted to her before he had started dating Kylie. Like my feelings for Natalie and James's for Kylie, it was likely that Peter would have a soft spot for Serena still and may not give me the most impartial advice about how to deal with her. That seemed even more likely now that he was single again, but at the same time, I was curious about him and Siobhan. He didn't seem to treat her any differently from the rest of us, yet she certainly seemed interested in him. If Peter was lonely, and surely he must be since the events of a week ago, then why hadn't he allowed her to comfort him as she probably wanted to?

Ignoring the curious looks from Siobhan and Serena (Natalie and Tommy barely looked up as we left), Peter and I went into the bedroom corridor and into my room. We sat down on the bed and there, I began recounting as much as I dared in front of him, not hesitating to bring Natalie, Amelia, and Lena into the tale, even though I had already decided that Amelia didn't factor into my romantic future in any way, and if I could control my imagination, Lena wouldn't either. Peter listened mostly in silence, though occasionally he chipped in with a question. He kept a straight face as I spoke, but by the time I came to a stop, having just told him of what I'd been thinking about the night before, he didn't look very happy. In fact, he looked both angry and disgusted—not a sight I found comforting.

"Jesus, John," he muttered, looking away for a moment.

"What?" I said indignantly. "I know I'm not doing this thing right, but until I find my way—"

"Who are you kidding? You know what you want," he snapped. "You want Natalie, you always have, but you're too spineless to tell Serena you've been playing her for a fool for two months."

"I haven't been playing her for a fool."

"Sure you have. Don't you remember ages ago? How she was chasing you and you kept avoiding her? Why on earth did you suddenly decide to let her catch you?"

"Er," I said, brought up short, thinking back to that first night of March. Now that I looked back on it, I realised what had gone wrong that night: I had been lonely and depressed and I had simply responded to Serena because it had come naturally. The truth of the matter was terrible and undeniable.

"I'll tell you why," he went on. "It was because you were there and she was there, and maybe you had become sick of being single and watching the rest of us—"

"Hey, come on," I protested. "There was nothing wrong with it at the time. How could I know things wouldn't work out with Serena if I didn't at least give it a try?"

He sighed. "That's true, I guess, but then why didn't you get out of it when you realised it wasn't working? You had several opportunities to break up, and never mind wanting other girls, but you kept finding excuses to stay. What on earth for?"

"I dunno." I shrugged. "I guess I just really wanted it to work somehow."

"You just couldn't bear to tell her the truth," he said coldly. "Telling her about Tulip is barely scratching the surface. She probably knows that Natalie likes you, and she certainly knows about Lena liking you—everyone does. Why didn't you just break up with her before doing what you did with Lena?"

"You know, if things had happened in a different order, I probably would have," I said truthfully. "I just felt really guilty the next day and —"

"That's really pathetic," he muttered. "Well, I won't say anything about it to Serena, but only 'cause you're my brother. If you wanted my opinion, I reckon what you're doing is really gutless, and how you handled the whole Lena situation, even if it was necessary to get us here, was as bad as anything Underwood did. You really have to make up your mind about this 'cause it's so unfair on Serena to keep stringing her along. She probably believes you still really like her."

"I will," I muttered shamefully, feeling a little resentful, yet knowing everything he said was true. "I guess you're right. I do still want Natalie, and more than any of the others, but how do I know I haven't just lost my chance with her?"

"If I were you, I'd take the chance," he told me. "If you miss out and have to be single, at least you won't be screwing with someone else in the process. Now that you mention it, though, what on earth is going on with those two anyway?"

"Beats me." I shrugged gloomily. "He said something to her on the boat, something about asking her if she wanted to come and sit with him. She blew him off that time, but ever since, she's just been looking at him more and more. Beats me why she's suddenly interested in him again after what he did to her last time."

"And 'cause she's supposed to like you, going by that thing she did a couple of weeks ago," said Peter. "Interesting, you know. I thought Tommy had got over her by now. Looks like he never really lost interest in her but was just waiting for her to get over it. Smart move." He looked at me with interest of his own now. "How far do you reckon he would go to get her back?"

"Who knows," I said bitterly. "Maybe not to any length, though. I mean, he had the Sien-Leoard Crystal with him in those early days, and I was definitely worried he might use it against her to make her sleep with him. That wasn't the main reason I took it off him, but it was a relief to get it away from him."

"Exactly, you *took* it *off* him," said Peter, and I recognised his expression—he was on to a theory of some sort. "How do we know what he might have been planning on doing with it if things had kept going like that?"

"He might have used it," I said, hoping he wouldn't have. It was not a nice thought to have about a guy who, apart from this business with Natalie, I liked quite a lot. "Or maybe he would have just kept screwing her sister. Who knows."

"True, we don't know," said Peter, shrugging, "but the point is, he doesn't have the Sien-Leoard Crystal with him this time, so even if he might have considered doing it last time, he couldn't have done anything to her this time."

He was staring hard at me, and I knew I was supposed to pick up the hidden message, but I was completely stumped. "Maybe he's just really persuasive," I suggested. "Who knows. Girls often get attracted to the wrong sort of guys."

"That must be why they like you," Peter grumbled, "but that's not the point. Don't you get it, John? Tommy doesn't need the Sien-Leoard Crystal to screw with Natalie's feelings. He's already got what he needs."

"Good looks?" I said blankly.

Peter shook his head. "Wake up, John. When you took the Sien-Leoard Crystal off him, what did you give him in return?"

"The Light Crystal," I answered, trying to think ahead to whatever Peter was getting at—and then, in a stroke, I understood. "You think he used the Darkness Crystal?"

"Maybe," he said. "I mean, it's as good of an explanation as any for why it's taken so long for him to have another go with her."

"I hope you're wrong," I said, a little shakily. Anger was there too, but for now, it was below the surface. "I mean, after all the things that crystal has done, killing all those people and directly murdering

Amelia's mother just last week, and then days later, Tommy goes and uses it to fulfil his own sexual appetite?"

"Doesn't sound good, does it," said Peter, a little shakily too, "but we don't have any proof, so let's not blame him just yet."

"Maybe not, but it's so damn likely now you've drawn my attention to it," I muttered darkly.

We sat in silence for a few minutes after that. It seemed we didn't have anything else to discuss, yet I had no desire to return to that room and watch those two at it again, especially with these new, dark thoughts. I searched for things to say and found something else I'd been meaning to discuss with Peter.

"Hey, what's going on with you and Siobhan anyway?"

He grimaced. "Nothing's going on," he muttered, then added quickly, "Well, nothing's going on at my end. I think she does like me a bit, even if it's—you know—not in that way exactly, since, you know, I brought her through and stayed with her that night while Marc was hurt, and then I told her about Underwood and all. Maybe that somehow helps with girls, I dunno, but I'm not interested. She's nice, but I guess it's too soon for me to just get with someone else. I just feel like being single for a while first."

"Oh. Okay," I said, thinking that his words sounded far more noble than anything I'd done for many weeks now. The feeling brought the shame rushing back and I was now one step closer to deciding that Serena and I wouldn't be together for too much longer. I was finding many reasons to break up and not nearly enough to stay, and the few of the latter were sounding more and more pathetic all the time. I still intended to wait until we got back from Rock Haulter, though, before doing anything. Lena would probably still be an option by then, and one I would have to consider, but only if it was too late to have the one I really wanted. I could only hope that I wouldn't miss my chance…

Chapter 34: War of Old

The ten of us were back in the cave of memories by seven o'clock that evening. Fewul, as earlier, was stationed outside the room, guarding the hovercars and making sure no unfortunate Russians came up this way. The first thing I had done when I entered the room was walk around with the Sien-Leoard Crystal, creating a number of softly cushioned armchairs for us to sit on, including one right next to the playback device for whoever would be pushing the button. Marc, who seemed to have been given custodial rights over the box of memories, was given the task once again.

"Are we all ready?" he asked us when he had put the third memory inside the device and seated himself in his armchair. The rest of us were already seated.

"Go for it," said James.

Marc pushed the button, and a moment later, we were all seized once again and hurled away from reality. In this memory, Smiley was watching, from his shadow, Lillian Woodward and her father, Roger. They were sitting in an office that looked similar to the one Mr. Woodward used today, though perhaps older and a little larger. Both of them looked older than I had seen them last. Roger looked like he was nearing eighty or so, while Lillian had greyed somewhat since Tankom had come to visit her in her home at the Christmas of '77.

They were both poring over various notes on the desk before them and looking extremely tired when a loud knock sounded on the door and they both started.

"If that's you, Graham, come in," Lillian called through the door. "If not, come back later."

The door opened, and if I'd been a physical form, my jaw would have dropped. It certainly was Graham, the Graham I knew, though much younger than I had ever known him. He might have been in his late twenties or early thirties in this year. I had already deduced that this memory was well into the war, exactly how far in I felt sure I would find out soon.

"Oh good," said Lillian approvingly as Graham shut the door carefully behind him. "Come and sit down, Graham. What has happened down there that could cause you to come running so urgently?"

"I don't really understand it all," he said, sitting down beside Roger and looking somehow out of place. "There was an intruder there, just sorta materialised out of nowhere in the middle of the crowd. Everyone saw it. Tankom went at him right away and—and he did some strange stuff."

"He had magic?" asked Roger.

"Maybe, not sure," said Graham, struggling to find the right words. "Tankom made him bleed, but people kept getting in the way. None of us knew who he was, yet people kept jumping up and running to get between him and Tankom. He got out of there pretty quick once he realised what was going on, but—but I don't think he knew who Tankom was. I'm not even sure he's human."

"You call it a he, though," said Lillian cautiously, "so he must look close enough to human, yes?"

"Well, yeah, I guess," said Graham, still awkwardly. "He was very tall, about seven feet maybe. And he was—well, beautiful." Graham grimaced. "I know how weird that sounds, but it's true—he was beautiful. Really strong too. When Lester made their guards try to restrain him before he could get to the street, you know the sort of guards they have down there, this guy just grabbed one with each hand and hurled them over his shoulders like they were as light as— as pillows or something, I dunno."

Lillian and Roger exchanged confused looks. Finally, Roger said, "Do you know any more?"

"Only that he got away," said Graham, hanging his head and looking slightly ashamed, perhaps thinking that he had jumped at a fly, that this information was hardly worth the Sorcerers' time. Lillian and Roger, however, looked interested.

"You think we should try to find this person?" Lillian asked.

"Perhaps," said Roger quietly. "I've never for a moment entertained the idea that there were other intelligent beings in the world, but if this is true and this person has some characteristics that aren't quite human, it might be a good idea for us to at least find out who he is and offer him protection. The Hammersons will be after him now, not just because he got away but because he got away after seeing one of their exclusive functions. Thank you, Graham, you've done well. Anything else to report?"

"Nothing since this morning." He shrugged.

The two Sorcerers got to their feet. Roger took command. "Lil, you round up a few people and set out to find this man. Graham, could you go and fetch Frederic? I'll need him to help me with these papers."

The memory faded away as Lillian and Graham left the room, leaving Roger alone beside the table, but this time we did not return to our armchairs. Instead, we seemed to skip from one memory straight to another. For the first time, Smiley was observing something that had taken place outdoors. Lillian was standing at the head of a small group of soldiers. They had all been armed, but now their weapons lay on the ground before them. About twenty feet away stood a man—a very tall man—surely the Honnie Smiley had spoken of. Yes, he did look vaguely human, I saw, but of an ethnicity that couldn't possibly exist in this world. And, like Smiley had done, he seemed to shimmer a little around the edges. His attire was a little unsettling: He was wearing what I could only think of as a long, brown robe, so long that it covered his feet. Graham had been right; he was nothing short of breathtaking in a way that I couldn't put my finger on. He looked slightly nervous but not scared. He and Lillian were staring at each other, telepathic communication clearly taking place between them.

"Who the hell is he?" grunted one of the blokes behind her.

"Hope my wife never catches sight of that bastard," grunted the man next to him.

"Do you speak English, mate?" another soldier called out to him.

"He doesn't speak English," Lillian said quietly. "He doesn't speak any of our languages. He has his own, but he can still communicate as well as anyone."

"You lost me," yet another soldier muttered.

The Honnie was watching the group, but most of his attention was on Lillian. He must have been looking into her mind and had determined that she was the leader of this group. Perhaps he had also realised that she was the only one in the group who didn't want to either shoot him or run away. Slowly, carefully, Lillian raised one of her hands into the air before her and began beckoning him to come forward. Even more carefully, the Honnie took a few steps forward, closer to the group. They then stood still for several seconds before the Honnie took a quick step back, apparently frightened by something Lillian had thought.

The Sorcerer was not fazed. She simply continued to let her honest mind do the talking, and after several minutes, when I wasn't the only one starting to get bored (the soldiers were looking most impatient with this course of events), the Honnie began to move forward again. Lillian motioned to her charges to remain perfectly still, an order they respectfully obeyed. Finally, there was only three or four feet between the Sorcerer and the interdimensional being.

The telepathic communication continued for a few more minutes, during which the time the Honnie became more and more relaxed. Finally, he raised his own hand and reached for Lillian's. They grasped hands for a few minutes before the Sorcerer raised her other hand, and in an instant, she, the Honnie, and all the soldiers vanished, teleported to some other location.

Smiley didn't bother hanging around any longer either. The memory faded away again and, for the second time, moved straight into another memory. This time we were in some sort of meeting room, not the one I knew from the Woodward base but one fairly similar. Lillian and Roger were there, as were a select bunch of others. Graham was not among them, nor was Frederic, but a much younger Rafael Smiley was. He looked to be in his mid to late fifties in this time, perhaps. Unlike the Smiley of today, or the Honnie, who was sitting by Lillian's right hand, this Smiley did not shimmer. The Honnie, meanwhile, was sitting back in his seat with his head back and his eyes closed. He looked like he might be sleeping, but Smiley's thoughts informed us that he was in fact listening in on the conversation by dipping into the minds of every person in the room.

"This may be what we have needed for so long," Roger told them all confidentially. "We have whittled the Hammerheart army down considerably from where it had stood three years ago, but their influence in many areas is still far too great for us to swoop in ourselves. This man, or whatever he is, has agreed to assist us in the process of—his own plans?"

He looked enquiringly at Lillian, who shrugged. "He claims to have been intending to take over the world himself, but he wasn't counting on coming up against magic. He appears to have reconsidered his plan and has decided to assist us in taking down the Hammerhearts. In return, we are to provide him with protection from the Hammersons and their magic while he is here."

"How can he help us?" asked the woman sitting on Smiley's left.

"This man has a special ability," Lillian told everyone in the room. "He has an ability to read minds, both the protected and unprotected, as apparently his technique doesn't use earthbound magic that Sien and Leoard tapped. More importantly, though, he can influence people by planting thoughts into their minds, like the influential charm but much more powerful. I know this because he has used his mind to communicate with me. He cannot speak English, but by placing thoughts in my head, he has been able to tell me a small amount about himself and what he can do. The communication is on his terms because I cannot use my own powers to read his mind."

"What is he?" asked Smiley. "Is he human?"

"I don't know," said Lillian. "He has defined himself as a—a Honnie, but beyond that he refuses to tell me any more. I don't even know if he will stay with us after we've attempted our plan, or if he will return to wherever he came from, or if he will return to his original plan. I sincerely hope not."

"So what is the plan?" asked the woman who had spoken earlier. "Do we even have a plan yet? Or is that what we're here for now?"

"We have the makings of a plan," said Lillian, "and that is what you're here for. The important thing here is to keep it secret from everyone so that the Hammersons don't get wind of it until it's too late. So much of it hinges on them believing that we are acting alone here, that our new friend is not involved in any way. It involves setting up a large place where we can store a large number of people. It can be anywhere the Hammersons cannot reach, perhaps in bushland somewhere. If we have to build an auditorium of some sort, then that is what we'll do.

"The plan is for our friend here to gather a large number of Hammerhearts, roughly ten thousand and as many of the important ones as we can find, and bring them to that place. We can send the Hammersons video footage of the group to make them see what we have done, perhaps emphasise it by showing as many of them in uniform as we can, and hope that they will take the bait. We must make them believe that we will execute them all unless they agree to a ceasefire. If that doesn't work, our friend here can perform the executions himself. If they don't take the bait initially, I don't believe they will be stupid enough to take us on after losing such a large number of their army."

"This may be our last chance," said Roger grimly. "This will be our D-Day. If this fails and the Hammersons launch further attacks on us, if they regroup, even after losing such a large number, I don't believe we will have enough firepower, nor any special tricks, left to defend ourselves. So much hinges on this plan working."

They began making arrangements to go out and begin looking for a suitable location, as well as setting a date and time for the Honnie to begin his work, but Smiley didn't hang around for that. The memory faded, but it seemed that this particular reel just kept going and going. The next memory took place in an enormous hall with rows of lights across the ceiling and a large stage. Smiley, farther back in his shadow than he had been in any of the previous memories, was on the stage, looking out at the enormous crowd of people before him. On the stage with him were Roger, Lillian, the Honnie, and the Smiley of '81, as well as a few other important Woodward soldiers. They had set up a camera, behind which a man of about thirty-five crouched, moving it carefully around the crowd. The Honnie, of course, stood well out of the way of the camera.

"Are we ready to go?" Roger asked his daughter.

"Hold on," she said. "I'll just let Frederic know it's time to make his move."

Silence fell, a silence that echoed in its completeness. Not a single person in the crowd below moved a muscle, and it was only as I watched this phenomenon that I realised the enormous power this Honnie must have had. What sort of human, even a Sorcerer, could completely still a crowd of ten thousand?

"No, no!" Lillian cried out very suddenly, making everyone around her start. "You can't! Not now!"

She had wheeled to face the Honnie, who had moved from his original position to the edge of the stage. He looked back at her, looking slightly confused by what she had said but quickly grabbing the meaning from her mind. A quick telepathic exchange took place between the two of them. The Honnie looked quite expressionless, but Lillian had lost her composure completely.

"Traitor," someone near Smiley muttered.

Both Sorcerers, Roger and Lillian, seemed to decide that the only way to save this situation was to use magic, but the Honnie was one step ahead of them. A moment later, the two Sorcerers had frozen, just like all the Hammerhearts on the floor. Yet another moment later, everyone else on the stage went rigid as well. Slowly, they all got on their knees and cowered on the spot, none of them saying or doing anything more. The Honnie turned his attention from them to the Hammerhearts on the floor, the enormous pack of humans he was about to take back to his own world.

He leapt gracefully off the stage into the space between it and the nearest Hammerhearts. Nothing seemed to happen for about twenty seconds, but Smiley's buzzing thoughts informed me that he was escorting humans through a gateway in the fourth dimension into his own world. Eventually, as he moved forward, we began to see it: The Honnie would take hold of two people while forcing as many more as possible to hold onto him; they would all fade, as though turning into ghosts, only the fading would continue until they were completely gone; and then, a couple of seconds later, the Honnie would fade straight back in again, alone.

The hall emptied out very slowly indeed, and as it did, I saw a few terrible things. The Honnie took most of them through but some of them, perhaps two or three dozen, he kept for himself. The way he disposed of them was quick and efficient. The human would first collapse as all their brain power was sucked out of them, but the Honnie would have him or her in his clutches before they hit the ground. He used his tongue to strip the flesh off their bodies, barely spilling a drop of blood as he sucked everything up—everything but the bones, which, once they were all that remained, he tossed aside. The scariest thing about it was his tongue. From this distance, it looked pointed, perhaps sharp as a pin at the tip.

Smiley decided to skip most of the procession, jumping forward in the memory to the point where about twenty humans remained. The Honnie was still taking them through, and the humans on the stage still crouched and did nothing to stop him. When the last humans disappeared from this world and the Honnie was the only one left on the floor, not counting the small piles of human remains scattered around the place, he looked back up at the stage and seemed to release those up there from their mental binds. At least, they all came back to life at the same time. The two Sorcerers were quick on their feet but not as quick as the Honnie, who vanished from existence one final time. This time, he did not reappear.

"Wait!" Lillian called, knowing it was pointless.

"It's too late," said Roger solemnly. "Too late. I guess he must have believed our deal was too thin, that he wouldn't get anything he wanted out of it."

"If he got that from our minds, he must have been right," said Lillian, shaking her head miserably and staring at the floor below. "Did we believe that strongly that the Hammersons would take the bait?"

"Did we have a backup plan?" asked a woman standing close to the Smiley of '81.

"Maybe we can still make something of this," said Lillian, considering the enormous space where all the Hammerhearts had stood not too long ago. "The Hammersons will soon know they've lost an enormous number of their army; it might still be enough to plant the seed of fear if we can make them believe we did it. Now that our friend has left us, at least they shouldn't make the link between him and us."

"I think I understand what you're saying," said Roger. "You think we should claim that we have already killed them all and will kill more if they don't give up?"

"Exactly," she said. "They won't know immediately that we're serious, but they'll find out soon enough when they start getting reports of missing Hammerhearts. We might as well go back to base."

The memory faded quickly and promptly returned for what I hoped would be the final time. Roger and Lillian were back in the room in which they had organised this plan, but this time the room had been cleared of furniture and there was only one other person with them—the man who had operated the camera back in the hall, and it appeared that his job would be the same here. He stood in the very centre of the room, pointing the camera at Roger and Lillian. They were to Smiley's left. To Smiley's right was an enormous television screen that was presently blank.

"He is ready," Lillian said quietly. "Go ahead, establish the link."

It became clear how this interaction would take place. It was a rather advanced video link for the early eighties (so I thought anyway), but then again, this was magic we were talking about. The screen flickered to life seconds later. Apparently Frederic was controlling it from the other end. Through a speaker I couldn't identify, I heard him say, "Okay, I've made the telepathic connection and all three of them have agreed to meet me. Er, I'm a little nervous they might use the chance to gang up on me and attack but—well, at least you'll know."

He moved backwards, facing a dark brick wall ahead that was littered with graffiti. I had a feeling I knew what was hidden in that wall, and sure enough, the three Hammersons materialised out of the invisible door only moments later. The camera jerked slightly, and I knew Frederic had flinched at the sight of them. Lester had aged considerably, and like Roger, he looked exhausted, but unlike Roger, he didn't look defeated. Tankom looked almost exactly as she did in my time, though perhaps less wrinkled and grey. Arnold, meanwhile, was a tall, strapping young man, perhaps nineteen or twenty years old, and (I hated to admit to myself) a reasonably good-looking guy.

"What on earth are you—" Lester growled at Frederic, then stopped dead, staring above the young Sorcerer's head. All three Hammersons looked up at it in astonishment. I didn't need Frederic to turn his camera around to know that he had created a television screen exactly like this one for them to see through the camera at our end.

"Good afternoon, Lester, Dorothy, Arnold," said Roger pleasantly, "or whatever time it is wherever you are. We are sorry to have interrupted you from whatever mad plans you have been concocting lately, but we have an important matter to discuss with you."

"Is this a message of surrender?" Lester asked, trying to hide his excitement. "If so, we will accept it if you teleport to us now and make the gesture in person. It is not too late for you to join forces with us, Roger. We would welcome you graciously."

"Am I to seriously believe you mean that?" Roger asked coldly.

"You should, for as I told you long ago, six Sorcerers are much more effective than three," said Lester. "Very well, if it is not surrender, what is this important matter of yours?"

"The matter is this," said Roger. "We have taken some of your people hostage—approximately ten thousand of them, in fact. I believe that is greater than half your army. We understand well that you would not give this much credence, that you would believe you could get them back at any time, and perhaps up until now, you could. That is why Lillian and I have taken it upon ourselves to murder each and every one of them. Several of your favourites too, I'm led to believe."

"*Good Lord*," said Frederic, sounding both impressed and disturbed.

"I don't believe you," snapped Lester. "Killing has never been your style, Roger, and you now expect me to believe you have murdered ten thousand people?"

"I didn't think you would," said Roger, "which, as I said, is the reason why we have done just that. Now, Lester, Dorothy, Arnold, this is the deal. You will soon learn of these disappearances, so there is no hurry. Four weeks, I think, is ample time for you to consider your options, but let it be known, we have decided that it is time to stop the silliness. If you do not agree to throw down your arms and sign a treaty of peace, we will repeat what we have just done, stripping down your entire army."

"Also let it be known that continuing to recruit at this point would be pointless," Lillian added. "We are prepared to kill them all, so you must ask yourselves: Is it worth losing so many innocent lives when all you may end up with at the end is a rule over a world with barely anyone left in it?"

The three Hammersons gawped at the screen over Frederic's head. I would have liked to see Frederic's face at that point. He probably would have been gawping too.

"We will continue as we are, I think," said Dorothy coldly. "We are not about to take any bluffs, you two, but if we find that you are telling the truth, we will consider your threat seriously. Once again, we are still very disappointed that you refuse to join forces with us."

"Good, very good," said Roger pleasantly. "That is all, then. We will be in touch, you three, and remember what we have spoken of. Oh, one more thing: While you are considering your options, I don't want to see any more attacks on anyone. If I get wind that you are still continuing with your plans while you should be worrying about more important things, the deal will be off and we will be in action again."

"Noted," said Lester coldly. "Get the hell out of here, kid," he snapped at Frederic, then to his daughter and grandson, "Come on, back to base."

The three Hammersons moved backwards into the wall and vanished. Roger started to say something, but before he got more than a few words out, Smiley had had enough. The memory faded again and, yet again (I had lost count by now), was replaced by another memory. All six Sorcerers were sitting at a large table, the Hammersons on one side and the Woodwards on the other. Tankom and Lillian were both holding piles of paper in their hands.

"Well, I suppose you can guess what we're all doing here," said Lester bitterly. "Tankom?"

"I've never understood that name," Frederic started.

"Be quiet," Lillian snapped, flinching.

Tankom didn't look at all happy with the situation. Rather than look across at the Woodwards, she chose to read directly from her notes. "We have deliberated and have now decided that we cannot afford to take any more risks. We are prepared to agree to a conditional ceasefire."

"That is not acceptable to us," said Lillian, flicking through her notes to find what she was looking for. "No conditions shall be set by you. We will not agree to any conditions you might have. It is our conditions you must meet in order to make this ceasefire work."

"Lucky for you, we expected that," said Lester. "And even luckier, we are prepared to agree to that, depending on what these conditions are."

"Condition the first," said Lillian, looking down at her notes. "There are to be no magical or non-magical attacks from you or any of your *Hammerhearts*—(she said the word as though it put a sour taste in her mouth)—on any form of authority, whether it be political or otherwise. We will retaliate immediately if we get wind of any attacks from you or yours."

"We agree," said Tankom bitterly.

"Condition the second," Lillian went on. "We are aware of the underground structure you have constructed over many years. We do not expect you to tear it down, but we expect you not to continue using it. You are to choose a location in which to settle down and shut down the rest of your bases."

"Go on," Tankom went on, glancing sideways at her father.

"Condition the third," Lillian continued. "Your army is to disband. You are to cease ordering non-magic people around for your bidding. You are not to intimidate any of them with your powers into doing what you want. In short, there must be no more Hammerhearts from today onwards."

Tankom merely nodded this time, clearly liking this progression less and less.

"Condition the fourth. You are no longer permitted to experiment with dark magic. You are from here on denied access to any open terminals of magic and will be held accountable for any overt signs of magic not performed by any of us or ours, whether it be sinister or recreational."

None of the Hammersons responded at all to this.

"And condition the fifth," said Lillian, putting her papers down —she had clearly memorised this last one. "We have received intelligence recently that you have been planning on bolstering your powers, making yourselves more powerful than us, by acquiring the Magic Crystals. You are not to lay a hand on any of those crystals, wherever they are hidden. Their magic is far too powerful to be meddled with, especially by the likes of you. We will not tolerate so much as a consideration to hunt after any of the Magic Crystals."

The three Hammersons exchanged furious looks.

"Those are the conditions," Roger told them firmly. "You must accept them and accept them now. Fail to do so and the war will continue. Fail to do so and we will attack like you haven't seen yet. The choice is yours, but I dearly hope you are not stupid enough to make the wrong decision here. So much is counting on it."

"I don't think we have a choice," said Tankom bitterly.

Lester nodded. "The conditions make sense, and I agree. If it takes this much to make you believe we are backing off, then this is what we will do. We only ever wanted to do the right thing, but we cannot risk doing even more damage than has already been done. Where is your contract?"

Lillian produced it from the top of her pile and handed it across to Tankom. I saw briefly that it had written the conditions as Lillian had read them out. Lester signed it first, then Tankom, then Arnold, who passed it back across to Frederic. The Woodwards also signed it, and just like that, the first war had ended.

That was all she wrote, finally. The memory faded and we landed back in our armchairs in the cave of memories. Nearly two hours had passed since we had started observing that memory. It took us several moments to pull ourselves together after it. I had sunk so low in my armchair that my back felt extremely stiff.

"That Honnie looked weird," was the first thing Peter managed to say. "Stunning, maybe, but weird."

"I thought he looked pretty normal," said Serena. "I was expecting something much more different."

"Smiley did say they looked pretty similar to humans," James reminded us. "The only major differences I noticed were his eyes and his height."

"And his tongue," I said shakily. "Did you guys see—"

"It was pointy," Peter finished my sentence. "I tell you one other thing too. I know he looked reasonably strong, but the way he killed those people—he turned out to be so much stronger than he looked."

"Well, we know how it ended now," said Tommy, "and how it started, but guys," he looked around at us all, "there's something I don't get. We know for a fact that the Hammersons broke nearly all those conditions before this war started. Why didn't the Woodwards retaliate like they said they would?"

Nobody seemed to have an answer to this. James started saying, "They probably thought…" then considered for a little longer.

"They went soft," Marc told us. "That's all there was to it. It's like a guy over in the States said when we were over there: It's been too long since 1981, and they've forgotten how to fight. They've forgotten how to be tough. They must have known the Hammersons were up to no good, but they probably thought that as long as they weren't actually publicly attacking anyone, they could just let it slide."

There was too much truth in this to be ignored.

* * *

That was it for the day. We were all starting to feel tired, so we took the hovercars back to the garage and hung out in Group E's campsite for the next couple of hours. The conversation went mostly along the same lines as it had that afternoon, but I wasn't paying much attention to it. I was sitting between Serena and Marc, but I had retreated into myself, returning to my conversation with Peter from earlier. It was notable that Serena was sitting beside me, yet I felt not a single urge to reach out and touch her. She made no physical contact either, but that was normal for her. She normally kept to herself when we were in public and wouldn't dare touch me under the intense gaze of Lena, who had once again positioned herself so that I would have to look at her every time I looked up. The tension between Tommy and Natalie seemed to be thickening too, making me feel that despite what had happened two months earlier, just about anything was possible now.

I went to bed at around half past eleven but didn't go to sleep. I had felt tired before, but right now I didn't feel like sleeping at all. I knew I would regret it, especially since I wanted to be up and about again in a few hours, but my mind was buzzing too unpleasantly to allow sleep. It wasn't helped by Serena taking advantage of my privacy to come into my room, wanting to spend some time with me, but where normally I would grudgingly allow it, tonight I told her that I wanted to sleep and preferred to be left alone. She may have been slightly put out by that, but I forced myself not to care too much. This was such a bad time for me to be intimate with—well, pretty much anyone.

I fiddled with the alarms first, using the crystal to wake me up at two o'clock, then using it to change the alarms in everyone else's bedrooms to eight o'clock. A sleep-in tomorrow morning might help all of them, but especially me. Then I just sat there, rolling the crystal from hand to hand and trying to think what to do—what could be done. The only thing I knew I wouldn't do was use the crystal. I wouldn't stoop to Tommy's level, if that was what he had done to make this happen. I wished I knew a way to find out. If he had used the Darkness Crystal, it could probably be undone by the Light Crystal. It could also be undone by the Sien-Leoard Crystal, but surely it depended on whether anything had been done in the first place. If I tried to undo magic that had never been done, how could I be sure that I wouldn't accidentally perform dark magic against Natalie? The Light Crystal wouldn't have allowed it, but the Sien-Leoard Crystal also contained the evil power of the Darkness Crystal. I just wished I could know what was really going on.

I soon began hearing people coming into the hallway outside my room and was struck by an idea. If I just waited until they were all in their rooms, I could probably go out right now. I wouldn't be able to do a lot if the Russians were still up, but I would worry about that later. Getting out of here now would be better than falling asleep and risking sleeping in too late again. I therefore sent my crystal out from my mind so that I could watch their progress. Serena and Marc were already in their rooms. Peter and Tommy were in the boys' bathroom while Siobhan, Lena, and Erica were in the girls'. Natalie had gone into her room to change into her nightclothes (I sped away from this vision against my will), and James was still in the Group E house, cleaning up a few things he'd left in there.

I continued to watch as they slowly drifted into their rooms so that eventually the only one left in the Group E house was Fewul. This hardly bothered me at all since he had kept his mouth shut so far. Unfortunately, however, one person seemed in no hurry to go to his bedroom. Tommy had gone back into the Group E house while Peter and James had taken care of business in the bathroom, and then he had gone back in there despite the fact that he had already brushed his teeth and washed up for the night. He was stalling for something, and I had a very bad feeling about what it could be. Sure enough, he was waiting for the same thing I was—for everyone else to be safely in their bedrooms. Once the hallway was empty and silent, he tiptoed down to Natalie's door and softly knocked.

"Hey," she said when she had opened it and seen him standing there, taking a step back in what looked like surprise.

"Hi," Tommy said, taking her backward step to be an invitation into her room. He shut the door softly behind him and said, "How are you?"

"What are you doing here?" she asked quietly, looking totally wrong footed.

I could read the trend of this scene far too clearly for my liking. Perhaps the crystal was giving me an ability to see exactly where this was going, even though neither of them could see it properly. Tommy had chosen this moment to make things happen between him and Natalie. He had been keeping track of her increasing desire as closely as I had over the last two days and had apparently decided that there was enough of it there for him to score. Whether he only wanted sex or something that would last longer, I couldn't be sure, but I supposed it was probably the latter. Natalie's desire was great, greater than it had ever been for anyone before—not a thought I took comfort in. Yet she was also scared of it. She wanted him very much, but at the same time didn't want him at all. For her, it came down to a battle between her morals and her physical desire. I dearly hoped her desires weren't quite strong enough to make her forget herself completely.

"Just wanted to see you," he said, moving to her bed and sitting down on it.

He patted the spot beside him, the implication all too clear. Natalie still stood by the door, staring at him. Then, slowly, as though in a trance, she came to him and sat down beside him.

"Er, okay," she said vaguely. "It—er—it's late, you know."

"Just after midnight, I know," he said. "That's not too bad. It's not like it'll matter too much if we sleep in a little late. Are you tired?"

He put his arm around her as he spoke, and that seemed to distract her from the question. Finally, she managed to say, "Yeah, I am tired."

"You don't look too tired," he said smoothly. "If so, it can only be mental, 'cause mostly all we've done today is sit around and watch mental TV."

He tightened his arm around her so that she was leaning against his shoulder. His touch seemed to have paralysed her to such a degree that she could do nothing but move with him—yet another bad sign.

"Comfortable?" he asked her, smiling to himself.

"No," she moaned, and my heart leapt for a moment. Her morals finally got a look in, if only a brief one.

"Oh, really?" he said, still grinning. Now he turned his body so that he could put his other arm around her and press her into his chest. Again, she just went along with him, the side of her face resting very close to his heart. "How about now?"

"Don't do this, Tommy," she moaned, barely audible now.

"Just relax," he whispered. "No need to be so tense. That's why I'm here, you know? You've been so tense lately, and why? There's no point."

He was right about that. She may have been leaning on him, but she was certainly tense. She was still clenching her arms to her body, as though resisting a powerful urge to throw them around him, and now her legs were clenched tightly together too, suppressing the itch that must be screaming down there. I groaned aloud and barely noticed my own voice.

"I don't want," she moaned again, trying to move away from him.

To my surprise, Tommy allowed this, but only for a moment. He even helped Natalie sit up straighter, but once she was upright, he drew her back into his arms, and this time, she was unable to stop herself hugging him back. Thankfully, though, she became aware of herself again about ten seconds later and promptly drew back with a jerk, looking ashamed, annoyed, and—what else? Vulnerable? I thought so.

"No, no," she gasped, wiping her hair out of her face and scuttling away from him. "I don't wanna do this, Tommy. I don't want to."

"Yes, you do," he said firmly, pulling himself into a sitting position and looking very pleased with the way this was going. "You do want it, Natalie. You wouldn't have done what you just did if you didn't want it. You're just resisting because it's your instinct to do so. Why not give in this time, Nat? There's no reason to hold back."

He moved on her, and once again, it seemed to paralyse her before she could retort. He moved nimbly up beside her and took her in his arms again. She tried to push him away, but it was a feeble attempt.

"Relax," he whispered tantalisingly, and kissed her. "Come on, Nat, just relax. I know you've been imagining this while you've been here. Believe me, I have been too. We've held back for way too long. Come on, just relax."

Back in my room, my fists were clenched tightly as I watched this struggle continue. It didn't matter that she wanted him physically. All that mattered was that he was ready to take her against her will, that, despite being a good guy in most areas, he couldn't seem to get his head around the concept of "no means no." I had no idea how the law would work if she went at it just as hard in the end, but in my book, this was no different from rape, pure and simple. What was I to do? I wanted to stop it—I didn't want Natalie to have to go through anything like what Amelia was dealing with—but I didn't want to humiliate her in the process. I clenched the crystal, knowing that if it continued any further and she couldn't prevent it, I would have to step in. I couldn't let this happen.

And so it didn't. Tommy decided to take a chance, a chance that both he and I thought would pay off. He slowly lifted her body off him, allowing her a certain amount of freedom, enough for her to turn around and face him, though he never actually took his hands off her. Indeed she did turn around, and there was an instant where I knew that if Natalie couldn't resist now, all was lost.

She *did* resist.

"No!" she said very loudly, and I noticed, in my bodiless form, that several people in neighbouring rooms had started at the sound.

He had been about to pull her back towards him, but now she struck out, pushing him away from her, hard. He fell back against her pillow and she fell backwards, almost off the end of the bed. She was still burning with desire, her body feeling like it had been denied a great treat (the crystal was telling me this), but her mind full of a number of emotions I couldn't begin to identify with, humiliation and self-disgust chief among them. Tommy had been taken by surprise, apparently realising that he had put a single foot wrong and it might be about to cost him everything.

He reached for her again, but this time she slapped his hand away. "Don't you touch me again!"

She scrambled off the bed, turning her back on him so that he couldn't take in any more of her body. Tommy sat there on the bed the whole time, gazing at her back in great disappointment and annoyance, probably thinking that there was just no way to get in her pants, that she were simply too prudish to allow it.

"Nat," he said quietly, apologetically almost, when she had turned back to him.

He reached for her again, but she backed away. "Don't you touch me again or I'll use magic on you."

She did that to herself, performing a spell that seemed to be meant to clear her head. Once it had, the moment of desire had passed. Physically she would still have felt let down, but now she had complete control of herself again. For Tommy, the battle had been lost, and I couldn't remember ever being more proud of Natalie than I was right now. If she had just fought and beaten the work of the Darkness Crystal, it spoke volumes about the sort of person she was. If she had just fought off enormous physical urges, urges that had been brought on by dark magic and would have surely been stronger than anything any person should be capable of beating, that surely made her the complete opposite of the sort of person I was. It was perhaps then that I realised just how much I wanted her, how much I desired her, how much I even idolised her. I was cautious about using the word 'love' in connection with my feelings, but I was definitely starting to wonder now.

"Nat," Tommy started to say, but Natalie had had enough.

"Just leave," she said shortly, jerking her head at the door. "Don't come back again, Tommy. Don't even try, or you'll regret it."

Tommy gazed at her for a few seconds before deciding that he couldn't take any more chances. Anger crossed his features now, and for a moment I felt scared that he would hit her, but instead he turned his back, slid off the bed, slouched for the door, opened it, and swung it shut behind him. The noise it made was loud, and again several people around started at the sound. I didn't watch Tommy's progress along the corridor but kept watching Natalie as she sank back onto her bed, her mind now an emotional wreck.

She sat there for some time, not getting under the covers but sitting on top of them, her arms around her raised knees, staring at the wall opposite her. What was she feeling now? Shame? Disgust? Anger? Did she feel that she had let herself and her morals down in a big way tonight? I thought she was probably feeling all that and more. Her mind was still transparent, I noticed, so it wouldn't be too difficult to find out exactly how it was making her feel. I could have slapped myself. Come on, John, if you really care about her, then surely you wouldn't invade her privacy in such a way as that, even if you've done it once before.

That was my moral conscience kicking in, and I'd never been more pleased to hear it. Of course I cared about Natalie, and of course I would never do something so invasive to someone I cared about so much. At least I wouldn't now. Curiosity killed the cat, I remembered, and I would continue wondering about this until I found out, one way or another. Curiosity killed the cat, satisfaction brought him back, and once I knew I would be satisfied, because I already had an idea that whatever it was would work against Tommy. She would work very hard not to let this happen again.

I retreated back to my body, put the crystal down roughly on my bedside drawers, and slid under my own covers. I lay down and rolled over, thinking of Natalie, wondering how I was supposed to sleep now, wishing I could do those things Tommy had done to her but have her enjoying them all instead of trying to resist. I just wished I knew, knew exactly how she felt, but no. It would be much better if she could tell me these things and I could hear them straight out of her mouth than grab them from her mind.

Curiosity killed the cat, satisfaction brought him back. Screw the cat, I thought savagely; I'd never liked cats anyway.

Chapter 35: Through the Years

I had completely forgotten my plan to wake up at two o'clock and head down to the main hall, and lay in bed quite confused for some time as to why I had suddenly woken up and couldn't get back to sleep. When the memory of my using the crystal to set an alarm for myself returned, however, I scrambled quickly out of bed, checked the time, saw that some twenty minutes had elapsed since the time I should have got up, and proceeded to dress quickly. I fumbled for the invisible crystal on my bedside drawers, eventually located it, pocketed it, and left the room quietly.

I had so far forgotten what else had happened only a couple of hours earlier, but it all came flooding back as I stepped into the corridor and glanced down towards Natalie and Tommy's rooms. I couldn't help imagining them both, sleeping behind those closed doors, wishing I had done more to spare Natalie from that experience, despising Tommy for honestly believing he and her were so meant for each other despite her continual rejections. I pushed the thoughts away. I would worry about Natalie's condition and what (if anything) I ought to do for her later. Right now, I had a job to do.

The Group E house turned out to be empty. Perhaps Fewul had gone to guard somewhere else, most likely outside the car park since the other entrance into this place would be extremely difficult for anyone unfamiliar with the setup to get to. The door Natalie had linked from this room to the car park was on the opposite side of the room from the one I had linked to the bedrooms. It was beside the original door, in fact. I headed for it down the side of the room where, in past times, the eight beds had been lined up. But just past the halfway point, giving me an enormous fright, someone spoke.

"What are you doing?"

I started guiltily and looked around, wishing I'd checked the place out a little more carefully. My heart skipped a beat. For reasons best known to herself, though ones I could probably guess at, Natalie was curled up in the very seat she'd been sitting in several hours earlier. It had a tall back and was facing away from the bedrooms, which explained how I had missed her. She looked somehow cold by the way she seemed to be hugging herself.

"What are *you* doing?" I retorted, stunned into the reaction.

"Just sitting," she replied meekly.

"Why?" I asked, taking a couple of steps nearer and stopping behind another seat, watching her. Careful, John. Don't push her.

"Just feel like it," she said, still in that same vague sort of tone. Without being entirely sure, I thought maybe she herself had been stunned into this reaction. "What are you doing?"

I hesitated. So far, I had avoided mentioning my night-time excursions to anyone, but now that I was faced with the question, I wondered why I'd bothered to take such precautions. Obviously the reason why I did it at night was because it was the only time I could be sure the hall would be free, but that didn't explain why I had kept it secret from the others. The only reason I could think of was that I couldn't possibly explain the reasoning.

"I've just got stuff to do," I said lamely.

I felt torn in several directions at once. I wanted to wrap this up so I could get down to the main hall. I wanted to sit with Natalie and talk to her while she obviously needed someone to set her right. I wanted to talk about her, not me, though. Yet how could I get her to talk about herself? She seemed to be either pushing me away, despite the fact that she did need someone with her (or so I thought), or pushing other things away. I thought it might be a bit of both.

"Stuff?" she repeated, uncurling a little and forming a more conventional sitting position. "What stuff?"

Great. What now?

"I'd rather not say just now," I told her. Might as well be honest about it, I supposed. "Er, are you okay, Nat?"

I knew she wasn't, of course, but I'd got a good look at her face just then and her eyes were very red indeed.

"Yeah," she said unconvincingly.

I knew I still had a few hours of darkness left and so made my decision, and for once, I felt it was the right decision. I moved around two seats so that I could get to her, knelt down beside her seat, and hugged her. The way she responded was all the proof I needed that I'd been right. She almost pulled me down on top of her, and I would be lying if I said it didn't hurt my back at least a little. We clung there for several seconds before, needing a more comfortable position, I let her go so that I could get on my knees beside her. She was actually sitting on one end of a couch, and I could easily have sat on her other side, which would have been far more comfortable, but I had a feeling that doing so might put me closer to Natalie than I could really afford to be at the moment. Oh, John, exactly what is the definition of the word 'right' anyway?

"What's wrong, Natalie?" I asked her, hoping this time she would be more likely to answer, but apart from the brief outpouring of emotion, she was still holding back.

"I—well—" she said falteringly.

"I know there's something," I persisted. "I mean, what other reason could there be for coming out here and just sitting for a while? But you don't have to say if you don't want. I just thought it might make you feel better."

She shrugged. "Maybe. I guess I do wanna, but—" She shook her head, and I resigned myself to the fact that she wasn't about to talk about Tommy. Perhaps it was too soon for her to do so.

"All right," I said quietly. "Well, I'm always happy to listen, okay? I've gotta go out now, though, so are you gonna be okay here?"

"Wait," she said quickly, and my heart skipped a beat. I had hoped for but certainly not expected her to stop me. "Hey, can I ask you something?"

"Sure."

"Do you—do you ever miss Nicole much?"

My stomach turned over. "All the time," I told her.

It was perfectly true. Barely a day went by when I didn't think of Nicole, imagine that she was with us, imagine what her input into a discussion might be.

"Yeah," Natalie sighed. "I really miss her now."

I couldn't think of anything to say to that. Nicole was certainly the person Natalie would be most likely to open up to, but Nicole had gone where none of us could ever speak to her again. I made to get up, not really wanting to leave but knowing that I had to, but Natalie caught me by the arm.

"Where are you going, anyway?"

"Er, the main hall," I said, far too honestly, knowing what was coming. Sure enough…

"Can I come?"

What? That was the last thing I had expected her to say. I was completely taken aback and for several moments was unable to articulate a response or even consider the idea.

"You'll probably be bored," I told her eventually, "and you can't say a word to me while I'm doing—what I'm doing, but—yeah, I guess you can come."

She hesitated for a moment, clearly wanting to ask questions, but then she shrugged and pulled herself up out of her seat.

"Can we walk?" she asked, again taking me by surprise.

"I guess so," I said, knowing it would increase the travel time and give me less time to see what I could do down there, but right now I was prepared to enjoy as much time with her as I could. Perhaps the walking time would give us a chance to talk.

So that was what we did, zigzagging through the cave, the Sien-Leoard Crystal lighting our way, then down the side of the mountain, and then down the track, past the tree house, and towards the main hall. Natalie hadn't even bothered to change out of her pyjamas into something a little warmer. She still wasn't wearing a bra, I had seen back in the camp where there had been some light, and I wondered why she hadn't asked if she could change her clothes first. Where had her self-consciousness gone? I devoutly hoped that it hadn't gone the way of whatever else she thought she'd lost tonight.

She stayed close beside me as we walked, and on several occasions I had seriously considered putting an arm around her as we went. We never spoke about anything as we walked, but I hadn't given up hope. Things were already looking pretty good, and as long as Tommy didn't turn his attention back to the Darkness Crystal before I could take it off him, I felt I could move slowly. Slowly enough to, hopefully, do things in the right order with Serena. Amelia was well and truly out of contention now, my mind completely made up by what the James in my head had said the other night, and if I stayed true to what I'd thought back in Graham's room, Lena shouldn't be a factor either.

By the time we reached the front of the main hall, I thought I probably had perhaps two hours at most before we would have to leave again. Also, by then I was feeling very tired. I was going to be very sleep-deprived through the rest of the day, probably through the rest of my time on the Rock, but at least for now I wouldn't be the only one. Natalie, who had probably not slept at all tonight, wasted no time energising us both with her magic before we entered. I supposed it was a good thing. At least I could relax with less chance of just dropping off to sleep.

"What do you want me to do?" Natalie asked. She looked very nervous indeed in the very little I could see of her.

"Just stay close to me and be very quiet. Don't even move if you can help it," I told her.

I unlocked the door, slid in, left enough space for Natalie to slip in under my arm, and shut it quietly behind us. The place was dark and shadowy, but using the crystal to sharpen my vision, I saw that nothing seemed to have changed in here since the previous morning. I tried to turn my mind to what I was about to do. If I was going to attempt to go back and see what had happened in this room, I would need to be able to see as much of it as possible. The best place to do that from was surely out the front where the stage used to be. I took Natalie by the wrist and led her into the darkness, around the side of the hall opposite the doors, and towards the front. She stuck close to me the whole time, turning her head around and around, her quick breathing sounding much more terrified than I felt.

Once out the front, I let her go and simply stood, about a foot from the wall, looking into the darkness. Natalie stood beside me, close enough that I could have put an arm around her, but to her credit, she stayed completely still. Now all I had to do was relax, but that was more difficult than I had anticipated. It was hard to forget that she was so close, that she had chosen to come with me, that she must want my company. I kept imagining that she would be using this chance to think more freely about things that had happened back at the campsite. I had no idea if that would happen, but if it did, hopefully it would mean that she might be ready to talk about it.

Snap out of it, John. You can worry about that all you like later, but right now, you have a job to do.

I moved back slightly so that my back touched the wall behind me and tried to clear my mind. It turned out to be easier than I had thought. All I had to do to take my mind off Natalie was just reflect on the fact that she was close to me. If I looked at it without adding desire to the mix, it seemed to fill me with serenity. I leaned back against the wall behind me and stared blankly ahead of me. My mind was beginning to lighten and I welcomed the sensation, allowing myself to loosen up to a point that I could possibly have moved, yet somehow I didn't.

It happened very quickly this time, almost effortlessly, although later I would reflect that the whole idea of this business was that it was supposed to be effortless. I felt myself disconnect from my body in that weird, directionless movement again and was able to make out echoing sounds again—quiet sounds, busy sounds. I had no doubt about what it was—students and teachers or supervisors or whatever they were, hard at work, making use of the equipment filling the room.

I had thought about what I would need to do now. The moment of truth had arrived. I needed to induce that feeling of moving backwards through time, but I had to move well past the sounds I could hear now. I began to focus on them, to try to pick out individual voices, footsteps, keystrokes, but at the same time trying to hear past those noises to echoing sounds further back. I began to hear a male voice shouting in Russian and tried to focus on that; further back, sounds of heavy objects being moved around the room, and I focussed on those; then finally, as the sense of moving backwards sped up, I simply focussed on that.

I was completely lost to my current surroundings by now, the knowledge that Natalie was still standing behind me well swept from my mind, the realisation that she thought I had fallen asleep and was considering waking me non-existent until afterwards. My mind had entered the in-between, the place where time didn't run, and now I was moving along the time axis, speeding backwards faster and faster, hearing everything and now seeing flickering shadows and lights as days and nights sped by. I knew I could slow down and step off the time axis if I chose, but now that I was on my way back, I wanted to see if I could get all the way back to the time I desired. Additionally, now that I knew how to go backwards, I also wanted to see if I could go forwards as well without breaking the spell. I knew the time I needed would have been either November '95 or February '96, or sometime around then, but I was sure to go past it or land on the wrong time. Unfortunately, there was no calendar inside my mind.

It turned out to be easier than I had anticipated to count the Rock Haulter visits as I passed them, because they were all separated by long periods of emptiness. This returned me to the question of exactly when I had been here the first time. I tried very hard to keep count while I considered. I had been through three visits so far, which meant that the next visit would be in August 2009. So when exactly would I have been here last? The earliest possible time was November 1995. I would have been a couple of months old, and Marc would have been one and a third. The Hammersons would not have moved to Australia yet, for I believed that had probably been sometime in early 1997. The biggest clue, however, was the approximate date of my mother's death. Had Marc said how old he had been when she had died? Had he mentioned a date? I seemed to remember him saying 1997, and I tried to remember where I had heard those words from.

Seven visits now. That meant the next one I heard would be August 2008. This was slow work, but it was preferable to rushing by them too fast to count. I thought back to the day in Moran's room when I had learnt that ghost woman had been my mother; had Marc mentioned when she had died then? I couldn't remember, but somehow I didn't think so. The time prior to that, we had spoken of her outside the lounge room on the evening of Lisa's death. Yes, he had said it then: "She was twenty-seven when she died back in '97."

So what did that mean? It meant that I could narrow the events down to nine possible Rock Haulter visits—the last in 1995 and all four in 1996 and 1997. I wished I had more information to go on, but that was probably the best I could do. I would just have to check the February 1997 one, since it seemed the most likely in my mind, and see what I got. If I didn't learn anything useful, I decided, I would go up to the eastern side of the rock and ask Smiley when Moran had given me to him. In the meantime, I settled into counting the visits, trying to speed up the process. Fourteen visits down. That meant the next one would be November 2006.

On and on it went, not seeming to speed up at all but stay at a regular speed that was easy to follow. I was able to recognise some of the sounds I heard as I passed, most of them in other languages, although the November visitors up until 2005 were Americans. I could also recognise the vice principal's voice in the February visits. After the twenty-second visit, the noises changed. I remembered Lisa once saying, indirectly, that Chopville High had been coming to Rock Haulter since 2005. It seemed that all the institutions changed over that year. Apart from the August visits, which were again done by Americans, the rest of the visitors spoke other languages that I couldn't identify among all the echoes.

On and on it went, the effort required to keep count and not relax too much growing more and more all the time. Thirty visits and it was late 2002; forty visits and it was mid-1999; forty-five visits and it was early 1998. After I had passed the forty-sixth visit, the next group of people would be the visitors from November 1997. I was on high alert now, ready for the next wave of voices, ready to attempt to pick out a voice I recognised—Hammerson, Tankom, Moran, or just about anyone else American.

The November visit yielded nothing at all, which didn't surprise me. It was fairly later than I would have expected, probably after Smiley's plane crash, too. The August visit was more challenging, though, so I attempted to slow down and focus on certain voices. A loud male voice was instructing a group of girls to take samples of something or other from the cave they had marked N76. There was also a gaggle of female voices behind his, and I felt sure they were the girls he was instructing. There were no voices I recognised, though, so I continued moving backwards, more slowly now.

More and more American voices passed me by until they eventually faded and died. Okay, I thought, not that one. Seven more visits to look at. I sped up my backwards flight again until more voices reached my ears. Again, they weren't speaking English, so I attempted to pick out any English sounding words amongst the incomprehensible jabbering. Soon enough, that visit had passed me by too, and now I was wound to the point of snapping. If my mother had died in 1997, this visit was the most likely time it had happened, even if the voices I had heard from this visit in the later years had sounded Japanese or something similar.

I flew backwards, more and more long-gone days passing me by, until finally more echoing voices reached my ears. I almost groaned aloud when I noted that I couldn't understand a word any of them were saying. I moved slowly, so slowly that the words I was hearing seemed unnaturally elongated. It was only at this point that I realised that the whole time I had been doing this, I had actually been stopping and allowing myself to move the other way whenever I tried to focus on a voice. It made sense now, but I couldn't believe it had taken me this long to work it out. If I kept going backwards the whole time, then of course I wouldn't understand anything. It would be like a tape being played backwards at high speed.

I might have spent close to half an hour on this visit, which really wasn't very long considering it had probably lasted a week or two, and I was surely missing a few things, but what I did hear gave me nothing at all to work with. By the time the voices had faded again, I'd had enough. I could probably keep going back and look at the visits from 1996 (now that February 1997 was out, all of them could have been likely), but it seemed smarter at this point to give up this fruitless search, go and visit Smiley, and find out exactly when it had happened. Then, tomorrow night, I could return here and have another look. I may have been dispirited by my failure to learn anything useful, but I was still feeling pretty good about the extent of my capability.

I broke the spell by raising my right hand to my face. For a fraction of a second, it felt like I had been hurled across a wide expanse at breakneck speed, before a moment later my surroundings returned to me in their completeness. The main hall was still as dark and still as it had been before. To my left, Natalie was still watching me, now looking mightily relieved that I had returned to my senses.

"Oh, thank God," she moaned. "I know you said not to disturb you, but I was almost about to. It's nearly half past six."

My stomach lurched. I'd estimated it around five o'clock. I'd stayed way longer than was safe. We had to get out of here quick-smart.

"Come on," I muttered, taking hold of the crystal in my pocket in one hand and her wrist in the other and beginning to lead her back around the side we had come by. "I've just got one more thing I need to do tonight."

"Can it wait? It's really late, and the others would be wondering where we are."

"Not yet," I told her, and added more quietly, "I mucked with the alarm so they can have a nice little sleep-in."

"Oi," she said indignantly. "Fine. What else have you got in mind?"

"I need to see Smiley."

"At this hour?"

"He won't mind. It'd be around lunchtime for him, remember?"

"Oh yeah," she said, "but—but what for?"

I didn't answer right away. We had reached the front door and I proceeded to open it quietly and allow enough space for Natalie to slip through, then a slightly wider space to admit myself. I shut it softly behind us, used the crystal to lock it, and gave a sigh of relief; out of the danger zone once again with no trouble.

"I've got something to tell him and something to ask him," I told her. "You'll see if you wanna come along."

I didn't expect her to. She'd had hours now to recover from the business with Tommy, and surely she would be feeling very tired. I myself was pretty tired, and as we began to walk, I dipped my hand to the crystal and gave myself a familiar energy boost from it.

"Yeah, I'll come," she said, surprising me, "but can we stop by camp first? I wanna change into something else."

Understandable, I thought, and nodded. I suppressed the satisfaction. She was still self-conscious about what she wore, at least enough not to want Smiley to see her without a bra, but apparently she didn't mind so much with me—or maybe it was just that it was getting lighter now. "We'll have to stop by there anyway to get the cars," I added. "We can't get up there on foot."

We set off up the track towards our campsites, the Group E one because we still had the magical rod used to enter it, even though Group F's would have been easier. The air was fresh and rather cool, cool enough that before long my hands and face felt icy. Once again Natalie stuck close to me, so much so that our shoulders kept bumping every ten feet or so. If I was cold, she must have been positively freezing. I didn't put an arm around her, but what I did do, on a sudden stroke of courage, was reach out (not very far) and take hold of her hand in mine. It was as cold as mine, and I thought, perhaps, I had felt her give it a little squeeze. She certainly didn't pull away, though, and we didn't let go until we had reached the entrance to Group E's cave.

While she was in her room changing, I had time to reflect that being alone with her for this long had finally made up my mind. It wasn't much different from what Smiley had said two days ago: Knowing is not enough, understanding is not enough, only acceptance will do. I had known since at least the boat ride that Serena wasn't right for me, and probably before then, and I had probably come to understand it when I'd lain in bed, contemplating my dilemma, but now I thought I could accept what had to be done. I would break up with Serena. It would be one of the first things I did when we got back from the Rock, because I didn't think it would be sensible to do it any sooner.

I thought I now knew something else as well—knew, and understood, and if the acceptance hadn't come already, I hoped it wouldn't take long. It was the most liberating and illuminating thought I'd had in some time and could very well set me free of this problem entirely, as it applied to every girl who had ever been attracted to me, or I to them: Not with anyone else—not Amelia, Serena, Lena, or even Stella in that short period when she could have been interested—did I feel as right as I did with Natalie. Never mind how they were all pretty and attractive in varying ways, never mind that they were all good people with good intentions, never mind that they all made me feel good in varying ways—none of them felt quite as right as Natalie.

* * *

The sun had well and truly risen by the time Natalie and I entered Smiley's cave. It was almost half past seven by then, and the east side of the rock was as bright as if it were high noon. It now looked as though we would have to come up with some sort of explanation to the others for why we had been out of the campsite when they woke up. We took our hovercars into Smiley's home and parked them beside the black-and-silver cars already parked there. I had forgotten about Underwood until I saw that black thing, but I supposed there was a chance he wouldn't be out of bed yet, anyway. Who knew what sort of stuff Smiley had him doing in there.

I unlocked the door, and we entered Smiley's sitting room (the entrance to the rest of the house, for lack of a better word). Natalie lifted the veil (none of the others would notice) and took a seat while I moved across to the other door and put my ear to it, listening. How had Smiley known we would be here when we were last time? He had responded almost immediately to the intercom when Tommy had called, as though he had been sitting right by it, waiting to hear from us. I couldn't hear anything through the door now, though, so I knocked once and pressed on the intercom.

"Morning, everyone," I called into it. "Rise and shine, lovely red wine, crack your spine, kick your bony behind."

Natalie groaned. I stood there, grinning at my own daring, waiting.

"Well, good morning to you too, young man," came Smiley's crisp response. He sounded both wide awake and highly amused. "What a nice surprise to hear your dulcet tones again, whichever one you are. To what do I owe the pleasure of your company?"

"We need to chat about something," I told him. "I need to know something, and I've found out something that—well, I sort of understand it but you might be interested to know. I'm John, by the way, and Natalie's here too."

"Only two of you?" Smiley cried out, and I could just imagine him pointing wildly at a refrigerator as he spoke. I almost burst out laughing. "Very good, very good. I shall join you shortly. Please wait out there for me and make yourselves comfortable."

I stepped back and sat down beside Natalie in the seat Tommy had occupied the other day. We simply sat and waited, not saying a word, not even looking at each other. I was busy preparing myself for what was about to happen, to make sure I knew what I was going to ask and tell. I also had to resist a brief urge to take Natalie's hand again, but this time it was easier while my mind was busy working. Smiley kept us waiting for nearly ten minutes, but eventually, the door to our right clicked open.

"Good day to you both," he said, staggering around us and sitting down on my other side. He pointed his remote control at the door and pressed a button. The door obediently swung shut. "It is rather early for you both, I believe. What brings you out at this hour?"

"I've been up all night," said Natalie wearily.

"Most of the night for me," I added. "I've been up and out every night—in the main hall."

"Indeed you have," he cried, pointing at me. "You have wasted no time beginning your personal quest for discovery, I see. So tell me, young John, have you learnt anything so far?"

I took a deep breath and said, "Yeah, I'm learning more and more every night, but I still haven't actually found out what happened in there. That's one of the reasons why I'm here. I need to know exactly when Moran gave me to you. Was it in '96 or '97, and which portal did they use?"

"Ah, I see," said Smiley, more solemnly now. "It was in October of 1996, which suggests that it was most likely the Atlantic portal that they had used. How long they were here is not knowledge I possess, whether they had been here for two months, whether it took your father a long time of running before he found me, or a bit of both."

August 1996—I supposed that made sense. I hadn't gone back that far. It could only mean that my mother had managed to evade the Hammersons for several months between the time they ran for it and her death.

"I still don't get why you think it was the main hall," said Natalie. She looked like her exhaustion was really catching up with her now.

"It might not be," I admitted, not really believing my words, "but it's the one lead I've got. I kept dreaming of the place, even once before I'd ever seen it. Don't you reckon that's a little odd?"

"It is, of course, but it seems that you are no stranger to odd dreams, young John," said Smiley, "and that, perhaps, is yet another special ability you possess. So tell me, what have you learnt so far? What progress have you made?"

I hesitated for a moment. How on earth was I to explain this? "Well—er—the other night, I sort of accidentally did something that I didn't understand until later that day when you told us about the fourth dimension."

"Indeed," he replied, and I knew he was attempting to predict where I was going with this in order to help me get there. "You do have a perception of the fourth dimension, after all, as I explained to you on Wednesday."

"Yeah," I agreed, "but you also said that you didn't know much about what I can actually do."

"Also true," Smiley agreed. "I only know for sure that you cannot access the fourth dimension in the same sense that I can. Have you learnt otherwise?"

"No, you're right about that," I said. "I can't go into it the way you can, but I can access it mentally. That's what happened on Tuesday night. I didn't understand it at the time, but I kind of separated from myself and started hearing voices in my head, mostly Russians but I also picked out our vice principal from three months ago."

Natalie was completely astonished by that revelation, and Smiley's eyes lit up with excitement. "My dear boy, you have tapped into the time axis! You must have allowed your mind to drift along the fourth dimension far enough that you were able to perceive moments along the time axis. The voices you were hearing may have been in both the past and the future. Of course, perceiving anything from the future may be dangerous, as any sorcerous seer can testify to."

The future—I hadn't even considered that one, but I supposed it made sense.

"That was the first night, though," I told him. "Once I thought I'd worked out what was happening, it sort of got easier."

I tried to explain the corridor analogy I had come up with yesterday, got myself all confused, shrugged, and said, "Well, anyway, I managed to move along the time axis as well and got a look at stuff that happened the previous evening—actually saw it as well as heard it. It was like I was standing right there, except to the Russians, I wasn't there at all. I couldn't move physically, though. When I did accidentally, it just broke the spell."

"Well done," Smiley cried, pointing at me. "You are a very resourceful young man, John. I take it you now intend to attempt to go all the way back to August of 1996 and see what took place in the main hall?"

"Yeah, that's the plan," I said. "I guess I'll go back there tonight again and see what I can do."

"Be sure you let me know how it goes, won't you," Smiley told me. "I would be very interested to hear what it is you can learn from this."

"Sure, I'll stop by again tomorrow. Same time, or maybe a little earlier. We should probably get back to camp before the others go nuts."

* * *

They hadn't gone nuts, exactly, but they were most definitely curious and, in Tommy's case, suspicious. They were all up and most of them dressed by the time we got back, only Siobhan still in the shower. They gathered around us as we entered the Group E house, regaling us with questions and accusations. Fortunately for us, they hadn't got too worked up yet. It was only just before nine o'clock by now and they seemed to think that they should only start worrying if we weren't seen before lunchtime. We did have magic, after all.

"What's the deal, you two?" James asked us. "What were you doing taking the cars out this early? And without telling us or leaving a note or anything?"

Natalie shrugged and looked at me. I supposed this was my responsibility, after all.

"Well, to be honest, I never even thought of leaving a note," I said, feeling a little stupid. "Guess I should have done that. As for why we went out, well, we had to see Smiley."

"Smiley?" Peter repeated. "Why? What's happened now?"

I hesitated again. How on earth was I supposed to explain this? Did I have to do it all now? For a moment, I thought I didn't have a choice, and then I thought: No, how silly of me. Of course I have a choice.

"Nothing's happened as such," I told them. "I've been working on something privately at night that Natalie came along for this time, just coincidence, and I needed Smiley's help with something. I'm not explaining it all now, though. Shower's calling."

That gave me a few minutes of reprieve as I barricaded myself in the bathroom. Siobhan was just getting out of the girls' room as I was shutting the door, so I supposed Natalie would be taking my lead. I didn't get away with it for too long, though, for the others deliberately held off breakfast until Natalie and I had re-joined them so that I would have no choice but to sit with them, during which I was once again subjected to a torrent of questions. Mostly I let them ask away while I ate, shrugged, nodded, shook my head, and occasionally muttered something or other. Natalie, who was also being interrogated, said nothing at all and was once again pretending that Tommy didn't exist as she had done in the short time after their breakup.

Soon enough, though, the time came where I had to explain myself. I told them as much as I could, about how I had been in the main hall every night, how I could mentally move along the fourth dimension and the time axis, and my plan to use it to work out what had once happened to me in that place when I had been a baby.

"Wow, time travel," said Erica, amazed. "You can go back and see anything in the past."

"Not anything, I don't think," said Peter. "He said you could only move to points within your lifetime. John couldn't see anything that happened before September 17, 1995, or anything after his date of death in 2100."

"You're saying John will live 'til he's a hundred and five?" Marc asked. "Well, I guess that makes sense."

"What? That I'll live 'til I'm a hundred and five?" I grinned.

"No, I mean it makes sense that you can only see stuff in your lifetime," he corrected. "Well, I still don't think we can be sure whatever happened to you has anything to do with the main hall, but I guess there's no harm in finding out. I think it was good that Natalie went with you, though, and I think someone should come with you tonight. It is in enemy territory, after all, and from your description, it sounded like you don't perceive much of the present while you're doing this thing."

"I don't mind doing it again," Natalie volunteered. "I was a little worried this morning, but at least I know what's going on now."

Marc shook his head. "You could, but it would make more sense for someone else to do it. After all, you shouldn't go two nights in a row without much sleep when you don't have to."

"John doesn't mind getting little sleep—"

"He doesn't really have much choice. Maybe he can catch up on sleep this afternoon while we're having our break. Or better yet, we can get all the memories out of the way in the afternoon so that he can have a nice early night."

"Actually, I already have something else I wanna do this afternoon," I cut in, and with a heavy heart and an enormous effort to control my bitterness, I turned my attention to Tommy for the first time since I'd entered the campsite. "We've gotta hide that Darkness Crystal somewhere around here. I thought later today, the two of us could go out there and build a place in one of these caves for it."

"Sounds good," he said, looking like it wasn't so good after all, all the proof I needed that he was getting a little too fond of that evil object.

"If you say so," said Marc. "But then are you sure you'll be able to keep yourself going? It's no good to be running so low on energy all the time and have to keep using magic to keep yourself going."

"I'll survive," I said heavily. "I'll still have time for two or three hours tonight if I go to bed early enough, then maybe two or three more if I can get back here early enough. We'll see."

"And I'll come with you," said Serena quickly before anyone else could jump in.

I sighed, unable to think of a good enough reason to knock her back. "Okay."

Chapter 36: The Unwanted Child

By eleven o'clock, we had all been wrapped in another invisibility veil along with our cars and were back in the cave of memories, ready to dip into the fourth episode in the series of Smiley. We all took our places in the seats that I had left there from the previous evening, except for Marc, who was once again loading the fourth memory into the playback device. Once we were all comfortable, he pushed the button to begin the episode. He just had time to seat himself before our surroundings faded once again and we zoomed back into the past, though not quite as far back as we had on previous occasions.

We came to rest in a room very similar to the one in which Lillian had been knitting when Tankom had come to call to declare war long ago. The single occupant of the room told me all I needed to know about how much time had passed. Lester Hammerson, who had been tired and elderly enough in 1981, had almost withered away to nothing in the intervening years. He was resting in a large armchair, his head back, appearing to be asleep except that his eyes were wide open. He was completely bald, his skin so wrinkly that it seemed to hang off him, and so frail that it looked like a gust of wind could blow him over.

A loud knock sounded on the door. Lester jerked slightly, made a croaky noise deep in his throat, cleared it harshly, and said, in an extremely trembling voice, "Come in."

Arnold Hammerson entered the room, a man in his thirties by now who looked not too much different from the man who now wanted me dead more than almost anything else. The most noticeable difference was his hair; it was still entirely dark brown, whereas nowadays you could see liberal streaks of grey through it. Based on the ages of the two men, and knowing that for Lester to be alive it must have been prior to Stella's birth, I estimated this to be in the early nineties. He shut the door behind him and moved across the room towards his grandfather.

"You wanted to see me, Pop?" Arnold asked in a gentle tone I had never heard him use before. It made him sound so much more human.

"I did," Lester replied weakly. Arnold had to move in very close and pull a chair up right beside him just so that he could hear the old man's words. "We can drop the formalities we normally observe, can't we?"

"Of course, that's why I just called you pop. Can I do anything for you to make you more comfortable?"

"Some water would be very useful."

Arnold waved his hand and a glass of water appeared. He created a straw for it and held it out toward his grandfather. The old man did not take it, though. Instead, the younger man brought the glass right up to the old man's lips so that he could drink from it. It was a very sorry sight. When Lester had had his fill, Arnold set the half-full glass down on the small table beside the old man's chair and settled back beside him.

"So for what purpose did you call me here?" Arnold asked. "After all, we both know that you never specifically request any assistance unless we offer it to you."

"I have a very important matter to discuss with you, Arnold," said Lester, and although he still looked very weak, the water seemed to have made his voice rather stronger. "This is a very important and top secret matter that is just between you and me. What we discuss here and now cannot be repeated to anyone outside these walls, especially your mother."

"You want me to keep secrets from Mom?" Arnold asked, raising his eyebrows and looking as astonished as if his grandfather had just asked him to masturbate live on international television. "That goes against just about everything we've been about for my whole life."

"I agree, but I've known your mother a lot longer than you have," Lester told him, "and believe me, if she became aware of this plan while she had a chance to stop it, she would do all she could to prevent it. It would hurt her like nothing else possibly could, which is why we must move quietly for now."

"So you're saying she's allowed to know eventually?"

"She will learn eventually. The whole world will learn eventually."

Arnold bit his tongue and waited for Lester to elaborate.

"So much has changed for me in recent months, Arnold," said Lester philosophically. "I held to a certain line of values all my life, for nearly a century, in fact, and for half of that time, I was forced by my elders not to act upon my beliefs. After all this time, however, I have come to realise that I was wrong about at least one very important thing."

"Like what? Are you saying all that we went through in the seventies, all the work we have been doing since, is a mistake?"

"No, not that," said Lester quickly. "No, we have always had the right idea about that, but I believe we were mistaken in another area."

"What might that be?" Arnold asked doubtfully.

"The three of us," he said, his voice now starting to weaken again, "have always worked so well together, but I'm afraid our idea that our Sorcerous chips will enable us to rule for eternity was unfounded. Do you understand what I'm saying, Arnold?"

"Does this have something to do with the Magic Crystals?" Arnold asked.

Lester made a disgruntled noise. "You really are slow sometimes. Always focus on the trivial things. Arnold, look at me. Look into my eyes and tell me I'm not dying."

Arnold did look at him—and said nothing. Lester smiled faintly.

"You see it too," he rasped. "It is as plain as day, is it not? Sure, my crystal chip will keep me alive, but it cannot make me strong again. I have run out of energy, Arnold. I have run my race. At this rate, I will soon fall into an irreversible coma from which no magic can bring me back. The time has come for you, Arnold, to continue the circle of life."

Arnold looked away from his grandfather and fixed on a spot on the wall just above the back of the large armchair. He did not respond for some time. Lester sat still, watching him and waiting patiently for his grandson to swallow the truth of the matter. Through Smiley's rambling thoughts, I came to understand that Arnold was extremely unwilling to go along with this plan, that he did not want to let go, but that he also knew that Lester was right and that, soon enough, he would have no choice. Why was he so unwilling to have a child? Was it the simple notion of being a parent? Was it the entirely understandable reason of knowing that you would be performing an action that would ultimately kill your grandfather, rather like flicking the life-support switch? Was there more to it?

"I guess I don't have a choice, do I?" he said finally.

"Of course you have a choice, young man," said Lester faintly. "You always have a choice, but you know as well as I do that the right choice is not always the easier one."

"Are you saying I have to go out there and have a child?"

"That is generally how one continues the circle of life," said Lester amusedly. "Could you give me a little more water, please?"

Arnold obliged, bringing the straw back to his grandfather's lips.

"I don't think that will work," he said as Lester sipped through the straw. "Women don't like me, they never have, and I've always been hopeless at socialising with—well, with just about anyone. How can I pull this off?"

"Arnold, you are an attractive man more capable of putting a beautiful young woman into a trance than anyone else—quite literally," Lester said as the straw came away from his lips again.

"Your obligation is to have a child, and if that means going out there and searching for a woman to enchant into being yours, then bringing her into hiding in solitary confinement during her pregnancy, it is what you must do. There is no reason why you can't enjoy the experience, Arnold, or are you telling me that at your age you're still a virgin?"

Arnold went red at that, and if I'd had control over the physical form I was feeling, I would have burst out laughing. "That's not up for discussion," he said coldly, "and before you ask, no, I'm not homosexual."

"Your sexual preference is irrelevant. As I said, you have an obligation to continue the Hammerson line, Arnold, and it is what you will do. I believe some of your closest advisers have had recent success with women? Hignat, Wilwog, and Moran? Why don't you ask one of them to assist you in finding the most worthy young lady out there to bear your child?"

This discussion was clearly well outside Hammerson's comfort zone, but Lester would not let up. He continued to stare at the younger Sorcerer until, finally, Arnold folded.

"Fine," he said despondently. "I'll go out on Friday night and see what I can do. You're saying I should definitely use magic?"

"I would advise you to disguise yourself appropriately," said Lester. "As far as using magic against a woman goes, I suggest you use your best judgement. Remember, though, once you bring her in here, she cannot return to her previous life. Her only purpose will be to our cause."

"Understood," said Arnold bitterly.

Lester looked at him in some surprise now. "Come now, Arnold, you're in a position here that so many men out there dream about. You have an opportunity to go out and have almost any woman you desire, so long as she is fertile, and the option of doing anything you want to her and have her do anything you want to you."

"I really don't care about that," said Arnold, still bitterly. "I just don't want to lose you and have to raise another in your place. How can I know that he will be as great as you have been? How can I know that he will even share our beliefs?"

"It is a life experience that you need to have, Arnold," said Lester firmly. "I was able to raise Dorothy to my belief system, despite grandparents who did their best to brainwash her into thinking that Sorcerers must never use their magic to make a great impact on any situation. She and I were then able to raise you, despite the increasing enmity that was growing between ourselves and our transatlantic rivals. I think you, Arnold, have much more going for you than either of us did. You have yourself, your mother, and a global network of loyal Hammerhearts, all of whom can combine to raise your child to be, perhaps, the most powerful Sorcerer in the history of magic. As for raising him to share your beliefs, that will be determined by your ability to raise him. Maintaining order among the army is all well and good, maintaining authority is fine, but neglecting the next generation will most likely cause results you will not desire, Arnold."

"Couldn't we just get Tankom to raise him? Or maybe 3M27 and his new wife? I mean to say, it is a lot of work I have to put in, and I really don't have time to be changing diapers and reading bedtime stories."

Lester shook his head. "You must put your priorities in order, Arnold. Dorothy is perfectly capable of maintaining order around here while you put the majority of your time into your child. You have many loyal Hammerhearts you can delegate certain duties to if you have no time to perform them yourself. Delegating parenthood? No, Arnold. That is the wrong attitude to take, considering that by the time you're ready to take on Frederic Woodward, your child will be old enough to participate."

That idea didn't sit too well with Arnold, I knew by both the look on his face and the prior knowledge that he would indeed neglect Stella in the coming years.

"Very well," he said heavily. "I suppose I can find some magical solution that will allow the best upbringing for my child."

He stared at Lester for several seconds, then said, "You know something, Pop?"

"I should hope that after more than ninety years, I would know a few things."

"I'll really miss you."

"I'm glad to hear you say that, Arnold," said the old man, and to my surprise, a single tear fell from his eye and ran slowly down his cheek. "Remember, Arnold, not a word to your mother, unless you wish to break her heart."

"She'll be devastated anyway."

"I know, but I believe she will accept it more readily if the process is already in motion. She understands the situation."

The two men sat in silence for perhaps three or four minutes after that, neither looking at each other but lost in his own thoughts. Finally, Lester broke the silence by saying, "Could I finish the water now, please?"

"Sure," Arnold replied, and then as he held the drink to the old man's lips again, added, "I guess I'd better go and find 3M27—and maybe 3H42. They could probably help me pick the right woman."

"Well done," said Lester vaguely. "Do not stall, Arnold. There is no point delaying what must be done."

Once the glass was empty, Arnold vanished it and turned to leave. Before he had shut the door behind him, the old man had already fallen into a deep sleep, snoring dully. Smiley didn't linger any longer but zoomed forward slightly into another memory.

I knew immediately that this must be the Friday night Arnold had mentioned. We were now in some sort of nightclub, and Smiley was doing his best to tag three tall men not too far from him. People kept moving right through Smiley as though he wasn't there, and since he was far enough in his shadow, to them he really wasn't there, and apparently nobody around here was blessed (or cursed) with an ability to se ghosts. The loud old-school R&B music thumping through the venue gave Smiley a headache in seconds that I had to bear, even though I would have felt more comfortable in my own body in an environment like this.

Smiley moved right up to the three men in time to catch one of them saying, "You two hang back while I go and see what they're about."

It was Moran who was speaking. My father, I reminded myself, back in the day when he had not betrayed the Hammersons, back in the day when he had a wife and probably a son as well (surely Lucien would have been born by now). The other two men were Hammerson and Hignat Senior, though in this memory he looked quite young, even though I knew him to be around the same age as Moran. Moran had just set off for a group of young ladies lurking by the bar while Hammerson and Hignat were attempting to conceal themselves in the midst of a group of drunken blokes. Judging by their accents, Moran and Hignat had come all the way across to the United States just to help Hammerson in this mission, a task that would only have taken about twenty seconds by the Hammerheart Highway, anyway.

Smiley stood right behind Hignat and Hammerson and watched on as Moran engaged one of the women in conversation, a petite blond thing with disproportionately large breasts. She was attractive, certainly, and sexy, most definitely. Desirable to just about any red-blooded man, even if she probably was ditsy—in line with the most common stereotypes of such girls anyway. I didn't think she was the three men's target, however. Moran was probably speaking to her in order to get a foot in with the rest of the group. I looked at the other girls and tried to pick out the likely target. It wasn't difficult. There, right there in the very centre of the group, as though protected by her friends. She looked very like Stella except that her eyes were a darker shade of blue (they hadn't been hardened from years of misery as Stella's had) and she wasn't quite as tall. Still, with her slender waist, pretty face, modest chest, and long, dark hair, she was very attractive indeed. It may also have been a stereotype, but she also looked like the smartest out of the group, the one with the most self-respect.

"Is it time?" Hammerson asked quietly.

"Almost, just wait for the signal."

Wow. Moran and Hignat were actually leading the charge in this operation, and for once, Hammerson was quite happy to be the follower. The two of them hung back for about a minute longer before Moran turned and addressed another girl, a redhead this time. This was clearly a signal that he and Hignat had agreed on. He nudged Hammerson and the two of them moved forward, focussing not on the girls but on Moran, as though they had just come out of the men's room and were looking for their mate. As they neared, Moran looked around at them so that the girls would notice them too. A well-thought-out plan so far.

"Oh, these are my mates," Moran told the redhead, gesturing at them. "Arnie and Tom."

Arnie? Seriously?

"Well, hi there," she said, addressing the two men before switching her gaze back to Moran immediately. The big-breasted blonde beside her only briefly acknowledged the other two before she too turned her attention back to Moran. He was no better looking than Hammerson, and perhaps no more smooth-talking than Hignat (when he wanted to be), yet the women seemed more interested in him than the other two. Why was that? Surely it couldn't all be that very slight French accent…

The remainder of the group had been halved as two of the girls had departed, to where I didn't know, but the target of the evening still remained, and Hignat wasted no time in engaging her in conversation. The one remaining girl, who kept shooting flirtatious glances at Moran, addressed Hammerson instead, though not looking particularly interested in him. Hammerson certainly didn't do a good job at keeping her attention either, keeping his responses to a bare minimum and barely making eye contact. She quickly got bored with him, but before she could turn her attention back to Moran, Hignat drew her into conversation instead. That left Hammerson and the target alone, but neither said a word to each other. Instead,

Hammerson cut between her and Hignat, circled the group, and stopped right at the bar, where Hignat, Moran, and the other three girls separated him from the girl he was after.

Smiley and I watched on with interest as Hignat and Moran continued to chat up the women. Although they were both in their thirties, these women—and they all had to be in their early twenties—all seemed very interested in them. Granted, they were a little tipsy, but that didn't seem to change the fact that a lot of women liked older men. Maturity and experience pay off, John. Just remember that when you're 105 years old.

"So you're from Australia," the girl talking to Hignat was saying, "and your friend Berny is French? What a multicultural lot you are."

"I guess you could say that," Hignat replied, smiling pleasantly. "We all came together in one place and had enough in common to want to keep in touch ever since."

Moran, meanwhile, seemed to have gotten himself into a situation he hadn't anticipated. He was clearly becoming aware that these women were far more interested in him than he had intended them to be. I supposed he was now beginning to remember that he had a wife and son at home, and that if he didn't change this course of events soon, he might end up doing something he would regret very much later. Not that he had any way of knowing that later was very limited. He was surrounded by three girls at this stage: the blonde, the redhead, and the target, as I was beginning to think of each of them. As I watched, the other two girls returned to the group, looking refreshed, and while one of them spoke to Hignat, the other jumped in the crowd of Moran fans.

Hammerson had his opportunity. This seemed to be part of the plan. He watched his target closely as she clung to the conversation, adding very little to it herself. Smiley and I watched him as he raised a hand in front of his face. The woman jerked slightly and went very still, but only for a moment. Her friends didn't even notice as she returned to herself almost immediately, though she had certainly been distracted. The only person to notice was Moran, who chose that moment to say loudly to Hignat, "Don't forget where I parked the car, Tom."

"You brought a car?" one of the ladies asked. "What are you, the designated driver or something? No fun."

"No, Tom's the designated driver," Moran assured her smoothly.

It was another signal. Hignat abruptly broke off his conversation with the two women and turned to Hammerson. The result was that Moran now had the entire group of six to attend to. This motley collection of girls seemed to include both the outgoing and the shy, which seemed to make Moran's task a little easier, and even the outgoing ones looked as though, despite being clearly interested in him, they would play hard to get. They hadn't realised that this particular fish was only humouring them and had no interest in taking the bait.

Hignat, meanwhile, moved right up to Hammerson and said very quietly, "Her name's Lindsay. According to her friend, she's very shy unless you get her talking about classic romance novels. The most I could get out of her is that she enjoys reading and quiet walks, and the fastest way to her heart is with a box of chocolates. Have you done the magic yet?"

"It's done. It shouldn't matter what we talk about."

"Good," he said. "You go for it, then, while we distract her friends."

He turned away and circled the gaggle of girls so that he wound up at Moran's left shoulder. This left Hammerson alone and unattended. Nobody was paying any attention to him. Moran and Hignat had their hands full, and the women no doubt thought that Hammerson was too dull for them. Just lucky for them they didn't recognise him, I thought, although admittedly I barely recognised him myself. It was only because I knew what to look for and because I had become so familiar with him in recent months. He had done a good job disguising himself—his hair was a lighter brown, his nose a little higher on his face and slightly crooked (it was normally very straight), his eyes a little rounder, his chin a little more rounded, and, most noticeably, he was dressed up. Nearly all the times I had seen Hammerson in my life, he had been wearing either blue-grey or dark jeans and a black leather jacket. This new smart-casual outfit, which Moran and Hignat had also implemented, although perhaps a little more naturally, was so far outside his character that it was hard not to think of him as a different person.

As he stood there, hesitating for who knew what reason, an argument sprang up amongst the group of women. One of them, the redhead, had departed the group for the ladies' room (maybe), but two of the other women wanted drinks. None of them wanted to be the one to go and get them, though, and I didn't have too much trouble working out why. Hammerson moved forward after about twenty seconds of it, by which time Moran and Hignat were looking rather alarmed, and started to say, "I don't mind—"

Why would he volunteer? Perhaps to give himself a chance to regain composure, or perhaps as a way of getting back in with the group. Or perhaps he had been reading Lindsay's mind, because a moment later she said, "I'll get them for you."

"I'll come with you," Hammerson offered before anyone else could interrupt. "Does anyone else want something while we're away?"

They did, of course, all four remaining women, now that they knew they didn't have to leave Moran to the others. Hignat seemed on the point of asking for one too before remembering he was playing the role of the designated driver tonight. Lindsay had seemed slightly taken aback by Hammerson's offer, but she didn't say anything. They set off together, down the bar to where the barman was quickly and skilfully juggling drinks as he handed them around a large group of men.

"So are you from here, Arnie?" Lindsay asked while they waited.

"Am now, yeah," he said. "Florida originally, though."

It was only a very simple collection of words, but Lindsay's reaction to them was quite surprising, or at least it would have been for anyone unaware that she had recently had magic performed against her. The question had only been to make conversation initially, but as soon as Hammerson began to speak, Lindsay's expression seemed to become vague and distant. Something disturbing crossed her features, a kind of desperate longing, and she never took her eyes from Hammerson's face in the following seconds. It made my heart hurt somehow to see such a beautiful woman fold so easily.

"Wow, Florida," she sighed, swaying slightly towards Hammerson and seeming completely unaware she was doing it. "So what made you come all the way over here?"

"Tom," said Hammerson, gesturing at Hignat's back some fifteen feet away. "He owns a printing business out here and he offered me a job a few years ago when I was a little down on my luck."

"Oh? What was wrong before?"

"Just—got in a spot of bother with the banks, debt collectors and all, because I was an idiot and kept losing every job I got."

"Oh yeah. You gotta have a good job."

It would have been funny if the situation hadn't been so serious. That woman had lost just about all her common sense by now. What on earth had Hammerson done to her? It wasn't the domination charm, and I doubted it was the influential charm either. It looked more like some sort of spell that caused crippling desire. Probably a common enough piece of magic, but not one I had ever seen before. The pattern was becoming more and more predictable now—five more minutes like this and Hammerson could do just about anything with her. As long as Hignat and Moran kept her friends busy enough, he could take her out of this venue and teleport her to a

Hammerheart base before anyone noticed there was anything going on.

"What do you do, then?" Hammerson asked her now.

"What I do when?" she asked, and it was barely a sigh now as she continued to drink him in with her eyes.

"I mean your job, your work," he pressed her, exercising great patience (well, great patience for him, anyway). "What sort of job do you have?"

"Oh yeah," she sighed again. "I fly."

"You fly?" he repeated incredulously.

After about a minute, he deduced that she was in fact a flight attendant.

"You must see a lot of interesting places in a job like that," he said, "and meet a lot of people."

"Yeah, it's nice to meet people," she said vaguely.

There was space in front of them now, and Hammerson took her by the arm and moved her forward, towards where the barman stood, watching them. Shielding her from his gaze for what reason I didn't know (the man had already seen everything), Hammerson ordered the four drinks for the women. As the barman busied himself, he leaned in towards Lindsay and said quietly, "How would you like to continue this conversation somewhere a little more quiet?"

An expression of bliss crossed Lindsay's features, and for several seconds, she made no reply. By the time she had got her voice back, four drinks were sitting on the bar before them.

"I tell you what," said Hammerson quietly. "You go and wait by the door for me. I'll give these drinks to your friends and let them know what's going on."

"I'll wait for you," she said vaguely and began moving slowly towards the exit. To anyone watching, she would have looked pretty drunk.

Hammerson gathered the four drinks up in his arms and carefully carried them back down the bar to where Hignat and Moran were still keeping the group of now five women distracted, Smiley following along behind in his shadow. Alarmingly, I saw that there were other people in the vicinity now too—other women, some as young as these girls and others closer to Hignat's and Moran's ages, as well as several jealous-looking blokes, all watching on and ready to break up the scene for their own.

"Where's Lindsay?" one of the girls asked as she took one of the drinks from Hammerson's arms.

"She had to go to the bathroom," he lied, beginning to hand the drinks out. "Er, listen, you two—"

He turned to Hignat and Moran and leaned in close so that he could speak to them without the girls hearing. Before he could say a word, however, Moran said urgently, "Get me the hell out of here. I know they say it's impossible for a woman to rape a man, but I think it might happen to me tonight if I don't escape soon."

"Okay, but you listen to me first," Hammerson said, a little more loudly, obviously signalling that this was an act for the women's benefit. "I'm a bit tired, think I'll have an early night. I'll take a cab, though, so, Tom, you're still responsible for the car." Then more quietly, he added, "Do whatever you have to. You know where the nearest entrance to the Highway is, so just get there as quickly as you can, and who gives a shit if you have to break a few hearts in the process."

"See you on Monday," Hignat said loudly to Hammerson, then added quietly, "Or tomorrow."

Hammerson backtracked from the group, said good night to a few of the women (they barely heard him), then headed in the general direction that Lindsay had gone a minute earlier. Smiley watched him out of sight but didn't follow. This surprised me because I would have thought we would be following Hammerson all the way through this episode. Perhaps Smiley had no desire to see how he went about doing the deed with that woman; it wasn't difficult to fill in the gaps from here on, anyway. Instead he turned his attention back to Hignat and Moran and, perhaps for my and Marc's benefits, observed the two men's efforts to break free of the situation they had landed themselves in.

The efforts began after about ten minutes, by which time Hammerson and Lindsay had surely cleared the vicinity. It started with them both telling the women that they needed to go somewhere. When forced to say where, Hignat grudgingly admitted they needed a bathroom break. They set off, but a couple of the women (the blonde and the redhead) followed closely behind without them being aware, at least until one of them pointed out that the men's room was the other way. Unable to get through the exit, they had been forced to change course for the men's room where, once inside and safely away from the females, they conferenced.

"What the hell are we gonna do?" Moran asked. "They're not gonna let us go. I think they've already got some sort of bouncy naked yummy foursome in mind for tonight."

"You could tell them you're gay," Hignat suggested, "and I could tell them, I dunno, I have herpes or something."

"You think they'll believe us now?" Moran said frantically. "They've already lost most of their minds. They probably won't care by now."

"I don't mind taking your place," a gruff voice muttered from one of the locked stalls, causing both men to jump in surprise.

"Get your own women, jerk," Hignat snapped. "Fine, what are we gonna do, then? I still think pretending to be gay is a good idea. Maybe you and I should walk out of here, arms around each other and kissing and not noticing anyone else."

Moran grimaced. "If you wanna make me throw up all over your shirt, then that's a pretty good plan."

Hignat's face lit up. "That's an even better plan. You pretend you're sick and I say I have to get you out of here. If they say they wanna come and help us out, I'll get a couple of their numbers and promise to call them back, and then—surprise, surprise—guess who turns into a jerk?"

"It'd work much better if I really was sick, but it's probably the best we can do," said Moran heavily. "Why don't we just tell them to fuck off? It would be so much simpler."

"I don't mind doing that," said Hignat amusedly, "but do you? The nice, polite Frenchman that you are?"

I could have snorted at that. A lot had changed in seventeen years, that was certain.

Moran stared at Hignat for a few seconds before shrugging. "Just give me a minute."

"What are you doing?"

"Sticking a finger down my throat."

The scene deteriorated somewhat after that, losing some of its interest. Moran did indeed make himself sick, and although it wasn't convincing by the time they got out of the toilet, they used it anyway as an excuse to get out of the club. Hignat did indeed take a few numbers down before leading Moran through the crowd towards the door. Smiley watched them out of sight before deciding that he'd had enough too. His head was throbbing worse than ever by now. The memory faded and was replaced by another, apparently on a different day for Smiley because his head had cleared completely.

We had returned to the room where Lester had lectured Arnold on his future responsibilities. Lester himself was resting in the same armchair he had been in on the last occasion. Where Arnold had sat last time, Tankom now sat, looking extremely despondent. Her expression suggested that she was now aware of the plan to replace Lester with a new Sorcerer, but the evidence in the room suggested that perhaps the plan hadn't quite gone ahead yet. Hammerson was there, but he hadn't taken a seat beside Tankom yet. He was presently using magic to bind Lindsay to another armchair in front of where the three Sorcerers would sit. She was struggling weakly and whimpering, but she was no match for him, probably wouldn't have been even if he didn't have magic.

"What do you want me for?" she sobbed. "Why you lie—why you bring me here?"

"Spare us the dribble, if you please," said Tankom bitterly. "None of us are in a mood to deal with a bitch like you right now."

"Stop being so ungrateful," snapped Hammerson. "You should be honoured that you've been chosen to breed a Sorcerer, that in the next generation, someone with your blood may well rule the world."

"I thought you liked me."

"Liked you? How much did you drink last night?"

"Please be quiet," said Lester calmly. He was the only one who looked at peace with the current situation, or maybe he just didn't have the energy to get worked up. "I have been told that your name is Lindsay. Is that true?"

"Yes," she moaned. "You're going to hurt me, aren't you?"

"Nobody is going to hurt you, Lindsay," said Lester firmly. "We value you too much for that. Keeping you in good health for the next nine months is one of the most important things to us now. You have nothing to worry about."

"You're keeping me here for nine months?"

"Of course not," said Tankom, raising her head slightly now and looking at Lindsay with heart-freezing dislike. "We're keeping you here forever. You have an obligation to us now. Your son or daughter will be perhaps the most important person to walk the Earth in the history of mankind."

"But my parents—my friends—my career—"

"None of that matters anymore," said Lester firmly. "Perhaps down the track, we can arrange for you to see your family again, but the rest of your life means nothing to us and will soon mean nothing to you either. Remember, we have ways of making you comply."

Lindsay whimpered again.

"Will you stop making that pathetic noise," snapped Hammerson, and he raised his hand, about to perform a spell, but before he could, either Lester or Tankom blocked his magic, as I had once seen Stella do to Amelia.

"Do not harm her, Arnold," Tankom snapped. "I agree with this no more than you do, but it does have to be done. If you end up accidentally killing her, you'll have to go back out and find someone else. Is that what you want?"

"Should just get 3H42 and 3M27 to do it for me," he muttered, not making eye contact with his elders.

"Arnold, has the insemination happened yet?" Lester asked. That was a rather impersonal way of asking if he'd knocked her up yet, I thought, but wasn't particularly surprised by it.

"Isn't it too early to know for sure?" Hammerson retorted. "I did try, though. Guess it did feel kind of nice, but way too close to be really comfortable."

"Good, very good," said Lester. "You know, if you do enjoy it, you do still have a few more months in which you can make the most of it."

"It did not work," said Tankom bitterly. "She won't say it, but look at her mind—she is a pill popper."

A silence filled the room as the three Hammersons stared at the poor woman trussed before them. She herself was too terrified to even make a sound now.

"No matter," said Lester calmly. "There will be no more contraception for you, Lindsay. Arnold, it just means that you will have to keep trying, but we will perform regular tests on her to determine when she has caught."

"Where are we keeping her?" asked Tankom. "The Basement?"

"I don't think so," said Lester, his voice beginning to weaken again. "Those are perhaps not the most appropriate conditions for a woman with child. Dorothy, you can create a room for her off the side of Arnold's room. It only needs to be comfortable and secure, and it means that Arnold can go in there anytime he likes and do whatever he likes with her—except hurt her, of course."

"Very well," she said, getting to her feet. "Come, Arnold, we should move her."

"I don't want—" Lindsay started, but Hammerson slapped her across the face.

"What you want means nothing to us, bitch," Tankom hissed at her.

Instead of untying her, Tankom levitated Lindsay's chair into the air and made it follow her from the room. In her wake, Hammerson was left staring at Lester in dismay.

"Well, this is a happy little situation we've landed ourselves in, isn't it?" he said bitterly.

"It can certainly be so," said Lester, smiling faintly. "You just need to come to terms with the fact that it is necessary. Besides, Arnold, there is no reason why you can't care for your child just as you care for your mother."

Hammerson shook his head in disbelief. "Perhaps, but I'd be much happier if it didn't have to be so."

"Don't waste your time and energy brooding over things you cannot change, Arnold," said Lester firmly. "Lindsay looks like a very nice girl who you could probably have a good time with during her stay with us. It might be good for you to actually make a real friend for a change, Arnold, even if we do have to use the influential charm just to make her happy."

"That's *my* decision," said Hammerson shortly, and he turned and left the room. Lester sighed deeply as the door swung shut behind him.

The memory faded again and was replaced by another one. I hadn't expected it since this one had already gone on for what felt like a very long time. Once I realised what it was, I didn't even understand why Smiley had included it as part of this tape; it would have made more sense to package it separately. He hadn't bothered to show us Hammerson's attempts to impregnate Lindsay, nor any of the months of her pregnancy. We had skipped right to the finale. February 21, 1994—I knew it to be the date of Stella's birth.

What else surprised me, for about two seconds anyway, was that it wasn't by Lindsay's bedside that Tankom and Hammerson sat. This was obviously a private hospital that the Hammersons owned or had created underground like everything else of theirs. We were only in one room with a single bed, but it felt fairly small. I knew Lindsay was close by, however, because I could hear her screaming bloody murder through the wall. In this room, however, Lester occupied the bed. Around him sat Hammerson, Tankom, Moran, and Cornish. His code at this stage was 3C50, which must have meant that he was only promoted to level two once Hammerson had taken over Tankom's position of family leader.

"It is almost time," Lester whispered, "so I must say this now before it is too late. Arnold, Dorothy, I have only one final request."

"Anything," Tankom whispered back. She was crying.

"I am given to understand that Roger's time is almost up," he said. "Frederic Woodward's daughter is due a month from now. That will leave the Woodwards down on strength and defence—a perfect time to strike them, those leeches who have made my final years such a misery with their ridiculous restrictions. I want you to avenge me. Find all of the Magic Crystals and take them down."

"Wouldn't that go against the treaty?" asked Hammerson. "What would happen to us if we put a foot out of line?"

"After this long, I believe nothing drastic, as long as you're careful about it," Lester replied. "That is my final request. Don't make all my work over the last three decades worth nothing."

"I promise it will not be," Tankom sobbed. "We will finish your work, Father."

Somewhere nearby, a clock struck. Through the wall, the screaming reached a whole new pitch. Lester sighed deeply and closed his eyes. Seconds later, he appeared to have fallen asleep for the final time. Tankom couldn't control herself; she broke down where she sat, crying uncontrollably. Hammerson maintained his composure a little better. He moved toward the bed and gently straightened his grandfather's head on his pillow. Wiping a trickle of blood from the corner of the deceased Sorcerer's mouth, he said to Moran and Cornish without looking around, "One of you, go and check if it's happened yet."

Moran did the honours, muttering something darkly as he headed for the door.

"I heard that, Berny," Cornish said loudly, "but just between you and me, I actually agree with you."

Neither Tankom nor Hammerson paid any attention to the exchange. Once he had given his grandfather the appearance of comfort, he turned his attention to his distraught mother and began comforting her. Cornish watched on, frowning slightly and appearing to be attempting to listen to the noises in the next room. The screams had stopped and it was now very difficult to hear what was going on in there. Moran didn't take long to return, though. About a minute later, he reappeared in the doorway and spoke to the room at large.

"It's happened. Boss, would you like to meet your daughter?"

He didn't want to, it was clear, but with an effort, he disengaged himself from Tankom and got to his feet. "You stay here," he told her. "3C50, take over, and do a damn good job."

Cornish nodded and got up from his seat. Hammerson followed Moran out of the room, Smiley close behind them both, and down the corridor to the next door. The room in which Stella had been born looked very similar to the one in which Lester had just died, except that there was more medical equipment around it. Lindsay lay in the midst of blood-soaked sheets, a Hammerheart nurse standing over, her making sure that she was comfortable. The poor woman looked distraught, and the reason was clear enough: she wasn't allowed to hold her daughter. Two other Hammerhearts, one of them surely a doctor, had laid Stella down on a trolley and were examining her. Even as a baby, she was tall, although at this stage it looked more a case of being long. Moran and Hammerson stopped in the doorway until one of the Hammerhearts gave them clearance.

"How are you, Lindsay?" Moran asked smoothly, adopting that same tone he had used to chat up the women at that nightclub many months earlier.

I barely heard her reply, if she even made a coherent reply. Hammerson had stopped beside the trolley and was staring down at Stella. The look on his face at that moment put so much into perspective for me: He despised her. It was clear that he blamed her for this whole unfortunate series of events that had put his family into disarray, had reduced his mother to tears, and, on top of all that, given him the responsibility of a parent. Stella could never have understood all the reasons why she had been dealt such a bad hand, but I certainly did.

"Congratulations, 1H3, sir," said the doctor. "You have a healthy baby daughter."

"Final decision, sir," said the nurse beside the doctor, who was preparing to write out a birth certificate. "What should she be called?"

"Stella," Lindsay cried out before anyone could stop her. "She's Stella, my Stella."

"Whatever." Hammerson shrugged. "I really don't care anymore."

"Stella it is," said the nurse, beginning to write. "Stella Lindsay Hammerson."

"Let me hold her," Lindsay cried out.

Hammerson's patience snapped like a twig. Before anyone could stop him, he spun around and raised a hand over the bed. There was no flash of light, no crack of sound as Lindsay slumped on the bed, her life expired. Moran and the nurse beside him yelled in surprise and leapt backward, lucky not to have been in the way. Hammerson simply stared at her lifeless shell for a few more seconds before turning to the doctor and saying, "Move her to our living quarters when you're ready. Let me know if you need me for anything else."

Without another word, he strode from the room, Smiley tagging along behind, and went back into the room where the rest of his family was. Smiley's mind told me that we had seen just enough to work out the rest for ourselves, to understand just how unwanted Stella had been right from the start, before the memory faded once again, and this time, reality returned. It was already after one o'clock.

"What a bastard," said Erica. "Hammerson—such a bastard, doing that to that woman and then just walking out on Stella like that."

"It does explain a fair bit, doesn't it," said James. "I wonder how much Stella knows about that."

"My guess is very little," I said. "She knows her mother's name— it was the same name she gave Underwood—but I doubt they would have told her all that other stuff that went on."

"But he's an idiot," said Tommy, rather unnecessarily, I thought. "I mean, if they wanted Stella to replace Lester, they should have done a better job."

"But that's exactly the thing—they never wanted her to replace Lester," said James. "I agree, though. Common sense says that once the deed has been done, you would move on and raise Stella to be like them. She could have been totally horrible if they'd done a good job. As it is, though, she's just confused."

The scene I had just observed only served to make me feel even more sorry for Stella than I had been already. It had been bad enough before knowing how horrible they had treated her all her life, but now, actually knowing the reason why it had all started, it made me want to avenge her, to stand up for her, as she had never been able to stand up to them herself. This memory on its own probably didn't cover the whole reason why Hammerson had mistreated Stella (the possibility still existed that he knew what was between me and her), but this was where it had all begun. Stella had never been wanted, was probably still not wanted, yet in spite of all that, she was still with them now. The thought filled me with a great sadness.

Chapter 37: Fear Factor

About an hour later, Tommy and I took our hovercars around to the south side of the island where, we had earlier agreed, we would hide the Darkness Crystal. Before we had set off, I had taken the crystal from him (he hadn't looked too happy about giving it up, but to his credit, he hadn't hesitated) and concealed it inside a box similar to the one the Hammersons had hidden it in. I had performed a spell on it that would prevent magic being used to unlock it or break it open, although I knew that any determined person with magic could probably find a way around that. I had also made it so that the box would prevent any non-magical efforts to open it. The job now was to find a place to put the box and set up a decent amount of protection around it.

I had given it some thought over lunch, and now I tried to lead Tommy to the place I had in mind. It hadn't been as easy to find this time as it had on Wednesday, but eventually I spotted the smiley cave above us and the track above it.

"We're going up here again?" Tommy asked, steering his car after mine, around the cave and up to the track.

"Yeah," I said, "just up to that hole again."

"We're throwing it in the hole?"

"Not throwing—putting," I told him. "We can go down there and make a nice little home for it."

"You're sure that's not dangerous?" he asked tentatively.

"Not if we're careful," I said. "And remember, what's in that box ain't the only crystal we've got here."

"We should have brought Marc with us," he said nervously.

"We'll be fine," I said firmly. "Look, there it is. Start looking for a good parking spot. At least up here we can't be booked by dodgy parking officers."

"Very funny," he said drily.

I slowed my car up and stopped it just before the hole. There really wasn't enough space off the track to park it there. At best it would have been on a forty-five-degree angle. I let the car drift back to the ground, then, when I felt the gentle thud of its landing, climbed out and waited for Tommy. He had pulled his car up just behind me and was looking at the narrow strip of track he would have to sidestep along to get past my car.

"I'll pick you up, trust me," I told him.

It turned out not to be necessary, though. By hanging onto my hovercar, Tommy was able to get past it with no trouble—didn't even have to slow his pace down. When we were together, I turned and looked down into the depths of the hole. I had forgotten until now that there was water down there, which ruled out the idea of going right to the bottom, unless we wanted this to be an underwater adventure. I personally didn't, though. The alternative was to create a new cave in the wall down there somewhere and hide it inside. That idea was much more appealing. Lisa had told us once upon a time that all the caves on Rock Haulter were created by generations of Sorcerers since Sien and Leoard had created the Rock itself. Now I, as the user of the Sien-Leoard Crystal, had a chance to add my own mark.

"So what's your plan?" Tommy asked.

"We need something to lower us into it," I said vaguely, trying to think. "Something like that thing Fewul made us to get under the water up there, remember?"

"You mean like an elevator?"

"Yeah, exactly."

I squeezed the crystal and a square block of wood appeared in the hole before us, floating on our level so that we could step onto it. A few spells later and the wood would be strong enough to support our weight and would be able to rise or fall on voice commands, just in case. I stepped onto it experimentally, and perhaps rather bravely, but it held up fine. Looking back at Tommy, I said, "You coming?"

He didn't look at all keen about it, but he gritted his teeth and stepped carefully onto the wood.

"Just stand still and keep your balance," I told him, "we're going…*down*."

Obediently, the wood began to descend, a little more slowly than I had expected it to, but there was no harm in being too cautious. The rock closed in around us so that before too long, we could barely see each other's faces.

"How far down before we get to the water?" Tommy whispered.

"I don't know, but this thing will let us know when we do. We won't have to get wet. Then when we do, we can just go back up a bit—*down*," I added, for, as I had spoken the word 'up', the wood had halted its downward progress.

We continued to descend, and now I had to admit to myself that despite the calming presence of the Sien-Leoard Crystal, I was at least a bit scared. There didn't seem to be a logical reason for it; it was more a case of being surrounded by darkness, coldness, and silence. That, along with the knowledge that we were heading deeper into it, increased the fear of the unknown, for surely it was no more than the unknown that we feared. Tommy stood close to me, but by now I could barely see him and couldn't hear him at all. It was as if he had turned himself to stone to block out his own emotions.

My plan to go all the way down and back up didn't eventuate. I looked up at one point and could barely see any light above me and decided then that we might as well stop here. I said "stop," then began feeling my way around the block of wood, trying to find the nearest wall of rock.

"Thanks," sighed Tommy, "but I still reckon it'd be much simpler to just throw the damn thing in the water."

"If we're gonna hide this thing here, then we might as well do the job thoroughly," I said firmly.

It seemed that at this depth, the hole had become narrower, so much so that it was probable that the block of wood wouldn't have been able to go all the way down to the bottom anyway. I was able to touch the rock surrounding us on all four sides. If this was the south side of the island, it made sense to dig into the north side of our current position. The trouble with that idea was that I could no longer tell my directions, and since I had moved around so much already, I couldn't remember which way I had been facing to start with. The only thing I could do was pick a side at random and see what—

"What the hell was that?" gasped Tommy.

The fear in his voice sent a terrible chill down my spine. I froze, listening hard. Yes, I could hear it too—a faint gurgling sound coming from directly below us.

"Did we touch the water?" I whispered.

"No, you told it to stop. There's something down there."

I would not entertain that idea. My mind would not—could not —accept it.

"Let's just do this," I said and raised the crystal again.

I picked the wall to my left and used the crystal to carefully dig an indent into it, making sure that the rock above it would remain in place. The hole in the wall, which would be large enough for me to climb into (at a crouch at least), stretched farther and farther into the rock until, quite suddenly and surprisingly, it opened into a new room. Beside me, Tommy gasped in horror.

"Geez, John, close that thing up. You never know what's in there."

I agreed with that and quickly placed a strong shield of rock over the entrance to that cave, whatever it was. There was still enough room in the hole for the box, though. I took it out of my pocket, leaned into the hole, and placed it carefully on the rock. I then retreated back onto the wood and used the crystal to fill the hole back in. Make it appear exactly as it had before I started, I thought at it, and the crystal obliged.

"A successful mission," said Tommy. "Now let's get out of—"

It was the splash that made him break off, but the reaction had barely happened when something crashed into the block of wood from below. It was hard enough to lift the block by about five feet, sending Tommy and I flying and yelling in terror. The magic of the wood prevented the wood from falling all the way down; it simply sank to the level it had been at before impact. We both landed hard, Tommy on his backside and me on my knees. From below the wood, we heard a splash as the thing sank back into the water.

"Jesus H. Christ, there really is something down there," Tommy moaned. "Damn, my fucking arse. What is that?"

"What's your fucking arse?"

"No, that thing down there."

"I don't know, but I'm not staying around to—"

Too late. It leapt from the water again, but this time, instead of thumping into the wood, it seemed to snap at it. The floor shuddered, and we both fell over again. Large cracks appeared in the surface, and we both heard pieces of wood splash into the water below as the creature descended once again. This thing had been damaged pretty badly and probably couldn't take another blow like that, but that wasn't the worst of it. The worst—the very worst—was that as much as I wanted to speak the word 'up', the one word that may well have been our saviour, I couldn't. The last impact had dislodged the Sien-Leoard Crystal from my hand. I'd heard it roll away from me a short distance, but I didn't think it had gone over the edge. I hoped to God it hadn't.

"Shit, help me find the crystal," I hissed at Tommy. "But don't move too much in case it rolls over the edge."

"You lost the crystal?"

"Just help me!"

I was almost delirious with panic. That thing would be back any second, and once it struck, if we didn't have the crystal, not only were we goners, but the Sien-Leoard crystal would also probably be lost for good. I crouched down and began feeling all around myself, not in sweeping motions but more like tapping motions so that I wouldn't accidentally knock the crystal over the edge. Tommy crouched down and began doing the same thing on the other side of the wood. Below us, I could hear the water churning as the thing below did who knew what, prepared what assault I had no desire to find out.

We were extremely lucky. At least, we were lucky for about three seconds. I managed to place a finger on the smooth, round rock and grab it up just as another splash sounded below. We felt the shudder as the thing made contact with the block of wood again, but this time, it wasn't so much a strike. Instead, it seemed to have grabbed onto it, and now it was—it was—

"*Up! Up!*" I bellowed.

The floor began to rise, but the thing rose with us. The bottom part of the block, which had already been fractured, was now being splintered by something that was far too strong for my liking. We continued to rise through all that, but now the top part was feeling the strain as well. Large cracks were appearing and quickly deepening beneath our feet, and it was becoming increasingly difficult to keep our balance.

"*Do something!*" Tommy shouted, his face transported.

This was the ultimate test, concentrating hard enough to use the right magic while trying desperately to keep my balance, knowing that at any moment we could fall to the mercy of whatever was trying to attack us. I squeezed the crystal and thought at it—make us go up, make us go up. Indeed the wood shot up into the air so that the light suddenly appeared and grew around us. We shot out of the hole and dived. The block of wood continued to rise without any specific instruction from me to slow it down (perhaps it would keep going until it left the Earth's atmosphere, and then beyond), but Tommy and I managed to jump off not too far above the ground. We fell down on either side of the track. I tumbled several feet down the hill and landed on a small ledge. Tommy was lucky; he had fallen on the up side of the track, so he only rolled into a ditch. I on the other hand had almost tumbled right over the edge. A few feet farther and I would have fallen thirty or forty feet onto the ground below.

I raised myself up painfully and wiped blood from my face. I was stinging in several places. Looking down at myself, I saw that I was a mess, having ripped skin off my arms and legs, my pants and shirt torn. I had barely a few seconds to dwell on it, though, because a noise that sounded a bit like a propeller sounded from the track above me. Looking up, I caught sight of something that made my insides cringe in revulsion. It looked a bit like some absurd starfish made of goo. About three quarters my height, it seemed to stand on two of its points while two more of its points looked a bit like arms. The fifth point, which stuck vertically up, might have resembled a head, but its face (if it could be called a face) was in the centre of its body—long, horizontal eyes, no nose at all, and a large, lopsided mouth that looked quite capable of swallowing just about anything.

It moved quickly, doing a cartwheel along the track (that explained the noise I'd heard) until it reached our hovercars. It wrapped itself around the back of Tommy's car (it was hardly big enough to cover it completely but it did a good job all the same) and began sucking on it. I stared in horror. By all the normal rules of magic, it shouldn't even be able to see the cars, what with them being separated from it by the invisibility veil. Slowly the back of the car disintegrated and disappeared into the thing's mouth, and as the car got smaller and finally disappeared, so the monster grew. By the time it was done, it was perhaps as big as Tommy and I put together. I thought it would proceed to my car next, but instead, it dived off the other side of the track.

"Tommy!" I yelled as I heard his terrified scream from the other side of the track.

I scrambled to my feet and, ignoring the terrible pain, raised the crystal, which had miraculously not flown out of my hand again. I made Tommy levitate into the air, clearing him from the reach of the starfish. I saw him float up into the air and tried to direct him over to where I was, all the while trying to think how we were gonna get away from this thing. I saw it leap into the air, higher than I had expected it to be able to jump but not enough to reach Tommy. It spun in the air like a ridiculous fan before falling back down on the other side of the track. I could hear it cartwheeling back up the other side, though. It would come for me now.

I sprung up an invisible shield around the two of us and watched as the starfish collided with it. It spun off the top and cartwheeled through the air down the mountain. Good, I thought. That gave us a bit of time. Tommy was huddled on the ground beside me, and now he staggered back to his feet.

"We have to get rid of it," he panted. He looked no better than me but knew he had to grind this thing out before he could rest and lick his wounds. "We can't just let it stay loose. It could do all sorts of damage."

"And follow us to the edge of the Earth," I muttered, watching as it spun and twirled below us, making its way back up the mountain.

It was true. Now that it had got out of the hole it had been trapped in, it could do all sorts of damage. The question was how did I get it back in that hole? I squeezed the crystal and tried to freeze it in place—that didn't work. I tried to tie it in ropes—the ropes appeared but the way it spun and twisted around made it impossible to get hold of. It spun back towards us and, this time, landed right on top of the shield. To anyone watching, it would have looked like the starfish was hovering in mid-air, curled around nothing. To the starfish itself, it probably felt simply like landing on top of something solid that it could see through. To me, it felt like being beneath a glass roof and looking up at something terrifying.

"Any ideas?" Tommy asked.

"We have to get it back in the—"

"What the hell is it doing?"

It had wrapped itself around the top of the magical shield as though it were a solid object (I supposed from that angle, it must be) and was opening and closing the hole of its mouth repeatedly. I thought I knew what it was doing: The shield wasn't as big as the hovercar it had eaten, yet somehow the magic of the thing was preventing the monster from getting it into its mouth. Still, I had no idea how long our luck would last, and we couldn't do anything in this position.

"Can we move?" Tommy asked.

"I think I can."

I turned and began climbing back up the slope towards the track. The shield moved with me, dragging both Tommy and the starfish along with it. The monster, seeming to realise it was up against something beyond its ability to penetrate by force, leapt back into the air, landed on the track, and jumped again, cartwheeling through the air directly at me. It propelled itself back off the shield, but that didn't stop me cringing as one of its fierce points came within a foot of my face.

We reached the track. I turned to help Tommy stagger up beside me, watching over his shoulder as the starfish rolled its way up the slope and stopped beside us. For a few seconds, the three of us just stood there looking at each other, separated only by an invisible barrier. Staring into the terrible slits that resembled eyes, I could see that basic primitive intelligence it possessed. It meant to have us. It meant to swallow us just for disturbing the peace of its dark, wet lair. I had a feeling that the only sure way to defeat it was to put it in a place where it could not get out, and the only place that could probably stop this creature was the place that had been designed for that specific purpose by whichever Sorcerer had put it here—its home. The question was how to trick it into dropping back into the hole?

"Why can it see us?" Tommy hissed at me. "Or do you reckon it's got other senses it's using?"

"Probably the latter," I muttered, "or maybe Natalie's magic only applies to humans. We'd better clear that up with her later on."

Only half my mind was on what I was saying, though. I kept trying to look around the thing before us, trying to think of a way to get it to spin back towards the crevice from which it had come.

"What on earth are you waiting for?" Tommy hissed in my ear. He didn't seem brave enough to look at the thing standing right beside us. "Do something about it."

"Shut up. I'm trying to think."

I took a few steps along the track, hesitated, then took a few more. My hovercar was about six feet ahead of me, and beyond that, the dark slit into which I thought I would have to go to get the starfish to follow me down, but the monster had other ideas. Proving that it must have had a greater intelligence than a basic instinct to hunt down those who disturbed its absurd tranquillity, it cartwheeled past me and onto the track ahead of us, blocking our access to the hole. I had no idea if it knew what my plan was or not. It seemed to understand that any plan I had was one it had to fight.

Now what? I couldn't teleport around it, nor could I step around it (it would simply move with me), and having a coward beside me didn't help the situation. I tried once again to shift the beast aside, but the magic of the Sien-Leoard Crystal had no impact on it. I felt sure that the crystal would be capable of destroying it utterly and on the spot, but for whatever reason, I couldn't work out how to make it happen. I considered the possibility that the starfish was an illusion, and the damage it was doing was possible only because of our mental insistence that it was there. It was a plausible explanation for why it could see us and also why direct magic against it had no effect. It sounded plausible, if only I could accept that it was something I couldn't understand, but I couldn't make sense of it. It must have been something to start with; otherwise, we never would have heard those splashes in the hole—or would we?

"What are you doing?" Tommy hissed. He was barely moving his lips now, and it was very difficult to hear him.

I tried to make sense of the possibility I had just stumbled over. I had no idea where it had come from; after all, I had never once before considered that something I was seeing with my own eyes wasn't real. The best I could do was—

I was distracted by Tommy, who nudged me hard in the side, almost knocking me sideways off the track. I regained my balance quickly and whirled on him. "Will you cut it out! I'm trying to work out what to do but the most I can work out is that it's responding to our fear. You know, I don't even think it's real."

"Have you lost your mind?" he hissed at me. "Look at it. It's—"

He made the mistake of glancing sideways at it, and the terrible sight froze him on the spot. The starfish seemed to leer at him, daring him to come closer.

"Snap out of it!" I hissed back. "I can't get rid of it with the crystal, but I think we can get rid of it if we show that we're not afraid of it, or that we don't believe in it."

"What's not to believe in?" he squeaked, and I was starting to realise that even after all that we'd been through, Tommy was still lacking a good deal of courage.

If our only hope of getting rid of this monster was to conquer our fear of it, I had no hope of getting anywhere while I had Tommy stuck beside me. My only other idea at that point was to continue with my original plan. I therefore leaned in close to Tommy and whispered, "I'm gonna try to send it back that way. When it moves, be ready to run straight at the hole. Get as close to it as you can without falling into it. Got me?"

He looked terrified, but to my relief, he nodded. I looked back at the starfish and made eye contact with it (or at least as close to eye contact as you could get with something that didn't really have proper eyes). Its response to my cheek was to leer still more threateningly, but in response to my lack of fear, it seemed unsure of itself, or perhaps that was merely my imagination. I then turned deliberately away from it and took a few steps down the track, past Tommy. The monster reacted just as I'd hoped it would. It spiralled past me, tried once again to break through the shield, failed, and settled itself on the track before me. I abruptly turned away from it and, Tommy ready and waiting beside me, we both tore off up the track.

What happened next was something that hadn't even occurred to me as a possible option. The starfish leapt over us and settled back on the track ahead of us, but we couldn't slow down in time. Instead, our shield pushed the starfish backwards. It leapt sideways, forced on by the magic but apparently in some control of its direction. It spiralled into the ditch where Tommy had fallen earlier and wheeled around to come back at us. I had come to an abrupt halt as my shin collided painfully with the rear of my hovercar while Tommy, who had been aiming for the gap between the car and the ditch, was brought up short by the magical shield.

"What are you waiting for? You said get to the—"

"Too late now," I muttered.

The starfish had rolled up past Tommy and had settled itself precariously between the hovercar and the hole I wished we could drop it into. It seemed to know that I was aiming for the hole and was merely positioning itself to stop me from getting there. Tommy was closer to it than I was, and now he shrank away from it, looking rather pathetic in my view, but I barely had emotion to spare for him. My all was concentrated on what I could do to get into a showdown with this monster without Tommy's fear working against me.

"If you can't make it vanish or whatever, just throw something large at it," Tommy moaned. "Look at it—it's almost in there."

I had doubts about that idea. Was it the right way to defeat this monster? All the same though, Tommy's idea wasn't a bad one, at least to try. I squeezed the crystal and a large bolder (about Tommy's height in diameter) appeared in mid-air between us and the monster in what little space there was. I squeezed the crystal again and sent the rock tumbling directly at the starfish. It cartwheeled out of the way, and the rock rolled away into the ditch. Moments later, the monster had spiralled back up the slope and resumed its position guarding the hole.

"What now?" I asked ironically.

"Let's just get the hell out of here."

"We can't really do that."

"Then what's your idea, smart guy? How you gonna get rid of that thing?"

"Come back down here," I told him, and I turned and took a few steps away from the hole.

Tommy followed gladly enough, since we were moving away from the monster. Predictably, it came cartwheeling past us to block our path again, probably thinking to itself that it had us good and trapped up here now. I'd almost given up on the idea of sending it back into the hole but not on the idea of defeating it with courage. The main problem now was Tommy. I knew now that the only way to move forward with this battle of wits was to remove the protective shield around us and expose myself to the monster. If I did that, though, would the starfish feed on Tommy's fear and use it to destroy us both?

"I'm going to put you in a separate shield," I told him. "Then I'm gonna try and guide it back into the hole. Stay out of the way, but be ready to help me out if I need it. You've got the Light Crystal with you, don't you?"

"Yeah, but I'm not sure that would help much here."

"Just be ready, okay, in case I get in trouble."

I gripped the Sien-Leoard Crystal and placed a new shield around Tommy—the magic knocked me sideways slightly and seemed to squeeze me against the old shield. I thought at the crystal to remove it, and suddenly I was completely unprotected, completely exposed to the monster before us. To my way of thinking, and I would soon find out if I were right, the monster would firstly go for Tommy because he was the one more afraid of it. As soon as it realised it couldn't get to Tommy, it should theoretically turn its attention to me. Then, when it realised that I was unprotected, it would try to destroy me. This was incredibly risky, and if my theory were wrong, then I would be a goner, but for some strange reason, perhaps brought on by knowledge fed to me by the crystal, I felt confident that I was on the right track.

I made eye contact with the monster again (it leered at me but once again seemed unsure of itself), then, very deliberately, turned away from it and walked back towards my hovercar. To my left, I saw Tommy turn and follow me, slightly off to the side of the track. Predictably, the monster leapt past me and settled itself on the track before me, between the car and the edge of the track. Apparently it thought I was aiming for the hole again. I saw it there, but I tried to imagine the path ahead of me contained nothing but the hovercar.

It seemed to work for a moment (the monster almost did become nothing), but before it became a reality, it leapt into the air, bounding straight at Tommy. He yelled and almost fell back. The starfish struck his magical shield and was once again propelled into the air. Tommy was cowering slightly, but it didn't take him long to recover. He seemed to trust his magical shield. That was good, I thought, but not good enough. I had almost destroyed it, or so I thought, before it had gone for Tommy. What to do now?

I knew the answer to that well enough. I wheeled around and set off down the track again, past Tommy and heading down towards the smiley cave. Some distance ahead of me, the monster came cartwheeling up the side of the track and settled itself there, leering at me, daring me to come closer. What it didn't seem to realise was that I was daring, because I knew, was almost completely sure now, that it was not real. It had merely been created by our fear, most particularly Tommy's, but I had to admit that even I had been afraid for a short time while in that hole. We had created it, and as long as we were unaware of that fact, we could never destroy it. But I was aware now.

When about six feet separated me from the illusion, however, I was distracted by a noise behind me. I turned, hoping that Tommy was ready to join me, hoping against all hope that he had not created another illusion for me to deal with. What I saw was none of that: Tommy had settled as best he could in my hovercar and was already steering it down the side of the mountain, away from the danger zone. I clenched my fists in anger. Was this Tommy's idea of 'be ready to help me'? Get rid of his magical shield, I thought angrily at the crystal, and felt it oblige. He wouldn't need it now.

My insides were jangling and my head was spinning with unpleasant thoughts, theories, possibilities, and conspiracies waiting to be explored, but I knew I had no time for that now. I turned back to the track ahead of me and the monster standing there. Since it was only me up here now, and since I knew it was not real, it would have no way of surviving. Since I didn't have a hovercar anymore now that Tommy had stolen mine, I would have to walk all the way back to one of the campsites or, better yet, go back across the hole and acquire a new one.

Deciding that was my best avenue now, I turned my back on the monster and set off back towards the hole. Behind me, I heard the monster leap into the air, but I didn't really expect too much to happen now. It was perhaps this realisation that caused—nothing at all. The monster did not land on the track ahead of me. There were no cartwheeling or propelling noises off to either side to suggest it was running away. It had simply vanished. So after all that, Tommy had done me a favour by chickening out and, to his knowledge, leaving me for dead, for he would still be believing even now that I was struggling with a very physical monster.

That didn't stop me from being furious with him, though. It wasn't so much the result I cared about but the intent. I knew he was scared, but I also knew that he was protected. He was in no danger from the starfish. Yet he had taken my hovercar and left me up here to deal with it on my own. Why had he done that? Was a small part of him hoping that I wouldn't make it back? Was he perhaps hoping that something would happen to me up here so that he wouldn't have any more competition for Natalie? That was a ridiculous theory, surely, but was it? I was really starting to wonder about Tommy. He had been generally a good friend, most of the time, but anyone capable of using the Darkness Crystal for his own means surely wasn't completely honest. Not that I was completely honest by any stretch of the imagination, but I would never have done something like that to any of my friends.

I reached the hole and recreated the bridge we had used to cross it the last time. I took the L-key from my pocket (I hadn't really expected that we would need it but had brought it along anyway just in case), turned it in the lock, entered the chamber beyond, and a few minutes later was directing a new hovercar (a deep crimson one this time) through the door and back across the bridge. Once I had vanished the bridge again, I began the familiar ride down the track, back down to the ground, and around the rock toward our car port.

There were less cars in there than I had expected. Only seven, I realised, after I had done a quick count around. My new car would make that number eight, but it still meant that a couple of other cars were missing. I looked around, taking note of the cars that were here. I registered that apart from Tommy's old bright green (jealous) car, Marc's bronze and James's canary yellow cars were also missing. Neither of them had said they were going out, but I decided it really didn't matter. The sight of my old, faithful red car parked behind Lena's shiny gold car had filled me with rage once again, and I headed for the three campsite doors with blood pounding in my ears.

They turned out to be in the tree house this time—at least, most of them were. Peter was sitting at the round table with Serena, Erica, and Natalie. Siobhan was on her feet by the window and there, beside her and ironically closest to me, was Tommy. They all looked around at me as I entered, but it was only Peter who recognised my expression, only Peter whose eyes widened in panic, only Peter who jumped to his feet and launched himself forward—but not quickly enough. Before I even knew what I was doing, I had drawn a closed fist back and, for the first time in my life, driven it squarely into Tommy's gaping jaw.

The room rang with surprised and alarmed yells. Tommy, who had been on the verge of saying God knew what before I had struck, staggered backwards and was only spared falling out of the window by Siobhan grabbing him by the shoulders. At the table, the other three girls had jumped to their feet, just about ready for anything. Serena and Peter had launched themselves forward to restrain me, but there was little point. The aching in my knuckles had driven a bit of sense back into my boiling brain, but not enough to extinguish the fire entirely.

"What are you playing at?" I bellowed at him. "Were you trying to get me killed down there? Steal my car and leave me for fucking dead—is that what you do to a guy who saves your pathetic arse?"

"John, calm down," said Serena franticly, tugging at my arm. "You don't know what you're saying."

I wrenched my arm away from her, glaring at Tommy, who was staring at me in alarm, rubbing his lower jaw. I hoped vindictively that it was hurting him like a son-of-a-bitch.

"You're just so goddamned lucky I got out of there," I spat at him. "You are pathetic! You're a coward! Can't even back me up."

"John," said Peter quietly, but I ignored him.

"Fuck you!" spat Tommy, who had apparently got over the initial shock. "I was doing you a favour. I was holding you back while I was there. You were only five minutes behind me, so don't go blaming me for helping you out."

"You did nothing!" I roared at him, causing Erica, Natalie, and Siobhan to cover their faces in utter horror. I probably looked ridiculous to them, but right now I didn't give two hoots. "You had protection—you even had a fucking crystal—and all you did was whimper! You're pathetic!"

"Shut up! Okay? Shut up!" Tommy roared back, and for a moment I thought he was going to strike back. I even hoped he would, and perhaps he would have if Siobhan hadn't grabbed his arm again. "I'm not like you—I have sense. I didn't even wanna go down in that stupid hole. It's your fault that thing came."

"No—it's—not," I spat at him, not nearly as loudly anymore. "You created that monster by your own stupid fear. You know how I got rid of it? By turning away from it. It just disappeared. It was your monster, not mine."

"Then you should be thanking me for leaving," he said stubbornly.

"Give me that crystal," I shot back at him. "You don't deserve it anymore. Its power's wasted on you. Give it here."

"I'm not giving it to you! You already have a—"

"If you don't hand it over, I'll *force* it off you!" I shouted, staring around at the others for some support, which didn't come. "Where the hell is Marc, anyway?"

"He went somewhere with James," said Serena, trying to take my arm again. "John—"

But I had well and truly had enough. I squeezed the crystal in my pocket and caused the contents of Tommy's pockets to spill out onto the tree house floor. He yelled in alarm, but I was too quick for him. I snatched up the blindingly bright crystal, stuffed it in my pocket, and, ignoring the astounded looks of the others, wheeled around and marched through the door to our bedroom corridor. My rage was starting to cool down now, but my head was still reeling from the confrontation.

Part of me knew that Tommy was right, that his leaving had done me a favour, but I also knew that it wasn't his primary reason for leaving—nor his secondary. The primary was surely fear, but the secondary? Whatever it was, it was very unpleasant, but he certainly wasn't about to admit to it. Whatever story he had given the others, they had clearly swallowed it in its entirety. I knew I would have to explain my actions to the others at some point, but how could I explain something like this? None of them would believe I was in the right, but perhaps they would agree that I had good enough reason to be angry. I didn't know and I didn't really care. All I knew was that Tommy could not be trusted with power in the future, not after his behaviour this afternoon. Next time I saw James, I resolved as I softly closed my bedroom door, he would become the new holder of the Light Crystal.

And by shutting myself in my room, I thought after I'd been there for a few minutes, I had pretty much conceded social defeat. What on earth was going to happen now? Tommy was out there, perhaps having any pain I'd inflicted removed by Natalie's magic (the thought of her touching his face was enough to make me want to punch something again), while I was stuck in here, knowing that I hadn't done anything wrong out there yet still looking like the bad guy—or a sulking child, more likely. We would surely get through this as a group (Marc and James, probably the two most level-headed of us, would see that we did), but a certain amount of awkwardness would have to be negotiated. I sighed. That was exactly the reason why I didn't want to break up with Serena here on the Rock—there was just no way to get away from each other here.

And that had been long enough for me to cool down, in the opinion of the others. Bang on cue, there was a soft knock at the door, and Serena came in to see how I was going. Why her and not Natalie? I thought bitterly, and had to force myself not to think like that. Serena cared, for real, and regardless of what would soon become of our relationship, I had to appreciate that.

"Don't worry about him," she said, shutting the door and coming to sit with me on the bed, "or the others."

"The others?" I repeated incredulously. "What did he tell you? That I told him he should go because I had it under control? That's not how it happened."

Serena shrugged. "He didn't say it quite like that, but I think that was the implication."

"That thing could have killed us," I told her. "And yeah, I did have the crystal, but I couldn't use it to get rid of that thing. He couldn't have known what would happen to me after he left, just 'cause he was more scared of it than I was. He just chickened out and didn't think about me—didn't even tell me he was going—just nicked off with my car."

I was on my soapbox now, but it felt good to get it all out. I left out the possible motive, though. Again, not appropriate. Serena's eyes were very round as she stared at me.

"But—but why would he do that? That's just—that's not right."

It was my turn to shrug. "He was too scared, too much a coward, only worried about saving his own skin. He's probably sorry now, though. Well, yeah, he definitely is," I added, feeling a reluctant grimace forming on my face and remembering what I'd thought earlier: "I hope it hurt him like a son-of-a-bitch."

She opened her mouth to say something, then put her hand over it instead. She blushed slightly as she looked at me, and for a moment, I couldn't work out what she might be thinking. It was only when I took in her entire body, rather than just her face, that it hit me: She was turned on. I'd walked straight into the tree house and punched Tommy in the face, almost knocking him out of the window, and she was turned on by that. She'd crossed one leg over the other, probably suppressing a similar itch down there from the one Natalie had dealt with last night (though considerably less so), and although she was wearing a bra, I could see the tips of her nipples pushing against her shirt.

It wasn't the first time I had seen that (her nipples often showed through whatever she was wearing when they were erect, probably because her breasts were so nicely large and perky), but it was the first time that I hadn't been fetched by the sight. Rather than acknowledge it (didn't want to give her the wrong idea, possibly leading to a sexual encounter right here on the bed while I was planning on breaking up with her), I closed my eyes and leaned back against the wall, hoping I looked as though I were considering the issue.

"I'm sure he'll get over it," she said, a little dismissively. "He deserved it—perhaps even more. He'll be okay, though, and there's no reason why you need to feel bad about it."

"Trust me, I don't," I said, opening my eyes again and making sure to look directly at her face. I would not be fetched by her body again. "I reckon I can guess how the others will be about it, though. Since they weren't there, they'll probably say we shouldn't be fighting, whatever happened out there."

She bit her lip. "Yeah, and maybe there's merit in that. I dunno. Someone should go talk to him."

"Marc can do it whenever he gets back to camp," I said, getting back to my feet. "Listen, I think I'm gonna go out for a bit. Don't follow me—I need to be alone with my thoughts for a while."

"Oh, okay," she said, looking disappointed as she followed me from my bedroom and back into the tree house, which was now completely empty.

Chapter 38: Danger

By the time five o'clock came around, I was very tired indeed. The events of the day, as well as the lack of sleep from the night before, had combined to make me exhausted and very surly. I ate very little over dinner and, for much of the time, had a hard time keeping my head up. I was looking forward to getting back to the cave of memories in the next couple of hours (that would wake me up for a bit), but in the time I'd had to think things through since the episode with Tommy, I came to realise that I would not get anywhere if I attempted any tricks in the main hall tonight. It would have to wait until tomorrow night.

The atmosphere in the tree house, where the ten of us sat eating our dinner around the round table, was very tense indeed. My confrontation with Tommy seemed to have divided the whole group. While I thought Tommy had been in the wrong, and he thought I had totally overreacted, everyone else seemed somewhere in the middle. Most of them were annoyed with me though because, in the words of Erica, my attitude may cause fighting amongst the group, which was the last thing we needed if we were to take down the Hammersons. It was Serena who defended me the most, probably on the back of our earlier conversation. As for Natalie, she had kept most tight-lipped about the drama. I had no idea what she thought of it all.

Only one really good thing happened that afternoon: While I'd had possession of the Light Crystal, I had used it to see if Tommy had done anything to Natalie. It seemed that he had indeed done something, and the Light Crystal had freed Natalie from whatever dark magic had been set against her, but as I felt it happen, I got a vibe from the crystal that the magic hadn't gone the way Tommy had intended it to go. Where Tommy had wanted nothing more than to regain Natalie's interest, the Darkness Crystal had turned interest into obsession. That didn't excuse Tommy's behaviour, of course, but it was nevertheless a relief to know that he had never wanted to hurt her.

Marc and James, who had taken the S-key (which I had left behind) out that afternoon, had returned to the campsite about half an hour before dinner. When asked what they'd been doing, Marc had merely shrugged and looked at James, who had shaken his head, saying that it might have been nothing but he wasn't entirely sure. His expression said otherwise, though—he looked troubled. Marc had spent the time since on the phone to Amelia, catching up on whatever was going on back at Woodward HQ, while James, along with Peter and Lena (who had been reading alone in one of the other campsites during the confrontation) had come to see me to get the story of what had happened out there. I had then given James the responsibility of the Light Crystal, telling him that I didn't think Tommy deserved it until he grew something resembling a backbone, though of course, I had another reason for keeping it off him as well.

In order to lift some of the tension over dinner, or perhaps to replace it with new tension, or to distract us from thinking about the drama, Marc spent much of dinner filling us in on what had been happening over the last few days back in Chopville and around the world. It was only listening to him and trying not to drift off that I was becoming aware just how isolated and cut off from the world we were here on the Rock.

"All the resistance now is from guerrilla combat," Marc told us. "Most of Europe and Asia is still full of wild fighting. They're saying that since so many of those countries had been going through political turmoil before all this started, all this war is doing is refocussing their fighting on a common enemy. The United States is doing okay because the Hammerhearts who are given door-knocking duties keep getting shot by civilians, so they're having trouble rounding people up around there. It's our area that the Hammerhearts have the most control over. There is some resistance, of course, but not a lot by comparison. Australians aren't used to this sort of thing."

"So what are the Woodwards doing about that?" asked Peter.

"Probably nothing yet," said James bitterly. "Mr. Woodward's probably sitting back saying, 'Just wait a little longer, 'til the fighting dies down, then we'll go in and start reclaiming territory.' Is that about right, Marc?"

"Actually, they're working on a top secret plan," said Marc. "Amelia wouldn't say much about it—we'll learn more when we get back to base—but it involves setting up an ambush for Tankom."

That took people by surprise. Was that more than what the Woodwards were usually about?

"Only Tankom? What about her son?" asked Erica.

Marc shrugged. "Maybe they'll get him too, I'm not sure. Amelia didn't say. Perhaps they think it'll be easier to get him if they only have one Hammerson to worry about."

"What about Stella, then?" asked Natalie. "Have they got any plans for her?"

"Only one," said Marc, "and it's a pretty basic one: Wait until the other two Hammersons are out of the way, then capture her and find out from her mind just whose side she's on. Maybe they know a way to make sure she'll do the right thing, or maybe they'll use the influential charm to keep her in line—who knows. I get the impression that they're not worried about her at the moment, though."

Once dinner was finished, we packed up and set off once again to the cave of memories and another evening in the mind of Smiley. I had been one of the first in the car port and had taken my old, faithful red car before Tommy could get near it, not that I knew if he would or wouldn't. As I parked it up beside the entrance to the cave and waited for the others to come piling in, I saw that he had taken the crimson one I had collected earlier that afternoon. Good, I thought, although I still thought green suited him better.

We all seated ourselves in the soft armchairs while Marc busied himself with loading the fifth memory into the playback device. As I leaned back in my seat in preparation for the moment where my mind would leave my body, I felt as though I were sinking right into the chair. At that moment, I could have happily closed my eyes and dropped off to sleep. The quiet noises the others were making wouldn't have disturbed me in the slightest. Once the memory started, however, my mind was swept away from my exhausted body and I was able to concentrate once more.

Rafael Smiley, a man who was elderly yet not quite as old as the Smiley I had visited twelve hours earlier, was leaning back in a comfortable-looking recliner, listening to easy-listening music on the radio and reading the newspaper, holding the print inches from the bridge of his wrinkled nose. The room was clearly the sitting room of a man who had been retired for some time now, but most of what I gathered from this scene came out of Smiley's buzzing mind. This was the home he had bought shortly before his retirement and had owned up until 1998. He had lived alone for that entire time. The first three quarters of that time had been, perhaps, the happiest of his life, what with very little to worry about other than consistently insufficient pension cheques. Today, however, was the day that all changed. If I'd had my own body, my stomach would have lurched and my heart would have skipped a beat, for I knew what this memory must contain.

Sure enough, a doorbell rang from the hallway behind us, and I knew what was coming. As the Smiley of '96 put down his paper and began to heave himself out of his chair, the Smiley of 2010 turned and preceded the younger man out of the sitting room and into the hallway where, right at the end, was the front door, and I knew what was coming. Smiley moved towards the front door and stood off to one side so that the younger (though still old) man could access the door without walking right through him, and I knew what was coming. The Smiley of '96 approached the door and peered through the peephole at the man outside, the man who was holding a baby in his arms, and I knew what was coming. Through the door, I clearly heard the sound of an unhappy baby, followed by a hushing sound, and I knew what was coming. The Smiley of '96 smiled most appropriately before he opened the door, and I had most certainly not expected this. If I'd had my own body, my jaw would have dropped halfway to my knees.

"So you've finally made good on your word, after nearly a year?" Smiley cried, pointing at him through the wire door. "How much did Frederic have to do with this?"

"Apart from the teleportation, nothing at all," said Charlie Thomas, grinning back at the old man. In his arms, baby James, who would have just turned one, appeared to grin back at Smiley too. "You gonna let us in or what?"

"Come on, come on," Smiley cried, unlocking the door and flinging it open. "In you come, in you come now. Do take a seat and talk to me. How is Marge doing?"

"Pretty good, but she wasn't happy about me coming here," said Charlie, nudging the front door shut with his foot before following Smiley back down the hall to the sitting room. In his shadow, the older Smiley followed behind him. "She thinks that coming over here was putting myself in the line of fire, no matter how many times I told her the war's been over for fifteen years."

"That it has been," Smiley agreed, "and we both know that as much as the Hammersons would no doubt like me pushing up daisies, they would not dare hunt me here, so close to the Woodwards' home."

"I told her that too, but..." He shook his head sadly.

"And how are the girls? Jessica and Felicity?"

The conversation proceeded along those lines for quite a while. Smiley asked how Charlie's family life was coming along and how they were coping under the stress of having three children under the age of three years old. He enquired after the Playmans and told Charlie to give Dad (before he had been my father) a punch in the stomach for not bothering to bring Nicole and Peter around for him to meet. Charlie also asked after Smiley's family and how their events were coming along. Apart from Jacob Underwood, who only got a single mention, I didn't recognise any of their names. Smiley was just describing his latest work correspondence from Gerald Fick when the doorbell rang again, and this time I really knew what was coming.

"Excuse me a minute," Smiley told his guest and heaved himself out of his recliner once again.

The Smiley of 2010 stepped out into the hall as the younger Smiley left the sitting room and headed for the door, but he did not follow this time. The Smiley of '96 peered through the peephole once again but this time, instead of smiling and opening the door immediately, he frowned and backtracked down the hallway to the sitting room.

"Not answering it?" Charlie asked.

"Take young James and hide behind that door," said Smiley quietly, pointing a withered old finger at a closed door on the other side of the room. "Don't make a sound, but listen closely, in case there's any trouble."

Charlie looked clearly confused by this, but he nodded and, James still in his arms, being obediently quiet, got up and headed for the door. I caught a glimpse of a dark dining room behind the door before it shut quietly behind Charlie, leaving Smiley alone in his sitting room, to the best of his knowledge anyway. Smiley stared at a walking stick in the corner of his room for several seconds before shaking his head and proceeding back into the hallway without it. I supposed it was the sight of the baby out there that convinced him that he probably wouldn't need a weapon. Both Smileys headed for the door once again, and if I'd had my own heart, it would have been banging very hard now. I supposed Marc's would be too.

"What is your message?" Smiley asked curtly as he opened the front door wide enough to stick his nose out. We couldn't see any of the Morans outside, but Smiley pictured them in his mind for our benefit: Bernard, looking anxious and frantic; his wife, looking terrified, her eyes flying in every direction; the baby in her arms, looking rather expressionless; and, to my slight surprise, a confused-looking toddler that had to be Lucien. Marc alone of the Morans seemed to be absent, and I wondered vaguely where he was.

"Not a message," I heard Moran snarl from beyond the door, sounding as though he were barely moving his lips. "For Christ's sake, let us in!"

Smiley hesitated for a few seconds that seemed to hang in the air. Perhaps it was nothing more than the knowledge that my life would have been so much different (and probably shorter) if Smiley's decision had been otherwise. Then something in one of their faces seemed to make up his mind. Slowly, he opened the door wider and unlocked the screen door to allow the family entrance. As the four of them entered and the man closed both doors quickly behind them, my mind flicked first to Marc, wondering what he would be making of all this, and then to Charlie in the next room, wondering how much of this he was about to hear, or if he would interfere.

"If it is not a message, what business of the Hammersons' could possibly bring you to me?" Smiley asked coldly, directing the question to Moran. From his mind, I picked out that he was deliberately not looking at my mother in case her expression should cause him to lose his composure. There was still enough suspicion in him to proceed cautiously.

"Not their business," he said, a little more calmly than he had spoken on the doorstep. "They don't know we're here. We've—er—left them for the time being."

"Indeed, and I am expected to believe that, am I?" said Smiley scornfully. To confuse the issue a little further, he added blandly, "Come and sit down, all of you. I don't believe I know this young man. What's your name, youngin'?"

"Lucien," he said nervously, confirming my assumption.

"We've come to ask a favour," Moran said as they proceeded back into the sitting room, unaware that an old school enemy was standing just beyond the dining room door. For a moment, Moran's gaze seemed to linger on the Smiley of 2010, as though he could see him, but a moment later it had returned to the man he was speaking to. "It won't be much to you, I don't think, but it would mean the world to us."

"A favour?" Smiley repeated, looking surprised but still managing to give off an air that he was still dictating the terms of this meeting. "What favour could a Hammerheart possibly ask of me?"

"Arnold has decided to—to kill our son," Moran told him, twisting his hands in his lap and looking almost as wretched as his wife. "He says it's—well, he won't accept any compromise. It's very important to him. We need to hide him from them, and we think the Woodwards are the best ones for it because it's the last thing they would expect. Can you help us?"

Smiley's surprise was more evident now. He opened and closed his mouth several times, staring at Moran, his eyes ready to bulge out of his face. Finally, he managed to say, "You're asking me to take your boy and take him to the Woodwards?"

The tone in his voice suggested, not disbelief, but suspicion still, as though he were trying to work out where the trick lay.

"Yes, that's what we're asking. Can you help us?" Moran repeated impatiently.

Smiley continued to stare at Moran. Both Smileys seemed to be focussing mostly on him and barely anything else, but I wished the

Smiley of 2010 would pay a bit more attention to my mother. She was just visible in the corner of his vision, sitting still and rigid and terrified, the baby still in her arms. It was the only time I had ever or probably would ever see her in the flesh, and I wanted nothing more than to drink her in.

"Why?" Smiley finally asked. "Why does Hammerson wish to kill your boy?"

My imaginary stomach lurched. Could Moran know anything I didn't already? The idea was brief and wonderful, but it was eclipsed almost immediately by the knowledge that Smiley would have told me days earlier if Moran had told him.

"He sees him as a threat in the future, apparently," Moran told him curtly

"He knows something about the boy that he hasn't told you?" Smiley asked.

Moran scoffed. "He's jumping at shadows is what he's doing. There is nothing dangerous about a baby, and no one can know how he'll turn out when he's older, whatever Arnold might think. I don't believe it for a second, but that doesn't matter. What matters is that he believes it, and he intends to stop it at any cost."

"I see," said Smiley slowly, and it looked as though he was coming close to making a decision. "So you want your boy hidden away from the Hammersons so that he won't be harmed by them. Has it occurred to you at all that if Arnold Hammerson is right, your boy might rise up one day and strike your masters down before you?"

"Honestly, after this, I wouldn't care," said Moran bitterly. "We only want him to live and be safe, that's all. What comes later doesn't matter. The way he treats people, it wouldn't surprise me if someday, someone comes along and takes him down. He's certainly looking for enough trouble."

"And this is definitely not a trick?" Smiley enquired casually, watching their faces carefully, clearly the final test for them.

The moment was almost lost right there as Moran, the strain of the last couple of months showing, and apparently never one to maintain patience easily, opened his mouth in a snarl of impatience; but before he could fire back the sort of retort that would have had him kicked out of the house immediately, his wife spoke to Smiley.

"Please help us," she said quietly in a voice that throbbed with emotion. Beside her, Moran reached out and touched her elbow lightly, and it was all the evidence I needed that Smiley had been right, that she was the only thing that kept him grounded. It was the first time, and perhaps the only time, I would ever hear her voice, and I stored it away in my memory. It wasn't a happy voice at all, but it spoke volumes about her love for me. I was glad I had no body now. I probably would have balled like a baby if I did.

The effect of the exchange, meanwhile, had thrown Smiley off his game completely. It was just about impossible not to believe a woman when she looked and spoke like that, no matter the prior knowledge you possessed about the man's acting ability. Even Lucien, who seemed mostly clueless about the situation, looked uncomfortably up at his mother.

Smiley deliberated for only a few moments before sighing. "I'll see what I can do. Leave the child with me and I'll contact Frederic as soon as possible. However, if you seriously wish to keep the boy safe, I ask only one favour in return."

"What would that be?" said Moran at once, his relief almost tangible in his face.

"Don't try to find him," Smiley said solemnly. "I'm sure you understand that your movements will be closely monitored by the Hammersons from this point on, assuming they let you live. What happens between you and them is not my business, but if you lead them to your son in the future, you will be endangering not only him but whoever is chosen to raise him. You will be held accountable if that happens. Do you understand?"

The two exchanged a look that showed no surprise. Clearly they had accepted that they would probably never see the baby (me, I thought furiously at myself) again. Still, hearing it put in those terms didn't sit all too comfortably with them. Moran nodded reluctantly, sadly.

"Very good," said Smiley, pointing at them both and added in an apologetic tone, "now, I'm sure you would like to say good-bye, but I'd just as soon prefer you leave us."

The scene that followed was one I tried my utmost to tune out, but unfortunately, I had very little control over what I took in. Smiley was paying close attention to just about every detail, perhaps thinking he was doing me a favour, but all the same, the good-bye scene was not one I wanted to remember. My mother cried, my father almost broke down, and even I started crying, although since I was a baby, who knew what the cause of that would be. Even poor little Lucien began to cry, clearly in response to his parents' distress, and as part of the background noise that none of the other seemed to hear, beyond the wall, I heard baby James making a few crying noises as well.

Within a few minutes, thankfully, my mother had handed me over to Smiley and the Morans took their leave, moving carefully out into the street and then hurrying away, trying to stay as much under cover as possible. Smiley watched them out of sight before closing the door and returning to the sitting room where he had left me sitting in his rocking chair. Charlie had emerged and was staring incredulously at Smiley as he re-entered the room.

"The spirits have done it all in one night," he said, stunned. "What are you gonna do?"

"Call Frederic," Smiley replied. "Don't touch the boy. I don't think there is any trick going on here, but we best wait for Frederic to examine the situation for himself."

"Find a family for him," Charlie said slowly and quietly, and there was obviously something going on behind his eyes, an idea forming, and I had a feeling I knew what it was and where it would lead. "Well, I know somebody who seems to think the kid's a bit of all right. Here ya go, little fella."

He put James down in the rocking chair beside me, and the look on both of our faces was almost comical. The two babies took a long look at each other before appearing to grin at each other, as though sharing some sort of private joke. Charlie threw his head back and roared with laughter. The way it happened would have been worthy of a home video, and with some amusement, I imagined what the Charlie of 1996 would have said if someone had told him about YouTube.

Smiley had left the room during this and returned only a few minutes later, looking relieved. "He'll teleport to us in a few minutes. He's got a few things to take care of in Japan first. What the man's doing in Japan baffles me."

"Did you have time to tell him what's up?" Charlie asked.

"No, just that a Hammerheart had been to see me and I required his assistance immediately. He's probably thinking of things much worse than this, but at least he'll come prepared for anything."

"He can't think it's too urgent if he's prepared to leave you for a few minutes," Charlie grumbled. "You think Freddy would put him up for adoption?"

"I can't predict what he will think is best," Smiley said, "but if he determines that the child isn't dangerous, I imagine he would."

"But then, who would adopt him, knowing what we just heard?" Charlie mused, and his thoughts were clearly ticking over—neither Smiley knew it, but he was most likely trying to measure my dad's (Chester's) reaction to all of this.

"Perhaps we won't tell anyone other than Frederic, then," Smiley concluded. "In fact, I think it may be a good idea to keep this entire meeting a secret. The knowledge that the boy had come from a Hammerheart family, I mean."

"You think that just about anyone would turn him away for that?"

"Perhaps, and especially if they learn that Arnold Hammerson may find him and kill anyone who tries to protect him, but there is yet another reason also. How do you think the poor boy would feel growing up and knowing that he was spawned by a bad family? Well, one bad parent, anyway," he amended.

"So you're saying that I have to take this secret to the grave," said Charlie, smiling grimly.

"It mightn't be such a bad idea," Smiley said, just as the doorbell rang, announcing the arrival of Frederic Woodward.

To my surprise, however, Smiley didn't hang around to watch this part of the scene. The memory faded and was replaced by something much gloomier indeed. I took a second to take in the room before me. Once I had, it was as though an ice cube had slipped down my throat and frozen my very soul. How much time had passed since I had been handed to Smiley? A few months at least, for the Morans had been tracked down, taken into custody, and brought to this place. I knew where we were, not because I had ever seen this room but because Smiley's thoughts had connected my mind to a place I had been once before. This was the base the Hammersons had used before moving to Chopville, and this was the room on the very bottom floor—the execution chamber.

The room was dark. The walls were black and bare. The only source of illumination came from an old-fashioned gas lantern hanging from the ceiling in the very centre of the room. I cast my mind around but couldn't think of any other time I had ever seen an actual light inside any of the Hammerson bases. They normally just used magic for this purpose, making it clear that the single purpose of the lantern was to add to the ambiance of the place. The effect it had was to cast all the walls into shadow. The corners were so dark that a person could have stood there and been almost completely invisible to anyone in the light.

Smiley was standing against one of the walls with a clear view of almost all of the room but for the deepest shadows. There were eight people before us: Hammerson and Tankom, standing directly opposite Smiley; Cornish and Hignat, both off to the left and closest to the one and only door; and, in the centre of the room directly below the lantern, the four remaining Morans. Marc was there this time, sitting on a seat beside Lucien. Their parents were standing, tied to a five-foot-high post with their backs to their sons, the pain of not being able to see them no doubt part of the torture. There was no immediate indication of exactly how the deed was done in this room yet.

"You made a big mistake, 3M27," Hammerson told him, his voice throbbing with anger but not yet taking on the maniacal tone I knew it capable of reaching. "I'm not surprised—I always knew your loyalty was flaky—but I am most deeply disappointed."

"Of course you would be," Moran snarled. "You would never have done something like that for your child, would you?"

A moment later, he was screaming and writhing in his binds. It wasn't the agonator this time, but Hammerson using his own magic to administer the pain. His wife began to scream as well, as did both of the children. The cacophony was deafening, each sound bouncing off the walls and seeming to amplify each time. Cornish and Hignat covered their eyes rather than watch while Tankom, the scene clearly not to her comfort, stood back and tried her best to keep a neutral expression on her wrinkled old face. The torture lasted perhaps twenty seconds, but it took nearly a minute afterward for the room to fall into silence once again. Hammerson waited patiently.

"There's no need for this to become personal, 3M27," he said mildly, as though he hadn't just watched a family in agony before him. "Those implications mean nothing to me, as you well know. What does mean a lot to me is that you may have put our entire future in jeopardy by your actions, and even if that means nothing to anyone else in this room, directly disobeying orders and running from us for nearly six months most certainly does. Let me ask you this: Did you ever bother to read our policy on truant Hammerhearts?"

"Oh, no doubt you are to kill the offender," scoffed Moran. "It's very original, don't you think?"

His wife gasped and screwed up her face as though wishing to take his words back.

"Don't do that, man," said Cornish weakly, and to my surprise, I saw that he seemed to value his old friendship more than his loyalty to Hammerson.

He, meanwhile, had been taken slightly by surprise by Moran's response. Clearly death was exactly what he had planned for Moran, but something in his face suggested he was reconsidering his options. Tankom gaped at him.

"What are you thinking, Arnold?" she asked.

"He may be right," Hammerson said slowly. "Yes, I think he may be. You see how he has already accepted his own demise? It will not be a punishment for him."

"It can be if you take him out slowly," she retorted. "Also, did you see the reaction a moment ago? Killing him today would certainly torture his family."

"It probably would," Hammerson agreed, "but it's not the others I'm interested in torturing—they are not Hammerhearts. It was his decision to disobey my orders."

"I'm pretty sure they all went in together, Arnold."

"Be that as it may," he said slowly, beginning to pace up and down the room, clenching and unclenching his fists as he went, clearly in deep consideration.

"Ah, so you're going to step outside the square this time," Moran jeered, but he looked more apprehensive now.

"Cut it out," snapped Cornish, who was looking more and more alarmed as events progressed.

"Stay out of it," Hignat muttered to him, but Cornish continued looking edgy, rocking back and forth on his heels as though ready to take a long dive.

"If killing him would torture his family," Hammerson said slowly, coming to a stop and staring at my mother now, "then is it possible that the process could work in reverse? That is to say, would killing his family—or part of his family—torture him? They do say that living in pain is worse than death, especially if that pain can never be reversed."

If the couple before him had been better actors, they could perhaps have prevented Hammerson from settling on this plan, but the alarm in both their faces was all too unmistakable. Tankom's eyes were wide and she was smiling now, clearly happier with this plan. Hammerson smiled too, a terrible grin indeed, worse than any I could ever remember seeing on his face. Apparently he was impressed by his own plotting.

"Yes, I think so," he said slowly, moving forward toward the place where they were trussed. Moran began to struggle frantically against his binds, snarling incoherently at Hammerson all the while. "Marc is indispensable, of course, but I believe there was nothing particularly special about Lucien. I'm sure doing away with him would be acceptable, except—"

He hesitated for a moment, long enough for Tankom to say, "Just kill the boy and be done, Arnold. I'm sure losing two of their sons would be enough."

Hammerson shook his head. "I like the look of Lucien, though. He looks like he'll grow up to be a strong man. He is Hammerheart material—I don't want to hurt him."

"You can't know he'll grow up to be a Hammerheart," Tankom snapped. "There may not be enough of the right influence in his family after this. Just kill him already. It's nearly lunchtime."

"Then, perhaps we'll just have to remove the negative influence," Hammerson said softly, his eyes flicking from Moran to his wife and resting there. She blanched beneath the spooky light of the lantern. "Actually—"

He sidestepped the Morans and moved around behind them, stopping before Lucien and kneeling down so their faces were level. Lucien tried to pull away from him, but Hammerson stilled him with a look.

"Now what are you doing?" Tankom snapped. She was in a very bad mood today.

"Setting up Lucien's future for him," Hammerson said, and Lucien seemed to fall asleep as he spoke.

Tankom's eyes widened. "Is it—that curse? But what are you going to make him do? When?"

"Those things are for me to know," said Hammerson, straightening up, the magic complete, "but with a bit of luck, we need never see it."

He moved back around to face Moran again, smiling unpleasantly.

"What have you done to my son?" he growled.

"He'll be fine," Hammerson assured him smoothly. "You'll be able to leave with him in just a few minutes. Only a couple of things to take care of first. 3H42?"

"Yes, sir," Hignat said automatically.

"Give us—(he considered)—ten clicks on slot two."

This statement meant nothing to me whatsoever, and judging by his quietly jabbering thoughts, Smiley had no understanding of it either, but it caused an instant uproar in the room before us. Moran opened his mouth and bellowed; the words were incomprehensible, but I felt sure it contained a lot of profanity. Cornish took a couple of quick steps backward, then turned away, facing the wall. Beside Moran, my mother tried to ask what was going on but not a word of hers could be heard. Marc began to cry again, as did Lucien, who had been woken up by the noise. Only the two Hammersons kept their composure, waiting on Hignat. He gaped at Hammerson for a few seconds before moving slowly past them to a control panel on the back wall, throwing an apologetic look over his shoulder as he did so.

"*Traitor!*" Moran roared at Hignat's back, freezing him on the spot for a moment, just a few feet from the panel.

"Traitor?" Hammerson repeated, turning to look at Hignat also. "Well, 3H42, I guess you have to choose, don't you, bearing in mind that if you don't do it, I'll get 2C7 to do it, and if he refuses, I'll do it myself. Would you betray an old friend who is, for all intents and purposes, washed up, or would you betray the future rulers of the world?"

Hignat looked imploringly at Moran for several seconds, who stared him down agonisingly. Finally, he said, "Nothing personal, man."

Moran closed his eyes but made no other reply. He wriggled slightly so that he could reach out a hand to touch his wife's arm. By that simple gesture, she seemed to understand what was about to happen. She closed her eyes and went rigid, but not a sound did she make. Hignat set a switch and pushed a button on the control panel before putting his hands over his face. A low humming started up, and it seemed to be coming from the room itself, from the walls, floor, and ceiling. The ropes tying my mother raised up into the air, pulling her up with them. They splayed her out in the air directly below the lantern and hanging about eight feet off the floor.

For a few seconds, nothing happened. And then, to my utter horror (I had no idea what I'd expected her death to be like, but it certainly hadn't been this), the ropes began to tighten. They did not strangle her (that would have made more sense); they ripped her apart. The ordeal took exactly ten seconds, a break occurring on every second. The ropes would twist and squeeze so quickly and sharply that her body was torn to pieces in the air. The pieces fell down to the floor around the place where the rest of her family was tied, but still not a sound did she make. No blood, though. Some magic in the ritual made sure that blood didn't fly in every direction. The final break was her neck. Her head came completely loose and fell to the floor with a horrible cracking sound, rolling forward slightly so that her vacant face stared directly up at Lucien.

Unsurprisingly, the child screamed at the top of his lungs, filling the room with yet another terrible cacophony of echoing sound. Hammerson shot a spell at him, but apparently the shock of what he'd seen prevented the magic touching him—now that was something Hammerson would no doubt never get his head around. Moran didn't scream but he was clearly distraught. He merely hung limply in the ropes, his eyes still closed.

"Why didn't you just do it yourself?" Cornish shouted, turning back to face the room and then quickly turning away again.

"I'm sure I could have," Hammerson said, "but sometimes killing outright gets boring. When you have a lesson to teach, the manner of delivery matters. Hopefully 3M27 has learnt his lesson now."

The room began to quiet. Sound continued to bounce off the walls, but it was no longer being amplified by new sound. Lucien had fainted. He fell off his seat and landed on the floor beside his mother's head.

"Thank goodness for that," said Hammerson. "Now that that's settled, we have much to sort out."

"You mean there's more?" said Tankom incredulously.

"Of course there is," snapped Hammerson, and it was only now that he was starting to lose patience. "Marc is very important to us. We must make sure that he is kept well under observation so that 3M27 can't take him and run again."

"So we'll just raise him ourselves," she said. "He and Stella could be good playmates."

"I don't think so," said Hammerson, staring at Moran. "No, he'll rebel against us if we did something like that. No, he should be allowed to raise his son, both of his sons, and they will grow up believing that he killed their mother, won't they, 3M27?"

Moran made no reaction whatsoever. Hammerson took that for assent.

"I think it is time," Hammerson said, turning to Tankom, "for us to pick up stakes and move to that little pissy town he comes from."

"But, sir," said Hignat in a strangled voice. I'd almost forgotten he was there, "Chopville's population is like two thousand or something. We don't have a base there."

"Then we'll just have to build one, won't we?" he said calmly. "The time of reckoning begins from here. We will move to Chopville, where we will prepare to take on the Woodwards once again. We have much to organise, but first, I think it might be a good idea to clean up the mess, don't you?"

Smiley decided enough was enough at that point. If I'd had a choice, I would have pulled the pin on that one much sooner indeed. He retreated from that scene, and the memory faded. We all returned to our bodies and, in my case, one so deeply asleep that it wasn't until Peter shook me that I stirred back to consciousness. I had clean forgotten how tired I was, but it all came rushing back to me now, mixed with a tangle of terrible emotions left over from the memory.

The room was very quiet indeed. When I came back to myself enough, I saw that they were all staring at me, waiting to see my reaction, my own shock mirrored on all their faces. I tried desperately to sort through my thoughts, blocking all those terrible thoughts of my mother. I knew I would have nightmares about that tonight, and probably Marc would too. Finally I was able to fix on the thing that had jammed my thoughts up right from the start.

"Charlie," I said, and couldn't add any more to it.

"He knew," said James bitterly. "I can't believe that. Why on earth didn't he say something all this time?"

"He thought we wouldn't wanna know," said Peter. "We never did tell him what we've been doing the last two months, and we never asked him if we knew anything. We just assumed since our dad didn't, he wouldn't. My God."

"You gonna be okay, John?" Serena asked gently.

I shook my head. "Dunno. Probably, eventually."

I looked over my shoulder to where Marc was still sitting by the playback device, his face strained and terrible to look at. "I mean to say—we'll be okay."

Marc nodded in agreement. "I always knew it was bad. I just wish Smiley hadn't shown it to us. Did he think he would be doing us a favour? I mean, apart from that thing with Mr. Thomas, there wasn't anything in that memory we didn't already know or couldn't have guessed."

"He must have thought we might pick up something in there that would matter," Erica said shakily.

"Yeah, sure," he said and checked his watch. "You know, we've only got four memories left now. That means we should only be here for another two days at most."

Changing the subject if ever I saw it.

"Not necessarily," said Serena. "John might need more time in the main hall."

"That's true," I said, "'cause I've decided not to go down there tonight. I'm too goddamned tired, and honestly after what I've just seen, I reckon I deserve a rest."

"Sure," Marc said distractedly. "Well, it's eight o'clock now. Maybe we give it away for tonight and be back here tomorrow morning?"

That was pretty much it for the night. We all left the room and headed back to the car park without a word to each other. I got out of my car very slowly when we got there, only partially faking my exhaustion, waiting for the others to go into the Group F campsite where they would no doubt sit up talking for a while, except perhaps Marc, who couldn't have been doing any better than I was. Once they were all in, I headed quietly for the tree house instead, where I sat alone at the round table, lost in my thoughts of my parents and their sacrifice, taunted by periodical visions of my mother's headless corpse, only in those visions it was a burning corpse, surrounded by thick black smoke, impenetrable shadows, and glowing flames. Eventually, I fell asleep there and woke up at some stage in the night, cramped, uncomfortable from my sleeping position, and sweating profusely after having relived my mother's death in my dreams. I got up and headed for my bedroom instead, my eyes filling with tears, but as tired as I still was, I lay awake for quite a while before sleep took me.

Chapter 39: Talent

I felt thoroughly unrested the following morning, despite the fact that I must have gotten five or six hours of uneasy sleep during the night. The first thing I did was give myself an energy booster from the crystal before giving my head a little shake and leaving my room, ready to have to talk to the others again. I dearly hoped that none of them would be insensitive enough to try to talk about last night's memory, but unfortunately, just as I was leaving my room, a snatch of conversation from a scattering of people gathered around the bathrooms caught my ear. Erica appeared to be in the middle of a spirited argument with James, and the two of them were being watched on by Peter, Tommy, Natalie, and Lena, all of whom seemed to be enjoying the spectacle.

"I wasn't the only one in there," James was spluttering, red as a tomato.

"Maybe not, big fella, but it's not the others we're talking about here," said Erica, grinning broadly.

"I am not a cute baby!" James nearly shouted.

I almost laughed before remembering exactly what they were talking about, and the memory brought me back to Earth with a hard thud. I didn't have long to think about it, though, because Serena came out of her room a little farther up the hall a moment later and, looking around and spotting me, changed direction and came down to meet me.

"How are you feeling?"

I shrugged. "Okay, I think. A little tired, though."

"I wanted to see you last night when you didn't come into camp," she said in a bit of a rush, "but Peter wouldn't let me, said you probably needed to be alone. I hope you don't mind."

She faltered, gazing anxiously at me, more worried about my reaction than I would have expected. I shrugged again.

"That's fine. I wouldn't have been great company last night anyway. Reckon I needed the alone time."

"Sure, sure," she said. "Still, though, I would have preferred to be a bit more supportive."

"How was Marc after we got back?" I asked, wanting to change the subject.

She hesitated for a moment and said, "Very quiet. He only stayed for maybe half an hour, and we knew better than to try to talk to him or about anything while he was there. Then he just got up and went to bed, and actually it was sort of a relief, 'cause he was making the rest of us nervous."

I glanced back down the hall to where James was still trying to defend his childhood. Marc wasn't there, but his bedroom door was open—that meant he had managed to snag the first shower. I wished he hadn't. Now I'd have to have breakfast with the others sooner. On top of that came yet another stab of guilt for Serena. I really was being unfair towards her, but again, I reminded myself, that wouldn't last much longer. We would only be here a few more days at the most.

I turned and walked through the door into the tree house, now thinking about what I would eat, but was distracted only a moment later by Serena's voice from the other side of the doorway. "Hey, John! Where'd you go?"

I was on the point of replying when I remembered: Of course she wouldn't be able to see or hear me now. I thought for a moment of staying in here anyway and having my own private breakfast, then decided that was cowardly. She, along with a few of the others, had already gone into the Group F house and were taking seats when I entered from the car park.

We settled down to a subdued sort of breakfast while waiting for Marc and Siobhan to free up the showers. Marc came out first, and James, desperate to get away from Erica's radiant grin, was quick to claim it. It was around that point when I started feeling the involuntary urges and not having any idea what they were. At first, I thought they were my imagination playing tricks on me, no doubt brought on by sleep deprivation, but as they became progressively stronger, I was forced to accept that something was going on with my body. I was sitting down, but my legs kept twitching, wanting to be upright. Soon my arms also began to twitch and spasm, as though desperate to engage in the act of lifting myself out of the seat.

"What's up with you?" Peter asked, looking concerned.

I shook my head, unable to voice the absurd thoughts racing around in my head. I made a supreme effort to control the urges and for a short time, it seemed to work.

A few minutes later, Siobhan emerged from the bedrooms and Erica, who had just finished her breakfast, leapt to her feet immediately. Siobhan took the breakfast Marc provided her and sat down beside Peter, looking rather content, having missed most of the awkwardness of the morning. Seeing them together made me think again of what I'd thought was going on between them. Certainly it seemed apparent that Siobhan felt happy around Peter. Not entirely happy, perhaps, as it would be very difficult for anyone who had been through what she had to be completely happy, but happier than she was without him. As for Peter, it didn't seem to make much of a difference. He looked like he was starting to get over losing Kylie, though, and I had to wonder how long it would be before he became proactive in the matter, however he felt.

"Where are you going, John?" Serena asked, looking up from her breakfast.

I jumped, startled out of my reverie. To my surprise and slight horror, I was no longer sitting but firmly on my feet and halfway towards my bedroom. I hadn't even known I had gotten up and was walking. It was the urges, I knew instinctively, and even now that I'd stopped and looked back, every part of my body was urging me to turn away and continue towards my bedroom. What on earth was going on here?

"Er, my bedroom," I said awkwardly. "Be back in a sec."

"You okay, mate?" Peter asked, looking concerned.

"I'm fine. Just be a minute."

I hoped that was the case. All I knew was that something I'd never felt before was wanting me to be in my bedroom. I could have continued fighting it, but I knew I couldn't possibly win. The urges were getting stronger with every second, and all I would achieve by fighting now was to make a complete fool of myself in front of the others. Shrugging, I turned away and set off again, my body apparently on autopilot.

It was as I reached my bedroom door that the comprehension finally hit me in two great bursts. The first was brought on by the sight of the life assistant sitting innocently on my bedside table, and I knew instinctively that it was causing this somehow, that Smiley was doing this. The second burst came with the memory that I had told him I would come back to see him this morning. I hurried toward it and picked it up, feeling the urges settle to nothingness the moment I had made contact with the little object.

The thoughts that Smiley had been attempting to send to me through the devices crashed upon me the moment I'd made contact with the life assistant. Of course he was wondering where I was, was I coming down to see him, and how had it gone last night. After I had absorbed his thoughts and regathered my own, I sent a quick response back, telling him that I had been too tired to go down to the hall the previous night and would do so tonight instead. His relieved response came almost immediately, relieved that I was okay and apologetic for the reaction he had caused me. Some of my shock must have seeped through with my thoughts. Feeling considerably better, I went back into the camp to let the others know what had just happened.

* * *

By ten o'clock, we were back once again in that memory chamber and Marc was loading the sixth roll into the playback device. We all took our seats and moments later were sinking back out of reality once again, emerging seconds later into something resembling a plane crash site. I had a second of confusion before understanding what this must be, and horror rose up inside me. It didn't resemble a plane crash—it *was* a plane crash. What on earth was wrong with Smiley? Why did he make a point of showing us such devastating scenes from his past? The only good thing about it was that he had at least gone to the trouble of revisiting the scene through the fourth dimension rather than recording his own painful memories of the experience. That would have been just too much.

Smiley was standing on the side of a mountain looking down on the devastation below. It appeared to be night-time, but the flames around him were so bright that he had no trouble seeing the wreckage of the aircraft around him. A siren echoed far in the distance, approaching this spot, but they would have trouble reaching the plane here. The mountain upon which the bulk of the wreckage lay was thick with trees and bushes, and right now so many of them were on fire. The heat rose in stifling waves all around Smiley, and the smoke made it difficult to see too far into the distance, but he knew he would be safe. He did not need to breathe here, and the fire could not burn him, no matter how hot it felt.

There were other sounds as well, coming from the spot directly below Smiley's feet, from a small part of the fuselage that was not burning yet. A child was crying (Tommy, in one of his forms, anyway), and there were desperate struggles that had to be the injured Smiley. The older yet fitter Smiley backed away from the spot and watched as his younger self tried to pull himself from a small opening in the wreckage. He was covered in blood and was sporting a broken collarbone, dislocated shoulder, and several broken ribs (I could see some of this but mostly it was Smiley's thoughts as he recalled the feeling). As he finally dislodged himself and rolled away from the spot, screaming in agony as he went, I saw that his legs, incredibly, looked unharmed, apart from rips in his jeans.

Then, as he had done when the Honnie had been escorting the Hammerhearts into his world, Smiley skipped over the next few minutes, landing on a point in time when the rescuers were on the scene. The fire appeared to have intensified, but rather than trying to land in the death trap, the rescuers were winching the old man up into a chopper hovering far overhead. How they had located the only survivor with all that smoke up there was anyone's guess. Tommy had emerged too, crawling from the same opening Smiley had come from. He was also bleeding profusely, but it was clear that he was not the Tommy we knew. His skin was as white as our Tommy's was dark. The other Tommy had apparently been thrown from the wreckage earlier because another man in a winch was already seeing to him, perhaps pointed out to them by Smiley. They were too far to see clearly, though.

Then it happened again. The memory skipped forward and we were inside the chopper. I had a moment to wonder how Smiley had managed to get up there in the fourth dimension. Perhaps he had climbed on board before the chopper had taken off. Smiley was lying back in a seat, apparently unconscious while a paramedic of some description was seeing to him. The dark Tommy was asleep beside him while the light Tommy was screaming bloody murder on the child's other side. Interestingly, and this gave me serious food for thought later that day, the dark Tommy looked older than the light Tommy. He would have been three years old, assuming the crash had occurred later than April in 1997, but the dark Tommy looked like he might have been five or six years old. I had never considered that Tommy looked older than his age. Taller, sure, but not older. Could that be part of the reason why he had been able to survive on his own before being adopted? In my mind, it provided evidence to the idea that this body had belonged to another child. If it had been created, then surely it would look the same age as the original Tommy.

This scene held for perhaps twenty seconds before the memory faded out and back in once again. We were now in a hospital room. Six weeks had passed since the accident (ha-ha, what accident?), and three of the room's four occupants appeared to have mostly recovered. The light Tommy was in the bed directly opposite Smiley while the dark one was fast asleep in the one closest to the door. The bed to Smiley's right was occupied by a man who looked to be in his mid-thirties, and I couldn't work out just from looking at him what illness he exhibited. Smiley's thoughts answered that for me: He was a Hammerheart, placed in that very bed by Tankom. She had hurt him in some way, then used her magic to ensure that he would end up in the same room as those who survived the plane crash. How much had she learnt about the survivors in the six weeks that had passed? Remembering what Smiley had said, I supposed she had figured out quite a lot, and that this man's job was to find a way to take one or both Tommys out of their beds without any of the staff (or Smiley) being able to stop him. How Tankom had been able to get him in here and not been able to get in here to do it herself was not knowledge Smiley possessed.

The first thing I noticed was that the Smiley in the bed knew of the existence of the older Smiley. His eyes kept darting sideways to exactly where the older Smiley stood safely in his shadow. Smiley's thoughts told me that he had a clear memory of wondering if he were losing his mind and deciding, for now, to make like nothing unusual was happening. The second thing I noticed was that at some point between my parents handing me to him and now, the younger Smiley had acquired his shimmering quality. He was sitting up in his bed, eating his breakfast, and looking generally healthy and was probably ready to get out of here. As we watched, a doctor entered the room and came to sit beside him.

"Herr Smiley," he said, smiling at him. He had an accent that sounded a bit like German. "How are you feeling?"

"Restless," Smiley replied irritably.

"Any pain?" the doctor prodded gently.

"Stiffness," said Smiley, "from sitting still too long. I'm an old man—my joints, you know."

"Of course," said the doctor. "We would like to see you walk around for a bit this morning first, and if that goes well, you can leave this afternoon, but we need to ask you a few questions first."

Smiley grimaced. This was apparently something he had put off until now. The doctor noticed his reaction and quickly added, "It's a necessary procedure. We need to make sure you will be okay after you leave."

"Go ahead," said Smiley, continuing to eat his breakfast. Across the room, I could see that the Hammerheart was listening intently as he stared at the ceiling.

"You live in England?"

"Yes."

"You were on your way back there?"

"Obviously that's where the plane was supposed to be going."

"You were in Germany because…?"

This was where Smiley hesitated, and I found myself wondering the same thing: What had Smiley been doing in Germany? Had he been on Woodward business? That seemed most likely somehow if Harry and Simon's parents had been in the same place, but then if that had been the case, how was it that they had been doing two different jobs?

"Holiday. I've earned it."

"I think you've earned another one after this. Is there anyone who can pick you up?"

"From here? No, I'm on my own."

"Ah," said the doctor thoughtfully. "Herr Smiley, you are healthy enough to fly again, but do you think you feel ready?"

I knew he was not referring to Smiley's physical health this time.

"Yes, I think so."

"Good," said the doctor, getting to his feet. "Herr Smiley, we would be happy to arrange for you to fly back to London, but it might be that you'll have to wait until tomorrow. That being the case, we would prefer you remain here until the time. Do you have a preferred airline?"

"The cheapest you can find so long as it's not the bastards who put me here."

"Fair enough," said the doctor. "I'll pass that on and will see you later this morning."

"Hang on," Smiley said quickly as the doctor turned to leave. He turned back, eyebrows raised. "Those two," he said, jabbing a finger at the two children on the other side of the room, "what's going on with them? Will they be okay?"

The doctor hesitated, then said, "Herr Smiley, I am really not at liberty to talk about that."

"Sure you are," said Smiley, smiling up at him. "It's just between us? I'll never see them again after this, and I guess I kind of—well, we were the only survivors, weren't we?"

The doctor hesitated again, glancing sideways at the Hammerheart, who was currently feigning sleep. Finally he lowered his voice.

"That one," he said, nodding at the light Tommy, "lost his parents in the accident. He has been adopted by a childless couple in Berlin and will be flown out day after tomorrow. That one—(he nodded at the dark Tommy)—we could not identify at all. He may have been part of an African family who had been on board, but his DNA does not seem to match theirs. He will also be adopted just as soon as a suitable home can be found for him."

"You haven't been able to find a home for him?" Smiley asked, looking confused.

"There has been interest," the doctor said confidentially, "from a young American couple, but those left in charge of his future for now thought they seemed unsuitable. I'm sure a home will be found for him soon."

This apparently meant plenty to Smiley, but he did his best to hide it. "Thank you," he said to the doctor and lowered his head back to his nearly finished breakfast, closing the subject.

That was it for that scene. It faded out again, but Smiley wasn't done with us yet. The next scene that followed didn't seem to make any sense for a few moments. Smiley was sitting in a private compartment on a train with the sleeping child on the seat beside him. The older Smiley was leaning against the wall only a few feet away from the seat. The younger Smiley, the real one for all intents and purposes, looked extremely jumpy as the train carried him and the dark Tommy southward. I knew this only because Smiley happened to be thinking it. There was no other proof because it appeared to be very late at night (perhaps even after midnight). It seemed that this was the train from Sydney to Melbourne. Smiley had skipped over the part where he had fled from the hospital with the child in Germany and escaped halfway across the globe.

The train was just pulling out of a rural stop, by the look of it, leaving the lights behind, suggesting that the train had left Sydney probably a few hours ago. Smiley faded backwards, actually moving partially into the wall but keeping his face on the other side so that he could continue watching the interior of the compartment. Again, the younger Smiley met his eyes and looked confused, even alarmed, but he made no movement. The train continued to pick up speed until it was rattling along at a decent clip, and both Smileys seemed to be waiting for something. How far would Smiley get from Sydney before the Hammerhearts caught up with him? Considering Tommy ended up in Sydney, surely not too far. Smiley's buzzing thoughts weren't any help; all he was thinking was that it must be soon and wondering if he had arrived here a little too early.

After maybe half an hour of this, footsteps reached our ears from just outside the compartment. Both Smileys looked around to see a man pass by through the glass door and continue up toward the back of the carriage. Smiley had left the curtain open deliberately so that he would have forewarning if any Hammerhearts were approaching. It never occurred to him that he would also be making it easier for them to find him that way. It also meant that with the lights coming in from the corridor outside, he wouldn't be able to sleep, but that wasn't such a bad thing. The younger Smiley had stiffened at the sight of the man but relaxed when he had passed, no doubt thinking he was either a guard riding at the back of the train or a passenger using another of these compartments. There was nothing to suggest the man was a Hammerheart; he was casually dressed, unmasked, and unarmed. He couldn't have been hiding anything either because as far as I knew, weapons such as solid-outliners, stunners, bludginators, and agonators hadn't been invented until the last couple of years.

A tense calm settled in the compartment for another couple of minutes until someone else came by the compartment, this time stopping and tapping on the glass. He was dressed well enough to pass for a staff member, well enough for Smiley to make a great mistake by unlocking the door and allowing him to open it. Didn't it occur to him that a real staff member would have had a key to the compartment? Probably not, but I knew how it must have been for him. When you're under that sort of pressure, you can easily make a mistake that you wouldn't be stupid enough to make on any other day. I had done that very same thing by telling Tulip to fly under the hanging cage on the night she had been killed.

"How are things, Mr. Smiley?" the man asked pleasantly enough, ducking his head slightly so that he could enter through the small doorway.

"Very comfortable, thank you," Smiley replied. "Just a quick question—at what time will I be allowed to use this bed?"

He gestured to the wall behind him and I found, from Smiley's buzzing thoughts, that it was the bottom of a bed that could fold out into the compartment. The whole setup was quite compact and I had to admire the way it all came together.

The man hesitated, and I hoped it would be enough to give him away, but then he said, "Anytime you like. It's nearly eleven now, so feel free to rest. Just close the blinds and we'll know not to disturb you. He's rather well behaved, isn't he?"

"Oh yeah, he's a dream," said Smiley, but even as he spoke, the man had bent and scooped Tommy up in his arms. "Hey, what are you—"

"Just need to check something, Mr. Smiley. I'll be back in a few minutes."

Smiley was no fool. He lunged for the man, ricocheted off one of the door frames, and came to rest in the hallway outside between the two slanted doorways of the compartments. He staggered to his feet and looked up and down the corridor. To his right, the man who had walked past the compartment earlier was standing about ten feet farther down, ready in case Smiley attempted to come down that way; to his left, the man carrying Tommy had just passed by a third man and was heading for the next carriage. I wasn't completely sure, but I thought that maybe, just maybe, that third man was Ugine Wilwog's father. There was a distinct resemblance, and not just because they were both built like a brick shithouse.

Smiley stumbled forward, almost blind with panic, but was easily stopped by Wilwog's maybe-father. Beyond him, Smiley caught sight of the man with Tommy again. He was already in the next carriage, moving quickly and carefully up the aisle between rows of travellers who didn't suspect a thing. They were his only hope now. He opened his mouth, but before he could make a sound, Wilwog's maybe-father raised his elbow right into his face, shutting his mouth in a very final way. The two men continued to struggle together, and now the man from the back of the carriage came to assist. They restrained Smiley between them and dragged him (practically carried him) back up the carriage to his open compartment.

Once inside, with the door shut and the curtains drawn, a session of something like torture began. Smiley was tied to his seat, gagged, and cut in several places by knives that the men had been concealing in their pants. Didn't they have metal detectors on these trains? Perhaps not. Smiley struggled and tried to make any number of noises but was unable to do anything to raise the suspicions of anyone else on the train. He was bleeding terribly all over his face, his arms, his legs, and his torso, his clothes cut almost to ribbons, before the men had had enough. The session ended about fifteen minutes later when a voice came over the speakers, announcing the train's imminent arrival in Goulburn. The two men undressed right in front of Smiley and, completely naked, left the compartment, leaving their bloody clothes behind. A second set of clothes for each of them had been left just inside that carriage, as it turned out, and once they were dressed, they hurried up the train towards the door that would be opening at the next stop, their mate with Tommy no doubt waiting for them there.

That was it for that memory. Everything faded and was replaced by reality once again. Like last night, I found myself almost asleep in my seat, but this time I was able to pull myself back without assistance. Everybody was looking at Tommy for his reaction, but he merely shrugged. "Nothing in there we couldn't have guessed."

"He wasn't very smart, was he," said James. "I mean, he could easily have prevented that from happening in several places. I mean to say, of course the Hammerhearts would have been watching Sydney Airport, for a start. How stupid can you get?"

"He probably thought the Hammerhearts would be watching Melbourne more closely," Marc said reasonably, "since it's geographically closer to Chopville. He probably should have come through some other airport altogether, or by boat even."

"Easy for us to say," I said, remembering my thought from earlier. "It's a lot harder to think clearly when you're under that sort of pressure. Take it from someone who knows."

Everyone looked at me in surprise and—what? There was something else in their expressions I couldn't quite identify, but I thought it looked a bit like admiration, as though they were all suddenly remembering all those dangerous situations I had found myself in, situations that most of them had never faced before. Shrugging, I said, "Don't ask. Just take my word for it."

"But even if he was under pressure, why didn't he just go into his shadow to get away from them?" asked Lena. "He could have got all the way up the train without them even knowing where he was."

"He hadn't had a chance to explore that talent yet," said Marc. "Maybe he hadn't worked out exactly how to do it properly. Also, you probably need to concentrate to do that, judging by what John was telling us yesterday, so maybe he was too distracted."

"You got the time, Marc?" Peter asked.

"Yeah, half past eleven," he said. "We've probably got time for one more before lunch. You guys up for it?"

We all were, so we settled back in our seats as Marc replaced the memory in the playback device with the next one and hit the play button. Seconds later, reality was swimming away from us to be replaced, mostly, by bushes. For the first time, Smiley was not in his shadow. For the first time, he had taken us back to one of his own memories, not just a time he had revisited in his shadow. He was pacing up and down in the bushes, thinking about the turn his life had taken over the last nearly four years. From the day Moran had landed on his doorstep, his life had been nothing but trouble.

The Hammersons had learnt from Moran's mind that he, Smiley, had been somehow involved in the transfer. They did not know that he had no idea where the boy had ended up (as if it would have made a difference to them), so they had come after him with a vengeance, causing him to move away from his home and out into the great wide nothing. Frederic Woodward had attempted to help, of course, but that was exactly what the Hammersons expected him to do, which was the reason why he had rejected the offer. If they were to catch Smiley, they would learn from his mind, not the exact location, perhaps, but the most probable course of action Frederic Woodward had taken (assuming Charlie Thomas had had been right in his estimations that day), thereby ruining the whole plan. It was all so carefully guarded because even if he hadn't, Charlie was the only other person who knew the whole story. Nobody else, not even Frederic himself, knew where the boy had come from, and nobody else knew that Charlie had been there, for Smiley had made him leave the house through the back for his own safety before allowing Frederic to enter.

Then came the plane crash nine months later. He had since learnt that he hadn't been the target, that the Maivises, who had been in Germany on a different assignment for the Woodwards, had stumbled over something about Arnold Hammerson's daughter that they wanted kept secret. Smiley wished he had asked for the information before the plane had gone down, not that they would have given it. Confidentiality was of the utmost to those working for the Woodwards. As it was, the result of the crash was his own messed-up talent and the young boy who had been snatched by the Hammerhearts. He had taken that news back to the Woodwards, and they, in turn, had tried to learn what had become of the boy, but all their spies came up empty-handed. He didn't want to believe the boy was dead now, but unfortunately, it seemed the most likely outcome.

And so everything Smiley had spent his whole life working towards, a peaceful retirement, had been screwed up by those godforsaken Hammersons, who couldn't have given a damn what became of a poor old man like him. He had been forced to move away from the country he loved and go into hiding. He had been forced to run from almost every person he met, not knowing if they were Hammerhearts or if they would recognise him, or if they would offer him help in the belief that they were doing the right thing, never knowing that every bit of attention given to him increased the chances of the Hammersons pinpointing his location.

The only respite came in the form of the curse that the Hammersons had unwittingly fitted him with: the ability to move along the fourth dimension. He had begun to experiment with it and had given it much thought. That sort of stuff had, up until this point, been well outside his field of interest. (There was enough crap going on in the first three dimensions to deal with, as far as he had always been concerned.) What he had learnt was that if he moved a short way to either side, he could become invisible to those around him. He could still plant his feet on surfaces if he imagined those surfaces being there, but he could also step through them. He could not pick things up, though, meaning that to eat and drink, he had to return to his usual position. He didn't need to breathe when he became invisible because there, his body didn't seem to run the way it normally did—also, there was no air to breathe. He also knew that if he continued to move along the fourth dimension, he would move away from the world to a place where time no longer ran and the first three dimensions no longer existed, or at least, to move along them meant nothing. He had been scared of these places and since having learnt of them, he had put in a supreme effort never to leave the world behind again. Nevertheless, being invisible for the majority of the time served to provide him with great protection and security, even if it did diminish the quality of his life.

He was thankful for this, but he had to admit, he would be much happier without it. All he wanted was a place he could call home, a place where he wouldn't need to depend on his talent to protect him. He had spent his entire career on the side of the law, fighting to ensure justice came to those who flouted it, although occasionally he would be forced to defend a man or woman he knew full well had committed a crime simply because it was his job; he was sure to put in an entirely half-arsed effort in these situations. Yet at the end of this, he had become an outcast, stealing from others in order to live. Stealing was easy when you could walk through a solid wall into a deserted building in the dead of night. He was always sure to steal from those who couldn't possibly notice something had gone missing, but that didn't make him feel much better about it. Then, at the end of all that, he would lie down to rest in some clump of bushes or in a shadowy doorway.

For a man who had lived most of his life as an upper-middle-class citizen and who could have been looked upon by some as a war hero, this was no way to live out his twilight years. Understandably, he thought, he had become most bitter towards the entire world that had forsaken him. More than once he had contemplated suicide, but the ghost of his strictly Catholic mother kept returning to him in these moments, ensuring that his soul could never get into heaven if he chose that path, and now that he had seen the place where time and space didn't exist, he was inclined to think she may have been onto something.

Now he stopped pacing and stared unseeingly ahead of him, thinking of that place he had been so frightened of. He had only been there once, and the feeling had been most surreal indeed. Even remembering it now was difficult. He had had a body, but he had not been able to feel it, nor had he been able to move it in any way. Only two directions had been open to him: the fourth dimension, which required more mind activity than physical movement to step along (only because adjusting to the direction was difficult after having not had access to it for most of his life), and another direction which hadn't been perceptible to him before. He supposed it was time, since it didn't run there, but he had never experimented with it.

What was there to lose in having a look now? It wasn't as though he was missing anything here, and his mother couldn't call it suicide because he had no idea if death awaited him beyond this world. He took one last look around, cursed the world as he had always known it (how shallow it was, how the human race had destroyed it as they were willing to destroy each other, obsessive over the smallest things, never contemplating how much existed all around them), and finally began to move away. What he felt next was similar to what I had felt when I had disconnected from my body, except that Smiley's body came along with him. There was that tug in no particular direction, except that this time Smiley was forcing it to happen rather than allowing it to force him along. I also had the benefit of Smiley's thoughts, and I realised that he had chosen one of two ways he could have moved along the fourth dimension, and I had a moment to wonder: What world would he have come across if he had chosen to move the other way?

The immediate reaction to Smiley's movement was pretty much what I had imagined. All sounds faded to nothing, as did Smiley's vision. In fact, all of his physical senses quickly numbed. His mind was wide open, though, and he knew he had found the place again. He stopped moving for a moment and turned back the other way; his senses immediately returned a small amount. He was in his shadow now, but farther back than he had been all the other times, so far back that it was as though he were standing in a long tunnel, looking at a spot of light at the end. He turned back and headed deeper into the nothingness.

I found myself remembering my corridor theory as Smiley contemplated what he could feel around him. Before, he had been standing in the middle of the corridor, or perhaps at the edge, looking into one of the alcoves. Now, he was moving across the corridor to the alcove on the other side, the entrance into the Honnie world at this particular point in space and time. It seemed that he was unable to see and hear around corners as I had done in the main hall, but otherwise it was the same deal. He was able to operate it more at will than I was. Smiley too was thinking about the back and forth movement he knew he would be able to do, the time axis he now had access to, but now the idea of continuing along this path was firmly in his mind. He would come back to testing the time axis another day, should he have the chance.

All this happened very quickly. There wasn't much distance along the fourth dimension between worlds, it seemed, for moments later (I could have counted ten seconds, although such things as time only existed in the mind now), Smiley's senses began to return, slowly at first and then more rapidly. Once again he was looking down a long tunnel toward a spot of light ahead of him. He couldn't hear anything yet, but that seemed only to be because there were no sounds coming from that new place. Smiley's excitement increased. Maybe, just maybe, he had found a place where he wouldn't have to live as an outcast, a place where he would be able to finish his existence. He clearly hadn't given the matter enough thought, hadn't even contemplated that the world could contain anything whatsoever. Perhaps if he had read more science fiction books, his mind would have been more open to possibilities.

He moved quickly down the tunnel so that his senses sharpened with every second that passed, for time had started up again. Moments later, he broke through, his body finding that it required oxygen once again, and he gasped it down willingly, relishing the clean air, cleaner than any he had ever inhaled before. A few seconds passed before he looked around the new world he had entered. It didn't look much different from our world. In fact, the surrounding bushes looked very similar to the ones he had just left behind. He had a terrible moment of misery as he imagined that after all his wandering, he had ended up right where he had started, but that feeling disappeared the moment he caught sight of the figure sitting in the grass some twenty feet away. The tall, thin man, shimmering around the edges in a way I recognised all too clearly, was staring at Smiley, a look of complete surprise on his face (fairly beautiful, though not in the same league as the man from 1981), and when Smiley recognised the man for what he was (not *who*, for it wasn't the same one he had seen nineteen years earlier), comprehension hit him with the force of a charging bull.

He had one second to marvel at the prospect that there were creatures in existence who knew of and utilised his talent as he now did, before he felt something wrap itself around him like a rubber glove. He tried to struggle with it, but only for a second. In the next moment, his will to struggle had been wiped cleanly from his mind. He simply stood still, staring ahead of him at the Honnie, who stared calmly back at him. He could no longer feel the rubber glove, but he knew it was still there, and it was just loose enough for him to realise that it was around his mind, not his body. Thoughts raced across his mind, but they weren't the sort of thoughts that would have made sense in this situation. Smiley was remembering his name; he was thinking about England, not in a longing way but simply in a reflective way; he thought of all the people he had ever known, and finally of how and what had possessed him to come here in the first place. Only when the slideshow stopped did he realise that the Honnie had dipped into his head and deliberately pulled those thoughts forward in an attempt to learn his identity. He remembered what Lillian Woodward had said many years earlier: "He can influence people by planting thoughts into their minds, like the influential charm, but much more powerful. I know this because he has used his mind to communicate with me."

Smiley moved slowly forward toward the Honnie, carefully lest the creature spring into attack. He knew it would be strong enough to dispose of him in seconds if it chose. That was Smiley's reasoning for moving forward, but I knew better. The Honnie had made him come forward by placing the thought in his head. The only way to know this was by the thought pattern that had preceded it: Smiley had been thinking he ought to back out of this world immediately, before disregarding that thought more quickly than would have been natural in any other situation. He stopped before the Honnie and sat down in the grass in front of him so that they were face-to-face, just a few feet apart, staring at each other.

The sharing of knowledge began. It was very difficult to keep up with the trading of thoughts as they zoomed from Smiley to the Honnie and back again. I stopped focussing on each one and simply attempted to take in as much of the knowledge Smiley was gaining from the Honnie. Much of it was information Smiley had already given us, but there were a few interesting things that he hadn't imparted. Honnies knew of humans, but intelligent humans, those who had been educated in our world, were highly valued in this world, for their brain power could be used to feed a Honnie's mind, thereby making it stronger. They also fed on human bodies, mainly because they were there and humans were of little use once they had been drained of their brain power, but also for the nutrients they contained—nothing Smiley hadn't already told us.

There was much else too that was of little use but I still found interesting. For instance, Honnies and humans were capable of mating together (at least, male humans and female Honnies; the reverse would often be the death of the human female), although the practice only ever occurred in order to produce half breeds. Such creatures were usually large and stupid but highly useful in performing the low-end jobs in the Honnie society, such as construction. Each and every Honnie was also required to mate with another Honnie to produce two children. They would each take one and raise it alone, often never seeing the other again. Each Honnie also had what humans would call a 'speciality'; it would be the equivalent of a career path in any normal society. It would be up to the parent to discover their child's speciality and find ways to train them in order to hone their skills.

There was one other thing that Smiley learnt that he hadn't mentioned to us the other day, and it positively gave me the creeps. All Honnies would develop an ability (some earlier than others) to charm humans into absolute submission. It would only work on the opposite gender, but once charmed, a human would be irrevocably bound to follow that Honnie everywhere. Everything else in that human's life would cease to matter but the Honnie that had charmed him or her. Once charmed, there would be no use left for the human but to be used and then destroyed by the Honnie. Honnies didn't often use it, though, because they normally didn't need it. Their minds were usually enough to beat a human into submission, as Smiley could now testify, but also because it was a respected custom never to charm a human who was in the possession of another Honnie, for that was exactly how Honnies viewed humans, as nothing but possessions.

They were there for about half an hour before the Honnie allowed Smiley to return home. He told Smiley that while he could always have used another human, he had enough respect for him as a being rather than an object. He did emphasise that it was highly unusual for a Honnie to do that, though, and advised Smiley never to return here unless he wished to be slaughtered like a cow (the analogy he used after learning about human eating habits from Smiley's head). He never released Smiley from his mind but gave him enough self-control to move back along the fourth dimension, through the nothingness, across the corridor, and into the adjacent alcove. A minute later, Smiley was back in the bushes in which he had begun, not far from the spot he had started from.

That was the end of the memory, and moments later, reality returned. My body was heavy once again, but I recovered myself fairly quickly this time and without any real effort. All around me, the others were looking a little disturbed but mostly intrigued by what they had just seen.

"They're an interesting lot, aren't they," said Lena.

"Scary lot," said Serena.

"That was interesting," said James, "and I guess I'm glad he showed us that, but I can't see how that would be any use to us now."

"It's not," said Marc, getting to his feet, "but seeing it is better than not seeing it. I know I would have been very curious about it if I hadn't. Well, it's after midday. Who's up for some lunch?"

Chapter 40: Impending

With only two of Smiley's memories remaining, we decided to take the afternoon off and return to business that evening. We had lunch back at the campsite (the tree house this time), then split up for the afternoon. Most of them stayed at the campsite: I knew that Peter and James were playing cards; Lena was reading; Serena, Erica, and Siobhan were doing who knew what female business; Natalie was on the phone to Amelia, who had just finished her dinner and was now filling her in on whatever was going on outside the portals; and Marc and Tommy had left the campsite in their hovercars to do some exploring.

I could have stayed at the campsite (Peter and James had certainly wanted me to join in their card game, and Lena had thrown me a seductive look on her way out as though she'd hoped I might follow her to Group F's campsite), but I hadn't really been in the mood. I took my hovercar out and, with the Sien-Leoard Crystal, set off around the mountain, looking for something to take my mind off the unsettling thoughts that had been occupying it since lunch. I didn't really find anything, though, and before too long, I had gone farther up the mountain than I had ever been in the hovercar. I crested a hill and found myself drifting towards the deadly mote that circled the peak of the mountain. I knew from my previous experience that any contact with the water would be a very quick death for both me and my car, so I turned and set off around the mountain in search of the tunnel that led under it.

A few minutes later, I was at the very top of the mountain, looking out over an incredible view. It was a little duller than it had been last time due to the overcast conditions, but there was still plenty to appreciate. I turned the hovercar off and hopped out, settling myself on a slope just below it so that I could look out over the rock, the trees at the bottom of the mountain, the sea beyond. It was nice being there, but it didn't take long to realise that if I stayed here too long, I would probably catch a cold. I used the crystal to cast a spell around myself so that I wouldn't feel the chill in the air, making the scene extremely comfortable indeed.

In spite of my comfort, however, I had achieved the complete opposite of what I had intended, for there was nothing to distract me from my disturbing thoughts. My misery over my mother's death was beginning to pass now; perhaps the closure I'd been looking for ever since learning of her identity was finally upon me. No, what I was feeling now was a gloomy apprehension I had only ever felt twice before. The first time had been after learning of Daniel's death and had lasted right up until our Young Army meeting had been raided. The second time had been five days later, after Daniel's funeral and in the hours preceding the Hammersons' first escape from the Woodward base. I hadn't recognised it for what it was then, other than simple apprehension, but now, I thought I knew what it meant: Something bad was in the offing.

The feeling wasn't unreasonable, I told myself. There were only two remaining memories to see, and I had to wonder at the possibility that Smiley's tale may be building up to some sort of dreadful conclusion. Then, later tonight, I would return to the main hall where I would, hopefully, see whatever had taken place in there fourteen years ago. That would probably be enough to set me back again, but it wouldn't be the end of my gloom, for then I would have to see Smiley again and recount what I had seen, and he would no doubt be able to add further unpleasantness to my overall mood. Then, assuming I survived all that, we would be returning home sometime tomorrow or the day after. Somehow, that made me more nervous than anything else. If anything dangerous were coming, it would be waiting for us on the other side of the portal.

I couldn't deny that overall, this war had probably changed me for the better. I was certainly more courageous now than I had been before all this began. I could remember, clearly, how much I had just wanted to turn and run from Moran when he had been a Sorcerer. I doubted I would think twice about fighting him now. Even taking into consideration my indecision when it came to the girls in my life (if not for this, I would probably still be a single, horny, fourteen-year-old virgin) and my tendency to complicate matters for myself when I thought too deeply about it, I had certainly done a lot of quick growing up over the last three months. Yet, all that aside, what I wouldn't have given for everything to just quit and let things go back to how they had been before I had met Marc and Tommy. I liked them both fine enough, especially since Marc was my biological brother, but I couldn't deny that their involvement in my life had turned it upside-down.

Thinking about how it had been before the war was enough to distract me and lift my mood somewhat. An interesting twist to psychology, I supposed, since those times were gone forever. Without Nicole beside us, or Kylie for that matter, things could never be quite the same again, but reminiscing over those good times was a pleasant thing to do. Quite suddenly, I found myself feeling rather homesick. Most of the important people in my life were here on the Rock with me: Marc, Peter, James, Natalie, Serena, and even Tommy to a certain extent, but there were so many others I wanted to be back with: Felicity and Jessica, who were like my two remaining sisters, even though I didn't see as much of them anymore as I used to; Amelia, who I missed very much, even with my decision not to pursue her any more; Harry and Simon, who I wished very much I had invited along on this trip (they would have added the X-factor that would have kept us all cheerful through all that had happened); and most of all, Stella, who I wanted desperately to seek out and bring to safety as soon as I could.

I had been up there for about an hour when I caught sight of the one thing I'd most wanted not to happen: Someone was coming up the mountain to join me. I had been leaning back, almost daydreaming, when movement caught my eye from farther down the hill. I sat up straighter so that I could get a better look at the hill below, right down to just past the mote. A hovercar was moving around the circumference of the mountain. It was too far away to see who was in it, but that didn't matter. I recognised the colour. Not Marc or Tommy, both of whom I knew to be out and about this afternoon, although I probably wouldn't have minded if it was. Marc couldn't have been doing much better than I had been over the last twenty-four hours, and Tommy? Well, since I'd seen his abduction that morning, some part of me had wanted to bridge the gap that had formed between us since the previous afternoon. Even better, not Serena or Lena, either of whom could have been problematic up here, alone, with nothing but each other to keep ourselves warm. No, it was Natalie who was coming up to see me.

I adjusted my position slightly, not out of necessity but rather preoccupation. The sight of Natalie coming to me had temporarily driven away the melancholy but had instead replaced it with nerves. This was the first time I would be alone with her since two nights ago. There was something about the idea of being alone with her up here, before this magnificent view, so far isolated from everyone else in the world, that made me both nervous and excited. Add to that the fact that she would be freezing before too long and I would have to warm her up… Okay, now I was getting carried away, and I spent the remaining couple of minutes before she reached me trying to compose myself. I had to remind myself that there was probably some perfectly grounded reason why she was coming to see me, and that it was just too much to hope that she simply wanted nothing but to be close to me. Besides, if I could avoid overlap, I still wanted to. This could be just as problematic as if it were Serena or Lena.

"Hi," I said simply as she lowered her hovercar to the rock beside mine and jumped out.

"I was wondering where you were. Nobody seemed to know. How come you came up here?"

She seemed to regret the words the moment they were out of her mouth because she added quickly, "Not that there's anything wrong with it. It's just a bit strange, not to mention cold."

"I didn't plan to come up here. I was just looking for a good place to be and ended up here. What's going on down there?"

"Nothing really," she admitted, seating herself beside me and wrapping her arms around her raised knees. "The boys are playing cards and the girls are gossiping, and I have no idea where Marc went."

No mention of Tommy or Lena, I thought, and no direct mention of Serena either. Interesting.

"He's out there somewhere," I said, looking across the landscape. "What did Amelia have to say?"

"Well…" She hesitated before proceeding. "She's looking forward to us getting back. I'll tell all the others later, but they've got a plan and they wanna put it into action in the next few days."

"Is this the one about Tankom?"

"She didn't say on the phone, but it probably is. It sounded big."

I sighed, wondering if this big plan was the reason for my feeling of impending danger.

"Something wrong?" she asked, and I jumped. Had I been that obvious?

It was my turn to hesitate. What would she say if I told her what I was feeling? Probably she would just think I was going crazy, but it could also scare her if she took me seriously. What made me decide to tell the truth was the knowledge that I wanted her to know what was on my mind. Perhaps if it had been Serena up here, I would have kept tight-lipped.

"Do you feel like something bad is coming?" I asked her.

"Bad?" she repeated in some confusion. "Like what?"

"I don't know. I just have a feeling that something bad is coming. I've had it before. It's making me a little jumpy."

"It's probably nothing," she said in an attempt at reason. "I've had bad feelings often enough, like when I haven't done my homework."

I laughed in spite of myself. "I had that before every English class this year, and French class last year, but this is different. Last time I had this was the day before Tulip died."

That wiped the smile off her face. "Bloody hell. Are you precognitive or something? What's going on?"

Precognitive? I hadn't considered that one, but I dismissed it almost immediately. "Honestly I don't know what I am—that's sort of what I'm trying to find out—but I don't think it's that. It's probably not that unusual to feel these things coming. Last time I'd already been nervous about taking her along. I just proved myself right. This time I've got another couple of memories to look forward to, and they've certainly given me more than I bargained for, not to mention what I might see tonight. And now you tell me there's a plan for when we get back."

Natalie shrugged. "This one will be different. Mr. Woodward is planning it very carefully. He won't let any of us get ourselves into positions that could be dangerous."

"I'd like to believe that, but it could all go wrong if he doesn't leave at least some room for improvisation. I don't suppose Amelia told you who would be involved in this plan?"

"We will be," she said, "plus Marc, and possibly Tommy—(she scowled)—and probably some of his people. That's probably it, though. I can't see him wanting to put any other teenagers in."

"I hope it works, whatever it is. We really need something to go our way for once."

I checked my watch. It was nearly four o'clock. I thought maybe we had another hour up here before we would have to head back down. I looked sideways at Natalie, wondering again why she had come all the way up here just to sit with me, and saw that she was beginning to shiver. The thought of warming herself with magic apparently hadn't occurred to her yet.

"Here," I said, and extended the magical warmth around myself sideways so that it enveloped her body. "Sorry, I should have done that when you sat down."

"Hey, thanks," she said gratefully, shifting her body. Whether accidentally or intentionally, the movement brought her very close to me. Our shoulders were actually touching, if only very gently. The position made me nervous and excited all over again. It would have been so easy to put an arm around her here and now, but I resisted the urge. If all went as I intended it to, I would be able to do that soon enough (assuming Natalie herself didn't have other ideas), but now was not the time, not while I was technically still in a relationship.

"You know," she said suddenly, "it's been more than two weeks now and I can't believe you still haven't asked me."

My heart skipped a beat. "W-what? What do you mean? What was I supposed to ask you?"

I could hardly believe my ears. Was she about to take the matter completely out of my hands? I scrambled to convince myself that she was referring to something else, hoping against hope that she hadn't recognised my start for what it really was, but her grin suggested that she knew exactly what internal struggle I had just been through.

"I just assumed it would have been a sharp point of curiosity for you since that night you got me and Amelia out of that tight spot."

"You mean Moran and Lucien?"

"And Stella, don't forget Stella," she went on, still grinning.

"I haven't forgotten Stella. I was just thinking about her before you turned up."

"Are you sure? I spent a whole twenty-four hours with her, and not once have you bothered to ask me what I might have heard out of her mind."

"Er—" I faltered. That had thrown me off completely. I had a split-second of relief (this wasn't about me and her), but it was immediately followed by a different kind of nervousness. What on earth was Natalie about to tell me? Was this the sort of thing I would want to hear from Natalie, of all people? "I never even thought of it," I admitted. "There's been a lot of stuff going on."

"You could say that," she agreed.

I shook my head. "I already hear her thoughts for myself, so I guess it just never occurred to me that you could tell me anything I didn't already know."

"You think so?" she persisted. "I got a pretty good look at her, plus I was actually with her and she talked to me a bit, so I could turn her thoughts where I wanted to. That's a little better than seeing her for a few seconds at a time when you sleep. Have you seen her lately?"

"Just once since we got here, three nights ago. Her father was mad at her for not being able to get Sebastian out. At least I think that was it. I can't actually remember what he was saying."

"Ah," she sighed. "I don't know why she doesn't just do a runner. Surely they can't have someone watching her all the time."

"I wouldn't be surprised if they do. Her father seems to really want her on his side. I can't think of a good reason why he hasn't used a boggler on her yet."

"Oh, I can," she said, surprising me. "Those things are designed to make people follow the Hammersons. Hammerson wants her to lead, not follow. What's the betting he'll get her with an influential charm first thing if he ever gets his own magic back?"

"Well, that is a pretty good reason," I admitted. "How did you know that about the bogglers?"

"I asked her," she said simply.

I hesitated before speaking again. "So—what sort of stuff was she thinking about, then? You really think you can tell me stuff I don't already know?"

"Maybe. I got a pretty good look at her."

"What sort of stuff was she thinking about, then?"

"What she'd been up to since her family let her go. She only got caught up with Moran and Lucien when she got back to Chopville. She left the tunnel through their place and they intercepted her. It was either join or fight them. Guess she did the right thing, considering."

"Right, and you reckon she got it out of my head that we were dealing with Underwood?"

"Yeah. She wasn't trying to cause trouble, though. She planned to give the life assistant to us like she did the Darkness Crystal once she got it. She seemed to think that since we screwed up the first time, we'd have a lot more trouble the second. She was pretty low about failing and—well, she didn't like him at all."

I knew what she wasn't saying. Stella was disgusted by what she'd done to him and what she could have done further.

"And…" She hesitated for a moment before going on. "I guess she hasn't done much since then, but she had every intention to try to get back in with us."

"She did try once," I said, remembering the note she had tried to leave in the Woodwards' house a week ago. "I got the idea from her head that she felt like she'd lost everything when we let her go."

"Yeah, I got that too. Seemed like she saw us as her only ticket to a life she could enjoy. You know, since she's had such a crappy life with her family. That's what she wants most out of all of this—for the Woodwards to take her back and forgive her. I dunno if she wants to fight against her family or not, but she certainly doesn't wanna be with them."

"Yeah, but give her credit. From what I've seen, she's standing up for herself more now than she ever did before."

"Yeah, well, she's more grown-up now than she ever was before. I suppose we all are. I know I've changed a lot since I got magic."

"Yeah, I was just thinking that before you turned up, that we all had to grow up quickly since all this started. Hey," I said, struck by a sudden thought, "I don't suppose, when you were with Moran and Lucien and Stella, did you notice anything unusual going on?"

"Such as?"

"Anything that might suggest there was a ghost in the room?"

"Oh, right." She went quiet for a few moments, and I was glad she was at least taking my question seriously. Finally, she said, "I don't know. I can't remember noticing anything particularly unusual. Both their minds were protected, and Stella knew nothing about a ghost. Only thing is…" She hesitated again. "Amelia was pretty hysterical at first, but then she went really quiet. At the time I thought it was Moran's doing, but if you're so sure ghosts can mess with our emotions, maybe she had that calming effect or something. Other than that, though, she stayed out of the way. Maybe she wouldn't have wanted anything to do with what he was doing, anyway."

"Probably not, but from what Smiley said, she never tried to stop him doing these crazy things."

"Hmm, yeah," she said and lapsed into silence, apparently awkward with discussing my ghost mother.

"Did you get anything else from Stella?" I asked.

"Er." She hesitated yet again. "Well, she thought about you a lot."

I could have groaned. Exactly the thing I'd been nervous about. To hear this sort of thing from Natalie… I made a supreme effort to maintain my composure.

"What sort of stuff did she think?" I asked cautiously.

"Well." She hesitated yet again, and I found myself wondering just how honest she was about to be. "She—she really wants to get back in your good books. She wants the Woodwards to take her back, like I said, but she especially wants you to take her back."

"Take her back?" I repeated, slightly startled. "Take her back? That makes it sound like I—I had her or something."

The words sounded silly in my ears, but Natalie understood what I meant. "That's how she thought of it," she said. "When Underwood let her use the life assistant, Smiley pointed something out to her about you. I'm not sure what it was, because she wasn't thinking about the details, but it was something along the lines of not understanding herself. She reckons you let her go that night, and she's wanted you to take her back ever since. I got the impression there's not much she won't do to make that happen."

Now I really did groan. I wasn't sure which part of that disturbed me more—Stella's belief that she was, for all intents and purposes, my girl (whatever that meant in her mind); the lengths she would go to be back by my side; or the fact that I was getting this from Natalie, that Natalie had known all this for nearly three weeks now.

"Well," I said, floundering for words. "Well—thanks for letting me know."

She laughed, then sighed. "I dunno if I like everything she thought about, but she deserves a lot better than she's getting now. I don't care what Mr. Woodward says. Once we get back and through whatever plans they've got, I'm gonna find a way to get her back."

"Yeah, I'll help out, and probably a few of the others will want to as well," I said. "Do you think Amelia wants her back? Somehow I really can't tell with her."

"Don't know either. She wasn't really with us that day. Don't think she paid any attention to Stella's mind like I did, or even what we were saying most of the time. She was a bit—lost in herself."

I didn't say anything. What I wanted more than anything else was to just say whatever I thought to Natalie, but the way this conversation was going, I kept finding myself at sharp little turns that seem to cut me off. Talking about Amelia was almost as awkward as talking about Stella had been because the logical direction of the conversation, if I were to be honest with Natalie, would be to tell her exactly how I had tried to help Amelia with her problems. I still had no idea just how much Natalie even knew about Amelia's problems. Whose mind could she have read who would know what Hignat and Wilwog had done to her? No one I could think of.

"What are you thinking?" Natalie asked quietly, and I started. Her tone sounded more suggestive than I'd ever heard, yet it was probably my own imagination. I hesitated for only a moment before deciding on the truth—or part of it.

"Just thinking about Amelia," I told her. "How was she doing, anyway? After all that stuff, I mean?"

"She's doing better," she replied. "I think the shock of what happened to her mum is starting to wear off now. What she really needs is a holiday, I suppose, but it's hard to see where that's gonna come from. The Hammersons certainly aren't looking for a holiday."

"Yeah. Well, we're sort of having a holiday. It really would have been good if she had come."

"Yeah, but that was her choice."

Another silence followed. I leaned back against the rock, assuming the position I'd had before Natalie had turned up, and she leaned back beside me. It was very relaxing. The rock was a long way from the most comfortable surface I'd ever rested on, but it really didn't matter. What mattered was me and the girl sitting/lying beside me, the fact that we were alone, and the intimacy of the situation. How good it would have been to put an arm around her and pull her even closer than she already was, but I knew it still wasn't the time. The time may come very soon, but until it did, I had to abstain. Some (perhaps myself included if I were on the outside) would say it mattered not since I had already decided to break up with Serena and try my luck with Natalie, but mainly for Serena's sake, I wanted to do it in the right order. I didn't like the idea of there being overlap. It just made the thing feel more dishonest than it already was.

* * *

The general mood of the group was very cheerful over dinner that night. Natalie and I had returned at around five o'clock, me worrying about the questions that would fly at us from just about everyone in the group about what we had been doing together and why we were so late, but as it turned out, Marc and Tommy didn't return until nearly six. When asked by the others, Serena and Lena both looking appropriately suspicious, we just said we'd been up on the mountain, chatting and not really exploring. Most of them accepted the story, except James, who continued to look suspicious, and Serena, who looked more resigned to something than anything else. Her expression made me feel both sad and guilty. Why on earth was I being so cruel to her? Was there any other way I could handle this situation, other than break up with her immediately? Sometimes, it was hard to get away from one simple fact: Dating sucked.

The girls had spent the entire afternoon in the Group E house, chatting and listening to music; Lena, who hadn't been with them, had sat alone, reading in the Group F house; James and Peter had started off playing cards (Peter's preference) and ended up playing chess (James's preference); but it was Marc and Tommy who returned to the tree house, where we were to eat dinner, with news of the most exciting afternoon.

"I know we might be going back tomorrow," Marc told us, "but before we do, I reckon you should all come with us to check something out, either tonight or tomorrow morning."

"We were just checking out some caves in the mountain," Tommy told us, "and we followed one in pretty deep. It was close to the one that led down to the swimming pool you guys used when you were here last time, so Marc tells me, anyway. You wanna know what we found down there?"

"Nah, let's eat our dinner first," said Peter sarcastically. "Honestly, what do you think we're gonna say to that?"

A few people laughed, including Tommy. "Fine. Tell them, big boy."

"Big boy?" Marc repeated, taking a badly aimed swipe at Tommy. "Well, what we found down there was—well, let's just say

I'm gonna try and create one of these for my bedroom when we get back home."

Tommy burst out laughing. "You never said anything about that on the way back. Who are you planning on inviting in there?"

"*Oi*," said James loudly. "Either tell us what you're on about or we really *will* start dinner."

"Okay, okay," said Marc quickly. "The chamber had a bunch of smaller rooms off it, right, and in each of those smaller rooms was a hot tub, all different and varying sizes and the like. We tried a couple of them."

"Together?" grinned Peter wickedly. "Geez, Marc, I didn't realise you'd jumped the fence. What is it about our dark friend here that so entrances you?"

"Oh, shut up, we didn't jump in together," said Marc, but there was something wrong with the way he'd said that. I wondered if I was the only one who noticed. I made a mental note to ask him about it later. "Anyway, we were thinking that the rest of you could go down there too. They're really nice and warm and—well, you'll see."

"And they're private too," Tommy added, "in case you don't wanna be seen by anyone else."

"I'm up for it," said Erica eagerly. "We can share one, what say you, Jamesy?"

"Well, I guess that would be like living out a fantasy of some kind," said James, smiling slightly, "as long as you promise to never call me that again."

I looked around the group to see how the rest of them were reacting to this. All positive, by the look of it. Serena was staring pointedly at me, of course, and I winked back at her, pretending not to notice Lena giving me exactly the same look. Marc and Tommy were both looking pleased with themselves, but while Marc's eyes kept darting to Lena, Tommy was determinedly avoiding looking at Natalie. She, meanwhile, was going about getting dinner ready without showing much interest in the hot tubs at all. Would it be so bad if I asked Natalie to join me in a hot tub? Would I get another opportunity? I discarded this idea almost the moment it had occurred to me. What greater insult could I give Serena than that? On the other hand, how could I justify sharing a bath with Serena at this point? Yep—dating sucked.

As we sat down to our dinner, Natalie began telling the rest of the group what she had already told me about what Amelia had said. As there wasn't much new about it other than the plan to ambush Tankom, I didn't listen too closely. The others didn't have much to say about this. It was as though they had been expecting a break now that the Smiley hunt was almost over. I still had plenty of room to wonder what was to come next for me, but I wouldn't know that until I'd seen the last two memories and what had happened in the main hall. Perhaps the next most important thing was to get Stella back. Perhaps I would need her in order to work the rest out.

When my mind next returned to the conversation, it had moved around to the order of events this evening.

"No, memories first," Marc was saying sternly.

"Aw, come on," Erica pleaded. "The memories aren't going anywhere."

"Look, we wouldn't be proving ourselves as responsible adults if we delay our return home just so we can sit around snuggling in a hot tub," Marc told her.

"They're waiting for us so they can attack Tankom, anyway," Lena said. "That plan could make a lot of difference in the war, so it'd be pretty selfish for us to consider creature comforts before the war."

Erica looked slightly embarrassed. "I just think it's better to do that sort of stuff after dark."

"I agree, but let's be grown-up about this," said Marc. "The memories might be short, if we're lucky. I can't think of much that's happened between 2000 and now that he would need to show us. Most of the stuff happened when we were babies. We'll probably have time once we're finished to get our toes wet."

"You're only getting your toes wet?" said Serena amusedly.

"You know what I mean," he said shortly.

"Hang on," I protested, suddenly realising what this would mean for me. "I've gotta go to the main hall tonight. If I don't sleep, I mightn't be able to make it work when I get there."

"You're not as tired now as you were this time yesterday, right?" Peter asked.

"No, but—"

"You know, I don't think that'll matter, John," said Marc. "I can't say for sure since it's you, not me, but it's not a case of how tired your body is. Once you detach from it, it won't matter how tired you are."

"That's true, John," said James. "It sounds like you've had a pretty light-on day, so you shouldn't be too tired that you can't at least get it started. Besides, what better way to get yourself ready than a couple of hours in a hot tub?"

"He's got that right," said Serena, grinning at me. "I'll make sure you're ready to go at one or so."

"That reminds me of something," said Marc, a little warily as he glanced at Serena. "I was thinking earlier today and—I know this isn't gonna go over too well, but, John, I actually think it would be better if either myself or Natalie came with you tonight."

"Hey! What? Why?" Serena protested, almost getting out of her seat, such was her indignation. "I said I'd do it first. You can't just take it off me."

"Your funeral," I told him, trying not to grin. "How come you don't want Serena to do it?"

But I thought I already knew the answer. The whole point of someone coming with me was just in case something went wrong and I was discovered by the Russians, and what could Serena do to prevent the Russians from accidentally walking into me? Stun them —that would be her only option. If it were either Marc or Natalie, they would be able to do more, more that would probably go completely unnoticed by anyone else.

"You only have your magical devices," Marc told her. "What happens if someone comes walking along the wall where John is standing, what are you gonna do? Attack them with a bludginator?"

Serena bit her lip, thinking. Then she said, "I could just use John's crystal. He won't mind giving it to me for a few minutes while he's in another world."

"Maybe not, but since you've never used it," said Marc, not unkindly, "it'd be better for someone with more magical experience to take this one. There's too much to be lost if something goes wrong. So, either myself or Natalie—who's your preference, John?"

"I don't really have one," I said automatically, trying to give Serena an apologetic look, which she missed.

"I don't mind doing it again," Natalie offered, maybe a little too eagerly. Serena's eyes narrowed, Tommy frowned, and Peter and James swapped amused grins.

"Or maybe it's Marc's turn, since you did it last time," said Erica quickly, and I knew she was jumping to the aid of one of her best friends.

"That's true, I guess," said Marc. "So around one, John?"

"I dunno," I said, a little startled at how the last minute had played out. "We'll just check with the crystals if it's empty and go down there when it looks like they're done for the night."

Chapter 41: Bare Hands

Dinner was done by just after seven, and little more than fifteen minutes later, we were all seated back in the cave of Smiley's memories, ready to dip into the last two rolls of tape left to us. Our cars were piled up around the entrance as usual and Fewul, who was going more and more unnoticed as the days wore on, was once again standing by them, ensuring that nobody stumbled across what we were doing. It was still assuming the form of Lucien, although on Marc's commands it seemed to be making itself invisible more and more often. It meant that none of us other than Marc knew where it was at any given time, but as long as it was doing the job assigned to it, nobody really cared.

Marc loaded the second-to-last memory into the playback device and hit the button. We all zoomed away from reality as usual and came to rest in the body of Smiley, who was standing in his shadow again in a place I knew very well indeed. I had been in this room twice before, both of those times in terrible danger. The old man was standing just behind the Hammersons' kitchen bench, looking across the room towards two doors, one leading out into a corridor to the rest of the base, the other leading back to their bedrooms. There were two people in the room. Tankom looked exactly the same as she did now—old, wrinkled, and grey-haired. Stella looked very similar in this memory to today too. Even here she was taller than her grandmother, perhaps taller than some of us already. Based on the development of her body, I estimated her to be perhaps thirteen or fourteen, meaning that this memory could only be two or three years in the past.

It only took me a few seconds to deduce what was happening in this memory, perhaps because I knew how it had been from Stella. She had once mentioned that this sort of stuff happened to her. Tankom was seated quite comfortably on the couch while Stella was on her feet, side-on to her grandmother, ready to leap into some sort of action. It looked as though Tankom was teaching her something magical.

"Concentrate hard on what I told you, Stella," Tankom said firmly. "If this were real, you would have already given your opponent plenty of opportunities to get the jump on you. As soon as you see it, attack."

"Just do it," she said through clenched teeth. "I'm ready."

Silence fell. Stella stood, poised and ready to strike, at what I had no idea, and Tankom lounged back, quite at her ease. What exactly was going on here? Smiley's mind wasn't helping me at all this time; apparently, he had no idea what was to happen now. Something more important would happen a bit later. The scene hung, suspended for perhaps fifteen seconds, before something grey, a bit like a cloak, appeared out of thin air across the room from Stella. What followed happened so quickly that I could barely mark the movements. The grey thing shot straight at Stella, who ducked before sending it into the air. It hit the roof, and that was all I knew. The battle ensued for several more seconds, during which I saw fire, water, ropes, and several other things I couldn't even identify. Both Stella and the cloak were wrapped up in the fight, and it was impossible to see which of them was doing what. It ended as suddenly as it had started. The cloak had been sliced several times and now lay in pieces. Stella was also on the floor, burnt and nursing what was clearly a broken arm.

"A win," Tankom said in a bored voice, "but if you were facing more than one, you would be in a world of trouble. Fix yourself up, Stella, and we'll try one more time."

Stella took several seconds to overcome the pain of her predicament enough to fix her arm and repair the burns to her face. Then she clambered back to her feet, looking as though she wanted nothing more than for this to be over. I was struck, both by how well Stella had just fought with magic and by how unimpressed Tankom had been with it. Whatever she believed, I thought Stella had done extremely well. She probably could have killed both Marc and I several times over in those few seconds.

As she readied herself for another fight, however, voices began echoing from outside the room. Men, three or four of them, were climbing the stairs up to the living quarters. Tankom looked around at the sound and said, without looking at her granddaughter, "Stella, off to bed with you."

"But weren't we going to have one more try?" said Stella, trying to hide her relief.

"Tomorrow night. Go, now."

Stella didn't argue but strode quickly around the couch and headed for her bedroom. No sooner was she out of sight than the owners of the voices entered through the other door. In the lead was Arnold Hammerson, who also looked the same here as I knew him in life. He looked very tired but pleased with whatever he had been doing. Behind him came Cornish, Hignat Senior, and (my stomach did a backflip at the sight of him) Moran. They too looked exhausted, as though they had walked for miles and not slept properly in days.

"Evening, Tankom," Cornish said, bowing to her and then needing Hignat's assistance to straighten up again. He and Moran too bowed to her before Hammerson, who had sat himself down opposite her, spoke.

"It is done, at last," he told her. "I hoped very much that we would not need to go out again, and I'm relieved to say that it won't be necessary."

"You found it, then?" she asked, her own excitement evident now.

"We certainly did," he said. "3M27, show her."

Moran reached into his pocket and pulled from it something round that was wrapped in foil. He leaned forward and passed it across to Tankom, who accepted it with trembling hands. Slowly, she removed the foil from around the smooth, deathly black crystal and held it up to the light. It was not the Darkness Crystal as I knew it; this had to be the Villain Crystal. It was pure black and seemed to glint, but it didn't cast a shadow on things around it as the Darkness Crystal did.

"Yes, it certainly does look evil," she said admiringly, "though not as evil as the Darkness Crystal, if I may say so. Was it difficult to find?"

"Well, as I'm sure he will gloat the house down over the coming days," said Hammerson, looking sideways at Moran, "why don't you tell her, 3M27."

"It wasn't as difficult as the Light and Darkness Crystals had been," he told her, "but I certainly had some luck in locating it. It was buried deep."

"How did you find the place, though?" Tankom asked, addressing her son again.

"Research is a valuable tool," he told her. "It disappeared in the same manner as the Light and Darkness Crystals over a thousand years ago, and for the same reason—all traces of magic must be hidden to protect those in possession of it. We found it buried beneath a monument in Medina, Saudi Arabia, and it took some tricky magic to extract it. A bit of magic helped us narrow down the search, but it was 3M27 who detected the pulses of magic generated by the crystal."

"Very good," said Tankom softly, rolling the Villain Crystal between her hands. "So we have three out of the five now."

"We do," said Hammerson, "and I think now we ought to begin moving into action against the Woodwards. By taking possession of these crystals, we have put ourselves into a more advantageous position than they can possibly know. It really has been so easy since that old bleater died—"

He broke off suddenly, his face darkening as he glanced over Tankom's head towards the door through which Stella had gone before he had arrived. "How has she been going? Is she showing any more aptitude, or are we going to have to go on without her?"

"Better, but she needs more time," said Tankom firmly. "I don't think it's wise to jump into action until Stella is ready."

"I'm not sure that will ever be the case, and meanwhile that Woodward girl is getting stronger by the day. I've heard a lot about her, and I honestly think if it came down to a fight between her and Stella, she would win with her hands tied behind her back. She's much more focussed."

"Stella will be fine," said Tankom, still firmly. "Her loyalty is still an issue, but if the time comes and that's all we have to worry about, a good influential charm will be the solution. Besides, I still believe that the Woodwards have gone soft. However focussed the girl may be, I doubt Frederic or Lillian have put the same time into her that we have in Stella. Now, what to do with the Villain Crystal. Put it with the Darkness Crystal, I suppose?"

"I thought of that," said Hammerson, "but it occurred to me that if Frederic Woodward were to suspect that we have these crystals, he may make an attempt to steal them from us. If he were to succeed, I would prefer he only get his hands on one, rather than two. So, separately would be better, I think."

"Any particular hiding place, sir?" Cornish asked. "Or is it better that we not know?"

"Somebody will need to know, of course," said Hammerson, "if it is to be guarded. The Darkness Crystal is safe because it is right under our nose. What to do with this one, though?"

"The Pacific base?" suggested Hignat. "The Atlantic base? Maybe even one of the Antarctic bases? Or are you thinking of doing what you did with the Light Crystal and handing it to a Hammerheart to keep?"

Hammerson considered this before shaking his head. "The Light Crystal is, perhaps, the quietest of all the crystals. Letting 3K17 hold onto it is, I think, quite safe, given that she isn't likely to do much with it. The Villain Crystal, though, the temptation to use it for one's own ends will be too great for many Hammerhearts, I—"

"I think 3M27 should hold on to it," said Tankom suddenly, and all four men goggled at her.

"Why him?" spat Hammerson, glaring sideways at Moran, as though it had been his idea.

"Because he was the one who found it," said Tankom, raising her eyebrows at her son. "As long as he promises not to use it until the time is right."

"But where will he keep it where it will be safe?" Cornish asked, looking over at Moran. "You got anywhere safe, Berny?"

"I have a safe," said Moran, but he didn't look convinced.

"I think he has earned the right to guard it," said Tankom firmly to her son, giving him a 'don't argue' look that made me curious. Why was Tankom so determined that Moran should get the Villain Crystal?

"Fine, fine," snapped Hammerson, a little disconcerted now. As Tankom rewrapped the crystal and passed it back to Moran, he added, "3M27, I want you to make a pact with me."

"Oh?" said Moran warily. "What sort of pact?"

"I want you to swear to me," said Hammerson, gesturing to Moran to move in front of him, "that you will not use the Villain Crystal to prevent us using the Seventh Sorcerer when the time comes."

The silence in the room now was almost quantifiable. All eyes were on Moran, who looked visibly shaken. He gulped and said, "And if I break it, I'll die?"

"That's how magical pacts work," said Hammerson dispassionately. "Either that or no crystal."

"I thought the Villain Crystal couldn't do stuff like that anyway," said Hignat suddenly, and everyone looked at him now.

"Excuse me?" said Hammerson gruffly.

"Well, the research we did suggested that if he were to use the Villain Crystal to protect someone, it wouldn't work because the magic isn't evil enough."

"I'm aware of the research," said Hammerson, "but the fact is, there are always loopholes around that sort of magic. If he were to do it with the sole intention of setting us back, the magic would work perfectly. So it's no pact, no crystal. Are you in, 3M27?"

Moran considered for several seconds before saying, "Yes, I'm in."

He got off his seat and crouched down in front of Hammerson. The Sorcerer stretched out his hands and placed them over the top of Moran's, sending what looked to be a tingling force through them. Smiley, who had moved closer to the action in the last few minutes to get a better view, couldn't see anything in the air, but I had a vague memory how it had felt when Stella had done it to her father and grandmother. The process lasted for several seconds, during which the other three in the room watched in silence as the two men stared into each other's eyes, staring each other down almost. Finally it ended, and Moran scrambled quickly back to his seat.

"Bear that in mind, 3M27," said Hammerson, looking happier now. "Use that crystal to protect your son and you will die. Remember that."

"Of course, we're also giving you the order not to use that crystal at all," Tankom reminded him. "You said you have a safe? Lock it in there and guard it with your life. I guess it won't help much if the Woodwards came to call, but as long as you don't draw attention to yourself by using it, they'll have no reason to go near you."

"It's a deal," said Moran flatly.

And quite suddenly, that was it. We floated out of the memory and came to rest back in our seats in the memory chamber. I straightened up in my seat and looked around at the others. Most eyes were on Marc, who looked a little uncomfortable.

"So now we know how he got the Villain Crystal," said Peter, "and I'd be prepared to bet that that's why they ordered him to find the Sorcerous Crystals earlier in the year—he'd proven that he was capable of locating crystals. When did that happen, do you think? Stella didn't look much younger than she is now."

"Couldn't tell you exactly when," said Marc, "but probably two or three years ago. Let's just say January 2008, give or take a few months. Should we look at the last memory?"

"A couple of questions first, Marc," said James, holding up his hand.

"Go on," said Marc, looking wary.

"It sounded like the mission they went on to get the Villain Crystal took a few days," James said, "and it sounded like they went on quite a few of them, for the Light and Darkness Crystals as well. What happened to you and Lucien in that time if your father wasn't around?"

"We got left with Hammerhearts," said Marc. "Probably on Hammerson's orders, now I think of it. I didn't know that then, of course. I just assumed they were Dad's friends, but I never really spoke to any of them, anyway. It happened fairly often, so I can't remember who we were with that time."

"Okay," said James. "And also, someone said in there that 3K17 had the Light Crystal. What happened there? How did your dad get it if she was supposed to be guarding it?"

Marc shrugged. "I have no idea. They might have been friends and maybe she decided to give it to him or something. Maybe Lucien would have a better idea of that than me."

"Well, it doesn't look like these memories are gonna tell us that," said Tommy, "unless it's in the last one. Should we have a look?"

"Sure," said Marc, removing the memory from the playback device and fishing in the box for the last one. "We're lucky that didn't take too long. If this one's reasonably short, then we'll probably be out of here before nine."

He found the last memory, placed it in the playback device, hit the button, and quickly took his seat again. Once again, we left our bodies and re-joined with Smiley in his shadow, this time in a room on the other side of the Chopville base—the den. Smiley was standing to the side of the doorway watching the three Sorcerers, who were sitting around the table in silence. This time, all three of them looked exactly as they did today; this couldn't have been more than a few months ago. Tankom and Hammerson, who were sitting directly across the table from where Smiley stood, both looked impatient. They both kept glancing up at the clock (which showed it was nearly one in the morning) every few seconds and spent the rest of the time twisting their hands or tapping their knees. Stella, who was sitting to Smiley's right, looked bored, tired, and probably just wanted to go to bed.

This scene held for about five minutes, but it wasn't until I heard the footsteps outside the room that the déjà vu hit me in one powerful blow. I had seen this before, in a dream that hadn't really been a dream at all. It had been on the night before the first day of school this year, and as usual, when I had dreamt of the Hammersons in those days, I had buried the memory of the dream almost as soon as I woke up. It was better that way. Seeing this scene now made me think back to it, and as the footsteps approached the door, I tried to remember what was about to happen.

A moment later, two people entered the room—Cornish, and Moran right behind him. Of course, I wouldn't have known who either of them were back then (though perhaps Stella's knowledge of them had hidden that fact from me), but I certainly recognised them now. All three Sorcerers straightened up at the sight of them, and Hammerson and Tankom swapped relieved looks.

"Sorry about the delay," Cornish said as he took the seat to Hammerson's right, Smiley's left, and directly across the table from Stella. "I had trouble getting hold of him."

"My bad," said Moran as he took the seat in front of Smiley, to Stella's left and directly opposite the other two Sorcerers. "I wasn't aware that it would be tonight."

"Well, it is," said Hammerson, his frustration at being kept waiting so long becoming evident. "Or rather, today. You understand what it is you need to do?"

"Indeed I do," said Moran. "You are—er—quite sure the Woodwards won't have protection around them?"

"Certain," said Hammerson. "However, if they become aware of what we're doing and decide to use our own plan against us, I think it a good idea that you keep these as well."

Hammerson looked sideways at Tankom, who pulled what looked like a small bag from her pocket and held it out for Moran to take. I thought I knew what it was just by the shape of the things inside it—three lumps, three very circular lumps. Moran took the bag from her and pulled the drawstrings to open it. As he looked inside, his face lit up with comprehension and excitement.

"Keep them protected, won't you," Tankom said firmly. "Put them in the safe with the other two."

"But of course," replied Moran, and the look on his face (which Smiley had moved sideways so as to get a good view of) made it quite clear that he had his own idea about what he was going to do with the contents of the drawstring bag. I couldn't believe everyone in the room had missed it.

"Now, 3M27, have you spoken to your son today?" asked Hammerson.

"Yes, he told me of the promotion," said Moran. "I must tell you, in case it slipped his mind, that we are both exceptionally honoured that you have granted him such a privilege. I have to wonder, though —why? I was under the impression that he wasn't entirely trustworthy."

"You remember why he is, I'm sure," said Hammerson, giving Moran a very sharp look. Moran returned the stare with interest, and my own curiosity rose. What was that about? "Well, the reason," Hammerson continued, some of his colour gone now, "is because we want him to bring H4 to us, and it might be easier on you to only have one job at a time."

No, it wasn't, I suddenly knew, for Smiley's mind had given me a prod in the right direction. What was the real reason why Hammerson believed Lucien would be trustworthy? There could only be one reason that could have caused the exchange between Moran and Hammerson that we had just seen—the time bomb curse.

"All the more reason why you must keep those," Tankom pointed at the drawstring bag, "away from the boy. Understand?"

"Of course," said Moran curtly. "Anything else?"

Tankom and Hammerson swapped looks again. "No," Hammerson said finally. "You have everything you need. Tomorrow, you will set off, and I want you to report back to us on Thursday evening. Good luck."

"Thank you," Moran replied, and after waiting a few moments for a nod from both Sorcerers, got up and left the room with the bag.

"Stella, you're free to go too," said Hammerson curtly. "And remember, not a word to anyone about what you have just seen, and stay away from that Woodward girl. Don't let her get close enough to read your mind. Got it?"

"Sure, Father," said Stella as she got up from the table. She looked dead on her feet.

Once she was gone and the sound of her footsteps had faded to nothing, Tankom said to her son, "So what's this big plan of yours you were so excited about earlier?"

"Ah, yes," said Hammerson, pulling himself up straighter in his chair. "Now this is very exciting, I think you'll agree, and top secret. Nobody but we three can know about it."

My stomach—or what represented it—seemed to twist at these words. Everything up until now had come back to me as it happened, but this was completely new. I must have woken up before this bit.

"Are you sure I should be in on it?" asked Cornish, who in any case looked as though he didn't want to leave.

"Yes, I think we can trust you with this knowledge," said Hammerson, "as long as you swear not to tell anybody."

"My lips are sealed," said Cornish, his own excitement starting to show.

"Good. Well, I've been thinking very hard about contingency plans lately," Hammerson told them both, "like for instance, what we will do in order to maintain our own security should we somehow lose our magic in the coming months."

"You really think the Woodwards will finally take our magic?" Tankom asked him. "Or are you having reservations about placing our powers in 3M27's hands?"

If not, he should have been, I thought.

"Yes, and probably not," said Hammerson firmly. "3M27 would know better than to defy us in such a way, unless he wants to lose yet another family member. I am more concerned about the Woodwards, unless of course everything we've planned so far goes perfectly. However, I think it would be foolish for us not to expect that eventually, something will go wrong. I am confident that as soon as we make one open move against the treaty of '81, Frederic

Woodward will attempt to strip us of our magic. He will want to stop us before we can really get started."

"But haven't we been more or less planning for that for years?" Cornish asked. "All those magical devices you have created—surely they will be enough to continue if they took your magic?"

"To a certain extent, yes," said Hammerson, "and of course, with the three crystals we still have, as long as we have them, we will be able to put up a fight. What I'm worried about is one simple fact: If we lose our magic, we become mortal, and if they can kill us, it will throw the whole organisation into turmoil. What is to be done if that happens? In order to continue our philosophy of magic rule over all, all Hammerhearts will have to rally around the Woodwards and whoever else has been given our magic and persuade them to continue with our plans. Do you see the problem?"

"I see *a* problem," said Cornish dully. "Rally around the Woodwards? That's not gonna happen."

"That's what I thought," said Hammerson, "but more importantly, the Woodwards would not allow themselves to become a centre of power. That, right there, is the entire problem of the thing. So what we need is to ensure that we can't be killed for as long as it takes us to get our magic back if they take it from us. As long as the Sorcerous Crystals exist, the possibility will always remain that we can find a way to take them back. Now, I have been thinking long and hard about ways we can ensure our lives are protected for as long as it takes to get our magic back should we lose it. I have experimented with some of the darkest kinds of magic and now, finally, I have an almost perfect solution."

"Immortality?" said Cornish, his eyes widening. "You can make yourselves immortal without it depending on your crystal chips?"

"Not just us," said Hammerson, "but you too, Hank. I think you have earned this right. More importantly, though, you will hold a very high position in our new regime once it comes into effect. Many will see you as a top target, and they will be right to do so. Killing you would do a lot of damage to our structure. It is important to us that your life be protected too."

"Well, I'm honoured, really," said Cornish, doing his best to look humble, "but can I just ask, if it's not too impertinent, what about your daughter? Does 1H4 get this privilege?"

"Surely she will," said Tankom at once. "She is our future leader. She will have to be protected with whatever this plan of yours is, Arnold."

"I did think of that," said Hammerson, "but on the whole, I think it best if Stella doesn't know about this for now."

"Arnold, have you lost your mind—"

"Hear me out," he said, holding up a hand. "When I tell you what I have in mind, you will understand why it is absolutely paramount that the Woodwards, or anyone affiliated with them, don't know what we have done here. Quite apart from not knowing for sure whether Stella will be truly loyal to us, the truth of the matter is far too visible in her mind. We cannot allow this knowledge to fall into the wrong hands. The time may come when we can protect her, too, but that time isn't now."

"Surely you can give her the protection without her knowing what it is," suggested Cornish.

Hammerson considered this but shook his head. "That may or may not be possible. Knowing Stella's inquisitive nature, she probably won't allow us to protect her without knowing exactly what it is. Besides, there's another reason why I'd rather not tamper with her just now, though I intend to change that as soon as I can."

He meant me, of course, and it made perfect sense. Hammerson didn't know exactly what was between Stella and me, H3, but he knew there was something, and as long as it was there, he wasn't going to risk doing anything to her that might have unexpected consequences.

"Fine, if you say so," said Tankom, though she didn't look very happy about it. "So what is this plan of yours, Arnold?"

Hammerson reached into his pocket and withdrew the Darkness Crystal. Cornish recoiled at the sight of it.

"You've been carrying that around with you?" Tankom asked, startled.

"Only for the last few hours," he said. "Now, what I am going to do is place upon the three of us an enchantment far too powerful to be done with my own magic. That's why we need to use this. I haven't been able to find any spell that will make us completely immortal, sparing nothing whatsoever, but I have worked the magic far enough around that we can come very close. The trouble is that some of the most basic methods of killing—strangulation, for example—cannot be protected against by any kind of magic, unless we were to put iron bands around our necks or something similar. This enchantment will make it impossible for us to be killed, even without our own magic, and completely regardless of what harm may come to our bodies, unless the method of killing is performed directly by another person. We cannot be shot dead, burnt to death, thrown from a cliff, asphyxiated, or drowned, and, most importantly, we cannot be killed by magic, any magic at all."

"Arnold," said Tankom, and there was awe in her voice, "that would protect us against—well, anything. Certainly nothing the Woodwards would consider throwing at us would get around an enchantment like that."

"What about the Light Crystal?" Cornish asked. "If the magic is performed by the Darkness Crystal, wouldn't the Light Crystal be able to undo it?"

"That's the best bit," said Hammerson, now looking positively gleeful. "Quite apart from them not knowing what to do should they get their hands on the Light Crystal, it wouldn't work anyway. The Light Crystal is too good for its own good; it wouldn't want us to be killed any more than it would want them to be killed. No, I'm convinced no magic will lift this enchantment. Neither the Light nor Darkness Crystals would do it, and if that's the case, then not even the Sien-Leoard Crystal could do it. I think we've got this one wrapped up good and proper. As long as the Woodwards don't know about it, they can't begin to find a way around it."

"Arnold, this is some of your best work yet," breathed Tankom. "Are you sure you can do this?"

"Positive," said Hammerson, raising the Darkness Crystal in front of his eyes. "I know the theory. Now it's a simple case of putting it into practice."

"What do we have to do?" Cornish asked nervously.

"Probably nothing," said Hammerson, "but just so that it makes it easier for me, everyone sit still now."

They all went still and quiet. Smiley watched in horror as the room darkened as the Darkness Crystal began to work its evil magic. His horror was all-consuming so that I felt like I wanted nothing more than to turn and sprint from the room, but Smiley wasn't going anywhere. He was determined to see this through. That it was the last thing he would need to watch, he already knew. The evil emanating from the crystal now was so concentrated that it was obscuring the light in the room. Cornish and the two Sorcerers were cast into such deep shadows that it were as though they themselves had become products of the darkness. Hammerson, the one operating the magic, now looked more evil than anything I had ever seen before—he could have been Satan's human counterpart.

It held for perhaps twenty seconds, during which something about the trio seemed to alter. By the time it had finished and the darkness began to subside and retreat to where it had come from, they looked normal again but with a new undefinable air of durability around them, though that could have been Smiley's imagination.

"Did it work, Arnold?" Tankom asked quietly.

"It worked," Hammerson replied just as quietly, and I suddenly realised that the process had drained him almost completely of energy. "We are now as close to immortal as it is possible to be."

"So now if they take your magic—" Cornish began.

"If they take our magic, they still won't be able to kill us," Tankom finished the sentence, her grin almost as evil as the darkness had been.

Smiley didn't need to see any more. For the final time, we lifted from the memory and came to rest back in our bodies in the chamber of memories. I straightened up in my seat and looked around. Everyone was swapping horrified expressions.

"Holy crap," Peter whispered finally. "Holy crap."

"We're in big trouble," said Natalie, almost too quietly for me to hear. "The Woodwards can't possibly know about this. What plan of theirs ever involved strangling the Hammersons?"

Nobody answered. The shock and horror at what we had just seen was almost like a physical presence in the room with us. I felt numb with it, firstly trying to get my head around the enormity of what Arnold Hammerson had done to his own life form, and secondly trying to think of a way that we could finish them off. Whoever did it would need to use their bare hands to accomplish the task. Who among any of us would have the nerve to do that?

Silently, Marc removed the last memory from the playback device and stowed it back in the box with the other memories. Turning to the rest of us, he said, "So what should we do with these memories now?"

"Destroy them," said Natalie firmly. "We've seen all we need to see and nobody needs to know we've seen them. The less people know about this, the better."

"Are you sure?"

"She's right," said James suddenly. "It would be a very bad thing for us if the Hammersons knew how much we know about their secrets. We have to destroy them. I'm sure Smiley would tell us to do the same thing."

Marc put his hand in his pocket and a moment later, the box with all its memories had vanished into thin air. "We should probably get rid of the chairs too," he said, and once we had all got up off them, he vanished them too.

For several seconds, we continued to stand around, just staring at each other. It was as though we had finally reached the end of a long path and now that we were here, we had no idea where we were to go next. I checked my watch. As Marc had predicted, it was almost nine o'clock.

"So, who's up for a hot tub?" Tommy asked the room loudly, and the tension broke immediately.

* * *

As Tommy had told us, the cave containing the hot tubs was close to the one we had used for the water sports when we had camped here three months earlier. We drove our cars all the way into it (they handled the stairs exceptionally well) and ended up in a long, dimly lit chamber well below ground level. The hot tubs were in alcoves off either side of the chamber, each of them with a sliding panel before them to give its occupants privacy if they wanted it. Everyone parked their cars along the chamber, and with Fewul standing guard in the entrance to ensure no one else tried to take a bath, everyone picked out a tub and got in. Most of them went in alone; only Erica and James shared, predictably. Since only some of them had swimwear (Siobhan, Natalie, James, Marc, and I hadn't thought to pack any), I supposed most would be uncomfortable being naked around each other. Still, I wondered how many of them would get out and join someone else in a tub before the night was out.

I was one of the only ones not to get in a tub at all. Despite my earlier misgivings, I had planned to spend the intervening time with Serena anyway, perhaps to take one last sexy memory away from the relationship (and there had been plenty of good times along the way, complications aside), but it was only when we were down there that I realised, I didn't want to share anything with her. It should have occurred to me earlier, since I had already decided to break up with her when we returned, it would be base treachery to be naked with her now. It was harder to decide who I would be insulting more, her or Natalie, who I still hoped I would have a chance with once all this was over. Serena had been most unhappy when I told her I didn't feel like going in a hot tub. She hadn't shouted at me, but I knew that was only because there were people around. She flounced off to take a bath alone, leaving me with Marc, who had also decided not to take a bath.

"I thought there'd be a bit more sharing," he told me quietly. "I mean, isn't this what teenagers dream of? Why aren't they taking advantage of the opportunity?"

"Well, someone wanted to," I muttered, my eyes moving towards the place I knew Serena to be. She had closed her panel so that we couldn't see her. She wasn't naked in there; she'd brought her bikini, perhaps with an idea to go back to that swimming pool we had used last time, but once again, I wasn't fetched.

"I thought Tommy would have wanted to share with someone," he muttered, "and Siobhan and Peter."

"It doesn't matter," I said. Who was sharing with who wasn't very important to me at the moment, though admittedly I was glad that Tommy wasn't trying to get naked with Natalie again. "Listen, I've been meaning to ask you something."

"About tonight?"

"No, about this afternoon. What really happened when you came down here?"

"Eh? What do you mean?" he asked, but I knew I had caught him out.

"I dunno. It just sounded strange when you said you and Tommy didn't take a bath together. You didn't, did you?"

"Come on, do you really think we'd do that?"

"No, but I'm trying to work out exactly what you really did do."

"Aw, damn," he muttered, shaking his head. "I'm not a very good liar, huh."

"Guess not. So what happened?"

He sighed. "When we came down here, there were already a few people checking the place out."

I swore under my breath. "Did they see you?"

I thought they must have, but I didn't want to assume anything just yet.

"No, 'cause of the invisibility veil, but they heard us," he said shiftily as he glanced towards where we both knew Fewul to be standing guard. "I ordered him to stay back at the campsite and guard that, so we didn't get any warning. We might be invisible now, but Natalie never put that soundproof barrier back up after you saw Smiley the second time."

"Damn. Who were they? Was there any trouble?"

"No trouble," he said, shifty as ever. "They weren't Hammerhearts or even Russian officials, just a couple of students, doing the rounds."

"You mean they were in the hot tubs closest to the door?"

Marc nodded, and I thought I knew where this was going.

"They had the panels open?" I prodded, and he nodded again. "Were they girls?" Nod. "Were they—" Now it was my turn to be awkward. "Were they naked?"

"Bare as the day they were born," he said, and I felt my own grin starting to surface.

678

I thought I knew what must have happened, and it was hard to feel bitter towards Marc after all he had been through. "So are you saying that you and Tommy got in with these two Russian girls?"

"It's not as bad as it sounds," he said, almost defensively. "We didn't use any magic. If anything, they persuaded us. They were intrigued by—you know—not being able to see us. That was the thrill for them. There were three or four others farther down, but they wouldn't have seen or heard anything because we closed the panels."

"They didn't see your hovercars?"

"Course not. They're under the veil, too."

"How old were these girls? I thought the Russians were older than us?"

"Yeah. I dunno how old they were, couldn't be more than a few years older than us, but we never troubled them with that information. They won't tell anyone what happened 'cause it'll land them in a whole load of trouble, probably more than us."

"So you spent the afternoon with these two girls," I said, trying to imagine exactly what Marc and Tommy could have been doing for several hours with a couple of foreign girls in a hot tub. "How long were you with them?"

"A few hours," he said. "Their classmates left earlier than them, so we got to move around a bit. You know, it was kind of funny. They knew we were there 'cause they were—you know—touching us, but they couldn't see a thing."

"Wow." What he was describing sounded very exciting indeed. Perhaps he and Tommy had both left their morals at the campsite (assuming Tommy ever had any), but other than that...

"Were they...hot?" I asked, trying to sharpen my mental image of these two girls.

"What? The girls or the tubs?" he asked, grinning broadly.

"Which do you reckon?"

"One was steaming; the other was smoking."

I burst out laughing. I couldn't help myself. Part of me, the frustrated-with-my-love-life part, felt jealousy towards Marc and Tommy for what they had experienced—an experience that I could have replicated with Lena if I only cared about my penis. Perhaps Marc deserved the adventure, but Tommy certainly didn't. Most of me, though, was a little relieved. Perhaps this experience here today would help Marc get over Amelia, if he hadn't already. Perhaps Tommy too would move on from Natalie now. That could only be a good thing. As long as there were no bad consequences of their actions, I couldn't find any reason to complain.

Chapter 42: Along the Corridor

Marc and I left for the main hall at around a quarter to midnight, by which time we knew the hall to be empty and most of the Russians retired for the night. The possibility still existed that one or two could come downstairs and disturb us, but Marc would be ready for them if they did. Most of the others were still bathing at that stage; only Peter and Tommy had so far become bored and retired back to the campsite, each alone; and other than Erica and James, nobody else got in a tub with someone else. I was distinctly nervous about Serena, though. I knew I had upset her, and I wondered if she had spent all that time sitting in her tub, sulking and thinking of ways to pay me back for what I had done. I wondered if she would dump me before I had a chance to dump her. I wasn't petty enough to be upset by that, but I still preferred to do the thing on my own terms.

We didn't speak as we took our hovercars down from the mountain and parked them in front of the main hall. I used the crystal to let us both in, and we moved around to the front of the hall where I had stood with Natalie two nights earlier.

"You ready to go?" Marc asked in a whisper. "Not too sleepy?"

"A little," I conceded, "but I think I'll be fine. You just stand by and make sure nobody comes near me, and for God's sake, don't touch me unless it's an absolute emergency. I wanna do this right so I don't have to come back here again."

"Got it," he hissed back and fell silent.

I leaned back against the wall and tried to relax. It wasn't easy, given that my mind had so many directions in which to turn—Serena, Natalie, Lena in her bikini, the Hammersons and their almost immortality, what I might be about to see here in the main hall. It was a lot, and it was hard to clear my mind of it all. I rested my head against the wall behind me (it wasn't very comfortable) and began counting in my head. One Mississippi…two Mississippi…three Mississippi…four…

I counted to ten and stopped—it was all I needed to do. The counting had driven all else from my mind, and a moment later, it happened. I felt that tug in no particular direction. I heard a young male voice speaking in Russian (he sounded irritated, although it was hard to tell given that I couldn't understand the language) and I tried to hear past him, to any other voices. I remembered that Smiley had said I could also move forward in time, but as I listened, I felt myself moving backwards. I caught a glimpse of a man walking quickly through the door opposite me (walking backwards) and the sensation of moving backwards began to speed up. I concentrated on the feeling of going back in time (the visions before me were also speeding up and the sounds were becoming more distorted and impossible to recognise), and as I did, I began moving even faster. The process was underway.

Keep count, keep count, I demanded of myself. It was absolutely imperative that I know exactly what point in time I am watching before me at all times. This May 2010 visit was just fading out now, so the next one would be February 2010, our camp. I would have to count from that. If February 2010 was visit one, then February 2000 was visit forty-one, and so August 1996 would be visit…fifty-five? Did I have that right? I sure hoped so.

The silence echoed all around me, as did the ever-empty main hall as I continued to zoom backwards through the months during which nothing happened in this place. I passed through our visit, then the next, never stopping to listen or watch what was happening. I saw a lot of rapid movement before me as I stood in a position I was becoming more and more familiar with after having spent so much time in Smiley's shadow lately, but I never concentrated on what I was seeing, only the sense of continuing to move backwards and keeping count of the number of visits I had passed.

As the November 2009 visit faded and I fell once again into silence, my mind turned to the other world Smiley had visited, the one the Honnies inhabited. If my corridor theory was correct, I could probably see just as easily into that dimension as this one if I turned and faced the other way along the fourth dimension. The only problem with that idea right now was the fact that I was on Rock Haulter, a place that probably didn't exist in any form in any other dimensions. Maybe sometime when we returned home, I would have to try that.

Two more visits passed and that was four down. Another year gone and we were now eight down. I felt as though the sensation were speeding up even more now and I actually had to concentrate on slowing down a bit. The February 2008 visit (nine down) went by in a matter of seconds, and I knew that if I kept this up, I might lose count, and then I'd be in trouble. I slowed up a bit and got by the next few years in what would have been perhaps twenty minutes to my physical body. I could still feel myself standing there, now propped against the front wall of the main hall, my head resting uncomfortably against it (I wished I hadn't done that), but it was a distant thing, a very minor part of my overall sensation. It was easy to forget that I even had a body and concentrate much more on what was happening within my mind.

November 2004 gone…that's twenty-two down, thirty-three to go. May 2002 gone…that's thirty-two down, twenty-three to go. November 1999 gone…that's forty-two down, just thirteen to go now. I thought my fifty-five had probably been on the mark now, and I was becoming more and more tense as August 1996 drew ever closer. August 1998 gone…that's forty-seven down, eight to go. One —two—three—four—and there goes August 1997. I had probably been standing there for the best part of an hour now, and I had to remember how much time I had back in the real world. If it was one o'clock now, let's say, I had up to five hours to spend perusing the August 1996 visit for what I hoped to see. I also had to remind myself that I mightn't see anything. What proof did I had that the thing that had caused Moran to flee with me from the Hammersons had happened right here in the main hall? Only the dreams, I supposed, and that would have to do.

Shut up and concentrate, John. There went two more visits, and the one I'm flying by now is November 1996. Just get through this one and to the start of the August 1996 visit and then I'll be ready to start looking. Silence once more as I found myself again between visits, during which time I supposed my parents were on the run and I was just being handed over to Smiley somewhere else in the world. Then I began hearing and seeing things before me and my heart skipped a beat. This was it. I began slowing up again so that now I was able to identify things that were happening around me. The voices were American, I realised, not because I could understand what they were saying but because I identified that they were all speaking quite loudly.

It took a while to locate the start of the visit, but eventually I found the silence again, at which point I stopped and began skipping forward instead until I saw people in the hall again. I stopped altogether this time so that I floated along at the normal speed of time, able to watch and listen to everything around me as though I were standing right there in the hall with them. Or, almost so, excepting the sensation of standing in a tunnel, watching activity from outside it, though I noticed that since I had slowed up, I had moved farther along the tunnel so that I was almost standing in the entrance.

There may have been anywhere between twenty and thirty people in the hall, all facing the front—or rather, all facing the big, blond bloke who appeared to be in charge of the group. The students looked similar to the Russians of today. At least, they were around the same age and, judging by what the man up front was saying, here for much the same purpose. I scanned the crowd for any familiar faces but couldn't see any. Perhaps the Hammersons and whatever entourage they had brought with them would get use of the main hall later.

I sped up my forward movement a bit, watching as the Americans moved upstairs, then came back down and set up their equipment. Again it looked very similar to the Russian setup, although I noticed they had left an open space out the front, where I was standing. The Russians also had a space out the front, but it was significantly smaller than this. It was as though the Americans intended to use it the same way that Chopville High had used it—as a stage.

I continued to skip forward, now passing through the first night of the August 1996 visit. Where were the Hammersons? They had to be here somewhere. They could only have come through with the Americans. Perhaps they were staying somewhere else on the island, like the Hammerhearts who'd come with the Russians? That seemed likely given their reputation, but if that were the case, when would they be coming up here, and for what purpose? I thought back to what Smiley had said: "I believe the tests are done in various places around the mountain. My suspicions with regard to you do involve that hall, however." If that were the case, then maybe the Hammersons wouldn't come to the main hall until after these tests had been performed.

I watched as, the next day, the Americans came back downstairs and congregated towards the front of the hall. The blond man was there again, and I listened as he began directing his students, first dividing them into groups of five, then sending them off to do certain tasks in different areas of the island. It was towards the end of this process when I finally glimpsed a familiar face. The front doors had been opened when the first students had left through it, and as the second last group was about to leave, Hank Cornish walked through it from the outside and positioned himself out of the way to the side of the door, staring pointedly at the blond man who was still barking instructions to the final group of five and who hadn't noticed Cornish yet. Some of the students had, though, and they must have had an idea who he was, or at least who he was working for, judging by the looks of anxiety they were swapping.

The blond man looked up as he sent the last group on their way. He caught sight of Cornish standing there and beckoned him forward nervously. Cornish moved forward, giving the students a wide birth as he skirted around the edge of the hall towards the front. The blond man moved too so that when they came together, they were a good distance to my right. I reminded myself quickly that I couldn't move along the first three dimensions without returning to the present, so I instead strained my ears to pick up their quiet discussion.

"Everyone's out," the American was saying. He sounded very nervous indeed, as though a single mistake on his part could be the death of him. "I've organised a lunch up on the mountain, so the hall will be empty until four o'clock at the earliest."

"Good," said Cornish, whose voice by contrast sounded extremely confident with his position, more so than he usually sounded. I wondered if he had been instructed by the Hammersons to put it on in order to add further intimidation. "Our plans are to organise ourselves in here today, then go out and utilise the mountain for—(he considered)—probably seven or eight days. We'll let you know the exact details later. I trust you have been given a map outlining the areas of the mountain that are, to you, out of bounds?"

"Yes indeed, sir," the American said emphatically. "None of our people will be going anywhere near those areas. Our students are under the strictest instructions."

Not to mention that they'd be terrified for their lives if they stepped out of bounds with the Hammersons around. I was sure that was his subtext.

"Good," Cornish repeated. "You will have access to the main hall most of the time except between two and four o'clock each afternoon while we're using the mountain. Once we're done here, you will have full use of it, but the rules we gave you earlier will still apply. Do you have any questions?"

"Just one," said the American, trying to inject some firmness into his tone. "What will your people do if any of our students do cross your path?"

"I'm afraid that won't be my decision," said Cornish curtly. "There are people much bigger than me in this, and they have expressed their wish for complete privacy. If that is compromised by any of your students, then I can't promise it will be just the offending students who will be punished."

I couldn't see either of their faces from my position, but judging by the short silence that followed these words, the American had paled considerably.

"I'm glad you understand," said Cornish approvingly. "You had better get going, then. My colleagues will be here in less than ten minutes, and believe me, you don't want to be here when they arrive."

I had to admire Cornish's tactics. If he had been instructed to place the fear of Sorcerers in the Americans right from the off, he had done the job flawlessly. The American wasted no time in vacating the building once Cornish had finished, leaving Hammerson's deputy standing alone at the top of the hall. He moved slowly toward the centre of the stage so that he passed right in front of me and stopped, a metre or so to my left. He leaned against the wall beside me while he waited, in almost exactly the same position I had left Marc fourteen years in the future.

I moved slowly forward so that I didn't have to wait for as long as he did, and soon enough the hall was filling up again. There were perhaps fifteen people moving through the hall towards the front, and as I should have expected, nearly all of them were carrying babies. The cacophony of wailing now filling the large space, echoing off the stone walls and ceiling, was enough to bring tears to several people's eyes. I scanned the crowd of Hammerhearts as they approached Cornish, still waiting out the front, careful not to move my head even a fraction of an inch. Arnold Hammerson was there, and he was one of the few not carrying a child. Tankom was right behind him, and she was holding Stella by the hand. Stella would have been two and a half by now, and she already came up to Tankom's waistline. She could walk already and she looked eager to go and explore the hall; her bright blue eyes were darting left, right, and centre, full of innocent curiosity. I also recognised Moran, Hignat, and Wilwog (yes, he had been the one on the train), each of whom was carrying a baby boy.

"Everyone set your children down at the front!" Hammerson bellowed over the din. "Then move over to this side of the stage."

The Hammerhearts took a few minutes to organise themselves, by the end of which the children (around a dozen of them) were sitting on the floor, completely silent due to the spell Hammerson had cast upon them once they were all together (Ather Hignat, Ugine Wilwog, Stella, and I were all in amongst that bunch) while a few feet away, Arnold Hammerson and Cornish stood out the front of a group of Hammerhearts, addressing them.

"Okay, everybody listen up and listen good," Hammerson said to the group, and several people laughed. That seemed to be some sort of Hammerheart joke. "Yeah, yeah, I know I was a little off, but at least this time we can hear each other."

This time there was a great shout of laughter. Apparently the Hammerhearts' sense of humour left a lot to be desired.

"Right, let's be serious now," said Hammerson, and the crowd went silent at once. "You all know the schedule. We have fifteen tests to perform on each child, and if we can keep on top of it, we can get two done each day, perhaps more. Nobody wants to be here for two whole weeks, do they?"

There was a noncommittal muttering.

"Good, very good," he said. "Today, though, we will be remaining in here for a few more hours so that we can verify all the children and straighten out all the details. Everybody pick up your child, and don't worry, they'll stay silent."

Another ripple of laughter.

"Yes, yes, and line up along this wall here. 2C7 and I will get the database ready. Tankom, you just make sure she—(he jerked his head at Stella)—doesn't get in anyone's way."

"Sure, Arnold."

As they began moving again, Hammerson called over the renewed hubbub, "3M27, a quick word."

My heart skipped a beat. Could this be the start of something? I'd been on the point of skipping forward (I knew that nothing could have happened regarding me until I had been tested at least once), but perhaps there would be something worth hearing in this conversation. Hammerson took a few paces farther to the left so that he was even farther away from me, and Moran followed him. It became extremely difficult to hear what they were saying in their new position, especially over the Hammerhearts moving around nearby, but I strained my ears anyway and managed to pick up some of their conversation.

"Who is he with?" Moran asked Hammerson in a tone that sounded close to anger.

Hammerson recited a code that I didn't quite catch, then said more loudly, "Your son, Lucien—" then something else I didn't catch.

"At home," Moran replied, then something else, and then, "Being looked after. He is perfectly safe."

He asked Hammerson another question, and Hammerson replied, "Very soon, 3M27. He is too young to be used now, but as long as we can make use of him when the time comes."

Moran responded angrily, and Hammerson replied, more loudly so that this time, I had no trouble hearing, "He will do as he is told, as will you, 3M27. No buts. He has an invaluable position in our structure now and he will do what is expected of him."

Moran swore audibly and several nearby Hammerhearts chuckled. I felt sure that they were talking about Marc. By the sound of it, he had already been tested here the previous year, and now Hammerson had plans to use him in the future, plans that Moran wasn't particularly happy with. It also sounded like Marc was being kept away from Moran for the time being. Perhaps he was being held somewhere safe within the Hammerson bases until he had grown up a little. It would explain why he hadn't been with the rest of the family when they had gone to find Smiley. As for Lucien, judging by what I had just heard, I assumed he was at home with our mother, so it looked like I was the only one out of the three of us to make the trip down south this year.

That seemed to be it between Moran and Hammerson. The former had gone to get me while the latter had re-joined Cornish and was now interviewing a female Hammerheart whom I didn't recognise. I tried to look around for a sign of Tankom or Stella but couldn't see either of them, so I skipped forward, stopping occasionally to check what was happening around me. The process of checking the babies lasted for the rest of the day. Then, not long after the Hammerhearts had vacated the building, the American students re-entered it, many of them carrying various things from around the mountain, others carrying things they had left with. They stayed in there for the rest of the evening, then went up to bed, emerging early the next morning and setting to work again almost immediately. Some of them left during the morning to do who knew what around the mountain while others stayed in the hall, measuring things on scales or with rulers, while still others busied themselves on computers, entering data or writing reports, again who knew what. Those who had gone out in the morning returned around lunchtime, and then everyone left again, as they had been instructed by Cornish.

I skipped forward until once again I saw Hammerhearts entering the hall through the doors in front of me. The scene was almost exactly the same as it had been when they had entered the previous day, with everyone winding their way through the desks towards the front, and all the babies attempting to raise long passed spirits from who knew what distant realms. Hammerson and Cornish once again took the lead out to the front and waited for everyone to assemble themselves around them before Hammerson silenced the children with a wave of his hand.

"A good morning over all," Hammerson said, looking around at them all. "I'm sorry we only had time for one test today. We'll have to get up early to try and squeeze three in tomorrow. At least almost all of the children have been proven trustworthy—" he threw a nasty glance at Hignat and Wilwog, both of whom seemed to be skulking near the back of the pack. "But just because your child is trustworthy, don't get complacent. It doesn't necessarily mean they will grow to become loyal Hammerhearts; it simply means they will be loyal if they are raised to believe that our way is the right way. Some effort is still required on your part. Each of you remember the statistics given to you from your child's test, I trust? Line up along the wall here so that 2C7 can copy them down one at a time."

And that was all there was to it. They went through this process, with the Hammerhearts lining up along the wall where I was, each of them walking right through me towards where Cornish sat at a computer, copying all the details down as the Hammerhearts recited them. Once that was done, Cornish shut the computer down and the Hammerhearts left the hall again, and nothing more to it. I was disappointed, but I still took a moment to appreciate the irony of Hammerson's words. How he could accuse any other Hammerheart of not putting in the effort to raise their child to believe in the Hammerheart philosophy…

I began skipping forward again, becoming a little impatient now. At what point had things started to happen where I was concerned? How long had it taken them to get around to the test that had identified something odd about me, causing Moran to flee from the island with me? All I had to go on was that the only times they used the main hall were between two and four o'clock each afternoon. It wasn't much but since it was all I had, I skipped forward through the rest of that day and night and the following morning, slowing down as I noticed the Americans hurrying out of the hall again.

I didn't have to wait long for the Hammerhearts to enter the hall again and set themselves up, but as it turned out, there was nothing interesting to report from this second day of testing, nor was there anything worth noting the day after. Finally, on the fourth day of testing, the first of my unusual talents had been unearthed.

"His boy can see ghosts," I heard Hammerson telling Cornish, gesturing to Moran. "I shouldn't be surprised, since 3M27 himself can see ghosts, but I never knew such a talent could be inherited. Certainly neither of his other sons picked up the ability."

But not until two days later—the sixth day of testing—did I finally stumble across a piece of the knowledge that I was seeking. As Moran reached the front of the line with me, Cornish said, "1H3 told me you had the odd result from all the others on that second test. What was it?"

Moran shrugged. "I've never heard of something like this, and let's just say I'll believe it when I see it in action, but apparently, he is able to connect to an external source when he falls asleep."

My insides squirmed at those words. Could this be the beginning of an explanation into the connection between me and Stella?

"What external source?" Cornish asked sharply, typing rapidly.

"John Leoard referred to it as the 'Enlightener.'" Moran spat the word as though it put a sour taste in his mouth. "It's supposed to show him things that are important to him but that he doesn't realise are important in a particular sense. Apparently it can sometimes show him things that he wouldn't understand but are supposed to be treated as warnings. Sometimes it only shows things metaphorically, but most of the time, it is quite clear with its visions." He said all of this as though he had memorised a piece of text that he didn't much value. "Have you ever heard of this 'Enlightener'?"

"No, but I agree with you—all a load of baloney," said Cornish. "Even if it's true, doesn't sound like it can help him in any way, but I'll put it down anyway. Maybe the Hammersons can find some use for it. Do you think it's connected with his ability to see ghosts?"

"Don't see how it would be. For one thing, I'd have it too, but all I ever dream about is—"

"Girls, girls, girls," Cornish finished the sentence, and they both laughed.

So I was connecting with the Enlightener. I wondered if either Lisa or James had ever read about that one, or if any of the girls had stumbled over it during their history of magic projects. It didn't explain my connection with Stella, no, but it explained all the other crazy dreams I'd ever had, like the one in which I had seen Fewul for the first time before ever seeing it in life, or all those dreams about this place, the main hall. Even the visions of fire and darkness I'd been having could have possibly been attributed to the Enlightener, even though I hadn't been asleep the first time I had seen it. As I watched Moran leaving the line and the next Hammerheart moving forward, I made a mental note to do some investigating into the Enlightener once I had returned home.

I skipped forward a little to see whether Hammerson would talk to Moran about me again, but when they began packing up and leaving, I decided it wasn't going to happen and began moving faster forward. If there were any other conversations, they could just as easily happen somewhere else, like wherever the Hammerhearts were sleeping. Through the rest of that day and night and the following morning I went, not slowing down to watch whatever the Americans were doing. Soon enough, I was watching the Hammerhearts enter the hall after their seventh day of testing. Seventh, I reminded myself—seven is supposed to be a lucky number—maybe this would be the day.

It seemed apparent very quickly that I may have been right, too, because all the Hammerhearts were casting curious, nervous, and even worried looks in the direction of Moran, who looked rather nervous himself as he carried the baby towards the front of the hall. Even more notably, neither Tankom nor Hammerson were present yet. Stella was there, but she was by the side of Cornish this time. Apparently this was before she had developed her hatred of him.

"Everybody be quick," Cornish called to the Hammerhearts around him, letting go of Stella and settling himself down by his usual computer. "1H2 and 1H3 will be here soon, and they want the data part done before they get here."

The Hammerhearts hurried into a line, Moran placing himself at the back of it so as to avoid the stares of his fellows. Even so, they still kept looking over their shoulder at him, still looking curious. Most of them had very little to say to Cornish and the line moved rather quickly, but none of them made any effort to move out of the way when their time was done. When Moran reached Cornish, there were still a dozen people lurking nearby, trying to listen to what Moran had to say.

"You all go out the doors and wait for the Hammersons there," Cornish barked at them all, and they didn't dare disobey. Several of them swore under their breath as they traipsed out of the hall.

"So," Cornish now said quietly to Moran, "what's happened to get 1H3 all worried about this one?"

Moran sighed deeply. "You know he thinks he's the most powerful Sorcerer of all time, right?"

"Yeah, he probably is. So what?"

"So Sien and Leoard made a prophecy regarding the most powerful Sorcerer ever," Moran said, and my blood went ice cold in my veins, "and about how only one ordinary boy will be capable of bringing that Sorcerer down."

"So you're saying the test has revealed that this boy is connected with that prophecy," said Cornish, guessing where Moran was going. "Well, you're no stranger to having your sons connected with prophecies, eh, Mr. Seventh Sorcerer?"

"This isn't funny," snapped Moran. "You do realise what will happen now, don't you? He's gonna come back here and murder the boy, and probably me too."

"Are you sure?" asked Cornish, not nearly as worried as Moran. "Because surely if he is the most powerful Sorcerer of all time, and this child is destined to bring him down, 1H3 won't be capable of killing him."

"That won't work," said Moran, "because the prophecy only said that he 'can,' not that he 'will.'"

"Ah," said Cornish, comprehension coming slowly to him. "So what are you gonna do?"

"I—I don't know," Moran almost whispered. "I might just have to—to—"

"To let him do it?" Cornish asked, raising his eyebrows. "Well, it's your choice, but I see a lot more trouble for you if you try to get in the way, Berny. You don't wanna put your life in danger when you don't necessarily have to, do you? Or the rest of your family?"

"Maybe some things are more important than self-preservation," Moran said quietly, and Cornish gaped at him.

"The only things more important than self-preservation are loyalty and courage," Cornish hissed. "You have to be loyal to those you have sworn loyalty to and courageous enough to let go."

"Or loyal to my family and courageous enough to stand up for them," Moran retorted, and Cornish looked almost frightened now.

"Don't do this, man," he whispered, but Moran shook his head.

They were the only two people left in the hall now. Everyone else was outside the doors, their babies currently in the process of scaring all the animals away from the vicinity of the main hall.

"So what are you gonna do?" Cornish asked, still in a whisper.

"Run for it, I guess," he said. "Then find a safe place to keep him. I guess I'll have to give him away if he is to be truly hidden."

"He'll kill you for doing that," Cornish said, a little more loudly now. "He'll kill you, and probably your wife and oldest son too. The Seventh Sorcerer will be safe, but the rest of your family will be seen as dispensable."

"Then we'll all hide if we have to."

No, I suddenly realised, they weren't the only ones in the hall. Stella was still there. She had been behind a couple of desks, wandering around on her own before, but now she came sidling back into view, looking curiously around here, wanting to explore this maze of desks and boxes. There was someone else in the hall too, someone who had, up until that point, been keeping himself deliberately hidden. Arnold Hammerson had been crouching low as he moved carefully and quietly around the far edge of the hall, working his way towards Moran and Cornish out the front. Moran had his back to the place where Hammerson lurked, but Cornish, who was facing the computer but kept turning his head sideways to look at Moran, was the first to catch sight of the big boss over his shoulder. He froze, knowing that Moran's plan to run had just been overheard, and Moran, apparently seeing the look on his face, spun around to look. Hammerson was smiling. It was almost the most evil thing I had ever seen. It would have been if not for what I had seen him do with the Darkness Crystal in Smiley's last memory.

"Is there anything you would like to tell me now, 3M27?" he asked calmly, straightening up and striding forward a few paces.

There were only ten feet or so of clear space now between the two men.

Moran's face was very white. He opened his mouth but was unable to articulate any words. He held the baby in his arms to him even tighter (I had to remind myself that that baby was in fact me). Hammerson smiled still more broadly at him.

"You know, it never struck me until today just how much I value my position," said Hammerson conversationally. "I have known for many years now that I am the best, the most powerful, the most skilled ever to hold a crystal chip, that I compare favourably to both Sien and Leoard, as I possess the extraordinary talents of both, excepting the useless abilities that have no practical use in my life. Yet I never realised until today just how much it mattered to me to have all obstacles removed from my path, to be sure that there can be no threat to my life or my powers from anyone at all. I was always so careful of Frederic Woodward and his family that I never stopped to consider that threats may come from other places, but now that I know, and more importantly that there is only one threat, and still more importantly that it is within my power to eliminate that threat right now—"

"I don't give a damn about your threats," Moran spat, finally finding his voice. "But my son has done nothing to you—none of my sons have done anything to you—and you will not hurt any of them just because of some silly prophecy."

"So you think that Sien and Leoard's prophecies are not to be trusted, do you?" Hammerson asked in a dangerous voice. "My, what a nonbeliever you are. I have studied the prophecies of Sien and Leoard extensively for many years and not one of them do I doubt. Now, 3M27, I advise you to drop that child on the floor before me. There is no reason for you to die along with him. Unless, of course, you give me a reason."

"I will not!" he shouted.

"Good, then do it."

"I mean I won't let you kill him!" Moran roared, and he actually looked like he wanted to fly at Hammerson, to attack him with his bare hands. What on earth could have been more foolish? Hammerson simply stood where he was, smiling at Moran's struggles, and over Moran's shoulder, Cornish watched the exchange nervously, not daring to interrupt.

"Is that so?" Hammerson asked, and now he did take a step toward Moran. "Well, then, since I never gave you a say in the matter, you leave me no choice."

He waved his hand, and Moran was knocked sideways to the floor. Cornish yelled in alarm but none of the magic touched him. Moran had thrown out an arm to break his fall, using his body to protect the baby. He rolled over onto his back, but before he could scramble to his feet, Hammerson struck him again. He spun around in a dizzying circle, and this time the baby flew out of his arms, skidding along the slippery floor to a point about halfway between Moran and Hammerson. My heart was in my stomach because even as Moran roared and attempted to scramble back across the floor to where I lay, I knew there was no hope for him, and therefore no hope for me. How on earth had I survived?

Understanding, full and complete comprehension, hit me in one almighty blow as I saw Hammerson raise his arm to cast the spell that would claim my life, because neither Hammerson nor Moran had seen that I was not the only one on the floor between them. Unnoticed by all, the two-year-old Stella had sidled across to where I lay, apparently curious to investigate the funny looking person who had just gone sliding across the floor in front of her. She reached me at almost exactly the same time as Hammerson cast his curse. It was not the sort of curse that generated a jet of light, like the ones that came from such devices as agonators, stunners, solid-outliners, and others similar, but I knew almost before it happened that the curse that had been meant to kill me had actually hit both of us.

There was a dreadful scream and an explosion of light. The scream could have come from either me or Stella, but as far as I could tell, it only sounded like one voice. Moran and Cornish both screamed too, and even Hammerson let out a yell of despair when he realised what had happened. He and Moran both bounded forward into the light and tried to pull each of their children from it. That didn't work, however, because when it faded, I saw that the two children had been fused together by the head. They were two different people, and yet in that moment, their minds were the same. When the two men realised this, they both roared in dismay.

"Fix them up!" Moran bellowed in Hammerson's face. "Fix them up, you monster!"

"What the hell is this?" Hammerson shouted back, trying to pry the two children apart, looking confused by what had just happened.

"Stop that! You'll kill them both!"

"Stella won't be killed—she's a Sorcerer. Just let me—"

Stella won't be killed because she's a Sorcerer. That had to be it, I thought. I had no way of knowing for sure, but I doubted anyone alive, even Hammerson, would have had a better idea. Stella couldn't be killed by the curse because of her crystal chip, and in that moment when we had been so close and the curse had taken us both, her chip had protected me too. Now it seemed to have fused us together, although as I watched, Hammerson began performing spell after spell to attempt to separate us both. I knew he must have done eventually, since Stella and I were each our own person now, but he hadn't done it completely right, and the only possible reason for that was that he hadn't understood the full extent of what he had done. So consequently, Stella and I had remained bound together all this time, bound by the mind rather than the body, and the full understanding of what he had done could only have come to him very recently, when he attempted to use the undoer to set things to rights. All this understanding came to me in a matter of seconds. Much of it was assumptions, but it made sense. It fit together.

Meanwhile, Hammerhearts outside the hall were banging on the doors, which seemed to have been closed at some point. I couldn't remember seeing that happen but knew that Hammerson must have done it to make Moran's job of escaping just that little bit closer to impossible. They couldn't not know that something was going on in here, even over the racket the babies were probably still making, but the doors were locked up tight and nothing they did made any difference. I wondered if Tankom was out there. She would be able to open the doors, but on the other hand, Tankom didn't know the full story of why Hammerson wanted me dead, so for whatever reason, she must have been off doing something else and Hammerson had never bothered to tell her what had happened here, right down to what he had done to Stella. But if that were true, what about Moran and Cornish? They both knew about this prophecy that had predicted me as a threat. How could neither of them have bothered to tell anyone, not even Smiley, what had happened here? Because he didn't believe, a small voice whispered in my head. Moran didn't know that I was still damaged, and he didn't believe in the prophecy, so he didn't bother to tell Smiley about it.

At last, Stella and I had been separated by Hammerson. He pulled Stella towards him and was now checking her over to make sure she was okay. Moran, on the other hand, didn't stop to make sure I was okay, but scooped me up and took off towards the closed doors. Hammerson, busy with Stella, didn't notice what had happened until the doors flew open and Moran streaked out into the afternoon sun, startling the Hammerhearts out there.

"*Stop him!*" he bellowed, leaping to his feet. "Don't let him get away."

694

Cornish straightened up and made to get out of his seat, but Hammerson rounded on him. "You," he said angrily, "must not know what has transpired here."

"What?" Cornish said, startled.

"This information is for nobody but myself. Nobody must know of my vulnerability, nor must there be any way of retrieving the information from anyone else. You will remove 3M27's record of this test from that database, and then you will not remember any of what has happened here."

He waved his hand at Cornish, whose eyes went suddenly vacant. I knew he had been placed under the domination charm. Cornish turned back to his computer and hit several keys, removing the information he had most recently entered. Hammerson waved his hand at Cornish again, this time removing the memory of the last five minutes, no doubt. He didn't wait for Cornish to recover from the magic but turned and sprinted for the doors, yelling at the Hammerhearts out there as he ran. "Don't let 3M27 get away! Round up the students and force them to search too—he must not get off the island!"

I watched for perhaps another five minutes as the Hammerhearts outside the doors quickly organised themselves into a search party and set off, then for another few minutes as nothing happened, trying to take in the enormity of what I had just seen and trying to think if there was anything more I needed to see. Deciding after a while that there probably wasn't, that the only things left to see now were Hammerson's fury and his attempts to track Moran down, I raised my hand to my face, returning myself to the present-day main hall. I felt once again as though I'd been thrown across a great expanse of nothingness before landing in my body with a dizzying sense of vertigo. I then ran my hand through my hair, feeling that all my muscles were very stiff from being kept so still for so long. I checked my watch and saw that it was nearly four o'clock.

"You're done," said Marc from beside me, and he sounded relieved. "Blimey, John, you look freaked."

"Yeah, you could say that."

"Did you get anything from it? Did you see?"

"Come on, we gotta go see Smiley," I told him. "I'll tell everything when we get there."

Part 6: Villain

Chapter 43: Lure

The day following that fateful night should have been a contemplative one for me. Marc and I had spent a little under an hour with Smiley, not bothering to wake any of the others to come join us (we would catch them up later), and although I had been tired when we had returned to the campsite, I had been unable to get any sleep until nearly six in the morning, and perhaps Marc wouldn't have done much better. However, there was little room to even consider all that I had seen and then discussed with Smiley the next day for the calamity that had taken place while we had all been sleeping.

"Oi, everyone shut up!" James bellowed, staring around at the eight of us present. Only Tommy hadn't risen from his bed yet, and I knew well and good that the chances were fair that he may never do so again. "John, just tell us what happened."

"I don't know how," I said, my whole body trembling with the shock of what I had just seen, "but they've got him—they've got Tommy. They're—they're torturing him."

By 'they', I meant Tankom and a couple of henchmen. Arnold Hammerson hadn't been present.

"What?"

"How?"

"Where?"

"In Germany, probably," I stammered. "They must have got him while he was sleeping there, 'cause they're only two hours behind us where we are now, so it must have been easy. They've already killed his parents over there, Tankom said, and they'll keep torturing Tommy until he gives them what they want, and they won't let him sleep so he can't come back to us."

"But what do they want from him?" Marc whispered.

I remembered back to the things Tankom had said, the threats she had made. "They want—they want this Tommy to hand himself over to them."

"No way, we can't listen to her," said Peter at once.

"Come on, Peter, what do you think Tommy would want us to do?" James asked. "Remember, he's being tortured over there."

"How do they expect him to tell us what they want if they won't let him come back?" Erica asked. "That's just…stupid. We'd be none the wiser if John hadn't just seen it."

"We'd know that Tommy was stuck over there, though," said James. "No, they probably just wanna rub the message in as hard as they can. He'll have to sleep eventually, or faint or whatever. They can't stop him coming back altogether, but if they make it as hard as possible for him now, he'll be more willing to comply when he gets back here. That's probably their thinking."

I shook my head and tuned their voices out, thinking of Tommy and the terror he was in at this very moment. It seemed so stupid that we were still sitting in this campsite while, thousands of miles away, Tommy was enduring unbearable agony. Why on earth hadn't we packed up and set off for the portal already? There was nothing else here for us on the Rock, and meanwhile, one of our Young Army fellows needed us. Fortunately, Marc was in line with my thinking.

"We've gotta get going," he said. "Everyone go pack up your stuff. Nat, you call Amelia and let her know what's happened—the Woodwards will need to know—and John, you set the vessel up so it's ready to go when we get down there. The rest of us will make sure the campsites are good and secure. Everybody move!"

We all scrambled out of our seats and everyone other than Natalie headed for their bedrooms. Most of my stuff was already packed up so my job was very quick. I stowed the life assistant back in my bag, thinking that I would probably never need it again now, and took from the same pocket the shrunken vessel. Through the walls, I could hear all the others hurrying to pack up their things as fast as they could.

"Everyone remember your bags probably won't be invisible," I bellowed as I left my room. I wasn't completely sure about that, as they had been under the invisibility veil when we had arrived, but Natalie had cast it again since then and probably hadn't included the bags. Better not risk it. I heard several unintelligible responses but didn't try to make sense of them.

I gave the two keys to Marc, told him to put them back in the panel in the tree house, and hurried out through the Group F campsite, theirs being the easiest by far. I sprinted down the path towards the main hall and jetty, my mind full of the dream I'd just had. Marc and I would have only had about two or three hours sleep; it wasn't even ten o'clock in the morning yet. I should have been tired, and soon enough I would be, but anxiety for Tommy kept me moving. The dream I'd seen had been set in a chamber of some sort, no doubt one the Hammersons operated, but that gave nothing of its location away. There had been six people present: Stella (obviously), Tommy (the white Tommy, who looked so very unlike the Tommy I knew), Tankom, and three other Hammerhearts, none of whom either I or Stella recognised.

Tommy had been chained to the back wall of the chamber, his arms held out horizontally from his body and each of his feet in stirrups tied to the floor at forty-five-degree angles to his torso. Tankom stood several feet in front of him, agonator and bludginator in hand, and her reinforcements just behind her. Stella was huddled in the corner behind all these Hammerhearts, as though not wanting Tommy to see her there, though that would have been an impossible endeavour. I couldn't remember much of what Tankom had said, but I would never forget seeing Tommy's terrible pain as he was tortured with the agonator, his skin and clothing torn by the bludginator, again and again. I could never forget the sound of his screaming bouncing off the walls and floor, deafening all their ears. Most of all, I couldn't forget the whole point of the operation—lure the dark Tommy to her, so that she could kill him, thereby completing whatever she had messed up thirteen years earlier.

As for Stella, I got most of her position from her babbling thoughts. Tankom had been most displeased that Stella hadn't been able to make any inroads into freeing Sebastian, so had brought her along to this to teach her a lesson. She intended to have Stella torture Tommy some before he fainted or drifted off or whatever, and Stella intended to make her stand right there and simply refuse to do it. She knew Tankom would probably torture her, or at least order one of the other Hammerhearts to do so, but Stella didn't care. She would not turn on one of the people who had once considered her a friend, even if that person already believed she had done just that.

She was also considering ways to get out of there and escape from her father and grandmother for good, but she kept thinking that there were just too many armed and dangerous Hammerhearts around her, and they probably had orders to make sure she didn't try anything. That made me think now that they must be in one of the Hammerheart bases, but where? In Germany still, assuming they had a base in Germany? Or had they perhaps gone all the way back to Chopville? Unfortunately, Stella hadn't been thinking about that, but if Tankom stayed true to her plan, Tommy would know exactly where they were and how to get there.

I reached the main hall, whose doors were wide open but whose interior appeared deserted by the brief glimpse I caught. I didn't stop but swung around to the left and kept running down the path leading to the jetty. When I got there, I saw, clearly for the first time, the ocean liner the Russians had used to get to the Rock. It was tied (or perhaps anchored, I couldn't tell) to one side of the jetty and was considerably larger than the one we had used three months ago, despite their numbers being less than ours had been. I slowed down as I left the firm ground and walked more slowly out onto the jetty, staring out at the waves ahead and thinking again of Tommy.

The rest of the group turned up about ten minutes later, all running down the path from the main hall as I had been, Peter and James in front, Marc and Lucien (Fewul) at the rear, with Tommy floating along on a stretcher behind them along with several bags.

"We're all ready to go," Peter told me as he skidded to a halt on the jetty. "Marc sorted out the campsites so that they'll be secure until the next time we come back here—if we ever do—and Fewul's made sure the Hammerhearts will be able to look after themselves."

"Good," I said distractedly, counting around to make sure they were all here, then withdrawing the vessel from one pocket and the crystal from the other. In one movement, I threw the vessel out into the water and used the crystal to normalise its size. A moment later, it was floating in the water about three feet from the edge of the jetty.

"Everybody just get in and get down," I told them as I moved it right up beside the jetty. "James, you get back to the front. I hope you've got coordinates to get us home."

"Er, close enough," he said shiftily, "or maybe I'll go back on the net and get some more accurate."

I could have sworn. After all the work James had done to work out how to get here, he hadn't given any thought as to how we'd get back. It would have been laughable if the situation hadn't been so serious.

As they all clambered up onto the top of the vessel and raised the trapdoor, I took care of the floating luggage, making it hover along behind me as I too climbed up onto the vessel and headed for the trapdoor. Climbing down, I found that all the others apart from James were just standing around in the dining room, as though waiting for orders. Again I could have laughed on any other day.

"We're ready to go," I said, closing the trapdoor and proceeding to store the luggage away in the lockers. "Anyone wanna get up there and help James?"

"Erica," said several people, and she didn't need telling twice.

"Perhaps you too, John," said Marc, looking at me seriously. "You know there's a chance they'll have people outside the portals, waiting for us to come back out."

My stomach lurched. I hadn't even thought of that.

"Maybe, but it would be a long wait, wouldn't it?" I said, trying to sound reasonable. "I mean, they can't have any idea when we'll be coming back out."

"True, but are you prepared to risk it?"

"Okay, okay, but do me a favour and put him down on one of the beds," I said, nodding at Tommy.

"Sure," said Marc, and he headed for the ladder to the lower level, Fewul following like an obedient dog, the stretcher in his wake.

I found James and Erica in the control room, where Erica appeared to be using the camera again.

"I'm sending this out first," Erica told me. "It was James's idea. He says we have a huge advantage in case there really is someone out there, because we can attack them from this side of the portal but they can't attack us."

"Wow, that's true," I said thoughtfully. "Good thinking, James. So is there anything out there?"

"Haven't seen anything yet," she said, "but I'm not sure if I've left the portal yet."

"How will we know when the camera leaves the portal?" James asked, looking down at the control panel. "I don't suppose there's anything on here that would tell us that, is there?"

"It hasn't," I said, dipping my hand to my crystal to make sure, "but it shouldn't be hard to work out. Just look for a sudden change in the water or the sky. James, shouldn't you be working on the coordinates?"

"I'll do that once we're out," he said. "Get this part over first, and then I can go downstairs."

"Right," I said, sitting in the seat I had occupied last time and leaning back, becoming a little impatient again. Tommy was being tortured as we sat here so sedately.

It took perhaps ten minutes for Erica to determine that the coast was clear for us to leave after all ("Unless they're invisible, but how we can plan for that," said James nervously), by which time we had made the ship invisible again and were moving slowly away from the jetty, due north. As I was no longer needed up front, I found myself unsure what I ought to do with myself. If I'd had my way, I would have teleported myself straight to Tommy and launched an attack on Tankom and those working with her, but I knew I'd be in awful trouble if I did that, even if I could. I supposed the thing for me to do right now was go downstairs and just hang out, like the others were doing, but the thought of who was down there was enough to turn me off that idea. Natalie and Lena were down there somewhere, and so was Serena. I hadn't said a word to Serena since the incident of the night before, and through all that had happened, she hadn't made any attempt to come and talk to me. Yet I still found

I wanted to wait until we had returned home before breaking up with her, and I thought I had a good reason to remain on the back foot this time—such an event couldn't possibly go unnoticed by all the others in such an enclosed space, and I didn't want a big deal to be made of the demise of our relationship. Perhaps Serena would anyway, but if I could have my way, I would prefer Natalie (and especially Lena) not to be around at the time and not to know until after my initial shock had worn off, because I had no idea how I would feel after the deed had been done.

So in the end, I just stewed over these unpleasant thoughts right up to the point when James said, "Okay, we're out. Let me just get us a distance from the portal, and then I'll go downstairs."

"Sure," said Erica, resetting the camera so that it followed automatically above the vessel, then sat back in her seat as I was doing and folded her hands in her lap. "Boy am I relieved we got out of there without any trouble."

"I'm a little surprised by that, actually," said James, looking at me now. "I'd have thought the Hammersons would be almost desperate to know when we would be leaving the Rock."

"I'm not sure the Hammersons even know we're here, though," I said reasonably, only half my mind on what I was saying. "It's not like the Hammerhearts actually saw who we were. They can only know we're with the Woodwards. Also, they're probably relying on the Hammerhearts they've stationed on the Rock to let them know when they think we've left. Not a very good plan, huh."

"No, it's not," said James thoughtfully, "which makes me think that they aren't taking the matter as seriously as they ought to."

"Why would they?" Erica asked. "I mean, what do they think we're doing here? They can't possibly know we were seeing Smiley; otherwise, they'd be putting their efforts into finding him there rather than us. They probably think that as long as we're out of the way, they need not worry about us."

"They won't like it if we suddenly turn up and ruin their plans, then," said James, "which is probably what we're gonna have to do."

I tuned out again, my mind returning at his words to Tommy. I marvelled at how a situation like this could make everything else seem so insignificant. After everything we had been through recently, after the disagreements, the fights, after I had almost knocked him out of the tree house—none of it seemed to matter anymore. The whole lot of it had been thoroughly eclipsed. Now all I cared about was getting Tommy back, rescuing him from the terrible place in which he was now being held, and making those responsible pay for what they had done. At the end of the day, Tommy was still my mate, and whatever else went on between us, mates had to pull together at times like this. He and I were in the same boat, after all: We were both being hunted, and we were both on the same side in this war.

My mind whirled around these thoughts, and many others concerning Serena, Natalie, Lena, Stella, and even Amelia a little, not to mention all that I had learnt about myself and the things Smiley had told me that morning. Amazingly, I was so preoccupied that I barely noticed how quickly the time flew. It seemed like no time later that James said, "I think we're far enough away. Forty miles, that ought to do. I'll go get some coordinates for somewhere close to the west coast. Be back in a bit."

"I might as well come down with you," Erica said, and the two of them left me there, quite alone. I didn't mind. I still preferred to be up here than down there, even with the possibility that any of them could come and find me here if they chose. I decided to move across to James's seat, then just sat there as I had been doing for a while now, thinking again, occasionally coming out of my reverie to look briefly out the window at a whole load of nothing before sinking back into my thoughts again.

It was time to think practically about what lay ahead for me. Everything Smiley had told me was very important, of course, but in light of everything else going on, that would have to take a backseat now. The business with Serena too, that would have to wait until after we had dealt with the current crisis, as would working out how to deal with Lena, or even working out if I really wanted to deal with Lena. I only knew that I couldn't stand to let it—all of it—drag on much longer. Who knew what sort of state we would all be in once this was over? Who knew how Tommy would be feeling? That thought led to another, most alarming possibility that I hadn't considered until now: What if this business somehow made Tommy seem more attractive to Natalie all over again? Certainly it had done enough for me to feel I could forgive Tommy his past misdeeds. Would Natalie be feeling the same? Worse, could she be feeling regretful over what had happened between them, was perhaps sitting down there blaming herself for their argument of a few nights previous?

I shook my head hard, trying to rid it of these thoughts, trying to get back to what I wanted to think about.

"What are you shaking your head for, hey?" a voice asked behind me, making me jump.

It was Marc, probably the one person in the world I could handle speaking to at the moment (well, perhaps Peter would fall in that category, too). He squeezed himself between two seats and plonked himself down in Erica's vacated seat. Lucien, who had followed him up, took the seat on my other side. I had to remind myself yet again that it wasn't really Lucien.

"Ignore him," said Marc quietly.

"What's going on down there?" I asked, preferring to ask rather than answer at the moment. "Were you bored enough to come up here?"

"Actually, I was wondering why you never came down," he said, "but yeah, I was kinda bored."

"So what's happening down there?" I repeated.

"Nothing, really," he said, a little hesitantly, and my mind strayed to Serena. "James is on a computer, and Erica's with him. Peter was teaching Siobhan how to play some card game, and the others—" He broke off, and I knew who the others must be. There were only three people left unaccounted for. "Well, I was sitting with Lena before, but she was just reading so I didn't bother staying."

"Oh," I said, my mind ticking over. Marc had thrown Lena plenty of interested looks over the last few days, and he had been just as affected by her bikini display the previous evening. Could he, possibly, solve one of my problems for me? If Lena's attraction to me was based on something physical (and I had no proof that it wasn't), Marc, who looked a lot like me, only a bit older and a few inches taller, ought to be more appealing to her. The idea that she could move off me and onto him was like a kick to the groin, but not a kick I didn't feel I thoroughly deserved. It came back to what I'd been thinking in bed a few nights earlier—I was still holding onto a fantasy of being with Lena even though I wanted to be with Natalie more, even though I knew that as long as they were both in the picture, I probably wouldn't be able to settle for either, or anyone else. It should be simple, so why wasn't it?

More for something to do than because I really cared, I checked my watch. It was nearly midday. For the first time, I began to notice two things I hadn't felt up until now, that my brain had refused to acknowledge. I was tired, very sleep deprived, and also very, very hungry, having eaten nothing whatsoever since dinner the previous night.

"Has anyone bothered to eat out there?" I asked now.

"No, but perhaps we ought to call lunchtime, since we missed breakfast. Or actually," he said thoughtfully, "maybe we should call it dinner, since we're about to lose six hours."

And so we did, or rather, Marc did. Part of me would have liked to stay in the control room keeping watch, but my stomach was ready to start singing Ave Maria and I knew I had to put it first. So I followed Marc out into the little dining room where we were eventually joined by all the others, except James, who was still downstairs on a computer, and Tommy, who had been placed comfortably enough on one of the beds. I knew the possibility still existed that he could pass out in Germany and re-join us at any time, but none of us really believed that would happen while we were on this vessel.

Lunch, or dinner, or whatever meal it was, was an extremely quiet affair. The eight of us present (nine if you counted the Beast of Magic, who sat quietly beside Marc and barely moved an inch the whole time) didn't speak to each other at all but simply ate in silence. I was sitting between Marc and Peter and avoided eye contact with all the others, not only because of my own internal turmoil regarding three out of the five females on board with us but because a feeling seemed to be running through the room that I was responsible for the current predicament, whether because I had led the group to the Rock in the first place or because I had returned with news of Tommy. It was probably my imagination, I hoped, but the idea that some of them were blaming me for placing them in this position was both unfair and hurtful.

I was extremely relieved when James came to me half an hour later back in the control room and told me he was ready to go with the teleportation. Erica followed along right behind him, gazing at her boyfriend with an expression somewhere between pride and envy.

"It's probably not the same spot we teleported from last time," he said, "but it's close enough. I used Google Earth to find another secluded beach and get the coordinates for it. We'll be able to get out there and teleport to the shore. Is that okay?"

"Do you hear me complaining?" I asked. "Come on, let's do this thing."

We took our seats at the controls, James and I swapping so that he would have access to the teleportation device. He entered his coordinates, braced himself, and pressed the teleportation button. For the second time, we went through that feeling of being suspended, unable to move an inch, for several seconds, before everything returned to how it had been before. I raised my head and looked out the window, but apart from the sun, which had moved rapidly across the sky during the teleportation, these choppy waves didn't look much different from what we had left behind. I lowered my eyes to the display screens and saw a different story. We appeared to be facing north, but Erica's camera, which she was already swivelling around to get a good view of all directions, picked up a not-too-distant coastline off to the east.

"Good stuff," I said, taking the controls and turning the vessel around to face the coast. "How close do you reckon we can get to it?"

"Well, logic suggests that you keep going until you find yourself beached like an unfortunate whale," said James, smirking slightly.

"Be serious, man."

"I am. Just go as far as you can. This thing won't get damaged. It doesn't matter since we'll be teleporting onto the shore, anyway. That's how we got on here in the first place."

And so we did, getting rather closer than I had expected before feeling the bump that meant we had made contact with the ground beneath the waves. Ten minutes later, we were all standing firmly on that ground, after having made ourselves visible, both by way of the vessel and Natalie lifting her invisibility veil. I had used the crystal to teleport all of us along with our luggage from the top of the vessel onto the shore and to shrink the vessel as I had done on the Rock. Like the flying capsule I had used to penetrate the Hammerheart base, I thought the possibility existed that I could need it again, though I couldn't be bothered putting a button on it to shrink it at the moment. Now that we had returned to the country, the most important matter was Tommy and those terrible people torturing him.

Natalie teleported us this time, from that secluded beach straight back into Hamster's Stretch Reserve, where the sun had already set in the east and it was much darker than it had been on the opposite coast. As I looked around myself, I experienced an unexpected feeling I couldn't quite identify. I only knew that I was extremely glad to be back home again, although I had to remind myself that I probably wouldn't be here for very long. The ten of us turned and, without a word, hurried down the path through the park to the eastern end where the Woodwards' home overlooked the river. To my surprise and perhaps pleasure, we found Amelia waiting for us just outside the study. It was great to see her again, but I had to suppress the wave of desire I felt. Thankfully it was smaller than I had expected it to be. She could be my best female friend, but no more than that.

"Hey, you all," she cried, leaping forward and hugging Natalie. "Come straight through. Dad wants to know exactly what happened over there."

"You haven't told him?" Natalie asked, somewhat surprised, as the rest of us followed her into the study.

"Yeah, but he wants to hear it from you," she said, with half a glance at me, and I wasn't entirely sure if they were talking about Tommy or what else had happened on the Rock.

She grabbed on to James and Peter first and marched them through, while Natalie took Erica and Serena, leaving the rest of us standing around in the study, just looking at each other.

"So what do you reckon?" Marc asked me.

I shrugged. "Guess it's good that she was waiting for us, but it's hard to tell if they're panicking in there like we are."

Marc scowled. "Probably not. I can imagine Mr. Woodward won't be too urgent about the whole thing, knowing him. He didn't mind leaving you in the Basement for nearly two days so long as he could get you out quietly. He'll probably wanna wait 'til Tommy wakes up before deciding how to act."

"I hope you're wrong," I said uneasily.

The two Sorcerers returned a moment later. Amelia latched onto Lena and Siobhan while Natalie took me and Marc. Fewul followed along independently behind Marc, bringing with him our luggage and the stretcher upon which Tommy was lying again. The rest of them were milling around at the head of the corridor. There was no reception committee waiting for us this time. Probably news of our return hadn't made its way around the base yet.

"I was just saying to the others," Amelia said, "you all take your bags up to your rooms, then come straight back down to our living quarters. You'll get a chance to unpack later. Try not to get held up. I can take Tommy up to his room; that's probably the best place for him to be kept."

So we sorted through the bags, which Fewul obligingly crashed to the floor for us (I clearly heard something break inside one of them), taking that which belonged to each of us and lugging them down the corridor to our living quarters and up the stairs to the third floor. Amelia brought up the rear, now levitating Tommy's stretcher as Fewul had been doing, and Fewul himself followed as ever right along behind Marc. I would have liked a moment to sit in my room and gather my thoughts, and I did in fact take a moment in the toilet before going back downstairs, but my exhaustion was catching up with me again, and as desperate as I was to do something for Tommy, it was becoming increasingly difficult to keep myself going.

Five minutes later, we were in the Woodward living quarters, which had been left open to admit all of us, where we found Mr. Woodward, Mr. Fletcher, and both their mothers waiting for us all.

"Good to see you all back safely," Mr. Woodward said, somewhat ironically in my opinion. "It's a pity it had to go like this, though. I could ask plenty of questions about what you got up to while you were away, but it looks like there is a more urgent matter at hand. John, go on."

"Tankom's got Tommy," I told him. I assumed Amelia had already told him, but I had to go over everything I had seen. "I don't know where. I only know that it was in some sort of chamber and it was probably underground. There were a couple of Hammerhearts with her, as well as Stella. They killed his parents and were torturing him. She kept telling him that when he passed out or she let him sleep, whenever that was, he had to bring himself—the body he has here—to her, so that she can kill him. She's gonna keep torturing him if he doesn't do it. Will probably end up killing his German body as well."

The others had all heard this story before, but hearing it again seemed to make everyone pale. Amelia looked fearfully toward her father, and I was pleased to see that he too was looking rather tense. He considered for several moments before speaking again.

"It's going to be very difficult to act without knowing exactly where they are. Are you quite sure that Stella didn't give any hint of her location away in her thoughts?"

"Positive. The only thing she was thinking that might help is that she knew she was surrounded by Hammerhearts, because she was thinking about trying to make a run for it. Other than that, though—" I shook my head sadly.

"Do you think," he said, and he looked very awkward now, "that perhaps you might be able to go back to her and see if she gives any more away?"

"What?" I said, startled. "You mean make myself see into her mind? I don't think I can. I've never been able to make it happen on command. I can't control it at all."

But a small selfish part of me felt suddenly hopeful. Would he let me go back upstairs and sleep? It seemed like a bit much to hope for, and I had to mentally chastise myself harshly for even thinking it.

"Never mind," said Mr. Woodward, pulling himself together and turning to Marc. "Not all is lost. There are ways of tracking people down. Even if Tankom has somehow made herself untraceable, I doubt very much that Tommy is. Marc, do you think you could help us out?"

"Where are they keeping him, Fewul?" Marc asked the beast, who was sitting placidly beside him, still in Lucien's form.

"He is being held in the execution chamber on the bottom level of their base in Berlin, Germany," he told us. "Tankom is no longer with him. She is currently preparing her preferred method of execution for when this Tommy has reached her. She intends to let him rest within a few hours of now."

"Is Stella still with her?" Natalie asked.

"I believe not, although since she is untraceable, I cannot be sure."

"Okay," said Mr. Woodward, pulling himself into a more upright position and looking at Mr. Fletcher. "We will need to assemble a small group of people to go over there and find a way to get him out. We won't be able to get inside because of the spells set up to stop Sorcerers entering their network, but we may be able to help from the outside. Perhaps Chester and Charlie? They're both free at the moment."

"Greg Pont," Mr. Fletcher suggested. "Er, who else? We should probably have at least six of them."

"I could go," Marc offered, raising the Hero Crystal. "They won't be able to stop this kind of magic getting in."

"That's a brave offer, but I think you've done enough for now," said Mr. Woodward, surprising us all. "A job this dangerous is best left to those of us with a little more experience."

"I have experience," Marc retorted angrily, "and I've got a better chance—"

"No," said Mr. Woodward very firmly indeed. "I'd much rather all of you remain behind today. This is too dangerous for teenagers to be involved in, and I see no reason why we need any more of you to put yourselves in deadly situations when more experienced fighters could do the job just as effectively. In any case, we need someone to let us know when Tommy wakes up and what he has to tell us. That could be very useful information."

My mind was reeling. This was a complete backflip on the policies Mr. Woodward had carried prior to now. He'd never had a problem sending us off on potentially dangerous jobs before, something that James wasted no time in pointing out at that moment.

"True, James, but this is slightly different," said Mr. Woodward, firm as ever. "We are talking about a dwelling that, by the sound of it, is loaded with watchful Hammerhearts, ready for the slightest sign of trouble. Many of us have been in positions like that in the last war, but that is experience you haven't had."

"Maybe I haven't, but Marc and John have," said James calmly.

Mr. Woodward shook his head, stubborn as ever. "They will be expecting trouble, James. All the times Marc and John have infiltrated their bases have been when the Hammersons weren't prepared. They were only prepared once, and in case you've forgotten, it cost a young girl her life."

Now that was way below the belt. They all looked quickly at me for my reaction. It could have been just about anything, but before I could say or do anything, Lillian spoke quickly.

"Frederic is right. It's easy to think you know what you're up against at your age, but the fact is there are a multitude of situations that you probably haven't even contemplated. Too many of your friends have already been taken by this. There is no reason why any more of you should follow."

I still wanted to fire something back, mainly because they were laying the blame squarely on my shoulders, but at the same time, I knew she was right. It was very similar to what Dad and Charlie had told us months earlier, and they had certainly been right, for two weeks later, Amelia, Peter, and I had found ourselves held hostage in the Basement. Now, though—now it meant that we had to sit back here tonight, not knowing what was going on, not knowing if Tommy had been rescued or if the Woodwards' fighters, perhaps Dad and Charlie themselves, were in mortal danger. It was grossly unfair.

"Good," said Mr. Woodward, clapping his hands and getting to his feet. "So, Brian, you go and gather up the best fighters in the base who you can find. The rest of you are free to go—oh, except you, Marc. You remain here for a moment longer. We need more information about where we should go. You stay back a moment too, John; I have a job for you too."

Good, I thought, because there would have been a lot of grumbling from me if I hadn't been allowed to do anything to help. The others trooped out of the living quarters, and I distinctly heard Peter muttering to James, "…should just go over, anyway."

Mr. Woodward waited until it was just he, Marc, Fewul, and me left in the room before speaking again. "John, a situation seems to have arisen inside the prison yard you created."

I groaned aloud this time. It had nothing to do with Tommy after all. "What's happened?"

"I'm not quite sure," he said. "Brian has been keeping an eye on them while you have been away, and two days ago, something happened in there that he's not quite sure about. The prisoners are refusing to tell anyone. They say they want you to sort it out because you were the one who created their yard. They're getting pretty edgy, so you had better go and fix it before we have a revolt on our hands."

I felt angry now. I couldn't think of any reason why a Sorcerer couldn't have fixed just about any problem inside that prison. Trying hard not to sound accusing, I said, "Why didn't he examine their memories? I put that feature in there for exactly this purpose."

"Because he does not wish to mess anything up," said Mr. Woodward firmly. "Don't look at me like that, John. It should only take you a few minutes, and then you will be free for the rest of the evening."

"Yeah, 'cause that's exactly what I was looking forward to," I muttered darkly, turning on my heel and leaving the room.

Chapter 44: Lifeline

Dealing with a bunch of resentful Hammerhearts was the last thing I wanted to be doing tonight, especially as what I wanted more than anything was to be on the other side of the planet, knocking Hammerhearts aside to get to Tommy. It didn't look as though I had a choice, though, so grudgingly I left the Woodward living quarters and proceeded down the corridor to the entrance to the prison yard, thinking about how I ought to do this. Mr. Woodward had made it sound as though I would need to find out from the prisoners what had happened in there, which would mean having a civil conversation with at least one of them. Who would I talk to? Who, in fact, would want to talk to me?

When I entered the dark prison yard (dark because it was dark outside), I saw that it was almost completely deserted but for a group of Hammerhearts in the far right corner. There might have been half a dozen of them over there. Everyone else appeared to be inside the building, which was probably sensible of them. I made my way over to them, noticing that they hurried to form a tighter group as they noticed my presence, as though worried I would attack stragglers. I was already halfway there before I saw the one person in the yard who hadn't grouped up with the rest of the Hammerhearts, and hatred rose inside me at the sight of him: Sebastian. When he saw that I had seen him, he raised a hand and beckoned to me to join him. Great, I thought sourly. Instead of rescuing Tommy, I got to have a conversation with the person who had betrayed my sister to the Hammerhearts. Oh goody.

"John," he called pleasantly to me, as though no death had ever come between us, "I'm glad you're here. Something's come up we're not quite sure about."

"What would that be?" I asked coldly as I reached him.

Sebastian jerked his thumb in the direction of the cluster of Hammerhearts. "Old Patty Striker got a bit depressed lately. He was talking a lot about how his family wouldn't know where he was and probably thought he was dead and that no one gave a damn about them. Anyway, a couple of days ago, he—he went and took a high dive."

My stomach lurched. "What? He—he jumped from a window?"

"Went right through it," said Sebastian, pointing up to a window that was too dark to see.

I felt a mixture of disgust and guilt. Not guilt that he had taken his life but guilt that his family, who could have been completely innocent for all I knew, were probably worried about him.

"Anyway," Sebastian went on, "there are a couple of things here. We had to leave his body over there because we're not sure what will happen if we try to bury him, just in case there are any spells to prevent us trying to dig our way out."

"You wouldn't be able to," I said, remembering the way I had designed the box. "The ground probably goes down maybe a few feet before you can't go any farther. Maybe—" I considered the problem. What was the best thing to do about this? I scowled because it looked like the problem would take a while to sort out after all.

"Well, we can get to that later," Sebastian went on. "The other thing we wanted sorted out was the window. I expect he probably tried to open it before he went through it—I dunno. In any case, it's smashed now and—well, we don't need a broken window in the place, do we? People will be using the broken glass to do themselves in next."

"Guess you're right about that." I shrugged bitterly.

Sebastian turned and strode quickly away, and I had to hurry to follow. He headed straight for the group of Hammerhearts, who all scattered out of our way. As they moved, I caught sight of the body lying at the base of the building—thank God it was dark, was about all I could think. Meanwhile Sebastian had pushed open a door and was climbing the stairs just inside it. I followed almost at a run. Sebastian was walking very quickly indeed, quicker than was necessary, I thought, taking long strides so that I had to put on a bit of extra speed just to keep pace with him. Up three flights of stairs we went, and still he didn't slow down. Along an empty corridor we went now, most of its doors closed but a few farther down standing ajar. Sebastian didn't go far before pulling sharply into the second door on the left.

"In here," Sebastian called loudly as I followed him into the room.

I looked around him and saw that most of the glass in the window was missing, although large, jagged shards still clung to the frame. I stared at it in revulsion. How could I have been so stupid as to forget to make the glass unbreakable? It should have come naturally, especially after what Marc had said about the prisoner diving off his bed.

"You reckon you can fix that?" he asked, taking me by the arm and dragging me around the bed to the window.

"Sure," I said, "but—"

I stared at the broken window, my mind turning over, trying to work out what the prisoner must have done. A lot of glass seemed to be missing from the window, I thought. Too much? If he was going to die, surely he wouldn't have cared how much glass was in the window as long as there was enough for him to fit through it. Moreover, the part he would have gone through was the bottom of the window. There was nothing for him to use to climb higher up the window, yet long shards stretched upwards from the bottom of the frame, at least five or six inches up. It hardly made sense. I honestly couldn't imagine how he had jumped from the window, leaving it in this state, but now wasn't the time to dwell on this. Sebastian was waiting just behind me and I could tell that he was starting to lose patience too.

"Yeah," I said more strongly, dipping my hand to my pocket and the Sien-Leoard Crystal that rested there, "no problem. This should be easy to—"

Blinding white light, the Light Crystal times a thousand, filled my world and overloaded my senses as something large, hard, and heavy smashed into the back of my head. I lurched forward involuntarily, almost falling out the window myself in fact, but hands grabbed my shoulders and threw me roughly backward into the centre of the room. I felt my back hit the bed and slid sideways onto the floor, where I came to rest, my whole world spinning horribly and my head aching fit to split. I scrambled to get back to my feet, but a large foot came down hard on my chest, forcing me back to the floor, upon which I hit my head again. I shook myself hard and tried to squint up into the room, into which I could hear people pouring. There, standing right above me, his foot pressing down on my chest, a horrible grin on his stupid face, was none other than Ugine Wilwog, looking more pleased with himself than I had ever seen.

"*You!*"

Horrified, I scrambled to reach the crystal in my pocket, but too late. Hands grabbed my wrists and forced them above my head, and although I struggled with all my might, heaving my shoulders and kicking my legs and moving every part of my body I could, it was no good. They had no intention of letting me go.

"Sorry about the ruse, Playman," drawled a most unpleasantly familiar voice somewhere above my head, and rolling my eyes upward, I caught sight of Ather Hignat standing above me, looking exceptionally pleased with himself. His grin was as broad as Wilwog's but nowhere near as stupid. "You," he barked at someone, "get that crystal out of his pocket and give it to Sebastian, and don't drop it; apparently it's invisible."

"Why me?" Sebastian asked from some distance away. It looked as though he didn't want to come near me now that he had betrayed yet another person.

"We've discussed this. You're the one who knows best how to use it, being in with the jerkoffs for as long as you were," said Hignat smoothly.

I felt a hand rummage in my pocket and remove the Sien-Leoard Crystal. I squinted sideways at the person. It wasn't someone I recognised, but he was leering delightedly at me. I blurted out a string of obscenities that would have made Mum and Marge faint, but above me, Hignat and Wilwog grinned even more broadly.

"We ought to wash your mouth out, Playman," sneered Hignat. "You," he addressed the person who had stripped me of the crystal, "go get a cake of soap and a cup of water from one of the bathrooms and bring them back here."

Wilwog laughed loudly above me, but my insides went cold. "You—you—" But that was all I could say.

Hignat ignored me completely. As a pair of footsteps left the room, he turned to Sebastian, to whom the crystal had now been handed. "We have to act quickly, before the Sorcerers realise something's wrong. You know the deal."

"Sure," said Sebastian. He sounded unwilling, but I knew he would go along with whatever their plan was now that it had progressed this far.

"The rest of you go round up the others and tell them to wait in the yard," Hignat called, and there was a great scurrying as everyone left the room so that only Hignat, Wilwog, and Sebastian remained to hold me in place. Nobody was holding my arms anymore, but it hardly mattered—Wilwog's foot was keeping me firmly in place. I knew that my only hope of throwing it off was to settle down for now and take him by surprise in a minute or so, so I rested my arms by my sides and glared up at Hignat.

"You're so dead," I growled at him, but I knew they were empty words. They had unknowingly picked the best possible time to escape, while four of the six Sorcerers were out of the base. I could only hope that Fewul would think to tell Marc that there was trouble.

"On the contrary, Playman," drawled Hignat, quite at his ease with the situation, "the three of us will be rewarded most handsomely when we hand over that invisible crystal to the Hammersons. I've heard that it's the most powerful out of all of them, certainly more so than any of the Sorcerers. Promotions all 'round, I daresay. Hurry up with the bag," he added to Sebastian.

I couldn't see Sebastian from where I lay, but at Hignat's words, the plan they had concocted was falling into place in my mind. Sebastian would leave the base alone, invisible and with the crystal, probably through one of the level-two rooms he had become so adept at using prior to his discovery, with the rest of the prisoners inside an extender-case on his back. I had to admit that as long as they acted quickly, they would probably be well clear of the base before anyone thought to come and check up on me.

"You'll get caught before you get out," I snarled at him, knowing it probably wasn't true but only trying to plant the seed of doubt in their minds.

"You don't seriously believe that, do you?" Hignat asked, almost laughing. "Sebastian could probably knock a few of them off as he passed and still they'd have no idea what's going on."

"Dunno about that," said Sebastian uncertainly. "I thought the plan was to do it as quietly as possible."

"Of course it is!" Hignat snapped. "I'm just saying, if it has to come down to a fight, what chance do they stand against the almighty crystal you hold?"

Sebastian didn't answer, and the room fell into an uncomfortable silence, during which I contemplated how I could possibly cause enough of a disturbance to make Wilwog raise his foot. I could only see one possibility: If I could just raise my right arm high enough, I may be able to punch him in the nuts, but I didn't think my arm was long enough, and one failed attempt would just about be the end of me. My leg would probably be long enough, but the angle at which I would have to raise it to point my foot in the right direction was extremely acute. I could try to knee him there, but that presented the same problem—I probably wouldn't be able to reach, and one failed attempt…

The silence was broken by the return of that person who had been sent to the bathroom. Above me, Wilwog was grinning piggishly, and Hignat said, "Excellent. I'll take those. You hold his wrists for me."

I attempted to beat his hands away, throwing everything I could into the blows. It almost unbalanced Wilwog, but he steadied himself and pressed down harder on me, taking my breath away long enough for the person to grab my wrists and hold them above my head as they had been earlier. Hignat then knelt down beside me and pinched my nostrils shut, and of course, stupid me actually thought he was only doing it to humiliate me further and automatically opened my mouth so that I could breathe. I realised my mistake a split-second too late. A moment later, there was soap in my mouth and Hignat wasn't about to let it go. It tasted revolting, and my stomach cringed at the thought that I might have to swallow it.

"Very good, Playman," Hignat drawled, letting go of my nose and picking up the cup of water. Holding the soap firmly in my mouth with one hand and the cup in the other, he very carefully poured the cold liquid into the tiniest gap between the soap and the side of my mouth. Some of it ran down my cheek and chin, but I barely noticed. It was well beneath the rest of my discomfort. As the water mixed with my saliva, the free space inside my mouth became more and more moist, and it was having an effect on the soap. I had managed not to swallow so far, but I wouldn't be able to hold it together for long.

"Just a little longer, Playman." Hignat grinned down at me. "I can see that your mouth is already a little cleaner. We just need to let it sink in a little more. If you'd given us liquid soap instead of solid stuff, this would have been done more quickly, but I guess you didn't think of that."

It was too much. There just wasn't enough room left in my mouth for any of the expanding liquid, and the fact that I was lying on the floor made it even worse. It swished to the back of my mouth, my throat opened reflexively, and the game was lost. Hignat saw my Adam's apple move, and his expression became satisfied.

"It's done," said Sebastian from several feet away, and I had actually forgotten about him, what with everything else going on.

"It works?" Hignat enquired.

"Yep."

"Well, good work. Now, I think it might be a good idea to put Playman completely out of action so he can't attempt an escape before we leave the prison."

At this point, I would have welcomed it.

"Oh right," said Sebastian, and a few moments later, I felt my whole body freeze solid. It felt a bit like being stunned in place, something that had only happened to me a few times in my life. It was very uncomfortable being held in that position for more than a few seconds, uncomfortable enough that I actually noticed it beneath what was going on in my mouth (and now beyond), but there was nothing I could do about it. The only things I could move were my eyeballs, and by that I attempted to cast Hignat and Wilwog the dirtiest look imaginable.

"Nicely done," Hignat said, sneering down at me. "Well, this is certainly a most agreeable position of power, is it not, Playman? Perhaps not quite as fun as watching you and your friends in those cages, but close enough. You can probably let him go now," he added to Wilwog and the person holding my wrists, and they obliged. "Come, all of you, we'd better get a move on."

He, Wilwog, and the wrist-holder left the room and headed for the yard, where I could now hear plenty of noise issuing through the broken window. The prisoners were all cheering, celebrating the escape they were about to make. If only someone would come in now, I thought bitterly, and catch them right in the act.

"Sorry about this, John," said Sebastian, who seemed to have remained behind. "Nothing personal, mate, but let's face it, we weren't really any use to anyone, locked up in here. High time we got out and started doing some good in the world again. I know Patty would have been all for it. I suppose you guessed he didn't really jump, but his sacrifice has thrown a lifeline to the rest of us. Here," he said, and he bent down and took the soap out of my mouth for me. "I wish I didn't have to leave you there like this, but you'll just try and stop us and we can't have that. Someone will find you eventually, I'm sure. Take care, buddy."

And he left the room, leaving me in one of the worst fixes I'd ever been in. What on earth was I to do? I knew I wasn't in any danger of being killed right now, as I listened to the prisoners cheering Sebastian as he emerged into the yard, but I knew that the situation could get so much worse: What if Hignat, in his infinite wisdom, decided to send Sebastian back up here to load me into the bag as well? Not only would I be back in front of Arnold Hammerson before too long, but I would be facing Arnold Hammerson in possession of the Sien-Leoard Crystal as well. Meanwhile, how long was it going to take the others to realise that something was wrong and investigate why I was taking so long to sort out the prisoners? Most of them didn't even know I was in here. Marc was the only one who had been there when Mr. Woodward had assigned me this task. To top it off, I was stuck lying on the floor with my arms over my head and my mouth jammed open and full of soap suds.

Now I understood everything, the whole dirty plan, and resentment swelled up inside me. Not just at the prisoners, but Mr. Woodward and Mr. Fletcher, who could have so easily avoided this catastrophe if only they'd been more forceful with the prisoners. They had wanted me, not because I was the only one who knew the technical details of the prison, but because I was the only one whose magic they could strip. Perhaps they would have preferred Marc, but there were less excuses for getting him to come in here than me. The man who had been killed...now I understood what had really happened with him: He hadn't jumped at all, he had been thrown.

Judging by the remains of the window, someone—probably Wilwog —had actually picked him up and used his skull to break the glass right in the centre of the frame. I wondered if the man had agreed to sacrifice his life or if the other prisoners had simply agreed that he was the most expendable.

How could such a thing have happened, though? How could they have come up so quietly behind me and caught me off guard like that? I would never have put Wilwog's name and the word 'stealth' in the same sentence, but apparently that was what had happened this time. It took several seconds to work out, but the more I thought about it, the more it made sense. Sebastian had walked so quickly so that I wouldn't have a chance to look around the place thoroughly. He had almost shouted at me when I had entered the room, not for my benefit, but as a signal to those hiding behind all those doors that had been left ajar. They had then crept up behind me, and next thing you know, I'm on the floor with a foot on my chest and a mouth full of soap. I had to give them credit, they had got into position extremely quickly. They wouldn't have had any warning that I was coming, couldn't have known when I would be returning, yet they were all ready when I had shown up.

It was Hignat, I thought savagely, and the fury built inside me. This had been Hignat's plan, all Hignat's—I would have staked my life on it. It had Hignat's fingerprints all over it, and he had certainly been pleased at how successful it had been. He had been the person I hated most in the world for a very long time, and I had to admit that since this business had started, and particularly since he had been locked up in here, I hadn't spared much thought for him. Most of my animosity had been directed towards Hall, Sebastian, and Hammerson himself, when I should never have forgotten my number-one enemy, the person who had troubled himself to make my entire schooling an utter nightmare.

Of course, for most of that time, I doubted that Hignat really understood why he didn't like me, and until very recently, I hadn't understood why I didn't like him either, except that it was mostly based on the simple fact that he didn't like me. He had always been a sneering little boy who most people, teachers included, hadn't thought much of. He had then hooked up with Wilwog a few years into primary school, and his confidence hadn't taken a backward step since.

I had been raised by Dad and Charlie to believe that the Woodwards had been the good guys in the war. I hadn't known very many stories because Mum and Marge had been very strict about how much our innocent ears should be allowed to hear, but I knew enough, perhaps more than most children, since many people didn't like to talk about the war anymore, knowing that the Hammersons were still around and still powerful. No story they had ever mentioned, however, had included either Hignat's or Wilwog's names, so all along I had never known that they were descendants of Hammerhearts, not until very recently anyway, but it hadn't surprised me to learn that Stella knew who they both were and was able to give them orders.

Perhaps I would have known better right from the start, though, if it weren't for the fact that it had been Mum and Marge who had seen us to our first day of school, rather than Dad and Charlie. For many years, the memory of that first day had been buried in more memories, but now, forced to acknowledge the animosity once again, it all came flooding back. Peter, James, and I had just been standing around together, the three of us nervous and excited, because of course we had no idea how much we would grow to despise school before very long. We were surrounded by other children and parents, but our own had departed briefly to speak to one of the prep teachers. Hignat had sidled up to us in that time and attempted to talk to us. It was too long ago for me to remember all that he had said. I could only remember James bursting into childish tears and Hignat telling him he looked like a loser.

I had been just about ready to hit him, as had Peter, before Mum and Marge turned up to break up the fight. Upon hearing of what Hignat had done from James, Marge had spoken firmly to his father, asking him to have a word with his son, whereby she was promptly told to go and jump off the Main Street bridge because he didn't need to be told by "a miserable, unkempt, layabout old bat" how to raise his son. I could remember those words clearly. Tom Hignat had probably known who she was, but she hadn't recognised him. Whether or not Charlie had told her later was something I had never found out.

Either way, none of us had ever got on with Hignat since that very first day. He had, in fact, made many enemies in his first year of school just from his attitude. It hadn't taken the three of us long to make friends with Harry and Simon, a friendship of which our parents had been extremely proud, and they too turned on Hignat along with us, having been thoroughly insulted by him about their dead parents (a fresh wound back then) already. Hignat had tried a few times to make up for his behaviour on that first day, by apologising to James and insisting they hang out from time to time. As it turned out, he had only wanted to get into James's good books after working out how smart he was and that he seemed to be just about every teacher's favourite student. He had abandoned his attempts upon learning of James's surname because, to a family such as the Hignats, anyone who had fought against the Hammerhearts in the war wasn't worth befriending. At least, that was what I had come to deduce in the plenty of time I'd had to think about it.

And speaking of plenty of time to think things over: The next time I paid attention to the noises around me, I realised that the yard was completely silent. It looked as though the prisoners had all climbed into Sebastian's bag and he had made his escape from the prison. It didn't look as though anyone was coming just yet, which probably meant that he wouldn't be stopped on his way up to one of the second-floor rooms. If I could have groaned, I probably would have done. It looked almost a foregone conclusion now that Arnold Hammerson would very soon have the Sien-Leoard Crystal in his hands. All hell was going to break loose very soon once he had command of that sort of magic, entirely separate from the hell that was already breaking loose inside my stomach. He would be able to tear this place apart in no time. Even with Marc and the Sorcerers, there would be only so much we could do to stop him. He wouldn't even need the Villain or Darkness Crystals anymore because of course he would have the power of both in one. I now found myself wishing that I had shut the Sien-Leoard Crystal away with the Darkness one on Rock Haulter. Who cared if I didn't have it. At least they wouldn't. Now I fully understood why Mr. Woodward had placed such high importance on the crystals. I had known, of course, but knowing isn't always the same as understanding, but I certainly understood now.

My brain disengaged. Unable to move, with nothing to hear but the silence of the yard, nothing to see but the ceiling of the room in which I was stuck, and nothing to concentrate on but the seemingly endless torture of my current predicament, I lost track of time. I only knew that sometime later, it could have been as little as twenty minutes or as much as several hours, I jerked back to awareness as the sound of running footsteps echoed up through the broken window from the yard. It was hard to tell, but I thought it sounded like more than one person. They were sprinting along the exact route Sebastian had led me into the building. I would have yelled to them to find me here, no longer caring if it was help or an unfortunate prisoner who had been left behind, but of course, neither my mouth nor my throat were operative.

Now they were thundering up the stairs, coming closer and closer, and I felt sure, now, that it must be help. The urgency in the footsteps was unmistakable. Moments later, they reached this floor and came straight to the second room on the left. One person stopped right outside the door, but the other (there were definitely two of them) came hurtling into the room.

"John! Oh, my God!"

It was Marc, of course, the one person who could have rescued me from this horrible predicament. A moment later, I felt the stiffness suddenly leave my body and I was able to clamber onto my hands and knees and look around, knocking the cup over and spilling the little remaining water onto the floor. Marc was standing just inside the doorway, his face white with shock, and Fewul stood behind him, almost hidden in the darkness of the corridor, still in Lucien's form.

"I only just found out something was wrong. What happened?" he asked, grabbing my arm and pulling me to my feet.

I opened my mouth to tell him, but that was when my internal hell really broke loose. It was as though my body had been precariously balanced, and me standing up so suddenly had destabilised everything. A moment later, I hunched over and vomited onto the floor between us.

"Holy crap," Marc said, looking enquiringly over his shoulder at the Beast of Magic.

"They washed his mouth out with soap, master."

Marc swore in a fashion strikingly similar to how I had landed myself in this mess in the first place. A moment later, just as I was ready to vomit again, everything cleared up. My stomach settled down, all the nastiness in my mouth and throat cleared, and I could only taste my own saliva again. It was an enormous relief.

"Thanks. That was—my God, never again."

"What happened here?" he asked again.

"They got the crystal," I muttered shamefully. Among everything else, I had to take responsibility for the way I had been so thoroughly deceived. "They led me up here, distracted me with the window, and Wilwog king-hit me."

Marc swore again, this time under his breath. "So it was a plot all along?"

"Hignat's plot, I reckon," I muttered as the two of us left the room and headed for the stairs. "Marc, they got the crystal, and they've probably used it to get out of the base by now."

"Have they?" Marc asked the beast over his shoulder.

"They have already entered the Hammerheart network," said Fewul monotonously.

Marc swore again. Three times in less than a minute. "How could this have happened?"

"It's my fault," I told him. "I should have taken my own advice and looked at their memories. They tricked me, and I took the bait. How long have I been stuck in here?"

"About two hours," he said, and it was my turn to swear.

"What's been going on out there?" I asked urgently. "Has there been any news about Tommy?"

"No. Nobody's come back and he hasn't woken up yet. We're going out to get him ourselves."

"What?" I said, stopping in my tracks. We were halfway across the prison yard now. "What do you mean we're going out? Who's going out?"

"All of us," he replied, looking surprised. "We couldn't not go, you know it. The Young Army is back in business," he said proudly.

I shrugged and continued walking. I would go with them, of course, because I couldn't just sit back here feeling guilty and sorry for myself for what I had allowed to happen, but all the same, all my senses had been dulled by the calamity of losing the Sien-Leoard Crystal.

"We're meeting in Amelia's lounge room," he told me as we left the prison yard and started down the corridor. "There are still some adults in the base, including your mothers, and we can't let any of them know what we're doing or they'll try to stop us. The Woodward living quarters are empty apart from Amelia now, so we're meeting in there. We're gonna work out a plan there."

I muttered incoherently. Perhaps my sense of adventure would reawaken once a plan had been worked out, but right now, it was hard to get into the spirit of things after what I had just been through.

"He's here," Marc called to the unseen people in the lounge room as we turned the corner and approached the Woodward living quarters, which stood open and waiting for us. Yet another security hazard, I thought savagely. People around here were never going to learn.

When we entered the lounge room, I saw that Marc hadn't been lying about the Young Army being back in business. They all seemed to be here: Peter, James, Felicity, and Jessica; Amelia, Natalie, Harry, and Simon; Erica, Serena, Katie, and Sophie; Liam, Lena, Darcy, and Jane; and a whole bunch of other people who hadn't been involved in the Young Army at all, such as Siobhan; Natalie's sister, Rebecca, and her friend Candice; Lena's younger brother, George; and Harry and Simon's older sisters, Misty and Michelle. All up, there would have been at least thirty people crammed into the lounge room, including me and Marc.

"John, my boy," boomed Simon merrily when he saw me, having no sense of the occasion.

"What's up with you?" asked Peter as I sat down beside him.

"Something very bad," Marc told them. "The worst thing that's happened all day, including Tommy, but we'll talk about that later. We have to work out what we're gonna do tonight."

There were several looks of frank curiosity, but Marc raised a hand to stall any questions before they could really get going. "Not now, okay? John can tell the story later if he's up to it. We need to work out a plan."

"Well, that is easily managed, now that our fearless leader has joined us," said Harry, grinning broadly at me.

I shook my head. "I dunno why you keep thinking of me as a leader. I'm just gonna let Marc take this one, I think."

There were several looks of alarm swapped between some of them, but I didn't bother trying to work out what they were thinking.

"John, what on earth happened to you?" James asked sharply.

"Right, well, we need to make sure that we can get around there without getting in the way of the adults," Marc proceeded loudly, and I felt a rush of gratitude towards him. "They'll have their own plan, but we don't want to accidentally prevent it from working, in case it's a good one. Fewul, where are they now?"

"They have been able to locate an entrance into the base in question through one of their supporter's houses," Fewul told him, "but they have not been able to get very far in due to the sheer number of Hammerhearts guarding the place. The base is rather larger than the one here in Chopville and is currently being occupied by no less than a thousand Hammerhearts, many of them with no business there except to occupy space."

"And what about Tommy?" he asked tentatively.

"Still being held in the execution chamber," Fewul went on, "but no longer being tortured. The three Hammerhearts currently guarding him are under orders to keep him awake but not to torture him unless they have to. They are waiting for Tankom to give them the word that they can let him rest."

"And where is Tankom?"

"Currently addressing some of the Hammerhearts, but that shouldn't take long. She wants to prepare the base for Tommy because she fully expects him to come to her once they let him rest."

"She's not really giving his bravery any credit, is she," Marc muttered darkly, but privately I thought Tankom had a point. "Okay, and is Stella still in the base?"

"I believe so, although she is not revealing herself to me in any way."

"All right," said Marc, looking around at the rest of us now. "Seeing as it is in one of the Hammerheart bases, it means that you two—(he jerked his head at Natalie and Amelia)—wouldn't be able to come with us under normal circumstances, but I think we might be able to change that this time."

"How so?" Amelia asked, looking hopeful.

"Fewul," he said, turning back to the beast. "I'm sure the Hammersons made it so that no ordinary Sorcerer would be able to undo the magic they cast, but we have a bit more magic than that on our side."

"That's good."

"Marc," I muttered, for I was starting to see a gaping hole in the plan. He looked nervous as he turned back to me. "Don't you think there are too many of us? If it's hard for six people to move around undetected in there, how on earth are we gonna manage?"

"You're also forgetting who we've got on our side," said Marc, jerking his head yet again at Fewul. "Now, what sort of protection should we go with? We used capsules last time—Fewul, is that a good idea?"

The Beast of Magic shook its head. "This base has even more lines on the floor than the one in Chopville, and all of them are presently turned on. You would be exposed immediately if you flew over one of them."

"Damn," Marc muttered. "What about an invisibility veil, then?"

Again, the beast shook its head. "The spell you call the invisibility veil only works because it includes a binding spell. The drawback of such spells is that if one of you is revealed, everyone else under the same spell will also be revealed."

"So…" Marc gulped. "So you're saying that we all have to be under separate invisibility spells?"

The beast nodded. "That would be the safest option, although each one of you may still get into trouble if you step over a line."

Marc sighed. "Well, we knew it wasn't going to be easy. I guess we'll just have to hang onto each other to stick together. Now, the base is pretty big, so even with Hammerhearts all over the place, we'll probably need to split up in order to achieve anything. We need to get to Tommy, find a way of rescuing him, and find a way of guiding him from the base without anyone realising something has gone wrong. That will probably be the hardest part. Also, assuming she's there, do we wanna get Stella out too?"

"Yes," said Natalie firmly. "It's high time she came back to our side."

"But don't you think it was useful having her with Tankom when —" Erica started, but broke off when several people gave her furious looks. I knew she'd been on the verge of mentioning my connection with Stella, but there were still so many people who didn't know about it, and perhaps information like that was best kept to a select few.

"All right, okay," Marc said quickly, bringing the meeting back under his control. "So how do we wanna do this?"

Everybody continued looking at him, waiting for him to tell him exactly how they were going to do this, except for those few who still expected me to take a more active role in the planning. I determinedly avoided their eyes.

"Okay then," Marc went on, a little coolly now. "We need a small group to go and find Stella and find a way of whisking her from the base. She'll probably have people around her, but if she sees us and they don't, I imagine she'd wanna fall in with whatever we're doing. John, perhaps you should be in that group with"—he raised the Hero Crystal in his hand, as though letting it decide who I would be grouped with, "Darcy, Serena, and Jane. Is that okay?"

"Guess so," I muttered. I could see the sense in it, though. If Stella thought I had come to get her out, she'd probably follow me without questions, unless I was banking too much on what Natalie had told me the day before.

"Right, then we'll need another group to get down to the execution chamber and deal with the Hammerhearts guarding the place," Marc went on.

Slowly, the group divided up into several smaller groups who would have separate tasks. I didn't pay much attention to who was doing what. I knew my own orders were to take Serena, Darcy, and Jane into the base and look around for Stella. If I'd had the Sien-Leoard Crystal, as all but Marc still assumed I did, it would have been easy. As it was, we would have to have a good look around for her, all the while making sure not to be discovered by any of the watchful Hammerhearts around the place. Once we had her, we were to get out as quickly as we could, again without being discovered. I was almost certain that it wouldn't be as simple as that, was fairly sure we would have to fight at least some of the way, but hopefully we would be up to it. Fewul was ordered to be on the watch if anything went wrong with any of the groups, and James, whose group would be concerned with making sure Tankom couldn't get in the way while Tommy was escaping, was to use the Light Crystal at regular intervals to make sure we all stayed safe.

Then at last, when the clock on the wall told us it was nearly midnight, we were ready to go.

"Everybody who's got weapons, hurry upstairs and get them," Marc told us all. "The rest of you, stay behind so I can use this to arm you. We'll all meet up in Amelia's house, through the wall. There'll be someone there to let you out. Try not to take more than five minutes. We've gotta get a move on."

Everybody hurried out of the room, packing the corridor down to the living quarters to bursting. Being one of the last into the lounge room, I was one of the first in the pack.

"Where are you going?" Peter asked as I turned sharply and took off up the stairs, several people climbing close behind me. "You don't need to be armed."

"Yes, I do," I told him as we turned off on the third floor and hurried along to our respective rooms. "Long story—tell you later."

In my room, I searched my drawers and loaded my pockets with the devices I hadn't needed to use in a long time but which I would certainly need now. I already had the solid-outliner on me (I barely went anywhere without it these days), but now my stunner, agonator, bludginator, and invisibility toggle joined it. I almost put my signaller in as well before deciding that it would be pretty pointless. With Fewul on the scene as a danger alarm, it probably wouldn't be needed. I was almost ready to go when I spotted the unboggler at the bottom of my drawer. I couldn't think how I could need that tonight, but I packed it anyway. If any Hammerhearts started attacking us and we could reduce their numbers without hurting them, it would probably make fighting the rest of them easy.

I felt extremely vulnerable without the Sien-Leoard Crystal in my pocket. Remembering what Tom Hignat had said back in the gym, I had to accept now that I had simply become too used to having that privilege, taken it too much for granted, and now that I didn't have it anymore, I had no choice but to deal with it.

Chapter 45: Tankom's Method

Marc teleported us all from Chopville into the middle of a park in Berlin, in which the guest entrance to the Hammerheart base was hidden. Fortunately for us, the park was empty, as it appeared to be late afternoon here. Half the group had already been helped through the tree that held the entrance by Fewul, those groups who would be concerned with attracting and distracting the Hammerhearts first. The rest of us were to wait a few minutes to give them time to get farther into the base. The task that lay ahead promised to be a difficult one. The place was supposed to be big, and although we knew that Tommy was being held on the bottom floor, getting down there wouldn't be as simple as stepping through this door and crossing a platform to a lift, as had been the case in the Chopville base.

Serena, Jane, and Darcy were gathered around me, but none of us spoke to each other. Marc stood just ahead of us with Peter, Katie, and Sophie, whose job it would be to free Tommy from the binds holding him and escort him from the base. I sincerely hoped they would do well, but my mind was full of my own task for the evening. How on earth were we going to find Stella in a place like this without being discovered by anyone else? We were all invisible, of course, and had to link arms in order to stay together, but being invisible certainly didn't make it impossible for us to be discovered. The sound barrier was out completely because that would make communication impossible. I was very nervous about it all, but now that I was here, I felt calmer and more ready than I had back in the base. Any sort of action would feel better than doing nothing, particularly after what had happened in the prison yard.

A few minutes later, Fewul assisted the rest of us through the hidden entrance and into the base. This part of the base, to my surprise, was no different from the Chopville base. No fewer than fifty Hammerheart cart tracks stretched across the room, a bridge leading over all of the tracks to a door directly opposite, sets of steps between each track leading down to where Hammerhearts could call their carts. The only two noticeable differences were the increased volume of traffic in this base—far more than there had been in the Chopville base—and the increased volume of Hammerhearts—not just those getting in and out of carts but those standing guard at regular intervals along the bridge, not to mention the ones standing just in front of us, apparently guarding the entrance we had just come through.

We edged very carefully around the two nearest Hammerhearts and, the four of us holding on to each other, made our way slowly across the bridge, sticking to the wall to stay out of the way of any passing Hammerhearts. Marc's group was just ahead of us, and I hoped very much that they were moving faster than we were—bumping into them would not be good for any of us. It took nearly five minutes to get all the way across the bridge and through the door at the other end, where we found ourselves in a large foyer-type area. There were eight lifts in here, not to mention a single stairwell that was packed with people. Getting to the upper and lower floors was going to be a nightmare in this.

"Any ideas?" either Serena or Jane hissed on my left.

"Look at that first," I suggested, pointing at a sign between two of the lifts before realising that they couldn't see me. "Er, that floor map there. Which floor do you reckon she would be on?"

There were twelve floors in this base, and according to the number on the wall opposite the lifts, this was level nine. I assumed there must be two levels of the Basement in this base. Perhaps they had more people to imprison in a city this size. As for the upper levels, it looked as though three of them were residential, and levels six and seven were completely unlabelled. Stella didn't normally come to this base, I had to remind myself, so she wouldn't have her own office here, nor would there be a living quarters on the top floor for her to go to, so where could she be now?

"Let's get in that lift," Darcy muttered, and I didn't need to see where he was pointing to know what he was talking about. A lift had just opened almost directly in front of us and it looked as though the four people on board were all getting off on this level.

So we edged around a pack of Hammerhearts, all of whom were conversing in German or some language that sounded similar, and headed for the lift, getting in just in time as the doors closed right behind us. Thankfully we were the only ones on board.

"Now what?" asked Jane in a normal voice as the lift began to ascend.

"Stop it on level—er—seven," I suggested, trying to think. That would be one of the unlabelled levels, and we had to at least have a look on those.

This floor was the most open area I had ever seen in a Hammerheart base. It wasn't a worship hall, or dining hall, or any sort of hall. All it contained, as far as I could tell, was an enormous glass tank standing in the centre of the cavernous room. There were Hammerhearts standing around it, up to twenty of them, I thought, but I couldn't see all the way around it, so I had no way of knowing if Stella was in here. None of the Hammerhearts were watching the lift, however, so I didn't mind sticking my arm out to stop it closing on this floor.

"We should split up, I reckon," I hissed. "Search more floors at once. I'll take this one with Darcy, and then, if she's not here, we'll move up to level five. You two do level six, and if we don't find anything, we'll meet up on level four just to the left of the lift doors."

They all muttered assent and I stepped off the lift, now linking arms with only Darcy. Behind us, the doors closed as the girls headed up to the next level.

"How do you get in the tank?" Darcy asked in a whisper. "It doesn't have a top. Can you see if there's anything in there?"

I took a closer look at the tank. Now that I came to have a better look at it, it looked less like a tank than a window in an aquarium. It didn't look as though there was anything in there, though—certainly no water or fish or anything. I wondered what on earth it could be, but that hardly mattered now.

"Never mind it, let's just have a look for Stella."

"Split up or stay together?"

"Stay together. It'll be quicker if we don't lose each other."

All that in whispers and luckily for us so far, nobody had heard anything. The place was very quiet because apart from a few scattered words passed here and there, nobody was speaking. Now I started to wonder what they were all doing here. I had never seen anything like this inside the Chopville base. What was the significance of that glassed off area? And why were there so many Hammerhearts standing around it, apparently waiting for something? The aura in the place seemed, to me, to be a mixture of impatience and fear. What did that mean?

Darcy and I moved well away from the glass walls and began to edge sideways around the room, watching the Hammerhearts in front of us carefully, me looking for a sign of someone I would recognise. All the Hammerhearts here were wearing the uniforms I recognised, and although I only saw a few of their codes, which were emblazoned over their right breasts, they all seemed to be level threes. We continued to move sideways along the wall adjacent to the lift doors, then around the corner, where we were able to see some of the Hammerhearts we hadn't been able to see when we had first arrived on this level. Again, none of them seemed to be familiar to me. Most of them seemed to be men, although there were a few women mixed in with them. Most of these women were shorter than Stella, or their hair was blond or light brown as opposed to her dark, almost black hair, and their eyes—well, nobody had eyes anything quite like Stella's.

We were almost to the next corner and about to turn around it, now able to see the final group of Hammerhearts, when a tangible silence fell over the Hammerhearts. They all seemed to be looking towards the lift and stairwell, and although those things were so distorted from where we stood, they seemed to know who had just arrived on this level. Apparently it was someone very important to have inspired that reaction. Maybe it was Stella, I thought wildly, squinting in that direction, but I really didn't think so somehow. A man began to speak from the opposite corner of the large room, and although I couldn't make out a word, I thought it sounded like English. I tugged on Darcy's arm and we began to move back the way we had come, more quickly now and a little more carelessly. The Hammerhearts' attention seemed to be focussed so exclusively upon the new arrival that it seemed not to matter.

We reached the first wall we had moved along, able to see straight ahead to the lift and stairwell now and able to see, quite clearly, who had joined the group of Hammerhearts on this level, now moving towards the glass walls, apparently about to check them over. Not Stella—Tankom. I was not pleased to see her after what I had watched her doing to Tommy some fifteen hours earlier (had it been that long?), but I couldn't deny that her presence up here was good for us. It looked as though James's group wouldn't need to do much as long as the others downstairs got a move on, because as long as Tankom stayed up here, she would be out of the important action.

"Blimey, it's her," Darcy hissed. Of course he would recognise Tankom just as quickly as I had, having captured her weeks earlier. "You reckon James's group is up here too?"

"If they are, I hope they stay out of our way," I hissed back. Although I supposed there were worse things in the world than walking into invisible people, the possibility existed that such a slip up could give away our position if any Hammerhearts were paying attention.

We moved slowly along the wall again so that we came to stand about ten feet behind Tankom as she looked through the glass into the centre of the room within, whatever it was. The inside of it looked rather peculiar. The ceiling and floor were the same colour as the ceiling and floor we were standing upon, and the glass was just plain old glass as far as I could tell, yet a strange light seemed to emanate from the place. It was an odd, light blue colour that lit the floor around the glass for a few feet in every direction and silhouetted the Hammerhearts darkly against it. It wasn't bright, exactly, but it was slightly brighter than the rest of the place. In short, it stood out. It was impossible to miss. I still had no idea what its purpose was, but I was getting an ominous feeling about it. Now that Tankom was up here looking in it, I especially knew it couldn't be good news.

And then, just as I was having these unsettling thoughts, the very worst thing in the world happened right in front of us. Tankom was still watching the inside of the glass room, apparently considering something unimaginable, and the Hammerhearts were standing around the edges of the glass, all staring at Tankom, when part of the ceiling of the glass room suddenly fell inward, causing several Hammerhearts to yell in surprise and alarm. I knew at once what must have happened on the floor above to cause that, and apparently Tankom did too, for she cried, "The switch! Everyone around here knows where not to go—flick the switch!"

All the Hammerhearts were simply too astounded to obey orders, so Tankom went ahead and did it herself on some sort of remote control that she snatched from the nearest Hammerheart. There was a flash of light within the room, a blinding blue light that unfocussed my eyes for several seconds. When I returned to my senses, I saw that it was already too late. Beside me, Darcy let out a cry of dismay as he realised what was happening a second before I did. The Hammerhearts were withdrawing all sorts of devices from their pockets and firing them at the glass. I saw familiar jets of gold, orange, and white light, as well as several unfamiliar colours, along with several flashes as a number of completely unfamiliar devices were set off. It was all pointless, of course, as none of the magical devices were able to penetrate the glass, but it hardly mattered, because the button Tankom had pushed had been a revealer of some kind, and it was Jane and Serena who had been exposed, trapped inside the glass room and looking around themselves in horror. They were relatively unhurt from the fall, but that was the only good thing that could be said for them.

"Intruders!" Tankom cried dramatically, pushing another button on her remote control, this time causing the roof above the girls' heads to repair itself.

I wrenched myself free of Darcy and dipped my hands to my pockets, withdrawing the solid-outliner and bludginator. The alarm would go up now, so we might as well be ready to fight, but unfortunately, the real alarm for us had been set off seconds earlier by Darcy. Quite a few of the nearest Hammerhearts had heard him, and before either of us could prevent it, several jets of semitransparent light came flying across the room towards us. We both popped back into visibility before I had time to think, oh shit.

Because I had been ready to attack them before they had registered our appearances, I got in a few good hits first, trapping three of them in thicky prison and knocking a few more to the floor. Darcy, not quite as experienced in this kind of battle as I was, had only managed to take down one Hammerheart before the white stuff caught hold of his leg and began working its way up his body. I shot at it quickly with my own solid-outliner, but the time taken had cost me the chance to defend myself. A stunner froze me in place for several seconds, during which time several bludginators went to town, ripping most of my shirt to ribbons.

We were under a complete assault now, as those Hammerhearts on the far side of the glass hurried around to help out. They didn't bother trying to attack Jane or Serena anymore, each of whom had her own weapons out and was attacking the glass with no more success than the Hammerhearts had had. It was impossible to communicate anything to Darcy while we were so thoroughly surrounded, but my idea was to make Darcy invisible and let him attack them with an unboggler while I tried to hold the rest of them off, but I knew even that wouldn't be any good. There were simply too many of them. I used mostly the solid-outliner, as it was the only one I could really count on to put them out of action quickly, but before long, both Darcy and I were caught up in the thicky prison too. In the end, it was Tankom who put an end to the battle.

"Stoppen!" she screeched, and for a wonder, they ceased their attack immediately, backing away and beginning to set each other free from the thicky prison. I had just enough mobility left to set Darcy and myself free in turn, before looking carefully around to see what was happening.

The Hammerhearts were still armed and ready to launch back into the assault the moment Tankom gave the command. Behind them, Serena and Jane were standing beyond the glass, watching the proceedings they had no control over in terror. To my surprise, I also saw James and Rebecca, who had also been revealed by the jets of flying light. Apparently they had followed Tankom to this floor in readiness to distract her should the need arise. It would have been much more effective if they had been invisible, but as there were only two of them, that could only mean that the rest of the group (Erica and Siobhan, who had never experienced a fight like this, other than the one that had taken her family) hadn't yet been revealed.

I turned my attention back to Tankom, who was looking at me with a curious expression on her wrinkled old face. "Well, well," she said very quietly, and she smiled. It was an evil thing. "H3, I believe."

The room went very still as these words sank in. Although most of these Hammerhearts plainly didn't speak much English, they knew all too well what 'H3' meant. I could see that quite a few of them had half a mind to launch back into the attack, to bind me good and proper so that they would be given credit for catching me. None of them did so, and I found myself feeling glad that they still respected (or feared) Tankom enough not to dare disobey an order right in front of her.

"I think I can guess what brought you here," she said conversationally, glancing briefly at Darcy before returning her gaze to me, "but I think you are friendly with this one."

She half turned so that she could look from me to Serena and back again. Serena took the opportunity to flip Tankom the bird, and several people chortled. How on earth had Tankom known that, I wondered. Only Hall could have told her, I supposed, but it was still something for Tankom to have recognised Serena as the person Hall had referred to.

"So what if I am?" I retorted. There was no reason not to talk back now that we were good and trapped, and previous experience had taught me that dialog could work as a good distraction if used correctly.

"So I think you need to be punished soundly for coming here tonight," she told me, smiling at me again, and I shuddered involuntarily at the look. That expression practically dripped evilness. "It's been a long time since I've been able to have my idea of fun. I was saving this for your nigger friend, but now that you're here, this seems even better. After all, he can't be held responsible for the trouble he has caused. But you, on the other hand, had the balls to attempt to defy me."

"What on earth are you talking about?"

Her eyes widened in slight surprise. "But surely you know the story? Or does Frederic Woodward think you too young to hear it?" she asked. "Yes, that sounds like the sort of thing he would do—keep you too overprotected for your own good. 'Tankom' (she enunciated each syllable heavily) is not just some ridiculous name given to me to make me sound more impressive. I earned it in fair—killing."

I had known the name 'Tankom' for as long as I had known that there were Sorcerers, but although I had asked Dad and Charlie on several occasions, they hadn't told me where the name had come from. I had wondered plenty of times recently, too, but hadn't asked any questions about it. The name hardly seemed important compared to the person to whom it referred.

"You mean there's such a thing as 'fair killing'?" Rebecca said scornfully. I had almost forgotten about her and James, still standing where they had been revealed, unable to move for the weapons pointing at them.

"Well, of course there—" Tankom began, looking around at her, and then she froze, her eyes widening in horror. "A Sorcerer!" she shrieked, making several people jump and look wildly towards the stairs, perhaps expecting to see one of the Woodwards striding towards them.

Tankom, however, had withdrawn an agonator from her pocket, and quick as a flash, she brought it to rest pointing directly at Rebecca. A moment later, Rebecca dropped to the floor and began screaming terribly, writhing and thrashing and knocking into James, causing him to stagger backwards. Tankom kept her agonator pointing at Rebecca for a very long time. I had only twice before seen a person tortured for this long without a pause—Tulip and Eric, Kylie's killer. Eventually she released her, by which time Rebecca lay prone, barely able to move, barely conscious even. Tankom wore a very satisfied expression as she said, "Bind that girl up. I must know how a Sorcerer managed to get into this base."

"She's not a Sorcerer, you stupid old woman," I spat at her, anger giving me the courage (or perhaps stupidity) to take a step towards Tankom. "She's Natalie's sister."

My anger came from two places—the fact that Tankom had clearly enjoyed causing Rebecca that amount of pain and the fact that she had intended that pain to be Natalie's. If that really had been Natalie, I probably would have flown at her.

"That," she spat right back, "remains to be seen. Bind her up!"

Not like Rebecca was going anywhere in a hurry, I thought darkly. One of the Hammerhearts shot ropes at her, which twisted and snaked around her, tying her arms to her sides and her legs together, then finally bringing her knees up to her chest so that she now lay balled up on the floor. Tankom watched this process up to its conclusion before turning back to me.

"Well, since you haven't heard the story, H3, perhaps I should show you. I couldn't think of a better opportunity."

She turned and appraised, not Serena or Jane, but the glass behind which they were trapped. Without looking at me, she said, "In January 1978, I committed the first killings of the war in a way that history will never forget. There were a dozen of them, and they were close friends of the Woodwards, as well as a few family members, including Frederic Woodward's father. I don't think Lillian ever forgave me for murdering her husband, but—(she shook her head tragically and sighed)—such is life."

Slowly, she replaced the agonator in her pocket and withdrew again the remote control with which she had revealed Serena and Jane. Now her eyes moved to Serena, who glared insolently back at her. Again without looking around, she said, "I don't suppose anybody has a video camera handy? 2H9 has been very faithful lately, and I'm sure he would like to see what I am about to do. Er— hat jemand eine videokamera?"

My stomach lurched. I couldn't know exactly what was coming, the unpleasant details, but I knew what the end result would be— Serena and Jane's deaths. I looked wildly at Darcy, who seemed to have realised the same thing. His fists were clenched and his expression was one of great anguish as he stared at Jane. To my left, James stood over Rebecca as though caught in the beam of several spotlights, his eyes darting desperately from left to right, looking for a way he could interrupt proceedings, but still he didn't dare move. He would have been struck down half a dozen times before he could take a single step. The same held true for me and Darcy, but I had almost reached the point where I didn't care.

"This is less of a tank than what I used last time," Tankom said, and now she looked at me, "but it has the same dimensions, the same properties—it will serve the purpose."

"And what might that be?" I snarled.

"Why don't you see for yourself, H3." She leered, turning back to face Jane and Serena, who had both resumed their pointless attempts to break out of the tank. Serena had resumed swiping her bludginator at the glass while Jane kicked at it repeatedly, swinging her leg back and throwing all the force she could muster into the blow. It made no mark upon the glass, of course.

Tankom began walking sideways around the perimeter of the glass room, or tank, if that was how she thought of it, and pressed a button on the remote control. Jets of electricity shot down from the ceiling to the floor all around the edges of the room. Serena had leapt backward in time, but Jane, who had just taken another furious kick at the glass, had been less lucky. Her leg broke one of the jets, electrocuting her and sending her reeling backwards into the centre of the room with a loud cracking sound. Serena hurried to see if she was okay, but before she reached her, Tankom had pushed another button on her remote control. A panel in the ceiling suddenly opened, almost at the point where the two girls had fallen through, and wasps began dropping through it. Perhaps it wouldn't have been such a big deal if the number of insects had been relative to the size of the hole through which they had entered, but they just kept streaming downward, more and more of them in an apparently never-ending flood. Predictably, they went straight for the two girls, who tried desperately to bat them away but were overcome within seconds.

"*No! Jane!*" Darcy howled, hurling himself forward towards the glass.

I expected him to be beset upon immediately, but to my surprise, the Hammerhearts held back. In fact they even moved backward, giving Darcy plenty of space and a clear path to the tank. Apparently watching the suffering of those on the outside, who were forced to helplessly watch the suffering of those on the inside, was all part of Tankom's grand plan. They weren't so generous for James, though, whose close proximity to the exit caused them to keep him under arms the whole time. I could hear terrified whimpering from that direction, though, and knew that Erica, who must have been over there with James, was almost ready to fly at the glass as Darcy had just done.

Tankom had reached the corner of the tank and was moving around it, moving up the side of it now, still walking sideways so that she could watch the drama within. The two girls were on the floor now, thrashing and still trying desperately to free themselves from the wasps as they were stung repeatedly—not just on their exposed skin, but in the time I had watched, I'd seen them fly down both girls' shirts and pants, and at least one went into Serena's gaping mouth. Not much sound penetrated the glass, but I could just hear small whimpering noises coming from within. Between the jets of electricity around the edges and the wasps, now covering just about every inch of the two girls' bodies, it was very difficult to see them at all, and still the wasps continued to stream downward from the open panel on the roof.

Tankom wasn't done. She pushed a third button, and this time, the two girls let out long, piercing screams.

"*No!*" I cried out, and now it was my turn to fly at the glass.

Jane and Serena had just been subjected to the very worst thing I had feared during those long hours I had spent locked up in the Chopville Basement. Nails, each about two inches long and spaced just inches apart from each other, had popped out of the floor all over the room, and the two girls, prone on the floor and unable to get up due to the wasp attack, had been pierced all over. Through the glass, I clearly saw Serena attempt to get up off the floor, but pushing herself up only impaled the palm of her hand on yet another long nail. The screaming was muffled through the glass, but the pain of it came through clearly.

Hardly knowing what I was doing, I began to run up and down the side of the room, banging desperately on the glass and yelling, and I couldn't have said later what on earth I might have said. Several feet to my right, Darcy was doing exactly the same thing, and on the floor behind me, Rebecca had resumed screaming, not in her own pain this time but in anguish at what was happening inside the glass and her inability to come to the glass as we had due to the ropes still binding her. The Hammerhearts around us weren't laughing as the ones in Chopville probably would have been, but they were clearly enjoying watching the struggle.

With the next push of a button on her remote control, Tankom withdrew the nails back into the floor. Both girls were able to stagger to their feet, trailing blood behind them, but as the wasps came up with them, they fell straight back down again. They were both still screaming and thrashing as they were stung, again and again, by the wasps. Darcy and I were both sobbing now, banging hopelessly on the glass in sheer desperation. I hardly knew what I would have done if I could have broken through—probably nothing, except perhaps get myself killed—but at that moment, such thoughts hadn't occurred to me, nor had the idea of simply running up to the floor above and trying to fall through to reach them as they had done. The only sound in the large room, other than our yells, Rebecca's screams, and those that penetrated the thick glass, came from Tankom herself. She had now reached the opposite side of the tank altogether, and she screeched at us, the sound travelling around both sides of the glass to reach us, "Watch this, boys! See how I finish the job!"

"*No!*" we both howled, and I was ready to sprint all the way around the room to Tankom, to reach her, to attack her before she could press one more button on that remote control. I knew I would never reach her, though. That was probably the reason why she had moved around to the far side.

As we watched in horror, another panel opened over the girls' heads, this one closer to where Tankom stood, and something began to drift downward from it, though I couldn't see very clearly what it was. It looked like wispy-white smoke tinged with yellow. It descended slowly from the open panel, thinning and spreading out sideways so that it drifted towards the sides of the room, all the while descending painfully slowly towards Jane and Serena.

"*No!*" The yell wasn't from either of us this time, but James, who seemed to have recognised the gas, now covering the entire ceiling within the glass room.

We all got a good look at what was to come for the girls before it happened because some of the wasps, those closest to the roof, were the first casualties. The moment it touched them, they simply fell, clearly dead, to the floor. It didn't stop there, though. Something else happened to them once they hit the floor, or perhaps on the way down, but given their tiny size, it really wasn't possible to see what. As for Jane and Serena, it was hard to know if either of them were even aware of the gas descending towards them. Both were still on the floor, trying to beat off the wasps as the stinging went on and on. Indeed, Serena looked as though she was barely conscious.

"Besorgen Sie sich die kleinen helden," Tankom called as she came back around the side of the room towards us, and I didn't give a damn what that meant in English. "Lassen Sie sie nicht entkommen, aber lassen Sie sie das Ende der Show zu sehen."

That was the trouble with not knowing how to speak the language—you couldn't know when they were about to attack again. I didn't even know it was coming until I was seized, my wrists grabbed and held high above my head so that I had no chance of reaching my own weapons. Another Hammerheart used his stunner on me, freezing me in place, making it impossible for me to turn away from what was about to happen inside the glass room. Beside me, I heard, rather than saw, Darcy being beaten into submission, and knew that James was being held too. Meanwhile, in the room, I knew the end was coming. The gas had sunk low enough that the two girls would have been taken by it if they had been able to stand upright. I didn't want to see it, yet I had no alternative, because although I could roll my eyes, I could not close them, so I did the next best thing—rolled them up as high as I could.

The result of this was that I didn't see, until after it had happened, the source of the explosion off to my left. Yells of panic shattered the air from Tankom and all the Hammerhearts along that side of the room. Those holding me in place didn't do more than flinch, but rolling my eyes sideways, I saw that the left side of the glass room had completely blown outward. All the Hammerhearts along that wall ducked and covered their faces as glass came flying at them, followed swiftly by that lethal gas. More yells of panic as those closest to it realised what had happened. Many of them tried to run from it, knocking into each other and falling to the ground. Only Tankom kept her cool, first vanishing the gas altogether with the press of a button on her remote control, then shrieking at her charges, "Es ist wirklich ein Zauberer hier! *Revealers!*"

And out they came, jets of semitransparent light flying in every direction. A couple of them hit me with no effect. I squinted in the direction where most of the mayhem was taking place and saw that they had successfully revealed Siobhan and Erica and were quickly attempting to bring them under control, but whoever had caused the glass to blow out had evaded the revealers so far. I struggled desperately against my own binds, knowing this was perhaps our only chance, but whoever had stunned me hadn't released the button, and I couldn't move so much as a fraction of an inch.

To my right, I heard Darcy, who had not been stunned, let out a low, despairing moan, and as I rolled my eyes back towards him, I saw why. Jane had managed to clamber, not entirely to her feet, but just high enough that she had come into contact with the gas moments before it had been vanished. Whether or not she was dead now was hard to tell, but she was back on the floor, sprawled and completely immobile, and worst of all, she appeared to be wasting away before our eyes. The yellow tinge of the gas was now showing on her skin, and the flesh beneath it, what part of it I could see, appeared to be either rotting away or compressing in on itself. The effect was utterly sick.

Serena was still alive, though. Her own injuries had perhaps saved her life by preventing her from getting very far off the floor. She was presently crawling agonisingly towards the glass wall that no longer stood there, and the Hammerhearts nearest her were too distracted in locating the Sorcerer, attacking Siobhan and Erica, or simply treating their own injuries to notice her. Tankom saw her, though, and no way was Tankom going to leave a job like this unfinished, Sorcerer or no Sorcerer. She took a few careful steps over the fragments of glass, withdrawing a bludginator from her pocket as she went. She met Serena perhaps six feet from where the wall had stood, and most unluckily for Serena, though she probably couldn't have escaped anyway, she hadn't even realised Tankom was there. The old woman finished it all with a single stab to the neck. Serena convulsed for only a moment before falling flat on her stomach and moving no more, blood beginning to spread in a little pool around her.

"Nehmen Sie diese—(she counted the six of us)—sechs personen in den Basement," Tankom barked at the Hammerhearts around her, giving no sign that she had done anything more interesting than swatting a fly, and the only word of that she spoke in English was enough for me to know what must be coming for us. "Ich brauche Zeit um über das was ich mit ihnen zu tun zu denken. Sie," she barked at some others, "gehen die Treppe hinunter und sehen, dass H2 ist immer noch in Gefangenschaft; es könnte mehr sein Eindringlinge. H3 must not be harmed," she said, more to herself than anyone else. "He is Arnold's business." Then, more loudly, "*Ich muss nach unten gehen, ich werde bald eine Rede. Gehen!*"

They all began to move around. I felt myself raised from the floor, not by the person who had been holding my arms but by the one who had stunned me. The Hammerheart stunning devices had two buttons on them—one small circular button that sat in the middle of a larger circular button, so that together they looked a bit like a doughnut. The smaller button simply stunned the person at whom the device was aimed, but when the larger button was also pushed (for it was impossible to push the larger one without pushing the smaller one at the same time), it enabled the person holding the device to direct the stunned person as they themselves moved. The person directing me turned me and headed towards the stairs. As we went, I got a good view of most of the others: Rebecca was being moved the same as I was while James, Erica, and Siobhan had all got caught up together in thicky prison. Nobody bothered to do anything about Jane or Serena, and I found myself wondering if we would be able to come back up here and retrieve their bodies before we left. Tankom was just ahead of me. She had her back to me and was already waiting for a lift, but as I stared at her, I imagined my gaze could drill holes in the back of her head.

She didn't get a chance to leave the seventh floor, however, because the person responsible for blowing out the glass hadn't finished causing trouble. The four Hammerhearts who had been carefully lifting the contorted forms of James, Siobhan, and Erica suddenly found themselves without protective gloves, and a moment later, the thicky prison began spreading up their arms. They yelled in alarm and tried to wrench it from them, knowing full well that it wouldn't work. A moment later, I lost sight of them as the person holding me was flung to the floor. I was momentarily released from my stunned state and wasn't about to waste my chance, but where in the past I would have attacked those closest to me, or those who were about to attack me, the only person I wanted to attack had just spun around and aimed a revealer of her own at a spot somewhere behind me.

"*Sorcerer!*" she shrieked, and fired.

This time, her aim was true, and as I scrambled around to look, I saw Natalie pop into plain view but only for a moment, as she was quick to hide herself again. The Hammerhearts were alert this time, and they launched an assault unrivalled by anything I had so far seen. Not even a Sorcerer could have got out of the way of this in time. Several more revealers found Natalie, as well as a few solid-outliners, stunners (which had no effect), bludginators, and even one of those devices designed to disable a Sorcerer's magic (which also had no effect). She was up to most of this, of course, except for the thicky prison, which once again proved to be the Achilles' heel of the Sorcerer.

"How dare you," Tankom snarled, hurrying forward and stopping just short of where Natalie had been struck down. "You must tell me how you got in here, but only after—"

And to my horror, she jumped into the air with more energy than I would have believed any eighty-year-old woman could possess, coming down hard right on Natalie's face. Blood spattered everywhere but fortunately for me, I never caught sight of the damage Tankom had done, for a moment later, she had withdrawn two more devices from her pocket—an agonator, which she fired at Natalie's face, followed immediately by a solid-outliner, which cut off her screams before they could really get going.

"Take her downstairs with the others," Tankom barked at the nearest Hammerhearts, not bothering to speak their language for their convenience this time. Perhaps this part was for our benefit rather than theirs. "And don't release her from the agonator until she is in her cell. She can have this all the way down for daring to come in here."

Yes, it definitely was for our benefit. White-hot rage burst forth inside me, but before I could act on it, I was stunned again by the same person who had held me earlier. There was nothing to stop the Hammerhearts this time. Darcy had now been stunned as I had and was being directed towards the lifts in the same way, while two Hammerhearts carried Natalie between them (she was now unable to operate any magic at all, whether because of the thicky prison or the pain, I knew not). A large group of Hammerhearts dealt with the rest of them, deciding not to free those trapped Hammerhearts just yet but to instead carry the whole lot of them in a separate lift. Tankom took the stairs down, giving us all a furious but gloating look as she went.

We were bustled into the lifts and taken down to the Basement, level ten or eleven, I didn't know which. I had been facing the wrong way when the button had been pushed. It appeared to be much the same as the Chopville Basement. Perhaps it was larger, but other than that I couldn't see any difference as we were taken past the cluster of guards around the entrance and into the rows of cells. Natalie was thrown into the first cell and Darcy the second. The third cell was to be mine; the Hammerheart walked a short distance into the cell, released the larger button, then backed out, only releasing me from the stunner altogether as the door was swinging shut.

Chapter 46: Revenge

Alone in the darkness, I felt my way over to one side of the cell (much the same position as where I had spent most of my time in the other Basement cell) and leaned against the wall there. Through the wall, I heard more footsteps as more prisoners (James, Erica, Siobhan, and Rebecca, probably) were taken to cells farther down from mine. Minutes later, they retreated back from whence they had come, leaving the seven of us alone down here.

I wasn't worried about myself at all (it would only be a matter of time before Marc or Amelia found out we were down here and came down to get us), but I did have enough space inside my mind to wonder if anyone other than Jane and Serena had been seriously hurt (or killed?) in the act of freeing Tommy. Had they even succeeded? If so, they had done it very quietly indeed, since nobody up on level seven had been aware of anything. I didn't have to wonder about what had happened to draw us all to the spot: James's group had simply followed Tankom up or down from wherever she had been before, ready to put up a fight against her should she attempt to go down to the bottom level, while Natalie had been told to go there, probably by Marc, who would have been told by Fewul that there was trouble upstairs.

As for us, though, we had failed in our job. Not only was Tankom on the loose and aware of our presence, but we hadn't been able to find Stella either, although she was probably aware of our presence by now too. Maybe she would come down to rescue us as she had done from the Chopville base? Probably not, I told myself. As much as she might want to get back in our good books, she would probably reason that it would be too dangerous for her if she was caught. True enough, I supposed. Certainly in the dream I'd had, her priority had been not to hurt Tommy, then to find a way to escape. Finding a way to free Tommy had only been her third priority, which didn't really make it a priority at all.

These thoughts led me to think about the dream itself, and as I pondered it, something new came to me, something that hadn't occurred to me until this moment, and it had nothing whatsoever to do with burning bodies or the Enlightener or any of that stuff. Shock froze me in place for several seconds as I tried to digest the very end of the dream, the thing that had most likely woken me up in the first place. The final words that Tankom had said to Tommy—they would have meant nothing to me if I'd heard them anywhere else, but Stella, whose knowledge of both magic and Tankom herself outweighed mine, understood at once what Tankom had meant, and her shock had been as great as mine was now.

"And once I have killed you both," she had hissed, "I will be whole again, and you will be nothing, just as you should have been from the moment that plane went down. My error is almost repaired."

Well, it wasn't really, I would have said on any other day, because Smiley had been just as affected by that crash and he still lived, but I knew now, because Stella had known, that she wasn't referring to Smiley at all. It was the 'whole again' comment that had been most significant, and the more I thought about it now, the more it made sense. It explained why Tankom had been so determined to hunt Tommy right from the start. It didn't explain why she still sought him now, since she didn't have magic anymore, but then I reminded myself that the Hammersons fully expected and intended to have their magic back in the near future.

What it seemed to mean was that when Tankom had attempted to bring down that plane and failed, she had left a small portion of her magic in its wreckage. I remembered what Smiley had said about loose magic floating around, and it made more and more sense. As long as Tommy and Smiley had their respective talents, Tankom would be (or had been) using impaired magic. She believed that killing Tommy (or perhaps undoing the magic as Hammerson had tried to do to me) would restore her magic to what it had been. That was Stella's interpretation of what Tankom had said, and I felt sure, as sure as she was, that she was right. It made so much sense. It even explained why Moran had been unable to control Fewul on that one occasion when he had tried: One Sorcerer would need all six chips in order to do it, but if Tankom's chip wasn't working properly, he would have fallen just short of the required power.

Tankom… Now that I was thinking about her, I felt a cloak of coldness begin to settle over me. The anger I had felt as I had watched Tankom doing those terrible deeds up on the seventh floor had been hot, boiling hot, but something, perhaps my isolation, had turned it freezing cold. I was now able to consider it as it was without wanting to hurl myself at her. For reasons that didn't make much sense, I had always felt that Tankom was the more level-headed of the Sorcerers (evil like her son, perhaps, but with enough control that she wouldn't explode with anger if things didn't go right). That was probably still the case, but apparently I had underestimated her capacity for evil. If I had known that story about how she had killed Mr. Woodward's father, I probably wouldn't have made that mistake.

Serena and Jane were both lying dead upstairs, and I had no idea what was going to happen to their bodies now. Would we have a chance to go up there and get them before leaving? I hoped so because it hurt terribly to think of leaving them both behind. Not being able to bring Tulip back had been bad enough. The Hammerhearts would eventually clean up the mess up there if we didn't get to it first, but that thought was even worse. Anything those people would do to the two bodies couldn't possibly be good. I wasn't surprised that Tankom had ordered their deaths; she probably would have ordered that the rest of us be dropped into the tank after them if Natalie hadn't wrecked it. What did surprise me (and horrify me) was the manner in which it had been done, and the extent to which Tankom had enjoyed it, not to mention the fact that she had finished the job so brutally. Again, it shouldn't have, because the way Tulip had died should have removed any and all reservations I'd once had about these people.

That would have been enough for me to hate her, to swear a vendetta against her as I had her son and Hall, but she had gone further than that. Torturing Rebecca as she had, and particularly given that she had meant to do that to Natalie, had created the dark thoughts I was thinking now. Then when Natalie had really turned up, Tankom had kept her in unendurable pain for not just a few seconds (all that it was designed for) but several minutes, and she had even stamped on her face, by God.

"It's personal," I whispered into the darkness, the sound (particularly the S sound) echoing around the dark empty room, and I felt the coldness envelop me. It was the absolute truth. She had killed my girlfriend (never mind that we had been about to break up), then launched the worst attack possible on the one I wanted as my girlfriend, the one I was becoming increasingly sure I loved. Seeing Serena's death had been bad, but seeing Natalie in that kind of pain had been somehow worse. If I had seen what remained of Natalie's face after Tankom had stepped on it, I probably would have gone crazy with my own anger, but now that I hadn't, I was glad. It enabled me to focus my thoughts, to control them.

There was only one thing for it, I realised as I stood there, thinking thoughts I never would have imagined I would think. I had believed for some time now that every human had at least a small portion of evil inside them somewhere. I couldn't think of a single person who hadn't done something influenced by an evil aspect, including myself, but most good people did their best to bury the evil inside them. If they had nasty thoughts, if they felt mean, most people would choose not to act on those thoughts. Not all, of course, but even mean people weren't necessarily cruel people. That, right there, was the difference between the Hammersons and most other people: Even a nasty person wouldn't have enjoyed watching another human being tortured. The Hammerhearts had, of course, but then those who weren't as cruel as the Hammersons themselves had since been indoctrinated to believe that we deserved it, that it was only right and proper.

I remembered back to when Tulip had been killed, and the resolution I had made after my lucky escape from Arnold Hammerson. Back then, I had only felt terrible guilt for leading Tulip to her death and had, for myself, only cared about making sure I would never do that to another person again. What a striking difference that had been compared to the resolution I was making to myself now. I felt slightly guilty for Jane's and Serena's deaths, but I didn't blame myself in the same way as I had for Tulip's death. Even though I had told them to go up to level six, I didn't believe I had made any other decisions that had contributed to their deaths. Most of all, though, when Tulip had died, avenging her hadn't even occurred to me. Perhaps it should have, especially given that Hammerson was so desperate to have me killed. I could only reach one conclusion: All the deaths I had watched happen around me, losing several of my friends now, not to mention my sister, had broken something inside me. It had released my evil aspect, and in that moment, I gloried in it.

I lost track of time as I brooded, but after what seemed like no time at all (perhaps something in my mind was protecting me from the passage of time), I heard a disturbance somewhere outside the cell. People were walking and talking, not directly outside my cell but farther down the corridor, around the front of Darcy's cell, I estimated. I couldn't recognise the voices, but I felt sure that it wasn't the Hammerhearts; they didn't sound aggressive, as far as I could tell. I moved away from the wall, watching the door, or where I assumed the door to be, waiting for it to open. A few minutes later, it did, and sure enough, it was Marc and Fewul outside it. Fewul was still in Lucien's form and his expression was completely blank, but Marc was looking extremely grim.

"What's up?" I asked him before he could say anything to me.

He shrugged. "Well, we've got him. The others are all hanging around the entrance. Just go down there and I'll be with you in a few minutes."

He stepped back and locked the cell shut when I was outside it. Without another word, he proceeded along the corridor to where James, Erica, Siobhan, and Rebecca had been taken. I looked around and saw at once where the others were. It was a straight line from where I stood to the door into the room with the lifts. It was open, and the guards who had been lurking around it were now lying unconscious just inside the doorway. I examined who was among them as I drew nearer. Darcy was closest to me, and although he looked unhurt, he didn't seem to be with them at all; his mind was a long way away, and I thought I knew what he was thinking about. Natalie was there too; she looked very unsteady on her feet indeed, but she had managed to fix up her face at least, or perhaps Marc had done that for her. Most of the others seemed to be there too. Amelia was farthest from me, watching the stairs and lifts, ready to attack anyone who might come out of either, and Felicity, Jessica, Katie, Sophie, and Peter were with her, pointing various weapons into the doors of the lifts. I saw that Tommy was with them. He was a complete stranger to me in this body, but I recognised him well enough from the dream. He was being supported between Harry and Simon and seemed to be only semiconscious. I scanned the group carefully, trying to see if anyone was missing, but other than those I knew to be in the cells past mine, the only two I couldn't see were Jane and Serena.

Most of the group didn't even look around when I joined them. I could tell that they all knew what had happened on the seventh floor and were in shock as I had been. The only ones who noticed my return were Amelia and Peter (who caught my eyes briefly before returning to their tasks), and Lena and Natalie (both of whose eyes I avoided). I mostly stared at my feet, not because I was miserable, shocked, angry, or utterly exhausted (all of which would have been true enough), but because I didn't want them to see my face. I worried that they would see the change in me, and I didn't want any of them (especially Natalie) to attempt to talk me out of my current state of mind. I wasn't in any mood to argue with them, but nor was I going to be told what to do.

The others (Rebecca, Siobhan, James, and Erica) joined us gradually over the following five minutes, followed again by Marc and Fewul.

"Okay, you all," he said, drawing most of our attention. "They think there are only seven people here, and that they're all locked up and defenceless, but now that they know we're onto them, there's no point in trying to get anything else done. We have to get out of here as quickly as possible. I don't think it matters if they see us on the way through; there's not much distance between here and the visitors' entrance. Fewul, are there many Hammerhearts between here and there?"

"There are a few," he said, "and they each have an alarm that will alert all those in the Worship Hall if you try to make an escape. Tankom doesn't believe you will, though. She thinks she's got you all locked up."

"Okay," he said shortly. "What about the adults—Mr. Woodward's people?"

"They were ordered to retreat immediately when Frederic Woodward discovered that you were inside the base," said Fewul. "He knew it would not be safe for any of them to be here once the Hammerhearts became aware of your presence. He is trusting you to guide everyone out safely. He is very angry that you disobeyed his orders; there is likely to be a lot of trouble when you get back to base."

"We'll deal with that when the time comes," said Marc, turning back to the others. "Okay, here's my thought. Fewul and I will go up at the front of the group and attack all the Hammerhearts in our way, hopefully before they have a chance to call for reinforcements. Amelia, Natalie, you two go at the back of the pack and make sure we're not attacked from behind. The rest of you just try to stay between us and stay orderly and all that. We want to get out quickly but we don't want any carelessness either, not falling over each other or anything."

"How are we going up?" asked James.

"Er, the stairs," he said, deciding on the spot, and Harry and Simon glared at him. "Let's all get into two lines, me and Fewul at the front."

And so we did. It felt rather like being back at school as we arranged ourselves into two careful lines. I ended up being close to the back of the pack, which was exactly what I had wanted, with Peter to my left. There were only four people behind me (the two Sorcerers, James, and Erica), which was the best thing for me. I still didn't know whether we would need to go up one flight of stairs or two, but either way, I would be going up at least one flight more than the rest of them.

The door to the stairwell was closed. Marc pushed it open and we slowly began to filter through it. We moved slowly forward (slower than Marc would have wanted but such was always the way with groups like this). By the time Peter and I got in the stairwell, Marc and Fewul would have already been at the level of the Hammerheart Highway, perhaps already examining the scene across the bridge. We were halfway up the first flight when we heard the shouts and knew it was the Hammerhearts, alarmed as rabbits in a spotlight as Marc and Fewul came bearing down on them.

"Hurry up," Amelia hissed behind me, and the two lines began to move more quickly.

We had reached the next level, and I saw that it was here where the two lines were exiting the stairwell through the door to the left—even more perfect. If the door had been on the other side, I would have had to cut right across Peter in order to keep going. As it was, I simply turned and hurried up the next flight of stairs. I heard alarmed voices behind me as Peter, James, and the three girls realised what I had done, but hopefully, for their sake, they didn't have a chance to follow me. Not the case, I knew, for I could hear at least one of them sprinting up the stairs behind me.

I burst through the open door on the next level, hearing concerned shouts behind me and ignoring them completely. A passageway stretched off to my left with doors along it (offices, by the look of it), but straight ahead of me was a wider corridor, and the first door on the left led, I saw, straight into the Worship Hall. I hurried forward so that I was directly in front of the door, able to see right across the hall, but far enough back in the corridor that those seated in there wouldn't be able to see me. Unlike the Chopville Worship Hall, whose seats faced the front doors, here the seats faced the wall to the left of the doors. This gave me a clear view of the entire stage, and as I had hoped, there she was, directly in my sights, and so far, she hadn't seen me.

I looked around as Peter, James, and Natalie came skidding to a halt beside me.

"What the hell are you doing?" James hissed, his eyes darting between me and the open door. "We got off on the level below here. Come on."

I found myself feeling very glad that I hadn't let any of them see my face downstairs. I gave the three of them a very level look and knew that I had been right to do so. As they watched my face, their expressions changed, firstly to concern and then to what I assumed was fear, only it wasn't fear for me—it was for themselves. They were actually scared of me.

"Don't tell me what to do," I said in a very even voice.

The words sparked another change in them. Natalie looked even more scared, not to mention hurt, and I wondered what part of her wanted to take my hand and lead me away from this before I could do anything stupid, what part of her wanted to get the old John back. Peter took a step back from me, his eyes widening as though he'd never suspected this side of my personality. James, on the other hand, became angry.

"What are you playing at?" he hissed venomously. "We almost got out clean, and now you've gone and ruined everything."

As though to confirm his words, Amelia emerged from the stairs and hurried over to where we stood. She took one look at my face (I saw her eyes widen in alarm) and addressed nobody in particular instead. "The others are turning around and coming back up here."

"You see what I mean?" James hissed, but I barely heard him.

In fact, I barely even noticed the four of them there as I turned my head slowly back to face the doors ahead of me, and Tankom some way beyond them. That hall was sure to be packed with Hammerhearts, and there were a good twenty feet at least between Tankom and the doors. It would take some time to do what I needed to do, given the protection she, her son, and Cornish had set around themselves, and I was sure to be struck down a thousand times by the Hammerhearts in the hall. I thought again of Serena's body, of Rebecca being tortured, of Natalie being stamped on, and all other concerns disappeared from my mind. The rage that I had kept cold all this time suddenly broke. Like a bomb, its insides exploded outward as they were released, white-hot, burning. I had a single moment to notice that the other four had noticed the sudden change in my expression, but none of them had time to pull me back.

I was off like a cork shot out of a champagne bottle. I covered the distance between the wall and the doors into the hall in about one and a half seconds, but later, I would play that moment back in slow motion, again and again. James threw something at me, hard enough that I was actually able to snag it as it flew past my left shoulder. The reaction had been instinctive and not until a few seconds later did I realise that I was holding anything at all. I also felt some unknown magic whoosh over me from behind as either Natalie or Amelia cast some sort of spell. I later discovered it to be both of them—Natalie had put a magical shield around me (not a physical one, but one that would deflect other spells) while in the prior instant, Amelia had protected me with something entirely unfamiliar. I knew almost immediately what it was, for as I burst over the threshold, I felt a pleasant warmth surround me. The insides of the Worship Hall in Chopville were magically heated so that anyone who entered without a Hammerheart uniform would be immediately burnt to a crisp. I had completely forgotten about that but was later glad that Amelia hadn't. It was just lucky for us that they used the same protection in this hall. I didn't feel anything burn, but I knew that it was hot around me. It just felt nice.

I heard alarmed yells around me as the nearest Hammerhearts saw me. Their yells attracted everyone else in the hall, and a moment later, they all knew I was there. Ahead of me, I saw Tankom look around in surprise. I saw her eyes widen in recognition and alarm. Jets of light flew around me in the last few feet, ones I recognised and all manner of others that I had never seen before, but even with the shield, none of them hit their target. Some unknown force greater than that kind of magic seemed to want nothing to stop me reaching the old woman before me. My instinct had been to hit her across the face, knocking her to the ground, at which point I would proceed to strangle her, and if I could stomp on her face in the process, all the better. I never got a chance to act upon those instincts, though, because as I raised my hand to strike, I realised that there was an unfamiliar device in it—the thing that James had thrown at me, which I had never seen in my life.

My momentum prevented me from being able to change my course. I struck her hard with my right hand (an open-handed slap to the face) and followed it up with a blow from my left hand, knocking her back the other way. The object in my left hand collided with Tankom just under her chin and she screamed in apparent agony. The blow should have been strong enough to knock her to the ground, and indeed she did fall a moment later, but as I raised a foot to accelerate the process, I noticed something else.

Something unusual seemed to be happening to Tankom. She was still screaming, writhing on the ground, clutching her neck where I had struck. Her skin appeared to be turning a faint shade of yellow. I heard the alarmed yells around me, but nobody attacked now. They were as paralysed by what was happening as I was. Blood began oozing sluggishly out from under the old woman's clutching fingers from the wound in her neck. The screams were already becoming weaker as she appeared to be choking on her own blood. What on earth had I done? There was just enough sanity left in my mind to register that although I certainly wasn't complaining, I couldn't possibly have done this much damage just by hitting her.

I looked down at the thing in my left hand, the thing which James had thrown to me, which had most likely caused this bizarre turn of events. It was about the same size as the life assistant and the side pressed against my palm had been completely smooth. The other side, however, that which had struck Tankom, was really not that much different, except that it was rougher—and, more importantly, it was a different colour from the rest of the device. Where the other side of it was a shiny silver, as were each of the four edges, the rougher side was a light shade of yellow. I looked back at Tankom. Not only was her skin turning yellow, but something seemed to be happening to the old flesh beneath it, and suddenly I understood. This device, whatever it was, had somehow poisoned the old woman with exactly the thing she had used to kill Jane. That had been in the form of a gas, and who knew what form this was in.

As good as that was, however, I knew it wouldn't be enough. Tankom would live through this, however bad it got, because of the magic that prevented her from being killed by any means other than the direct hand of a human. I therefore crouched beside her and, allowing my fury at Serena's death and Natalie's torture to overcome me one final time, brought the device down squarely in her face. I'd been prepared for that not to kill her, for another blow or two to be required. I hadn't counted on the thing sinking right into her face, shattering all the bones and flattening her skull. It had sunk through as though she had been made of a much more fragile substance. Blood spurted everywhere, drenching me and the floor all around us. I knew the job was done this time. Not only was her body damaged beyond repair (without magic, anyway), but given that I had used my hand to deliver the final blow, that should get around the magic she had used to protect herself. I certainly hoped so, anyway.

An odd hush had fallen over the assembled Hammerhearts at the moment I had struck the second time. Then, slowly, the volume swelled as they realised what had happened. The noise grew and grew until it became a roar of absolute outrage. I scrambled back to my feet, pocketing the poison device and withdrawing my bludginator and solid-outliner. I had no intention of trying to fight all these people; there were probably hundreds of them there, and the ones at the front were already taking aim. I turned and took off for the doors, running low and feeling several spells bouncing off my shield, thankfully leaving it intact. I reached the doors just in time. The stage had been flooded with Hammerhearts by now; they were giving chase.

Amelia, Natalie, Peter, and James were still there, and they had now been joined by a few others—Marc, Fewul, Harry, Simon, and Tommy. As I burst through, one of them caused the doors behind me to slam shut, locking the Hammerhearts in. Loud bangs filled the corridor as people crashed into them on the other side, but none were able to break through. I looked from the doors to my friends and saw that although they still appeared a little fearful, there was a considerable amount of admiration in their faces too.

"You are so, so stupid!" Amelia cried out, and she actually looked like she wanted to hit me. "Don't ever do that again!"

"It's not gonna hold them for long," Marc said, watching the door nervously. "Come on, we gotta go while we still can."

We moved quickly, but I saw a problem looming just ahead of us. The rest of the group, probably unsure where they were supposed to be, had piled into the stairwell and were now blocking our quickest way out of the place. Marc was already beckoning and shouting at them to move down, and they did so, but just as we reached the door into the stairwell, an explosion shattered the air around us. The Worship Hall doors had been blown out; one of the Hammerhearts on the other side of it must have had a very powerful weapon on him or her indeed. I looked back in time to see them charging up the corridor toward us, and I knew there was no time. They'd get us halfway down the stairs. There was only one option.

"Down!" I bellowed at Amelia, and I actually pushed her down the stairs after the others before tearing around the corner and sprinting up the next flight instead.

The others followed not a moment too soon. The doorway prevented the Hammerhearts all getting in at once, but they came quickly, and most of them came for us. Marc and Natalie brought up the rear of our pack, moving backwards up the stairs as they deflected spell after spell, and I hoped Amelia had the sense to do the same for the larger pack heading for the Hammerheart Highway. I couldn't see Fewul anywhere and assumed that he had gone to help the rest of them get out of the base.

I reached the seventh floor and hesitated. This was not somewhere I wanted to be, but I considered the place and thought it would probably be a good place to attempt to hold them off. I went through the door, turned to help the others through, and stood ready to attack the first Hammerhearts to reach the landing, Marc, Natalie, Peter, and James right with me now. I had a clear memory of the first Chopville High battle and how the build-up of unconscious bodies had made it difficult for us to access the gym. My idea was to create a similar scenario here, and given the narrow space in the stairwell, I thought it would probably work.

About five Hammerhearts reached our level first, and Marc and Natalie knocked two of them out in an instant. Peter, James, and I used solid-outliners and stunners respectively to firstly trap the others, then prevent them from bursting through the door and catching us up in the white stuff too. Those Hammerhearts behind them tripped, fell over the top of the bodies, and were immediately trapped in with them. Quite a few more got caught up in it too, so that by the time they had the sense not to move any closer, the pile was almost as high as it was wide. Of course, it only took one halfway intelligent Hammerheart to release the whole lot of them at once, but by then, Marc and Natalie had knocked quite a few more of them unconscious, and Peter, James, and I were ready with our solid-outliners. It took a few repeats of this before the build up of unconscious Hammerhearts on the landing was too great for any of them to get past. No more tried, and with a sigh of relief, James slammed the door shut on them.

I took a quick and unwilling look around the room we were in. Very little had changed. Nothing had been cleaned up since we had been here last. It was completely empty, thank God, except for a whole load of dead wasps and, of course, Serena's and Jane's bodies. Beside me, I heard Peter let out a low moan of misery as he too took in the scene. He would have known of Serena's fate before this, but apparently seeing it for himself had made it so much more real to him.

Marc, too, looked a little sick at what he saw, but he was able to pull himself together more quickly. He moved forward, away from the rest of us, magically creating a bag as he went. I knew what he intended to do and felt grateful to him for it. He moved carefully through the broken glass and stopped beside her, using magic to lift her body into the air. I couldn't watch this bit. I looked around to see how the others felt. Peter and Natalie both had their hands over their eyes, while James appeared to be watching the lifts, probably waiting to see if any Hammerhearts would think to get at us that way. Harry and Simon were a few feet from us and they were simply looking at each other, having taken in the scene while the rest of us had been fighting and having no desire to watch it now.

Marc returned to us a minute later with the bag over his shoulder and no sign of Jane or Serena outside it. "We ready to go?" he asked. "I suppose we just take the lift down to the Hammerheart Highway."

"Er," said James nervously, "I think it's a little late for that."

He was watching the little screens above the lifts. I looked at them too and saw that all eight of them were moving, and all eight of them were coming up towards this floor.

"Oh shit," Peter muttered, pointing his solid-outliner at the doors to one of them, but I knew it would be no good. Even if Harry, Simon, and Tommy were all able to fight, that left each of us to take on a lift full of Hammerhearts on our own. We would be far too outnumbered. There was only one option.

"Stairwell," I said, hurrying to it and wrenching open the door.

Looking down, I saw that there were simply too many bodies for us to get down safely. We would probably trip and tumble right down to the bottom if we tried. That meant we would have to go up yet another level. I had a horrible feeling that the more we went up, the more we were closing ourselves in, making it more difficult to escape, but what choice did we have? I scrambled over the bodies, knocking as many aside as I could and gaining the stairs on the other side of the room, those that went up to the next level. The others came clambering along behind me, Harry and Simon grunting with the effort of helping Tommy get past the bodies. Most unfortunately, we had carved a path through them (not a very clear one but a path all the same), and only seconds later, as Hammerhearts began flooding out of the lifts and grouping around the door, we saw just how great a mistake that was. Marc and Natalie brought up the rear once again, filling that little path with yet more unconscious bodies as they attempted to follow.

The rest of us left them to it, hurrying up the stairs to the sixth level, stopping on the landing and looking out. It was deserted, thank heavens, and we hurried through the door, stopping and resting against the wall just outside it. I had a look around. I had no idea what was supposed to be on this level. There was a corridor to my right, and there was a corridor straight ahead of me, and they both had a number of other corridors leading off them, but not one single door could I see, nor any of the markings that indicated hidden doors that only those privileged could get through.

"Look what they're doing," James said, pointing once again at the lifts.

I looked up at the little screens, expecting to see them rising to this level, but none of them were moving. All of them were sitting on the seventh floor, their doors open wide, not giving any indication that they were about to move anywhere. That felt like a good thing, I thought, so why did James look resigned.

"Doesn't look too bad to me," said Peter.

"They're holding them there deliberately," said James, "so that we can't use them to get back down. Someone's probably standing in the doors of each of them."

He was right, of course, and my sensation of closing ourselves in increased. How on earth were we supposed to get out of this one? If Marc could get Fewul back, he could probably teleport us out of here, unless Marc himself could think of a way to do it, otherwise we would have to be more creative about it. We couldn't use the lifts. That meant we would have to use the stairwell, but how could we get past the seventh level in the stairwell with all those bodies there? They would be there for another twenty-four hours, most likely. Would we have to wait twenty-four hours before we could escape? Or was there a third way down that we didn't know about? There were still five levels above this one, so I supposed anything was possible. I wondered if Stella was up there somewhere. I had forgotten about her since I had been in the Basement, but now I wondered if she was still in this base, and if so, did she know yet that her grandmother was dead? How would she feel about it, especially knowing who had done it?

This made me remember something, and I removed the device I had used to kill her from my pocket.

"What is this thing, anyway?" I asked James. "Where did you get it?"

James shrugged as he took it back from me. "Long story, but basically it's got that stuff in it—"

"That killed them, yeah, I worked that out," I said crisply. "How did you get hold of something like this, though?"

James started to say something but broke off as the device was taken carefully out of his hand. Tommy appeared to have returned to some form of consciousness. He was still in a bad way and still depended on the twins to keep upright, but he had some awareness now, and he looked mightily interested in James's little poison device.

"Well, it was real risky throwing it to me," I said, shuddering at what might have happened if I'd caught the wrong side of it, "but I'm glad you did."

Marc and Natalie emerged from the stairwell at that moment, looking around them as they joined us.

"Where are we?" Marc asked. "This doesn't look like anywhere in the Chopville base."

"That's 'cause we're not in the—" Peter began, but broke off in horror as Tommy raised the device high over his head.

I had a moment to see that his eyes were wide with what could only be described as madness before one of the others grabbed me and hurled me out of harm's way. All seven of us had dived for cover, fearful of what Tommy was doing, and without the support of Harry and Simon, he propped back against the wall as he brought the poison down, firmly, to sink into his own skull.

Chapter 47: The Way Out

The dull thud of Tommy's body hitting the wall and sinking to the floor seemed to resound, long after the echo had bounced off the nearest walls and faded away. The rest of us were on the floor in various crouches. I couldn't speak for the others, but I couldn't find any strength in me to move a muscle. For me, the enormous shock of what I had just seen had more to do with the sudden violence of the suicide than the fact that it had been one of my friends who had done it. Even when he had been alive, this version of Tommy had felt like a stranger to me, and now that he was lying a few feet from me, completely lifeless and, from the shoulders up, not even recognisable as a human being (I closed my eyes hard at this point), it was hard to connect the scene with any personal loss.

It may have been seconds, or perhaps several minutes, before the others began stirring, pulling themselves into sitting positions and looking around at each other in horror. Peter and James were pale with shock; Natalie looked on the verge of tears; and Harry and Simon had rarely been so lost for words. It was Marc who looked thoughtful as he stared, not at Tommy, but at the open door to the stairwell where he had only just come from.

"Why?" he said finally. "Was it so bad?"

I shrugged, knowing what he meant but unable to think of any response. Yes, I supposed that most of Tommy's life would have been so bad. Just the thought of never being able to sleep, of living every single hour of every single day, of never having the time to mentally recharge, never being able to dream—I could hardly contemplate such an existence. Other than that, though, I couldn't think of anything else so bad about Tommy's life. He wouldn't have even needed to worry about being hunted anymore, now that Tankom was out of the equation, and yet…

"Too much," James said weakly. "It was too much for him. He'd had enough."

"Enough that he'd do—that?" said Peter, refusing to look at Tommy's body. "Surely, if he just laid back for a while—"

"You can't get away from what he was dealing with, Pete," said James simply.

Marc got slowly to his feet, using the wall for support. Loosening the bag from one shoulder, he used the crystal to lift Tommy's body into the air (we all looked away pointedly, because in the moment I had looked, I'd seen more dripping than I cared for). When we looked back, Tommy had disappeared into the bag with

Jane and Serena. Marc was already looking back at the stairs and the lifts and looking thoughtful again.

"We still have to get out of here," he said. "We can mourn when we're back with the others."

"Sure, sure," said Peter distractedly. "Maybe you should have a look around, Marc, see what's going on."

"How are we gonna get out?" James asked as Marc gripped the Hero Crystal and began looking at things we could not see. "The lifts are stalled on the floor below us and the stairs are blocked."

"Maybe there's another stairwell somewhere?" Harry suggested doubtfully.

"Maybe we can just teleport out," I suggested, almost as doubtfully. "Or at least teleport down to the Hammerheart Highway so we can go through the door."

"That might work," said Marc vaguely, only half with us, "but I'd rather not unless we have to."

"What's going on, Marc?" Simon asked.

"Well, all the others are out," he said. "The stairs are just as packed with bodies below the Worship Hall as they are above. Fewul's not in the base anymore; he's helping the others to safety. I can call him back, but I'd rather wait some time, just to make sure he's not interrupted."

I felt a great relief—the others were out. That meant that we seven were the only ones left that could possibly get hurt. That in itself wasn't a comforting thought, but at least there would be no other deaths on this night unless it was one of the people standing around me. I shuddered at my own pessimism.

"What about us?" James asked. "What's the best way to get out? And where are the Hammerhearts?"

"Right below us," Marc said slowly. "Not all of them, though. There are a lot of them on the seventh floor, guarding the stairwell below us, waiting for us to come down. They're holding the lifts on that floor so that we can't use them."

"Not all of them?" I repeated. "Well, it looked like there were at least a thousand of them in that hall. How many you reckon are down there?"

"Not that many," he said. "I think some of them have left the base. Maybe they're gonna tell Hammerson what's happened here."

That seemed likely. I shrugged indifferently. The man already wanted me dead, so if he turned up here, it probably wouldn't make much difference, unless…

My insides went icy cold with dread as I suddenly realised how much danger we were potentially in. If Sebastian had already caught up with Hammerson and handed over the Sien-Leoard Crystal, and Hammerson took it into his mind to come here before we could leave…nothing we could do would protect us. He had been, supposedly, the most powerful Sorcerer of all time when he had possessed a single crystal chip—imagine his might with the Sien-Leoard Crystal, the greatest of them all. I shuddered again and decided, for now, not to mention this new threat to the others. There was already enough for them to worry about for now.

"Also," Marc went on, "ah, you're right, Simon. There is another stairwell—"

"Oi, I said that," snapped Harry, but James gave him a hard shove.

"But it doesn't go all the way down to the Hammerheart Highway," said Marc. "It only goes as far as the back of the Worship Hall. Looks like an easy way in for the people who live on the upper levels of this base."

"So you're saying we have to go through the Worship Hall to get out?" Peter asked. "Well, I can think of worse things. You reckon you know how to protect us from the heat in there? Or turn it off altogether?"

"Won't work," said Marc bitterly. "There are already Hammerhearts coming up that way. They've blocked the stairs on this level and every level above us up to level two because they're not sure which floor we're on now. Some of them are coming across level two to block all the doors in this stairwell too."

"So what are you saying?" asked Natalie slowly.

"I'm saying they've got us good and cornered, that's what," said Marc. "There aren't any ways out up there anyway, but—there are just so many of them. As soon as they work out exactly where we are, they're gonna work us into a position where they can attack on all sides and we won't be able to get through them."

"Brave of them," muttered Simon darkly.

"So what do we do?" asked James, looking around. "What's on this level, anyway? Looks like nothing to me. Is there anything on any of the upper floors that could help us, other than the stairs?"

"This level seems to be a maze of some sort," he said vaguely, "and I can't tell if there's anything here."

"Unless we're not careful," I said, "and drop through the floor like Jane and Serena did. We have to watch out for any lines on the floor if we're gonna walk around up here."

"Level two is the same as level two in the Chopville base," Marc said, "and so is level one, by the look of it—just offices, and nothing of use up there. Level three looks like living quarters for some of them, and it doesn't look like there's much for us up there."

He was speaking very slowly now, as most of his concentration went into looking around with eyes far distant from his body, but at that moment his physical eyes, vacant as ever, widened in what would have been surprise if there'd been any life in them. "Hey, I think I may have just found Stella."

"What?"

"How could you have, Marc?" Natalie asked. "Stella's untraceable—she told me so herself—and nobody—not even Fewul —has been able to find her since."

"I know, but one of the beds," he said. "All the rooms up there are identical, right down to the furniture, but in one room, the bed is missing altogether. If she's lying in it, then it would have become untraceable too. She's probably having a good long sleep after everything they made her do earlier, so she wouldn't know any of what's going on around her."

"Unless she's dreaming right now," said James, staring into my eyes, perhaps looking to see if he could detect Stella's presence in them. I shrugged. If Stella was watching me now, I couldn't feel a thing.

"Anything else up there?" Harry asked. He looked confused by what James had just said but had wisely decided not to ask questions.

"No," Marc said, "and levels four and five look the same, except perhaps not as luxurious, and they're both completely empty. So it's just us here."

He returned to himself in those last few words and pocketed the Hero Crystal. "So we've got two options. We can try to find that other stairwell, knock out the Hammerhearts guarding it, and go down through the Worship Hall to get to the Hammerheart Highway. Trouble with that idea is by the time we get back to this stairwell, all the others will know exactly what we're doing, so we'll have even more to fight off. The other option is to just go straight back down through here, but then we have the original problem of trying to get through all those bodies. I'd suggest going invisible again, but it's a bit hard not to give ourselves away while we're climbing over bodies or moving them aside. Once they know, they'll all come piling out of level seven. There are still at least a hundred of them there, waiting for us, because they know we'll most likely cross their path there."

"That's still the better option," said Peter, "but you're right. Being invisible won't work at all. A shield would be better—that means we won't have to worry about being attacked—and then you and Nat can focus on knocking out more as we go past while the rest of us make a path through the bodies. Blimey, that sounds gross."

"You realise we'll all have to stay really close if we do that," I told him, "like we did that time we got shot at. That'll be hard getting down the stairs."

"Don't see why it would need to be like that," said Natalie. "I could just make it the same as the invisibility veil."

"But it will need to deflect physical stuff as well as magic, in case we get shot at again."

"I'll just make separate shields for each of us," said Marc. "I can't think of any reason why that would be a—"

He broke off, and as silence fell once again, we all knew why. Footsteps were hurrying closer, and they were coming from above us. There were no voices, but there had to be—who knew how many Hammerhearts coming down. We had run out of time. Marc swore under his breath and hurriedly beckoned to us to follow him along the corridor parallel with the lifts. The feeling of closing ourselves increasing horribly, we went with him, along a bare corridor with nothing but a few other corridors branching off to the right, and each of these just as uninteresting as this one.

"So your idea now is?" James asked pointedly.

Shouts echoed behind us as Hammerhearts emerged onto the landing where we had been moments ago and saw us along the corridor. We should have turned into one of these side ones by now.

"Turn around and fight," Marc muttered as he and Natalie wheeled around and stepped in front of the rest of us.

Jets of light volleyed back and forth as the Hammerhearts launched a disorganised attack. Marc and Natalie blocked most of them so that the rest of us were able to duck sideways into the nearest corridor where, out of sight of the Hammerhearts, we withdrew our own weapons and turned back, ready to fight. Marc and Natalie were backing slowly in behind us, still deflecting spells from Hammerhearts, who were drawing nearer and nearer up the passage. The attack ended when the gap through which we had come suddenly filled with a wall just like those on either side of us. We heard shouts from behind it as the Hammerhearts came skidding to a halt, probably trying to think of a way through.

"We're in trouble now," James moaned. "They know this place better than we do. They're probably using some other corridor to corner us as we speak. What's the purpose of this maze, anyway?"

"I don't know, probably just to confuse intruders like us or something," said Marc, and then he shook his head. "Nah, it must have a purpose, but the way I see it, we have to now find another way out of it. I'm sure there are Hammerhearts waiting at all the exits, but we'll just have to get through them when we find them. Nat, maybe you should put an invisibility veil around us now."

"And everyone be careful not to step over any lines on the floor," I pointed out as Natalie waved her arms over her head to perform the magic.

We made our way deeper into the maze, an idea that I thought was probably the worst of the whole night. The sensation of closing ourselves in was becoming ever stronger. Now they knew, not only which floor we were on, but how to keep us trapped in here. Marc was right, of course. They would be standing guard at every exit out of the maze now. There would be no reason for them to stand guard anywhere else in the building if they hurried. If only there were some quicker way of getting out of here... I would have suggested capsules again, or some other magical means of transportation that would provide both protection and speed, but therein lay the same problem: If we went over a line, we would be in all sorts of trouble.

We passed passages on both sides. All the ones on the right seemed to lead to dead ends while the ones on the left either stretched straight ahead or turned off to either side. I was concentrating more on the right-hand side because if we could find a straight corridor there, it would take us straight out again, but it seemed that we weren't about to have that much luck. Within a couple of minutes, the corridor along which we were walking came to an end, and we had a choice of corridors on the left and right.

"Which way, Marc?" Harry asked. "You reckon you can use the crystal to work out the best way out of here?"

"I can certainly try," he muttered, putting his hand in his pocket and rolling his eyes up once again.

We stood in a tight group around him, looking nervously around us as we waited for Marc to tell us what was going on around us and to identify, hopefully, the quickest way out of the maze. It took a few minutes for him to speak, and when he did, it was a low oath.

"What's up?"

"They must have hidden cameras or something," he said slowly, "because they're coming in, exactly towards where we are. They know we're here. They've got all the exits blocked, and they're blocking every passage we could use to get away from this spot. They're closing in."

"But how can they know where we are?" James asked, looking accusingly at Natalie. "We are invisible, right?"

"Yeah, we are," said Natalie, looking around at us, as though to check the strength of her own magic. "I don't know why cameras would be able to see us."

"Maybe they can't," Peter suggested. "Maybe they sense us stepping over lines or something. Not sight, but sensing—I dunno—disturbances in the air or something."

"It's possible," said Marc vaguely. "Either way, the quickest way is back here. We went past it just before, but we're gonna have to fight to get through."

He broke out of the pack and led us back the way we had come, eventually turning left into one of the passages I had disregarded earlier, because all I could see ahead of me was a dead end. It didn't seem to faze him though. The rest of us exchanged confused looks but followed his lead. He stopped about halfway down, indicated to us to be ready, and pulled open a door to the left, diving sideways immediately as a jet of red light came flying in at him. Even if we were invisible, there was no way a group of watchful Hammerhearts could miss a door opening all by itself right in front of them.

Three men hurried through the door, shooting jets of revealing light all around them, while others on the other side of the door raised an almighty din to alert the others in the area to our location. We all ducked to avoid the revealers and, miraculously, the invisibility veil remained in place. Marc scrambled to his feet and dealt quickly with the three attackers, while Natalie busied herself with keeping the veil in place. Moments later, however, more people were entering the door Marc had not long opened, and the rest of us were forced to join in the attack. None of us used solid-outliners this time, even though they would have been highly effective, because they would have prevented us from being able to use this door to escape. Instead, it was bludginators and stunners in use, and although they didn't take any of the attackers out on their own, they slowed them down long enough for Marc to deal with each of them in turn.

We might still have been able to get through that door, even with the unconscious Hammerhearts piling up all around it once again, if it weren't for the attack that came from behind. All seven of us had been busy preventing Hammerhearts getting too far through the door that we hadn't been paying attention to the corridor from which we had just come, but of course, the Hammerhearts knew our exact location now, and plenty of them had known other ways to get to this part of the maze. The only warning we had were sudden footsteps from the corridor behind us. Peter, James, and I looked around just in time to see several jets of light from no fewer than a dozen Hammerhearts come flying down the corridor towards us. We ducked, causing at least one jet to hit one of the twins, who yelled in surprise as blood spurted from his back, but there were simply too many spells coming at us to get out of the way completely.

Peter went down under an agonator, and while he made a superhuman effort not to make any noise, there was still enough there to pinpoint his position to the enemies. James and I had both been knocked backwards by bludginator swipes. James knocked into Simon and they both went down, while I staggered into Marc, knocking him down as well. It didn't really hurt me due to the shield around me, which Natalie hadn't gotten around to removing (a good thing), but I felt the force of the magic all the same. By the time we had all regained our feet, someone had finally succeeded in breaking through Natalie's invisibility veil. I could tell from their eyes that they could now see exactly where we were, and that some of them even recognised us.

"Shield!" I bellowed at Marc, using up one of the three seconds we had before we would be overwhelmed completely.

But it was too late for that. No fewer than six Hammerhearts jumped right over the top of their unconscious fellows in the doorway and seized Marc. The Hero Crystal flew out of his hands before he had a chance to perform any magic with it. The Hammerhearts saw it and several of them lunged, but I got there first. I got both hands on it and had almost pocketed it when disaster struck. The crystal separated in my hands, became the six smaller Sorcerous Crystals, and let me tell you, I had never been any good at juggling in my life, and this was no exception. I kept hold of two, and fortunately, James managed to grab another two.

Harry and Simon flanked us both as we pocketed them, withdrawing our weapons once again, but Marc was still struggling with the six holding him—they were now beating up on him. I looked around for the last two crystals and saw that nobody had grabbed them yet. They were on the floor very close to where Natalie stood, but she too was struggling with a number of Hammerhearts. They had lifted her off her feet, pinned her arms, and were attempting to draw her legs up behind her, perhaps for the convenience of carrying her. She dealt with them a moment later by appearing to burst into flames. They all jumped back, howling in pain, all their exposed skin burnt roar red, but Natalie herself seemed to be fine. She landed on her feet, snatched up the two crystals, and turned to deal with the group holding Marc.

All this happened in no more than five seconds, but by now, we were completely surrounded by Hammerhearts. Peter hadn't yet been released from the hold of the agonator, and now he was trampled as the enemies closed in. I stood with James and the twins and we were doing our very best to hold off the advance, using our solid-outliners now (to hell with a pile up of bodies) but it wasn't enough, because as quickly as we were capturing them, someone would set them free again. We copped bludginators left, right, and centre. All our clothes had been ripped to ribbons (mine weren't being cut now, again thanks to my private shield, but they hadn't been much to begin with after the episode on the floor below) and blood was flying in all directions, but not once did any of us fall down.

Eventually, though, there were simply too many of them too close for us to attack any longer. James was thrown to the ground and kicked around while Harry and Simon were beset upon by who knew how many. I'd lost sight of Marc and Natalie now. He had clearly been overwhelmed, and she was probably too busy just trying to keep them off her to be able to do anything for the rest of us. As for me, perhaps they knew better than to hurt H3 too badly, but all the same, I was knocked to the ground as James had been, my shield not protecting me from the physical assault, buried in a tide of Hammerhearts and unable to pull myself up. The most I could do was grab a man by the ankle and watch with amusement as he went down, dragging three of his fellows with him.

The situation changed only when the whole room exploded. I never saw how it happened. I only knew that the whole world erupted in a blaze of light and a deafening roar of noise. The force of it seemed to dull all my senses, but later I could remember the feel of the floor shifting and collapsing beneath me, the weight of the Hammerhearts all falling down on top of me as they lost their footing, and a sense of falling through empty space with noise and bodies all around me. The next thing I knew was that I was lying on the floor again with bodies on top of me, barely able to breathe.

What made the situation so different from before was that while I had suffered comparatively little in the ordeal, most of the Hammerhearts had been far more exposed to the explosion than I had, and judging by the horrible moaning all around and above me, many of them were pretty badly hurt. I struggled pointlessly beneath the weight of them for several moments before my own strength ran out and I simply lay there, trying to breathe and barely able to get any clean air into my lungs. I may have been there for some thirty seconds, but those were some of the thirty darkest seconds of my life. Trapped beneath a mass of bodies, unable to move, unable to breathe properly, my body aching from the fall, I seriously thought I could possibly die in this if nothing happened soon.

Fortunately, something did happen. Magic came to my aid, shifting the bodies aside as though deliberately looking for me. The moaning bodies fell sideways onto other moaning bodies and the weight was suddenly gone from my back. I took in a great lungful of air before looking up to see that Natalie had come to my aid. She helped me to my feet before moving away to free Peter. I couldn't see any of him, but I thought I knew approximately where he would have fallen. I turned and stepped slowly and carefully over prone Hammerhearts to join Harry, Simon, James, and Marc, all of whom were white, bloody, and apparently in as much pain as I was.

The scene in which we stood was truly horrible, easily one of the worst things I had ever seen in my life. No, I had to revise that. I had probably seen things worse than this, but at the moment I couldn't think of any. Not even the plane crash in Smiley's memory could compare to this, because at least then there hadn't been many bodies visible to look at. Most of the Hammerhearts were alive, but I could see some who were surely dead, and those who were alive were seriously hurt. There had to be at least a hundred of them, piled high in a space perhaps two or three times the size of my bedroom at home on Lopher Lane—I had no idea why I thought of that.

We had fallen through to the seventh floor as Serena and Jane had done, except that this time, it hadn't been by design. For one thing, we had landed just outside the glass wall (one of which still stood) almost exactly where Darcy and I had been pacing during Jane and Serena's torture. For another thing, and this was the topper, we were surrounded by wreckage—not just that of the wall that Natalie had blown out, but great chunks of steel and concrete from the floor above. A great big hole had been blasted in the roof, right where we had been. It had taken out, not just the floor on which we had been fighting, but the walls on either side. I could see very clearly through it to the inside of the maze above and was busy thanking the heavens that it hadn't blasted through the roof of the floor above as well (if that had come down on us, we would have all been killed without a shadow of a doubt) when Natalie returned to us with Peter.

He was unconscious from his ordeal. Natalie had removed the power of the agonator from him, but he had been under its hold for so long that it was unsurprising that he had tuned out. She was levitating him beside her as she walked, and she, I noticed, was the only one of us who looked almost completely unhurt. Her clothes were pretty much in one piece, apart from what looked like a small burn from the explosion, and she was hardly bleeding at all.

"What on earth," Harry said, but he couldn't find any more words.

Not that he needed to, of course. The same question was written on all our faces: How had that just happened? Who, or what, could have caused such a massive explosion? I seriously doubted that the Hammersons had ever installed a feature like that in any of their buildings. All I could think of at that moment was the way the doors to the Worship Hall had been blasted open. Perhaps it had been the same person with the same weapon who had done this? If so, I hoped he was dead now. Weapons that dangerous shouldn't belong in the hands of fools.

We became aware of other activity around us and instinctively went for our weapons. The Hammerhearts who had been on this level prior to the explosion (there hadn't been many of them, no more than ten) had come to investigate the condition of their fellows. None of them were armed anymore, and although they looked at us several times, none of them made any moves to attack. Meanwhile, the lifts that they had been holding open on this floor had rediscovered their freedom to roam and were closing their doors.

"Let's go," said James, pointing up to the hole in the roof. "They'll be coming down in a minute."

We looked up to see that Hammerhearts were approaching the hole, seeing what lay below, and hurrying away. James, was right, of course. They would be coming straight down here to recommence the battle, and never mind the fate of their friends.

"Guys, I lost the crystal back there—" Marc began, but we didn't give him time to finish. James had already pushed his two Sorcerous Crystals into Marc's hands, and Natalie and I hurried to follow his lead.

"A bit of luck for a change," Harry remarked. "Let's see if it can continue."

The six of us hurried towards the lifts and the stairs. The door to the stairwell was still open and I could see bodies beyond it. We might have to wait for a lift, but in the state we were in, that definitely seemed like a better option. Marc hit the down button and we stood, waiting, watching the screens of all the lifts as they moved, ominously, up to the sixth floor, where they remained with their doors open, probably admitting Hammerhearts.

Simon swore under his breath. "Even the computers in this joint are against us."

"We gotta take the stairs," said Natalie, looking through the doorway onto the crowded landing.

"Any ideas how we're gonna get through that?" Marc asked.

"We always knew we'd have to climb over more bodies," said Harry nervously. "Let's just get it over with before—"

Too late. Several Hammerhearts were already pushing their way down the stairs from the floor above, and they were followed by several more. At the same moment, one of the lifts to our right opened, revealing a group of perhaps a dozen Hammerhearts, all of whom were just as ready to fight as those on the floor above had been. Marc and Natalie dealt with them while the rest of us attended to those in the stairwell with our solid-outliners, holding them up, trapping them in with those who were lying unconscious there, and making it more difficult for those behind them to make any further progress. Again, they used their own solid-outliners to free their fellows, meaning that we had to remain on the offensive.

The situation once again became out of control as more lifts arrived and the number of Hammerhearts around us multiplied. Additionally, more came streaming in from a door I hadn't seen on the other side of the room, skirting the pack of injured people and joining in the attack from behind. I barely had any energy left (both physical and mental) to spare for this now, but fortunately, Marc had an opportunity to cast a protective shield around all of us as they closed in —a physical one this time, which seemed to automatically remove my private one (whether accidentally or on purpose, I wasn't sure). It prevented them coming within six feet of us and deflected all their spells, causing them to hit other people. It enabled Harry, Simon, James, and I to deal with them a little more easily since we didn't have to worry as much about defending ourselves, and it became slightly easier still when Peter was finally able to return to the attack.

Within seconds, as they began to realise what was going on, a standoff ensued, where they could not approach any farther due to the shield, and we could not move due to them pressing in around the shield. I thought back to the starfish monster on Rock Haulter. That had been forced to move as we came at it, but then that hadn't been quite as physical as these Hammerhearts were, and there were so many of them on all sides. Marc was stuck in the middle of the shield, unable to move but at least able to continue attacking the Hammerhearts around us. They were up to the task, though, for whenever one dropped, his or her place was instantly filled by someone else.

"You people had better get moving," Natalie warned them, pointing above their heads in the direction of the hole blasted in the roof, "in case we do that again."

A few of their faces became nervous, apparently unaware that Natalie hadn't caused that at all, but one brave man said, in a strong German accent, "You vill pay for vhat you did to our friends."

"You vill pay even more," Marc retorted, throwing his accent right back at him, "for vhat you did to *our* friends."

"You vill not get out of—"

The rest of his words were cut off by an almighty *BANG*, whose sound I couldn't trace due to its sheer volume, nor could I see where it had come from or what it had done, but after my recent experiences, I would recognise it anywhere: a gunshot. Yells of fright followed the shot, and then they were extinguished by a second shot, then a third. Hammerhearts began running in all directions, desperate to get out of the line of fire, tripping and falling over each other and being trampled by others. It was horrible to watch, but fortunately, Marc wasn't about to let this opportunity slip. He beckoned us all to gather close around him as he proceeded to carve a path through the crowd towards the lifts.

"Oh my God—Marc!" James called, pointing over several heads at something none of us had seen yet. "You didn't tell us you called it back."

"What? Fewul?" Marc repeated, looking confused. "I didn't call it back, although now you mention it, it's probably safe to do so now if—"

And then, through the frantic crowd, I saw him for myself. The man with the gun, who had taken the form of Lucien, was also forcing his way towards one of the three lifts that still stood open, firing regularly into the crowd to hurry them out of his way. A few Hammerhearts were crouched not far from him with guns of their own, firing their own shots, but they were all somehow missing him. I gripped Marc's arm very hard because I felt sure I knew what was really going on here, for even if Marc really had called the beast back, there was no reason in the world why Fewul would need to use a gun to guide us to safety.

"Oh, blimey," I barely heard Marc whisper beside me. "But then, if he's here—"

I didn't need him to finish the sentence. Now I knew exactly how that hole in the roof came to be, and it hadn't been the man with the gun who had put it there. So if Lucien had managed to enter the base and was attacking Hammerhearts, where was his (our, I reminded myself) father? I received my answer to that question as we finally reached the nearest open lift at the same time as Lucien—he was already in the lift, and he looked similar to the way he had looked on the night he had cut his hand off. He was crouched on the floor, clutching his chest, very pale and barely able to breathe. Both he and Lucien were pushed backwards by Marc's shield as we hurried over the threshold, the former rolling backward onto the floor of the lift, unable to move anywhere else, the latter back out towards the mob of terrified Hammerhearts. Their terror was starting to transform into something more organised now, however, as they became aware that all their enemies were congregated in the space of a single elevator.

We all turned to face them and attacked as Marc took the brave step of removing the shield. Lucien continued to fire, stepping backwards through the doors as Peter pushed the button for level nine. As the doors began to slide shut, we were given one last glimpse of the seventh floor: Many Hammerhearts were still running in all directions, most towards the far stairwell, some for the closer, blocked up stairwell, but there were some who were preparing to launch one final attack on the group in the lift. Fortunately, they never got a chance, as Marc sprung up a second shield, this one across the doors, which he lifted the moment they had closed. The silence that followed was deafening in its completeness, caused both by its suddenness and the awkwardness of being stuck in a descending lift with Moran and Lucien. Lucien seemed to feel the same way I did, as he refused to look at any of us, but Moran didn't seem in tune with anything at all.

"What's up with him?" Simon muttered.

"Father," Lucien muttered distractedly, pushing his way past us to crouch down beside Moran. As the group parted, I got a better look at him. He was flat on his back and white as a sheet. He was barely stirring.

"I think he's—" Natalie whispered, but I knew as she spoke what was going on: The man was dying, clearly dying. What on earth had happened to him? He didn't look as though he had been attacked at all.

I saw his eyes open in the final moments. They moved from Lucien, who knelt beside him, to Marc, who stood above him, clearly unsure how to feel. He never saw me in those moments, and I could never decide later whether that had been a good thing or not. Maybe it would have been nice to receive some recognition, but then maybe it would have made it hurt so much more. As it was, the pain was minimal, given that I had despised him so much fairly recently and that I had always believed my parents were already dead.

"What happened to him?" James asked Lucien directly.

"I—I don't know," he whispered.

A moment later, it was over. The body fell still upon the lift floor. His hands, which had previously been clenched, relaxed and became limp. The eight of us were left standing (kneeling, in Lucien's case) and simply staring at each other, nothing but shock frozen on all of our faces.

Chapter 48: To the Death

The shock of the moment held for several seconds, but we snapped out of it as we felt the lift come to a stop on the level of the Hammerheart Highway. Peter slammed on the button to hold the door closed so that we had a few more moments to prepare for the sprint across the bridge and, most likely, more Hammerhearts attacking us. I was glad, because even if we were about to give them more time to prepare, at least we wouldn't be caught completely off guard, which we would have been if the doors had been allowed to open. The small enclosed space in which we stood seemed alive (or perhaps dead) with the suddenness of what had just happened. It almost felt as the room itself, which had become extremely claustrophobic now, was haunted by the spirit of the man who now lay dead upon the floor. This made me think of something to snap me out of my shock.

"Marc, the ghost—you don't reckon she's here too?"

"Course she's not," said James dismissively, and I felt my heart sink.

"How can you be sure?"

"John, all the Hammerheart bases are shrunken. If she were here, she'd fill the whole building."

Not necessarily, I thought. Perhaps magic like that would work on ghosts as well. Somehow, I doubted it, though. I had done a lot of research on ghosts as part of a project two years ago, and I knew that very few spells were capable of binding ghosts in any way at all. On the other hand, Smiley had been able to enter the Chopville base in his shadow…

Nobody else made any comment on the exchange that had just passed, not even Lucien, who was still by Moran's side and looked incapable of doing anything more, anyway. Another idea came to me as I watched him, and I gestured to the others to remain silent with one hand as I dug into my pocket for the unboggler with the other. If Lucien were allowed to walk alone from tonight on, he would return to Hammerson, who would promptly kill him for his betrayal. It was time he returned to our side. Balancing carefully to lean around James and Peter, I took careful aim and clicked the device. Lucien slumped forward, right across the chest of our dead father, and didn't move, but I knew I had done the job correctly.

"What on earth did you do?" Harry asked.

"Brought him back to our side," I said, feeling satisfied that finally, we had something other than death to take out of the night.

Lucien returned to himself a moment later, looking shocked, disoriented, and completely himself again. Marc grinned and helped him back to his feet. He was shaking, but not as though he had no idea how he had come to be here.

"Are we ready to move?" Peter asked, pushing the button to release the doors again.

"*No!*" Marc howled, but it was too late. The moment the doors had begun to open, Hammerhearts thrust their arms inside and wrenched them open the rest of the way.

The assault recommenced in earnest. Jets of light, hundreds of them by the look of it, flew into the lift. Natalie and Harry both went down under the influence of agonators while Peter, James, Simon, and I were all struck by jets from solid-outliners. Only Marc and Lucien remained untouched. The former took only a moment to raise another shield directly in front of us, throwing the nearest Hammerhearts backwards and preventing their spells ripping us to pieces. There was already so little of us left as it was. We weren't exactly naked, but our clothes were pretty much hanging off us (all except Natalie and Lucien, who were comparatively in one piece) and much of our exposed skin was either bleeding or covered in dry blood.

Lucien, meanwhile, fired a single shot into the crowd, directly between the ankles of two of the nearest Hammerhearts, both of whom scuttled backwards, waving their arms and toppling over. The shot didn't hit anyone, which was perhaps his intention now that he had returned to our side. Marc quickly extinguished Natalie's and Harry's agony before checking that he had the shield around all of us. Once he was free, Harry sprang to his feet and released the rest of us from our binds before shooting jets of white light into the crowd. They parted like the Red Sea before them.

"Let's move," Marc muttered, and he began to step out of the lift, the rest of us flanking him, keeping the crowd at bay with our own spells. A few feet from the lift, Marc looked back. Moran still lay there in the lift, and it seemed that both he and I remembered what lay with him at the same time, but before either of us could turn back, the doors slid shut on him. I groaned aloud. Another crystal had just fallen into the wrong hands, but then perhaps we were lucky and Lucien had managed to take it off him.

There was not a moment left to waste. The Hammerhearts around us had organised into a circle and were now moving along with us, firing spells into the shield but apparently not expecting them to break through. They simply walked with us, perhaps accepting that we were about to leave the base and resigned to it, but the looks on their faces told me that there was at least one more obstacle for us to pass, and I found myself wondering if anything that lay ahead could be as bad as what we had just left behind.

The answer to that question stood waiting for us on the other side of the bridge. As we pushed open the door and stepped out into the Hammerheart Highway, double file so that we could fit through, we came face-to-face with our reception committee. There were at least three dozen Hammerhearts standing there, all blocking our access to the door that would return us to the park in suburban Berlin, and I noticed quite a few familiar faces among them. Cornish was there, as was Chief Hall (it must be big business for those two to be pulled off their regular jobs), along with a number of Hammerhearts I recognised from the ambush at Chopville High. Both Hignats were there, both Wilwogs were there, and Sebastian was there, lurking at the back of the pack and looking like he would rather be anywhere but here.

And there, a few feet in front of the rest of them, stood Arnold Hammerson himself, smiling coldly at the sight of us, one hand by his side, the other hidden in his pocket, and I didn't have to wonder what it was doing in there. My worst fear had been realised.

The magic that followed happened so suddenly that it was a miracle that we weren't all blasted to pieces. Certainly Natalie hadn't saved us; she couldn't have read Hammerson's mind (so I thought anyway), nor did she know that he even had magic of his own now, but Marc knew and had only needed a fraction of a second of warning to prepare himself. Bright light, red and gold and blue and silver and a myriad of other colours, filled the air, blinding us all for no more than a second, accompanied by several bangs, so close together that they merged and became a single roar of noise. It lasted longer than the light, ringing in the air, bouncing off the stone walls again and again, deafening. Yet whatever Hammerson had tried to do hadn't had any effect at all. Marc had deflected every spell. No, he had neutralised every spell, and if he had cast any of his own, Hammerson had neutralised them just as effectively.

"Quick-witted, aren't you," Hammerson called over the fading echoes of the magic, his own voice adding to the cacophony but coherent all the same. His tone was amused, almost complimentary even, but his face gave lie to the idea that he was pleased to see how well Marc had equipped himself. "Very impressive, but do you really expect to outwit the likes of me, Seventh Sorcerer?"

"He's not alone," said Natalie fiercely. "He's got me too, and we've both got more power than you now."

"Incorrect, foolish girl," Hammerson jeered, removing his hand from his pocket and showing us all how it was clenched around what appeared to be thin air. I wasn't surprised, and neither was Marc, but the sight threw everyone else completely. Harry and Simon both leapt backward; Natalie let out a squeak of horror; and Peter and James both looked around at me, eyebrows raised, comprehension dawning in both faces. They had seen Hignat, Wilwog, and Sebastian, I knew, and probably would have said something if there had been a moment to spare. Now they understood everything, why I had been quiet since the episode in the prison yard and why I had fought with weapons of my own ever since.

"That won't help you now," Marc called back, his confidence admirable, I thought. He performed some sort of spell directed at the hand holding the Sien-Leoard Crystal, which Hammerson deflected just in time.

"And I think," Hammerson called back, now much easier to hear as the echoes of the magic had faded completely, "we can do without this too."

I felt something push outward from me, from all of us. The shield Marc had placed around us had vanished completely. Marc was quick to replace it, but just as quickly, Hammerson removed it again. Marc tried something different, but once again, Hammerson was able to neutralise it.

"You won't get away with that," Marc warned him. "Even if you won't let me use a shield, I'll stop anything you throw at us, and you're forgetting: There are two of us with magic, and only one of you."

"Maybe so, young man, but take a moment to look behind you and realise what could be without a shield to protect your friends."

I didn't need to look back to know what he meant, and neither did the others. All those Hammerhearts who had flanked us moments ago were now lined up along the wall behind us, across the bridge, blocking our way back into the building. Of course, they were all armed and all ready to attack the moment Hammerson gave the signal. They weren't the only ones either. All those behind Hammerson himself were also armed, mostly with stunners by the look of it, but they would do enough damage on their own given how many there were.

"My, how fortunes can turn so suddenly," said Hammerson softly, leaning forward slightly, apparently without thinking. "In a matter of hours, I have regained some of my most faithful supporters and the most powerful crystal of them all, and moments from now, I shall take possession of the Sorcerous Crystals too. As one chapter ends, another begins, and this next chapter promises to be a glorious tale indeed."

"You're forgetting one thing," said Marc loudly, waving his fistful of the Hero Crystal in the air. "You have to get this off me first."

"That," said Hammerson, smiling broadly, "will be the easy part."

A flash of purple light filled the air, but whatever it had been meant to do, Marc had forced it in another direction. It soared out over the tracks of the Hammerheart Highway and hit the far wall above the tunnels. I never tracked its progress, such was its speed, but I saw the end result in the moment before the light was extinguished: A great big crater had been left in the stone, perfectly round and about the size of half a basketball.

A second flash of light filled the air, exactly the same as the first one, only this time, it was Marc copying the piece of magic Hammerson had most recently performed. At least, I assumed that was what he had asked the crystal to do. The result was much the same, only this time, Hammerson sent it down into the bridge between us. It didn't leave a crater this time, but several jagged cracks spread outward from the place where it had hit.

"Do you really believe you can destroy me, boy?" Hammerson jeered. "You really think you have the power, or the knowledge?"

"I have both," Marc said calmly, "but no, I wasn't trying to destroy you."

This took everyone by surprise. Hammerhearts on both sides of the bridge muttered, and Hammerson's eyes widened.

"Then how," he asked softly, "do you intend to lead your friends to safety? As you are no doubt aware, there is only one way out of this base, and to get to it, you must get past me. So tell me, boy—"

He was right. I hadn't noticed until that point that unlike when we had entered, there wasn't a single Hammerheart cart to be seen, nor were there any sounds coming from any of the tunnels, and the cause of that were the lids that had slid down over them all, blocking each and every tunnel, sealing us in.

"Oh, we can get past you, no problems," said Marc, taking half a step forward so that he was slightly in front of the rest of us. "I only meant that I wasn't trying to kill you. I'll save that for another day, when it will be just you and me, one to one, man to man."

Hammerson gave this due consideration before nodding, apparently satisfied. "That sounds both smart and honourable, but there is one slight problem, Seventh Sorcerer."

"And what might that be?"

"I want to fight you *now!*" he roared, so loudly that everyone, including me, jumped.

An almighty cracking sound filled the air as the bridge ripped free of the rest of the building and went spinning across the room, all of us still on it. I staggered sideways into Peter and we both went down. Nearly everyone around us fell down too; only Marc managed to keep his balance as the bridge came to rest, floating ten feet above the tracks in the centre of the room. Hammerson stood at one end with only a few Hammerhearts still with him (most had been too close to the wall and had been left where they were as the bridge ripped free of the rest of the structure) and the eight of us were alone at the other end, those Hammerhearts behind us now moving quickly away from the wide gap that had suddenly opened up right in front of them. Slowly, we got back to our feet to face Hammerson once more, Marc leading the offense and Natalie popping up beside him.

"I intend to make you all pay dearly for coming here tonight," Hammerson told us, his eyes moving from Marc to Natalie and then fixing menacingly on me, "and especially for what you have done here."

"She deserved what she got," Marc said boldly. "Her life was worth four of ours tonight. She deserved it."

"Whatever it was that she got," said Hammerson coldly, "will only have made her stronger, and now that I have magic of my own, I shall see to that."

"Leave it," I muttered to Marc, quietly enough that with any luck, Hammerson wouldn't have heard. I knew Marc was on the verge of giving just enough away that Hammerson might guess how much we knew about the protection he had placed around himself, Tankom, and Cornish. If he believed we didn't know, that we had been lucky to strike Tankom in just the right way, that would serve us better in the future.

"Too late, buddy," said Peter bravely. "She's dead, and no magic can bring someone back from the dead, unless you'd be cruel enough to damn your own mother for eternity for two weeks."

"Would you like me to show you eternal damnation?" Hammerson asked Peter directly.

Whatever Hammerson had planned for Peter most certainly wasn't good. This time, Marc deflected the spell by placing a solid wall of metal in front of Peter. The jet of light, red this time, shattered the metal completely but did not have enough impetus to continue. Instead, Peter was sprinkled with fragments of metal. They may have added fresh blood to his face, but nothing worse than that.

"This isn't going to get you anywhere," Marc told Hammerson boldly. "I have no interest in standing here trying to prove who is better with magic. We'll be leaving here tonight, so—"

Another crack split the air and this time, we were all thrown completely. The stone upon which we stood separated from that on which Hammerson stood and flipped over backwards. All eight of us were thrown into the air, tumbling and screaming. I completely lost my sense of direction; I knew not which way I had been thrown, which way Hammerson was, or even which was up and which was down. I only knew when I hit the floor, landing on my outstretched hands and then coming down on my stomach, much more softly than I ought to have. Hardly shocked (I'd been through worse than that on this night), I jumped back to my feet, looking around for the others. Natalie was on her feet too, already helping the others up. I felt sure that it had been she who had cast that quick bit of magic to protect us. Above us, Hammerson and his loyal group of Hammerhearts (the Hignats and Wilwogs of this world) were laughing loudly. The only Hammerheart not laughing was Hall.

"You look like a fool, Seventh Sorcerer," Hammerson jeered. "Take your chance to hand over the Sorcerous Crystals now, and maybe you'll be allowed to leave. After all, you're nothing without them."

"You really expect me to believe that?" Marc called up to him. "That's an insult to my intelligence. Why don't you take your chance to go fuck yourself sideways with a twenty-foot telegraph poll—"

He was cut off, not by a flash of light or a cracking sound, but a deep rumbling that seemed to be coming from the walls, ceiling, and floor themselves. I remembered that this whole building was underground. That made me think of earthquakes, and in that moment, the floor on which we stood began to move. The whole room seemed to vibrate with the force of the rumbling as the tremor became more persistent. The Hammerhearts, all those not standing with Hammerson anyway, looked around them nervously. Many of the German ones backed into the building again, as though it could provide greater protection than the Highway, and in this case, I thought they were probably right.

I wasn't sure what Hammerson had been trying to do, until the floor began to open up, like some horrible stone mouth, the lips widening before us. The crack had appeared right down the centre of the group so that a few of us, myself included, had been, for a moment, standing with one leg on either side of the mouth. We were quick to jump aside to avoid falling into a hole who only knew how deep. The trouble was we had jumped to different sides, and by the time the fissure was six feet wide, there were four of us on either side—me, Peter, James, and Natalie on one side, and Harry, Simon, Lucien, and Marc on the other.

The crack stretched the entire length of the room and, by some twist of physics (or perhaps there was nothing scientific about it at all), only affected the floor. The walls and ceiling remained completely in one piece. I had a moment to wonder what had happened to the levels below this one, to the Basement and execution chamber, but the present situation demanded the rest of my attention.

"Any change of heart yet, Seventh Sorcerer?" Hammerson jeered. "Will you hand over the Sorcerous Crystals yet, or do I need to force one of your friends to take a high dive?"

"You know I won't let either of those things happen."

"Good luck to you. Very well, then, I think I'll start with the traitor."

On the other side of the great mouth, Harry and Simon moved forward so that they blocked Lucien from Hammerson's aim. Marc stepped sideways so that he was directly in front of them both, although he couldn't block them both from Hammerson's aim alone. I wished I could get over there too, and perhaps I could, but if I made a jump over that hole, I would be completely exposed to Hammerson for perhaps long enough to knock me straight down into oblivion.

Instead of repeating his words or trying to deflect Hammerson's attacks, Marc went on the offense himself. Before Hammerson had registered what he was doing, Cornish (who had been standing at Hammerson's right shoulder) was lifted into the air and thrown across the room. Marc didn't let him crumple against the stone on the far wall, but instead threw him upward again and suspended him against the ceiling. Hammerson made at least two attempts to break Marc's spell during the transfer, both of which failed. Once he was up there, Marc surrounded his body with the same metallic substance he had used to protect Peter, so that Cornish was locked in some horrible coffin.

"Hand over that crystal and I'll let him—"

He didn't even get a chance to finish this time. I had a moment's warning, enough to grab Peter and James and throw them away from the great mouth along with me, before a great wall of fire sprung from it, separating Marc's group from our group completely. The heat coming from it was dry, searing, and the four of us scuttled from it as best we could. I couldn't see anything of Marc, Lucien, and the twins on the other side of it, nor could I see Hammerson anymore, but I heard his words.

"The crystal will survive that, but you won't. Hand it over now before you're all toasted."

"This isn't getting anywhere," James muttered to the three of us. "We have to get up to that door somehow. Nat, make some stairs or something, while he's distracted."

"Are you suggesting we leave the others?"

"No, obviously we wait 'til they're ready to go, but we have to do something while we can."

There was one problem with that idea—we were on the wrong side of the hole in the floor. In fact, with the wall of fire (firewall, I told myself) beside us, we couldn't even see the door anymore. I was about to suggest to Natalie that she should teleport us to the other side, or get rid of the fire, or anything that would help us get over there, when either Marc or Hammerson obligingly did it for us. The fire vanished into the crack in the floor, and we were once again able to see what was going on.

Marc had managed to dislodge all the Hammerhearts from the stone they had been standing on. Hammerson had managed to guide them down to the tracks where they now stood in a group behind him, weapons out, ready to strike. Cornish had been rescued and was attempting to re-join his cohorts. The problem was the twins and their jets of white light—they had struck him in the back and the whiteness was spreading around him, but as long as his legs were free of it, he did his best to get out of the way of further spells.

"Give it away, boy," Hammerson called to Marc. "You know this won't end well for you, and I'm only just warming up. Don't give me a reason to get serious with you and your friends."

"I don't know why you bother to say that anymore. You must know none of us are cowardly enough to give in without a fight."

"There is a difference between bravery and stupidity, and that, young man, is the latter. Do the wise thing now or you and your friends can all take a ride together on the fast train to Ghost Town."

Both Marc and Natalie put their magic into operation at the same time. Natalie (at least I'm fairly sure it was her) created some sort of metal cover that slid over the crack in the floor, allowing us to step across it to join the others. Marc, meanwhile, sent some sort of spell directly at Hammerson, forcing the other to defend himself against whatever it was. I knew Marc wasn't aiming to hit him, perhaps knew he couldn't, and Hammerson knew that even if he were hit, it wouldn't kill him. Nevertheless, it achieved what Marc had wanted, and that was to engage the other.

Natalie, Peter, James, and I hurried over the crack as quickly as we could lest it open up again and crowded in behind the twins, whose solid-outliners were pointing into the group of Hammerhearts now. Lucien still stood behind them. He was unhurt but clearly in a state of shock, and after all he had been through in the last hour, it was no wonder. James, Peter, and I withdrew our own weapons and pointed them into the group of Hammerhearts, but it was no use even attempting to get a clear shot. Jets of light were flying around the space between us, so bright and so quickly that it was mesmerising.

Marc stood a few feet in front of us, ducking and weaving and never staying still longer than a fraction of a second, yet not a single spell of Hammerson's missed its mark. Each and every one of them was deflected back at him. He was likewise moving around, deflecting his own regurgitated magic and adding new spells to the mix, each in an attempt to knock Marc off his game. One wrong move by either of them would end the battle, yet neither looked like putting a foot wrong. The air was thick with the intensity of the magic and the effects of the spells as one or the other deflected them sideways. The stone on all the walls was becoming cracked, and I started to worry that the whole works might come crashing down on us if we didn't get a move on soon.

I wasn't the only one aware of the danger, either. While the rest of us kept the Hammerhearts across the room at bay, Natalie slipped away behind us and under cover of the battle, created a set of steps leading up to the little platform on which some of the Hammerhearts still stood, which led to the one and only door out of the place. The possibility existed that that door too had been sealed off, but I thought either Marc or Natalie would be capable of unlocking it.

I glanced back over my shoulder only once, when I heard a disturbance, and saw those Hammerhearts who had been trapped up there hurrying down the stairs. I thought I even heard one of them ask Natalie if she could make more stairs leading up to the other door—the one that led back into the rest of the building. She didn't oblige, of course, and they settled for attempting to climb up a huge chunk of stone (that which we had been standing on before it had flipped), which had fallen conveniently close to the place. Sebastian was among them, I noticed, and for a moment, I wondered if Natalie would curse him with something or other as he passed, but again, she didn't.

Neither Marc nor Hammerson noticed any of this. They were so thoroughly engaged in a battle that could easily destroy one or the other (not kill, in Hammerson's case, but certainly the possibility of completely disabling him existed if Marc could somehow remove the crystal from his hand). It was a miracle too that none of us had been killed. I felt sure that Hammerson was trying to get past him, to get a shot at any of us (probably I was his top priority there), but so far Marc had done well to deflect everything.

His Hammerhearts, however, had seen what we were doing. Hall was watching, through the battle, the Hammerhearts attempting to escape the Highway, probably marking their identities as cowards (if Hammerson believed that, they would all be killed most likely), and Cornish, who Hall had set free moments earlier, was communicating the message to the others that we were on the verge of escaping. Fortunately for us, they couldn't do anything to stop us, not with the space between us too dangerous to cross, and none of them were brave enough to interrupt the battle.

At that precise moment, however, the battle came to a standstill. It hadn't ended, as such; the two seemed to have hit a wall between them. What was happening now looked like an arm wrestle of the mind, where neither could afford to give an inch to the other. A blinding light lit up the room exactly halfway between them, a combination of red and gold, each colour trying to push against the other. Both their faces were screwed up with concentration.

"Your brother will be first," Hammerson snarled through gritted teeth in an attempt to throw Marc off his game. "I'll tie him up and have him ripped apart, just like your mother. If only you could have seen what was left of her…"

"Just you wait 'til you see what's left of your mother's head," Marc retorted in a snarl to match his. "That is—not much at all."

"But she's not dead, and when I've repaired her, she'll come after you like you've never seen before. We have the ascendency now, boy —you'd better believe it."

"Don't get ahead of yourself. I have one more trick left up my sleeve."

I thought I knew what was coming but wondered, with horror, if Marc would be able to pull it off without breaking his concentration. The thought had barely formed in my mind when an ear-splitting roar filled the room, an inhuman shriek that raised goose bumps all over. Sure enough, it did break Marc's concentration, but fortunately for him, Hammerson had been so thoroughly thrown by the noise that he hadn't been able to take advantage of the moment. The two lights between them flickered and went out, but not before they had illuminated, clearly, the figure that had appeared on the far side of the room. Fewul had finally returned to the battle, and he (it) had also returned to its true form, that of an enormous bear-shaped creature, dark, hideous, and every bit as dangerous as it looked, and then some.

Yells of alarm filled the room. The Hammerhearts already attempting to leave the place redoubled their efforts to climb the unsteady slab of stone, and even those behind Hammerson now looked extremely nervous. Several of them had lowered their weapons and seemed to be considering making a run for it—to where? I bet none of them knew. Only one person paid no attention to the Beast of Magic. Hall had apparently been waiting for the battle to die down enough for him to attack, and of course, it was me, Peter, and James for whom he went. Peter collapsed under the power of the agonator for the second time, yelling and almost knocking me and James over with his flailing feet, while James and I both let out involuntary cries as fresh gashes opened up across our exposed chests. With very little left of our shirts, the blow was even more painful than usual. Harry and Simon set on Hall with their own weapons, one stunning him while the other used a solid-outliner to freeze him in place, and Natalie used her magic to free Peter.

"We're on our way out now," Marc told Hammerson, glancing sideways at the beast but never completely looking away from the former Sorcerer. "I don't know when I'll be back, but I hope it's no time soon. Your hospitality is really nothing to boast about."

He cast another shield around us all, or rather, a shield around each of us. I knew it was so because James and I, who had been almost shoulder to shoulder, suddenly jerked sideways away from each other. Lucien was the first one to turn and sprint for the newly created stairs, and it was his initiative that enabled the rest of us to move. Harry and Simon turned next and sprinted after him, and Peter and James were quick to follow, the former being helped along as he was so unsteady on his feet. That just left me, Marc, and Natalie. Marc took care of the issue by looking sideways at the Beast of Magic, who launched into an attack of its own. The distraction was sufficient to prevent Hammerson from being able to pay us any attention at all.

"Meet us on the outside as soon as we're out," Marc called to it and turned, grabbing my arm and forcing me to move with him.

"*No—you—don't!*" Hammerson roared, sounding much more like he had the last time we had met than he had at any point until now.

He took the risk of taking half a mind off the Beast of Magic and paid for it when he was thrown through the air, hitting the stone wall directly opposite from Fewul and being knocked out cold. The Sien-Leoard Crystal would have been over there with him, I knew, but there was no chance to get it for two reasons. One was the Hammerhearts, all of whom were much happier attacking us than they were the Beast of Magic. The other reason was the spell that Hammerson had shot at us in the moment before he had been hit; it had probably been meant for both me and Marc, but as Natalie drew level with us on my left, I saw very clearly the result of it, what would have happened to us if his aim had been true.

The jet of red light (the same colour as that which the stunners generated, only this one seemed to glow almost blindingly) came to rest about three inches from Natalie's left shoulder. It paused there for a fraction of a second, halted by the shield that Marc had placed there, and then it burst through, shattering the shield completely. The scream that burst from her was as terrible as any other I had heard that night. Blood flew into the air, not in spatters but in one thick stream, more blood than I had ever seen come from a single person, and I had seen an awful lot of blood lately. And—and something else flew into the air with the blood, spinning and flipping and dripping along with it, and I knew what it was. My stomach turned over.

Natalie collapsed where she had been, and Marc and I, our momentum having carried us a few steps beyond, came back for her. Her shield was gone but both of ours remained. Marc removed them both and cast a new one around the three of us so that we could hoist Natalie back into the air, supporting her between us. I was lucky to be on her right side, the uninjured side. I placed her arm (her remaining arm) around my shoulders and heaved, and along with Marc, we managed to get her along to the foot of the steps.

All the others were waiting at the top of the steps for us, their mouths open in horror at what had just happened, at what they would have had a clear view of from where they stood. It looked as though I had been right about the door being sealed, and I looked sideways at Marc, whose face was screwed up with the effort of moving Natalie along without hurting her too badly. She was barely conscious, anyway.

"Unlock the door," I told him, stepping onto the first step and heaving again.

He obliged, and moments later, all five of them at the top of the stairs disappeared through the door. Good, I thought, only three of us left in here—we're almost out—we're almost through. We heaved again and managed to make a few more steps before trouble hit us once again. A badly aimed jet of gold light flew right between Marc and I. It would have hit Natalie if she had been completely upright. I knew, without having to look back, that despite the Beast of Magic to keep them busy, at least one Hammerheart was prepared to risk his life in an attempt to prevent us from leaving. I wasn't worried about him or her (Marc's shield would keep their magic out even if it hadn't worked against Hammerson himself), but if any of them climbed the stairs after us and got in our way, that would make things more difficult.

Thankfully, that didn't happen. Several more jets of light flew around us but none hit, and we were eventually able to reach the top of the stairs and the door to safety. Before we went through, I took one last look back at the scene we were leaving behind. I wasn't looking for anything or anyone in particular, yet my eyes almost instantly found Hall, who stood with the other Hammerhearts but was the only one not trying to either get to Hammerson or get out of the way of Fewul. He simply stood there, staring at the three of us, and as our eyes met, we reached an unspoken understanding between the two of us: The next time he and I met, it would be the end of one of us.

In the next moment, the Hammerheart Highway was gone. The three of us collapsed forward onto the cool grass in the park in which was located the entrance to the Berlin base. Marc jumped back to his feet almost immediately, but I remained where I was, holding onto Natalie and inhaling the smell of the grass, savouring the moment. All of a sudden, I was exquisitely exhausted. We had done it—we had got out of the base—all of us, every one of us. From the moment they had started coming after us, we had outrun them every step of the way. Of course, something had taken Moran's life, but somehow that didn't seem to count. I barely had room to worry about that now, though. I could barely think of anything except how lucky we were to be alive, and how I didn't think I could ever rise from this spot again.

Chapter 49: Burning

"Is everyone okay?" Marc called over my head.

"Oh yes, we're all thriving with life and vitality over here," said one of the twins very sarcastically.

"Oh, whatever. Shut up and get over here so we can teleport."

I raised my head and looked around as the others approached and gathered around us. None of us were unhurt, that was for sure (most of our clothes were hanging off us and the slashes were everywhere), but most of that damage seemed to have been done prior to meeting Hammerson. Lucien was in the best shape out of all of us and was the only one fully dressed. I looked sideways at Natalie and was horrified to see that she was still partially conscious but clearly in shock. It would have been much better if she had just passed out completely.

"Here," Marc said, and he knelt close to Natalie on her other side. He pressed the Hero Crystal against what was left of her shoulder and the gaping wound closed up. Her arm was still missing, but at least she wasn't losing blood anymore. Even the grass around us was splattered with blood when any normal person would have bled to death by now. I found myself wishing, for the first time, that Natalie wasn't a Sorcerer. The crystal chip was a curse more than a blessing in this case, especially if it was keeping her semiconscious.

"I'm not brave enough to fix it up here and now," Marc said apologetically, putting an arm around Natalie and, with my help, raising her half off the ground again, "but at least this will make it a little better until we get back to base."

I had a more careful look around us, taking more in. The others were all there. Peter, James, Harry, Simon, Lucien, and even Fewul, back in the bear form, all gathered around me, Marc, and Natalie, the centre of attention, but they were unable to come within a few feet of us due to the shield that Marc hadn't lifted yet. It was dead quiet and the dead of night. The only source of light came from the full moon almost directly overhead (how appropriate that there should be a full moon tonight). Behind me, the tree that had concealed the hidden entrance into the Hammerheart base had vanished completely.

"Er, where's the tree?" I asked, my voice sounding distant to my own ears, and I became aware that if I expended much more energy, I was likely to pass out.

"I got rid of it," said Marc, "just in case Hammerson comes around quicker than we want. At least with the entrance completely gone, it'll take him a while to get to this exact spot, and it won't matter if we get out of here right now. Everyone brace yourselves."

A moment later, we were gone from the park, and several more moments later, we rematerialised in Hamster's Stretch Reserve, within sight of the Woodward house. The first thing I registered was that it was dawn. The sun hadn't come up yet, but the sky in the east was beginning to lighten. Given the time of year, I estimated that to mean it was around six o'clock, give or take half an hour. My body wanted to collapse on the spot with the knowledge that we were back home, and indeed Peter really did fall to his knees, letting out a long, drawn-out moan of despair as he went down. Marc afforded himself no such luxury. He stiffened, looking around cautiously, and I knew why—if Hammerson was really on the ball, he would have sent a few people to this spot to wait for us to appear, in case we managed to escape. But the park was thankfully, blessedly deserted. All the same, we wouldn't be truly safe until we had gone through the wall in the Woodward study.

"Come on, guys, gotta get in the base," Marc told us. "Pete, you gonna be okay?"

"Sure," he muttered, getting back to his feet with an obvious effort.

We trooped to the house nearby, me and Marc leading the way, supporting Natalie between us. Fewul brought up the rear. Perhaps it had been ordered by Marc to make sure we weren't attacked from any side around. If so, it did its job, for nothing struck us all the way across the grass and through the back door. A small group of people were waiting for us just outside the study: Amelia, Rebecca, Jessica, Katie, Sophie, and Erica. They had been leaning against the wall, awake but not exactly attentive (not surprising, how long they'd been waiting already; they had probably assumed the worst already). When I released one hand to push open the door, however, they all started and, seeing who we were, hurried forward in a rush.

"Marc! John! Oh, my God!"

Of course, it was Natalie who drew most of the gasps, particularly from her sister. She and Amelia came forward and helped me and Marc get Natalie into a seat nearby. Under any other circumstances, I wouldn't have wanted to let go of her, but right now I was only relieved—she would be in better hands now. Katie, Sophie and Erica bounded into the arms of their exhausted boyfriends, and Jessica was left to stand close by, watching James with tears in her eyes.

"You—you all—" Amelia sputtered, taking us all in, our torn clothes, the blood drying on our exposed skin. Finally, all she managed to whisper was, "What happened?"

"Long story," said Marc, and there was a peculiar look on his face as he met Amelia's eyes, and I thought I knew what it was: He longed for her to give him a hug. Amelia may have noticed it, and maybe she would have obliged, but Jessica's voice drew our attention elsewhere before she could respond.

"Er, guys," she said slowly, and, looking around, I saw that she was the first person to register the fact that Lucien was with us—the real Lucien. The fact was obvious only because Fewul stood beside him.

"It's him," said James, "and he's on our side now. John sorted him out."

"What on earth happened in there?" Erica chided James. "You took so long to get back. We were so worried. We knew it couldn't be good after you guys went up a floor, but when we got back here, Mr. Woodward wouldn't let us come back. Refused it, point blank."

"Didn't stop us going in the first place," said Harry, but Amelia shook her head.

"Wait 'til you see him," she said in a low voice. "He was mad—angrier than I've ever seen him. He said that you guys got yourselves into that mess, so you had to get out of it. If you were going to disobey his orders, you were old enough to sort yourselves out. He said that you still had more magic than them, so you would be able to get out."

"He doesn't know about the last bit," I said, "about what happened at the very end."

"What happened?" Amelia repeated. "Is anyone going to tell me?"

"Let's go through the wall first," suggested Peter. "How much do you guys already know?"

"We know Tankom's dead," said Amelia, "and we know you guys went up a couple of floors after they started chasing you, and then Tommy killed himself."

We had been moving into the study, but I stopped dead at these words, and James walked into me from behind.

"John, what—"

"How did you know that?" I asked, and no sooner were the words out of my mouth than the answer came to me, and I exclaimed in wonder. "Tommy! He's—he's still here?"

"Oh, he's here all right," said Amelia, smiling weakly. "I wouldn't say he's exactly happy about things, but he's relieved for himself. He reckons maybe he'll be able to live a relatively normal life now."

I felt the relief touch me too. After all that had happened that night, we had come out with one less death. More than that. We had taken Tankom out and freed Tommy from whatever horror he had been living most of his life. Of course, what Tankom had done may not have been undone by Tommy's death in Germany (perhaps he would still be able to play the Maahoo, for one thing), but as far as Tommy was concerned, he was off the hook. If only he had thought to do that before this death, Serena, Jane, and Moran would all still be alive, but I couldn't blame him for that. He couldn't have known they would change tactics and go after him in Germany instead of here.

I mulled over these thoughts all the way through the study and up the corridor beyond. I could hear soft voices coming from the lounge room as we drew level with the door to the living quarters, but that was where the group was held up.

"We should all go up and change our clothes," Marc told us. "I know you all wanna sleep—believe me, I do too—but I'm sure Amelia's right, and Mr. Woodward will want to see us before we can rest. Lucien, you should probably go and see him right now; he'll wanna check you out for himself. And Amelia, can you help get Nat to the infirmary. I wasn't brave enough to sort her out myself, but at least you guys know what you're doing."

"I reckon you should fix her up yourself," Harry stated.

Marc rounded on him. "Why? You think it was my fault that Hammerson did that to her? You blame me for that? I did my best in there, you know."

I could only put his overreaction down to utter exhaustion, because it was unlike Marc to react like that to anything, even an intentional accusation.

"No," said Harry, surprised. "I reckon you should do it because you're absolutely fucking brilliant! I can't believe we got out of that."

Marc allowed himself to smile weakly. It was a feeble thing. "Me neither. We were so lucky. I couldn't have done that on any other day. Come on, let's go get changed."

"Hammerson came?" Amelia asked, but nobody answered. Marc in the lead, he, Peter, James, the twins, and I left her there and trudged up the stairs to our third-floor rooms. Several people came out of the lounge room to watch us up, but any questions they may have called to us were quelled by Marc, who leaned over the rail and gave them a facial expression that made them all cringe back; thankfully I didn't see it.

In my room, alone at last, I deposited my various weapons on my bedside table (I couldn't be bothered putting them away properly just now) and began removing what remained of my clothing, all the while staring longingly at my bed. That huge bed was an enormous luxury right now, and what I wouldn't have given to flop down on it and sleep. I'd probably be out before I could even get under the covers, but I resisted the urge. Believe me, it was a lot tougher to do that than it sounds. Slowly, I pulled on some fresh clothes. I would have gone for pyjamas, but I had no idea how long the rest of this night/morning would take.

As I changed, I cast my mind back to all that had happened that night, starting with the incident in the prison yard. For me, it all started there, and later, I would probably look back on that moment as my fall from grace. I had cost us all so much by falling for that trick. I had no desire to go down there and tell them all what had happened, but still, none of them knew the whole story, even those who had seen Hammerson with the Sien-Leoard Crystal. There were a couple of other explanations I owed them too: How Jane and Serena had come to be in danger in the first place, and more importantly, what had possessed me to take such radical revenge against Tankom. Also, I had something else to share with them, a theory that had come to me from nowhere, because I certainly hadn't spent any time dwelling on it. I felt sure that Moran had caused the explosion that had enabled our escape from all those Hammerhearts, and he had died shortly after it from means that had appeared, on the outside, completely unrelated to the magic he had performed. It was just too much of a coincidence. In fact, I could think of two possible links; he could have been killed by one or the other, or perhaps both at the same time.

By the time I returned to the stairs and was making my way down, quite a crowd had gathered in the hall below. Marc, Harry, and Simon had already returned and were busy trying to get to the door to the corridor. I made to follow them as soon as I reached the foot of the stairs but found my passage blocked almost immediately by Dad and Charlie.

"You okay, you big idiot?" Dad asked affectionately.

"Reckon I will be," I muttered. I was truly pleased to see him, Charlie too, but it was hard to be witty just at the moment.

"You've got a lot of explaining to do, young man," said Charlie in what might have been mistaken for a stern tone, if I hadn't known him so well.

"I'm sure I do, but I'm not up to it just at the minute."

"Course you're not, but Freddy's gonna wanna know."

"Well, Freddy can just wait 'til I'm ready," I said wearily. "I'm not exactly proud of myself just now, so don't expect me to take the limelight."

"You've never liked the limelight exactly, but it hasn't stopped you these days," Felicity pointed out. She was standing a few feet to the left of Charlie. I merely shrugged.

"Why aren't you proud of yourself?" Dad asked, genuinely curious. "You don't seriously blame yourself for what happened? From what Freddy gathered, it was Marc, Amelia, and Natalie who made the decision to go out tonight."

"I think it was, but I made a mistake of my own earlier."

"We know—"

"No, this is one nobody knows about yet, but I'm gonna have to tell. You mind letting me through?"

Fortunately, or not, I wasn't quite sure, Mr. Woodward appeared in the doorway at that moment. He looked around the crowd and beckoned Marc, the twins, and me to join him. The crowd parted easily then, allowing the four of us, plus James and Peter, who had been coming down the stairs, to get near him.

"We're in trouble, aren't we?" Peter asked, but he didn't look as though he cared one way or the other.

"Oh, really, really big," said Mr. Woodward, but it looked as though he was prepared to save his telling-offs for another day. I was extremely grateful. "I just want you all to come and talk about tonight. I need to know as much of what happened in there as you can tell me."

"How's Natalie?" I asked as we turned and headed up the corridor towards the Woodward living quarters. "Will she be okay?"

"She'll be fine. My mother has already seen to her. She's resting now, but we'll be able to wake her up in ten minutes or so. There won't be any lasting damage."

I felt another great rush of relief. I'd known that she would be fine, that not much Hammerson could have done to her would have been permanent, with her crystal chip resolutely keeping her alive, but it was good to know all the same.

"John," said James quietly, and I felt my stomach drop. The conciliatory tone made it clear that he was about to address just one of those things I wasn't proud of. "I think I can guess what happened, but the Sien-Leoard Crystal—"

"Yeah, you guessed right," I groaned. "My God, I'm such an idiot. I criticise you for not using the comprehensive memory I put in there," I tell Mr. Woodward, "and then I go and make exactly the same mistake. What on earth is wrong with me?"

"Hang on," said Mr. Woodward, stopping just short of the door to his living quarters. "What is this about, John? What else happened?"

I took a deep breath. "They got the jump on me. Tricked me. Wilwog hit me from behind, and then they grabbed me. I never even had a chance."

"This is when you were in the prison yard?"

"Yeah," I said. "It was all a trick. They wanted it to be me because they wanted to take the Sien-Leoard Crystal off me. It was a plot all along—and it worked."

"So you don't have the crystal anymore?"

I held out my empty palms for an answer, and his face went pale. "Well, maybe they won't have given it to him yet."

"Oh, Hammerson has the crystal now," said Marc hollowly. "If he didn't, Natalie would still have her original arm."

"Not really," said Peter, shrugging. "Didn't she lose her original body altogether in a bomb blast or something?"

"Shut up, Pete. You know what I mean."

"Come in, all of you," said Mr. Woodward briskly, magically swinging the door open before us. "We need to sit down and talk about all of this. I want to know everything that happened after you separated from Amelia. I've already got the beginnings of the story from her."

We settled down in the lounge room and began to talk. At least, Peter, James and the twins did the talking. Marc and I remained silent. I wasn't sure about him, but my silence was more out of shame than anything else. Of course I'd known I would have to talk. Mr. Woodward wanted to know, firstly, what had happened to Jane and Serena. He had already asked Darcy, but he had been too distressed to talk. I told him how they had gone up to the floor above and fallen into the tank and Tankom had executed them in there, but I left out the finer points, not only because I didn't want to relive them but also because of what Tankom had said. However bad we felt, we didn't need to drag Mr. Woodward down with us by reminding him of how his father had died. Judging by the look on his face, however, he guessed what I was talking about, anyway. Thankfully he chose not to interrupt.

Then, naturally, I was asked to explain why I had put all their lives at further risk by breaking from the group and going after Tankom. I told him, simply, that I had to do it. Perhaps I would have explained further except for one thing: It was almost impossible to reconstruct the arguments I had put together while locked in the Basement that had led to my decision in a way that would make them understand just how I had burned for revenge. Mr. Woodward told me, as though I didn't already know, that my move had been extremely foolish, that I was extremely lucky, as were my friends, to have gotten away with that, but in the next breath, he praised me for my bravery.

"I wouldn't call it bravery," James pointed out. "That implies that his decision to do that was rational. He was just acting on his feelings."

"Maybe so, but he still did it, and to have taken Tankom's life in the process makes it worth it," Mr. Woodward said firmly. "I always recommend taking calculated risks, because that's often the only way to get big things done, but I also recommend not taking them in situations like this. Having Tankom out of the way can only be good for us; it probably won't slow Arnold down, but it brings us a step closer to defeating the core of his army all the same. I still say you were very lucky, but very well. I'm given to understand that you went upstairs instead of down with the rest of your friends."

The discussion continued, with James and Peter mentioning how Tommy had gone about killing himself. Mr. Woodward had interrupted at this point to inquire, as I had done, what he had used to take his life.

"Well, it's like John said," said James, shrugging. "It poisons a person's blood."

"But from what you describe, it can shatter a person's skull on impact," Mr. Woodward pointed out. "How exactly does that work? And how did you come to possess this object?"

"That's what I wanted to know," Peter added.

"Hall gave it to me," said James, surprising us all completely. "Er, it was a prize for when I did so well on that spelling test. I didn't open it right away, though, and when we found out he was against us, I decided I wouldn't open it, 'cause I was pretty sure he intended for me to accidentally kill myself or do some other kind of damage with whatever it was. I reckon I was right about that, but when we were on the Rock, Marc and I took it out one day and investigated what it was. That's how I recognised the stuff when I saw it again. I don't know why it crushed Tommy's skull, or Tankom's. I assume it's just part of the magic of the thing."

"Must be," Mr. Woodward mused. "I'd never heard of a device quite like that, but it makes sense that the Hammersons would create one like it. How fitting that one of their own weapons should take one of their lives. Very well, please continue."

So James, Peter, and the twins went into detail about how we had been chased into the maze, how we had been cornered, how we had fought well for a while before being overwhelmed by sheer numbers, and of course, how the floor had exploded.

"Has Lucien confirmed it was your father?" Mr. Woodward asked Marc.

"We haven't had a chance to speak yet," said Marc, "but I don't see how it could be anyone else. I still don't understand how it killed him, though. He hadn't looked visibly injured."

"I think I know," I said quietly. The time had come for me to open my mouth again. "I was thinking about it before. I think he broke the pact that said he wasn't allowed to use the crystal to protect you, Marc, when he blew the roof out. Also, I think the crystal might have killed him—the Villain Crystal."

"It can do that?" Peter asked, alarmed. "I know it's an evil thing, but I just assumed all the crystals always had to serve the person holding them."

"They do," said Mr. Woodward, "but like all villains, the Villain Crystal would be prone to turn on one of its own kind. What idea did you have, John?"

"Well, if he was trying to help us get away," I said, "and I can't think of any other reason why he would do that, then it would have seen that as an action too good for itself—not enough evil in it. Obviously it performed the magic for him, maybe because it had a chance to hurt people in the process, but it didn't let him get away with the gesture. Does that make sense?"

"It does," Mr. Woodward agreed, "and you're right, the Villain Crystal would behave like that in a situation like that, as far as I am aware. Did you actually see the crystal on him?"

"We didn't get a chance to look," said Peter apologetically. "Er, that was my fault, but when he was dying, both his hands were empty."

"Just like they have been every time we've seen him since he came back," I added dully. "Do we have any proof he even has the Villain Crystal?"

"He had been able to perform magic of his own," Mr. Woodward said reasonably. "We know he was the last to have the Villain Crystal, and to this day, that is the only one of the Magic Crystals not accounted for. It's what we might call circumstantial evidence, even if it's not quite hard evidence. This pact you mentioned, John, how did you come to know about that?"

"Smiley told us," said Marc quickly, "but that's a story for another day."

Mr. Woodward stared at him for a few seconds before saying, "Very well. What happened when you left the seventh floor?"

"Only the best damn fight I've ever seen," said Harry admirably, tipping Marc a wink.

Marc shrugged. "After Dad died in the lift and John got Lucien back on our side, we ran into the people waiting for us in the Hammerheart Highway. Quite a few of them were Hammerhearts who had been locked up in here, and Hammerson was with them, and he had the crystal."

He didn't go on, so once again, Peter, James, and the twins described, in considerable detail, the progression of the fight, the taunts that had been exchanged, and the final exchange of magic that had led to Marc recalling Fewul to the battle.

"That was the diversion we needed," James said, "and we got out, but not before Hammerson took one last shot at Natalie. You can guess what happened there."

Mr. Woodward nodded. "Well, I know you don't look happy with yourself, Marc, and overall, I still say you've been extremely foolish this night, but you have to be proud of the way you fought tonight. You, Natalie, and Amelia may have cost two of our lives tonight—three if you count your father, which I suppose you would—but your magical skill saved eight more."

"Luck, you mean," Marc muttered, and when Mr. Woodward raised his eyebrows, he merely shrugged and made no further reply.

"If you say so," Mr. Woodward said, standing up. "That's all I need to know for now, I think, but you haven't heard the last of this. There will be a good amount of talking happening over the next few days, I think. I've let you all act quite independently over the months, but it's a privilege that may need to change after tonight, if it seems you cannot be trusted. Very well, I think you can all go and rest now. I'm going to the infirmary to see how Natalie is, and I'd also like a quick word with Lucien, if any of you want to come along."

We all did, but as it turned out, they were all out of the infirmary already. The time in Chopville was after seven o'clock in the morning now. Quite a chunk of time had passed while we had been recounting the night to Mr. Woodward, and in that time, Natalie's arm had been restored and she had recuperated just enough to leave the ward. We met her, Amelia, and Lucien in the corridor just outside the infirmary, one door down from the entrance to the living quarters. Even from where we stood, we could hear the babble of quiet chatter coming from behind the wall. As tired as many of them undoubtedly were, they were waiting for us.

"Does it hurt now?" Mr. Woodward asked Natalie. "Does it feel normal yet?"

Natalie was very pale, and while she was fully conscious now, she was still a little unsteady on her feet. Amelia stood close beside her, holding her arm and steadying her whenever she looked like overbalancing.

"Stiff," she said, trying to bend it at the elbow, "but it'll be fine in a few hours, probably."

"During which I'd like you to go and sleep," he told her. "All of you. Now, how about you, Lucien? How do you feel?"

"Pretty tired too," he said, smiling weakly.

"Not too upset about what's been happening to you?" he prodded gently.

Lucien shrugged. "A little, but other than the early stuff, there's not much I wouldn't have done even if I'd been with you guys."

"That's a story for another day," said Mr. Woodward. "Very well, since you seem to be good for us now, you might as well go get yourself a room. I believe Natalie's old room on the third floor is still empty if you'd like to take that one. I'm sure Amelia wouldn't mind making a key for you."

Amelia glared at him. "I've been awake for twenty-four hours."

"So have nearly all of us," her father told her, "and this poor young man has no bed in which to sleep. Please go and make him a key, Amelia."

She was too tired to argue. Weaving slightly, she moved around us and headed for her own living quarters. This left Natalie unaided, and after a few seconds, during which she looked like collapsing at any moment, I moved to her and resumed the role Amelia had just left behind. She turned to me and put her arms around me, surprising me completely, not just by her action but by the feeling that they inspired in me. Or should I have said feelings, because there were several of them. Gratefulness was the first, followed quickly by affection for Natalie, which was almost immediately followed by grief for Serena. Now that we were out of danger for the time being, I would have a chance to grieve for her, as Darcy would grieve for Jane, and Marc and Lucien would, I assumed, grieve for their (our) father. All these feelings were followed by enormous exhaustion, something I was becoming more and more familiar with in recent times, but I satisfied myself with the knowledge that soon, very soon, I would be allowed to climb those stairs and gain the comfort of my bed again.

We waited for Amelia to return with a key for Lucien. When she came back, her father headed for where she had just come from. She glared after him, no doubt thinking that he could have done the key since he was going down there, but made no comment. That left the nine of us crowding the corridor in front of the infirmary, so we moved instead for the living quarters, knowing the attention would come and knowing it had to be met before we could rest.

Of course, our re-entrance didn't go unnoticed. Once again, we found a whole host of people waiting to greet us, desperate to learn what had happened after they had been sent back. There were plenty of adults in the crowd as well, including several of our parents, who also wanted to know the full story. I was still supporting Natalie, now assisted by Amelia, but we were both relieved of this duty when her mother and sister arrived to examine her. This left me free to look for the cause of all of tonight's events, and after some searching, I located him. Quite a few people were standing around Tommy, including Felicity, Jessica, Lena, and Darcy. He didn't look nearly as tired as everyone else, but he did look as though some vitality had left him. I doubted it had anything to do with his own personal loss, though. More likely he felt guilty for what had happened tonight, perhaps saw it as partly his fault. When he saw me, he raised a hand and waved me over to him.

"Thanks, man," Darcy said quietly to me before anyone else could open their mouths, and I felt taken aback.

"Thanks? For what? I thought you'd blame me."

"You killed her," he pointed out, and it took me half a second to realise that he was referring to Tankom, not Jane. "She deserved it. I don't think anyone in here's sorry she's gone, but—(he shrugged)—thanks."

"I owe you one too," Tommy said, and now I was even more taken aback.

"No, you don't. Come on, man, do you expect anyone to expect you to pay them back for coming after you tonight?"

Tommy shrugged; my wording of the question seemed to have thrown him off slightly. "Not sure about that, but I know none of it would have happened if you hadn't seen it. I would have been left there," he added, paling slightly.

"Some of us know how it feels to be tortured," I told him, meeting Lena's eyes. She was another who had experienced the agonator on at least one occasion I could remember. "Trust me, we wouldn't have let anyone in this room continue going through that, especially knowing what Tankom had planned for you over there."

While I had been talking, something else had been happening around me. I only noticed it when I finished speaking. The room had fallen almost completely silent, and a dark sort of energy seemed to be building. I looked around and saw that the source of the energy was right in the doorway. Lucien, it seemed, hadn't been quite brave enough to step into the room with the rest of us, but he was by Marc's side now, and his reappearance hadn't gone unnoticed. Everybody was staring at him, and a few people had withdrawn weapons they hadn't got around to depositing yet.

"Holy geez," Tommy breathed. "That's seriously not Fewul, is it?"

"It's Lucien, all right," I murmured. Obviously Fewul imitated Lucien very well when it took his form, but somehow, when it was really Lucien, he appeared more human. He certainly didn't look like the Lucien I had become used to passing in the Rock Haulter campsites over the last few days (much less subservient and much more nervous).

"I swear, he's on our side now," Marc said loudly. He was also nervous about the potential of this situation. "John fixed him up with an unboggler."

"Then why's he got a gun on his back?" asked Liam, who should have been more understanding after what Sebastian had done to him.

"He had that before he got back to our side."

"Please, all of you," Lucien called over the renewed muttering, "what he says is true. I don't expect any of you to trust me after what I've been doing, what I did back in February, especially. I can only hope that you'll see in time that I'm back on the right side."

It was a reasonable speech, I thought. He didn't sound confident, and he certainly didn't look it, but you had to give him points for standing up straight and delivering it all the same. A long silence followed it, during which everybody stared at him, quite a few weapons remained pointing at him, and Marc stood ready to defend his brother should the need arise. Then somebody moved in the crowd. It was Candice Young, although I didn't see her clearly until she had broken free of everyone else and had reached Lucien. She reached out and embraced him, and he returned it in a distracted sort of fashion, and I understood. He was grateful for the support and the understanding she offered, no more than that.

"Wow, doesn't that beat all," Felicity remarked. "That's gotta mean it's bedtime."

It was. I was subjected to a few more hugs, this time from Lena, Amelia, another one from Natalie, Mum, Dad, Marge, and even Marc and Peter. Hugging other guys wasn't something I normally did, but this was no normal morning. Given the experience the three of us had shared, just about anything was acceptable this morning. Then, finally, I was able to climb the stairs, many other exhausted people around me, and gain the privacy of my bedroom. I changed my clothes again, getting into my pyjamas and not even bothering to put my dirty clothes away. Not that they were dirty, I supposed, since I'd only worn them for an hour or so. Then I climbed gratefully into bed and was out almost instantly. I only had time to decide that whatever happened now, whatever was going to happen in the next few days, and however royally I was about to screw my sleeping patterns, I would make this sleep last for at least fifteen hours.

Of course, when I had escaped from the Basement the first time and had counted on a good night sleep, I was subjected to seeing Stella instead. When I was exhausted after having stayed up all night and the following day only two days ago (really, only two days), I'd been haunted by what I had seen of my mother's final minutes. Between the Enlightener and my connection with Stella, it was foolish to think of sleep as any sort of refuge for me. Later, I would consider that what I went through wasn't much better than what Tommy had been through. At least I knew what it was to dream, but when I wanted peace the most, it always seemed to elude me. Naturally, this time was no different.

Whether Stella had woken up while we had still been in the building and had been unable to reach us was something I would never know, but I knew it had not taken the Hammerhearts long to get to her after we had left. They had examined the base thoroughly, turned it upside down practically, to make sure they knew the full extent of the damage in the aftermath of our visit there. Hammerson had regained consciousness almost immediately after Fewul had left and had repaired the damage to the Hammerheart Highway in about ten seconds. He had then gone through the base, repairing the damage on the sixth and seventh floors and attempting to repair the damage to his mother. The damage, it seemed, was far too extensive for her to be repaired, however, and this had left Hammerson extremely confused and worried, worried because he feared that some protective magic he had performed on her at some stage hadn't worked. Stella gauged this much, but she didn't know what the magic in question was. This was not information Hammerson had confided in her.

They had also found the one remaining body that we had left behind. Well, we had left a lot of bodies behind, but Hammerson had been able to bring them all around in short order, to clear the stairwell more than anything else. Quite a few of them had died on the seventh floor, but the ones who were still alive when Hammerson reached them had been restored to full health. They, plus most of the ones who had attempted to fight us, were now being held in the Basement, where Hammerson would punish each and every one of them for allowing us to do the damage we had achieved.

This left the base practically empty, for those who had not been locked up (mostly those who had stood with Hammerson in the final moments of the battle) were sent away. Only three people remained in the base—Hammerson, Stella, and Hall. Why Hall had been allowed to stay, when his job dictated that he ought to be somewhere in Australia, brushing his teeth and getting ready for work, was not knowledge Stella possessed, nor did she know why it was he who had been asked to remain behind and not Cornish. In any case, this was all information I gained from Stella when I entered her mind, and all in about three heartbeats.

She, her father, and the Australian chief of police were back in the room in which Tommy had been held—the execution chamber. It was dark, as it had been on all other occasions I had seen it, and a table stood in the centre of the room, a table that hadn't been there when Tommy had. Except it wasn't a normal table; it had the shape of a table, but the top of it looked more like the top of a drain than a table. Bernard Moran lay dead upon it, but by the way he was lying, he might have been sleeping. This was the sort of death Stella liked —a good death, if there was such a thing, and not the horrible violent deaths that had happened to others tonight.

"It is time," said Hammerson softly, placing his hand in his pocket. Stella had seen (or not seen) what was there, and it terrified her. This was the worst thing in the world, having that dangerous object in her father's hands, not just for the Woodwards and Fletchers but for herself as well, because it just about made escape an impossibility. The only way out now that she could see for herself was death.

"Would you like me to do anything, sir?" Hall asked respectfully.

"Stand, watch, and remember," Hammerson told him, "and be ready to accept the honour when it is given to you, for you have earned every bit of it. You watch this too, Stella, and remember it for as long as you live. This is the fate—the right fate—for those who dare to betray me."

Silence followed this. Stella was not required to respond, nor did she want to. His words were more warning than she needed. She was terrified of what was about to happen. Whatever this ritual was that her father had in mind, it was not one she had seen before. What was going on? Of course, I could have told her what was going to happen several seconds before it did, because I had seen it all before, seen it many times in fact. Even though I was in Stella's mind, and it was her thoughts I thought rather than my own, my own knowledge of what was about to happen seemed to filter through somehow. Stella didn't feel it, but I certainly did, and I remembered it clearly when I woke up.

Before Stella's eyes, the vision I had entertained for weeks became a terrible reality. The darkness in which they all stood suddenly exploded into bright, flickering light. Through the grate on which Moran lay, fire rose up, covering his body and setting him instantly alight. He burned where he lay, and it was all Stella could see, for the light the flames threw over his burning body cast everything else in the room into shadows. Smoke rose, of course, adding to the darkness and drying about the back of Stella's throat. She tried not to breathe it in, but she knew it wouldn't kill her. It was not her father's wish that she be poisoned by smoke inhalation, and he had the means to make sure it didn't happen, but that didn't stop it from being uncomfortable. He, meanwhile, along with Hall, watched the proceedings raptly, as though it were a film they were bidden to memorise.

Slowly, Moran's clothes burned away, revealing the blackened skin beneath. In many places, his skin began to flake away and crumble, revealing the melting flesh beneath. This seemed to happen mostly around his stomach as they watched, and after a few minutes of it, Stella began to understand why. As a gaping hole began to form in his belly, the flesh melting almost to the point of liquid, a sight Stella knew she would never forget, something else began to take shape there—a dark, round object. A thrill of terror rose in Stella as she understood what must be happening, but she knew she had no way of stopping it.

In the dancing light of the flames, Hammerson's expression was exultant as he used his own crystal to levitate the black crystal into the air, a foot above Moran so that it became separate from the fire. It hung there, unbound by any magic other than what Hammerson was doing to it, probably not even warm from the flames.

"The Villain Crystal," he whispered, "and who better to take possession of it than you, 2H9. I think that this will aid you greatly as you hunt down H3 and H4."

"You're right," breathed Hall, "this *is* a great honour indeed."

Slowly, the crystal floated towards him, and he stretched out his hand, careful not to reach too close to the flames, and closed his fingers around it. His expression was one of ecstasy, and although she hated to admit it, even to herself, Stella knew that her father was right. There was hardly anyone better than Hall for the Villain Crystal. Once upon an ignorant time, she would have said that Cornish was the greatest Villain she knew other than her own father and grandmother, but Hall's actions in recent months had surpassed anything Cornish had ever done. The worst of it was that he was also right about the damage that Hall would be able to do with it: A true villain would make the most of the Villain Crystal, just as, so she had been told, the true hero had made the most of the Hero Crystal already that night. With the Sien-Leoard Crystal in Hammerson's hands and the Villain Crystal in Hall's, nobody would be safe, not even the Sorcerers.

Chapter 50: The Quest Continues

There was no rising for lunch on that Monday, May 17, and dinner didn't happen until eight o'clock, more than an hour later than usual. I didn't manage the fifteen hours of blissful sleep I had promised myself, but once I had moved past that nightmare vision of Stella, I did manage nearly twelve. The hall was already half-full when I entered it alone, and in the time I was there, people kept drifting in and out at irregular intervals. It was the most disorganised meal I had ever seen within the Woodward base, including the very first night I had spent here nearly three months earlier.

I looked around when I entered the hall for someone to sit with. There were very few people I wanted to be near, and for the first time after one of our grand adventures, most people didn't want to be near me either. People had slept, true, but some had slept more than others, it transpired, and talk had passed around the base during those hours. The news of the fate of the Sien-Leoard Crystal had spread to most quarters by now, and it was clear that most people (the less understanding ones) blamed me for what had happened to it. Perhaps they blamed me for last night as well, seeing as I could have done more if I'd had it, and they were surely blaming me for whatever horrors were yet to happen. I saw them look at me and quickly away, leaning in towards their friends and whispering behind their hands as they glanced surreptitiously at me. I gritted my teeth and pretended I didn't see these things as I collected my dinner and headed for a table where Peter sat with James, Erica, Marc, and Tommy.

"The word's out," Peter said unnecessarily when I had reached them.

"I gathered as much," I said dully, sitting down between him and Marc and beginning to eat. "I don't suppose anything's been happening during the day that you guys know about?"

"I only just got up too," Marc told me. "I was knackered. He's the one who's been up all day," he said, nodding at Tommy.

He shook his head. "It's been really quiet," he said. "People have been coming down and keeping to themselves mostly, and I haven't seen any of the Sorcerers at all."

"They would have slept," said James wisely, "but I'm also betting Mr. Woodward's been doing some checking around with spies and such to see what changes there have been in Hammerson since this morning."

"I know of one," I told him, and when they all looked at me, I added, "I saw something when I slept last night, something big, but

I'll tell you later. We should probably call another meeting to talk about what happens next."

"Does anything happen next?" Peter asked. "We already found Smiley, unless—" He broke off, looking suspiciously at me. "You never did tell us if you saw anything in the hall back there, did you?"

"Never got a chance to," I said, meeting Marc's eyes for a moment and looking quickly away again. "Marc knows, and we saw Smiley before we left, but we got distracted before we could say anything to the rest of you."

"Are you saying there's more for us to do?" Erica asked.

"Not for you, there isn't," said Tommy, raising his eyebrows at her. "It was only an accident that you, Siobhan and Lena ended up involved in the first place."

"Well there's no need to take that tone with me," Erica huffed indignantly. "We care as much what happens to you and John as any of these guys."

"Whatever." Tommy shrugged dismissively. "It doesn't matter to me anymore, anyway. I'm pretty much normal now, and Tankom's dead. So far as I'm concerned, I'm probably gonna be okay now."

"Yeah, you probably are," said James, "unless Hammerson swears a vendetta against you for some ungodly reason after what happened this morning, but John's still got plenty to worry about."

"I do," I said and sighed deeply. The time had come for me to put it out there, to see what they would say. "I've still got more to learn, even after what I saw in the hall, but, you guys," I looked around at the five of them, "you don't need to be involved if you don't want. This is my business now."

"It was your business all along, bro," Marc pointed out, "and in case you haven't noticed, we're with you all the way. I'm sure Natalie and Amelia would agree if they were here."

"I know that," I said, and shrugged. "It's just—"

I broke off, trying to think. How did I explain to them what I was feeling? It was true that the hunt for Smiley had been my business all along, because it had been my past we were trying to uncover originally. What we had learnt about Tommy was useful for him, but it hadn't been the knowledge we were seeking. Now, though, after what I had discussed with Smiley before leaving the Rock, somehow it felt much more personal than it had before.

"I'll tell you guys everything I learnt later on," I told them, "but after that—well, it's more personal now, the stuff I've gotta do."

"We're gonna help you, mate," Marc told me firmly. "Just try and stop us."

I sighed deeply. Frustrating as it was, I couldn't deny that I had some of the best friends in the world.

* * *

That night was just as weird as the day had been, only now I was awake to see it for myself, as I had expected I would be. Once again my sleeping patterns were shot to pieces, but as I was to find out soon enough, it wouldn't really matter whether I slept in the night or day. The lounge room remained almost completely empty for the whole night; there were never more than three or four people in there at a time. The library was fuller, but of course all the people in there were as quiet as mice. Both the games room and the gym were completely deserted too. Most people, it seemed, were either able to sleep or up in their rooms doing who knew what.

I had planned to summon those who had been involved in the Smiley hunt (Marc, Tommy, Natalie, Amelia, Peter, and James were the only ones left from the original group, now that both Nicole and Serena had been taken from us). As the hours wore on, however, it became difficult to find any of them. I suspected I knew where James and Erica were, and I figured that Natalie and Amelia, if they were awake, were with their families. Marc too was missing, and I also thought I knew where he was. Lucien had sat alone at dinner and had looked extremely uncomfortable to be here. If anyone could ease him into the swing of things here, it would be Marc. I even thought it might be nice to invite him along to the meeting. Where one person fell, another could take over. Lucien had proven himself to be a good, sensible leader prior to the influential charm. If the others absolutely insisted on helping me with whatever came next for me, Lucien would probably be very useful.

At around one o'clock in the morning, I was leaning against the wall near the stairs, my back to the lounge room. This had been exactly where I had been standing when I had been spending my last pleasant moments with Stella, exactly where I had been when I had started a chain of events that had led both to Tulip's death and Stella's exile. I wondered if there was any significance in that because right now, it was Stella I was thinking of. Even after last night, she was still living in a hopeless, miserable situation. Perhaps it would become even more miserable now that Tankom was dead— there would be no one to stop Hammerson acting like a crazy person. I wished very much that we had been able to bring her back and wondered if there would be a way to do it now that we had two crystals working against us. It wasn't just getting her away from her family that I wanted to do, though: I missed her, I really missed her.

Also, now that I understood how we had come by our strange connection, I thought she deserved to know the story too.

It was as I was thinking these thoughts that I was interrupted from my musings by Tommy, who had just come down the stairs, and by Natalie, who had just come through the door from the hallway outside. Neither of them had seen the other, and they nearly walked into each other as they crossed paths. I had a moment of very slight amusement. That was one emotion it would take some time to regain.

"Sorry," said Tommy, taking a step back and looking wary, and I didn't have to wonder why. Although social mishaps came secondary to life and death situations, I knew they were both remembering all that had happened between them over the last week.

"Sure, sure," she said dismissively. "How are you, anyway?"

"I'm okay," he said cautiously. We both knew she was only asking out of politeness.

"You don't know where Marc and James are, I suppose?" she asked both of us. "Mr. Woodward asked me to find them. He wants a word."

"Upstairs, I think," said Tommy, jerking his head up toward the ceiling. "Not sure what they're doing, though, so if you're gonna interrupt them, you might wanna be careful."

"I guess I'll have to," she said sourly. "He's not in a good mood. I'm not sure what he's got to say to them, except that it's definitely got something to do with the crystals and it ain't good."

"Probably just gonna tell them they're not allowed to do anything stupid anymore," I said bitterly, remembering that I was no longer in that category, having done the stupidest thing of all. "Has he said the same to you and Amelia, too?"

"He did," she said, smiling weakly. "I didn't need to be told twice, but my dad—well, he went mad, really mad."

She shrugged and headed up the stairs without another word. Both Tommy and I watched her out of sight before he turned to me, that nervous expression still there.

"Hey, listen," he said nervously, and I was suddenly able to place his expression and knew what was coming.

"It's okay, mate. Really."

"No, it's not," he said stubbornly. "Seriously, I owe you an apology. I shouldn't have done it."

"I know, but it worked out okay, right?" I said, trying to smile. Now that he had the guts to admit he'd done the wrong thing, I felt all that bitterness I'd harboured for him ebbing away. "Just out of curiosity, though, why did you *really* leave?"

"I was scared," he said solemnly, "and maybe I was a little jealous. I knew you weren't gonna be hurt, but—I dunno—I guess I just thought you deserved to do it without support."

I breathed a sigh of relief. He didn't have to bring Natalie's name up for me to know that I'd been pretty much spot-on with my suspicions. "For what it's worth, you probably would have been better with that crystal in the end."

"Perhaps," he said, beginning to smile himself now, "but only because I would have been asleep with it, so no prisoners could have got near it. I guess it would have been worse if they'd gotten the Hero Crystal, though, wouldn't it?"

"Not really. They couldn't have changed the properties of any of them with Fewul out, and they wouldn't have had their own magic to get out."

"Ah, right."

We fell silent for a moment, and in the almost complete silence of the living quarters, we clearly heard voices three floors above—Natalie and, by the sound of it, Marc and Lucien. I was very pleased to have received the truth from Tommy about the starfish afternoon, but one matter was still left unresolved.

"While we're being honest with each other," I said to him, jerking my head upward, "you wanna tell me what was going on with you and Nat last week? It looked interesting, but me and Pete couldn't work it out."

"Ah," he said, looking suddenly shifty again. "Well, if we're being honest with each other, not nearly as much as I would have liked."

"You tried to get back with her?" I enquired. "I thought maybe you'd given up and moved on."

"I never stopped liking her, I just knew I had no chance before," he said, shrugging. "You know, 'cause of what I did."

I nodded. Cheating on Natalie with her sister had been bad, of course, but if I was going to be fair, I had no right to scold him for it after what I had done with Lena. Instead, I said, "What made you change your mind?"

"Well—" He looked more shifty than ever. "Well, I just thought maybe it had been long enough, and especially after what happened with you and Lena (my stomach dropped) and I'm sure she knew it, I thought maybe she would be willing to reconsider after that."

"Peter and I wondered if maybe you'd used the crystal to make her more interested again," I said casually. "While you had it, I mean."

He went slightly pale and swallowed, but to his credit, he didn't lie. "I didn't mean it to do what it did. I just wanted her to forgive me, and instead it made her all crazy. She's really strong, though. Not even magic can work against her that easily. She's an amazing person."

"Don't I know it," I muttered. He was speaking exactly what I had felt when I had watched her resist him that night.

Tommy took a deep breath and said, "Well, now I really am ready to give up. I'll never get her back. I'll always like her, but I guess it's time to find someone who'll take me as I am. She's all yours, mate, if you still want her."

"Sure I do," I said at once. "If she still wants me, that is."

"Oh, she does," he said, his eyes twinkling with amusement. "Trust me, she looks at you more than you realise, and she'll forgive you for what you did, even though she won't forgive me."

"How do you know that she knows?" I asked, straining my ears three floors above. If Natalie came down during this conversation, it wouldn't be so good for me.

"Sure she would. She can read minds, and she would have got a good look at Lena's mind before you and her left for England. Lena would have been thinking about it, and it doesn't take a genius to make the connection why she was suddenly willing to fall in with the plan. I'm betting Lena would have thought about it plenty since too. They've certainly been around each other often enough for Nat to have a good idea how Lena's mind works. Plus, she was pretty down that weekend while you were gone."

"She was?" I asked, my stomach falling horribly. "My God, nobody told me that, but then—how can you know she's forgiven me?"

"Oh, I'm pretty sure she has," said a different voice, and both Tommy and I jumped. Unnoticed by either of us, Amelia had just walked through the door from the corridor outside. "Sorry," she said, realising what she'd done, stopping a few feet from us and looking up the stairs. "I only just heard the last bit of what you said."

"Sure," said Tommy suspiciously. "What are you doing here? Natalie's already up there looking for Marc and James."

"And I'm looking for her," said Amelia. "My father just changed his mind. He'll see Marc and James later. I was just gonna tell them not to worry about it."

"They would have known that when they saw him."

"I know that. I just wanted to come down and see you guys."

"Oh," said Tommy, his eyes moving from her to me and back again, and he grinned at her. "Nice to see you too. So what makes you know that Natalie's forgiven him?"

I could have groaned. Having Amelia here right now was extremely awkward, especially as I remembered our last one-on-one conversation.

"Because I had a chat with her," said Amelia, looking back at me now, "a few weeks ago, about the ethical responsibilities of knowing what everyone around you is thinking."

"Ethical responsibilities?" I repeated blankly.

"Well, you know, pretending you don't know what people are thinking, for the sake of their comfort. People generally don't like it when their thoughts are public. Also, we have to try really hard not to judge people too harshly. I'm used to it because I've had it for so long, but Nat's still adjusting to knowing so much, and she's having trouble separating her opinion from people's unfiltered thoughts. She's getting better now, though, and I reckon she'll forgive you just about anything."

"Just like I thought," said Tommy, clapping me on the back. "So you've got no reason not to try your luck."

"May I respectfully point out that my girlfriend was murdered twenty-four hours ago," I said, feeling my face burn with embarrassment. This conversation had gone too far now. "I'm not doing anything just yet, if not because I don't want to, then certainly out of respect for Serena."

As I thought more deeply about it, though, I supposed that Tommy and Amelia were probably right. I hadn't detected any kind of hostility toward me from Natalie at all since I had returned from England with Lena and the life assistant. She had approached me days later and told me that she wasn't going to take anything for granted and that she wanted me to know how she felt. Then, of course, there had been the afternoon we had spent together at the top of Rock Haulter. Had that only been two days ago? It was incredible how much could happen in such a short amount of time, but as I remembered that afternoon, I remembered something else: I had sensed something dark approaching. I had sensed that something big and bad was coming, whether it would be in a memory, in the past I saw in the hall, or when we returned to the base. I had been right on all three counts.

* * *

That meeting I'd wanted to have happened at just after four in the morning. Everyone was awake, of course, and only Tommy was becoming really tired. He hadn't slept at all since his German body had died, and now that the time was coming, he was curious to see if he would be able to sleep at all and what would happen if he did. The rest of us were starting to become tired, but I thought I had at least a few hours left before I would become too tired to be productive. There were eleven of us in the meeting—me, Marc, Tommy, Lucien, Natalie, Amelia, Peter, James, Erica, Siobhan, and Lena. The latter three had insisted on being allowed to attend, now that they were up with pretty much everything that was going on. I suspected that quite a few more people would have liked to be involved, like Harry, Simon, Katie, Sophie, Felicity, and Jessica, all of whom had asked when they had heard there was going to be a meeting (such news got around quickly within the base), but feeling that there would be too much to explain and the night was too short for it tonight, we had told them no.

We sat on the circular couches at the back of my room and questions came at us almost immediately. Tommy, Erica, Siobhan, and Lena wanted to know the full story of what had happened twenty-four hours ago in the Berlin base. They also had plenty of questions for Lucien, who told us in more detail about the sort of things that he, his father, and Stella when she'd been with them, had been getting up to.

"Question for you, Lucien," I said to him, "before Marc and I tell you a little story about your father that you probably don't know. Were there any ghosts with you that you know of?"

He searched my face before he answered, "Yes."

"Thought so," I said and breathed a sigh of relief. "Do you know where she is now?"

"I'm not sure," he said, raising his eyebrows at me. "She didn't come with us to Germany. She's probably still in our house. That will be her haunt now."

"You saw her?"

"Yeah, I did," he said shortly.

"Okay," I said and breathed in deeply. "Well, Lucien, we've found out a lot of stuff over the last few months, about your family and about me. I dunno if your dad told you any of it."

So we told him all we had been doing. Well, not quite all we had been doing. The conversation resembled the one I'd had with Serena weeks earlier when I had brought her up to speed, only bearing in mind that Lucien was much closer to the action. We told him the important points, like that the ghost was our mother, which he already knew; that I was his brother, which he hadn't known; and the truth about why our mother had been killed. The only thing none of us mentioned was the time bomb curse Hammerson had placed upon him. I wasn't sure about the others, but I felt that was something Lucien would be happier not knowing. He couldn't change it, and it would only serve to bring him down. Lucien held up pretty well under the torrent of startling information, as well as Marc had that day, in fact.

"My God," he said in a hushed tone. "My God. I always thought there was some good in him somewhere, but I always thought it was out of guilt and regret for what he'd done."

"Are we done going over old stuff?" I asked. "Is there anything else you wanna know, Lucien?"

"Heaps," he said weakly, "but I guess I can catch up."

"You probably can. Here's a bit of something else for you to get your head around. Do you know anything about the connection between me and Stella?"

"Er—" He faltered, looking confused now. "I'm not sure what you mean. I know you and her used to get on, and—(he paused, thinking harder)—and I know Hammerson wanted her present when he tried to kill you."

"He did," I said, "and that's closer to the truth."

I explained briefly how Stella and I shared thoughts, then said, "It happened this morning when I went to sleep, and I saw something really horrible."

"Oh no," Peter groaned. "She would have been back there, and it would have been not long after we left. I bet Hammerson was running amok, was he?"

"He may have done," I said thoughtfully. "I know all those Hammerhearts who failed to capture us were locked up in the Basement, but when I saw her—"

And I told them what I had seen, how Moran had been burned and how the Villain Crystal had been taken from him and handed to Hall. Marc looked sick by the time I came to the conclusion.

"It was inside him?" Erica exclaimed. "*Yuck!* Well, at least we know where it'll be if we never see Hall using it."

"We're in trouble now," said James, horror-struck. "Hammerson with the Sien-Leoard Crystal is bad enough, but he'll be focussing on a bigger picture most of the time. Of course he wants John, but he's got the whole world to worry about. Hall, though, his job is to deal with us directly. He'll be on us every second of every day now. We'll have to be very careful about ever going out now because he'll always know, and he'll be able to use magic to spring traps on us everywhere."

"That's really sick, the way he did that," said Amelia, who looked almost as sick as Marc. "Really sick."

"Isn't there anything we can do to get those two crystals back?" asked Natalie.

"We have to try, don't we?" said Peter, looking around at us all. "We have a chance because even though they have the powerful crystal, we have more people with magic—seven Sorcerers, plus the Light Crystal and the Beast of Magic."

"I'm not so sure my dad will let us make any plans for that now," said Amelia dully. "He's really put-out about us disobeying him yesterday."

He, Mr. Woodward, hadn't got around to speaking to Marc and James yet. The suspicion was that he would pass down a stern warning to them both about how they were to use magic. It wouldn't have even surprised me if he asked Marc to get rid of the Beast of Magic, to call it back and send it wherever it came from. I certainly hoped he didn't do that because with Fewul gone, that made all of us, including the Sorcerers (especially the Sorcerers), much more vulnerable.

"So what if he doesn't," Peter shot back at her. "We have enough power. We don't need his permission."

"I know, but it's better if we have his permission," Amelia persisted, "only because we don't wanna muck up any plans he might be making."

"That's not hard, since he hardly makes any," Marc muttered, and, sensing the conversation approaching dangerous ground, James cut in swiftly.

"John, what else have you learned? What happened with Smiley the other morning?"

The focus in the room sharpened perceptively. I knew that all of them were very curious about what I'd learnt, because they knew I had learnt something. Marc hadn't let anything slip, and until now, there hadn't been an opportunity for questions.

"Well, what have I learnt," I mused. "Well, I know why I can see ghosts, I know how the connection with Stella came about, I know why I see weird stuff when I sleep sometimes, and I know why Hammerson wants to kill me. What I don't know, exactly, is what to do about it."

"You got all that from what you saw in the hall?" Tommy asked. "Wow, it must have been pretty comprehensive."

"Smiley did say they did all sorts of tests in there," James pointed out. "So start from the beginning, then. How come you can see ghosts?"

"Runs in the family," I told them. "We should have realised, since Moran could talk to the ghosts he summoned on camp."

"Marc and Lucien didn't get it, though," Peter observed.

"Lucien just said he did."

"No, I didn't," said Lucien quietly. "I was using Marc's ghost goggles to interact with her. Well, only see her; I couldn't interact with her. I could talk to her, but she couldn't talk to me."

"Ouch," said Tommy quietly.

I felt myself shiver too. What Lucien had just described sounded absolutely heartbreaking.

"How did you get ghost goggles?" Natalie asked.

"They were stored in the Chopville base when Dad and I went back in there," said Lucien. "I already knew that, but I hadn't bothered to get any until I was with Dad. He told me she was there and then regretted it; he didn't want me to have to see her, but I—I had to."

"I'd be the same," said Marc quietly.

"I couldn't even imagine it," said James. "So what else did you learn, John? What about these weird things you see?"

"Have you ever heard of the Enlightener?" I asked him. If anybody had heard of it, it would be James, but to my surprise, he shook his head.

"I've heard of it," said Lena, surprising us all. "It came up while I was doing some research for the history of magic projects we were doing earlier in the term. I don't remember anything about it."

"Well, I can't remember every bit of it either," I said, "but it's something like an external source I connect to when I sleep, and it's supposed to show me things that are important to me but that I don't realise are important. I've been dreaming for months about the main hall on Rock Haulter and they all had Stella in them—that was what led me to believe the answers lay in there in the first place. Also, remember that dream I had about Marc being the Seventh Sorcerer? It was all this Enlightener thingy."

"Wow," said Peter. "I wouldn't even believe in something like that if I hadn't already seen proof of it."

"Moran and Cornish didn't believe in it either," I remarked, "but I don't see why. So much of what we've been learning about has to do with external sources of some kind."

"Can you use it in any way?" asked Amelia.

"Not that I know of," I said thoughtfully. "I don't think I have any control over it at all; it just shows me what it wants when I sleep. I guess the only good it can do me is if I recognise it when it shows me something, then work out what's the meaning of it."

"Sounds dodgy," said Peter blandly.

"Does it have anything to do with your connection with Stella?" James asked, as ever pushing forward.

"No, that's completely separate," I said. "Actually, that is one of the reasons why he wants me dead—the connection—but it's not the only reason. You did say on the Rock, Marc, that there must be another reason why he wants me dead if he didn't know about the connection. Well, you were sort of right. If there hadn't been another reason, that connection would never have happened."

"And what is that reason?" asked James nervously.

"Apparently," I took a deep breath, "there is some prophecy or other that refers to me. Apparently, some test they did identified that I was the person it meant. Apparently, I'm supposed to be the one to defeat the most powerful Sorcerer who ever lived. Naturally, Hammerson assumed that the Sorcerer in question was him, so he came after me straight away."

I felt oddly separated from myself as I spoke, hardly able to believe the words as they flowed slowly from my lips. It seemed ridiculous that I could be destined to defeat Hammerson in any way, shape, or form, especially since the person sitting across from me hadn't quite defeated him in battle less than twenty-four hours earlier. The only way I had defeated Hammerson at all so far was by killing his mother, and that hardly counted. Or did it?

"Okay," said James in an overly reasonable tone after several seconds of silence. "I can see two things wrong with that. Firstly, if Hammerson knew you were destined to defeat him, why would he hunt you at all? Wouldn't it be wiser for him to avoid you altogether, to run from you?"

"I misspoke," I muttered. "It said I 'can,' not that I 'will.' Hammerson wants to prevent the can from becoming a will."

"Okay." James nodded. "Second problem. How can Hammerson know that he's the most powerful Sorcerer ever? He has no way of knowing that, unless there's a test on the Rock for that too. I would have said that either Sien or Leoard was the most powerful Sorcerers ever."

"I would have too, except for one thing: They're both dead," I pointed out. "I can't possibly defeat someone who's already dead, unless we bring either of them back as ghosts and they start causing trouble. No, it has to be someone who's alive today. As for him testing himself, I can only assume that it's not possible for whatever reason."

"But how can you know the prophecy is real?" asked Lena. "How can Sien and Leoard know these things thousands of years in advance? Surely they can make a mistake."

"They weren't wrong about Marc," Tommy told her. "And remember what Smiley said? 'Question Sien and Leoard's prophecies at your own peril.'"

"Maybe it's Tankom," said Natalie hopefully. "You certainly defeated her."

"I did," I agreed. "At least, I killed her, but do you really think she was ever more powerful than Hammerson is now? And besides, it doesn't change the fact that Hammerson believes he is the most powerful. It doesn't change the fact that he'll keep hunting me, believing he'll be preventing the prophecy from coming true."

"That's true," said James, "which means we have to keep protecting you until we have a way for you to defeat him, as the prophecy says. You have one thing on your side, though: He's tried to kill you once before, and it didn't work, remember?"

"Yeah, that's true," I said, my mind returning to Stella. "Anyway, about the connection, it came about because he tried to kill me right there, in the main hall, only Stella got between me and him right when he performed the curse that would have killed me. She was only a toddler then, so it was a complete accident, but it didn't kill either of us. Her crystal chip probably prevented it from doing that sort of damage. What it did do was sort of join us together—physically as well as mentally. Hammerson separated our bodies, but he probably didn't realise what had happened to our minds, so we've been joined up in the head ever since. We think he probably has to undo that damage before he can kill me. That's what he tried to do that night he killed Tulip."

I took a deep breath and let it out slowly. That had been a lot of talking, but now they all knew everything I knew. It was a relief to have talked about it again, even though I couldn't get anywhere here that I hadn't already gone with Smiley.

"Christ almighty," whispered Peter.

"Can you do anything about that?" asked Amelia.

"Undo it, maybe," I said thoughtfully, "but I don't see it as particularly urgent. I don't think Stella minds having it there, and if it keeps us both alive, then it's definitely worth something. Of course, if Hammerson can get into her mind again with the crystal, that won't be good for us. That's why we've gotta get her back here again. It's not a matter of trust anymore; she'll be a danger to us now if she's with him. Nothing she can do about it."

"Okay," said James slowly. "So, find Stella and bring her back here. That's one thing we've gotta do. If we can get the crystals back from them, that'll be helpful too. Is there anything else we can do that'll help you, John?"

"Yeah, there is," I said, sitting up straighter and looking from Tommy to Marc. "I need to do research on the Enlightener, really understand it. If there's so much weird stuff going on with me, maybe I'm supposed to use it. Also, I'd like to see the wording of this prophecy about me, really get to understand it as it's written. Those CDs you got from the magic display at school—where are they now?"

"Wow, those things," said Natalie, smiling slightly. "I have no idea where they are anymore. We never did get to finish those projects, you know."

"I don't have them," said Tommy, glancing at Marc. "I gave them to him way back before you guys went on camp."

"I gave them to Lisa," said Marc, "a few days after we got back from camp."

"Do we know if Lisa gave them to anyone?" asked James.

"She could only have given them to Jessica, Felicity, or Nicole," said Natalie. "They were the only other ones in with us for the projects."

She looked enquiringly up at Lena, as if asking if Lena knew where the CDs might be, but she shook her head. "Everything I used for research would be long-gone by now. I chucked it all when school was shut down."

"If Nicole had those discs, they might have been destroyed in that fire," said Peter nervously.

"Not likely. That was only the first time she went home, and I doubt she took them with her," I said. "She was never the type to study on holidays, Nicole. I guess I'll have to ask Felicity and Jessica if they have them. Otherwise, they're probably at the Ponts' house."

"We can go and check there, then," said Marc, and he too breathed a sigh of relief. "At least, we'll be able to whenever we're allowed out of this place."

"I can just let a few of us out," said Natalie. "There's nothing any of them can do to stop me."

"That's great," I said, "but listen, all of you—"

"This isn't the same crap you dished up at dinner, is it?" asked Peter, raising his eyebrows.

I ignored him. "I know all of you guys wanna help, but you honestly don't have to. This is more my business than anyone else's, but—"

"Are you snubbing us?" asked Amelia, smiling slightly.

"No, I'm giving you an out, if you want it."

"I think you know that none of us are going for that," said Marc, looking around the couches at all the others. When none of them disagreed, he said triumphantly, "There you are. We're with you all the way, mate. Besides, you need us. We have magic, and you don't."

"Thanks for the reminder," I muttered.

Part of me was slightly annoyed with them. My gut instinct was that as dangerous as things had been for me before, they were about to become so much worse. The last thing I wanted was another Tulip or Nicole, one more of my friends dead just because they were with me at the wrong time. Secretly, though, I was pleased that they were sticking with me, whatever the risks. Part of that was the truth in Marc's words—I would need them as much for their magic as their support—but the greater part was simply the fact that I didn't want to do it alone. I smiled weakly around at all of them, feeling that as bad as things were, as bad as they had become, compared to where they had been a few days ago, there was still hope for me yet.

Epilogue

Three weeks had passed since the dramatic events of that night, during which the lives of most of us in the Woodward base took a horrible turn for the dull. June had finally arrived, and outside in Chopville, the weather had turned bitingly cold and windy. I knew this due to the outdoor physical area that Mr. Woodward had created within the base (employing similar magic as that which I had used in the prison yard), but unfortunately, there was no opportunity to step out into the real world due to the new restrictions that had been imposed upon us.

It had started with Mr. Woodward finally getting hold of Marc and James on the Tuesday afternoon, two days after our return from Rock Haulter. I had been right in thinking that he might order Marc to call back the Beast of Magic, but what none of us had anticipated was that he also ordered both of them to turn in their crystals. James had handed the Light Crystal over reluctantly and without argument, but Marc had balked.

"I'm the Seventh Sorcerer!" he had roared, brandishing the Hero Crystal. "I was chosen! This crystal is *MINE!*"

"Magic is a privilege," Mr. Woodward had insisted. He hadn't been shouting, according to James, who had recounted the story for us later, but he had been very firm all the same. "It is not a right, and as far as many of us are concerned, Marc, it is a privilege you have abused. You can have the crystal back when you have matured enough to understand when magic should and shouldn't be used."

"*No bloody way!*" Marc had shouted. "What good is it going to be to anyone else? You can't use it for anything."

"Maybe not, but as long as it's not being used, it's staying out of trouble," he had replied coldly. "Hand it over."

The Hero Crystal had eventually been taken from him by force. Between Mr. Woodward and Mr. Fletcher, Marc hadn't been able to prevent the crystal flying out of his hands. As we understood now, Mr. Woodward was keeping the six Sorcerous Crystals on him at all times, and Mr. Fletcher was keeping the Light Crystal. So now we had no magic at our disposal except for Natalie and Amelia's, but Mr. Woodward had a solution to that problem (as it would have been for him) too. Perhaps he wouldn't have bothered if it weren't for the parents of most of us who'd gone after Tommy that night, but his own anger had caused him to agree with their demands very quickly.

I never knew how much Dad and Charlie had to do with this, but Mum and Marge were naturally leading the charge. Several families in their entirety were living inside the Woodward base now, and Mr.

Woodward had arranged for them all to move into the family suites on the first floor. Peter and I had both balked this time, but our keys had been confiscated while we were having dinner on Tuesday night (just vanished right out of our pockets), and we had been unable to enter our third floor rooms. There had been a lot of shouting that night, as you would expect, but we had been unable to sway them in any way. So Peter and I were now in rooms next door to each other, both of which were considerably smaller and less luxurious than those we had become used to. Mum, Dad, and Hilda had also moved into the suite, and although Dad had spent more time out of the base than within during the two weeks since that night, the setup enabled 'the parents' to make sure we couldn't get up to much dodgy. The Thomases hadn't survived the move either—they were in the suite next to ours—and the Maivises had all ended up in a suite too.

Meanwhile, and most depressingly for me, Natalie and Amelia were being prevented from entering our living quarters. Natalie's mother and Rebecca were somehow able to pass through the wall between the living quarters and the corridor outside (Mr. Woodward had turned that door into a magical wall to lock us all in), but Natalie and Amelia weren't allowed to come with them. Why? According to Rebecca, it was because they were extremely hard at work. Given the state of the war, with magic back in the hands of evil, all six Sorcerers needed to work together and practically around the clock. That was part of the reason, I was sure, but not the whole reason: Mr. Woodward didn't want the two girls to team up with Marc and get up to any dangerous business.

It was infuriating pretty much everyone, but perhaps nobody more than me. I had a path ahead of me, a path Smiley had helped me lay out. It wasn't a very clear path but a path all the same. Now, because of the adults' interference, I wasn't allowed to follow it. What made it even worse was that Natalie and Amelia were two people I wanted most to be around, and now, I had no idea when I would be allowed to see them again. My reason for wanting to be around them both wasn't what you're probably thinking, though: Where at one stage I would have thought that once I wasn't with Serena anymore, I would have jumped at the chance to be with Natalie. Now, though, because of the way I had lost Serena, my urge to be intimate with any girl at all had been pretty much snuffed out.

"It's guilt," said James wisely when I tried to explain the feelings to him and Peter over dinner about a week after Serena's death. "You're not set right in your head because you didn't get a chance to be open with Serena before you lost her. It's called closure, and you never got it."

"I don't think that's it," I said, though I wasn't entirely sure of that. "It's just—I dunno how to explain it. Losing her like that, I guess, just makes me wish we'd been better before it happened."

"That's more or less what I just said," James pointed out. "Help me out here, Pete. You know all about this, right?"

"Not from John's point of view," said Peter, looking up at me. "Me and Kylie were fine. I just needed time to move past her. You can't just turn feelings on and off like a switch. You shouldn't have to worry about that to the same extent I did because you—well—"

"Because I was already gonna break up with her," I said dully. "Yeah, I know, but that doesn't mean I didn't care about her."

"I know that," he said, and there was something extremely comforting in his understanding tone. "But you know what? You get over it eventually. I'm not completely over it yet, but I feel a little lighter in the heart than I did a couple of weeks ago. Besides, there are certain biological urges that can't stay turned off forever."

"That's one way of looking at it," said James distastefully.

My biological urges had been switched off, though, at least temporarily—obviously a mentally induced state. This virtual numbness had a surprisingly good side effect, however; it enabled me to look at what had been my love life with a less partial eye, and therefore made it possible to see why I'd had so much trouble letting Lena go, and Amelia too, to a certain extent. You could call it a life boat, or an insurance policy—it basically came to the same thing. I hadn't thought about it consciously, but part of me must have been prepared for the possibility that somehow I wouldn't be able to get Natalie. This applied to Lena more than Amelia, I reckoned, since I really had considered Amelia at various points along the way, but other than my dirty fantasies, I'd never seriously considered dating her. So why hadn't I let her go? Because if worst came to worst and I couldn't be with anyone else, Lena would still be there.

Even in my numb state post Serena's death, this was a sickening thought. Lena had only ever been good to me. Granted, she had been serving her own interests along the way, but every time I'd asked her to back off, she had done so—at least until the next time, and she had provided me with plenty of entertainment along the way. Yet through all of that, without even knowing I was doing it, I was treating her quite as crappily as Serena. Nobody deserved to be used like that, and it was mainly this thought, combined with lingering guilt for Serena, that caused me to let Lena go as I should have done a long time ago. Ironically, she really was my only option now.

Lena had backed off me immediately after Serena's death, respecting my need to grieve, I supposed, but she hadn't ignored me completely. Our contact, rather than flirtatious looks, now consisted of actual conversations. She didn't make a play for me until almost two weeks later, and when the moment came, I was prepared for it. I had, for the second time, asked Lena what she wanted from me, and the answer had been slightly different: Where last time she would have settled for what she could get, this time, she wanted it all. I was glad to hear it, but despite the incredibly sexy opportunity presenting itself to me, I stuck firm to my original decision. She was hurt, of course, but perhaps not as much when I explained, to the best of my ability (without the life boat thing), why I couldn't go there. I made sure to stop just short of saying 'it's not you, it's me', though.

She had continued to shoot me friendly looks after that, but I thought she'd made an effort not to. I'd been pleased by that, still feeling a sense of loss, still knowing what I was missing out on, but knowing that I'd done what I'd done for the right reasons. I could only hope that, despite the rejection, Lena would understand that this was better than being in a relationship with a guy who'd treated her the way I had. Lena didn't miss much, though, because of course, she was an incredibly attractive girl, and she had accidentally charmed at least one lucky bugger while she had been trying to seduce me. A girl like her would never have to go wanting for long.

We had held funerals for Jane and Serena three days after we had returned their bodies to base. Both were just as emotional for those who knew them as those funerals of Mrs. Woodward and Kylie had been. Serena had, in fact, been buried right beside Kylie in the private cemetery, and it made me extremely sad to look at their tombstones side by side. Jane had been buried closer to Mrs. Woodward's grave, and the body of the German Tommy had been laid to rest beside her. We hadn't held a funeral for him though because, understandably, he hadn't wanted one.

"How many people in history have attended their own funeral?" he had pointed out. "Besides, who would mourn for me? I'm still here, right, and everyone who knew me is still in Germany. I wish we could have found my German parents, though."

This last fate was something that haunted Tommy. He had asked on at least two occasions if someone could go and find out what had happened to them. He knew that they were dead, but he had no idea how they had died or where their bodies had been left. Mr. Woodward had told him that as much as he wished they could help, he had no resources to spare for a mission that wouldn't do the greater population any good. Tommy was generally happy, because it turned out that he could indeed sleep normally now, but even with that matter aside, he still spent a lot of time thinking about what he had sacrificed in order to let that happen.

"Try to think of yourself better off," Marc had advised him. "You can imagine that they were simply struck down and killed instantly. Some nice people stumbled over their bodies and notified the authorities, who were able to identify them. Their deaths were put down to some kind of health issue, and they were laid quietly to rest. Trust me, imagining something like that is often better than knowing. I wish I'd never found out what happened to my parents' bodies."

In Mr. Woodward's defence, he hadn't been lying when he had said they had no resources to spare. We were able to keep up with the progress in the war now entirely on the television and radio and in the newspapers. The adults tried to stop us achieving even that much, but there were some things they just couldn't control. People like Mum and Marge would have been happier if we knew nothing whatsoever about what was going on outside, but even they knew better than to deprive us of these things. It hadn't stopped them disconnecting the Internet, though. Mr. Woodward said it was just too risky, because he had heard word that Hammerson was developing a magical computer virus that, once inside the walls of the Woodward base, could damage a whole lot more than a computer.

Everything that was happening outside now came back to the fact that Hammerson had magic of his own now, and he wasn't afraid to use it. He slept very little, so we understood, and he moved all over the world, helping tighten the Hammerhearts' hold on power everywhere he went. Certainly the laws Cornish had put forward over a month ago were beginning to take proper shape now that he had magic to help him enforce them. In Australia, the public was adjusting very quickly to the new regime. Some laws were still causing problems, but Cornish had found a novel way of dealing with that. Now that Hammerson was able to assist with his own magic, many tasks were being performed much more inexpensively than they would have otherwise. The new government still had to pay contractors for certain tasks (to prevent the global economy from collapsing, if nothing else), but all the same, the fact that they didn't have to spend nearly as much money meant they could afford to introduce some pretty massive tax cuts. War or no war, the public loved that; at least they had after Cornish had also introduced some extremely restrictive policies to ensure that retailers didn't take advantage of the climate to bump up their prices.

Hall was on the rampage with his magic too. He had recruited a great army of experienced detectives, soldiers, and even assassins from all over the world whose job it was to find me, Marc, Tommy, and Lucien, only adding to the adults' desire to keep us all locked up. Unfortunately, we knew no more than that because the media had no interest in keeping up with his developments. We were still wanted criminals, but other than continuing to remind the public how dangerous we were, there was no new information to be provided. Hall would have been very busy, though. I had no doubt of that, but I had no way of knowing exactly what he was busy with. It was a scary thought.

Meanwhile, our great town of Chopville was dying. Both schools had been permanently closed down because, according to the Education Minister, they were too much of a target for trouble. That was true enough, I supposed, but it now meant that those who had been attending them (who weren't imprisoned in here) had to travel greater distances to attend schools in other towns. As they had planned to do since February, the Hammerhearts had taken over the grounds of both schools in Chopville and were operating an on-ground base from there. According to Charlie, it had put a great dampener on the vibe of the town. Partially for convenience and partially out of fear, many people had begun moving away from Chopville. The town was changing, and it was turning into something most people wanted nothing to do with.

Those schools that had reopened since the coup were now all bound to a specific curriculum that was designed to indoctrinate children into believing that the new regime was the right way to go, that it was better for mankind, and that all who opposed it ought to be taught just how wrong they were. Many in the public opposed what was being taught, but very few spoke up about it. Some stayed quiet out of fear (for those brave enough to be vocal usually didn't fare too well), but many, and this was a disturbing thought, had found one or two laws they did approve of. Like I said before, people were adjusting quickly.

I'm sure I wouldn't have liked those classes much, but I also felt sure that they would have been better than the ones I was currently attending. There weren't many people qualified to be teachers inside the Woodward base. In fact, that's putting it modestly: There weren't any, full stop. Yet they tried, for reasons best known to themselves (perhaps they just wanted to give us something to do, or perhaps they thought they were doing the right thing for us, or perhaps they had deluded themselves into believing we wanted things back to how they had been before the war). If it was the last one, then they were perhaps right, but they were most definitely going the wrong way about making it happen.

Every weekday, from nine in the morning until three in the afternoon, all of us still school-age (at least fifty of us, perhaps more) would sit down in the meeting hall, which, during those hours, became more like a lecture hall in a university, and we were taught. The subject matter included English, Math, History, Geography, Biology, Health, Commerce, Physics, Music, Drama, Information Technology, Art, and Sports. It sounds better than it was, believe me. Not only had they created a passage linking the meeting hall directly to the living quarters, so that none of us could get into the corridor, but they had also created a direct link to the outdoor physical activity area. It was a grassy field, about the size of a football field, and the edges were enchanted similarly to the sky so that it felt as though the town of Chopville were all around us. It was possible to see the town central, the school, the Jade River, and much of the southeast quadrant of town around us, but an invisible magical barrier prevented us from being able to reach it. I couldn't think of any greater slap in the face than to show us what we weren't allowed to go and enjoy.

And so all things combined to set me back a long way indeed. By the beginning of June, I found myself trudging pretty much everywhere I went. Others around me were disinterested in the setup too, but none of them were sinking quite like I was. Every morning when I woke up, I couldn't think of a single thing during the day to look forward to. Mum and Marge noticed that I was unhappy, of course, and they did honestly wish they could do something about it, but they weren't going to let me have any of the things I really needed to set me free.

Most important to me was my freedom, my future, my path, my quest—however you looked at it. I wanted my privacy back, that which came with my level-three room. I wished I could see Natalie or Amelia. That would cheer me up somewhat too, but again, not because I wanted to be intimate with either of them. I wished I could see Stella too. I had visited her mind twice in the last three weeks and had deduced that she had managed to escape from her father. I had no idea where she was except that she was outdoors, no cover, nowhere to go, and nothing she could do about it.

"Think of it this way," Tommy suggested. "Maybe you can't do anything about your so-called quest now, but as long as you're stuck here, Hammerson can't do anything about his either. That's gotta be worth something, right?"

It didn't do anything for me, though. Hammerson knew he had the ability to come after me and trap me here if he put his back into it. He would be capable of undoing just about any protection the Woodwards and Fletchers could put around us with the Sien-Leoard Crystal. The same may not hold true for Hall, but that wasn't something I had any way of knowing. Besides, it didn't change the fact that I was stuck here with no way of making any further progress at—well, anything at all. I'd never realised just how much I had depended on making forward progress before, but now, stuck here in the Woodward base, for all intents and purposes safe but with nothing else going for me, I came to realise that I had always taken it for granted.

Now, trapped and with no end in sight, I had to resign myself to the knowledge that until Mr. Woodward had a change of heart, or until something changed within the base, I wouldn't be able to do anything about my predicament, and with that knowledge came the darkness. I had avoided it after Tulip's death but only because I'd been able to do something about it. Now, stuck and with nowhere to go, I could do nothing but lie down and let the darkness take me. It washed over me, suffocating and debilitating, and I did nothing for it, because I could not. All I did was go where I was supposed to go and speak when I was supposed to speak, all the while dwelling on those things that had passed, those things that I had lost, those things that I wanted back. It was a dull, boring, depressing existence, but as May blended into June, and as June was to wear on, that existence became the story of my life.

The Magic Crystals Series

www.themagiccrystals.com